FYODOR DOSTOYEVSKY was born in Moscow on October 30, 1821. He was educated in Moscow and at the School of Military Engineers in St. Petersburg, where he spent four years. In 1844 he resigned his Commission in the army to devote himself to literature. In 1846, he wrote his first novel, *Poor Folk;* it was an immediate critical and popular success. This was followed by short stories and a novel, *The Double.* While at work on *Netochka Nezvanova,* the twenty-seven-year-old author was arrested for belonging to a young socialist group. He was tried and condemned to death, but at the last moment his sentence was commuted to prison in Siberia. He spent four years in the penal settlement at Omsk; then he was released on the condition that he serve in the army. While in the army he fell in love with and married Marie Isaeva. In 1859 he was granted full amnesty and allowed to return to St. Petersburg. In the next few years he wrote his first full-length novels: *The Friend of the Family* (1859) and *The Insulted and the Injured* (1862). *Notes from Underground* (1864) was in many ways his most influential work of this period, containing the wellsprings of his mature philosophy: the hope of gaining salvation through degradation and suffering. At the end of this literary period, his wife died. Plagued by epilepsy, faced with financial ruin, he worked at superhuman speed to produce *The Gambler,* dictating the novel to eighteen-year-old Anna Grigorievna Snitkina, who was to become his second wife. The manuscript was delivered to his publisher in time. During the next fourteen years, Dostoyevsky wrote his greatest works: *Crime and Punishment, The Idiot, The Possessed,* and *The Brothers Karamazov.* The latter book was published a year before his death on January 28, 1881.

The IDIOT

by
Fyodor Dostoyevsky

❧∾❧

Translated by
Henry and Olga Carlisle

with an Introduction by
HAROLD ROSENBERG

Revised and Updated Bibliography

Ⓒ
A SIGNET CLASSIC
NEW AMERICAN LIBRARY
TIMES MIRROR
NEW YORK AND SCARBOROUGH, ONTARIO

SIGNET, SIGNET CLASSICS, MENTOR, PLUME, MERIDIAN AND NAL
BOOKS are published *in the United States* by
The New American Library, Inc.,
1633 Broadway, New York, New York 10019,
in Canada by The New American Library of Canada Limited,
81 Mack Avenue, Scarborough, Ontario M1L 1M8

First Signet Printing, February, 1969

9   10   11   12   13   14   15   16

PRINTED IN THE UNITED STATES OF AMERICA

The IDIOT

Introduction

~~~~

The peculiarity of *The Idiot* is that its hero is almost a
spectator. "I'm really here only to meet people," explains
Myshkin on his arrival from Switzerland. From his first encounter with Rogozhin on the train, he has, however, stepped
into a complex underground intrigue involving Nastassya Filippovna, Ganya, the Yepanchin family, the Ivolgins, Lebedev, Totsky and, of course, Rogozhin himself. Unhesitatingly, Myshkin allows himself to be drawn into it, but without altering his onlooker's attitude. By the end of Part I, on
the very day of his return to Russia, he has offered to marry
Nastassya, become the "rival" of Rogozhin, aroused the interest of Aglaya and the impatience of Ganya, and has received
confidences from several quarters. Wrote Dostoyevsky in *The
Notebooks for The Idiot,* underscoring the entry *"The chief
thing is that they all need him"*—among other things as
their audience. He is the understanding listener, always available. Thus he attracts around himself all the personages of
the narrative in a perpetual round of comings and goings,
confessions and revelations, in pace not unlike that of bedroom farce.

Throughout the novel, Myshkin plays opposite a cast of
garrulous types, who amble about in episodes instigated by
self-delusion, greed, ambition, conventionality, desperation
and sheer love of absurdity and troublemaking. The reader is
dipped into twenty years of Russian debate on such topics as
the Russian character, capital punishment, religion, material-
ism, individual charity, the future of the aristocracy. Beyond
everything else, however, Dostoyevsky is a virtuoso of dramatic stagecraft, able to pull out of his hat a seemingly endless string of surprises. No sooner does a situation begin to
coalesce than it is blown apart again by a new revelation, an

unexpected arrival. Dostoyevsky's playing with Lebedev's purloined wallet or with the "case of Pavlishchev's son" are peaks of inventiveness in keeping the reader off balance—they match on the plane of comedy the buildup of tensions in the great passionate confrontations, such as Nastassya's unexpected visit to the home of Ganya or her showdown with Aglaya.

Myshkin's part in both the vaudevilles and climaxes is that of a sympathetic bystander ready to lend a hand; even when the action is aimed at him he commiserates with those who are trying to cheat him or to use him to settle emotional accounts. His self-abnegation makes him an impersonal witness even during his most earnest participation. For all his readiness to enter into everyone's life, he is and remains an outsider, an "idiot" in the classical meaning of a private or unrelated person. "He's as much of a stranger to me as to anyone else," exclaims Aglaya, his "fiancée," after Myshkin has spoiled their engagement party by throwing a fit. Rather than being engaged by the action of the novel, the prince "blesses" it by his presence. He hovers above the fatal pursuit of Nastassya by Rogozhin like an angel wringing his hands over the Crucifixion. In the end, his embrace of the murderer by the bedside of the immolated bride transforms the killing into a ritual sacrifice.

Myshkin's removed character is, as Dostoyevsky observes in *The Notebooks*, the *idea* of *The Idiot*. In him the reader was to see "how Russia is reflected." We know that it was Myshkin's sudden coming to life in Dostoyevsky's imagination that enabled him to start writing the work after half a dozen drafts centered upon an "Idiot" with a different (highly active) character had proved sterile: Dostoyevsky, too, "needed" Myshkin to bless his undertaking. Like that of Hamlet, the personality of the prince overflows the plot, a Dostoyevskian recasting of the familiar romantic tragedy of a passion-driven rich young man and a woman of blemished reputation. Myshkin is not shaped by the action—it is rather a background against which his uniqueness is revealed. For all its intensity, the love triangle, like the subsidiary intrigues spun through the narrative, is but an occasion for Myshkin to practice his irreducible talent for giving himself. "So as to make the Idiot's character more fascinating (more charming)," Dostoyevsky wrote, "he has to be imagined in a field of action."

The notion of a *field* of action is an interesting alternative to the traditional idea of a plot as a *structure* of actions. Instead of seeking to define its hero by the continuity of his deeds, *The Idiot* spreads outward to envelop as many aspects of his personality as possible. The "field" is made up of a mosaic of episodes that do not move toward a resolution or even bear any necessary relation to one another. Stressing multiplicity more than coherence, Dostoyevsky advised himself to "prepare many incidents and stories." The affair of Rogozhin and Nastassya is but one of the situations through which the prince's character comes to light; other sides of him are shown in his idyllic meeting with Aglaya in the park, his relations with Kolya, his responses to the machinations of Lebedev and the Burdovsky crowd and to the "protest" of Hippolite.

At bottom, Myshkin's feelings are directed past the framework of *The Idiot* toward events in Russia and the Russian folk. "In his most *tragic,* most *personal* moments," declares *The Notebooks,* "the Prince is concerned with solving general problems . . . *When at the end of the 4th Part* N. F. again deserts the Prince and runs away with Rogozhin on her wedding day, the Prince is wholly absorbed with the club [of the children]." I know of no other instance of a novelist planning to have his hero turn his back on the novel's greatest scenes. The detachment of Myshkin contemplated by this note would make Camus' *Stranger* seem like a passionate lover. In the completed work, Myshkin does not, of course, attain this degree of absence. Yet it is significant that Dostoyevsky thought him capable of it, and it is a fact that, as Dostoyevsky also notes, "the Prince has had *only the slightest effect* on their [the protagonists'] lives." (All italics are Dostoyevsky's.)

Myshkin's function is not to alter the course of the action but to disseminate the aura of a new state of being, let events occur as they will. *The Idiot* is Dostoyevsky's book of salvation, but Christ, too, saved without overcoming the implacability of destiny. As the personification of the highest potentialities of the Russian spirit, the prince illuminates (or "reflects") the Russian predicament in lightning flashes of grace. From abroad—*The Idiot* was begun in Geneva and carried to conclusion during disturbed wanderings in Italy—Dostoyevsky surveys the deepening chaos and depravity of Russian society, and to his unhappy country he dispatches Myshkin as the redeemer (as he hopes that *The Idiot* will redeem him from his creditors and allow him to return home). The mood of the novel is anxious—it occurs to Dostoyevsky that in its large cast of characters "everyone is a traitor" *(The*

Notebooks). Still, the author's nostalgia for the motherland and for Russians, even at their worst, comes through in the vivacity and good humor of his characterizations. Russia as represented in *The Idiot* is peopled by types in whom the corruptions of the European—lack of faith, vanity, boredom, fatuousness, lechery, lust for money—are heightened. Its Petersburg setting had long been for Dostoyevsky a dreamlike frontier where the grand wraiths of Western literature and history—the Iagos, Micawbers, Rastignacs, Richelieus, Napoleons, Marie Antoinettes, Camilles—mingled with the creatures of Gogol and Pushkin. In the capital there now also appeared new types born out of the materialistic ideologies of Europe, types out of whose midst Razkolnikov had sprung and who are represented in *The Idiot* by the group that accompanies Pavlishchev's son, characterized by Dostoyevsky in a letter to Maikov as "some types of the modern Positivist among the highly 'extreme' young men."

These alien presences are everywhere—the behavior of Russia's aristocratic, commercial, and intellectual classes is regulated by them. What makes matters especially desperate is Russian naïveté, the native genius for belief and enthusiasm, which causes Russians to carry out in action what the West with its coldness and caution only conceives in art or in abstract thought. "If one of us becomes a Catholic," cries Myshkin in his tirade at the Yepanchin party, "he is bound to become a Jesuit, and one of the most subterranean. If one of us becomes an atheist, he is bound to demand the uprooting of faith in God by force, that is, of course, by the sword! . . . And our people don't simply become atheists, they infallibly *believe* in atheism . . ." Rogozhin, Nastassya has told him, is "passionate in everything" and turns "everything to the point of passion"—he is thus a true Russian, a forerunner of Mitya Karamazov, and though Dostoyevsky sees his hunger for Nastassya as equivalent to his father's lust for gold pieces he respects him for the wholeness of his feeling. Dostoyevsky's conviction of the susceptibility of the Russians vis à vis their European models (he himself borrowed prolifically from French and British authors) gives his fiction its political edge, while his identification with Russian extremism as both a dangerous weakness and a sacred gift is the basis of his emotional nationalism. "Everywhere and in everything," he wrote to Maikov, "I go to the ultimate limit, all my life I have crossed beyond the frontier."

Dostoyevsky's hopes for Myshkin as a saving power rest on his theory of emulation which conceives dramatic fictions as constituting the roots of human action. In the opening pages of Part IV of *The Idiot*, which he jokingly compares to "the criticism one finds in periodicals," he presents the view that actual people are merely "watered-down" types out of novels and plays. Average persons are creatures of fiction reproduced in countless rough copies. Aware of their commonplaceness they acquire a character of their own—"the typical character of mediocrity which refuses to remain what it is and desires at all costs to become original and independent, without having the slightest capacity for independence." In sum, men prefer to imitate fictional models rather than seek their own reality. Social life is thus dominated by inventions of the imagination, by personages who are "perhaps exaggerated but . . . hardly unknown." Without fictional heroes nothing of significance takes place—after the death of Nastassya and the elimination of Myshkin and Rogozhin, there is only left to say that "Lebedev, Keller, Ganya, Ptitsyn, and the many other figures of our story go on living as before, little changed, and we have almost nothing to tell about them." Not only does life copy art but it derives from art its reason for being lived.

In *The Idiot* the supreme example of mediocrity is Ganya, whom Dostoyevsky detests for his smug and self-deceptive pretensions to distinction. Ganya enters the narrative as if he were made up for the stage, and everything about him is artifice. "He was a very handsome young man . . . Only his smile, for all its amiability, was somehow a trifle too refined, his teeth showing with somewhat too much pearly regularity." Confronted by Ganya's smile, the prince, despite his charitableness, suspects that when "he is alone he can't possibly look that way and probably never laughs at all." Whatever Ganya does is destined to be counterfeit. When Nastassya throws Rogozhin's rubles into the fireplace and offers them to Ganya if he will pull them out, Ganya, "in evening dress with his arms folded, hat in his hand and wearing gloves," adopts a noble stance and refuses to budge. His striving for dignity is more than he can endure, and as he watches the flames leap around the wrapping of the rubles "an insane smile wandered over his chalk-white face" and suddenly he falls forward unconscious. The fainting of Ganya, brought on by his inner conflict, is an imitation of the fit that seizes Myshkin when he tries to behave with dignity at the Yepanchin party in order to please Aglaya. Ganya's heroics gain him nothing. "He didn't pull it out, he held firm!" exclaims Nastassya in momentary admiration, then adds, "Which means his vanity is even greater than his lust for money."

Whatever course Ganya chooses, mediocrity remains his typical characteristic.

But though commonplace people are incapable of originating anything, Dostoyevsky insists that they cannot be overlooked, "because ordinary people are at every moment, by and large, the necessary links in the chain of human affairs." History is the conflict of types, each the personification of a passion and a fixed idea that drags in its wake hordes of self-deluded imitators. "It has been enough for some of our young to cut their hair short, put on blue eyeglasses, and call themselves Nihilists for them to persuade themselves that, in putting on their spectacles, they immediately acquire 'convictions' of their own." It is through equating the idea with the costume (the blue spectacles) that the masses of mimics become "links" between ideas and their realization. The Napoleonic idea gives rise to the image of Razkolnikov, upon the publication of whose story an actual student named Danilov promptly murders a pawnbroker out of "principle." *Crime and Punishment* is concerned with the privileges of the history-making archetypes as against the mere "links." In *The Idiot* Dostoyevsky undertakes to employ for his own ends the processes by which fictional types dominate human existence.

It is his grasp of the dynamics of these quasi-fictional beings, both unique and ordinary, as they appear in the streets and drawing rooms of Petersburg that constitutes Dostoyevsky's "realism." Somewhere Dostoyevsky denies that he is a "psychologist," but he claims deep insight into the states of the soul of typical characters. "I have my own idea about art," he wrote to Strachov shortly after finishing *The Idiot*, "and it is this: What most people regard as fantastic and lacking in universality, I hold to be the inmost essence of truth. Arid observation of everyday trivialities I have long since ceased to regard as realism. . . . Is not my fantastic 'Idiot' the very dailiest truth? Precisely such characters *must* exist in those strata of society which have divorced themselves from the soil—which are actually becoming fantastic."

Inhabited by dream personages—the Rogozhins, Nastassyas, Yepanchins, Princesses Belokonsky, Totskys, Lebedevs, Burdovskys, Ivolgins—Russia is plunging toward anarchy. Reason cannot avert the catastrophe, since reason itself only produces fantastic types of its own, the Positivists and Nihilists of the radical younger generation with their "logical" assumptions and their disregard of human feelings. The only chance for salvation is the appearance of a type of a different order, the embodiment of what to Dostoyevsky was "the Russian idea." In conceiving Myshkin as the "wholly beautiful man," the messiah of love and brotherhood alive in the depths of Russian piety, and manifesting himself under the conditions of contemporary Russian life, Dostoyevsky sought to demonstrate that Russian literature could take control of Russian history, and through it of world history ("the Renaissance of the whole of mankind and its resurrection by Russian thought"), by means of an original figure personifying the deepest national feelings undistorted by Western rationalism. The "idiocy" of *The Idiot* is a declaration of independence from alien philosophies and literary models, good or bad. The outstanding virtue of Myshkin is that he is "ours." "Any Russian who says, writes, or does something of his own, something that is his *by right* and not borrowed, inevitably becomes national, though he may not be able to speak Russian correctly. I regard this as an axiom." As the creator of a new Russian type Dostoyevsky did not hesitate to regard himself as a shaper of the future.

The messianic content of *The Idiot* is in contradiction to the dramatic form of Dostoyevsky's major novels. If the role of the tragic hero is to heighten the action and drive it toward its denouement, the mission of Myshkin is the reverse —to soften passions and to arrest the dramatic conflict or to divert it. He hopes to "rehabilitate" Nastassya by convincing her of her innocence, and to awaken compassion in the obsessed Rogozhin. He endeavors to sweeten the rancor of the "son of Pavlishchev" and his rowdy crew, to soothe Aglaya's hurt *amour propre,* to heal the break between Lebedev and General Ivolgin. Myshkin is less a dramatic figure than an edifying one. He offers an example of liberation from the centrifugal pull of self and of actions once they are under way. Nor was the continuing openness of Dostoyevsky's "Prince Christ" intended to affect only the characters of *The Idiot;* as suggested above, it was to extend to the readers of the novel as well. With Myshkin the art of fiction is redirected to serve an interest of the mind more urgent than art: the search for what man can be. This is the political substance of the novel, a politics that is inherently metaphysical. With his character reflected on many planes of experience, the prince projects out of *The Idiot* as a personage who could manifest himself in situations of actual life. Myshkin has brought into being the "Myshkin type," as an earlier relaxation, or opening out, of the contours of drama brought into being the "Hamlet personality." Fulfilling the design of his author, Myshkin has passed from literature into social history. He is a rival of those potent fictions—the Dandy, Superman, the Proletariat—

which the imagination of the nineteenth century provided as models for men reaching for new possibilities of conduct. He, too, is a "specter haunting Europe." He is the original of those who seek to persuade through self-renunciation, from the lover who "understands" his mistress' infidelities to Flower Children of the 1960's convinced of the perfidiousness of the adult mind. Although written one hundred years ago, *The Idiot* is an advanced instance of the modernist mingling of art and life. It is a work that is itself an action aimed at producing social, cultural and even political consequences. No doubt Dostoyevsky had in mind both the art of the novel and this potential force of *The Idiot* when he summed up his judgment of the work by saying that "there's much in the novel . . . that didn't come off, but something did come off. I don't stand behind my novel, but I do stand behind my idea."

Afloat between history and fiction, and only marginally related to the events of *The Idiot*, Myshkin is like a divine messenger in Homer or the Old Testament, but also a figure who seems about to turn into the abstract person of a religious or political tract. Dostoyevsky was acutely aware that to make Myshkin credible he had to prevent him from becoming the bearer of a philosophy, and he kept reminding himself to bring forth his hero's meaning through behavior, not through words. "N. B.," he enters in his *Notebooks*. "The Prince is like a Sphinx. He reveals himself without any explanations on the author's part, except perhaps in the first chapter." In this difficult effort to deliver his "idea" in the form of a living personality, Dostoyevsky is remarkably successful—the prince is an outstanding demonstration that Dostoyevsky's "types" have a dynamic reality different from those in other fiction. On occasion, Myshkin does fall into sermonizing ("You are a philosopher, and you've come to teach us," remarks Adelaïda, signaling Dostoyevsky's awareness that his hero has slipped into lecturing), and several of his speeches, notably the one preceding his fit at the Yepanchins, are in their aggressive class-consciousness out of character and unashamedly proclaim the political philosophy of his author. Yet so firmly has Myshkin been imagined that his very lapses confirm our recognition of him as an individual.

The vividness of Myshkin thrusts the central drama of *The Idiot* into the background. The romance of Rogozhin and Nastassya in which the prince has intervened is realized in three great scenes or "acts" that possess the unity of tragedy: the grand finale of Part I, in which Nastassya rushes off with Rogozhin and is pursued by the prince; the mysterious confrontation of Myshkin and Rogozhin and the latter's attempt to murder the prince in the dark hallway; and the concluding scene in which the murdered Nastassya is joined by her two "lovers." To focus the novel on these coherently related scenes tremendously heightens its poetic effect. But the poetry thus achieved belongs, for all the innovating chiaroscuro of the love intrigue, to the order of romantic drama; and it is gained at the expense of the new pathos represented by the figure of Myshkin and the state of the principal characters.

There is a tragic drama within *The Idiot*, but like the play within the play of *Hamlet* it is a set piece out of a more conventional literature. To read *The Idiot* as a tragedy or a "tragic novel" requires cutting across the vast disorder of episodes—from Myshkin's conversation with the Yepanchin butler to General Ivolgin's affair with the captain's widow—and the activities of subordinate and late-appearing characters (such as Hippolite) that constitute the real body of the novel and the "field of action" which supplies Myshkin's magnetism. The bitter affair of Rogozhin and Nastassya comes to the surface of the narrative on a few tense occasions, but it has a way of sinking out of sight the moment the prince is withdrawn from it—there is not a single scene in which the lovers are together without him. In substance and structure, *The Idiot* is closer to grand opera or to a chronicle containing ceremonial scenes than to tragedy. The pursuit of the self-doomed beauty by her single-minded victim-destroyer is a colorful leitmotif threaded through the scheming, drinking, lechery, gossip, matchmaking carried on as on a stage set of a village fair by a chorus of posturing society folk, matrons, marriageable daughters, eligible young men, mistresses, beggars, landladies, roughnecks, students and clowns.

The ineffable closing scene in which Rogozhin and Myshkin lie in each other's arms at the foot of the altarlike bed bearing the corpse of their slaughtered darling is a tableau composed of effigies that could be carried on a float in a procession—Edward Wasiolek, editor of *The Notebooks*, describes it as a "lyrical and deathly still life." The motionless vision becomes the emblem of Myshkin's transcendent power, a kind of inverted Heavenly Kingdom of love, madness and death where the emotionally disengaged prince attains final communion with the lovers purged of self.

That *The Idiot* is the most "musical" of Dostoyevsky's novels is related to the looseness of its action. Instead of pivoting on a single deed, as in *Crime and Punishment* or *The Brothers Karamazov*, the narrative rises and falls in tides of feeling keyed to the illuminated state of the prince. The poles of Myshkin's "idiocy" are the black despair and magical moments of release of the conversion experience. In Switzerland he was sunk in depression until his senses were awakened by the sudden bray of a donkey; then his feeling of being lost in a foreign place vanished and "all Switzerland became pleasing to me." The prince has looked at life through the eyes of the condemned prisoner facing his last minutes on earth. His uplifted condition is reaffirmed by his response to Adelaïda when she asks him to tell about being in love: "I haven't been in love, . . . I have been—happy in another way."

But Myshkin is not the only transformed person in *The Idiot*. All its leading characters have passed over into conditions that estrange them from their former selves, though on different psychic levels. Nastassya is breaking with her past with Totsky and is casting herself adrift. Rogozhin, like Myshkin a recent invalid and still running a fever, feels released by the death of his father and has set out on his hunt for love. Hippolite, the dying youth facing his brick wall, has, like Myshkin's prisoner on the scaffold, heard the hymn to life in the blackness of being deprived of it. Aglaya keeps changing before Myshkin's eyes from a "child-woman" to a "woman-child." Even secondary figures, such as Ganya and Lebedev, seem to alter their characters (at times as if by an afterthought of the author). A book of salvation, *The Idiot* is also a book of conversions, that is, of persons whose salvation is at issue. All are engaged in trying out in action the implications of a new position. Everyone is at the edge of an end and a beginning, whether through inheriting a fortune, getting married, or committing suicide. "The Prince and his activity:" we find in *The Notebooks*. "Aglaya *convertie*. Rogozhin cuts N. F.'s throat."

The characters are in a state of "enthusiasm" and gifted with clairvoyance. After scrutinizing the photo of Nastassya the prince declares that he can "read faces," and throughout the novel he arouses surprise by identifying the feeling hidden behind the social performance. He is a kind of investigating agent, a divine counterpart of the investigating magistrate Porfiry in *Crime and Punishment*. "Kolya and the Prince as spies," says an odd item in *The Notebooks*. Other characters, too, see into each other and reveal what they see with an absence of inhibition that often breaks out into scandal. Aglaya understands Ganya's calculations, and Nastassya is aware of every nuance of his motives. Rogozhin, too, is transparent to Nastassya, though she is helpless to make use of this knowledge. A wounding candor is achieved, which Myshkin is inclined to salute as the shock of newly attained innocence. His own charm consists in the first instance in acknowledging things to be as they are, undistorted by vanity or self-seeking, so that he offers an area of reality in which others are invited to inscribe their tentative identities. Everyone deceives him, but in encountering recognition instead of resistance they are compelled to confront themselves. It is this that causes Hippolite to hate Myshkin and Nastassya to run away from him.

Surrounded by indeterminate persons, semifictions striving to locate themselves in existence, Myshkin, the hero of light and quiet who was "happy in another way," yearns during recurring intervals of pressure to retreat from the world of adults to his peaceful kingdom of children and donkeys. In the perspective established by his presence, the action, though musical and full of color, is the sound and fury of people driven beyond themselves into abstract roles. "I'll go on the streets," Nastassya keeps proclaiming. "Or I'll be a washerwoman." In *The Idiot* action is questioned not philosophically, as in *Hamlet,* but in terms of its psychological reality. Herein lies the modernity of the novel and its continued relevance. The styles of action prevailing in Russia and the West are subjected to scrutiny and prove to contain a core of mental aberration. "It's not even an action, it's a psychological case," observes Totsky, after Ferdyshchenko has recounted the "worst action" of his life. A similar judgment haunts every action of the novel. Between the actor and his act falls the shadow of pathology. Is not Rogozhin's tracking down of Nastassya also a "case" and not an action? Telling Myshkin of the beginning of his love affair, Rogozhin implies that his passion is an obsession originating in his desire to destroy himself in order to escape his father's wrath. "And actually, before I went there [to Nastassya's] I never thought of coming back alive anyway." Nastassya's "scenes" constantly raise the issue of her sanity. When Rogozhin bursts into her party with his 100,000 rubles, General Yepanchin anxiously asks Totsky, who knows her best, whether she hasn't "lost her mind. I don't mean figuratively, but in the medical sense." Myshkin is convinced that she is demented and confesses to Radomsky near the end of the novel that he has been frightened of her from first sight. The narrator himself, reviewing the persons of his tale, refers to Rogozhin and Nastassya as a madman and a madwoman. The sickness of Myshkin is writ large in the title of the novel. He describes himself as an invalid who cannot marry, and his refusal to condemn violence and falsehood is as consistent with the attitude of a mental patient toward fellow inmates as with Christian forgiveness. In *The Notebooks* Myshkin's blending of saintliness and diagnostic concern is made explicit. "The Prince says of sinful persons: All sick people have to be taken care of."

Thus though *The Idiot* with its constant dramatic explosions is one of the most animated novels in literature, action in it is vitiated by the ambiguous condition of the actors, expressed in fantasizing on different levels, from Hippolite's nightmares to General Ivolgin's "memories." The motives of the characters tend to realize themselves in reverse. Rogozhin exchanges crosses with Myshkin, asks his mother to bless him, then tries to cut his throat. Nastassya, in love with Myshkin and frantic to escape Rogozhin, tries to induce Aglaya to marry Myshkin and promises to marry Rogozhin when this has been accomplished. The Dostoyevskian character cannot trust his feelings or decisions; some aberrant impulse may cause him to act contrary to them. At their height the conflicts of the characters reach an intensity beyond rhetorical formulation and hurtle into the physiological, as when Myshkin responds to Rogozhin's lifted knife by falling in a fit, or in the instance, given above, of Ganya's faint. The inability of the actors to sustain their identities in the face of the action dissipates their tragic pathos, as if Othello were struck down by a heart attack after smothering Desdemona. Instead of pity and fear, the slaying of Nastassya inspires tonal reverberations throughout the consciousness—the reader experiences not a resolution of the events but the feeling of being on the verge of a revelation.

In *The Idiot* a new kind of pathos appears; it arises not from the terribleness of the action as in tragedy but from the characters' desperate longing to act. This longing is dramatized by the consumptive Hippolite when, with but a few weeks to live, he decides to end his life by a public gesture, in order, he declares, "to take advantage of the last possibility to *act*" (Dostoyevsky's italics). The sole reason for Hippolite's presence in the novel is to bring up this issue of action in the face of its cancellation by sickness—to achieve authenticity Hippolite's act must eliminate the actor, that is, himself. Planning the part of Hippolite, Dostoyevsky designates him in *The Notebooks* as "the main axis of the whole novel," and advises himself to "center the whole plot on him." Like many other notions in *The Notebooks* this scheme for Hippolite is not carried out in the finished work. He is not the "axis" of the story; after his moment in the spotlight the plot passes him by and he all but drops out of sight. In respect to the action he is not a major figure but is rather a leftover of the "Idiot" of the early drafts, one of the "insulted and injured" who villainously avenges himself upon life, a male adolescent Nastassya. If Dostoyevsky is able to think of him as an alternative hero to Myshkin it is not because of his part in the novel but because Hippolite does come close to what he and the others yearn for, viz., a genuine act. This in itself gives him what Wasiolek calls a "finished character."

Hippolite's suicide does not come off. Like the other characters his longing to act is frustrated and he is left with his fever and his loneliness. Yet his attempt is not a "case," since his challenge to the world was a fit response to his hopeless situation and was conceived in full possession of himself. His public declaration followed by pulling the trigger would complete his life and define it in its wretched injustice. True, directed against himself, his act would change nothing except the quantity of time allotted him to live, and this emptiness of effect exposes him to the charge of showing off thrown at him by the reluctant witnesses of his performance. But if Hippolite's gesture is not quite an act, it is at least a demonstration, with something in it of finality, in short, as Hippolite himself calls it, a "protest."

Even this, however, Dostoyevsky will not grant him but prefers to drown Hippolite's intensity in a comical accident, his forgetting to insert the firing cap in his revolver, and in the end Hippolite, too, unable to bear the strain of his emotional conflict, falls unconscious and is cheated of his pathos. One might say that Dostoyevsky punishes Hippolite for his self-love in wishing to perform the act that will define him.

It is their awareness of the uncertain ground of their actions that causes the characters of *The Idiot* to hurl themselves toward a decisive event—a marriage, a crime—in the hope that the external situation thus produced will deprive them of choice and impose upon their personalities the unity of fiction. Dostoyevsky introduces reality with its irresolution into his novels so that his characters can fight against it. Myshkin, prepared to marry Aglaya or Nastassya, would, once the leap had been taken, have been compelled to renounce either love or pity but his nature is to cling hopelessly to both. To elope with Rogozhin and his gang is for Nastassya a final guarantee of degradation intended to lead unequivocally to what she calls her "proper place" as a streetwalker. But in Dostoyevsky's universe any proper place, even at the bottom, is unattainable. Like Hippolite's, Nastassya's final step turns out not to be final—soon she is living with

Myshkin in Moscow and appears at Pavlovsk among the fast set of the resort as she might had she still been Totsky's mistress. To the extent that it was to stamp her once and for all, Nastassya's act of self-destruction was not an action at all but a "psychological case," a piece of histrionics, felt yet put on for effect; and she has to perform her decisive act again at her wedding with Myshkin. Action is not accessible to Nastassya; she can go no farther than inviting Rogozhin's knife. By undermining the deeds of his characters Dostoyevsky forces us without arguing to assent to Myshkin's belief that "all sinners are sick people."

But though the personae of *The Idiot* are "cases," they are not mad in the ordinary sense; at least, not *only* mad in that sense. Descended from archetypal fictions, their pathology goes deeper than the mere aberrations of individuals. Their maladies are representative—the behavior of a Rogozhin or a Nastassya is "perhaps exaggerated, but . . . hardly unknown." Nastassya is hysterical and self-tormenting, but her dartings to the brink partake of a celebrated style, an aesthetic. Her moods are imposed upon her by the role of the femme fatale, the unpredictable lady in black whom men pursue, that she recreates. Nastassya originated in stories of the innocent virgin fallen under the power of a world-weary sensualist and corrupted by him, a situation psychologically injurious, to be sure, but one glorified also by romantic literature. If Nastassya is mentally ill it is as a creature of world fiction that she suffers, of poetry, as a universal being remade and recostumed by Russian sensibility. "Whether she was a woman who had read too many poems, as Yevgeny Pavlovitch had supposed, or simply mad as the prince was convinced" was a matter that could not be settled. But her poetic substance makes her irresistible as one already known and desired before being met, and lifts her madness and that of her lovers into realms of exaltation. Says Totsky reflectively as Nastassya departs in Rogozhin's "troikas with bells," "Who would not sometimes be captivated by this woman to the point of losing his reason and—all the rest?"

The substructure of Dostoyevsky's novels and stories is an extension of the continental stratum of romantic fiction with its solitary dreamers, idealistic maidens, self-centered wives, drunken ex-officers, servant girls falsely accused of theft, unexpected legacies. In *The Idiot* Dostoyevsky develops the insight, already introduced in *Notes from the Underground* and which he was to continue to harp on in *The Diary of a Writer*, that this world of introversion and half-serious playacting could no longer sustain great actions, not even the actions of great criminals, but is a breeding ground for hyper-distended egos. The malady of Russia, he finds, lies in the "segregation" of the romantic personality, in the passion of every Russian the moment he becomes conscious of himself to possess his own unique "idea." In opposition to this individualism, imported into nineteenth-century Russia in a decayed condition, *The Idiot* seeks the traces of a new collective substructure of feeling and imagination. Myshkin is the foe of segregation, the apostle of togetherness. During his sojourn in Petersburg and Pavlovsk, people are brought together and confront one another on a deeper plane of understanding, as in the instance of the "astonished footman" to whom Myshkin explains himself upon his initial visit to the Yepanchins, or of Madame Yepanchin lecturing the menacing adolescents seeking justice for Pavlishchev's son. In the Myshkin perspective of communion, the clairvoyance and uninhibited self-revelation symptomatic of the characters' mental disturbance are transformed into a social promise, as if what is sickness within present human relations will someday be the norm of healthy conduct. You are all "absurd," says Myshkin in a burst of prophetic inspiration before his epileptic collapse, therefore you are "superior people."

Myshkin is, of course, also a lone individual, moreover one who has come from abroad. "You are overardent—perhaps because of your solitude," says the old man at the engagement party, trying to calm him. Myshkin recognizes his isolation but claims, as he is about to be cast down, that he has made a start toward love and happiness. Before the new communion has been achieved all are sick, including the savior himself. Dostoyevsky can envision no cure for man in his present social condition, only possession by a higher spirit or Idea than the forces that now move him, a divine sickness as the alternative to the sickness stemming from the lust for sex or money.

But is there a "high" and a "low" in the domain of the abnormal? Confronted by the question of a hierarchy of metaphysical realms, Dostoyevsky demonstrates the toughness of his realism. For all his will to believe, he refuses to deny nature and take the religious way out. The good and evil effects of extreme experiences cannot always be separated. Meditating on his moments of illumination, Myshkin "often told himself that all these gleams and flashes of superior self-awareness and, hence, of a 'higher state of being,' were nothing other than sickness, the upsetting of the normal condition, and, if so, were not the highest state of being at all, but on the contrary had to be reckoned as the lowest." Like Freud or William Blake, Dostoyevsky is prepared to dissolve the distinction between highest and lowest. Myshkin *is* sick, as Rogozhin, Nastassya and Hippolite are sick, and all cures are for the future. The measure of their sickness is their departure from "the normal condition," that is, from the measure applied by medicine and by society. The last word in *The Idiot* is spoken by Madame Yepanchin as she turns away from Myshkin, now too far gone to recognize her. "Enough indulging our whims, it's time to be reasonable," she asserts, like a Chorus of Sophocles.

Yet for Dostoyevsky, Myshkin's higher experiences are justified by a value beyond society or its norms, including the norm of health. " 'What if it is a sickness?' he [Myshkin] asked himself. 'What does it matter if it is abnormal intensity, if the result, if the moment of awareness, remembered and analysed afterward in health, turns out to be the height of harmony and beauty, and gives an unheard-of and till then undreamed-of feeling of wholeness, of proportion, of reconciliation, and an ecstatic and prayerlike union in the highest synthesis of life?' " In the end Dostoyevsky's judgment is aesthetic—it is the "Beauty Will Save the World" theme that Aglaya warned Myshkin to avoid at the party. Myshkin's soliloquy on his vision of wholeness is a prose equivalent of Baudelaire's *"luxe, calme, ordre et volupté."* The highest attainment of life is not action but a condition of being in which the semifictional creatures that govern history give way before a harmony in which time has ceased and in which the instant expands itself indefinitely, as in the inspired state of the artist or in the eternal moment of the victim on the scaffold—that split second in which the epileptic Mahomet had "plenty of time to contemplate all the dwellings of Allah."

—HAROLD ROSENBERG

PART

ONE

Chapter ONE

About nine o'clock on a late November morning during a thaw, the train from Warsaw was nearing Petersburg at full speed. It was so wet and foggy that there was still hardly any light, and from the train windows it was difficult to distinguish anything ten yards on either side of the tracks. Among the passengers there were some returning from abroad, but the third-class compartments were the most crowded, mainly with ordinary people on business coming from no great distance. As usual, everyone was tired, everyone's eyes were heavy from a sleepless night, everyone was chilled to the bone, everyone's face shone with the yellow pallor of the fog.

By the window in one of the third-class cars two passengers had been facing each other since dawn, both of them young men, both with little luggage, both unfashionably dressed, both of rather striking appearance, and both wishing, finally, to open a conversation with each other. Had they known about one another and why they were both at that moment remarkable, they would certainly have marveled that chance had so strangely put them opposite each other in the third-class car of the Warsaw-Petersburg train. One of them was short, about twenty-seven, with black, curly hair and eyes that were small and gray, but ardent. His nose was broad and flat, his cheekbones high, his thin lips incessantly twisted into a sort of insolent, mocking, even malevolent smile, but his brow was high and well formed, and it redeemed the ignobleness of the lower part of his face. What was especially striking about his face was its deathly pallor, which gave the young man, despite his solid build, an appearance of exhaustion and at the same time a passionate, almost agonizingly passionate look, not in keeping with his coarse, insolent smile and his hard, self-satisfied expression. He was warmly dressed in a full, black, sheepskin-lined overcoat and had not felt the cold of the night, while his neighbor had received on his chilled back all the comfort of the damp Russian November night, for which he was obviously unprepared. He wore a rather large, thick cloak with an enormous hood, exactly like those sometimes worn in winter by travelers abroad, in Switzerland or, for instance, northern Italy, and who are not, of course, reckoning on such stretches as that from Eydkuhnen to Petersburg. But what was appropriate and completely satisfactory in Italy turned out to be not quite adequate in Russia. The owner of the hooded cloak was a young man, also about twenty-six or -seven years old, slightly taller than average, with very dense fair hair, hollow cheeks, and a narrow, pointed, almost white beard. His eyes were large, blue, and steady; there was something gentle but heavy in their gaze, something of that strange look by which some people can instantly tell an epileptic. The young man's face was pleasing, however; lean and fine-featured, though colorless, and, just now, blue with cold. From his hands there dangled an old and faded foulard knotted into a little bundle which apparently contained all his belongings. He wore thick-soled shoes and gaiters—nothing in Russian style. His dark-haired neighbor with the sheepskin-lined overcoat took all this in, partly from having nothing else to do, and at last —with that cold smile which can express with such casual indifference one's pleasure at the misfortunes of others—asked

"Chilly?"

And he tightened his shoulders solicitously.

"Very," replied his neighbor with great readiness, "and to think this is a thaw. What if it were a freeze? I didn't even think it could be so cold at home. I'm not used to it."

"From abroad, are you?"

"Yes, from Switzerland."

"Whew! Well, think of that!" The dark-haired individual whistled and laughed loudly.

They fell into conversation. The readiness of the fair-haired youth in the Swiss cape to respond to all questions put to him by his swarthy neighbor was remarkable, and he betrayed no suspicion of the utter unsuitability and pointlessness of some of them. In reply he made known that he had in fact been away from Russia for some time, almost four years, and that he had been sent abroad on account of sickness, some sort of strange nervous disease, like epilepsy or St. Vitus' dance, some kind of twitching and convulsions. The dark-haired person smiled unpleasantly several times as he listened, and he laughed outright when to his question "So they cured you?" the fair-haired one answered, "No, they did not."

"Ha! a lot of money must have gone down the drain, but we put our faith in them over here," said the dark one caustically.

"The veritable truth!" interrupted a shabbily dressed gentleman sitting nearby, the typical sort of functionary encrusted in the lower ranks of civil service, about forty, massively built, with a red nose and a pimply face. "The veritable truth, sir. All they do is milk us Russians, and what do we get for it?"

"Oh, how mistaken you are in my case!" said the Swiss patient in a gentle and appeasing voice. "Of course I can't argue because I don't know everything about it, but my doctor sacrificed to pay my train fare and had already kept me there on his own money for almost two years."

"So, no one to foot the bill, eh?" demanded the dark-haired one.

"No. Mr. Pavlishchev who had been supporting me there died two years ago. Then I wrote to a distant relative of mine, in Petersburg, a Madame Yepanchin, but I received no answer. So with that I've come back."

"Where are you coming back to?"

"You mean where am I staying? Well, the fact is I don't know yet. Wherever."

"Haven't made up your mind yet?" And both listeners burst out laughing again.

"And I suppose all you've got is tied up in that little bundle?" asked the dark-haired one.

"I'm ready to bet it is," put in the red-nosed functionary, highly satisfied. "And I'd bet he's got no more baggage in the baggage car—though poverty's no crime, as anyone ought to know."

This proved to be the case: the fair-haired young man admitted it at once with unusual readiness.

"Your bundle still has some significance," pursued the functionary when both had laughed their fill (it is noteworthy that the owner of the bundle himself finally started to laugh, gazing at them, which only increased their mirth), "even though one can bet there are no rolls of foreign goldpieces in it, no napoleons or ducats, as can plainly be seen if only by the gaiters over your foreign shoes, but if you add to your bundle the bonus of an alleged relative such as the wife of General Yepanchin, then the bundle takes on a rather different significance—assuming that Madame Yepanchin is in fact your relative, and that you haven't made an absentminded mistake, which is all too easy for anyone to do, out of—excess of imagination."

"Ah, there you have guessed right again," agreed the fair young man. "Indeed it is almost a mistake; that is, she is almost no relative. And so I was not at all surprised when she did not reply to me abroad. I expected it."

"So you threw away postage for nothing. At least you are direct and honest, and that's to your credit! As for General Yepanchin, I know him, sir; that is, he's a man everyone knows; as a matter of fact I also used to know the late Pavlishchev, who kept you in Switzerland, because there were two cousins. The other one is still in the Crimea. As for Nikolai Andreyevitch, the deceased one, he was a respected man and had connections and in his day owned four thousand souls, sir."

"That is right. His name was Nikolai Andreyevitch Pavlishchev," and, having replied, the young man looked intently and searchingly at the omniscient gentleman.

These omniscient gentlemen are sometimes, in fact rather often, found at a certain level of society. They know everything. All the restless inquisitiveness of their intellects is bent in a single direction, no doubt because of a lack of more important and more vital interests and opinions—as a modern thinker would say. By "everything," however, must be understood a rather limited area: where so-and-so works, who his acquaintances are, how much he is worth, where he was governor, whom he is married to, how much dowry she brought him, who his first cousins are, who his second cousins are, and other matters of this sort. Most often these all-knowing gentlemen go around out at the elbow and receive a salary of seventeen roubles a month. The people whose lives they know to the last detail would of course be at a loss to imagine what lies behind such curiosity, even though many such gentlemen take positive consolation from this knowledge, amounting, as it does, to an exact science, and derive from it not only their self-respect but the highest spiritual fulfillment. It is in fact a fascinating science. I have known scholars, writers, poets, and politicians who have found in this pursuit their loftiest satisfaction, their whole purpose in life, and owe to it alone the success of their careers.

Throughout the conversation, the dark-haired young man yawned, cast aimless glances out the window, and seemed impatient for the journey to end. He was preoccupied, in fact extremely preoccupied, almost perturbed, and even behaved quite strangely: sometimes he would seem to be attentive without hearing, then observant without noticing anything,

28

and sometimes he would laugh without the least idea of what he was laughing about.

"I beg your pardon," said the pimply gentleman, suddenly addressing the fair young man with the bundle, "whom have I the honor of—"

"Prince Lev Nikolayevitch Myshkin,*" replied the latter without the slightest hesitation.

"Prince Myshkin? Lev Nikolayevitch? Don't know it, sir. As a matter of fact I've never even heard of it," replied the functionary thoughtfully. "I don't mean the name of course; it's an historic name—you can certainly find it in Karamazin's *History*,* where it belongs—no, I'm referring to you personally, sir, for indeed there are no Prince Myshkins to be met anywhere now. You never even hear about them anymore."

"No, you certainly don't," replied the prince promptly. "There are no Prince Myshkins at all now, except myself. I seem to be the last one. As for our fathers' and grandfathers' generation, some of them only come down from peasant freeholders. My own father, by the way, was a sub-lieutenant in the army, after being a cadet. I can't tell you how General Yepanchin's wife came to be one of the princesses Myshkin; she also is the last one of her kind—"

"Ha, ha, ha," chortled the functionary. " 'The last one of her kind.' Ha, ha. How you put it!"

The dark-haired young man laughed too. The prince seemed somewhat surprised that he had made a joke, even a rather poor one.

"Believe me, I didn't mean to say it," he explained in bewilderment.

"Of course not! Of course you didn't, sir!" agreed the functionary gaily.

"Tell me, Prince, were you studying with that professor?" demanded the dark-haired young man suddenly.

"Yes, I have been learning—"

"Me, I've never studied anything."

"Well of course I only have a little," explained the prince, almost apologetically. "On account of my health they didn't feel a regular program of study was possible."

"Do you know the Rogozhins?" asked the dark-haired man abruptly.

"No. I don't happen to know them. Of course I know very few people in Russia. Are you a Rogozhin?"

"Yes I am. Parfyon."

* See Notes, page 633.

"Parfyon?" said the functionary with a marked air of importance. "Wouldn't you be one of the Rogozhins whose——"

"Yes, that's right, those, the very same," said the dark-haired young man with rude impatience, interrupting the pimply functionary whom he had not previously addressed, having spoken only to the prince.

"But—how can that be?" said the functionary, rigid with amazement, his eyes almost starting from his head, his whole face taking on an expression of mingled obsequiousness, reverence, and awe. "Then you must be related to the hereditary burgess* Semyon Parfyonovitch Rogozhin, who died last month and left a fortune of two and a half million?"

"And how do you know he left a capital of two and a half millions clear?" demanded the dark-haired young man, cutting him short without so much as a glance in his direction. "Look at him!" he winked at the prince, nodding at the functionary. "What do they get, suddenly falling all over you like that? It's perfectly true Father just died, and here I am returning home from Pskov a month later with practically no shoes on my feet. Neither my wretched brother or my mother send me either money or a word of news. Nothing. Treat me like a dog! I spent a whole month in Pskov in bed with a fever!"

"But now, just like that, you'll get hold of a sweet little million—at least. Oh my God!" exclaimed the functionary, clapping his hands together.

"What is it to him, I ask you!" said Rogozhin indicating the functionary with a gesture of angry irritation. "You wouldn't get a kopeck from me if you danced around on your head in front of me."

"I will! I will! I'll do exactly that!"

"You see! Well, I won't give you a thing, I won't—even if you danced around a whole week."

"Well, don't give me anything! It's just what I deserve. Don't! But I'll dance. I'll leave my wife and my children to dance in front of you. Oh, I'm making up to him!"

"Hang you!" spat the dark young man; then he turned to the prince again. "Five weeks ago I was just like you, with only a little bundle of things. I ran away from my father to my aunt in Pskov, where I took to bed with a high fever—and he kicked off without me being there. Just popped right off. Eternal peace to his ashes, but he nearly killed me that time! Would you believe it, Prince, so help me God. If I hadn't run away then he would have killed me."

"Did you make him angry somehow?" the prince asked, studying the millionaire in the sheepskin coat with particular

30

interest—though whatever fascination a million may have, as well as the fact of coming into an inheritance, it was something else that surprised and interested the prince. Besides, Rogozhin himself was taking special pleasure in conversing with the prince, more from a mechanical than any intellectual need, more as a pastime than from any true conviviality, from a state of emotional unrest, merely to have someone to look at and talk with about something. He could well have been still running a fever if not be actually delirious. As for the functionary, he was hanging on Rogozhin's every word, hardly daring to breathe, seizing and weighing everything he said as if he was hunting for a diamond.

"Oh yes, angry he certainly was, and perhaps for good reason," replied Rogozhin, "but it was my brother who really did it. I don't say a word about Mama. She's an old woman who reads the lives of the saints and sits with other old women—and whatever Brother Semyon says goes. And why didn't he send me word in time? I can tell you why! It's true that I was unconscious just then. They also say that a telegram was sent. Well, that telegram went to my aunt, who's been a widow for thirty years now and spends her days from morning to night sitting around with holy fools. Without really being a nun she's actually much worse. She was so terrified at the sight of the telegram she took it to the police station not daring to open it, and it's still there. It was Vassily Vassilitch Konyov who saved the day by letting me know what was going on. During the night my brother cut the gold tassels off the brocade over our father's coffin; 'Think how much money they're worth,' he said. Well, for this alone he could go to Siberia—if I wanted—because it's a sacrilege. Hey, you old scarecrow!" he said turning to the functionary. "What does the law say? Isn't that a sacrilege?"

"Sacrilege! Sacrilege!" agreed the functionary instantly.

"It'll get you to Siberia?"

"To Siberia! To Siberia! Straight to Siberia!"

"They all think I'm still sick," continued Rogozhin to the prince, "but without a word to anyone I climbed on the train, sick as I was, and off I go; you'll have to open the door to me, Semyon Semyonitch! He said bad things to my father about me, I know that much. Of course, as a matter of fact, I had got father good and mad with me over Nastassya Filippovna, that's true enough. There I'm to blame. I committed a sin."

"Over Nastassya Filippovna?" said the functionary in an obsequious tone, as if deliberating over something.

"But you don't know her!" Rogozhin shouted at him impatiently.

"But I do!" replied the functionary triumphantly.

"Do you now! Aren't there lots of Nastassya Filippovnas? And what an insolent creature you are, let me tell you! Well," he said to the prince, "I knew some bird like this would get hold of me!"

"Ah, but perhaps I do know!" teased the functionary. "Lebedev knows. Your Excellency is pleased to reproach me, but what would you say if I prove it? Yes, this is the very same Nastassya Filippovna for whom your father had the honor of caning you; her family name is Barashkov; she's highborn, you might say, a kind of a princess in her own way, and she is well acquainted with a certain Totsky, Afanassy Ivanovitch, and in unique relations with this gentleman, who is a landowner and a man of enormous wealth, a director of companies and syndicates, and on that account a great friend of General Yepanchin's—"

"Ah-ha! What's this?" said Rogozhin, genuinely surprised at last. "The devil if he doesn't really know!"

"Everything! Lebedev knows absolutely everything! For two months, Your Excellency, I went around with young Alex Likhachov, who'd just lost his father, too, and because I know my way around it finally got to where he couldn't take a step without Lebedev. Right now he's in debtor's prison. But for a while we had occasion to know Armance, Caralie, Princess Patsky, and also Nastassya Filippovna; there wasn't a great deal, in fact, that we didn't have occasion to know."

"Nastassya Filippovna? She and Likhachov were—?" Rogozhin glared angrily at him, his lips pale and trembling.

"Absolutely not!" said the functionary quickly, realizing what he had said. "There was nothing, absolutely nothing at all! What I m-mean is that for all his m-money Likhachov couldn't get anywhere. Nothing like with Armance. There's Totsky and only Totsky. Evenings she sits in her own box at the Bolshoi or the French Theater. The officers may talk about her a lot, but they can't prove a thing: 'Look, there's Nastassya Filippovna you've heard so much about.' But that's all. Nothing more. Nothing. Because there isn't anything more."

"That's how it is," confirmed Rogozhin, frowning gloomily. "That's exactly what Zalyozhnev once told me. One time, Prince, I was rushing across the Nevsky, wearing my father's three-year-old coat, and she stepped out of a shop and got into her carriage. Right then, the sight of her burned right through me. I met Zalyozhnev, he's not my kind at all, goes

32

around looking like a hairdresser's assistant, with a monocle stuck in his eye, while at our father's house we wore tarred boots and dined on thin cabbage soup. So Zalyozhnev says to me, 'She's not your kind, she's a princess,' he says, 'and her name's Nastassya Filippovna Barashkov, and she lives with Totsky, but Totsky doesn't know how to get rid of her, because he's fifty-five and he wants to marry the greatest beauty in St. Petersburg.' Right then he assured me that that very evening it was possible to see Nastassya Filippovna Barashkov at the ballet in her baignoire box at the Bolshoi Theater. At home at my father's just try to go to the ballet; it would be sheer agony—he'd murder you! Nevertheless I did run over to the ballet for an hour or so and saw Nastassya Filippovna again; I didn't sleep all night. The next morning my late father gave me two five-percent bonds worth five thousand roubles each and said, 'Go sell them. Then go to the Andreyevs' where you'll settle an account of seventy-five hundred roubles and bring me the rest of the ten thousand without stopping anywhere on your way back. I'll be waiting for you.' I sold the bonds, I pocketed the money, but instead of going to the Andreyevs' office I went straight to the English shop and for the entire proceeds picked out a pair of earrings, each one with a diamond almost as big as a walnut. I was short four hundred roubles but I told them my name and they trusted me for it. So off I go with the earrings to Zalyozhnev's: 'Let's go, old friend, come with me to Nastassya Filippovna's.' We went. Whatever happened on the way I don't have the slightest idea, I can't remember a thing. We went right into her main drawing room, and she came out to meet us, herself. At that point I didn't say who I was, but Zalyozhnev says, 'These are from Parfyon, from Rogozhin, in memory of meeting you yesterday. Do him the honor of accepting them.' She opened the box, took a look, smiled, and said, 'Thank your friend Mr. Rogozhin for his kind attention.' She bowed and left. Why I didn't drop dead at that instant I'll never know! And actually, before I went there I never thought of coming back alive anyway! What really mortified me was the way that beast Zalyozhnev came off so well. I'm short and I'm dressed like a lout and I just stand there not saying anything, with my eyes popping out at her, because I'm ashamed; while he's dressed up in the latest fashion, his hair pomaded and curled, rosy-cheeked, with a check cravat and bowing in every direction, and she certainly must have taken him for me. As we left I said to him, 'Don't be getting any ideas now, understand?' He laughed and said, 'And how are you going to explain things to your father now?' And as a matter of fact at that moment I wanted to jump in the river rather than go back home; then I thought to myself: what difference does it make?—and I went home like a damned outcast."

"Ah-ha!" cried the functionary in an exaggerated, squirming manner, actually shuddering. "The dear departed would have done a man in, not for ten thousand roubles but for ten!" he said, nodding his head to the prince.

The latter regarded Rogozhin with interest; Rogozhin appeared even paler than usual at that moment.

"Done a man in!" he said. "What do you know about it?" Again he addressed the prince. "My father found out about everything immediately, and Zalyozhnev went around telling everyone the whole story. He took me upstairs, shut us in, and gave it to me good for a whole hour. 'That's only a taste,' he says, 'I'll come back again to say goodnight to you.' And what do you think? The old fellow went to Nastassya Filippovna's, bowed down to the floor to her, begged and wept. Finally she brought the box and threw it at him. 'There,' she says, 'you old graybeard, there are your earrings! Now they're ten times more dear to me since Parfyon got them for me in the face of such a storm. Give my regards to Parfyon Semyonovitch, and thank him.' And meantime, with my mother's blessing I borrowed twenty roubles from Sergei Protushin to take the train for Pskov, and I arrived with a fever, and to cure me the old ladies started reading the lives of the saints to me, and I sat there drunk. Then I went around from tavern to tavern with the last money I had, and I lay unconscious in the street all night, and in the morning I had a burning fever, besides which the dogs had been taking bites out of me, and I barely came to my senses at all."

"Well, sir," chuckled the functionary, rubbing his hands, "now Nastassya Filippovna will be singing a different tune! Now what about the earrings? Now we will make it up to her with *such* earrings—"

"As for that," said Rogozhin, seizing him violently by the arm, "if you say one more word about Nastassya Filippovna I'll beat you, God help me, for all your running around with Likhachov!"

"And if you beat me it means you won't be getting rid of me! Beat me and you'll have me for sure! Beat me and you put your personal seal on me! But here, we've arrived."

They were, in fact, entering the station. Although Rogozhin had said he had come away secretly, several men were there waiting for him. They called out to him and waved their caps.

"Good Lord, there's Zalyozhnev!" said Rogozhin looking at them with a triumphant, somehow malevolent smile. Then he suddenly turned to the prince. "Prince, for some reason I've taken a strong liking to you. Perhaps it's because I've met you at a time like this; but then I met him too," he pointed to Lebedev. "And I've taken no liking to him. Come visit me, Prince. We'll get rid of those gaiters of yours, and I'll dress you up in a fine fur coat of martin. I'll have the best evening clothes made for you, with a white waistcoat—unless you prefer some other kind, and I'll stuff your pockets with money and—we'll go to Nastassya Filippovna's! Will you come or no?"

"Don't miss that, Prince Lev Nikolayevitch!" said Lebedev, with impressive solemnity, "Oh, be careful not to miss out on that!"

Prince Myshkin stood up, politely offered his hand to Rogozhin and said, "I shall come with the greatest pleasure, and I am very grateful to you for liking me. Perhaps I may even come today if I've time. Because I will tell you frankly that you appealed to me, too, especially when you were telling me about the diamond earrings. You had appealed to me even before the earrings, although you have a gloomy face. Thank you also for promising me the clothes, and the fur coat, for in fact I shall soon be needing both. As for the money, at the present moment I hardly have a kopeck."

"There will be money by evening. Come!"

"Yes, there will! There will!" echoed the functionary. "By the evening, before nightfall, there'll be money!"

"As for the female sex, Prince, do you care for that? Speak frankly."

"I—n-no. Of course— Perhaps you don't know, but on account of my illness I don't know women at all."

"Ah!" exclaimed Rogozhin, "if it's that way, Prince, you are a true holy innocent, and God loves people like you!"

"The Lord God loves people like you," echoed the functionary.

"As for you, scribbler, follow me," said Rogozhin to Lebedev, and they all got off the train.

So Lebedev ended up getting what he wanted. The noisy group soon left the station in the direction of Voznessensky Prospect. The prince was left to go toward Liteyny. It was damp and rainy. The prince questioned some passer-by; the distance he had to go was about two miles, and he decided to take a cab.

35

Chapter TWO

∽✵∾

General Yepanchin lived in a house of his own, not far from Liteyny, near the Church of the Transfiguration. Besides this (excellent) house, five-sixths of which was rented out, General Yepanchin owned still another enormous house on Sadovaya Street, which also brought him an important income. Besides these two houses, he had a large and very profitable estate near Petersburg and a factory of some sort in the same area. It was well known that General Yepanchin had participated in government monopolies in the past. At present he participated and had a strong voice in several substantial stock companies. He was known as a man of big money, big operations, big connections. In certain circles he knew how to render himself absolutely indispensable, among others, in his own branch of the administration. At the same time it was also well known that Ivan Fyodorovitch Yepanchin was a man of no education who had started as the son of an ordinary soldier, facts which undoubtedly reflected only honor upon him; but the general, although an intelligent man, was also not without his petty and quite excusable weaknesses and did not enjoy allusions to certain things. But intelligent and adroit he unquestionably was. For example, he made it a rule not to put himself forward when it was essential to stay in the background, and many people appreciated in him precisely this ingenuousness, precisely this quality of always knowing his place. Yet if those who judged him thus could have seen what sometimes transpired in the soul of Ivan Fyodorovitch, who knew his place so well! Though he did in fact have a practical sense and an experience with daily affairs, and some very remarkable ability, he liked to present himself not as an independent-minded man but as one who executed the ideas of others, a person of "devotion without flattery"* and—perhaps a sign of the times?—as a true openhearted Russian. In this connection some rather amusing adventures befell him—but the general was never the man to lose heart even in the face of the most amusing adventures.

Moreover he was lucky, even at cards, and he played for high stakes, intentionally not concealing this little weakness, as he called it, which had occasionally proved quite profitable to him, and actually playing it up. He moved in a mixed society, but of course one composed entirely of people of "influence." Yet everything was ahead of him, there was plenty of time, plenty of time for everything, and everything was bound to come in its own time. And too, General Yepanchin was still in what might be called full sap, he was no more than fifty-six, in the flower of manhood, when a man begins leading his *real* life. His health, his good color, his sound though discolored teeth, his stocky, vigorous build, his preoccupied expression in the morning at his office, his jovial one in the evening at cards or at His Grace's—all this contributed to his successes, present and future, and carpeted His Excellency's path with roses.

The general was the head of a flourishing family. To be sure, all was not roses there, but there was much upon which His Excellency's fondest hopes and aims had long been earnestly centered. And indeed, are there aims in life more sacred than paternal ones? What, after all, should a man devote himself to if not his family? The general's family consisted of his wife and three grown daughters. He had married a very long time before, when still only a lieutenant, a girl almost his own age, who had neither beauty nor education, with whom he took a dowry of only fifty souls that served, it was true, as the cornerstone of his future fortune. But in later years the general never complained about his early marriage, never attributed it to the rash folly of youth, and he so respected his wife, and at times so feared her, that he actually, in fact, loved her. The general's wife was a Princess Myshkin, a very ancient though not particularly brilliant family, and she had a high opinion of herself on account of her birth. A certain influential person, one of those patrons whose patronage costs them nothing, had consented to take an interest in the young princess's marriage. He caused doors to open for the young officer and pushed him inside, though no push had been necessary; a mere glance would have served and never been wasted! With a few exceptions the couple had lived the whole of their long and happy union in a state of harmony. In her very early years, the general's wife had known how to find certain protectresses in the highest circles, both because she was a princess by birth and the last of her house and possibly too because of her personal qualities. Later, when her husband had acquired wealth and administrative rank, she had even begun to feel at home in these exalted circles.

37

During these later years the general's three daughters—Alexandra, Adelaïda and Aglaya—had grown up and matured. True, all three were only Yepanchins, but through their mother they were of a princely line, with dowries that were by no means small, with a father who could reasonably aspire to a very high position one day, and—something which was also rather important—all three were remarkably good looking, not excepting the eldest, Alexandra, who was already twenty-five. The middle one was twenty-three, and the youngest, Aglaya, had just turned twenty. This youngest daughter was in fact a real beauty and was beginning to attract considerable attention in society. But this was still not everything: all three were distinguished by their education, cleverness, and accomplishments. It was known that they were remarkably fond of one another and rose to each other's support. People even spoke of sacrifices made by the elder two on behalf of the youngest, the idol of the household. They not only disliked putting themselves forward in society but were modest to a fault. No one could reproach them for being haughty or aggressive, though it was known that they were proud and knew their value. The eldest was a musician, the middle girl was a remarkable painter, though for many years practically no one had known about this and it had been discovered only quite recently by accident. In a word, many flattering things were said of them. But there was some criticism. People spoke with horror of the number of books they had read. They were in no hurry to marry, and while they valued the circle of society they belonged to, they did not overvalue it. This was all the more remarkable in that everyone knew of the attitudes, the character, the aims, and the desires of their father.

It was already almost eleven o'clock when the prince rang at the general's lodgings. The general lived on the second floor and occupied a fairly modest apartment, though one still in keeping with his importance. A liveried servant opened the door, and the prince had to enter into long explanations with this man, who had from the start regarded both his person and his bundle with suspicion. Finally, on his repeated and exact assurance that he was really Prince Myshkin and that it was absolutely necessary for him to see the general on a matter of urgency, the perplexed servant conducted him into a little anteroom between the reception hall and the general's study, handing him on to another man, whose function was to announce the morning visitors to the general. This second individual, dressed in a tailcoat, was past forty and wore a concerned expression. He was the special

38

administrative assistant who announced His Excellency's visitors and therefore had no doubts about his own worth.

"Kindly wait in the reception hall but leave your bundle here," he said, as he seated himself ceremoniously in his armchair, looking with stern astonishment at the prince, who had sat down on a chair next to his own with his bundle in his hands.

"If you don't mind," said the prince, "I'd rather wait here with you. What would I do in there all alone?"

"You can't stay in the anteroom, because you're a visitor, in other words a guest. Are you here to see the general himself?"

Evidently the servant could not reconcile himself to the idea of admitting such a visitor and was determined to question him once again.

"Yes, I have business—" began the prince.

"I am not asking you what business: *my* business is only to announce you. But as I said, without the secretary here I can't announce you."

The man's suspicions were obviously increasing moment by moment, so little did the prince resemble the everyday sort of visitor; and although the general received often, almost daily at a certain hour, visitors of the most varied description, particularly on business, the servant, despite this experience and the latitude of his instructions, felt the gravest doubts, and the intervention of the secretary appeared to him essential before he announced his visitor.

"And you are really—from abroad?" he asked almost involuntarily at last—and lost track of his thought. Possibly he had wanted to ask, "And are you really Prince Myshkin?"

"Yes, I just got off the train. It seems to me you want to ask, 'Am I really Prince Myshkin?' but did not, out of politeness."

"Hmm!" the astonished servant grunted.

"I assure you that I have not lied to you and that you will not have to answer on my account. And there is nothing surprising in my appearance, with this little bundle; at present my circumstances are not particularly bright."

"Hmm. You see, it's not that I'm worried. My duty is to announce you, and no doubt the secretary will see you, unless you—that is precisely it— You are not here to solicit the general for assistance, if I may venture to ask?"

"Oh no, you can be absolutely sure about that. My business is quite different."

"You must excuse me, but the question just came to me as I was—looking at you. Wait for the secretary; His Excellency is engaged with the colonel just now; after that the secretary will come—the secretary, that is, of the Company."

"Well, if I am to have a long wait, may I ask if there is anywhere here I could smoke. I have my pipe and tobacco with me."

"Smoke?" said the attendant with contemptuous surprise, looking at him as if he didn't believe his ears. "Smoke? No, you may not smoke here. and it's disgraceful even to think of such a thing. Oh, this is something!"

"Oh, of course I didn't mean in this room, I understand that; but I would have gone anywhere else you could have shown me. I am used to having a smoke and haven't had one for three hours now. But it's as you please. You know the saying, 'When in Rome—' "

"Now, how am I going to announce someone like you?" muttered the attendant, almost involuntarily. "In the first place you're not supposed to be here, you ought to be in the waiting room, because you're a visitor, which makes you a guest, and I'll have to answer for it— You're not planning on living with us, are you?" he added, glancing once again at the prince's bundle, which obviously still disturbed him.

"No, I don't think so. Even if they did invite me I wouldn't stay. I have merely come to make their acquaintance and nothing more."

"What? To make their acquaintance?" demanded the attendant in amazement, his suspicions redoubled. "Why did you say before that you'd come on business?"

"Oh, it's hardly business at all. That is, if you like I have one piece of business, a matter of asking advice, but mainly I want to introduce myself because I am a Prince Myshkin and the general's wife is a Princess Myshkin, the last, and besides her and myself there are no more Myshkins left."

"You're not a relative too?" said the servant with a start, looking frightened.

"Oh, hardly. Of course, if you stretch a point I am a relative, but so distant that it doesn't really matter. Once I wrote a letter to Madame Yepanchin from abroad, but she didn't answer me. Still, I felt I had to establish a connection on my return. I tell you all this to reassure you, because I see you are still worried: announce 'Prince Myshkin' and that in itself will make plain the reason for my visit. If I am received— very well; if not—that could be just as well. Only it doesn't seem to me they can refuse to see me. Madame Yepanchin will certainly want to see the last and only representative of her own line, and she values her own ancestry highly, I have heard that pointedly said of her."

The prince's conversation seemed to be perfectly natural, but this very naturalness made it all the more absurd in the present situation, and the attendant, who was experienced, could only feel that what might be completely suitable between one man and another was completely inappropriate between a guest and the master's man. And as servants are far more intelligent than they are usually thought to be by their masters, it occurred to the attendant that there were two possibilities: either the prince was some kind of cadger who had come to beg on account of his poverty, or the prince was simply a poor fool with no ambition; because an intelligent prince, with any ambition, would not have sat in the antechamber discussing his affairs with a servant. Consequently, in either case, wouldn't he get into trouble over him?

"Even so," he said as insistently as possible, "please wait in the waiting room."

"Yes, but if I was sitting in there I couldn't have told you all this," said the prince with a gay laugh, "and consequently you would still be worried at the sight of my cape and my bundle. But perhaps now there is no point in your waiting for the secretary, and you could go announce me yourself."

"I can't announce a visitor like you without the secretary, and what's more, His Excellency has just given orders he is not to be disturbed for anyone while the colonel is there. Gavril Ardalionovitch goes in unannounced."

"Some functionary?"

"Gavril Ardalionovitch? No. He serves with the Company on his own account. At least put that bundle of yours down here."

"I was thinking of doing that, if you'll permit me. And what do you think—should I take off my cape?"

"Of course. You can't go in to him wearing a cape."

The prince stood up and hurriedly took off his cape and appeared in a fairly acceptable, well-cut though worn jacket. Across his waistcoat ran a steel chain, on the end of which was a silver Geneva watch.

Although the prince was a sorry fool—the servant had made up his mind about that—nevertheless it finally appeared improper to the general's attendant that he continue in conversation with the visitor in spite of the fact that for some reason he had rather taken to the prince in a certain way. But from another aspect he aroused in him a very decided, very deep indignation.

"And Madame Yepanchin, when does she receive visitors?" asked the prince, sitting down again in the same place.

"That's not my business, sir. She receives differently ac-

cording to who the person is. The dressmaker would be admitted at eleven. Gavril Ardalionovitch is also admitted ahead
of others; sometimes he's even admitted for early lunch."

"Your rooms are kept warmer here in winter than they are
abroad," observed the prince, "but out of doors it's warmer
there than here at home. A Russian who isn't used to it finds
it impossible to live in their houses in winter."

"They don't heat?"

"No, and the houses are built differently. The stoves and
windows are different."

"Hmm. Have you been traveling long, sir?"

"Yes. Four years. But most of the time I stayed in the
same place. In the country."

"You've lost touch with us, sir?"

"That's true. Believe me, I'm surprised to find I haven't
forgotten how to speak Russian. Right now as I talk with you
I think, 'How really well I am doing.' Perhaps that is why
I'm talking so much. In fact, since yesterday I've wanted just
to go on and on speaking Russian."

"Hmm! Well! Did you used to live here in Petersburg before, sir?" (In spite of his efforts the servant found it impossible not to continue such a polite and proper conversation.)

"In Petersburg? Hardly at all, only passing through. And
in those days I knew nothing of what went on here, though
now they say that so much is new that whoever knew about
it before has to learn it over again. Right now you hear a lot
said about the new criminal courts."*

"Hmm! Courts. Yes, there are, certainly, the courts. Tell
me. how is it there? Is there more justice in the courts or
not?"

"I don't know. I have heard much good said of ours. And
besides we do not have capital punishment."

"Do they execute people there?"

"Yes. I saw it in France. In Lyons. Schneider took me with
him."

"They hang them?"

"No. In France they always cut their heads off."

"What do they do—scream?"

"Of course not! It's done in an instant. They lie the man
down, and this broad knife falls through a machine they call
the guillotine—very powerfully and heavily—the head flies
off before you can blink an eye. The preparations are horrible. When they read the death sentence, dress him and prepare him, tie him up and drag him onto the scaffold—all
that is dreadful! People crowd in, even women—they don't
like women to look on though."

"It's not their business."

"Of course not! Of course not! Such torture— The criminal was a middle-aged man, strong, fearless, intelligent. Legros was his name. Oh I tell you, believe me or not, he was white as paper as he was climbing the scaffold—and crying. Can this be? Is this not terrible? Who cries from fright? I didn't believe one could cry from sheer fright, not a child but a man who never cried, a man forty-five years old. What goes on inside a person at that moment, what kind of agony is he put through? It's an outrage to the spirit, nothing less! Does 'Thou shalt not kill' mean that because he has killed he shall in turn be killed? No, this cannot be. It is a month now since I saw this thing, and ever since it's been before my eyes. Five times I've dreamed of it."

The prince became quite moved as he talked, a faint color appeared in his pallid face, though he was speaking as quietly as before. The attendant followed him with interested attention, as if unwilling to stop listening. Perhaps he too was a man of imagination and a thoughtful turn of mind.

"At least it's a good thing," he observed, "there is little suffering when the head falls off."

"Do you know," said the prince feelingly, "you have just made that observation, and many people have said the same thing, and this was why they invented the machine called the guillotine. But the thought crossed my mind then: what if this was even worse? That will seem absurd and wild to you, but with a little imagination such a thought is possible. Think! When there is torture there is pain and wounds, physical agony, and all this distracts the mind from mental suffering, so that one is tormented only by the wounds until the moment of death. But the most terrible agony may not be in the wounds themselves but in knowing for certain that within an hour, then within ten minutes, then within half a minute, now at this very instant—your soul will leave your body and you will no longer be a person, and that this is certain; the worst thing is that it is *certain*. Just when you put your head under the knife itself and hear it sliding above your head, well, that quarter of a second is the most terrifying of all. Do you understand? This is no fantasy of mine, many people have said the same thing. I believe it so completely that I shall tell you frankly what I think. Killing someone for having murdered is a punishment infinitely more terrible than a murder by bandits. Whoever is murdered by bandits, knifed at night in the woods or somewhere like that, inevitably hopes until the very last moment that he will manage to save himself. There have been cases of people with their throats

43

already slit still hoping, or running away, or pleading. But here all final hope, with which it is ten times easier to die, is removed *for certain;* here there is a sentence, and in the very fact that there is certainly no escape from it all the horrible suffering lies, and there is no suffering on earth greater than this. Take a soldier and put him in front of a cannon in the midst of battle and shoot at him, he will still hope; but read this same soldier a death sentence which is certain, and he will lose his mind or begin to cry. Who could say that human nature can endure such a trial without slipping into madness? Why this ghastly, needless, useless outrage? Perhaps there is a man to whom the death sentence was read and who was allowed to suffer and was then told, 'Go. You are pardoned.' Perhaps such a man could tell us something. This was the agony and the horror of which Christ told, too. No, you cannot treat a man like this!"

Though he might not have been able to express these ideas in the same terms as the prince, the servant unquestionably grasped the essentials of what he was saying—if not everything—for his face showed plainly that he had been moved.

"If you really want to smoke, sir," he said, "it might be arranged, but you would have to be quick about it. What if he suddenly asks for you and you aren't here? Over there under that little stairway you see a door. Go in the door, on your right there's a little room where you can do it, but open the window vent because you're not supposed—"

But the prince had no time to go for his smoke. A young man suddenly entered the antechamber, carrying papers in his hand. The attendant went to help him off with his fur overcoat. Out of the corner of his eye, the young man examined the prince.

"Gavril Ardalionovitch," began the attendant in a confidential and almost familiar manner, "this gentleman has announced himself as Prince Myshkin and a relative of the mistress'. He has just arrived by train from abroad, carrying the bundle, only—"

The prince did not catch the rest that was said because the attendant began whispering. Gavril Ardalionovitch listened attentively, looking at the prince with much curiosity; then at last, ceasing to listen, he approached him impetuously.

"You are Prince Myshkin?" he asked him with extreme amiability and politeness. He was a very handsome young man, also about twenty-eight, slender, blond, of medium height, wearing a small imperial, with an intelligent and even beautiful face. Only his smile, for all its amiability, was somehow a trifle too refined, his teeth showing with somewhat too

44

much pearly regularity; and his way of looking at one, for all his gaiety and apparent sincerity, was somehow a trifle too watchful and searching.

"When he is alone he can't possibly look that way and probably never laughs at all," the prince could not help feeling. He rapidly explained all he could, almost exactly what he had already told the servant and, still earlier, Rogozhin. Meanwhile, Gavril Ardalionovitch seemed to be recollecting something.

"Was it not you, sir," he inquired, "who about a year ago or a bit less sent a letter—possibly from Switzerland—to Lizaveta Prokofyevna?"

"Yes."

"Then you are known here and certainly remembered. Do you wish to see His Excellency? I'll announce you presently. He'll be free in a moment. Only you— Only in the meantime please step into the reception room. Why is the gentleman in here?" he demanded sternly of the attendant.

"I tell you, the gentleman himself—"

At that moment the door to the study suddenly opened and a military officer carrying a briefcase bowed himself out the door, talking loudly.

"Are you there, Ganya?" called a voice from inside the study. "Well, come in here." Gavril Ardalionovitch nodded to the prince and hastily went into the study.

Less than two minutes later the door opened again and the sonorous voice of Gavril Ardalionovitch said affably, "Please do come in, Prince."

Chapter THREE

General Ivan Fyodorovitch Yepanchin stood in the middle of his study and looked at the prince with great curiosity as he entered the room. He even advanced two steps toward him. The prince approached and introduced himself.

"Very well, sir," said the general. "Now what can I do for you?"

"I have no pressing business of any kind. My purpose in

coming was simply to make your acquaintance. I wouldn't wish to disturb you as I have no idea on which days you receive or what your arrangements are for seeing people. But I have just come from the train. I arrived from Switzerland."

The general was about to smile but thought and checked himself; then he thought some more, squinted, and again surveyed his guest from head to toe; then he abruptly motioned him to a chair, sat down himself at a slight angle to the prince, and turned to face him with impatient expectation. Ganya stood at a desk in a corner of the room sorting papers.

"As a rule I have little time for making acquaintances," said the general, "but as you have no doubt an object in mind, I—"

"I did expect," interrupted the prince, "that you would look for some special motive in my visit. But apart from the pleasure of meeting you I have no particular reason whatsoever."

"It is of course an extreme pleasure for me as well, but pleasure isn't everything. Sometimes, as you know, there is business to attend to. Besides, up to now I fail entirely to find anything in common between us; that is to say, any reasons for—"

"There are certainly no reasons, and we have, of course, little in common. For if I am a Prince Myshkin and your wife is of the same family, this is obviously no reason at all. I understand that very well. And yet that is all that has brought me. I have been four years out of Russia—too long; and what's more when I left I was hardly in my right mind! I didn't know a thing then, and now it's much worse. I have need of good people, and there is a certain matter of business I don't know how to manage. Even back in Berlin, I thought to myself, 'They are the next thing to relatives, let me start with them; perhaps we can be helpful to each other, they to me and I to them—if they are good people.' And I have heard that you are."

"Much obliged, sir," said the general, astounded. "May I inquire where you are staying?"

"I am not staying anywhere as yet."

"Do you mean to say you have come straight from the train to me? And—with baggage?"

"Yes, though all I have in the way of baggage is one small bundle with my linen, and nothing else. I usually just carry it in my hand. I'll be able to find a hotel room this evening."

"Then you do intend to take a hotel room?"

"Oh, yes. Certainly."

"From what you said I thought you had come directly here to stay with me."

"That could be, but only with your invitation. Not otherwise. I confess, though, that even with your invitation I wouldn't have stayed, not for any reason in particular, except —it's the way I am."

"So it seems it's just as well I didn't invite you and that I'm not going to invite you. And allow me, Prince, so as to make things perfectly clear once and for all: since we're already agreed there can be no question of any family relationship between us—though naturally it would have been very flattering to me—but—"

"So I should get up and leave?" said the prince, rising, somehow managing to laugh with genuine good humor in spite of the difficulty of his position. "Really, General, while I know nothing of practical affairs nor of your customs nor even how people live here, I thought all along this is how things were bound to turn out between us. Well, perhaps it's the way it should be— And you didn't answer my letter. So good-bye and excuse me for disturbing you."

The prince's expression was so full of friendliness at this instant, and his smile so free of any hint of concealed resentment, that the general suddenly stopped and regarded his guest in a different manner, this transformation of the general's expression taking place in a single instant.

"But look here, Prince," he said in a completely altered voice, "I don't know you, after all, and Lizaveta Prokofyevna will probably want to have a look at a person bearing the same name as her own. Do wait if you like, if your time allows."

"Oh, my time allows, my time is entirely my own," (and the prince promptly placed his soft round hat on the table). "I confess that I was hoping Lizaveta Prokofyevna would perhaps recall that I had written her. Just now while I was waiting, your servant suspected that I had come to you for money; I noticed this; it must be that you have left very strict instructions on this subject; but I am really not here for that, I am really here only to meet people. But I'm afraid I have disturbed you, and this troubles me."

"Well then, Prince," said the general with a cheerful smile, "if you're really the sort of person you seem to be, then it will be a pleasure, I dare say, to make your acquaintance; only, you see, I'm a busy man, and in a moment I'll be sitting down again to look over some papers and sign them, then I'll be off to see His Grace, and then to the Department, so it works out that while I'm happy to see people—good ones, that is—still— However, I am sure that you are perfectly well brought up, so that— How old are you, Prince?"

"Twenty-six."

"Oh! I supposed you much younger."

"Yes, they say I have a young face. But as for disturbing you, I'll soon learn not to, because I hate to disturb people— And besides we seem to be so different—for so many reasons, that perhaps we can't have much in common, though, you know, I don't believe this myself, since it often only appears there is nothing in common when there actually is— Human laziness makes people pigeonhole one another at first sight so they do find nothing in common— But perhaps I am getting boring? I think you—"

"Two things: do you have any means at all? Or perhaps you intend to undertake some occupation or other? Excuse me for being so—"

"I beg you, sir. I perfectly appreciate your question, and I do understand it. For the moment I have no means whatever and also, for the moment, no occupation; though I need one. The money I did have was someone else's, given me by Schneider, the professor with whom I underwent treatment and studied in Switzerland. He gave me no more than the exact sum for my fare, so that the only money I have left now is a few kopecks. It is true that I have one business affair and I need advice, but—"

"Tell me, how do you intend to live in the meantime and what are your plans?" asked the general.

"I wanted to do work of some sort."

"Oh, so you are a philosopher! But, after all, are you aware of having any talents, or any aptitudes whatever, that is to say of the sort by which you can earn your daily bread? Once again, excuse me—"

"Oh, don't apologize. No, I don't believe I have any talents or special aptitudes; rather the contrary, because I am an invalid and didn't study regularly. As for my daily bread, it seems to me—"

Again the general interrupted and again began questioning. And the prince told him everything that has been already told. It developed that the general had heard of the late Pavlishchev and even had known him personally. Just why Pavlishchev had taken an interest in his education the prince himself could not explain; it was perhaps simply because of an old friendship with his late father. After the death of his parents when still a small child, the prince grew up and spent all his life in villages because his state of health demanded country air. Pavlishchev had placed him in the care of elderly country ladies, property owners and relatives of his; a governess was engaged for him, then a tutor; he declared moreover that while he remembered everything, there was little he could explain satisfactorily because there was so much he could not account for. Frequent attacks of his illness made him almost an idiot (the prince used that word: idiot). Then he told that in Berlin Pavlishchev had met Professor Schneider, a Swiss, whose specialty was such diseases and who had an institution in the Swiss canton of Valais, where he treated idiocy and insanity by his own methods of cold water therapy and gymnastics, educating his patients as well, and in general looking after their mental development; and that Pavlishchev had sent him to Schneider in Switzerland almost five years ago and had died suddenly two years ago leaving no provision for him; and that Schneider had kept him on for two years more and completed the treatments; but that he had not cured him though he had greatly helped him; and that, at last, at his own request, because of a particular situation which had arisen, he had now sent him back to Russia.

The general was very surprised. "So you have no one in Russia, absolutely no one?" he asked.

"No one now, but I hope— I have received a letter—"

"But at least," interrupted the general, having not listened to the mention of the letter, "at least you were trained for something and your illness wouldn't prevent you from taking some kind of easy administrative post, would it?"

"Oh, it certainly would not prevent me. I'd even like very much to take one because I'd like to find out what I am suited for myself. I've studied continuously for the past four years, though not quite in the regular way but according to his special system, and besides this I managed to read a great many Russian books."

"Russian books? Then you know grammar and you can write without errors?"

"Yes, indeed I can."

"Very good. How about your handwriting?"

"My handwriting is excellent. There you could say I do have a talent and that I'm even a calligrapher. If you'll allow me, I'll write something for you by way of a sample," said the prince eagerly.

"Please do. In fact it would not be a bad idea— I like this readiness of yours, Prince; you certainly are a very nice person."

"You have such fine writing materials, and how many pencils, and so many pens, and what fine thick paper. And what a fine study you have! There's a landscape I know: it's a view of Switzerland. I am sure the artist painted it from nature. And I am sure I've seen the place itself; it's in the canton of Uri—"

"Very likely, though it was bought here. Ganya, give the prince some paper. Here are pens and paper; please sit at that little table. What's this?" the general demanded of Ganya, who in the meantime had taken a large photograph from his briefcase and handed it to him. "Ah! It's Nastassya Filippovna! She herself sent it to you personally, herself, did she?" he asked Ganya excitedly and with great curiosity.

"She gave it to me just now, when I was there to congratulate her. I'd asked her for it a long time ago. I don't know, but it might have been an allusion to the fact that I arrived with no present on such a day," added Ganya with an unpleasant smile.

"Oh, no," said the general with conviction, "really, what a strange turn of mind you have! Why would she bother with allusions— She's completely unmercenary. And besides, what sort of present would you give her—you'd need thousands of roubles for that! Maybe your portrait? By the way, she hasn't asked you for your portrait yet, has she?"

"No, she hasn't yet. And perhaps, of course, she never will ask for it. Ivan Fyodorovitch, you haven't forgotten about the party this evening, have you? You are one of the people specially invited."

"I remember, I certainly do remember, and I am coming. I should say so—her birthday, twenty-five years old! Yes! You know, Ganya, I'm going to let you in on something; prepare yourself. She has promised Afanassy Ivanovitch and me that today, this very evening at her house, she'll say the final word: is it to be or not to be. So there you have it."

Ganya was suddenly so upset that he turned slightly pale. "She actually said that?" he asked, in a voice that seemed to quaver.

"She gave her word the day before yesterday. The two of us pressed her so hard she gave in. But she asked that you not be told beforehand."

The general studied Ganya intently; he was clearly displeased by his discomfiture.

"Remember, Ivan Fyodorovitch," said Ganya uneasily and with hesitation, "remember she has given me full freedom to decide up to the time she has made up her own mind; and even then I still have the final say—"

"Then could you—could you?—" The general was suddenly alarmed.

"I didn't say anything."

"Good Lord, what kind of a position do you want to put us in?"

"I'm not refusing. Perhaps I expressed myself badly."

"Refusing indeed!" said the general with an annoyance he did not even care to conceal. "Look here, my friend, it's not a question of your not refusing but of the eagerness, the happiness, and the delight with which you receive her consent— How are things getting on at home?"

"At home? At home everything goes my way; except that as usual, Father is playing the fool, but then of course he's turned into an absolute disgrace. I don't speak to him anymore, but I keep him under my thumb; and believe me, if it wasn't for Mother I'd show him the door. Mother, of course, is always crying, and my sister's in a temper, and I finally told them right out I was going to lead my own life and that at home I expected to be obeyed. In any case I made this all quite clear to my sister in my mother's presence."

"But my dear fellow, I still don't understand," said the general reflectively, with a shrug and a gesture of bewilderment. "Nina Alexandrovna was moaning and sighing when she came here the other day, remember? 'What's the matter?' I asked. It seems they find it would be a *dishonor:* Where's the dishonor in that, I ask you? Who can reproach Nastassya Filippovna with anything? What can they hold against her? Not the fact she's been living with Totsky, certainly? That is such absolute nonsense, especially under the circumstances. 'You wouldn't allow her in the company of your daughters?' she said to me. Well, Good Lord! That's Nina Alexandrovna! I mean, how can she fail to understand— How can she fail to understand—"

"Her own position?" Ganya prompted the general. "She understands it, don't be upset with her. But I did give her a good lecture about not meddling in other people's affairs. Still, so far everything is holding together at home only because the final word hasn't been said yet; but the storm will break. If the final word is said today, everything will be out in the open."

The prince heard all of this conversation as he sat in a corner of the room doing his calligraphic specimen. He finished, approached the table, and presented his page.

"So this is Nastassya Filippovna?" he said, looking with intent curiosity at the portrait. "She's astonishingly beautiful!" he added at once, with warm feeling. And indeed the portrait did show a woman of extraordinary beauty. She was photographed in a black silk dress of extreme simplicity and elegant cut; her hair, which appeared to be light brown, was arranged in a simple, casual style; her eyes were dark and deep, her brow pensive, her expression passionate and somehow haughty. She was rather thin of face and perhaps pale. Ganya and the general stared at the prince in astonishment.

"What? You say Nastassya Filippovna? Do you already know Nastassya Filippovna?" asked the general.

"Yes, I've only been in Russia twenty-four hours and I already know such a great beauty," replied the prince and thereupon told of his meeting with Rogozhin and repeated all that Rogozhin had told him.

"Here's something new for you!" said the general, uneasy once more, having listened to the story with the closest attention. He looked searchingly at Ganya.

"Most likely just vulgar talk," murmured Ganya, who was also somewhat disturbed. "A merchant's son on a spree. I've heard something about him before."

"I too have heard about him, my dear friend," pursued the general. "Right after the earrings affair Nastassya Filippovna told the whole story. Yes, except that now this is something else again. Maybe there really is a million sitting there and—a passion, a base passion perhaps, but a passion all the same; and everyone knows what gentlemen like that are capable of when they're roaring drunk! Hmm. What if it all leads to some sort of scandalous incident!" finished the general, thoughtfully.

"You're afraid for the millions?" asked Ganya with a grin.

"And you're not, of course?"

"How did he strike you, Prince," asked Ganya, suddenly addressing him, "like a serious fellow or just some sort of troublemaker? What's your opinion?"

Something was happening to Ganya as he asked this question. It was as if some particular new thought had suddenly kindled in his brain and was blazing impatiently in his eyes. As for the general, who was genuinely and frankly uneasy, he too looked askance at the prince, but as if he did not expect much from his reply.

"I don't know how to tell you," said the prince, "only it seemed to me that there was a great passion in him, actually a sort of morbid passion. Besides, he still seemed to be quite ill. It's very possible he will be laid up again, his first days in Petersburg, especially if he starts carousing again."

"Oh, you really think so?" The general seized at the idea.

"That's how it seemed to me."

"Things of this sort may well happen within a few days, or even by this evening; something might even happen today," said Ganya, smiling to the general.

"Hmm. Of course. It might, but everything will depend on her whim at the moment," said the general.

"And you know how she is sometimes."

"What do you mean, 'how she is sometimes'!" demanded the general, greatly agitated. "Listen to me, Ganya, please don't contradict her too much today, and do make an effort to be—you know what I mean—nice to her— Hmm! Why that expression on your face? Listen, Gavril Ardalionovitch, right now it's very much indicated that we ask ourselves what we are trying to do here. You understand that my personal advantage in this affair has long been guaranteed; one way or another I shall settle it in my favor. Totsky has made an irrevocable decision, which means that I too am completely in the clear. So if I want anything now it's only for your benefit. Think it over—don't you have confidence in me? Besides that, you are a—well, in a word, an intelligent fellow, and I have been counting on you; since that, in the present case, is —is—"

"—the main thing," finished Ganya, again rescuing the general, and he twisted his lips into a most poisonous smile which he now made no effort to conceal. With a fiery glare he looked straight into the general's eyes, as if he wanted the latter to read his full thoughts in that look.

The general turned crimson and burst out angrily, "Quite so, intelligence is the main thing!" he said, looking sharply at Ganya. "And what a strange fellow you are, Gavril Ardalionovitch! I notice you seem almost pleased about this young merchant as a way out for yourself. But it's precisely here that you should have started using your intelligence from the start, precisely here you should understand and—and act fairly and squarely with both sides; or else give some warning so as not to compromise others, particularly as there was enough time to do so, as there is, in fact, even enough time now," (the general raised his eyebrows significantly), "despite the fact that there are only a few hours left— Do you understand? Do you? Will you or won't you? If you won't, say so. Do as you like. No one is holding you, Gavril Ardalionovitch, no one is dragging you into a trap, even if you see a trap there."

"I will," declared Ganya in a low voice, but firmly. He lowered his eyes and lapsed into a gloomy silence.

The general was satisfied. He had lost his temper but he evidently regretted that he had gone so far. He suddenly turned to the prince, and his face showed his uneasiness at the thought that the prince had been there overhearing everything. But he was immediately reassured—one glance at the prince was enough.

"Oh ho!" cried the general, looking at the specimen of writing the prince had handed him. "That is calligraphy! That is, in fact, exceptional calligraphy! Look at this, Ganya. What a talent!"

On the thick sheet of vellum the prince had written in medieval Russian characters, "The humble Abbot Pafnuty set his hand hereto." "This," explained the prince with great pleasure and animation, "is the exact signature of the Abbot Pafnuty, taken from a fourteenth-century manuscript. They used to sign splendidly, those old abbots and bishops of ours, and with what taste sometimes, with what pains! Could it be you don't have Pogodin's edition,* General? Then here I have written in another hand: this is the full round French script of the last century; some of the letters were even formed differently: the script of the marketplace, of the public scribes, copied from specimens of theirs. I had one. You must agree that it's not without merit. Look at these round d's and a's. I have rendered the French characters in Russian letters, which is very difficult, but it turned out well. And here again is a most beautiful and original script, the sentence here, 'Zeal overcomes all.' That's a Russian script used by scribes or, rather, military scribes. An official paper to an important person would be written like this, another rounded script, a fine *black* script, written very heavily, but with admirable taste. A calligrapher would object to these flourishes or, rather, these attempts at flourishes, these unfinished tails—do you see?— but notice that on the whole they lend character, and there you have the soul of the military scribe peering through, the longing to give free expression to his talent; but the military collar is pulled tight around his neck, and discipline appears in the handwriting too—it's lovely! I was struck by a specimen of it lately; I came across it by chance, and where but in Switzerland! Now here is a simple, ordinary, clean English script; elegance can go no farther, it is pure charm, little beads, pearls; it's perfectly finished. But here is a variation, again French; I got it from a French commercial traveler; again it's the English script, but the thick strokes are slightly darker and heavier than in the English, and the balance and clarity are destroyed; and notice also, the oval is not the same, it's a trifle rounder, and also the flourish is admitted, and a flourish is a very treacherous thing! A flourish requires unusual taste, and if only it is successful, if proportion is achieved, then that script will be so incomparable that one could actually fall in love with it."

"Oh-ho," laughed the general, "you do go into the fine points, don't you. You're not just a mere calligrapher but an artist as well, eh, Ganya?"

"Marvelous," said Ganya, "and he even recognizes his vocation," he added, laughing sarcastically.

"You may laugh, but there's a career there," said the general. "Prince, do you know to what personage we'll have you writing official papers now? Why, we can fix your salary right off at thirty-five roubles a month to start with. But it's already half past twelve," he added, glancing at the clock. "To business, Prince, because I must hurry and we may not see each other again today. Sit down there a minute; I've already explained I can't see you very often, but I would sincerely like to give you a little help—a little, of course—in what is essential; after that you can work things out however you like. I'll find you a little place in the office, nothing too demanding but requiring accuracy. Now for another thing: in the house, that is, in the family of Gavril Ardalionovitch Ivolgin, this young friend of mine here, with whom I hope you will become acquainted, his mother and sister have set aside two or three furnished rooms, which they rent with board and service to specially recommended lodgers. I am sure Nina Alexandrovna will accept my recommendation. This will be a fine thing for you, Prince, because you won't be out on your own but, so to speak, part of the family, and in my view you shouldn't be alone at first in a city like Petersburg. Nina Alexandrovna, Ganya's mother, and Varvara Ardalionovna, his sister, are ladies for whom I have the highest respect. Nina Alexandrovna is the wife of a general who is retired, at one time a comrade of mine during our first service, but with whom, owing to certain circumstances, I have broken relations, a fact which, however, does not prevent me from respecting him for what he is. I am making all this clear to you, Prince, so that you will understand that I am recommending you personally, and so, in a sense, I am vouching for you. The rates are extremely modest, and I hope that your salary will soon be enough to cover them. Of course a man needs pocket money, too, however little; but I'm sure you won't be angry with me, Prince, if I tell you you'd be better off avoiding pocket money, and I mean any money in your pockets at all. I say this from my first impression of you. But since your purse is quite empty now, allow me to offer you these twenty-five roubles as a start. We shall, of course, settle later, and if you are the nice sincere person you appear to be, we can't have any difficulties there. And if I take this interest in you it's because I have a certain object in view; you will learn what it is later. As you see I'm being perfectly open with you. I trust, Ganya, you have nothing against the Prince being settled in your apartment?"

"Oh, quite the contrary! And Mother will be very pleased," agreed Ganya politely and obligingly.

"You have only one room occupied now, I believe; that fellow—what's his name? Ferd— Fer—"

"Ferdyshchenko."

"Oh yes. I don't care for that Ferdyshchenko of yours; he's some kind of filthy clown. And I don't understand why Nastassya Filippovna encourages him so much. Unless he really is a relative of hers?"

"Oh, no. All that's only a joke. There isn't the slightest relationship."

"Well, the devil with him! So how do you feel about it, Prince? Are you satisfied or not?"

"Thank you, General, you have been extremely good to me, especially since I didn't ask for anything—I don't say that out of pride; I really didn't know where to lay my head. It is true that Rogozhin did invite me."

"Rogozhin? Oh, no. I would advise you in a fatherly way, or if you prefer as a friend, to forget Mr. Rogozhin. And as a general rule I would advise you to limit your relations to the family you are entering."

"Since you are so kind," began the prince, "I do have one matter of business. I've had word that—"

"Excuse me," interrupted the general, "I haven't a minute more now. I'll go and tell Lizaveta Prokofyevna about you. If she wishes to see you now—and I shall try to present you in a way that she will—I advise you to take advantage of the occasion and make yourself agreeable to her, because Lizaveta Prokofyevna can be very useful to you; you have the same family name. If she doesn't wish to see you, never mind, we'll do it some other time, somehow. And, Ganya, you glance over these accounts in the meantime; Fedoseyev and I have just been struggling over them. Don't forget to include them."

The general went out, and the prince did not manage to tell him about his business, as he had been attempting to do for the fourth time. Ganya lighted a cigarette and offered one to the prince, who accepted it but did not open a conversation so as not to disturb Ganya, and he began examining the study. But Ganya scarcely glanced at the sheet of paper covered with figures, which the general had just indicated to him. He was preoccupied; his smile, his look, his thoughtfulness weighed all the more on the prince now that they were left

56

alone together. Suddenly he approached the prince, who at that moment was again by the portrait of Nastassya Filippovna, contemplating it.

"So a woman like this appeals to you, Prince?" he suddenly asked him, looking at him searchingly, as if he had some pressing reason for his question.

"An amazing face!" replied the prince, "and I'm sure that her life is no ordinary one. Her face seems cheerful, but she has suffered terribly, hasn't she? The eyes tell this, and the cheekbones that form two points under her eyes. It's a proud face, a terribly proud face; and yet, here I can't tell, is she a good person? Ah, if only she were! Everything would be all right!"

"And would *you* marry such a woman?" pursued Ganya, still gazing at him with his burning eyes.

"I can't marry anyone. I am an invalid," said the prince.

"And would Rogozhin marry her? What do you think?"

"I think he would marry her, he might marry her tomorrow—and a week later cut her throat—"

No sooner had the prince said this than Ganya suddenly shuddered so violently that the prince almost cried out.

"What's the matter?" he asked, seizing his arm.

"Sir," announced a footman, appearing in the doorway, "His Excellency begs you to see Her Excellency."

The prince followed the footman.

Chapter FOUR

All three Yepanchin daughters were tall, robust young ladies, in the full bloom of youth and health, with magnificent shoulders, powerful bosoms, strong, almost masculine arms; and of course, as a result of their strength and good health, they occasionally liked to eat well, a fact which they did not choose to disguise. Their mamma, Lizaveta Prokofyevna, sometimes looked askance at the honesty of their appetites, but as certain of her views, despite the outward respect they were shown by her daughters, had long since lost their former unquestioned authority among them, so much so, in fact, that the firmly established entente of the three young ladies had begun to prevail quite regularly, the general's wife, conscious of her own dignity, had found it more convenient to give in without argument. It is true that her temperament often prevented her from following the dictates of good sense. Lizaveta Prokofyevna was becoming more capricious and more impatient with each year and had even become a sort of eccentric, but as her submissive and well-trained husband was always at hand, she usually let all her accumulated bad humor fall on his head, whereupon harmony was restored in the family again and all went exceedingly well.

Madame Yepanchin herself, moreover, had not lost her appetite, and ordinarily at half past twelve she partook of an abundant lunch, which was hardly distinguishable from a dinner, together with her daughters. The young ladies had already taken a cup of coffee earlier, in their beds at the moment of their awakening, at ten precisely. They had grown fond of this custom and had adopted it as a regular habit. At half past twelve a table was set in the small dining room near the mamma's rooms, and sometimes the general himself made an appearance at this intimate family luncheon, if his time permitted. Besides tea, coffee, cheese, honey, butter, the special fritters which the general's wife adored, cutlets, and so forth, a sturdy, hot broth was also served. On the particular morning our story begins, the entire family was assembled in the dining room awaiting the general, who had promised to appear at half past twelve. Had he been late by so much as a minute, he would have been sent for, but he appeared punctually. As he went to greet his wife and kiss her hand, he noticed, on this occasion, an unusual expression on her face. Only the night before he had had a premonition that precisely this would happen today because of a certain "episode" (as he always put it) and had already worried about it as he fell asleep; nevertheless he now became very alarmed once again. His daughters went to kiss him, and although they were not angry with him, there was, nevertheless, something peculiar about them too. True, the general had because of certain circumstances become excessively suspicious, but as he was an experienced and resourceful father and husband, he promptly took appropriate measures.

It will perhaps not disturb the surface progression of our story too much if we introduce here some direct explanation of the relationships and circumstances in which we find General Yepanchin's family at the beginning of our tale. We have just said that the general, though a man of no great formal education, but on the contrary, as he described himself, "a self-taught man," was nevertheless an experienced husband and a resourceful father. Among other things he had adopted the "system" of not hurrying his daughters into marriage, that is, not hanging over them and upsetting them with the weight of his fatherly solicitude for their happiness, as so frequently happens quite unconsciously and naturally even in the most intelligent families in which there is a reserve of adult daughters. He had even succeeded in converting Lizaveta Prokofyevna to his "system," although this was no easy thing, because it was unnatural. But the general's arguments were extremely impressive, being based on solid fact. Moreover, left to their own wishes and decisions, the prospective brides would eventually be forced to come to their senses, at which time all would proceed nicely, because they would apply themselves voluntarily, putting aside their caprices and fastidiousness. All that would be left for the parents to do would be to keep a constant watch over them, as inconspicuously as possible, so they would make no strange choice or follow any unnatural inclinations, and then to seize the propitious moment to apply their full assistance and assure, with all their influence, the proper outcome. Finally, the mere fact that with every year their fortune and social position augmented in geometrical progression meant that the more time that passed the more the daughters were enhanced as prospective brides. But among all these incontestable facts there appeared still another fact. The eldest daughter, Alexandra, suddenly and completely unexpectedly (as it always happens) reached her twenty-fifth year. At about the same time, Afanassy Ivanovitch Totsky, a man of the best society, with the highest connections and extraordinary wealth, once again made known his long-cherished desire to marry. He was a man of about fifty-five, of exquisite character and extraordinarily refined tastes. He desired to make a good marriage; he was an exceptional judge of beauty. And as he had for some time been on terms of unusually close friendship with General Yepanchin, reinforced notably by their joint participation in certain financial enterprises, he put the matter to him, so to speak, asking for friendly advice and counsel. Would the idea of marriage to one of his daughters be considered or not? A definite change occurred in the quiet and attractive course of General Yepanchin's family life.

Now the beauty of the family was, as we have already said, unquestionably the youngest, Aglaya. But even Totsky, though a man of extraordinary egoism, understood that it was useless for him to look in that direction and that Aglaya's destiny was not to be an ordinary one but the highest ideal of earthly bliss. Aglaya's future husband was to have every perfection and achieve every success, not to speak of his vast wealth. The sisters had even agreed among themselves, with hardly any discussion, that if the need arose they would sacrifice their portions in the interest of Aglaya. The dowry destined for Aglaya was to be colossal and, in fact, unheard of. The parents knew of this agreement between the two elder sisters, and this was why when Totsky asked for advice and counsel they had little doubt that one of the elder sisters would not refuse to gratify their expectations, especially since Afanassy Ivanovitch could make no difficulties about dowry. The general with his exceptional experience in the world attached great value to Totsky's proposal from the start. So, since Totsky himself had for certain reasons to proceed with caution and merely explore the ground, the parents suggested the matter to their daughters only as a remote possibility. In reply they received from them the reassuring though not quite definite statement that the eldest, Alexandra, might not refuse him. This young lady, though firm in her ways, was good-natured, sensible, and easy to get along with; she might even marry Totsky willingly, and if she gave her word she would keep it faithfully. She did not care for ostentation, and far from causing trouble and violent disturbances she might even be expected to sweeten and soothe her husband's life. She was quite pretty, though not striking. What could be better for Totsky?

And yet the affair was still at the exploratory stage. Totsky and the general reached a mutual and friendly understanding that for the present they would avoid any formal and irrevocable step. The parents had not even opened the subject directly with their daughters; there were in fact signs of discord on the horizon: Madame Yepanchin, the mother of the family, seemed for some reason to be dissatisfied, and this was a very serious matter. There was one troublesome thing, one difficult and trying circumstance which could ruin the whole affair completely.

This difficult and trying "circumstance" (as Totsky expressed it) had arisen a long time before, eighteen years before, in fact. Next to one of Afanassy Ivanovitch's richest estates, in one of the central provinces, was the property of a poverty-stricken landowner, a man remarkable for his persistent and almost legendary run of bad luck. He was a retired officer of good family—better in fact than Totsky's own—whose name was Filip Alexandrovitch Barashkov. Burdened with debts and mortgages, he had finally managed by laboring almost as a peasant to get his small holding into a more or less satisfactory condition. The smallest success encouraged him inordinately. Radiant with hope, he went for a few days to the small district town to see one of his chief creditors and, if possible, reach an agreement with him. On his third day in town the elder of his village rode up to him on horseback, his beard singed and his cheek burned, and told him that the previous day at high noon his "country seat" had burned down and that though his children were unhurt his wife had "had the honor" of burning with it. This shock was too much even for Barashkov, accustomed though he was to the "blows of fate"; he went mad and died of brain-fever a month later. The burned property with its homeless peasants was sold to pay his debts. Barashkov's two daughters, little girls of six and seven, Afanassy Ivanovitch Totsky magnanimously undertook to support and educate. They were brought up together with the children of Afanassy Ivanovitch's steward, who was a retired government worker with a large family and was, moreover, a German. Soon only one girl, Nastassya, remained, the younger having died of whooping cough; and Totsky, then living abroad, soon forgot all about them. Five years later while he was traveling in the region it occurred to him to look in on his property, and he suddenly noticed in the family of his German an adorable girl of about twelve, lively, charming, and intelligent, who promised to become an extraordinary beauty; for in matters of this sort Afanassy Ivanovitch was undeniably an expert judge. On this occasion he spent only a few days at his estate but found time to make certain arrangements; a noticeable change occurred in the course of the girl's education. An elderly and respectable Swiss governess was engaged, a cultivated person experienced in the education of young ladies, who taught various subjects in addition to the French language. She took up residence in the country house, and the education of little Nastassya acquired much larger dimensions. Just four years later, this education came to an end, the governess left, and a certain lady came for Nastassya, a woman who like Totsky was a landowner and a neighbor of his but in another, very distant district, and on his instructions and with his authority she took Nastassya with her. On her estate there was a small recently built wooden house, exquisitely furnished, and the little village was, as if by intention, called "Consolation." The lady brought Nastassya straight to this quite little house, and as she was a widow without children and lived herself less than a mile away, she installed herself in the house with her. An old housekeeper and an experienced young maid attended Nastassya. In the house there were musical instruments, pencils, paints and brushes, an exquisite library for a young girl, pictures, prints, and a very handsome Italian greyhound, and two weeks later Afanassy Ivanovitch himself made his appearance. From that time on he somehow came to love this distant village of his lost in the steppes, and he would stop there every summer, spending two or even three months; and so a rather long time passed, four years of peaceful and happy life, in an atmosphere of taste and refinement.

It happened once at the beginning of winter, about four months after Afanassy Ivanovitch's summer visit to Consolation (which this time had lasted only two weeks), a rumor was circulated, or rather reached Nastassya Filippovna, that Afanassy Ivanovitch was to marry in Petersburg a rich and beautiful woman of noble birth—that he was, in a word, making a brilliant match. The rumor later turned out not to be exact in some details; the marriage was at the time only a project, the whole thing was still very vague; nevertheless, from that time on, a great change took place in Nastassya Filippovna's life. She suddenly showed extraordinary determination and a quite unexpectedly strong will. Without wasting time on reflection she left her little country house and suddenly arrived in Petersburg and, entirely alone, went straight to Totsky. He was astonished and started talking, but it was immediately clear, almost from the first word, that he would have to alter completely his language, his tone of voice, the subjects of agreeable, refined conversation he had used so successfully until now, even his logic—in fact everything, everything! Before him sat a completely different woman, in no way resembling the one he had known until then and whom he had left in the village of Consolation only the previous July.

It turned out first that this new woman knew and understood a great deal—so much that one could only wonder where she had acquired such knowledge and developed such definite ideas. Surely it wasn't in her library? Moreover, she had a fairly good understanding of legal matters and a positive knowledge, if not of the world at least of how certain things are done in the world. In the second place, her character was completely different; gone was the shyness, the schoolgirlish uncertainty that was sometimes so delightful in its spontaneous simplicity, sometimes so melancholy and pensive, wondering, mistrustful, tearful and uneasy.

No: here was an extraordinary new creature who laughed at him and stung him with venomous sarcasms, who declared to his face that she had never harbored any feeling for him but the most profound contempt—nauseating contempt which had seized her immediately after her first surprise. This new woman declared that she did not care in the least if he married at once anyone he liked, but that she had come to prevent this marriage, and to prevent it out of malice, simply because she wished to; so that was how it was going to be, "if only to have a good laugh at you, because I've finally decided I want to laugh."

This at least was what she said, perhaps she did not say everything that was on her mind. But as the new Nastassya Filippovna laughed and told him all this, Afanassy Ivanovitch considered the matter and tried to collect his rather scattered thoughts. His deliberations went on for some time; he weighed and considered for almost two weeks; but at the end of two weeks he had made his decision. The fact was that Afanassy Ivanovitch was then almost fifty, a man exceptionally secure and set in his ways. His position in the world and in society had been established long ago on the firmest foundations. He loved and esteemed himself, his peace and comfort more than anything in the world, as befits a man of eminent propriety. Nothing could be allowed to threaten or disturb this serenity which had been built up over an entire lifetime into so splendid an edifice. On the other hand, Totsky's experience and deep insight into things swiftly and accurately informed him that he was now dealing with a quite exceptional woman who would not merely threaten but would also, most surely, act, a woman who would not stop at anything, especially since she attached no value to anything in the world; so that one could entertain no hope of tempting her from her purpose. There was evidently something else here, some regrettable ferment of the mind and heart, something on the order of romantic indignation. God knew against whom or why, some kind of insatiable feeling of contempt that had become exaggerated beyond all bounds; in a word, something so totally ridiculous and intolerable in proper society that for a decent person to have to contend with it was a true judgment of the Almighty. Of course, Totsky with his wealth and connections could immediately rid himself of the nuisance by some trifling and completely innocent piece of villainy. On the other hand it was plain that Nastassya Filippovna was hardly in a position to do anything harmful through the avenues of justice for instance; nor could she even create much of a scandal, because it would always be easy to restrain her. But all this would be true only if Nastassya Filippovna chose to act as people normally act under such circumstances, without departing too far from accepted limits of behavior. But it was here that Totsky's precise power of judgment served him well; he was able to see that Nastassya Filippovna herself realized very well that she could do him no harm legally but that there was something else on her mind—and in her flashing eyes. Caring about nothing, least of all herself (it required great intelligence and insight for him, as a skeptic and cynical man of the world, to believe in the genuineness of this feeling), Nastassya Filippovna was capable of ruining herself, irreparably and most distastefully, facing hard labor in Siberia, merely to humiliate a man against whom she nurtured such an inhuman aversion. Afanassy Ivanovitch never disguised the fact that he was something of a coward or, in other words, that he was extremely conservative. Had he known, for example, that he might be killed in church during the wedding ceremony or that something of the sort would occur, something that would appear unseemly, ludicrous, and unpleasant to society, he would certainly have been frightened, but not so much of actually being killed or bloodied or having someone publicly spit in his face, or anything of the sort, but frightened of having a thing like that happen to him in such an unnatural and unattractive form. And this was what Nastassya Filippovna was counting on, though so far she had kept quiet about it; he knew that she had studied and to a large extent had come to understand him and that consequently she knew the weapon which would hurt him most. And since the wedding was still only in the offing, he resigned himself and gave way to Nastassya Filippovna.

He was helped in taking this decision by still another circumstance. It was hard to imagine how little the new Nastassya Filippovna physically resembled the old one. Formerly she was merely a very pretty little girl, but now Totsky for a long time could not forgive himself that he had seen her for four years and not noticed what she was beginning to be. It is true that much was due to the sudden interior change that had happened in their relation to one another. He could, moreover, recall moments of the past when strange thoughts would come to him as he gazed into those eyes, as if foretelling in them a sort of deep and mysterious darkness. Her eyes seemed to be asking a riddle. During the last two years he had often wondered about the alteration of Nastassya Filippovna's complexion; she became terribly pale and—strange to say—looked even prettier because of it. Totsky, like all gentlemen who have enjoyed the world in their day, felt contemptuously at first how cheaply he had obtained this inexperienced girl; but more lately he came to question this view.

He had in any case decided as long ago as last spring to lose no time in marrying off Nastassya Filippovna, with a dowry, to some sensible and decent fellow serving in some other province. (Oh how horribly and spitefully she laughed at that idea now!) But Afanassy Ivanovitch, fascinated by the new Nastassya Filippovna, went so far as to wonder how he could again use this woman. He decided to establish her in Petersburg and surround her with luxury and comfort. If not one thing, he would have the other. Nastassya Filippovna could be displayed and even shown off in a certain limited circle Afanassy Ivanovitch took pride in his reputation in this domain.

Now, five years of this Petersburg life had passed, and of course many things had become clear in that time. Afanassy Ivanovitch's position was not a pleasant one; the worst was that having been badly shaken once, he could not quite regain his confidence again. He was afraid, he himself did not know of what: he was, very simply, afraid of Nastassya Filippovna. For a certain time during the first two years, he had begun to suspect that Nastassya Filippovna herself wanted to marry him but that she said nothing because of her extraordinary pride and was awaiting his insistent proposal. This presumption would have seemed strange, except for the fact that Afanassy Ivanovitch had become suspicious; he frowned and he thought somber thoughts. To his great and (such is the heart of man!) rather unpleasant surprise, a certain event convinced him that even if he had proposed to her he would not have been accepted. For a long time he could not understand this. The only explanation that seemed to him possible was that an irrational woman's offended pride had reached the point where she would rather express her contempt in a refusal than secure her social position once and for all and attain inaccessible heights of grandeur. The worst of it was that Nastassya Filippovna had gotten the upper hand so dreadfully. She did not give in to mercenary inducements, no matter how large, and while she accepted the comforts offered her, she lived very modestly and had put aside next to nothing during the five years. Afanassy Ivanovitch attempted a very ingenious stratagem to break his chains: subtly and skillfully with able help, he tempted her with various ideal temptations, incarnated in princes, hussars, embassy secretaries, poets, novelists, even socialists; nothing of which produced any effect on Nastassya Filippovna, as if she had a stone for a heart and her feelings had withered and died forever. She lived a secluded life, she read, she even studied, and she was fond of music. She had few acquaintances; she associated mostly with the wives of functionaries, poor and ridiculous people, two actresses of sorts, certain old ladies; she was very fond of the large family of a respectable schoolteacher and was in turn very much liked by the family and always received a warm welcome from them. Quite often five or six people of her acquaintance, never more than that, came to see her in the evening. Totsky appeared frequently and regularly. Of late and with some difficulty, General Yepanchin made her acquaintance. At the same time, with no difficulty at all, a young civil servant also met her, a coarse, disreputable fellow named Ferdyshchenko who drank too much and thought himself amusing. Another acquaintance was a strange young man named Ptitsyn, a neat, modest person of polished manners and appearance, who had arisen from the depths of poverty to become a moneylender. Finally, Gavril Ardalionovitch Ivolgin had been introduced to her. The result was that Nastassya Filippovna acquired an odd reputation; everyone had heard of her beauty, but that was all; no one could say he knew her any better, no one had anything to tell about her. This reputation, together with her education and her elegant manners, her wit, all determined Afanassy Ivanovitch to pursue a certain plan. It was from this moment that General Yepanchin began to play such an active and important role in this affair.

When Totsky had so amiably turned to him for friendly advice in respect to one or another of his daughters, he had, in the noblest manner possible, made the general a full and candid confession. He disclosed that he had decided to *stop at nothing* to regain his freedom, that he would not be content even if Nastassya Filippovna herself would announce that from now on she would let him alone, that mere words were not enough, that he required the fullest guarantees. They had discussed the situation and decided to act together. The plan was to try the gentlest means first and appeal to, so to speak, the "finer chords of her heart." They both went to Nastassya Filippovna's, and Totsky proceeded directly to tell her of the intolerable horror of his position; he blamed himself for everything and told her that he could not repent of his treatment of her in the beginning because he was a hardened sensualist and could not control his actions, but that now he desired to marry and that the realization of this eminently desirable and distinguished marriage depended entirely upon her; in short, that he rested all his hope in the generosity of her heart. General Yepanchin then began to speak to her in his capacity of father, talking plainly and sensibly and avoiding all sentimentality, acknowledging that he fully recognized her right to decide Afanassy Ivanovitch's future: he cleverly made evident his own humility by disclosing the fact that the fate of his eldest daughter, and perhaps of his two other daughters as well, now also depended on her decision. In reply to Nastassya Filippovna's question, what exactly did they want her to do, Totsky confessed, with the same absolute frankness he had employed before, that she had given him such a fright five years before that even now he could not feel perfectly at ease—not until Nastassya Filippovna herself was married to someone. He added immediately that such a request coming from him would be completely absurd if he had not some basis for it. He had carefully observed and, indeed, knew for certain that a certain young man from a very good and respectable family, Gavril Ardalionovitch Ivolgin, whom she knew and received in her house, had for some time now been passionately in love with her and would of course give up half his life in the sole hope of winning her affection. Gavril Ardalionovitch had made this admission to Afanassy Ivanovitch personally some time ago, out of the friendly candor of his young heart; and General Yepanchin, who took an interest in the young man, had also known about it for a long time. Finally, unless Afanassy Ivanovitch was very much mistaken, Nastassya Filippovna herself was already aware of the young man's love for her, and he even had the impression that she looked on it indulgently. Of course it was harder for him than for anyone else to speak of it, but if Nastassya Filippovna would bring herself to admit that he, Totsky, had some thought for her own good quite apart from any selfish interest in arranging for his own welfare then she would see that he had for some time found it upsetting, and even painful, to think about her loneliness, her vague, dark loneliness, her complete lack of faith in the possibility of a new life, a life which could be reborn in her so marvelously through love and a family of her own and provide her with a new aim; that she was now wasting her abilities, which were perhaps most brilliant ones, in wanton brooding over her own distress, indeed in a sort of romantic sentimentality unworthy of her good mind and her generous heart. Emphasizing again that it was harder for him than for anyone else to speak thus, he concluded by declaring himself hopeful that Nastassya Filippovna would not reply with contempt to his sincere wish to assure her future comfort and offered her the sum of seventy-five thousand roubles He explained that this amount was in any case already left to her in his will; in short, that it was in no sense a compensation and that, anyway, why shouldn't she accept and excuse his all-too-human desire to ease his conscience, and so on and so forth, all that is ordinarily said on this subject in similar situations. Afanassy Ivanovitch spoke at length and with eloquence, adding in passing, as it were, the very interesting information that he was now mentioning the seventy-five thousand roubles for the first time, that even Ivan Fyodorovitch, sitting right there, knew nothing of them; in fact, nobody did.

Nastassya Filippovna's reply amazed the two friends. Not only was there no trace of her former sarcasm, her former hostility and hatred, her derisive laughter, the mere recollection of which even now sent cold chills up Totsky's spine, but on the contrary she appeared pleased to be able finally to speak to someone frankly and in a friendly way. She admitted that for some time she had been wanting to ask for friendly advice and that she hesitated only for reasons of pride, but that now the ice was broken nothing could suit her better. First, with a sad smile, then with a gay, spirited laugh, she admitted that there could be no such storm as there had been before, that she had for some time modified her views of things, that while she had undergone no real change of heart she had been forced to make allowances in the face of the facts, that what was done was done, what was past was past, so that it even seemed strange to her that Afanassy Ivanovitch was still so frightened. Then she addressed herself to Ivan Fyodorovitch and declared in a most deferential tone that she had already heard a great deal about his daughters and had come to hold them in deep and sincere respect. The very thought that she could in any way be of service to them filled her with joy and pride. It was true that at present she was depressed and bored, very bored; Afanassy Ivanovitch had divined her inner thoughts; she indeed desired to be reborn, if not through love at least through having a family of her own, and to find a new purpose in life. But about Gavril Ardalionovitch she could say almost nothing. It did appear that he was in love with *her,* and she felt that she might love him too if she were convinced of the firmness of his attachment; but he was very young, although probably sincere. It was hard for her to decide. What she liked best about him was that he worked hard and supported his family by his own efforts. She had heard he was a man of energy and self-respect, anxious to make a career and to succeed in the world. She had also heard that his mother, Nina Alexandrovna Ivolgin, was an excellent and highly estimable woman and that his sister, Varvara Ardalionovna, was a very remarkable and energetic girl; she had heard a great deal about her from Ptitsyn. She had heard that they bore their misfortunes bravely, and she would very much like to make their acquaintance, but there was the question of whether they would welcome her into their family. All in all, she would say nothing against the possibility of such a marriage, but she would have to think further about it; she did not wish to be hurried. As for the seventy-five thousand, there had been no need for Afanassy Ivanovitch to speak of it in such a round-about way. She knew the value of money and would of course accept it. In any event she had no intention of apologizing to anyone for anything and wished this fact to be made known. She would not marry Gavril Ardalionovitch until she was certain that neither he nor his family had any sort of hidden feeling against her. In any case she did not consider herself to blame for anything, and she thought it would be better if Gavril Ardalionovitch knew the conditions under which she had been living in Petersburg for the past five years and the nature of her relations with Afanassy Ivanovitch and how much money she had been able to put aside. Finally, if she was accepting a sum of money now, it was not to be considered payment for the loss of her maidenly virtue, for which she had not been to blame, but simply as a compensation for her wrecked life.

She became so emotional and upset in explaining this (natural as it all was) that General Yepanchin was highly pleased and considered the matter settled; but Totsky, having been frightened once, was not completely convinced and still feared there might be a serpent lurking in the garden. But negotiations had been opened, and the essential element in the two friends' scheme—the possibility that Nastassya Filippovna would show interest in Ganya—gradually seemed more definite and likely, so that even Totsky could sometimes bring himself to believe in the realization of success. In the meantime Nastassya Filippovna had discussed the matter with Ganya, in the briefest terms, as if her modesty suffered from the mere mention of it. However, she acknowledged and permitted his love for her but insisted that in no way did she wish to bind herself, that until the day of the wedding (if there was in fact to be a wedding) she would reserve the right to say "no," even at the very last minute; and she allowed Ganya exactly the same right. Quite by chance Ganya soon had definite knowledge that Nastassya Filippovna already knew in great detail about his family's hostility to the marriage and toward herself personally, which had manifested itself in family scenes. Though he expected it daily, she had never mentioned this matter to him. There was much more that could be told of the incidents and situations which arose during the negotiations over the proposed match, but we have now run ahead of the story, and some of these situations still took the form of rather vague, unsubstantiated rumors. For example, it was said that Totsky had learned somewhere that Nastassya Filippovna had entered into some sort of dubious secret understanding with General Yepanchin's daughters—a highly improbable story. On the other hand there was another rumor which he could not help believing and feared like a bad dream: he had heard for a fact that Nastassya Filippovna was perfectly aware that Ganya was marrying her only for money, and that Ganya had a foul, greedy, impatient, envious, and impossibly vain nature, and that while he had at one time tried in earnest to win Nastassya Filippovna's affection, the moment the two friends endeavored to exploit for their own purposes the passion that was incipient on both sides, to buy Ganya by selling him Nastassya Filippovna as his lawful wife, he had begun to hate her like a nightmare. Passion and hatred seemed strangely mingled in him, and while he had finally, after painful hesitation, consented to marry that "fallen woman," he had sworn in his heart to revenge himself cruelly on her and to "get at her" afterward, as he was supposed to have expressed himself. Nastassya Filippovna was said to know of all this and to be secretly preparing some countermeasure. Totsky was in such a panic that he had even stopped sharing his anxieties with Yepanchin; yet there were moments when, as it happens to weak men, he took heart and recovered his high spirits; for example, he was greatly elated when Nastassya Filippovna finally gave her promise that on the evening of her birthday she would give her final decision. On the other hand, the strangest and least credible rumor of all, which touched no less a person than Ivan Fyodorovitch himself, appeared—alas!—more and more accurate.

At first glance it seemed wildly preposterous. It was difficult to believe that Ivan Fyodorovitch, then entering years which promised him great respectability, with his superlative mind, his practical knowledge of the world, and all the rest of it, would be himself tempted by Nastassya Filippovna, and tempted to such a degree that this caprice was assuming the proportions of a passion. What exactly he was hoping for it was difficult to imagine—perhaps the cooperation of Ganya himself. Totsky suspected the presence of some sort of tacit agreement between the general and Ganya, based on their comprehension of one another. Of course it is well known that a man carried away by passion, especially a man getting on in years, becomes completely blind and is ready to find

70

grounds for hope where there is in fact none; moreover, he loses his judgment and acts like a foolish child, however intelligent he may have been previously. It was known that the general had arranged to present Nastassya Filippovna on her birthday with an astounding string of pearls, which had cost an enormous sum, and that he had put a great deal of thought into this present, even though he knew Nastassya Filippovna was not a mercenary woman. On the day of the birthday he was in a perfect fever, though he managed to conceal his emotion. It was of this very string of pearls that the general's wife had heard. True, Lizaveta Prokofyevna had long experience with her husband's footloose character, and she had to some extent even grown accustomed to it; but it was impossible to let such an incident pass; the rumor of the pearls interested her very much indeed; the general had discovered this in good time; the day before they had had words about it; he anticipated a major scene and dreaded it. This was why he had absolutely no inclination on the morning our story begins to take breakfast in the bosom of his family. Even before the prince made his appearance he had resolved to excuse himself on the pretext of having urgent business and stay away. And staying away was sometimes for the general identical to running away. He was very anxious that this day, and especially the evening of this day, should pass without unpleasantness. Then suddenly the prince had arrived so opportunely. "As if God had sent him," said the general to himself, as he went in to see his wife.

Chapter FIVE

Madame Yepanchin was proud of her family line. It was therefore a shock for her to hear that the last of the princes Myshkin, of whom she had already heard something, was nothing but a poor idiot and almost a beggar and ready to accept charity. The general had tried to create an effect so as to seize her attention and lead her thoughts in a different direction and, under cover of this distraction, avoid the question of the pearls.

In moments of stress Madame Yepanchin had the habit of opening her eyes very wide and, leaning slightly backward, staring straight ahead of her without uttering a word. She was a large woman the same age as her husband, with dark hair, still thick, though graying, a rather aquiline nose, sunken sallow cheeks, and thin pinched lips. Her forehead was high but narrow, her large gray eyes sometimes had a most unexpected expression. She had once been so vain as to fancy that her eyes were strikingly effective—a conviction which remained indelibly fixed in her mind.

"Receive him? You say I should receive him now? This moment?" Madame Yepanchin opened her eyes as wide as possible and stared at the general, who stood fidgeting before her.

"Oh, there's no need to stand on ceremony if you should care to see him, my dear," the general hastened to explain. "He's an absolute child and really such a pathetic fellow, he's subject to some sort of fits. He's just come from Switzerland, straight from the train. He's all done up like a German and hasn't a kopeck, he's almost ready to cry. I presented him with twenty-five roubles and want to find some little job for him in our office. And I ask you, *mesdames,* to offer him something to eat, because he appears to be hungry too."

"You amaze me," Madame Yepanchin went on as before. "Hungry? And fits? What kind of fits?"

"Oh, they don't happen too often and, besides, he's almost like a child, but well educated. I should like to ask you, *mesdames,*" he again addressed his daughters, "to give him an examination. It would be good to know what he's fit for."

"An ex-am-in-a-tion?" drawled his wife, again opening her eyes wide in profound astonishment as she looked from her daughters to her husband and back again.

"Oh, my dear, don't take it in that way. Of course, you may do as you please, I only wanted to be kind to him and introduce him to the family, because it would almost be an act of charity."

"Introduce him to the family? From Switzerland?"

"Switzerland has nothing to do with it; and besides, I repeat, it's as you please. I suggested it because for one thing he has the same name and might even be a relative, and for another he's got nowhere to stay. I even thought you might be rather interested because, after all, he is from the same family as ours."

"Of course, *Maman,* if there's no need to stand on ceremony with him. And he must be hungry after his trip, why not give him something to eat if he has nowhere to go?" said the eldest daughter, Alexandra.

"And besides, he's a complete child. We could have a game of blind man's buff with him."

"Blind man's buff? What do you mean?"

"Oh, *Maman,* please stop pretending," interrupted Aglaya in vexation.

The middle daughter, Adelaïda, who was quick to see the funny side of things, could not help bursting out laughing.

"Call him in, Papa," said Aglaya decisively. "*Maman* gives her permission."

The general rang and had the prince summoned.

"But on the absolute condition," insisted Madame Yepanchin, "that he has a napkin tied around his neck when he sits at the table. Let's call Fyodor, or Mavra, to have someone standing behind his chair to look after him while he's eating. Is he quiet at least while he's having his fits? Does he wave his arms around?"

"On the contrary, he is very well bred and has excellent manners. A bit simple at times. But here he is himself! Allow me to present the last of the Prince Myshkins, your namesake, and perhaps even your relative. Do welcome him and make him at home. Lunch will presently be served, Prince, please do us the honor. As for me, I must hurry off, I'm late."

"We know where you're hurrying to," announced the general's wife gravely.

"Must hurry, my dear, must hurry off. I'm late! Do give him your albums, *mesdames,* and let him write in them. What a calligrapher he is! Rare talent. In there he wrote for me in old script, 'The Abbot Pafnuty set his hand hereto.' So, good-bye."

" 'Pafnuty'? 'The Abbot'? Wait! Wait a minute! Where are you going, and who is this Pafnuty?" Madame Yepanchin called in vexation and some distress after her departing husband.

"Yes, yes, my dear, he was an abbot who lived in the old days. As for me, I'm off to the count's. He's been waiting hours for me, made the appointment himself. Good-bye, Prince."

The general quickly left the room.

"I know what count he's going to!" said Lizaveta Prokofyevna sharply and turned her eyes irritably upon the prince. "What were we saying?" she began in annoyance, peevishly trying to remember. "What was that? Oh, yes, what about that abbot?"

"Maman!" began Alexandra, and Aglaya stamped her foot.

"Don't interfere with me, Alexandra Ivanovna," admonished her mother, "I want to know too. Sit right here, Prince, in this armchair, across from me; no, here; move into the sun so I can see you. Now, what about this abbot?"

"Abbot Pafnuty," replied the prince, attentively and seriously.

"Pafnuty? That's interesting. Well, what about him?" Madame Yepanchin put her questions rapidly, impatiently, sharply, holding her eyes fixed on the prince; and when the prince answered she nodded her head at each word he spoke.

"Abbot Pafnuty was of the fourteenth century," began the prince. "He was the head of a monastery on the Volga in what is today our province of Kostroma. He was known for the holiness of his life. He visited the Golden Horde and helped in the management of public affairs and signed a certain document. I have seen the facsimile of this signature. I liked his handwriting and I learned how to imitate it. Just now when the general wanted to see how I wrote so as to find me a job, I wrote a few sentences in various scripts, among which was 'The humble Abbot Pafnuty set his hand hereto' in the abbot's own hand. The general liked it very much, and this is why he thought of it just now."

"Aglaya," said Madame Yepanchin, "remember: Pafnuty. Or better yet, write it down; I always forget. However, I expected it would be more interesting. Where is this signature?"

"I think it was left in the general's study, on the table."

"Send at once and bring it."

"Let me write it for you again, if you like."

"Of course, *Maman*," said Alexandra, "but now we had better have lunch. We want to eat."

"Quite so," agreed Madame Yepanchin. "Come along, Prince; are you very hungry?"

"Yes, I am suddenly very hungry, and I am most grateful to you."

"It's very good you are polite, and I notice that you are not at all so peculiar as some would say. Come along. Sit here, opposite me," she fussed as she seated the prince when they had reached the dining room. "I want to look at you. Alexandra, Adelaïda, offer the prince something. He isn't at all so—sick, is he? Perhaps the napkin is unnecessary. Prince, do you have a napkin tied around your neck when you eat?"

"I did a long time ago when I was seven, I believe, but now I usually put it on my lap."

"Properly so. And your fits?"

"Fits?" said the prince, mildly surprised. "I have them

74

rather seldom now. But I don't know. I am told the climate here will be bad for me."

"He speaks nicely," observed Madame Yepanchin to her daughters. She continued to nod at every word the prince uttered. "I didn't expect it. It seems that it was all stuff and nonsense, as usual. Do eat, Prince, and tell me where you were born and where you were brought up. I want to know everything. You interest me extremely."

The prince thanked her and, while eating with great appetite, once again began to relate everything he had had to tell several times already that morning. Madame Yepanchin appeared more and more pleased. The young ladies also listened fairly attentively. They compared relatives; it developed that the prince knew his family tree quite well, but for all their efforts it turned out that there was almost no connection between him and Madame Yepanchin. Among their grandfathers and grandmothers a distant relationship might possibly have been established. This dry subject particularly delighted the general's wife, who try as she would, seldom found occasions to speak of her ancestry, so much so that she arose from the table in a state of great animation.

"Come, let's all go into our sitting room," she said, "and coffee will be brought there. We have a common sitting room," she explained to the prince as she led him there. "It's really my little sitting room where we meet and each one does her own task. Alexandra here, my eldest daughter, plays the piano, or reads, or sews; Adelaïda paints landscapes and portraits and never finishes anything, and Aglaya just sits there doing nothing. I can't keep at anything either, and I get nothing done. So, here we are. Sit here, Prince, by the fire and tell us some more. I want to find out how you are at telling stories. I want to be completely convinced; and when I see old Princess Belokonskaya I shall tell her all about you. And I want them all to be interested in you. Now, tell something."

"*Maman,* that's a very odd way to have someone tell a story," observed Adelaïda as she adjusted her easel, took up her brushes and her palette, and prepared to work on a painting she was copying from an engraving. Alexandra and Aglaya sat together on a couch with their hands folded waiting to hear the conversation. The prince noticed that he had become the center of attention.

"I wouldn't tell a story if I were ordered to like that," remarked Aglaya.

"Why? What's so odd about that? Why shouldn't he tell something? He has a tongue. I want to know how well he speaks. About anything at all. Tell us how you liked Switzerland and what your first impressions of it were. You just watch: he will start talking right now and will begin beautifully."

"My first impression was a strong one," began the prince.

"There, you see," said the precipitous lady to her daughters, "he has begun."

"Do at least let him say something, *Maman*," said Alexandra, stopping her. She whispered to Aglaya, "This prince might be a great rogue and not an idiot at all."

"I'm sure of it. I saw it a long time ago," replied Aglaya. "And it is mean of him to play such a role. What does he expect to gain by it?"

"My first impression was very strong," repeated the prince. "When I was taken out of Russia we passed through various German towns, and I could only look in silence, and I remember not even asking questions. This was after a series of violent and painful attacks of my illness, and as always when the illness grew intense and the fits recurred several times in a row I fell into a complete stupor. I lost my memory, and though my mind worked I lost my logical train of thought. I could not keep what happened during more than two or three days in a row straight in my mind. That is how it seems to me. When the attacks abated I became healthy and strong again, as I am now. I remember the unbearable sadness I felt, I even wanted to cry, I was all bewildered and uneasy. What impressed me terribly was how *foreign* everything was. I understood this. This foreignness was killing me. I completely recovered from this depression, as I recall, one night after I had reached Switzerland and was in Basel, when I was awakened by the braying of a donkey in the marketplace. The donkey made a great impression on me and for some reason pleased me intensely, and at the same time everything seemed to clear up in my head."

"A donkey? That's strange," observed Madame Yepanchin. "But then it isn't strange at all," she added, looking angrily at her laughing daughters. "Any one of us might fall in love with a donkey. It happened in mythology. Go on, Prince."

"From that time on I developed a great fondness for donkeys; it's even a kind of special affection. I began to ask questions about them, because I had never really seen them before, and I was immediately convinced that it is the most useful of animals, hardworking, strong, patient, cheap, and long-suffering. And suddenly through this donkey all Switzerland became pleasing to me, so that my former feeling of sadness passed completely."

76

"All that is very odd, but I think we can leave the donkey and move to another subject. What are you laughing about, Aglaya? And you, Adelaïda? The prince has told about the donkey beautifully. He has seen it himself, and what have you seen? You haven't been abroad."

"I've seen a donkey, *Maman*," said Adelaïda.

"And I've heard one," declared Aglaya. All three girls began to laugh again. The prince laughed with them.

"That is very bad of you," observed Madame Yepanchin. "You must excuse them, Prince, they are good girls. I'm always quarreling with them, but I'm fond of them. They're flighty and frivolous and crazy."

"Why?" laughed the prince. "In their place I wouldn't have missed such a chance either. Still, I stand up for the donkey The donkey is a good, useful fellow."

"And are you good, Prince? I ask out of curiosity," said Madame Yepanchin.

They all laughed again.

"That miserable donkey again! I wasn't thinking about him," she exclaimed. "Please believe me, Prince, I intended no—"

"Allusion? Oh, I believe you implicitly!"

And the prince went on laughing.

"It's nice that you laugh. I see that you are an unusually good young person," said Madame Yepanchin.

"Sometimes I'm not," replied the prince.

"But I am good," said Madame Yepanchin unexpectedly, "and you might say that I am always good, it's my one failing, because one shouldn't always be good. I often get angry for instance at these girls, but especially at Ivan Fyodorovitch, but the bad thing is that I am especially good when I'm angry. A little while ago, just before you arrived, I got angry and pretended I did not and could not understand anything. That happens to me, just as it happens to a child. Aglaya taught me a lesson. Thank you, Aglaya. But of course all this is nonsense. I'm not so foolish as I appear or as my daughters would like to present me. I have a will of my own, and I'm not easily embarrassed. But I say this without malice. Come here, Aglaya, kiss me—here now, that's enough of that," she said when Aglaya had kissed her lips and her hand with great feeling. "Do go on, Prince. Perhaps you could recollect something more interesting than the donkey."

"I still don't see," remarked Adelaïda, "how anyone can tell a story like that. I could never do it."

"But the prince can because the prince is extremely clever, ten times cleverer than you, perhaps even twelve times cleverer. I hope you'll realize it after this. Prove it to them, Prince; do continue. You can surely leave out the donkey now. Tell us, what did you see abroad besides the donkey?"

"But he was very clever about the donkey," remarked Alexandra. "The prince spoke very interestingly about his illness and how everything seemed pleasant to him again after a single outside shock. I have always been very interested in how people go out of their minds and then recover again. Especially if it happens suddenly."

"Yes, isn't it so!" cried Madame Yepanchin excitedly. "I see that sometimes you can be clever, too. Here now, stop laughing! I think you were talking about Swiss scenery, Prince. So then?"

"We arrived in Lucerne, and I was taken around the lake. I felt how beautiful it was, but I was terribly depressed by it," said the prince.

"Why?" asked Alexandra.

"I don't know. I always feel depressed and unsettled when I look at such scenery for the first time; it affects me both with pleasure and uneasiness. But all that was while I was still sick."

"Oh yes, but I'd like to see it very much," said Adelaïda. "I don't understand why we don't go abroad. I haven't been able to find a subject to paint for the last two years. 'The East and the South have been painted long ago. . . .' * Prince, find me a subject to paint."

"I don't know anything about that. It seems to me that one should look and then paint."

"I don't know how to look."

"Why are you talking in riddles? I can't understand a thing," interrupted Madame Yepanchin. "What do you mean you don't know how to look? You have eyes, you look. If you don't know how to look here at home, you won't know how abroad. You'd better tell us how you looked at things yourself, Prince."

"Yes, that would be better," said Adelaïda. "The prince has learned to see things abroad."

"I don't know. All I did there was care for my health. I don't know if I learned to see. But almost all the time I was very happy."

"Happy!" exclaimed Aglaya. "Do you know how to be happy? Then how can you say that you didn't learn how to see? You can teach us."

"Do teach us, please," laughed Adelaïda.

"I can't teach you anything," said the prince, laughing also. "Almost my whole time abroad I lived in the same Swiss vil-

78

lage. Only rarely did I take short trips away from it. What could I teach you? All I did at first was not be bored; I soon began to get better. Later, each day became precious to me, and more precious as time went by, until I began to notice it. I went to bed feeling very contented and arose even happier still. But why this was so, it's rather hard to say."

"So you didn't want to go anywhere?" asked Alexandra. "You had no desire to go?"

"At first, at the very beginning, I did; and I used to be very restless. I thought all the time of what my life would be, what the future would bring. At certain moments I was particularly restless. You know, there are such moments, especially when one is alone. There was a waterfall there, not a very big one; it fell from high on the mountain in a thin thread almost straight down—white, splashing, and foaming. It fell from a great height, but it didn't seem high; it was a third of a mile away but seemed only fifty yards. I loved to listen to its sound at night, yet at those times I sometimes experienced a feeling of great restlessness. And sometimes also at midday when I wandered somewhere out on the mountains, I would stand alone on a mountainside surrounded by huge old resinous pines; above me on top of a steep rock cliff was an ancient medieval castle in ruins; our little village was far, far below, barely visible; and all around me bright sunshine, blue sky, and the terrible stillness. There I would feel I was being called away somewhere; and it always seemed to me that if I walked straight for a long, long time and reached that line where earth and sky meet, I would find there the key to the whole mystery, and I would at once behold a new life a thousand times more intense and turbulent than ours. I dreamed of a great city, like Naples, full of palaces, noise, uproar, life — What I didn't dream! But afterward I imagined that one might find a tremendous life in prison too."

"I read that commendable thought in my school reader when I was twelve," said Aglaya.

"This is all philosophy," remarked Adelaïda. "You are a philosopher, and you've come to teach us."

"You might be right," said the prince with a smile, "I might really be a philosopher, and—who knows?—I might really have it in mind to teach. That might possibly be true."

"And your philosophy is exactly like Yevlampia Nikolayevna's," Aglaya observed again. "She's the widow of a government clerk who comes to see us, and partly to live off us. Her whole concern in life is to get things cheaply, to live as cheaply as she can, and she talks of nothing but kopecks; but, mind you, she has money; she's a cheat. That is exactly like your immense life in prison and maybe also your four years of bliss in the little village, for which you traded your Naples, and at a profit, apparently, though it was only a very small one."

"There is still more than one opinion about life in prison," said the prince. "I heard a story of a man who spent twelve years in prison. He was one of the patients under my professor's care. He had fits, he was occasionally restless, he would weep, and once he even tried to kill himself. His life in prison was very sad, I assure you, but certainly not petty. His only acquaintances were a spider and a little tree which had grown up under his window— But I had better tell you of another encounter I had with a man last year. There was one very strange incident in his life—strange because a thing like this happens so very rarely. This man had once been taken with others before the scaffold and sentenced to be shot for a political crime. Twenty minutes later a decree of pardon was read to them, and a different punishment imposed. Nevertheless, in the interval between the two decrees, twenty minutes or at least a quarter of an hour, he had lived absolutely convinced that in a few minutes he would die. I was always anxious to listen when he recalled his impressions of that time, and I would often ask him about it. He remembered everything with extraordinary clarity and said he would never forget anything about those minutes. Twenty paces from the scaffold, where the soldiers and a crowd of people stood, three posts were planted in the ground; for there were several condemned criminals to be executed. The first three were led to the posts, bound, and dressed in death clothes (long white robes); and white hoods were pulled down over their eyes so they would not see the guns. Then a squad of several soldiers was formed opposite each post. My friend stood eighth on the list, which meant he would go to the posts on the third round. A priest went to each of them with a cross. It looked as if he had only five minutes to live. He told me those five minutes seemed an eternity stretching before him, a great abundance of time; he felt that in those five minutes he could live so many lifetimes that there was no need, yet, to think of the final moment; so he laid out his time. He allotted time to say farewell to his comrades, about two minutes; then another two minutes to think about himself for the last time, and then to look around for the last time. He remembered that he had carried out this plan exactly. He was dying at twenty-seven, a strong and healthy man. He remembered that as he said good-bye to comrades he asked one of them a rather pointless question and had been fascinated by the

80

answer. Then, when he had said good-bye to his comrades, came those two minutes he had set aside to think about *himself;* he knew beforehand what he was going to think about: he wanted to conceive, as fast and as vividly as he could, how it was that he was here and alive now and in three minutes he would be *something*—something or someone—but what? And where? And he thought he could resolve all this in two minutes! Not far away there was a church, and its gilt roof gleamed in the bright sun. He remembered that he gazed with terrible intensity at that roof and the rays of sun that sparkled from it; he could not take his eyes from those rays of light; it seemed to him this light was his new nature and that in three minutes he would somehow melt into it. His uncertainty and revulsion against this new thing which was bound to happen at any moment were terrible; but he said that nothing was more awful than the incessant thought, 'What if I was not to die! What if life was given back to me! What an eternity! And it all would be mine! I would turn each minute into a century. I would miss nothing. I would reckon each passing minute and waste nothing!' He said that this thought finally filled him with such rage that he wanted to be shot as soon as possible."

The prince suddenly stopped talking. Everyone waited for him to continue and to reach some conclusion.

"Have you finished?" asked Aglaya.

"Pardon? Oh, yes, I finished," said the prince, emerging from a moment's deep reflection.

"But what did you tell all this for?"

"Oh. It just came to mind. Something that was said—"

"You're wandering, Prince," remarked Alexandra. "You probably meant to make the point that no instant can be considered petty and that sometimes five minutes are more precious than great riches. All this is commendable, but let me ask you about this friend of yours who told you such horrors —he was pardoned after all; he was given this 'eternity.' So, what did he do with this abundance of time later? Did he 'reckon every minute'?"

"Oh no, he told me himself—I asked him about that. He didn't live that way at all and wasted many, many minutes."

"Well, that should show you it's really impossible to live counting every moment. For some reason it's impossible."

"Yes, for some reason it is impossible," repeated the prince. "I thought so myself. And yet somehow I can't believe—"

"And you think you can live more intelligently than everyone else?" said Aglaya.

"Yes, I've sometimes thought that."

"And do you still?"

"Yes—I do," replied the prince, looking steadily at Aglaya with the same gentle, timid smile. Then he broke into laughter again and looked at her gaily.

"Modest, aren't you!" said Aglaya almost irritably.

"But how brave you are. Here you laugh, and I was so struck by one part of that man's story that I dreamed about it afterward—I dreamed about those five minutes."

Once again he looked searchingly and intently at his listeners. "You're not angry with me about anything?" he asked suddenly, as if in embarrassment, but looking at them steadily.

"What for!" exclaimed all three girls in surprise.

"Because I seem to be preaching to you all the time."

Everyone laughed.

"If you are angry, please don't be," he said. "I know very well I've lived less than other people and know less about life than anyone. I probably talk very strangely sometimes—" And he was overcome by confusion.

"If you say you've been happy, then you've not lived less than other people but more. Why do you pretend and make excuses for yourself?" Aglaya persisted sternly. "And please don't worry about preaching to us, because you have nothing to be superior about. With your quietism one could live a happy life for a hundred years. Show you an execution, or one's little finger, and you will draw elevating reflections from both things and be as happy and untroubled as you were before. That is an easy way to live."

"I have no idea why you're always so cross," said Madame Yepanchin, who had for some time been watching the speakers' faces. "And besides, I can't understand what you are talking about either. What little finger? That's nonsense! The prince talks beautifully, even if a trifle sadly. Why do you discourage him? When he began he was laughing, and now he's quite glum."

"Never mind, *Maman*. It's a shame, Prince, that you haven't seen an execution; I had a question to ask you."

"I have seen an execution," replied the prince.

"You have!" exclaimed Aglaya. "I should have guessed. This is really too much. If you have seen one, how can you say that you've always lived happily? So, didn't I tell you the truth?"

"But do they execute people in your village?" asked Adelaïda.

"I saw it in Lyons. I went there with Schneider. He took me along. As soon as we arrived, there it was."

"Well, did you like it? Was it very enlightening? Was it a profitable experience?" asked Aglaya.

"I didn't like it at all, and afterward I was slightly sick. But I must admit it was as if I was rooted to the spot, I couldn't take my eyes off it."

"I wouldn't be able to either," said Aglaya.

"They don't like women to watch at all. They even write about such women in the papers."

"In other words, in saying it isn't women's business they say it is men's business, and they justify it this way. I congratulate them on their logic. But, of course, you'd agree with this."

"Tell about the execution," interrupted Adelaïda.

"I would much rather not just now." The prince seemed confused and frowned.

"You almost seem to grudge telling us," taunted Aglaya.

"No. It's because I've just been telling about that execution."

"Telling whom?"

"Your servant, while I was waiting."

"Which servant?" he heard from all sides.

"The one who sits in the entrance hall, with graying hair and a reddish face. I was sitting in the entrance hall waiting to see Ivan Fyodorovitch."

"That's strange," observed Madame Yepanchin.

"The prince is a democrat," said Aglaya sharply. "So now if you've told Alexey, you can't refuse to tell us."

"I simply must hear it," said Adelaïda.

"Well, as a matter of fact," the prince said to her, growing animated again (he seemed able to recover his spirits very readily and quickly became trusting), "it occured to me just now when you asked me for a subject to paint to suggest this: draw the face of a condemned person a minute before the guillotine blade falls, when he is still standing on the scaffold before he lies down on that plank."

"The face? Only the face?" asked Adelaïda. "That would be an odd subject. And what kind of a painting would it make?"

"I don't know. Why not?" insisted the prince eagerly. "Not so long ago I saw such a painting in Basel. I'd like to tell you about it. Someday I shall. It impressed me very much."

"You must certainly tell us about this Basel painting later," said Adelaïda, "but right now explain to me about making a picture of this execution. Could you tell me how you yourself

83

imagine it? How is the face to be drawn? Just that, the face alone? What sort of a face is it?"

"It's just one minute before death," began the prince with perfect readiness, carried away by his memories and apparently forgetting everything else immediately, "that moment he has just climbed the stairs and stepped onto the scaffold. There he looked in my direction, I looked at his face, and I understood everything. But how to tell it! I wish, oh, I really wish you or someone would paint it! You especially. I thought at the time that a picture of it would be useful. I mean, you would have to show everything that has gone on before—everything, everything. He has been in prison expecting his execution to take place at least a week ahead; he has been counting on the usual formal delays, on the sentence being sent somewhere and returned only in a week. But for some reason the procedure was cut short. At five o'clock in the morning he was asleep. It was the end of October, at five o'clock it was still cold and dark. The head of the prison came in quietly with the guard and touched him gently on the shoulder. He rose up on one elbow, he saw the light. 'What is it?' 'The execution is at ten o'clock.' Still half asleep he didn't believe it, he started to argue about the paper that was due only in a week, but when he was fully awake he fell silent—so I heard it told. Then he said, 'It's very hard this suddenly,' and he was silent again and didn't want to say anything more. Then three or four hours were spent on the usual things: the priest, the breakfast at which he was given wine, coffee, and beef. (Isn't that a mockery? You think how cruel it is, and yet, by heaven, those innocent people do this out of the kindness of their hearts and are convinced they're being humane.) Then the grooming and dressing of the condemned man (have you any idea what that is like?). Finally, he is taken through the town to the scaffold. I think that as he is being driven there he feels he has still an eternity to live. It seems to me he must have thought as he went through the town, 'I still have a long time, I still have three streets to live. I'll pass through this one, then there is that one, then the one with the baker on the right—it will be a long time before we reach the baker!' All around is the crowd, noise, and shouts, ten thousand faces, ten thousand eyes—all this has to be borne and, worst of all, the thought: 'Here they are, ten thousand of them, and not one of them is being executed—I am being executed!' Well, all that is just the beginning. There is a ladder leading up to the scaffold. There, before the ladder, he suddenly bursts into tears; a strong manly fellow who was said to have been a great criminal. The priest was with him every minute of the time; he rode with him in the cart, he talked without stopping, though it is doubtful if the other heard him; he would start listening, but after the third word he couldn't understand anymore. It must have been like that. At last he started up the ladder; then his legs were bound and he could only move in little steps. The priest, who must have been an intelligent man, stopped talking and kept giving him the cross to kiss. At the foot of the ladder he had been very pale, but as he climbed the scaffold and stood on it, he turned as white as paper, absolutely like white writing paper. His legs must have felt weak and wooden, and he must have felt nauseous, as if he was strangling, with a tickling sensation in his throat. Did you ever feel like that when you've been frightened, in moments of terror when your reason still functions but to no avail? I think that for instance if a person is faced with inevitable destruction, if a house is falling in on him, he must experience a terrific desire just to sit down, close his eyes, and wait—whatever happens! Just then when the weakness was beginning, the priest, with a rapid movement, silently presented the cross to his lips—such a little cross, a square silver cross; presented it to his lips again and again. And the moment the cross touched his lips he would open his eyes and his legs would move. He kissed the cross greedily, he hurried to kiss it as if he were hurrying not to forget to take something with him in case of need, but I doubt whether he had any religious feeling at this moment And it was like this until he was laid down on the plank. It is strange that people very rarely faint during those final seconds! On the contrary, the brain is terribly alive and active; it must be racing, racing, racing like a machine at full speed. I imagine how many thoughts must be throbbing together, all unfinished, some of them may be irrelevant and absurd: 'That man staring—has a wart on his forehead; and, here, one of the executioner's buttons has rusted.' And at the same time he knows everything and remembers everything; there is one point that cannot be forgotten, and he cannot faint, and everything turns around it, around that point. And to think that it must be like this up to the last quarter second, when his head is already on the block, and waits, and—*knows,* and suddenly he hears the iron slithering down above his head! He would certainly hear that! If I was lying there I would especially listen for it and I would hear it. It might be only a fraction of an instant, but one would have to hear it. And imagine, it is still argued whether as the head falls off it perhaps knows for a second it is falling off—what a thought! And what if it is for five seconds? Draw the scaffold so that

85

only the last step is clearly seen in the foreground, the condemned man has just stepped onto it; his head, his face is as white as paper; the priest holds out the cross to him, he seeks it avidly with his blue lips, and he looks and—*knows everything*. The cross and the head, there is the painting; the faces of the priest, the executioner and his two assistants, and a few heads and eyes below—all this could be painted in subdued tones to render the background. That would be the picture!"

The prince fell silent and looked at them.

"That certainly isn't like quietism," said Alexandra to herself.

"Well," said Adelaïda, "now tell us about how you were in love."

The prince looked at her in surprise.

"Listen," continued Adelaïda, as if she were in a great hurry, "you've still to tell about the Basel picture, but right now I want to hear about how you were in love. Don't deny it—you have been. Besides, the moment you start telling something you stop being a philosopher."

"As soon as you stop telling anything you immediately seem ashamed of what you've been telling," remarked Aglaya suddenly. "Why is that?"

"That's just silly," interrupted Madame Yepanchin, looking indignantly at Aglaya.

"Not the least bit clever," agreed Alexandra.

"Don't believe her, Prince," Madame Yepanchin told him. "She does it on purpose out of some kind of nastiness. She's not so foolishly brought up as that. Don't think it means anything if they tease you this way. Apparently they are up to something, but they love you already. I know their faces."

"And I know their faces, too," said the prince with particular emphasis on his words.

"How can that be?" asked Adelaïda, showing curiosity.

"What do you know about our faces?" asked the other two, more and more intrigued.

But the prince was silent and grave. They all awaited his answer. "I shall tell you afterward," he said, quietly and seriously.

"You're definitely trying to arouse our interest!" cried Aglaya. "And what solemnity!"

"All right," said Adelaïda, again as if she was in a hurry, "if you're such an expert on faces you've certainly been in love and I was right. Tell us about it."

"I haven't been in love," replied the prince as quietly and gravely as before. "I have been—happy otherwise."

"How? In what way?"

"All right, I shall tell you," said the prince, as though in profound meditation.

Chapter SIX

∽◆∾

"You are all looking at me with such curiosity," began the prince, "that if I don't satisfy it you might be angry with me. No, I am joking," he quickly added with a smile. "There were always children there, and I was with children all the time I was there, only with children. They were the children of that village, a whole crowd of them who went to school there. Not that I was teaching them, no, there was the school-teacher for that. Jules Thibaut; I suppose I did teach them too, but mostly I was just with them, and that was how I spent my whole four years. I had no need of anything else. I used to tell them everything, I hid nothing from them. Their fathers and relatives all were angry with me because after a while the children couldn't do without me and were always flocking around me, and in the end the schoolteacher became my chief enemy. I made many enemies there, and all on account of the children. Even Schneider tried to make me feel ashamed. What were they afraid of? A child can be told everything! I've always been struck by how poorly grown-ups know children, how poorly even fathers and mothers know their own children. Nothing should be hidden from children on the pretext that they are little and it's too soon for them to know. What a sad and unfortunate idea! And how quick the children notice it when their fathers consider them too little to understand anything, while they in fact understand everything. Grown-ups don't realize that a child can give extremely serious advice even about difficult matters. My Lord, when that pretty little bird of a child looks at you, so happy and confiding, aren't you ashamed to deceive it? I call them little birds because there is nothing better than a bird in the world. But everyone in the village was angry with me, mostly about something that happened— As for Thibaut, he was simply jealous of me. At first he just shook his head and wondered how the children understood everything from me and hardly anything from him, and then he began laughing at me when I told him that neither of us would teach them anything, but they would teach us. And how could he be jealous and speak against me when he lived among children himself! Through children the soul is healed. There was one invalid in Schneider's establishment, a very unhappy man. His was such a terrible unhappiness that I doubt if there could be anything like it. He had been sent to be treated for insanity, though in my opinion he was not insane, he only suffered terrible distress—that was all that was the matter with him. And if you only knew what our children came to mean to him. But I'll tell you about that patient another time; I'll tell you now how it all began. At first the children did not care for me. I was so big and, as always, so clumsy, and I know I am ugly; and then too I was a foreigner. At first the children would laugh at me, and later, when they saw me kissing Marie, they even began throwing stones at me. I only kissed her once. No, don't laugh," the prince hastened to check the derisive laughter of his listeners. "It was no question of love. If you only knew what an unhappy creature she was you would feel sorry for her too, as I did. She was from our village. Her mother was an old woman. One of the two windows in their little tumbledown house was partitioned off, with the permission of the village administration, and from this window she was allowed to sell shoelaces, thread, tobacco, and soap; all for tiny sums, which she managed to live on. She was an invalid, and her legs were swollen so that she could not move from her place. Marie was her daughter, a frail, thin girl of about twenty. She had been consumptive for a long time, but she still went from house to house hiring herself out by the day for menial work; she scrubbed floors, did laundry, swept yards, looked after cattle. A certain French commercial traveler seduced her and took her away, and a week later he abandoned her alone on the road. She walked back home, begging on the way, all mud-spattered and in rags, her shoes in pieces. She was a week walking back, sleeping in the fields at night, and she caught a terrible cold; her feet were covered with sores, her hands were chapped and swollen. And she hadn't been pretty before, only her eyes were kind, gentle, innocent. She was extremely quiet. One time—long before—she suddenly began singing during her work, and I remember that everyone was surprised and started to laugh. 'Marie is singing! What's this? Marie is singing!' And she was terribly upset and was silent thereafter. At that time people were still being kind to her, but when she returned, sick and in tatters, no one showed any pity for her! How cruel people are this way! What harsh ideas they have about these things! First the mother received her with spite and contempt: 'You have disgraced me!' She was the first to point the finger of shame at her. When the people of the village learned that Marie had returned, everyone ran to have a look at her; almost the whole village gathered in the old woman's shack: old men, children, women, girls, everyone—an avid, milling crowd. Marie was lying on the floor at the old woman's feet, hungry and with her clothes all torn; she was crying. When everyone crowded around she hid her face in her mussed hair and lay very still, face downward on the floor. Everyone standing around looked at her as if she was a reptile; the old men condemned and scolded her, the young people laughed, the women shouted abuse at her and glared at her as if she was some kind of loathsome spider. The mother allowed it all, she sat there nodding her head and approving. She herself was then very sick and about to die; in fact two months later she did die; she knew that she was dying, but right up to her death she didn't think to make peace with her daughter. She didn't even speak a word to her, she had her sleep out in the passageway and gave her almost nothing to eat. She often had to bathe her bad legs in hot water; every day Marie would bathe her legs and take care of her. The old woman accepted all her services in silence and never said a single kind word to her. Marie endured all this, and later when I became acquainted with her I saw that she herself accepted it as perfectly right and proper and considered herself the lowest creature on earth. When the old woman became completely bedridden the other old women of the village came in turns to care for her; that is the custom there. Then they stopped giving Marie anything to eat at all; and in the village everyone chased her off, and no one would give her work, as they had done before. Everyone virtually spat on her, the men no longer even treated her as a woman, and they would say obscene things to her. Sometimes, though quite seldom, when the men would get drunk on Sunday they would amuse themselves by throwing coins on the ground in front of her; Marie would pick them up without a word. By then she had already begun to cough blood. At last her torn clothes were nothing but rags, and she was ashamed to show herself in the village; she had gone barefoot since she had come back. And it was then that the children in particular, the whole crowd of them—there were about forty schoolchildren—began teasing her and even throwing dirt at her. She asked the cowherd to let her look after the cows, but he drove her away. Then, without permission, she began spending the whole day out with the herd. And as she made herself very useful to the cowherd he noticed it and no longer drove her away, and sometimes he even gave her the leavings of his dinner of bread and cheese. He considered this a great charity on his part. When the mother died the pastor saw fit to hold Marie up to public shame in church. Marie stood behind the coffin in her rags and wept. A large crowd had gathered to watch her weeping and walking behind the coffin; and then the pastor —who was a young man whose whole ambition was to become a great preacher—pointed to Marie and addressed them: 'Here is who caused the death of this respectable woman' (which was not true, because she had been ill for two years). 'Here she stands before you not daring to look up because she has been marked by the finger of God. There she stands barefoot and in rags, a warning to those who lose their virtue! Who is she? Her own daughter!' And so on, in the same manner. And just imagine, this vileness pleased almost everyone; but just then an extraordinary thing happened. The children took her part because by this time the children were already on my side and had begun to love Marie. This is how it happened. I wanted to do something for Marie; she was greatly in need of money, but I never had any money then, not a kopeck. I had a little diamond pin, and I sold it to a certain peddler who went from village to village trading old clothes. He gave me eight francs for it, though it was certainly worth forty. I tried for a long time to meet Marie alone; finally we met at a hedge outside the village, on a small path leading up the mountain, behind a tree. There I gave her the eight francs and told her to take good care of them because I would have no more; and then I kissed her and told her not to think I had any evil intentions, and that I kissed her not because I was in love with her but because I felt very sorry for her, and that from the very beginning I had not thought her guilty but only very unhappy. I wanted very much to comfort her then and to assure her that she should not consider herself beneath everyone, but she didn't seem to understand. I noticed this at once, though the whole time she scarcely uttered a word and stood before me with her eyes lowered, terribly ashamed. When I had finished she kissed my hand, and I took her hand and would have kissed it, but she pulled it away. Just then, suddenly, the children caught sight of us, a whole group of them; I learned later they had been spying on me for some time. They began clapping their hands and whistling and laughing, and Marie ran away. I tried to speak to them, but they began throwing stones at me. That same day everyone heard about it, the whole village, and again everyone was against Marie; they began disliking her more than ever. I even heard they wanted to have her tried and punished but, thank God, it didn't come to that. But the children would not leave her in peace, they teased her more than ever, they threw mud at her; they chased her, and she, with her weak lungs, ran away from them gasping for breath as they ran after her shouting insults at her. Once I even fought with them. Then I began talking to them, and I talked every day, whenever I could. Sometimes they stopped and listened, though they still abused me. I told them how miserable Marie was; soon they stopped insulting me and merely walked away in silence. Little by little we began to talk together; I kept nothing from them, I told them everything. They listened with great interest and soon began to feel sorry for Marie. Some of them took to greeting her in a friendly way when they met her—the custom there is that when people meet, whether they are acquainted or not, they bow and say a word of greeting. I can imagine how surprised Marie was. One time two little girls brought a plate of food and gave it to her, then they came to tell me. They told me that Marie had burst into tears and that now they loved her very much. Soon everyone began to love her, and at the same time they suddenly loved me too. They started to come to see me often and always asked me to tell them stories. I must have told them well, because they always liked to listen to me. And then I would study and read just so as to have things to tell them afterward, and during the next three years I talked to them about everything. Later, when everyone, including Schneider, took me to task for speaking to them like grown-ups and not hiding anything from them, I answered that it was a shame to tell them lies, that even if it was kept from them they would find out everything anyway, and they might learn it in a bad light, but would not from me. One has only to remember how it was in one's own childhood. But they did not agree. I kissed Marie two weeks before her mother's death; when the pastor delivered his sermon all the children were already on my side. At once I told them about the pastor's action and explained it to them. They all became angry with him, and some were so enraged that they threw stones through his windows. I stopped them, because this was wrong, but everyone in the village immediately learned all about it and began accusing me of corrupting the children. Then they learned that the children loved Marie, and they were terribly alarmed; but by now Marie was happy. The children were forbidden to be with her, but they ran off secretly to the herd, more than a quarter mile from the village, to see her. They would bring her treats, and some would simply run to her to hug and kiss her and say, *'Je vous aime, Marie!'* and then run back quickly. Marie was almost driven mad by such sudden happiness; she had never even dreamed of such happiness; she was abashed and she was full of joy. But what the children liked most, especially the girls, was to run to her and tell her I loved her and always talked about her. They told her that I told them all about everything and that they loved her now and would love her forever. Then they would run to me and with such bright, joyful faces tell me they had just seen Marie and that Marie sent her regards. In the evening I would walk to the waterfall; there was one spot there surrounded by poplars and completely hidden from the village. They would come to me in the evenings there, sometimes in secret. I think my love for Marie was an immense pleasure to them, and this was the only thing in which I deceived them. I did not tell them I didn't love Marie—I mean that I was not in love with her but only felt very sorry for her; I saw they wanted it to be as they imagined it among themselves; so I said nothing and pretended that they had guessed right. And how delicate and tender their little hearts were! For one thing it seemed impossible to them that their good Leon should so love Marie when Marie was so badly dressed and without shoes. Well, would you believe it? They managed to get her shoes, and stockings, and linen, and even a dress of some sort. How they did it, I don't know. The whole crowd of them worked at it together. When I questioned them they only laughed merrily, and the little girls clapped their hands and kissed me. Sometimes I too went in secret to see Marie. By now she was very sick and could hardly walk; at last she stopped working for the cowherd but still went out with the cattle every morning. She would sit by herself. There was a ledge on a certain sheer, almost vertical rock face there, and she would sit in a corner of the ledge out of sight, all day without moving, from early morning until the cattle went home. She was already so weakened by consumption that most of the time she sat with her eyes closed, her head leaning against the rock, drowsing and breathing heavily; her face had grown thin as a skeleton's, and perspiration stood out on her forehead and temples. This was how I always found her. I used to come only for a few minutes, and I too didn't wish to be seen. As soon as I appeared, Marie would give a start, open her eyes, and fall to kissing my hands. I no longer drew away, because it made her happy. All the time I sat there she would tremble and cry; sometimes she started to speak but it was hard to understand her. In her excitement and elation she seemed at times almost insane. Sometimes the children came with me. When they did they would usually stand a little way off to guard us against whoever or whatever might come, and this was a great pleasure for them. When we went away Marie would be left alone again, as still as before, her eyes closed, her head resting against the rock; perhaps she was dreaming about something. One morning she couldn't go out with the herd, and she stayed alone in her empty house. At once the children learned, and that day almost all of them went to visit her. She lay in bed, all alone. For two days only the children looked after her, who ran in to her by turns; but later when the village heard that Marie now was really dying, the old women came and took turns sitting with her. I believe the villagers had begun to pity Marie; at least they no longer scolded the children or prevented them from seeing her. Marie was drowsy all the time, but her sleep was restless; she coughed dreadfully. The old women would drive the children away, but they would run to the window, sometimes only for a moment, just to say, *'Bonjour, notre bonne Marie!'* And as soon as she caught sight of them or heard them she would revive and immediately, not heeding the old women, try to raise herself on one elbow and nod to them and thank them. They would bring her treats as before, but she ate almost nothing. I assure you that because of them she died almost happy. Because of them she forgot her deep misery; it was as if she had been pardoned by them, because to the very end she considered herself guilty of great wrongdoing. Like little birds, they beat against her window every morning and called her, *'Nous t'aimons, Marie.'* She died very soon. I thought she would live much longer. On the eve of her death I dropped by her house at sunset. I think she recognized me, and I pressed her hand for the last time; how dry it was! Then suddenly the next morning they came and told me that Marie had died. The children could not be restrained: they decked her coffin with flowers and placed a garland on her head. In the church the pastor did not hold the dead girl up to shame, and there were few at the funeral anyway, only a few who had stopped out of curiosity, but when the moment came to carry the coffin the children all rushed forward to carry it themselves. Since they could not carry it alone, they helped carry it, and they ran behind the coffin and they all wept. From that time on Marie's grave has always been tended by the children; they cover it with flowers every year and planted roses around it. But it was after the funeral that the villagers began their worst persecutions of me, on account of the children. The pastor and the schoolteacher were the chief instigators. The children were absolutely forbidden even to meet with me, and Schneider undertook to see that they didn't. Still we did see each other, and we communicated at a distance by signs. They sent me little notes. Eventually this was no longer necessary, but it was very nice at the time: because of the persecution I was actually drawn closer to the children than ever before. The last year I became almost reconciled with Thibaut and the pastor. But Schneider talked and argued a lot with me about my pernicious 'system' with the children. As if I had a system! Finally—just before my departure—Schneider put forward a very odd idea: he told me that he was entirely convinced I was a complete child myself, a real child, that is, and that only in my face and figure was I a grown-up person, but as for my development, my soul, my character, and perhaps even my intelligence, I was not an adult, and would never be one even if I lived to be sixty. I laughed a great deal; he was wrong, of course, for what kind of child am I? But in one thing he was right: I really don't like to be with grown-up, adult people—I realized that a long time ago—I don't like to be with them because I don't know how to behave with them. Whatever they say to me, however kind they are to me, it's always difficult for me to be with them for some reason, and I am terribly glad when I can get away the sooner to my comrades, for my comrades have always been children, not because I am a child myself but simply because I am drawn to them. At the very beginning of my life in the village, when I used to go off on solitary, brooding walks in the mountains, I would sometimes meet—especially at midday—that noisy crowd of children running home from school with their satchels and slates, with their cries and laughter and their games; then my soul suddenly went out to them. I don't know just how it was, but I began to have a kind of intense feeling of happiness every time I met them. I would stop and laugh from sheer happiness, seeing their little legs flashing in perpetual movement, the little boys and girls running together, their laughter and their tears (for many of them managed to fight, cry, make up, and start playing again, all on the way home from school), and I forgot all about my sadness. Later, in the last three years I was there, I couldn't understand how or why people could be sad and melancholy. I devoted my life entirely to them. I never expected to leave the village, and it never entered my mind that someday I would be returning home to Russia. I thought I would always be there. But I realized at last that Schneider could not keep me on forever, and just then a certain matter arose which was, apparently, so important that Schneider himself was anxious for me to go and replied for me that I was coming. I shall find out what it's about and get someone's advice. Perhaps the course of my life will be completely changed, but that's not what really matters. What matters is that my life is already changed. I left a great deal behind there—too much. It's all gone. I sat in the train and thought, 'Now I am going among people; I know nothing, perhaps, but a new life has begun for me.' I have decided to do what is to be done honestly and resolutely. It may be that I'll be bored and uncomfortable with people. But as a first step I've resolved to be polite and open with everyone: no one will expect more than that from me. It may be that I'll be taken for a child here—it can't be helped! For some reason everyone considers me an idiot, too, and it's true there was a time I was so sick that I could be taken for an idiot. But what kind of an idiot am I now that I understand people take me for an idiot? When I enter a room I think, 'Here they are, taking me for an idiot, yet I am intelligent and they don't realize it.' I have that thought often. It was only when I was in Berlin and received several letters from the children, which they'd managed to write me so quickly, that I knew how I loved them. How painful it was getting that first letter! How sad they were as they were seeing me off! A month before they had begun saying their farewells. *'Leon s'en va, Leon s'en va pour toujours!'* We met every evening at the waterfall as we had done before and always talked of how we would be parting. Sometimes it was all as gay as in the past; except that when they said good-bye at night they would hug me warmly, which they had not done before. Some of them came running to me in secret, one at a time, just so they could throw their arms around me and kiss me alone and not in the presence of the others. When the time came for me to leave, all of them, the whole pack, went with me to see me off at the station. The station was more than a half mile from the village. They tried their best not to cry, but many of them could not help it and wept loudly, especially the little girls. We were hurrying so as not to be late for the train, but suddenly one or another of them would run to me to embrace me, and this would stop the whole crowd of them; and though we were in a hurry everyone stopped and waited while he said good-bye. When I had taken my seat in the train and the train began to move they all cheered me, and they stood there for a long time until the train had gone out of sight. And I looked back at them—listen, when I came in here a little while ago and looked at your sweet faces—I observe faces very carefully now—and heard your first words, my heart felt light again for the first time since then. I thought then that perhaps I was really a person marked for happiness; for I know one doesn't often meet people one comes to like so soon, and I met you almost as soon as I got off the train. I know very well one should feel ashamed to speak of one's feelings to everyone, but I'm telling them to you and I don't feel ashamed. I'm not a sociable person and shall probably not come to see you again for a long time. You mustn't take it in bad part: I didn't say it because you don't mean anything to me, and don't think that I have been offended by anything either. You have asked me about your faces and what I saw in them? I'll tell you with great pleasure. You, Adelaïda Ivanovna, you have a happy face, the most likable face of all three. Besides your being very good-looking, one thinks as he looks at you, 'She has the face of a kind sister.' You approach a person simply and gaily, but you are also quick to understand him. That's how your face seems to me. You, Alexandra Ivanovna, you too have a lovely and very sweet face, but perhaps you have some kind of hidden sorrow; your heart is certainly the kindest, but you are not gay. There is something special about your face that reminds me of the Holbein Madonna in Dresden. There, so much for your face. Am I good at guessing? You said I was yourselves. But about your face, Lizaveta Prokofyevna," he suddenly addressed himself to Madame Yepanchin, "about your face I have not only an impression but I feel for certain that you are a perfect child in every single way, in every good way and every bad way, in spite of your years. You aren't angry with me, are you, for talking like this? Because you know what I think of children. And don't think that I've been speaking so candidly about your faces because I'm simpleminded. Oh no, not at all! It could very well be that I have something in mind."

Chapter SEVEN

When the prince stopped talking, they all looked at him gaily, even Aglaya, but especially Lizaveta Prokofyevna.

"Well, now he has passed your examination!" she cried. "Well, young ladies, you thought you'd patronize him like some poor nobody, but he scarcely deigns accept you as his friends, and then only on condition that he won't see you often. So we're the ones to look silly, especially, I am happy to say, Ivan Fyodorovitch. Bravo, Prince. He told us to put you through an examination. And as for what you said about my face, it's all absolutely true: I am a child and I know it. I knew it before you told me; you express my thoughts in a nutshell. I am certain you have a character exactly like mine, and I'm so pleased! Like two drops of water. Except you are a man and I am a woman and you've been to Switzerland, that's all the difference."

"Not so fast, *Maman,*" cried Aglaya. "The prince said that in making all these declarations he had some hidden purpose and was not speaking openly."

"Yes, yes," laughed the others.

"Don't make fun, my dears, for he may be shrewder than all three of you put together. You'll see. But, Prince, you haven't said anything about Aglaya. Aglaya is waiting, and I am too."

"I can't say anything just now. I'll say it later."

"Why not? Isn't she worth noticing?"

"Oh yes, she is worth noticing. You are extraordinarily beautiful, Aglaya Ivanovna. You are so pretty that one is afraid to look at you."

"And is that all? And what of her real qualities?" insisted Madame Yepanchin.

"It is difficult to pass judgment on beauty; I am not ready yet. Beauty is a riddle."

"That means you're asking Aglaya a riddle," said Adelaïda. "Guess what it is, Aglaya. She is beautiful, Prince, isn't she?"

"Extremely!" replied the prince ardently, with an impassioned look at Aglaya. "Almost as beautiful as Nastassya Filippovna, though her face is quite different."

They all looked at one other in astonishment.

"As who?" gasped Madame Yepanchin. "As Nastassya Filippovna? Where have you seen Nastassya Filippovna? Which Nastassya Filippovna?"

"Gavril Ardalionovitch showed her portrait to Ivan Fyodorovitch a little while ago."

"What? Did he bring the portrait to Ivan Fyodorovitch?"

"To show it. Nastassya Filippovna gave Gavril Ardalionovitch her portrait today, and he brought it to show."

"I want to see it!" cried Madame Yepanchin eagerly. "Where is this portrait? If she's given it to him then he must have it, and he, of course, is still in the study. He always comes to work on Wednesday and never leaves before four. Call Gavril Ardalionovitch at once! No, wait. I'm not exactly dying to see him. Do me a favor, dear Prince. Go to the study and get the portrait from him and bring it here. Tell him we want to look at it. Please."

When the prince had gone Adelaïda said, "He's nice, but really a bit too simple."

"Yes, a bit too simple," agreed Alexandra. "To the point of being rather ridiculous."

Neither seemed to be saying all she was thinking.

"Still, he got out of it quite well—about our faces," said Aglaya. "He flattered everyone, even *Maman*."

"Don't be so witty, please," cried Madame Yepanchin. "He did not flatter me—though I was flattered."

"You think he was being clever?" asked Adelaïda.

"I don't think he could be as simple as all that."

"There she goes again!" Madame Yepanchin cried angrily. "It looks to me you are being more ridiculous than he is. He is simple, but he has his wits about him—in the highest sense of the term, of course. Exactly as I do."

On his way to the study the prince felt a little guilty. "Of course it was wrong of me to have mentioned the portrait," he reflected, "but, it could be that I've done well to have spoken of it, after all." A strange, though still imprecise thought had flashed into his mind.

Gavril Ardalionovitch was still sitting in the study, engrossed in his papers. To all appearances he earned the salary received from the joint stock company. He grew extremely upset when the prince requested the portrait and told him how the ladies in the drawing room had learned of it.

"Oh, why did you go blabbering!" he cried in angry vexation. "You don't know anything. Idiot!" he muttered to himself.

"I'm sorry. I simply wasn't thinking when I said it. I was saying that Aglaya was almost as beautiful as Nastassya Filippovna."

Ganya asked him to tell in more detail what had happened; the prince told him. Once again Ganya looked at him sarcastically.

"You really have Nastassya Filippovna on your brain—" he muttered, breaking off his thought and falling silent. He was evidently very upset. The prince reminded him of the portrait.

"Listen to me, Prince," said Ganya, as if an idea had suddenly struck him. "I have a great favor to ask you—but I honestly don't know if—"

He became embarrassed and did not finish. He seemed to be trying to make up his mind about something, debating with himself. The prince waited in silence. Once again Ganya studied him with avid and searching eyes.

"Prince," he resumed, "just at present the ladies in there —on account of an absolutely absurd and ridiculous matter —which I'm not responsible for—actually, it's not even worth mentioning— Well, it seems the ladies in there are a little angry with me, so for the time being I don't want to go in there without being called. And right now I absolutely must speak with Aglaya Ivanovna. So on the chance, I've written a few words to her," (a small folded note appeared in his hand), "but I don't know how to get it to her. Would you, Prince, get it to Aglaya Ivanovna, now—but only to Aglaya Ivanovna herself; I mean so that no one sees, you understand? There's no great secret there, Lord knows, nothing like that—but— Will you do it?"

"I don't really like to," replied the prince.

"Please, Prince, it's extremely important to me," pleaded Ganya. "She will answer, perhaps— Believe me, I turn to you only in the most desperate of situations. Who else can I send it by? It's very important, terribly important to me."

Ganya seemed dreadfully afraid that the prince would not consent, and he looked into his eyes with timorous entreaty.

"Very well, I'll deliver it."

"And so that no one notices," insisted Ganya, delighted. "And look here, Prince, I can count on your word of honor, can't I?"

"I shall show it to no one," said the prince.

"The note is not sealed, but—" said Ganya fidgeting with anxiety, then broke off in confusion.

99

"Oh, I won't read it," replied the prince quite simply and, taking the portrait, he left the study.

Left alone, Ganya clutched his head.

"Just a word from her and I—I might really break it off!"

He was now so excited and anxious that he could not sit down to his papers again but began pacing back and forth from one corner of the study to the other.

The prince returned deep in thought. He was troubled by his errand and troubled too by the thought of a note from Ganya to Aglaya. But two rooms from the drawing room he suddenly stopped as if he had just remembered something, glanced around, walked over to the window, nearer the light, and began looking at the portrait of Nastassya Filippovna.

It was as though he was trying to penetrate some mystery hidden in that face, and which had struck him before. This earlier impression had scarcely left him, and he now seemed to verify it. This time he was struck even more forcefully by the face, which was extraordinary in its beauty and for something else in it as well. There was a sort of immense pride and contempt, almost hatred, in this face, and at the same time something trusting, something wonderfully artless. These two contrasting qualities aroused in him a kind of compassion as he looked at those features. This dazzling beauty was even unbearable; the beauty of the pale face with its slightly sunken cheeks and burning eyes—a strange beauty! The prince gazed at it for a minute, then suddenly, remembering where he was, he looked around the room and quickly brought the portrait to his lips and kissed it. When he did enter the drawing room a minute later his face was perfectly composed.

But, before this, just as he was going in the dining room (one room from the drawing room) he almost collided with Aglaya in the doorway. She was alone.

"Gavril Ardalionovitch asked me to give you this," said the prince, handing her the note.

Aglaya stopped, took the note, and looked strangely at the prince. There was not the least embarrassment in her expression, only a flicker of surprise which apparently had to do only with the prince himself. With her glance Aglaya seemed to be demanding an explanation from him—how he happened to be mixed up with Ganya in this affair—and she was demanding this explanation calmly and disdainfully. They stood facing each other a few moments, until at last a trace of mockery appeared in her expression; she smiled slightly and walked past him.

Madame Yepanchin examined the portrait of Nastassya Filippovna for some time in silence, with a certain contempt, holding it in front of her at arms' length, as far from her as possible, in a manner nicely calculated for its effect.

"Yes, she's pretty," she said finally. "Very pretty. I have seen her twice, only at a distance. So you appreciate that kind of beauty?" she said, addressing herself to the prince.

"Yes. That kind—" replied the prince with a certain effort.

"You mean particularly this kind?"

"Yes, particularly this kind."

"Why?"

"In that face—there is much suffering," said the prince, as though involuntarily, as though he was talking to himself and not answering the question.

"You are probably talking nonsense," decided Madame Yepanchin, throwing the portrait down on the table with a scornful gesture. Alexandra picked it up, Adelaïda moved close to her, both began to examine it. At that instant Aglaya came back into the drawing room.

"What strength!" cried Adelaïda suddenly, looking eagerly over her sister's shoulder at the portrait.

"Where? What strength?" demanded Lizaveta Prokofyevna sharply.

"Beauty like that is strength," said Adelaïda hotly. "One could turn the world upside down with beauty like that."

She walked away thoughtfully to her easel. Aglaya casually glanced at the portrait, squinted her eyes, pouted, walked away, and sat down a little distance away with her arms folded.

Madame Yepanchin rang.

"Ask Gavril Ardalionovitch to come in here," she ordered the servant who entered. "He's in the study."

"Maman!" exclaimed Alexandra significantly.

"I want to say a few words to him—that's enough!" said Madame Yepanchin bruskly, cutting short her protest. She was obviously irritated. "You see, Prince, everything in this house is secret now. Everything is secret! It's expected of us, a sort of etiquette—it's stupid. And this is just the sort of affair that requires the utmost frankness, clarity and honesty. Marriages are being concocted. I don't like these marriages—"

"Maman, what are you saying?" Alexandra hastily interrupted her again.

"What does it matter to you, daughter dear? Do you like them yourself? What if the prince does hear? We are friends. He and I are, anyway. God looks out for people—good people, to be sure; He has no use for nasty and capricious people, especially not for capricious ones, who decide one thing one day and say something else the next. Do you understand, Alexandra Ivanovna? Prince, they say I'm eccentric, but I know how to distinguish one thing from another. Because the heart is what counts and the rest is nonsense. Oh, the mind is important too, of course; indeed, perhaps the mind is the most important thing of all. Don't smile, Aglaya, I'm not contradicting myself; a fool with a heart and no mind is just as unhappy as a fool with a mind and no heart. It's an old truth. Here I am, a fool with a heart and no mind, and you are a fool with a mind and no heart, both of us are unhappy, both of us suffer."

"What are you so unhappy about, *Maman?*" Adelaïda could not resist asking, she being apparently the only one present who had not lost her good humor.

"First of all, about my clever daughters," said Madame Ye-panchin cuttingly, "and since this by itself is quite enough, there is no need to go into any of the rest. There has been too much talk already. We shall see how the two of you (I'm not counting Aglaya) will solve your affairs with your brains and your conversation, and whether you, esteemed Alexandra Ivanovna, will be happy with your respected lord and master. Ah!" she exclaimed, seeing Ganya entering the room, "here comes another matrimonial alliance. How do you do!" she said in reply to Ganya's bow, without inviting him to sit down. "You are entering into marriage?"

"Marriage? What? Into what marriage?" murmured the dumbfounded Gavril Ardalionovitch. He was terribly confused.

"Are you getting married? I'll ask it that way in case you prefer that way of expressing it."

"N-no. I—N-no," lied Gavril Ardalionovitch, his face coloring with shame. He glanced fleetingly at Aglaya, sitting apart from the others, then quickly away. Aglaya looked coldly, calmly, and intently at him, not averting her gaze, observing his distress.

"No? You said no?" insisted the implacable Lizaveta Prokofyevna. "Very well, I shall remember that today, on Wednesday morning, you said 'No' to my question. It is Wednesday today, isn't it?"

"I think it is, *Maman*," answered Adelaïda.

"They never know what day it is. What is the date?"

"The twenty-seventh," replied Ganya.

"The twenty-seventh? That fits in very well with certain plans I have. Good-bye, you must have a great deal to do, and I must get dressed and go out. Take your portrait. And give my regards to poor Nina Alexandrovna. Good-bye, my dear Prince. Come to see us often, and for my part I'll pay a call on the old Princess Belokonskaya and speak to her about you. And listen, my dear, I believe God has brought you from Switzerland to Petersburg especially for me. You may have other affairs, but mainly you have come for my sake. God planned it exactly that way. Good-bye, dears. Alexandra, come along to my room, dear."

Madame Yepanchin went out. Ganya, stunned, confused, and furious, picked up the portrait from the table and, with a twisted smile, addressed the prince.

"I am going home now. If you haven't changed your mind about living with us, I'll walk you there, since you don't know our address."

"Wait, Prince," said Aglaya, suddenly rising from her armchair. "You must write something in my album. Papa said you were a calligrapher. I'll get it at once."

And she went out of the room.

"Good-bye, Prince. I'm going too," said Adelaïda. She pressed the prince's hand warmly, smiled at him affably and graciously, and went out. She did not look at Ganya.

"It's you!" snarled Ganya, falling upon the prince the moment everyone had gone. "It's you who blabbered that I was getting married!" he muttered in a rapid undertone, with a frenzied expression on his face and an evil glint in his eyes. "You are a shameless gossip, sir."

"I assure you, you are mistaken," replied the prince, calmly and politely. "I didn't even know you were getting married."

"Just a little while ago you heard Ivan Fyodorovitch say how everything would be decided tonight at Nastassya Filippovna's—and you told them! You are lying! Who else could they have learned it from? Who the devil could have told them except you? Didn't the old woman even hint as much to me?"

"If you caught her hints, you should also know better than I who told them. I did not say a word about it."

"Did you give her the note? Did she answer?" Ganya interrupted him with feverish impatience. But at this very moment Aglaya returned, and the prince had no time to reply.

"Here, Prince," said Aglaya, laying the album on the table, "choose a page and write something for me. Here's a pen, a new one. Does it matter if it's steel? I've heard calligraphers don't write with steel pens."

Talking with the prince, she seemed not to notice that Ganya was there. But while the prince was fitting the pen,

103

looking for a page and preparing to write, Ganya went over to the fireplace where Aglaya stood just to the right of the prince and said in a broken whisper almost into her ear:

"One word, just one word from you—and I am saved."

The prince turned quickly and looked at both of them. There was real despair in Ganya's face; it was as if he had uttered these words without thinking, on an impulse. For several seconds Aglaya looked at him with exactly the same calm surprise with which she had looked at the prince; and it seemed that this contained astonishment of hers, this wonderment, this utter incomprehension of what was being said to her, was at that moment more terrible for Ganya than the most withering contempt.

"What shall I write?" asked the prince.

"I'll dictate it to you," said Aglaya, turning to him. "Ready? Please write, 'I don't bargain!' Now write the day and the month. Now show me."

The prince handed her the album.

"Excellent! You've written it marvelously; you have a wonderful hand. Thank you. Good-bye, Prince— Wait a moment," she added as if she had suddenly remembered something. "Come with me, I want to give you something as a remembrance."

The prince followed her, but as they entered the dining room Aglaya stopped.

"Read this," she said, giving him Ganya's note.

The prince took the note and looked in bewilderment at Aglaya.

"Of course I know you haven't read it and you can't be a confidant of that man. Read it. I want you to read it."

The note had evidently been written in haste:

"Today my fate will be decided, you know in what way. Today I must give my word irrevocably. I have no claim on your sympathy; I dare not have any hopes, but once you uttered a certain word, a single word, and that word illuminated the dark night of my life and has remained my beacon ever since. Say one such word again, now, and you will save me from ruin. Tell me only to break off everything, and I will break off everything today. Oh, what will it cost you to say this? I will read in it only a sign of your sympathy and compassion for me—that and only that! Absolutely nothing more! I dare not cherish any hope, because I am unworthy of it. But after this word from you I accept my poverty again and shall endure gladly my terrible situation. I shall take up

104

the fight, and welcome it; I shall prevail in it with re-
newed strength!

"*Give me, then, this word of sympathy (only sympa-*
thy, I swear to you!) Do not be angered by the imperti-
nence of a desperate man, of a drowning man, for dar-
ing to make a last effort to save himself from ruin. G.I."

"This man assures me," said Aglaya sharply, when the
prince had finished reading, "that to say 'break off everything'
will not compromise me or obligate me and, as you see, gives
me a written guarantee of this in his note. Notice how naïvely
he underlined certain little words and how crudely his secret
thought shows through. Besides, he knows that if he broke everything off by himself without waiting for any word from
me, without even saying anything to me, without placing any
hopes on me, I might then change my feelings about him and
possibly become his friend. He knows that for certain! But he
has a dirty soul; he knows that and cannot act on it; he
knows this and still asks for guarantees. He's unable to take a
risk on faith. He wants me to give him assurances about myself to make up for the hundred thousand. As for the word I
said previously, which he mentions in the note, and which
supposedly brought light into his life, it is an insolent lie. I
only took pity on him once. But he is insolent and shameless:
he immediately got the idea there was some hope; I realized
it at once. From that moment he has been trying to trip me
up, and he's still trying now. All right. Take this note and
give it back to him as soon as you leave our house—not before, of course."

"And what answer shall I give him?"

"Nothing, naturally. That's the best answer. It seems you
plan to live at his house?"

"Ivan Fyodorovitch himself advised me to," said the
prince.

"Then watch out for him, I warn you. Now he will never
forgive you for bringing him back his note."

Aglaya pressed the prince's hand lightly and went out of
the room. Her face was serious, and she was frowning; she
did not even smile as she nodded good-bye to him.

"I'll be right along," said the prince to Ganya. "I must get
my bundle, and we'll go."

Ganya stamped his foot in impatience. His face darkened
with rage. At last, both went out into the street, the prince
carrying his bundle in his hand.

"Her answer? Her answer?" cried Ganya, turning upon
him. "What did she say to you? Did you give her the letter?"

Without a word the prince gave him his note. Ganya was stunned.

"What's this? My note!" he exclaimed. "He hasn't delivered it! Oh, I should have guessed as much! Oh, d-d-damnation! Now I see why she didn't understand anything just now. But why, why, why didn't you give it to her? Oh, d-d-damnation!"

"Excuse me, but on the contrary I did manage to give her your note at once, only a moment after you gave it to me, and exactly as you asked me to. It is in my hands again because Aglaya Ivanovna just gave it back to me."

"When? When?"

"Just as I finished writing in her album, when she asked me to come with her. You heard her, didn't you? We went into the dining room, she gave me the note, asked me to read it, then asked me to give it back to you."

"To r-read it!" shouted Ganya almost at the top of his voice. "To read it! You've read it?"

And once again he stood dumbfounded in the middle of the sidewalk, so surprised that his mouth fell open.

"Yes, I read it just now."

"And she gave it to you to read herself? Herself?"

"She herself, and believe me, I never would have read it without her asking me to."

For a minute Ganya was silent, making a painful effort to reflect, but suddenly he cried, "Impossible! She can't have asked you to read it. You're lying! You read it yourself!"

"I am speaking the truth," said the prince in the same completely untroubled tone of voice. "And believe me, I am very sorry this is having such an upsetting effect on you."

"But, you miserable fellow, at the very least she must have said something to you about it? She must have answered something?"

"Yes, of course."

"Well, then tell me! Tell me! Damnation!"

And Ganya stamped his right foot, encased in a galosh, twice on the sidewalk.

"As soon as I read it she told me you were trying to trip her up, that you were trying to compromise her in order to obtain hopes for her hand in marriage, so that, relying on these hopes, you wouldn't risk anything by abandoning your other hopes for a hundred thousand. She said that if you'd done this without bargaining with her, if you'd done so on your own accord without asking her for guarantees in advance, she might have become your friend. That's all, I think. Oh yes: after I'd taken the note, when I asked what her

106

answer would be, she said that no answer was the best answer. I think that was what she said. Forgive me if I've forgotten her exact words, I'm telling you the way I understood it."

Ganya was seized by an ungovernable rage, and his fury burst out without restraint.

"Ah! So that's how it is!" he snarled. "My notes get thrown out the window! Ah! So she doesn't bargain, does she! Well then, I will! We shall see! I have plenty to fall back on— We shall see! I'll make her pay for that."

His face was contorted, he was pale, he slavered at the mouth, he shook his fist. They walked on a few steps like this. He paid no attention whatever to the prince, behaving as if he were alone in his room, because he considered him as a person of absolutely no consequence. But suddenly a thought occurred to him, and he collected himself.

"Just how does it happen," he said abruptly to the prince, "how does it happen that you," ("you idiot!" he added to himself), "are suddenly in such confidential relations two hours after your first meeting with her? How is that?"

Envy was the one torment he had not experienced then; suddenly it stung him to the heart.

"That is something I cannot explain," replied the prince.

Ganya glared at him malevolently. "It wasn't to make you a present of her trust that she called you into the dining room. She wanted to give you something, didn't she?"

"I can't understand it any other way."

"Yes, but why, damn it! What did you do in there? How did you make them like you? Listen," he said, overcome by agitation (at that moment his being was in such ferment he could not collect his thoughts). "Listen, couldn't you possibly remember exactly what you were talking about in there and get it straight, every word from the very beginning. Didn't you notice anything? Can't you remember?"

"Oh, yes, very well," replied the prince. "At the very beginning, after I went in and met them we started talking about Switzerland."

"Oh, the hell with Switzerland!"

"Then we talked about capital punishment—"

"Capital punishment?"

"Yes, to illustrate something— Then I told them about how I spent three years abroad and a story about a poor country girl."

"The hell with the poor country girl!" said Ganya, wild with impatience. "What then?"

"Then I told how Schneider gave me his opinion of my character and made me—"

"To blazes with Schneider and damn his opinion! What then?"

"Then something started me talking about faces, the expressions of faces, I mean; and I said that Aglaya Ivanovna was almost as beautiful as Nastassya Filippovna. That was when I mentioned the portrait."

"But you didn't tell them what you heard in the study this morning, you certainly didn't tell them that, did you? Did you?"

"As I said before, I did not."

"But how in the devil did— Bah! Aglaya didn't show the note to the old woman, did she?"

"I can assure you absolutely that she did not. I was there all the time, and besides, she hadn't time to show it to her."

"Yes, and perhaps you didn't notice. Oh, the damned idiot!" he shouted, completely beside himself. "He doesn't know how to explain anything!"

Having once begun shouting insults and meeting no opposition, Ganya gradually lost all restraint, as always is the way with some people. A little more and he probably would have spat in the prince's face, enraged as he was. And yet this very rage blinded him, otherwise he would have noticed long ago that this "idiot," whom he so rudely treated, was sometimes all too quick and subtle in understanding things and could give an extremely satisfactory account of them. But suddenly something quite unexpected happened.

"I must tell you, Gavril Ardalionovitch," said the prince suddenly, "that in the past I was indeed so ill I really was almost an idiot, but for some time now I have been completely cured, and this is why I find it decidedly unpleasant to be called an idiot to my face. And while you might be excused on the grounds of your misfortunes, you have in your state of vexation openly insulted me twice already. I don't like this at all, particularly as it happens on our first encounter. So as we are now at a crossing, wouldn't it be better if we parted: you to the right to your house, and I to the left? I have twenty-five roubles, and I will surely find some sort of hotel."

Ganya was terribly embarrassed and even blushed with shame for having been caught out so unexpectedly.

"Forgive me, Prince," he cried warmly, suddenly dropping his insulting tone for one of extreme courtesy. "For God's sake, forgive me! You see how miserable I am! You know almost nothing yet, but if you knew everything you would

108

surely excuse me a little. Though, of course, it was unpardonable—"

"Oh, I don't need elaborate apologies," replied the prince hastily. "I quite understand how very unpleasant it must be for you and that that is why you are abusive. So, let's go on to your house. I shall come with pleasure."

"No," thought Ganya to himself, "impossible to let him go like that now." He glanced with malice at the prince as they walked along. "This scoundrel has wormed everything out of me and now has suddenly taken off his mask. There's something behind it. We shall see! Everything will be settled. Everything! And this very day!"

They had by now reached the house.

Chapter EIGHT

∽✺∾

Ganya's apartment was on the third floor, accessible by a very clean, well lighted, spacious staircase. It consisted of six or seven rooms, large and small, quite ordinary rooms indeed, and yet still rather beyond the means of a functionary with a family, even one with a salary of two thousand roubles a year. But when Ganya and his family took it not two months before, the intention was to maintain rooms for lodgers, with meal service, to Ganya's intense annoyance and only at the insistent demand of Nina Alexandrovna and Varvara Ardalionovna, who wished in their turn to be useful and to contribute something to the family income. Ganya scowled and said that taking boarders was a disgrace, and thereafter seemed to be ashamed when he was in society, where he had become used to appearing as a rather brilliant young man with a future. All these concessions to his lack of fortune and the cramped conditions in which he had to live were wounds that touched his very soul. For some time he had begun to be irritable over trifling matters, intensely and all out of proportion to their importance. And if he still, for the time being, consented to put up with them and endure them, it was only because he had determined to change all this drastically at the earliest possible moment. But at the same time, this change, the very departure he had resolved to make, posed a considerable problem, such a problem indeed that its solution threatened him with more cares and complications and distress than all he had gone through before.

The apartment was divided by a corridor which led straight in from the entrance hall. On one side of the corridor were three rooms which were to be rented to "especially recommended" lodgers; besides which, on that same side of the corridor, at the farthest end near the kitchen, was a fourth room, smaller than the rest, occupied by the retired General Ivolgin, the father of the family, who slept on a wide sofa and was obliged to leave and enter the apartment by the kitchen and the back stairs. This same room was shared by Ganya's brother Kolya, a schoolboy of thirteen, who was crowded into these cramped quarters to study and to sleep on a second sofa, which was very old, narrow, and short, with a torn cover, and more importantly to keep an eye on his father, who was more and more dependent upon his attentions. The prince was to have the middle of the three rooms. In the first, on the right, was lodged Ferdyshchenko, and the third, on the left, was still vacant. But Ganya first took the prince to the family side of the apartment. The family half consisted of a drawing room, which as the need arose was transformed into a dining room, a smaller drawing room, which was however a drawing room only in the morning, since in the evening it became Ganya's study and his bedroom, and finally a third room, a small, confining room the door to which was always shut. This was the bedroom of Nina Alexandrovna and Varvara Ardalionovitch. In short, everyone in the apartment was crowded together. Ganya did nothing but grind his teeth. Though he wished to be respectful to his mother, one could see at once that under their roof he was the tyrant of the family.

Nina Alexandrovna was not alone in the drawing room; Varvara Ardalionovna sat with her, and both were occupied with knitting and conversing with a guest, Ivan Petrovitch Ptitsyn. Nina Alexandrovna looked fifty, with a thin gaunt face and heavy black circles under her eyes. She appeared sickly and rather melancholy, but her face and her expression were quite pleasant; from her first word it was clear that she had an earnest disposition and genuine dignity. In spite of her melancholy air, one could detect in her a firmness and even a determination. She was dressed extremely modestly in a dark dress, as if she was an elderly lady, but her bearing, her way of conversing, her whole manner betrayed a woman who was accustomed to better society.

Varvara Ardalionovna was a girl of twenty-three, of medium height, rather thin. Her face was not particularly beautiful but possessed a mysterious power to please without beauty and to inspire passionate attraction. She was very like her mother and was even dressed rather in the same way, being indifferent to fashion. The look in her gray eyes could be very gay and tender sometimes, yet more often was serious and thoughtful, sometimes excessively so, especially lately. Her face showed firmness and determination too, but one could imagine that this determination could be even more vigorous and enterprising than her mother's. Varvara Ardalionovna was subject to flare-ups of temper, and her brother was sometimes afraid of this temper of hers. The guest now sitting with them was also a little afraid of her—Ivan Petrovitch Ptitsyn. He was a man still fairly young, not yet thirty, dressed modestly but in good taste, with agreeable though somewhat heavy manners. His small dark brown beard showed that he was not in government service. He could talk intelligently and interestingly but was more often silent. On the whole he produced a rather pleasant impression. He was obviously not indifferent to Varvara Ardalionovna and did not conceal his feelings. Varvara Ardalionovna treated him in a friendly way but avoided answering certain of his questions and did not care for them. Ptitsyn, however, was far from being discouraged. Nina Alexandrovna was cordial to him, and lately had even begun confiding in him. It was known moreover that he was trying to make a fortune by lending sums of money for short terms at high interest on more or less good security. He was a great friend of Ganya's.

After an explicit, though abrupt presentation of the prince by Ganya (who greeted his mother dryly, did not greet his sister at all, and promptly took Ptitsyn out of the room), Nina Alexandrovna said a few friendly words to him, then asked Kolya, who had appeared at the door, to show him to the middle room. Kolya was a boy with a cheerful and rather pleasant face and a simple, confiding manner.

"Where's your baggage?" he asked, as he led the prince into the room.

"I have a bundle. I left it in the hall."

"I'll bring it to you right away. The only servants we have are the cook and Matryona, so I help out too. Varya looks after everything and gets cross. Ganya said that you arrived from Switzerland today?"

"Yes."

"Is it nice in Switzerland?"

"Very."

"Mountains?"

"Yes."

"I'll get your bundle in for you now."

Varvara Ardalionovna entered.

"Matryona will make your bed right away Do you have a suitcase?"

"No. A bundle. Your brother has gone after it. It's in the hall."

Kolya came back in the room.

"There's no bundle there except this little one. Where did you put it?" he asked.

"There is no other besides that one," replied the prince, taking his bundle.

"Ah! I was wondering whether Ferdyshchenko hadn't carried it off."

"Don't talk nonsense," said Varya sternly. She spoke quite dryly to the prince too and was barely civil.

"*Chère Babette,* you might treat me a little better. I'm not Ptitsyn."

"You can still get a whipping, Kolya, you're so stupid. Anything you need you may ask Matryona for. Dinner is at four-thirty. You can either dine with us or in your room, as you prefer. Come, Kolya, don't be in the way."

"Let's go, you determined female!"

On the way out they ran into Ganya.

"Is Father home?" Ganya asked Kolya, and upon receiving an affirmative reply whispered something into his ear. Kolya nodded and followed Varvara Ardalionovna out of the room.

"Just a word with you, Prince. I forgot to tell you something about all that—business. I have a certain favor to ask, if it's not too much of an imposition. Please don't discuss here what passed between Aglaya and me just now. And don't say anything there about what you'll learn here, because there are plenty of disgusting things going on here too. But then, the devil with it! At least for today, try to restrain yourself."

"I assure you I'm much less talkative than you think," said the prince, rather annoyed at Ganya's reproaches. Their relations were obviously becoming more and more strained.

"Well, I've already been through enough today because of you. All I ask is you don't say anything."

"I'd still like to point out to you, Gavril Ardalionovitch, that I wasn't in any way bound just now. Why shouldn't I have mentioned the portrait? You didn't ask me not to."

"Ah, what a foul room this is," observed Ganya, looking

around contemptuously. "It's dark and the windows open onto the court. In more ways than one you've come to us at the wrong time. Well, it's not my business, I don't rent out the rooms here."

Ptitsyn looked in and summoned Ganya, who left the prince and hurried out of the room. There was something more he wanted to say, but he was obviously ill at ease and seemed ashamed to mention it. He had found fault with the room only to cover his confusion.

No sooner had the prince washed and made himself somewhat more presentable than the door opened again and a new person looked in. He was a gentleman of about thirty, of more than average height, broad-shouldered, and with a huge, curly, reddish head of hair. His fleshy face was red, his lips thick, his nose broad and flat, his eyes small, almost lost in fat, mocking, and, so it seemed, perpetually winking. His whole appearance gave an impression of insolence. He was rather dirtily dressed.

He first opened the door only far enough to put his head in. The protruding head inspected the room for about five seconds, then slowly the door began to open, and the whole figure of the man appeared in the doorway. Yet the visitor still did not enter but, narrowing his eyes, stood on the threshold studying the prince. At last he closed the door behind him, approached, sat down on a chair, firmly took the prince by the hand, and made him sit on a couch near him.

"Ferdyshchenko," he declared, looking intently and searchingly into the prince's face.

"So?" replied the prince, almost laughing.

"A lodger," Ferdyshchenko now declared, studying him as before.

"Do you want to make my acquaintance?"

"Hah!" declared the visitor, ruffling his hair and sighing. Then he began to stare into the opposite corner of the room. "Do you have any money?" he suddenly asked, turning to the prince.

"A little."

"How much exactly?"

"Twenty-five roubles."

"Show me."

The prince took the twenty-five-rouble note from his waistcoat pocket and handed it to Ferdyshchenko. Ferdyshchenko unfolded it, looked at it, turned it over, then held it up to the light.

"It's very strange," he said, apparently lost in thought. "Why do they turn brown? Sometimes these twenty-five-rouble notes turn a horrible brown color, while others fade completely. Take it."

The prince took his note back. Ferdyshchenko got up from his chair.

"I came to warn you, first of all, not to lend me any money, because I'm sure to ask for it."

"Very well."

"Do you plan to pay here?"

"I do."

"Well, I don't, thank you very much. My room here is the first door on your right. You've seen it? Try not to call on me too often; I'll come to you, don't worry. You've seen the general?"

"No."

"Haven't heard him either?"

"No, I haven't."

"Well then, you're going to see him and you're going to hear him, and what's more, he even borrows money from me! *Avis au lecteur.* Good-bye. Is it possible to live with a name like Ferdyshchenko? What do you think?"

"Why not?"

"Good-bye."

And he went to the door. The prince learned later that this gentleman took it upon himself to astonish everyone with his originality and high spirits but somehow never brought it off. Upon some people, indeed, he produced an unfavorable impression, and this fact genuinely distressed him—but did not cause him to abandon his efforts. In the doorway he recovered his sense of importance upon colliding with a certain other gentleman, unknown to the prince, who was just entering. Letting this new visitor into the room, Ferdyshchenko winked at the prince in warning, behind the other's back, several times, and so managed to make his exit with no loss of self-assurance.

The new gentleman was a tall and rather corpulent man of fifty-five or more, with a fleshy sagging purplish face, set off by thick gray side-whiskers, a moustache, and rather protruding eyes. His whole appearance would have been rather impressive, had it not been for something ravaged, shabby, and even soiled about it. He was dressed in an ancient frock coat that was almost out at the elbows; his linen, too, was dirty—he was dressed for staying at home. Up close he smelled a little of vodka, but his manners were impressive, somewhat studied, and obviously intended to impress people with his dignity. The gentleman approached the prince without haste and with an affable smile silently took his hand and,

114

holding it in his, examined his face for quite some time as though he was recognizing features familiar to him.

"It's he! It's he!" he declared softly but solemnly. "His living image! I heard them repeating a name familiar and dear to me, and it brought back the past that is forever gone. Prince Myshkin?"

"Yes."

"General Ivolgin—retired and unhappy, sir. Your name and patronymic, if I may inquire?"

"Lev Nikolayevitch."

"Yes, that's it! The son of my friend—I might say of my childhood friend—Nikolai Petrovitch?"

"My father's name was Nikolai Lvovitch."

"Lvovitch," the general corrected himself, still without haste and with complete assurance, as if he had never forgotten the name but only made a slip of the tongue. He sat down, and he too took the prince by the hand and had him sit near him. "I used to carry you in my arms."

"Indeed?" said the prince. "My father died twenty years ago."

"Yes, twenty years. Twenty years and three months. We went to school together. I went straight into the service."

"Yes, my father was in the army, a second lieutenant in the Vassilyevsky regiment."

"In the Belomirsky. His transfer into the Belomirsky regiment occurred almost on the eve of his death. I was with him and gave him my blessing when he died. Your mother—"

The general paused as if overcome by a sad memory.

"She died too, a half year later from a chill," said the prince.

"Not from a chill. Believe an old man, not from a chill. I was there and buried her too. From grief for her prince—not from a chill. Yes, sir, I remember the princess. Because of her, the prince and I, friends of childhood, nearly became each other's murderers!"

The prince began to listen, though somewhat incredulously.

"I was terribly in love with your mother even when she was engaged to be married—to my own friend. The prince noticed it and was overwhelmed. He came to me between six and seven in the morning and woke me up. I got dressed in consternation, sir; not a word from either of us; I understood everything. He took two pistols from his pockets. Across a handkerchief. No witnesses. What's the good of witnesses when in five minutes we would be sending each other to eternity? We loaded, spread the handkerchief, stood with the pistols pointed into each other's hearts, and we looked at each other. Suddenly tears flooded our eyes; our hands trembled. Both of us, sir, both together. Well, then, naturally, we embraced and tried to surpass each other with kindness. The prince shouted, 'She's yours!' I shouted, 'She's yours!' In short— In short, sir— You've come to live with us?"

"Yes, at least for a while," said the prince, rather hesitantly.

"Prince, Mamma would like to see you," called Kolya, looking in the door.

The prince rose to leave, but the general placed his right hand on his shoulder and amicably made him sit down again.

"As a true friend of your father, I would like to warn you," said the general. "As you can see for yourself, I have suffered a tragic catastrophe—and without a trial! Without a trial! Nina Alexandrovna, sir, is a rare wife. My daughter Varvara Ardalionovna is a rare daughter. Circumstances force us to rent out rooms—an incredible comedown. And I, who was about to become governor-general! But we are always glad to have you, sir. Though there is tragedy in my house!"

The prince looked at him wonderingly, with great curiosity.

"They are arranging a marriage, a rare marriage, sir. A marriage between a questionable woman and a young man who might be a court chamberlain. This woman is to be brought into my house, where my wife and daughter are! But as long as I breathe, she shall not enter! I will lie over the doorway and let her step over my body! Ganya and I are hardly speaking now. I avoid meeting him. I warn you expressly, sir—though since you'll be living with us, you'll witness what's going on in any case; so it doesn't matter. But you are my friend's son, and I still have the right to hope—"

"Prince, will you do me the favor of coming into the drawing room," said Nina Alexandrovna, appearing in the doorway.

"Fancy, my dear," cried the general, "it appears I dandled the prince in my arms!"

Nina Alexandrovna looked reproachfully at the general, then inquisitively at the prince, but did not utter a word. The prince followed her but no sooner did they enter the drawing room and sit down, and no sooner did Nina Alexandrovna begin telling the prince something very hurriedly in an undertone, than the general suddenly made his appearance in the drawing room. Nina Alexandrovna stopped speaking at once and, visibly annoyed, bent over her knitting. The general probably noticed her annoyance but did not allow it to dampen his high spirits.

"The son of my friend!" he cried, addressing Nina Alexandrovna. "And so unexpectedly! I had stopped thinking about it. But, my dear, you must remember the late Nikolai Lvovitch? You were there then—at Tver?"

"I don't remember Nikolai Lvovitch. Was he your father?" she asked the prince.

"Yes, but as far as I know he died in Yelisavetgrad, not in Tver," the prince observed timidly to the general. "I heard from Pavlishchev—"

"In Tver," insisted the general. "He was transferred to Tver before his death, in fact even before he was seriously ill. You were still too little to remember his transfer or the journey. Pavlishchev might easily have been mistaken, though he was a splendid man."

"Did you know Pavlishchev too?"

"A man of rare merit, but I was a personal witness. I gave my blessing at the deathbed."

"My father was awaiting trial when he died," remarked the prince, "though I could never learn exactly what for. He died in the hospital."

"Oh, that was the Private Kolpakov affair, and the prince would most certainly have been acquitted."

"Really? Are you sure?" demanded the prince with marked interest.

"Of course!" cried the general. "The court broke up without reaching a decision. It was an absurd case! A mysterious case, one might even say. Staff Captain Larionov, the company commander, dies. The prince is appointed in his place for a time. Very good. Private Kolpakov commits a theft—steals some boot leather from a friend and drinks the proceeds. Very good. The prince—and notice this happens in the presence of the sergeant and the corporal—dresses him down and threatens to have him flogged. Excellent. Kolpakov goes to the barracks, lies down on his bunk, and fifteen minutes later dies. Splendid. But the case is unaccountable, almost impossible. In any event, Kolpakov is buried. The prince makes a report, and Kolpakov's name is dropped from the lists. What could be better, you'd wonder? But exactly six months later, at a brigade review, as if nothing at all had happened, Private Kolpakov is standing there in the third company of the second battalion of the Novozemlyansk infantry regiment of the same brigade and the same division."

"What!" cried the prince, beside himself with astonishment.

117

"It's not so. It's a mistake," said Nina Alexandrovna, turning suddenly to the prince with a look of anguish. *"Mon mari se trompe."*

"Now, my dear, it's easy enough to say *se trompe*, but how are you going to explain a case like this! Everyone was baffled. I was first to say *qu'on se trompe;* but unfortunately I was a witness and a member of the commission. Every confrontation showed that here was the very same Private Kolpakov who, a half year earlier, had been buried with the usual military formalities and the beating of drums. It is indeed an extremely rare case, almost an inconceivable one, I admit, but—"

"Papa, your dinner is ready," announced Varvara Ardalionovna, entering the room.

"Oh, that's splendid. Excellent! I'm quite hungry. But, it was, you could almost say, a psychological case."

"The soup will be cold again," said Varya impatiently.

"Coming, coming," muttered the general as he went out of the room. And he could be heard saying "and despite all the investigations" in the hallway.

"You will have to excuse Ardalion Alexandrovitch for a great deal if you stay with us," said Nina Alexandrovna to the prince. "He takes his meals alone. You must allow that everyone has his failings and his own little—peculiarities, some perhaps even more than people who are called eccentric. One particular favor I have to ask of you: if at any time my husband brings up the subject of the payment of your rent, you must tell him you have given it to me. Of course, anything you give Ardalion Alexandrovitch will be deducted from your bill, but I am asking you this to keep our accounts in order."

"What is it, Varya?"

Varya came back into the room and without a word handed her mother the portrait of Nastassya Filippovna. Nina Alexandrovna gave a start, then examined it for some time, at first, it seemed, fearfully and then with an overwhelming feeling of bitterness. At last, she looked questioningly at Varya.

"A present she gave him today," said Varya. "Everything is to be settled this evening."

"This evening," echoed Nina Alexandrovna half-aloud, in a voice of despair. "Well then, there's no more doubt, there's no more hope either. The gift of the portrait makes it all clear. But—did he show it to you himself?" she added with surprise.

"You know we've hardly said a word to each other for a

118

month. Ptitsyn told me everything. I found the portrait in his room, on the floor near the table. I picked it up."

"Prince," said Nina Alexandrovna, turning suddenly to him, "I wanted to ask you—it's why I had you come in to see me—have you known my son long? I believe he said that you have arrived from somewhere only today."

The prince gave a short account of himself, omitting the greater part. Nina Alexandrovna and Varya listened.

"I'm not trying to learn anything about Gavril Ardaliono-vitch in questioning you," remarked Nina Alexandrovna. "You must make no mistake about that. If there is anything he can't tell me about himself, I certainly have no desire to learn it behind his back. I inquire because when I asked him about you just now, first in your presence and afterward when you had left, he replied, 'He knows everything. No need to stand on ceremony!' Now just what does that mean? I mean, I should like to know to what extent—"

Suddenly Ganya and Ptitsyn came in. Instantly Nina Alexandrovna stopped talking. The prince stayed seated in the chair near her, Varya arose and went to the other side of the room. The portrait of Nastassya Filippovna was left lying in the most conspicuous spot in the room, on Nina Alexandrovna's sewing table, directly in front of her. Seeing it, Ganya frowned and in vexation swept it up from the table and threw it on his own desk, on the other side of the room.

"It's today, Ganya?" demanded Nina Alexandrovna suddenly.

"What's today?" said Ganya with a start, then suddenly flew at the prince. "Oh, I see you're at it again! What is it—some kind of a disease with you? Can't you restrain yourself? Can't your Lordship understand, once and for all—"

"Here I'm to blame, Ganya, and no one else," interrupted Ptitsyn.

Ganya looked at him questioningly.

"Yes, and it's better this way, especially since in one way the matter is settled," muttered Ptitsyn, and moving away, he sat down at the table, drew a piece of paper covered with penciled writing from his pocket, and proceeded to study it closely. Ganya stood sullenly, uneasily awaiting a family scene. It never occurred to him to apologize to the prince.

"If everything is settled, then Ivan Petrovitch is certainly right," said Nina Alexandrovna. "Don't frown, please, Ganya, and don't get annoyed. I'm not going to ask you about anything you don't want to tell me about yourself, and I assure you I'm completely resigned. So, please, don't worry."

She said this without stopping her work and, it appeared, with perfect calm. Ganya was surprised, but prudently he kept silent and looked at his mother, waiting for her to express herself more clearly. He had already suffered too much from family scenes. Nina Alexandrovna noticed this prudence and added with a bitter smile:

"You're still doubtful and you don't believe me. Don't worry. There'll be no tears and entreaties as in the past, not on my part at least. My only desire is that you be happy, and you know that I've resigned myself to fate, but my heart will always be with you, whether we are together or apart. Of course, I speak only for myself. You can't expect the same from your sister."

"Ah, her again!" cried Ganya, looking with derision and hatred at his sister. "Mother! I swear to you again, as I've promised already: no one will ever dare show any disrespect to you as long as I'm around, as long as I live. No matter who it is, I shall insist on the utmost respect being shown you —no matter who crosses our threshold."

Ganya was so disburdened he looked at his mother almost appeasingly, almost tenderly.

"I wasn't afraid for myself, Ganya, you know that. I haven't been worried and anxious for myself all this time. They say everything will be settled today. What is going to be settled?"

"She has promised to declare this evening at her house whether she consents or not," replied Ganya.

"For almost three weeks we've avoided speaking of it, and it was better so. Now that everything is settled, I shall permit myself to ask you just one thing: how could she offer her consent and even give you her portrait when you don't love her? How could you—with a woman so—so—?"

"—so experienced, you mean?"

"That's not what I meant to say. Can you really have taken her in so completely?"

Intense irritation was suddenly audible in her voice as she asked this question. Ganya stood motionless, thought for a moment; then, with unconcealed derision, said:

"You're carried away, Mother, once again you couldn't restrain yourself. That's always how these flare-ups begin You said there were to be no questions or reproaches, and here they've begun already! Let's drop it! Let's really drop it At least, you meant well— I would never leave you, not for anything in the world Anyone else would have fled from such a sister, at least—look how she's looking at me now! Let's put a stop to this! I was so pleased just now— And how

120

do you know I'm deceiving Nastassya Filippovna? As for Varya, she can do as she pleases and—that's enough! Oh, it's quite enough!"

The heat of Ganya's rage increased with every word he spoke, and he paced aimlessly around the room. A conversation like this immediately became a sore point with every member of the family.

"I said that if she sets foot here I shall leave, and I'll keep my word too," said Varya.

"Out of stubbornness!" cried Ganya. "And it's out of stubbornness you won't get married! What are you snorting at me for? I don't care a damn, Varvara Ardalionovna! You can carry out your plan immediately, if you like. I'm sick and tired of you. What's this? Have you decided to leave us, Prince, finally?" he shouted at the prince, seeing him get up from his place.

In Ganya's voice was that high pitch of irritability of a man beginning to take pleasure in his own anger, who abandons himself in it without restraint, with mounting enjoyment, no matter where it may lead him. At the door the prince turned to say something in reply, but realizing from the exasperated expression on the face of his insulter that another word would be the final straw, he turned and walked out in silence. A few minutes later he heard from the sound of voices in the drawing room that following his departure the conversation had grown even noisier and more outspoken than before.

He crossed the front drawing room and into the hall to reach the corridor on the way to his room. As he passed near the front door he heard someone on the other side making frantic efforts to ring the bell; but the bell must have been broken because it only shook without making a sound. The prince unbolted the door, opened it—and stepped back in startled amazement. Before him stood Nastassya Filippovna. He recognized her at once from the portrait. Her eyes flashed with annoyance when she saw him. She quickly entered the hall, brushed him aside, and said angrily as she flung off her fur coat:

"If you're too lazy to fix the bell, at least you might sit in the hall when people knock. Ah! And now he's dropped the fur, the clumsy oaf!"

The coat was in fact lying on the floor Without waiting for the prince to help her with it, Nastassya Filippovna had taken it off and thrown it to him without looking around, and the prince had not been able to catch it

"They ought to dismiss you. Go along and announce me."

The prince wanted to say something but was so struck with confusion that he could not utter a word and, carrying the coat which he had picked up from the floor, he went toward the drawing room.

"Well, now he's going off with my fur coat! What are you carrying the coat for? Ha, ha, ha! Are you mad, by any chance?"

The prince came back and looked at her in stupefaction. When she started to laugh, he smiled too, but he still could not utter a sound. At the first moment, when he opened the door to her, he had been pale; now, all at once, color rushed to his face.

"What sort of an idiot is this?" cried Nastassya Filippovna, stamping her foot at him. "Now, where are you off to? Whom are you going to announce?"

"Nastassya Filippovna," murmured the prince.

"How do you know me?" she asked him quickly. "I've never seen you before. Go on, announce me. What's that shouting in there?"

"They're quarreling," replied the prince and went into the drawing room.

He entered at a rather critical moment. Nina Alexandrovna was on the verge of forgetting altogether that she was "completely resigned"; moreover she was defending Varya. At Varya's side stood Ptitsyn, who had now concluded his examination of the penciled note. Varya herself was not intimidated (being hardly of the timid sort), but her brother's rudeness became grosser and less bearable with every word he uttered. On such occasions she usually stopped talking and merely stared in ironical silence at her brother, never taking her eyes from him. This habit, as she well knew, could drive him beyond all limits. At this very instant the prince stepped into the room and announced:

"Nastassya Filippovna!"

Chapter NINE

❦

Dead silence filled the room. Everyone looked at the prince as if they did not understand him—did not wish to understand him. Ganya was numb with fright.

The arrival of Nastassya Filippovna, especially at this particular moment, was the strangest and most distressing surprise for everyone. For one thing, she was calling on them for the first time. Before then she had borne herself so haughtily that in conversation with Ganya she had never even expressed the wish to be acquainted with his family, and lately she never mentioned them at all, as if they did not exist. Though Ganya was pleased to postpone so disturbing a discussion, still in his heart he had accounted Nastassya Filippovna's haughtiness against her and never forgot the debt. In any event, he had anticipated biting and sarcastic remarks about his family from her but not a visit to them. He knew for certain that she was aware of all that was happening in his house with regard to his engagement and what his family thought of her. Her visit *now,* after the presentation of her portrait and on her birthday, the day on which she had promised to decide his future, seemed to indicate what that decision had been.

The bewilderment with which they all stared at the prince did not last for long. Nastassya Filippovna herself appeared in the drawing room doorway, and again as she entered the room she lightly pushed the prince aside.

"At last I've managed to get in. Why do you tie the bell?" she said gaily, offering her hand to Ganya, who rushed forward to meet her. "Why do you look so upset? Introduce me, please."

Ganya, completely disconcerted, presented her first to Varya, and before they shook hands both women exchanged strange looks. Nastassya Filippovna however laughed and masked her feelings in a show of gaiety; but Varya did not care to disguise hers and fixed the visitor with a grim stare; not even the shadow of a smile required by ordinary politeness showed in her expression. Ganya was aghast. Already it was too late for entreaties, and he gave Varya a look so menacing that she understood from it what this moment meant to her brother. Thereupon she apparently made up her mind to give in to him and smiled, ever so faintly, to Nastassya Filippovna. (All the members of the family still did love one another very much.) The situation was somewhat improved by Nina Alexandrovna, whom Ganya—now completely at a loss —introduced after his sister, actually presenting his mother to her guest. But no sooner had Nina Alexandrovna begun to speak of her own "particular pleasure" in meeting her than Nastassya Filippovna, paying no attention to her, abruptly turned to Ganya and, without waiting to be asked, sat down on a small sofa in a corner near the window and exclaimed, "Where is your study? And—and where are the lodgers? You do take in lodgers, don't you?"

Ganya blushed deeply and stammered something in reply, but Nastassya Filippovna added immediately, "Where do you keep lodgers here? You haven't even got a study." She suddenly turned to Nina Alexandrovna, "And does it pay?"

"It is something of a bother," replied Nina Alexandrovna. "Of course, it ought to pay, but we've only just—"

But once again Nastassya Filippovna was not listening; she stared at Ganya, burst out laughing and cried, "What a funny look you have! Oh, my heavens, how funny you look at this moment!"

Her laughter lasted for some time, and Ganya's face was, in point of fact, quite contorted. Gone suddenly were his stupefaction, his cowardly and comical loss of composure; but he turned terribly pale; his lips worked convulsively; he stared malevolently and in silence at his visitor's face, while she went on laughing.

There was another observer too who had barely recovered from his astonishment at the sight of Nastassya Filippovna. But while he stood "like a post" in the same place near the drawing room door, he nevertheless noticed the pallor and the evil alteration of Ganya's face. This observer was the prince. Involuntarily he stepped forward, as if moved by fear.

"Drink some water," he whispered to Ganya, "and don't look that way."

It was evident that he had said this without premeditation or ulterior purpose on the spur of the moment, but these words produced a most extraordinary effect. All Ganya's spite seemed suddenly to surge against the prince. He seized him by the shoulder and glared at him in silence, vindictively and with hatred, as though unable to speak. General commo-

124

tion followed. Nina Alexandrovna even uttered a faint cry; Ptitsyn stepped forward in alarm; Kolya and Ferdyshchenko, who had appeared in the doorway, stood there in amazement. Only Varya continued to observe the scene with cold disapproval, yet she watched intently. She did not sit but stood near her mother with her arms folded in front of her.

But Ganya collected himself at once, almost the moment he seized the prince, and began to laugh nervously. He recovered his self-possession completely.

"What are you, Prince—a doctor?" he cried, trying to sound as gay and good-natured as he could. "He positively frightened me. Let me introduce him to you, Nastassya Filippovna. This is a rare fellow, though I've only known him since this morning."

Nastassya Filippovna looked at the prince, bewildered. "Prince? He's a prince? Imagine that! And just now I took him for a footman and sent him in here to announce me! Ha! Ha! Ha!"

"No harm done. Not a bit," put in Ferdyshchenko, rushing up to her, delighted that they had started to laugh. "No harm done. *Se non è vero—*"

"But I almost scolded you, Prince. Please forgive me. Ferdyshchenko—you here at this hour? I thought at least I wouldn't find you here. Who? What prince? Myshkin?" she again demanded of Ganya, who in the meantime, still holding the prince by the shoulder, had managed to introduce him.

"Our lodger," repeated Ganya.

It was plain that the prince was being presented to her as a sort of curiosity (and one useful to them all as the way out of a false situation) and was almost being pushed forward to her; the prince even heard distinctly the word "idiot" whispered by someone behind him, probably Ferdyshchenko, as an aside to Nastassya Filippovna.

"Tell me, why didn't you explain to me just now when I made such an awful mistake about you?" pursued Nastassya Filippovna, examining the prince from head to foot in a most unceremonious fashion. She awaited his reply impatiently, as if persuaded it would be so stupid that she would have to laugh.

"I was surprised to see you so suddenly," murmured the prince.

"But how did you know it was I? Where have you seen me before? Yet it's true I have the feeling I've seen him somewhere before! Do you mind telling me why you were so dumbfounded just now? Is there something so astonishing about me?"

"Come on, now! Speak up!" said Ferdyshchenko, with a clowning expression. "Oh, come on! Good Lord, the things I'd have said to a question like that! Come on! We'll have to take you for a dullard after this, Prince!"

"I would have said such things, too—in your place," laughed the prince, turning to Ferdyshchenko, then went on speaking to Nastassya Filippovna. "I was very struck by your portrait; later I spoke about you with the Yepanchins. And on the train early this morning, before my arrival in Petersburg, Parfyon Rogozhin told me a great deal about you. And then at the very moment I opened the door for you I was thinking about you—and suddenly there you were."

"And how did you know it was I?"

"From the portrait, and—"

"And—?"

"And because I imagined you exactly like this. I also felt I'd seen you somewhere."

"Where? Where?"

"I seem to have seen your eyes somewhere—but that can't be! I just say that. I've never been here before. Perhaps in a dream—"

"Well done, Prince!" cried Ferdyshchenko. "No, I'll take back my *se non è vero*." Then with regret he added, "And yet—and yet he is saying all that out of innocence."

The prince said the little he had to say in a troubled voice, often faltering and catching his breath. His manner, his whole person expressed intense excitement. Nastassya Filippovna looked at him with interest, but she was not laughing now. At this moment a new and very loud voice was heard suddenly behind the group crowded around the prince and Nastassya Filippovna, seeming to cleave through the company and part it in two. Before Nastassya Filippovna stood the father of the family himself, General Ivolgin, dressed in evening clothes and a clean shirt-front, his moustaches freshly dyed.

This was more than Ganya could bear.

Vain and conceited to a morbid degree, seeking constantly for the past two months something more solid to depend on, something by which to present himself in a more decent and honorable light, feeling still uncertain on the path he had chosen and recognizing that he might fail, deciding finally in desperate determination to behave at home, where he was already a despot, with the utmost insolence, but not daring to act in this way before Nastassya Filippovna, who was keeping him in doubt until the last minute, pitilessly holding the upper hand, calling him, as he had already been told, an "impatient beggar," having bitterly sworn by all imaginable oaths to make her pay for all this afterward, and at the same time occasionally indulging in a childish dream of making ends meet and settling his contradictory affairs, he had now on top of everything else to drink this dreadful cup and—worst of all—at such a moment! Still one more unforeseen torture, but for a vain man the most dreadful of all—the agony of blushing for his own family in his own home—had now fallen his lot. "Is the reward worth it in the end?" flashed through Ganya's mind at that moment.

What was happening at this very instant had been happening for the past two months as a nightmare and had frozen him with horror and burned him with shame; at long last the meeting between his father and Nastassya Filippovna, in the presence of the rest of his family, had occurred. Sometimes he had tormented himself by trying to imagine his father during the wedding ceremony, but he was never able to complete this agonizing picture and quickly put it out of mind. Perhaps he exaggerated this tribulation out of all proportion, but this is always the way with vain people. In these two months he had thought the matter through and resolved, whatever the cost, to keep his father out of the way somehow, for a while at least, if possible even to get him out of Petersburg, whether his mother agreed or not. Ten minutes before, when Nastassya Filippovna had come in, he had been so struck, so overwhelmed, that he had completely forgotten about the possibility of Ardalion Alexandrovitch appearing on the scene, and he had done nothing to prevent it. And so here was the general in front of them all, having solemnly attired himself in dress clothes, just at the time Nastassya Filippovna was "only looking for an occasion to heap ridicule on him and his family." (He had assured himself of this.) For what else did this visit mean if not that? Had she come to make friends with his mother and sister or to insult them in his own house? But from the attitude of both parties there could already be no doubt on that score: his mother and sister were sitting apart from the rest, looking thoroughly humiliated, and Nastassya Filippovna had apparently forgotten that they were even in the same room. And if she behaved like that she certainly had her own reason for it!

Ferdyshchenko took hold of the general and led him toward Nastassya Filippovna.

"Ardalion Alexandrovitch Ivolgin," declared the general with dignity, bowing and smiling. "An old and unhappy soldier and the father of a family which is gladdened by the hope of including such a charming—"

He did not finish. Ferdyshchenko quickly put a chair behind him, and the general, being rather weak on his legs so soon after dinner, sat down or, to be more exact, collapsed into the chair, a circumstance which, however, did not embarrass him in the least. He sat directly before Nastassya Filippovna and, assuming a pleasant expression, slowly and impressively raised her fingers to his lips. As a rule, it was rather hard to embarrass the general. Except for a certain air of untidiness he was still quite presentable, as he was well aware himself. It had been his lot in the past to move in very good society, and he had been irrevocably excluded from it only two or three years before. Since then he had given in too easily to certain of his weaknesses, yet he still retained an easy and agreeable manner. Nastassya Filippovna seemed delighted by the apparition of Ardalion Alexandrovitch, about whom she of course knew from hearsay.

"I've heard that my son——" began Ardalion Alexandrovitch.

"Your son, indeed! You're nice yourself, Papa. Why are you never at my house? Do you keep yourself hidden or does that son of yours hide you? You can certainly come to my house without compromising anyone."

"Children of the nineteenth century and their parents——" began the general again.

"Nastassya Filippovna! Please excuse Ardalion Alexandrovitch for a moment; someone is asking to see him," said Nina Alexandrovna in a loud voice.

"Excuse him! Why, I've heard so much about him and I've been wanting to see him for so long! Besides, what sort of business can he have? Isn't he retired? You won't leave me, will you? You won't go away?"

"I promise you he'll come see you, but now he needs rest."

"Ardalion Alexandrovitch, they say you need rest!" cried Nastassya Filippovna, pouting with displeasure like a frivolous little girl deprived of a toy.

The general did his best to make his position more ridiculous than ever. "My dear! My dear!" he cried reproachfully, turning solemnly to his wife, his hand over his heart.

"Won't you come away, Mother?" asked Varya loudly.

"No, Varya, I shall stay to the end."

Nastassya Filippovna could not have failed to hear this exchange, but it only seemed to increase her high spirits. She proceeded to shower questions on the general, who within five minutes was in a most ceremonious frame of mind and extemporizing amid the loud laughter of the company.

Kolya pulled the prince by his coattails.

"Do try to get him away somewhere! Can't you, please?" There were tears of indignation in the poor boy's eyes. "Oh, damn you, Ganya!" he swore softly to himself.

"It is quite true I used to be a great friend of Ivan Fyodorovitch Yepanchin's," the general was proclaiming in response to questions of Nastassya Filippovna. "He, myself, and the late Prince Lev Nikolayevitch Myshkin, whose son I have embraced today after a separation of twenty years, the three of us were inseparable, a regular cavalcade, you might say: Athos, Porthos and Aramis. But alas, one is in his grave, struck down by calumny and a bullet; another stands before you, still fighting on against calumny and bullets—"

"Against bullets!" exclaimed Nastassya Filippovna.

"They are here, in my chest. Received during the siege of Kars; in bad weather I feel them. In all other respects I live like a philosopher, I get about, take walks, play checkers at my cafe like a retired businessman, and I read *Indépendance*. But as for our Porthos, Yepanchin, I've broken completely with him ever since the affair three years ago on the railway about the lapdog."

"Lapdog? What's this?" demanded Nastassya Filippovna with marked curiosity. "About a lapdog? And, let me see, on the railway, too!" she added, as if she were remembering something.

"Oh, it's a stupid story, not worth repeating. Had to do with Princess Belokonskaya's companion, Mrs. Schmidt, but— it's not worth repeating."

"Oh, but I insist you tell it!" cried Nastassya Filippovna gaily.

"I haven't heard it either!" observed Ferdyshchenko. *"C'est du nouveau."*

"Ardalion Alexandrovitch!" again cried Nina Alexandrovna imploringly.

"Papa, someone wants to see you!" cried Kolya.

"It's a stupid story and can be told in a couple of words," began the general complacently. "Two years ago—yes, almost two—shortly after the opening of the—whatever-it-was railway, I—being already in civilian clothes at the time—I was taking care of some extremely important business about my separation from the service. I bought a first-class ticket, got on, sat down, started smoking. That is, I went on smoking the cigar I had lit already. I was alone in the compartment. Smoking isn't forbidden, but then it isn't exactly allowed either; that is, it's sort of half-allowed, as things like that usually are, and of course it depends on the individual. The window was open. All of a sudden, just before the whistle, two ladies sit down right across from me with a lapdog. They'd been late getting on. One of them was most elegantly dressed in light blue, the other more modestly in black silk and a cape. Not bad to look at, either one. Very haughty. Spoke in English. Of course I go right on smoking. That is, I did give it a thought but went right on smoking anyway, letting the smoke go out the window, since it was open. The lapdog is sitting there in the pale-blue-lady's lap. A little thing, no bigger than my fist, black with little white paws—quite an oddity. Had a silver collar with a motto. I pay no attention, except I do notice that the ladies are apparently displeased. By the cigar of course. One of them glares at me through a lorgnette. Tortoise shell. I go right on paying no attention—naturally, because they don't say anything! If they'd said something, warned me, asked me—because, after all, people are capable of speech! But not a noise from them. Then, suddenly—and, mind you, without the slightest warning, with absolutely no warning at all, just as if she had lost her mind—the pale-blue-one snatches the cigar out of my hand and flings it out of the window. The train is racing along, and I'm staring at her like a half-wit. The woman is savage, she's a wild woman; I mean she is absolutely primitive. What's more, she's a big round plump woman, a blonde with pink cheeks (too pink, in fact), and her eyes are flashing at me. So, without a word, I lean forward, and with exceptional courtesy, with perfect politeness, you even might say with elegance, I get hold of the lapdog with two fingers by the scruff of the neck and heave it out the window after the cigar. It let out just one yelp. The train was racing along—"

"You monster!" cried Nastassya Filippovna, laughing and clapping her hands like a little girl.

"Bravo! Bravo!" shouted Ferdyshchenko. Ptitsyn, too, was smiling, although he had been highly displeased by the arrival of the general. Even Kolya laughed and joined in, crying "Bravo!"

"And I was right, too. I was absolutely right!" the triumphant general continued, with great warmth. "Because if cigars are prohibited in railway cars, dogs are all the more!"

"Bravo, Papa!" cried Kolya in delight. "Splendid! I'd most certainly have done the same!"

"But what did the lady do?" demanded Nastassya Filippovna impatiently.

"The lady? Well, that's where the unpleasantness comes in," continued the general, frowning. "Without a word and without any warning whatsoever she slapped me across the cheek. A wild woman. A real savage!"

"And you?"

The general dropped his eyes, raised his eyebrows, shrugged his shoulders, pursed his lips, spread open his hands, paused a moment, then suddenly declared, "I got carried away!"

"Did you hit her hard?"

"No, by heaven, not very hard! There was a scandalous scene, but I didn't hit her hard. Just once, to defend myself, exclusively to defend myself. But it was the devil to pay, all the same. The pale-blue-one turned out to be an Englishwoman, a governess or even some sort of family friend of Princess Belokonskaya; and the one in the black dress was the eldest of the Princess Belokonskaya's daughters, an old maid of thirty-five. And everyone knows what terms Madame Yepanchin is on with the Belokonskaya family. All six princesses fainted, tears, mourning for the favorite lapdog, shrieks from the princesses, shrieks from the Englishwoman—the end of the world! Well naturally I went to apologize, expressed my regrets, wrote a letter. I was not received, nor the letter, and with the Yepanchins all was hostility, barred doors, and banishment."

"But excuse me, how can this be?" suddenly asked Nastassya Filippovna. "Five or six days ago I read in the *Indépendance*—I always read the *Indépendance*—exactly this story! But absolutely the same! It happened on one of the Rhine railways, between a Frenchman and an Englishwoman. The cigar was grabbed just the same way, the dog was thrown out the window just the same way, it ended just as it did with you. Even the dress was pale blue!"

The general blushed terribly. Kolya blushed too and clutched his head in his hands. Ptitsyn quickly turned away. Only Ferdyshchenko went on laughing as before. There is no need to speak of Ganya: he stood still all this time, suffering a mute and unbearable torment.

"I assure you," muttered the general, "the very same thing happened to me—"

"It's true that Papa had an unpleasant experience with Mrs. Schmidt, the Belokonskaya's governess," exclaimed Kolya. "I remember."

"What? Exactly the same? One and the same story at opposite ends of Europe, identical in all details, even down to the pale blue dress!" pursued Nastassya Filippovna pitilessly. "I'll send you the *Indépendance Belge!*"

"But observe," the general still insisted, "that this happened to me two years earlier—"

"Oh well, in that case!" Nastassya Filippovna laughed as if she was in hysterics.

"Papa, I beg you to come out for a word or two," said Ganya in an unsteady, harassed voice, mechanically taking his father by the shoulder. His eyes shone with infinite hatred.

At that moment there was a violent ringing of the bell in the hall—such a ringing that the bell might easily have been pulled down. It announced a most extraordinary visit. Kolya ran to open the door.

Chapter TEN

The entrance hall was suddenly full of people and commotion; from the drawing room it sounded as if a number of persons had come in and that more were still coming in. Several voices were speaking and shouting at once; there was talking and shouting on the staircase too, the front door having apparently not been closed. The visitation was an extremely strange one. Everyone exchanged glances. Ganya rushed into the large drawing room, but several people had already entered it.

"Ah, there's the Judas!" cried a voice familiar to the prince. "Hello, Ganya, you rascal!"

"It's him, there he is!" another voice echoed.

The prince had no doubt whatever: one of the voices was Rogozhin's, the other Lebedev's.

Ganya stood in the doorway as if stunned, staring in silence, doing nothing to impede the passage of ten or twelve people following Parfyon Rogozhin, one after another, into the room. The company was extremely diverse and distinguished not only for its diversity but also for its impropriety. Some entered just as they had come from the street, in their overcoats or fur coats. None of them, however, was completely drunk, though they all had apparently been drinking hard. They all appeared in need of one another to effect their entrance, since none would have been brave enough to enter alone; so they all seemed to be pushing one another inside.

Even Rogozhin at the head of the crowd walked warily; but he had some definite intention and looked somberly and irritably preoccupied. As for the rest, they were only a chorus, or, to be more exact, a gang of supporters. Besides Lebedev, there was Zalyozhnev, his hair pomaded in curls, who had thrown off his fur coat in the entrance and strode in with a show of ease and elegance; and there were two or three other gentlemen who resembled him, evidently rich merchants' sons; another in a semimilitary coat; a short and exceedingly fat man who laughed without interruption; a huge man over six feet tall, also very stout, extremely morose and taciturn, who appeared to place great faith in his fists. There was a medical student. There was an obsequious Pole. Two ladies looked in at the door but did not venture to come in. Kolya slammed the door in their faces and bolted it.

"Hello, Ganya, you rascal!" repeated Rogozhin as he reached the drawing room and stood in the doorway facing Ganya. "What's the matter? Didn't you expect to see Parfyon Rogozhin?"

But at that moment he caught sight of Nastassya Filippovna in the drawing room, directly in front of him. It was evident he had never dreamed of meeting her there because the sight of her produced an extraordinary effect on him: he turned so pale his lips went blue.

"So it's true," he said softly, as if to himself, appearing utterly lost. "It's all over!" He looked at Ganya with unchecked hatred and suddenly shouted, "You'll pay for this! Ah!"

He gasped for breath and could scarcely speak. He moved mechanically into the drawing room, but just as he entered he suddenly noticed Nina Alexandrovna and Varya, and he stopped somewhat embarrassed in spite of his emotion. Directly behind him came Lebedev, who followed him like a shadow and was quite drunk; then the student; the gentleman with the fists; Zalyozhnev, greeting everyone right and left; and finally the fat little man squeezed himself in. The presence of ladies still restrained them somewhat and obviously intimidated them; but of course this was only until something would *get them started*, until the first excuse to begin shouting and *get started*. Then all the ladies in the world would not stop them.

"What's this? You here too, Prince?" said Rogozhin distractedly, somewhat though not greatly surprised to encounter Myshkin. "Still in your gaiters. Ugh," he sighed, already forgetting the prince and directing his gaze once again to Nastassya Filippovna, moving toward her as if drawn by a magnet.

Nastassya Filippovna, too, looked at the new visitors with uneasy curiosity.

Ganya recovered himself at last. He looked severely at the newcomers and, addressing himself chiefly to Rogozhin, said in a loud voice, "Now will you kindly tell me what the devil this all means? You have not entered a stable, I believe, gentleman; my mother and my sister are here."

"We see your mother and sister," hissed Rogozhin through his teeth.

"Of course it's your mother and sister," seconded Lebedev.

The gentleman with the fists, apparently assuming that the time had come to use them, began growling.

"But look here!" cried Ganya, suddenly, in a somewhat excessive outburst. "First, would you kindly step into the main drawing room, and then let me know—"

"Ha! Let him know!" said Rogozhin with a malicious smile, not moving from his place. "You don't know Rogozhin?"

"I do think I've met you somewhere, but—"

"Met me somewhere! And only three months ago I lost two hundred roubles of my father's money to you. The old man died without finding out. You dragged me into it and Kniff cheated. You don't know me, eh? Ptitsyn here was a witness to it! All I'd have to do is pull three roubles out of my pocket and show them to you right now and you'd crawl on all fours to the Vassilyevsky district for them—that's the kind of fellow you are! That's the kind of soul you have! And I've come here now to buy you up for cash. Don't be surprised I have boots like this. I have money, my friend, and plenty of it—enough to buy up you and the whole lot of you, if I choose! I'll buy the lot!" Rogozhin grew excited and, apparently, more and more drunk. "Ah!" he cried. "Nastassya Filippovna! Don't chase me off. Just tell me one thing: are you going to marry him or not?"

Rogozhin asked this question as a man in despair to a divinity, yet with the daring of someone condemned to death with nothing more to lose. In mortal anguish he awaited her answer.

Haughtily, ironically, Nastassya Filippovna looked him up and down, but after glancing at Varya and Nina Alexandrovna she looked back at Ganya and suddenly changed her tone. "Certainly not. What's the matter with you? And what would lead you to ask me such a question?" she replied softly and gravely, and evidently with some surprise.

"No? No!!" exclaimed Rogozhin in a delirium of joy. "So it's to be no, is it? But they told me— Well, well! Nastassya

Filippovna! They told me you were engaged to marry Ganya! Him! But I told them all, I said: how can this be possible? When I could buy him for a hundred roubles; and if I gave him a thousand roubles, or maybe three, for him to step aside, he'd run off on the wedding day and leave the bride to me. And that's the way it would be, Ganya, you blackguard! You would take three thousand, wouldn't you? Here they are, take them! I've come here to get your signature on this. I said I was going to buy you—and I will buy you!"

"Get out of here! You're drunk!" cried Ganya, reddening and going pale by turns.

His outburst was followed by an explosion of several voices at once; Rogozhin's whole gang had been for some time awaiting an excuse to provoke trouble. Lebedev urgently whispered something in Rogozhin's ear.

"Right you are, you scribbling bureaucrat!" answered Rogozhin. "Right you are, you drunken sot! Ah!—here goes. Nastassya Filippovna!" he cried, looking at her like a maniac, losing heart, then suddenly emboldened to the height of arrogance: "Here's eighteen thousand!" and he threw down on a table before her a package tied in white paper. "There! And —there'll be more!"

He dared not finish what he had begun to say.

"No, no, no," Lebedev whispered to him once more, appearing greatly alarmed. It was easy to guess he was frightened by the size of the sum and had proposed trying a much smaller one.

"No. In this sort of thing you're a fool, my friend; you're way over your head— And it appears I'm a fool right along with you!" Rogozhin had suddenly checked himself and wavered under the flashing eyes of Nastassya Filippovna. "Oh, I've made a mess of it, listening to you!" he added in a tone of deep regret.

Observing Rogozhin's disconsolate expression, Nastassya Filippovna burst out laughing. "Eighteen thousand for me? There's the peasant in you coming out!" she added in a tone of insolent familiarity, rising from the sofa as if she were about to leave.

Ganya was watching the whole scene with a sinking heart.

"Then it will be forty thousand, forty—not eighteen!" shouted Rogozhin. "Ptitsyn and Biskup promised to get forty thousand before seven o'clock. Forty thousand! Cash on the table!"

The scene was becoming quite revolting, but Nastassya Filippovna went on laughing and did not leave, as though she was in fact intentionally prolonging it. Nina Alexandrovna and Varya had also risen from their places and in fearful silence awaited the outcome. Varya's eyes blazed, but the scene had painfully affected Nina Alexandrovna; she trembled and seemed to be about to faint.

"If that's the way it is—a hundred! I'll offer a hundred thousand this very day! Ptitsyn, help me out with it; it'll be well worth your while!"

"You've gone mad," whispered Ptitsyn, quickly coming up to him and seizing him by the arm. "You're drunk! They'll send for the police. Do you have any idea where you are now?"

"He's raving drunk," said Nastassya Filippovna, as if to taunt him.

"I'm not! You'll have it! Toward evening you'll have it! Ptitsyn, help me out, you money-grubber, take what you like, but get a hundred thousand by evening. I'll prove I mean business!" cried Rogozhin in an ecstasy of excitement.

"What's the meaning of this?" demanded Ardalion Alexandrovitch suddenly in a menacing voice, angrily approaching Rogozhin. The unexpectedness of the old man's outburst following his long silence made it very comic. There was laughter.

"Where did he come from?" laughed Rogozhin. "Come along, old fellow, we'll get you drunk!"

"That's so mean!" exclaimed Kolya, crying with shame and vexation.

"Is there no one among you who will take this shameless woman out of here?" cried Varya, trembling all over with rage.

"They call me a shameless woman," Nastassya Filippovna answered back with contemptuous gaiety, "when, like a fool, I'd come to invite them to my house tonight. Look at the way your sister treats me, Gavril Ardalionovitch!"

For some time Ganya stood as if thunderstruck by his sister's outburst; then seeing that Nastassya Filippovna was actually leaving this time, he rushed at Varya like a madman and furiously seized her by the hand. "What have you done?" he cried out, glaring at her as if he wanted to reduce her to ashes on the spot. He was completely beside himself and hardly knew what he was doing.

"What have I done? Where are you dragging me? You expect me to beg her pardon for having insulted your mother and for coming here to disgrace your family, you base creature?" cried Varya, looking exultantly and defiantly at her brother.

For several moments they stood this way, face to face.

Ganya still held her hand in his. Varya tried once, then again with all her might to pull free, but suddenly she lost all self-command and, in a fury, spat in her brother's face.

"What a girl!" cried Nastassya Filippovna. "Bravo, Ptitsyn, I congratulate you!"

Everything went blank before Ganya, and forgetting himself completely he aimed a blow at his sister with all his strength. The blow would have struck her squarely in the face. But instantly another hand caught Ganya's. The prince stood between him and his sister.

"Enough. Stop this!" he said forcefully, but also trembling as if from a violent shock.

"Will you forever be in my way?" roared Ganya, letting go of his sister's hand, while with his free hand in extreme rage he slapped the prince across the face.

"Oh!" cried Kolya, wringing his hands. "Oh my God!"

Exclamations were heard on all sides. The prince turned pale. With a strange, reproachful expression he looked straight into Ganya's eyes; his lips quivered as he tried to say something; a strange and utterly incongruous smile played across them.

"Well, it's one thing to hit me—but her—I won't let you!" he said softly at last; but suddenly he could not control himself, and leaving Ganya he covered his face with his hands, went to a corner of the room, stood with his face to the wall, and in a faltering voice said:

"Oh, how ashamed you'll be for what you've done!"

And Ganya did indeed stand there as if he was utterly destroyed. Kolya rushed to the prince and embraced and kissed him. Everyone crowded around behind Kolya: Rogozhin, Varya, Ptitsyn, Nina Alexandrovna, even old Ardalion Alexandrovitch.

"It doesn't matter. It doesn't matter," muttered the prince to everyone, still with the same incongruous smile.

"And he will regret it!" shouted Rogozhin. "You'll be sorry, Ganya, for having insulted such a—sheep!" (He could not find another word.) "Prince, my dear friend, leave them to the devil and come with me! You'll see how Rogozhin loves you!"

Nastassya Filippovna was also struck by Ganya's act and by the prince's reply. Her customarily pale and pensive face, which all along seemed so out of keeping with her affected laughter, was now clearly stirred by a new emotion; yet she seemed to wish not to betray it and endeavored to keep her expression of derision. "I'm certain I've seen his face somewhere!" she said, serious now, suddenly remembering her former question.

"And aren't you ashamed?" the prince cried suddenly with deep and heartfelt reproach. "Surely you're not what you're pretending to be now! How could that be possible?"

Nastassya Filippovna was surprised; she smiled, but as if she was concealing something behind her smile. Disconcerted, she glanced at Ganya, then started to walk out of the room. But before she reached the entrance hall she suddenly turned back, went quickly up to Nina Alexandrovna, took her hand, and raised it to her lips.

"It's true I'm not what I pretend to be. He guessed right," she said in a rapid intense whisper, then flushing hotly, she turned and walked out of the room, this time so fast no one had time to realize what she had returned for. They only saw that she had whispered to Nina Alexandrovna and apparently kissed her hand. But Varya saw and heard everything, and gazed after her in astonishment.

Ganya recovered himself and rushed to see Nastassya Filippovna out, but she had left already. He caught up with her on the staircase.

"Don't see me down!" she cried to him. "Good-bye until this evening. You must come, you hear?"

He came back, bewildered and thoughtful; a heavy perplexity weighed him down, even heavier than before. The figure of the prince flashed across his mind. He was so lost in thought he scarcely noticed Rogozhin's crowd thronging past him and pushing him this way and that in the doorway as they hastily followed Rogozhin out of the apartment. They were all talking in loud voices about something or other. Rogozhin walked with Ptitsyn, conversing intently about something important and evidently very pressing.

"You've lost, Ganya!" he shouted as they walked past him.

Ganya gazed after them in alarm.

Chapter ELEVEN

❦

The prince left the drawing room and shut himself in his room. Kolya ran in at once to comfort him. The poor boy seemed unable to keep away from him now.

"It's a good thing you left," he said. "There'll be a bigger row than ever in there now. Every day it's like this, and it all began over that Nastassya Filippovna."

"There's all sorts of suffering under our roof, Kolya," remarked the prince.

"Yes, a great deal. But we can't complain. It's all our own fault. But now I have a great friend, and he is even more unfortunate. Would you like me to introduce you?"

"I would indeed. Is he a comrade of yours?"

"Yes, almost like a comrade. I'll tell you all about it later. Nastassya Filippovna is beautiful, don't you think? I've never seen her until just now, though I tried hard enough. She's simply dazzling. I'd forgive Ganya everything if he did it for love. But why does he take money? That's the trouble!"

"Yes, I don't care very much for your brother."

"Well, I'd think you wouldn't! How could you, after— You know, I can't stand all these silly ideas. Here it's enough for a madman or a fool or some scoundrel who has lost his senses to slap someone across the face for that someone to be dishonored for life, and he can't wipe out the insult except with blood or if the other begs forgiveness on his knees. I think it's absurd and tyrannical. Lermontov based his play *The Masquerade* on this and—as far as I'm concerned it's stupid. What I mean is it's not natural. But then he wrote it when he was still almost a child."

"I liked your sister very much."

"The way she spat in Ganya's face! Varya's a brave one! But you didn't spit at him, and I'm sure it wasn't from any lack of courage. But here she is herself, speak of the devil. She's a fine girl, even if she does have her faults."

"You've got no business here," Varya at once said to Kolya. "Go to Father. Is he bothering you, Prince?"

"Not at all. On the contrary."

"So there, elder sister! That's the worst thing about her. By the way, I thought sure that Father would go off with Rogozhin. He's probably feeling sorry now. As a matter of fact, I should go and see how he is," added Kolya, leaving.

"Thank God I was able to get Mother away and put her to bed without any more trouble. Ganya is disturbed and very depressed. He has reason to be. What a lesson! I've come to thank you once again, Prince, and to ask whether you've known Nastassya Filippovna before?"

"No, I haven't."

"Then what made you tell her straight to her face she wasn't what she was pretending to be? And apparently you were quite right. It seems she really isn't like that. And yet I can't make her out! She must have come here with the intention of insulting us, that's clear enough. I've heard lots of strange things about her before. And if she did come to invite us, why did she begin acting the way she did with Mother? Ptitsyn knows her well and he said he couldn't make her out just now. And the way she was with Rogozhin! If one has any self-respect one doesn't speak like that, not in the home of one's— Mother too is very concerned about you."

"It's nothing!" said the prince, with a wave of his hand.

"And the way she listened to you—"

"Listened to what?"

"You told her she should be ashamed of herself, and suddenly she was completely changed. You have an influence on her, Prince," added Varya with a faint smile.

The door opened and, quite unexpectedly, Ganya entered. Even when he saw Varya he did not hesitate. He stood a moment in the doorway, then went up resolutely to the prince.

"Prince, I behaved like a scoundrel. Forgive me, dear fellow," he said abruptly with great emotion. There was a look of great pain in his face. The prince looked at him in astonishment and did not answer immediately.

"Well, forgive me, won't you? Come along, forgive me!" urged Ganya impatiently. "If you wish, I'll kiss your hand!"

The prince was overcome and, in silence, took Ganya by both his arms. They kissed each other with sincere feeling.

"I never imagined you were like this, never!" said the prince at last, drawing a deep breath. "I thought you—incapable—"

"Of apologizing? And what made me take you for an idiot before? You notice things other people never notice. One could really talk with you, but—one had better not."

140

"Here is someone else you should apologize to," said the prince, indicating Varya.

"No, they are all enemies of mine. You may be sure, Prince, I've tried again and again, but there's no real forgiveness there!" said Ganya with feeling, turning away from Varya.

"No, I will forgive you," said Varya suddenly.

"And you'll go to Nastassya Filippovna's this evening?"

"I will if you insist. But judge for yourself whether it's not rather out of the question for me to go now."

"She isn't at all like that. You see the kind of problems she poses! It's all tricks!" Ganya laughed viciously.

"I know very well she's not like that and that she's full of tricks—and what tricks! And Ganya, what do you think she takes you for? She may kiss Mamma's hand, but it's surely part of her trickery, but she is making a fool of you just the same! Brother, good Lord, this isn't worth seventy-five thousand roubles! You're still capable of honorable feelings, and that's why I'm saying this to you. Please, don't go yourself! Be careful. It can't possibly end well!"

Having said this, Varya left the room very upset.

"That's how they all are!" Ganya said with a laugh. "Don't they think I don't know all that myself? I certainly know more than they do."

Saying this, Ganya sat down on the sofa, obviously intending to prolong the visit.

"If you know this yourself," asked the prince somewhat timidly, "why have you chosen all this grief, knowing in fact it's not worth seventy-five thousand?"

"I wasn't talking about that," muttered Ganya. "But now that you mention it, tell me what you think, is this 'grief' worth seventy-five thousand or isn't it? I'd particularly like to have your opinion."

"In my opinion it isn't."

"No, of course not. And to marry like this is shameful."

"Very shameful."

"Well, then, let me tell you I'm going to marry her and now there's no doubt about it. I was hesitating before but now I'm not! Don't say a word! I know what you're going to say—"

"I wasn't going to say what you think. But I am quite surprised by your great confidence—"

"About what? What confidence?"

"Why, that Nastassya Filippovna is certain to marry you and that everything is settled; and secondly that even if she does marry you that the seventy-five thousand will go straight

141

into your pocket. Of course there is a lot I don't know about all this."

Ganya quickly moved nearer the prince.

"Of course you don't know everything," he said. "For why else would I accept all this burden?"

"I believe it happens all the time—people marry money, but the money stays with the wife."

"No. No, it won't be that way with us— In this case—in this case there are circumstances—" muttered Ganya, reflecting uneasily. "As for her answer, there's no more doubt about it," he added quickly. "What makes you think she will refuse me?"

"I know nothing except what I have seen, but just now Varya Ardalionovna said—"

"Ah! That's how women are, they have to have something to say. But she was laughing at Rogozhin, you can be sure of that. I could tell, it was perfectly clear. I was worried before, but now I see through it all. Or do you mean the way she behaved to Mother and Father and Varya?"

"And to you."

"Well, perhaps—but that's just a woman's way of paying off old scores and nothing more. She's a terribly irritable, susceptible, and vain woman. Just like a civil servant who missed his promotion! She wanted to show herself off and show all her contempt for them—yes, and for me, it's true, I won't deny it— And still she'll marry me anyway. You have no idea what sort of tricks human vanity is capable of. Here she thinks I'm a scoundrel because I take her, another man's mistress, so openly for her money, but she doesn't realize another man would have treated her far worse than that; he would have fastened himself on her with a lot of liberal and progressive talk, brought up the women's rights question, and gotten her completely in his power. He would have made the vain fool believe (and so easily!) that he was marrying her only for her 'nobility of heart' and her 'misfortune,' when right along he would be marrying her money. I'm not liked around here because I don't bother making pretenses, and that's what I ought to do. But what is she doing herself? Isn't it just the same? Why does she despise me for this, then carry on all these tricks? Because I won't give in and because I show some pride. Well, we'll see!"

"Did you really love her until this happened?"

"I did love her at first. But, never mind that. There are women good only for being mistresses and nothing else. I'm not saying she's been my mistress. If she wants to live in peace, I'll live in peace, but if she's rebellious I'll leave her at

142

once, and take the money with me. I don't want to appear ridiculous. Above all, I don't want to appear ridiculous."

"It appears to me," remarked the prince cautiously, "that Nastassya Filippovna is intelligent. Why should she walk into a trap when she can see beforehand the misery it would mean? She could marry someone else, couldn't she? That's what seems so strange to me."

"But she has her reasons for that! You don't know the whole thing, Prince. Besides— Besides that, she's convinced I'm madly in love with her, I swear it. And you know, I have a strong feeling she loves me too in her own way—like the proverb, 'He who loves well, punishes well.' All her life she'll treat me like a slave (perhaps that's what she wants), but she'll love me in her own way just the same. She's preparing herself for that, it's in her character. She's a real Russian woman, I can tell you. Well, I have a surprise in store for her. That scene with Varya a while ago was an accident, but it works to my advantage: now she's seen and convinced herself of my devotion and that I'll break all my ties for her. All of which means I'm no fool, you can be sure of that. By the way, don't imagine I'm usually such a chatterbox. Perhaps, my dear Prince, I'm doing the wrong thing by confiding in you. But you're the first honorable man I've come across and that's why I threw myself at you, literally. You aren't angry about what happened just now, are you? This is probably the first time in a whole two years that I've spoken out freely. There are so terribly few honest people around here—no one more honest than Ptitsyn. I think you're laughing—or aren't you laughing? Didn't you know scoundrels love honest people? And I am—but why am I a scoundrel? Tell me exactly what you think. Why do they all go along with her in calling me a scoundrel? And you know I go along with her and with them and call myself a scoundrel too! That's what's bad, that's what's really bad!"

"I'll never consider you a scoundrel again," said the prince. "A little while ago I took you for a wicked person, and suddenly you fill me with joy. There's a lesson for me not to judge people with no experience of knowing them. Now I see you're not only not wicked but not even particularly depraved. In my opinion you're simply a most ordinary man, capable of being very weak, perhaps, but not at all original."

Ganya smiled sarcastically to himself, but said nothing. Seeing that his opinion had displeased Ganya, the prince grew embarrassed and fell silent too.

"Did my father ask you for money?" asked Ganya suddenly.

"No."

"He will. Don't give him any. And to think he used to be quite a decent and proper person. I can remember that. He was received by nice people. And how quickly the end comes for all these decent old people! Let their circumstances change a little and there's nothing left of what they were, it's gone up in smoke. He never used to lie like this in the old days, I assure you; in the old days he was simply overenthusiastic, and—look what's come of it! Of course drink is the trouble. Do you know he keeps a mistress? He's no longer just a little harmless liar now. I can't understand how my mother endures it. Has he told you about the siege of Kars? Or how his gray horse started talking? Because it's gone that far."

And Ganya suddenly started roaring with laughter.

"Why are you looking at me like that?" he asked the prince.

"Because I'm surprised you laughed so openly. You really still have the laugh of a child. A moment ago you came in to make your peace with me and you said, 'If you wish, I'll kiss your hand'—that's the way a child makes up. That means you are still capable of talking and acting like a child. And then suddenly you start a whole speech about this dismal affair and those seventy-five thousand. Really, all that is somehow so absurd and impossible."

"And what conclusion do you draw from this?"

"I wonder if you aren't acting imprudently, if you shouldn't consider carefully first. Perhaps what Varya Ardalionovna says is true."

"Ah, morality! I know I'm still a little boy," said Ganya feelingly, "if only because I got into a discussion like this with you. I'm not in this miserable affair for mercenary reasons alone, Prince," he continued, speaking out like a young man whose vanity is stung. "If I acted only in a calculated way I'd certainly make a mistake, because I am still not strong in mind and character. I am driven by my passion toward a goal which is of the utmost importance to me. You may think that as soon as I get the seventy-five thousand I'll go right out and buy myself a carriage. No. I'll go on wearing my three-year-old coat and drop all my club acquaintances. There are so few persistent people among us, though all of us are usurers at heart. But I want to persevere. The essential thing is to hold on to the end—that's the whole problem! At seventeen Ptitsyn slept in the street and sold penknives. He started with a kopeck, and now he's worth sixty thousand roubles. But only after the most amazing acro-

144

batics! Here I'm going to skip the gymnastics and start right off with the capital. In fifteen years people will say, 'There goes Ivolgin, King of the Jews!' You tell me I'm not an original person. Observe, my dear Prince, that there is nothing more offensive to a man of our age and race than to be told that he is not original, that he is weak of character, without special talents, an ordinary man. You don't even give me credit for being a good scoundrel, and you know, I was ready to tear you apart for that! You offended me more than Yepanchin, who thinks me capable of selling him my wife—believing this, note well, without a lot of discussion and inducements, in the simplicity of his heart. This, my friend, has enraged me for quite some time—and I want money. Once I have money—then I will be extremely original. What is most vile and despicable about money is that it even confers talent. And it will do so until the end of the world. You will say all this is childish and perhaps romantic. That could be. It will be all the merrier for me, the affair will proceed in any case. I will persevere and see it through. *Rira bien qui rira le dernier!* Why does Yepanchin insult me like that? Out of meanness? Never. Simply because I am too insignificant to matter. Well, my dear sir, when the time comes— But that's enough, it's time to be off. Kolya has poked his head in twice already, he's calling you to dinner. I'm going out. I'll look in on you from time to time. You won't be badly off with us, they'll make you one of the family now. So be careful you don't give me away. I have the feeling you and I will either be friends or enemies. But what do you think, Prince, if I'd kissed your hand a while ago (as I sincerely offered to do), wouldn't that have made me your enemy afterward?"

"It certainly would have," decided the prince after thinking for a moment, then starting to laugh. "But not forever, because eventually you wouldn't have kept it up and would have forgiven me."

"Ah-ha! One must be on one's guard with you. The devil if you didn't put a drop of venom into that, too! And who knows, perhaps you are my enemy? By the way—ha! ha! ha! —I was forgetting to ask you: was I right in thinking that you were quite taken by Nastassya Filippovna, eh?"

"Yes—I was."

"Are you in love with her?"

"N-no."

"But here you are, blushing and miserable. Well, never mind, I'm not going to laugh at you for it. Good-bye. And do you know she's a virtuous woman, can you believe that? You may think she lives with that Totsky? Not at all! And not for a long time. And did you notice that she was extremely ill at ease herself and at times embarrassed? It's true. It's people like that who love to lord it over others. Well, good-bye!"

Ganya went out much more at ease and in a better humor than when he had entered. The prince sat motionless for almost ten minutes, thinking.

Kolya put his head in the door again.

"I don't want to have dinner, Kolya. I had a good lunch at the Yepanchins'."

Kolya came into the room and gave the prince a note. It was folded and sealed and it was from the general. It was evident from Kolya's face how he hated to deliver it. The prince read it, then got up and took his hat.

"It's two steps away," said Kolya in embarrassment. "He's sitting in there now over a bottle. How he manages to get credit there I can't imagine. Dear Prince, please don't tell them later that I gave you this note. I've sworn a thousand times not to pass on these notes, but I feel sorry for him. And please don't be afraid of hurting his feelings; just give him a little change and that will be the end of it."

"I was thinking the same thing, Kolya. I have to see your father—about a certain matter. Come along."

Chapter TWELVE

Kolya took the prince not far away to a cafe with billiard tables on Liteyny Avenue. It was on the ground floor and one entered directly from the street. Here, in a corner of a separate little room on the right, like an old habitué, Ardalion Alexandrovitch had installed himself with a bottle in front of him and, of course, a copy of the *Indépendance Belge* in his hands. He was expecting the prince. As soon as he saw him he put down the paper and launched into a long and heated explanation, of which the prince, however, could understand almost nothing because the general was already quite drunk.

"I haven't got ten roubles," interrupted the prince. "Here's a twenty-five-rouble note. Change it and give me fifteen back, otherwise I'll be left without any money myself."

"Oh, have no doubt, you may be sure that within this very hour—"

"I have besides come to you with a certain request, General. You have never been to Nastassya Filippovna's?"

"Me? Never been there? You're asking me this? Several times, my dear fellow, several times!" cried the general in a fervent burst of exultant and self-satisfied irony. "But I finally stopped going there myself because I didn't want to condone an improper alliance. You saw yourself, you were a witness this afternoon. I did everything a father can do—that is, a kindly and indulgent father. But now a different kind of father is about to step forth on the scene, and then we shall see, we shall behold, whether a meritorious old warrior will crush this intrigue or whether a shameless courtesan will enter a most honorable family."

"I was about to ask precisely whether you couldn't, as an acquaintance, introduce me to Nastassya Filippovna this evening? I must be there today; I have certain business, but I don't know how to get there on my own. I was introduced earlier, but I wasn't invited, and her party this evening is by invitation. However, I don't mind disregarding conventions, even if people laugh at me, if only I can get there somehow."

"That's exactly my own idea, my young friend—exactly!" the general exclaimed enthusiastically. "I didn't get you here just for this trifle!" he pursued, seizing the money nonetheless and slipping it into his pocket. "I got you here precisely to invite you to join me as brother-in-arms in a campaign against Nastassya Filippovna! General Ivolgin and Prince Myshkin! How will that strike her! And on the pretext of a courtesy call on her birthday, I will finally declare my will—indirectly, of course, not straight out, but exactly as if it was said straight out. Then Ganya will see for himself what he must do: will it be this meritorious father or—that is to say —and so forth— But what will happen will happen! Your idea is full of promise. At nine o'clock we shall set out. We've still plenty of time."

"Where does she live?"

"A long way from here, near the Bolshoi Theater, in the Mytovtsov house, almost on the square, on the first floor. There won't be many people there, though it's her birthday, and they will go away early."

It was already late in the evening and the prince still sat attending the general, listening to him as he began an incalculable number of anecdotes without finishing a single one. On the prince's arrival he had asked for a new bottle and finished it only an hour later, then he had asked for another and finished that one too. It may be assumed that in this space of time the general managed to tell almost the entire story of his life. Finally, the prince got up and said he could wait no longer. The general drained the last drops of the bottle, got up, and walked out of the room, walking very unsteadily. The prince was in despair. He could not understand how he could have been so overtrusting. In point of fact, he had not trusted the general at all; he was counting on him only as a way of going to Nastassya Filippovna's, even at the cost of a scene, though he did not anticipate a particularly scandalous scene. The general turned out to be completely drunk and at the stage of excessive eloquence. He spoke ceaselessly with much feeling and tearful emotion. He insisted again and again that the bad behavior of all the members of his family had made everything fall to pieces and that it was high time to put a stop to it. At last they reached Liteyny Avenue. It was still thawing. A warm wind, foul and depressing, whistled through the streets, carriages splashed through the mud, the horses' hooves struck the pavement with sharp rings. People on the sidewalk hurried to and fro in wet and dejected crowds. Here and there one encountered drunks.

"See those lighted first-floor windows?" the general was saying. "That is where all my old friends live, but I, the most deserving of the lot, who has suffered the most, am on my way on foot to the Bolshoi Theater to the apartment of a woman of dubious reputation! A man with thirteen bullets in his chest! You don't believe it? And yet it was on my account that Pirogov* telegraphed Paris and for a time left Sevastopol, then under siege, and Nelaton, physician to the court of Paris, obtained a safe-conduct in the name of science and came to examine me in Sevastopol. The highest authorities all know about it. 'Ah, there's that Ivolgin with thirteen bullets in him!' That's what they say, sir! See that house, Prince? There on the first floor lives my old comrade, General Sokolovitch, with his most distinguished and numerous family. This household, along with three on Nevsky Prospect and two more in Morskaya—there you have my present circle of acquaintances, my personal acquaintances, that is. Nina Alexandrovna resigned herself to circumstances long ago. But I still go on remembering, and, you might say, I relax in the cultivated society of my former comrades and subordinates, who still worship me. This General Sokolovitch (It's a long time, by the way, since I've seen him, and I haven't seen Anna Fyodorovna either)—you know, my dear Prince, when one doesn't entertain oneself one automatically stops visiting others. And yet—hm—I don't think you believe me. By the

148

way, why shouldn't I introduce the son of my best friend and childhood companion into this delightful household? General Ivolgin and Prince Myshkin! You will see an astonishing young lady, Prince; and not one but two, and in fact three, ornaments of our capital and of society: beauty, culture, purpose, the feminist question, poetry, all harmonizing in a pleasantly diversified combination, to say nothing of a dowry of at least eighty thousand roubles in hard cash for each of them, which never hurts in spite of all the feminist and social questions. In short, I am bound to introduce you and, indeed, must introduce you. General Ivolgin and Prince Myshkin! What a sensational effect!"

"Now? Right now? But you've forgotten—" began the prince.

"No, no, I haven't forgotten. Come along! Here, up this magnificent staircase. I wonder why there's no porter, but— it's a holiday and the porter has gone off. They haven't fired the drunkard yet. This Sokolovitch is indebted to me for the entire happiness of his life and his career—to me alone and no one else. But here we are."

The prince had stopped protesting against the visit and calmly followed the general to avoid irritating him, with the firm hope that General Sokolovitch and his entire family would disappear like a mirage, proving to be nonexistent, so that he and the general would presently be quietly descending the staircase. But to his horror this hope began to fade; he led him up the staircase as if he really did have acquaintances there, and at each instant he added new details, biographical and topographical, full of mathematical precision. At last, when they had ascended to the first floor, they stopped on the right in front of the door of a luxurious apartment and the general had reached for the bell-pull. The prince had by this time decided to make his escape, but one strange circumstance held him for a moment.

"You've made a mistake, General," he said, "the name on the door is Kulakov and you are going to see Sokolovitch."

"Kulakov—Kulakov doesn't mean a thing. This is Sokolovitch's. I spit on Kulakov. But here's someone opening."

The door, indeed, had opened. A servant looked out and announced that no one was at home.

"What a shame, what a shame! It would have to happen!" Ardalion Alexandrovitch repeated several times with profound regret. "Please convey to them, my good fellow, that General Ivolgin and Prince Myshkin wished to pay their respects personally and deeply, deeply regret—"

At that moment another person looked from inside the

149

apartment through the open door, apparently a housekeeper or possibly a governess, a woman of about forty in a dark dress. Having heard the names of General Ivolgin and Prince Myshkin, she approached inquisitively and doubtfully.

"Maria Alexandrovna isn't home," she said, looking at the general with special attention. "They've gone out with the young lady, Alexandra Mikhaylovna, to the grandmother's."

"And Alexandra Mikhaylovna went out with them too! Oh, Good Lord, what bad luck! Would you believe it, madam, that's always my luck! I humbly beg you to convey my compliments, and tell Alexandra Mikhaylovna to remember—that is, tell her I hope with all my heart she will realize her wish of last Thursday night during Chopin's Ballade. She will remember. My cordial wishes! General Ivolgin and Prince Myshkin!"

"I won't forget, sir," said the woman, more trusting now, bowing to them as they left.

As they descended the stairs, the general continued with undiminished fervor to regret that they had not found anyone at home and that the prince had been deprived of making a delightful acquaintance.

"Do you know, my dear sir, I'm something of a poet at heart, did you know that? But—but it seems to me we didn't exactly go to the place we should have," he suddenly concluded quite unexpectedly. "It now occurs to me that the Sokolovitches live in a different house and are in fact presently in Moscow. Yes, I made a slight mistake, but no matter."

"I'd like to know one thing," said the prince dejectedly. "Shouldn't I stop counting on you and go on alone?"

"Counting on me? Go on alone? But why, when this is an enterprise of such capital importance to me and on which the future of my family so greatly depends? No, my young friend, you don't know Ivolgin. To say 'Ivolgin' is to say 'rock'; you can rely on Ivolgin as on a rock, that's what they still say in the squadron in which I first served. We are only going to stop for an instant at a house where for several years I have found consolation after my trials and anxieties—"

"You want to stop by your house?"

"No! I want to go to Madame Terentyev's, the widow of Captain Terentyev, one of my subordinate officers—actually a friend of mine. Here at Madame Terentyev's I am refreshed in spirit, and here I bring my daily cares and family troubles. And as today I am weighed down by a heavy mental burden, I—"

"I'm afraid I've already been terribly foolish in troubling

150

you this evening," said the prince. "And now you're— Good-bye."

"But, my young friend, I can't possibly let you go!" cried the general. "A widow, mother of a family, who touches chords in my heart that resound in my whole being. The visit to her will take five minutes; I come and go in her house without formalities. I practically live there. I'll wash and tidy myself up a little and then we'll take a cab to the Bolshoi Theater. Rest assured I'll need you the whole evening. Here, in this house, we've arrived already. Ah, Kolya, you here? Do you know if Marfa Borisovna is home, or have you just arrived yourself?"

"Oh, no," replied Kolya, who had just run into them at the entrance way, "I've been here a long time, with Hippolite. He's worse, he was in bed this morning. I just went to the store for cards. Marfa Borisovna is expecting you. Only, Papa, what a state you're in!" Kolya concluded, carefully watching the general's walk and stance. "Well, come along anyway."

The encounter with Kolya induced the prince to accompany the general to Marfa Borisovna's, but only for a minute. The prince had need of Kolya; he had decided to give up the general in any case, and he could not forgive himself for having thought he could count on him. It was a long climb to the fourth floor, and they went by the back stairs.

"Do you want to introduce the prince?" asked Kolya on the way.

"Yes, my dear boy, I want to introduce him—General Ivolgin and Prince Myshkin, but what is—how is—Marfa Borisovna?"

"You know, Papa, it's better if you don't go up! She'll eat you alive. It's the third day you haven't been here, and she's expecting the money. Why did you promise her money? You're always doing things like that. Now you'll have to get out of it."

On the fourth floor they stopped in front of a low door. The general was visibly losing heart and kept pushing the prince ahead of him.

"I'll wait out here," he murmured, "I want to make it a surprise."

Kolya went in first. A woman of forty, heavily powdered and rouged, in slippers and a dressing jacket, her hair in braids, peered out the door. Immediately the general's "surprise" fell flat, for as soon as the woman saw him she screamed:

"There he is, that base and crafty man! I had a feeling he'd be coming!"

"Come right in—it's all right," said the general to the prince, continuing to smile guilelessly.

But it was not all right. No sooner had they entered through a low dark entrance passage into a narrow sitting room furnished with half a dozen wicker chairs and two card tables than their hostess immediately went on in a nagging whine that seemed to be her usual voice:

"Aren't you ashamed, aren't you ashamed of yourself, you barbarian, you tyrant of my family, you barbarian, you heretic! You've robbed me of everything, you've sucked me dry, and still you're not satisfied! How much longer will I put up with you, you shameless dishonest man!"

"Marfa Borisovna, Marfa Borisovna! This is—Prince Myshkin. General Ivolgin and Prince Myshkin," stammered the general, trembling and completely at a loss.

"Would you believe it," the widow suddenly addressed the prince, "would you believe this shameless man has taken no pity on my orphan children! He has robbed me of everything, stolen everything, sold and pawned everything, left nothing. What am I to do with your I.O.U.'s you shrewd, unscrupulous man? Answer, shrewd man, answer me, greedy heart! How will I feed my orphan children? Look at him—so drunk he can hardly stand up. How have I angered the Good Lord, you dreadful shrewd ugly man, answer!"

But the general was not up to answering.

"Marfa Borisovna, here are twenty-five roubles—all I can do, thanks to the help of my noble friend. Prince! I was cruelly mistaken! Such is—life. But now, excuse me. I am weak," the general went on, standing in the center of the room and bowing in all directions. "I am weak, excuse me! Lenotchka, a pillow, my dear!"

Lena, a girl of eight, at once ran for a pillow and put it on a hard sofa that was worn and covered with oilcloth. The general sat down on it, with the intention of saying much more, but no sooner had he touched the sofa than he turned on his side facing the wall and sank into the deep sleep of the just. Marfa Borisovna mournfully, ceremoniously motioned the prince to a chair at one of the card tables, then sat down opposite him with her right cheek resting on her hand and began to sigh noiselessly, looking at the prince. Three small children, two girls and a boy, of whom Lena was the eldest, came up to the table, all three put their arms on the table, and all three also stared at the prince. Kolya appeared from the other room.

"I'm very glad I met you here, Kolya," the prince said to him. "Could you possibly help me? I must go to Nastassya Filippovna's. A little while ago I asked Ardalion Alexandrovitch, but here he has fallen asleep. Please take me there, for I don't know the streets or the way there. I do know the address: near the Bolshoi Theater, the Mytovtsov house."

"Nastassya Filippovna? But she's never lived near the Bolshoi Theater, and father has never been to her place, if you want to know the truth. It's funny you should have expected anything of him. She lives near Vladimirsky Street, at the Five Corners, it's much nearer here. Do you want to go right now? It's now half past nine. If you like, I'll take you there."

The prince and Kolya went out at once. Alas, the prince had no money for a cab and they had to walk.

"I wanted to introduce you to Hippolite," said Kolya. "He's the eldest son of the captain's widow in the dressing jacket. He was in the other room. He's ill and has been in bed all day. But he is such a strange person. He's terribly sensitive and I figured he'd feel ashamed with you because you came at such a moment. Anyway, I wasn't as ashamed as he, because in my case it's my father and in his case it's his mother, and there is a difference, after all, because there's no dishonor for the masculine sex in situations like that. Of course it might be only a prejudice that one sex is more privileged than another in such cases. Hippolite is a splendid fellow, but he's a slave to certain ideas."

"You say he has consumption?"

"Yes, I think it would be better if he died soon. In his place I'd certainly want to die. He is sorry for his brother and sisters—the little ones you saw. If it were possible, if we only had money, we would leave our families and rent a separate apartment. This is our dream. And you know, when I told him just now what happened to you he actually flew into a rage, he said that a person who receives a slap without demanding a duel is a scoundrel. But of course he's terribly irritable now and I've stopped arguing with him. So I suppose Nastassya Filippovna invited you right on the spot, did she?"

"The point is she didn't."

"Then how can you go?" exclaimed Kolya, stopping in the middle of the sidewalk. "And in such clothes—when there's a party there?"

"Heaven knows how I'll go. If they let me in, well and good; if not—then my affair will have failed. As for my clothes, what can I do about them!"

"Do you have business? Or are you just going *pour passer le temps* in fine society?"

"No, in fact—I mean I have some business— It's hard for me to explain, but—"

"Well, I don't care exactly what it is—that's your affair. What does matter to me is that you aren't just inviting yourself for an evening in the delightful company of cocottes, generals, and usurers. Forgive me, Prince, but if this were the case I'd have laughed at you and despised you. There are so terribly few honest people here, there's almost no one one can respect. One can't help looking down on them, yet they all insist on respect. Varya especially. And have you noticed, Prince, that in our century everyone has become an adventurer? Here in Russia, among our very own people. How it happened I have no idea. It seemed that everything was so solidly established—and how is it now? Everyone writes about it. Everyone talks about it. Exposures! Everyone in Russia is making exposures. Parents are the first to retreat, and they're ashamed of the morals they once had. Right here in Moscow a father tried to persuade his son *to stop at nothing* to get money. It was in the papers. Just look at my father, the general. Well, what has he come to? And yet, you know, I think my general is an honest man—by God, he is! It's only his disorderly ways and the wine—he's an honest man! I even feel sorry for him—except I'm afraid to say so because everybody laughs—but by heaven it's a shame! And what is there to these intelligent people? They're all usurers, every last one of them! Hippolite justifies usury, he says this is the way it must be—economic crises, rises and falls— damned if I know! It makes me angry to hear this from him, but then he is so bitter. Would you believe it, his mother, the captain's widow, gets money from the general, then lends it back to him in little loans at high interest? It's a terrible disgrace! And do you know that Mother—my mother, Nina Alexandrovna—helps Hippolite with money, clothes, linen, and everything, and the children too, through Hippolite, because their mother neglects them. And Varya does the same."

"There, you see! You say there are no strong, honest people, that there are only usurers, but here you have people of strength—your mother and Varya. Isn't it a sign of moral strength to help people under such circumstances?"

"Varya does it from vanity, to show off, so as not to fall behind Mother, but Mother is really—I respect her for it. Yes, I respect it and I'll stand up for it. Even Hippolite is touched, and he is almost totally embittered. At first he would laugh and say it was ignoble of my mother, but now he sometimes begins to feel it. Now! You call this strength? I'll take note of

154

that. Ganya doesn't know about it or he would say she was giving them encouragement."

"Ganya doesn't know about it? It seems there is a great deal Ganya doesn't know yet," said the prince, thoughtfully.

"You know, Prince, I like you a lot. I can't forget the thing that happened to you this afternoon."

"And I like you very much, Kolya."

"Listen, how will you manage to live here? I'll soon get a job, and I'll be earning something. Let's the three of us rent an apartment and live together, you and I and Hippolite, and the general will come and see us."

"I would with the greatest pleasure. But we shall have to see. Right now I am upset—very upset. What? Are we there already? This house? What a magnificent entrance! And a hall porter. Well, Kolya, I don't know what will come of it."

The prince stood there looking completely lost.

"Tell me about it tomorrow! Don't be too afraid. May God bring you luck, because I share your ideas on everything. Good-bye. I'm going back there and tell Hippolite about it. And about your being received—don't worry, you will be. She's a terribly original woman. Go up those stairs to the first floor. The hall porter will show you."

Chapter THIRTEEN

As he went up the stairs the prince felt very uneasy and tried to take heart: "The worst that can happen," he thought, "is that they will not receive me and will think badly of me, or perhaps they will receive me and then laugh in my face— Well, it makes no difference!" And in fact it did not really alarm him very much, but he could find no reassuring answer to the question of what he was going to do there and why he was going. Even if he could catch a favorable occasion and say to Nastassya Filippovna, "Don't marry this man and ruin yourself, he doesn't love you, he loves your money, he's told me so himself, and so has Aglaya Yepanchin, and I've come to tell you this," this would hardly be the right thing to do when everything was considered. And still another insoluble question presented itself, one of such importance that the prince was afraid to think about it; he could not, he dared not even admit it, he was unable to formulate it, he blushed and trembled at the mere thought of it. Nonetheless, in spite of all his doubts and anxieties, he ended by entering and asking for Nastassya Filippovna.

The apartment Nastassya Filippovna occupied was not very large but was marvelously appointed. In the five years of her life in Petersburg there had been a period at the beginning when Afanassy Ivanovitch had been particularly liberal in spending money on her. At that time he had still been counting on her love and had sought to tempt her chiefly by comfort and luxury, knowing how easily habits of luxury are acquired and how difficult they are to give up after, little by little, they have become necessity. In this matter Totsky held fast to the good old traditions, not altering them in any way, having a boundless respect for the supreme power of sensuality. Nastassya Filippovna did not spurn luxury, in fact she liked it, but—and this seemed exceedingly strange—she did not succumb to it; it was as if she could do just as well without it; she even took pains to make a point of this fact on several occasions, which made an unpleasant impression on Totsky. But then there was much about Nastassya Filippovna which made an unpleasant impression on Totsky (and eventually aroused his contempt). Not even to mention the inelegance of the sort of people which she sometimes collected and with whom, inevitably, she became intimate, she showed a number of other extremely strange tendencies; there appeared in her a barbarous mixture of two tastes, a capacity for getting along with things and with expedients whose very existence would seem inadmissible for a person of propriety and refinement. Indeed, if Nastassya Filippovna suddenly displayed a pleasant and charming ignorance of the fact, for instance, that peasant women were unable to wear fine cambric undergarments as she did, Afanassy Ivanovitch would probably have been extremely pleased. Following Totsky's program, the whole early education of Nastassya Filippovna had been bent in this direction, and in this domain he was a person of subtle understanding; but alas, the result turned out curiously wrong. Nonetheless, there was still something in Nastassya Filippovna that now and then struck even Afanassy Ivanovitch with its rare and fascinating originality, a certain strength which sometimes won him even now, when all his former schemes concerning Nastassya Filippovna had fallen in ruin.

The prince was met by a maid (Nastassya Filippovna kept

only female servants) who, to his surprise, heard his request to be announced without a trace of surprise. Neither his dirty boots, his broad-brimmed hat, his cloak, or his embarrassed manner caused her the slightest hesitation. She helped him off with his cloak, asked him to wait in the reception room, and went off at once to announce him.

The company gathered at Nastassya Filippovna's consisted of her usual circle of acquaintances. There were even somewhat fewer present than on this day in previous years. First and foremost there were Afanassy Ivanovitch Totsky and Ivan Fyodorovitch Yepanchin; both were affable, but they both betrayed their secret apprehensions about the promised declaration concerning Ganya. Besides them there was of course Ganya—who was very gloomy, very thoughtful, and indeed almost completely *un*affable; most of the time he stood at some distance apart and did not speak. He had not ventured to bring Varya, and Nastassya Filippovna had made no reference to her; on the other hand she had no sooner greeted Ganya than she mentioned his earlier scene with the prince. The general, who had not yet heard of it, grew interested. Whereupon Ganya, dryly and with reserve, though with perfect candor, related everything that had happened earlier and how he had already gone to the prince and offered his apologies. He heatedly expressed the opinion that it was exceedingly strange and unaccountable that the prince had been called an "idiot," and that he personally thought it was quite the other way around, and that he had certainly "all his wits about him." Nastassya Filippovna heard this declaration with great attention and followed Ganya closely, but the conversation immediately turned to Rogozhin, who had played such a capital role in the afternoon's events, and in whom Afanassy Ivanovitch and Ivan Fyodorovitch also grew highly interested. It came out that particular information about Rogozhin could be furnished by Ptitsyn, who had been struggling over his affairs until almost nine o'clock that evening. Rogozhin had strenuously insisted on obtaining a hundred thousand roubles that same day. "It is true he was drunk," observed Ptitsyn as he told this, "but, difficult as it is to do, I think he will get the hundred thousand. Only I don't know whether it will be today or whether it will be the entire amount. But many people are working at it: Kinder, Trepalov, Biskup. He is giving any interest he's asked, all while drunk, of course, and in the first flush of joy," concluded Ptitsyn. All this news was received with interest, for the most part with rather somber interest. Nastassya Filippovna was silent, apparently not desiring to express her thoughts. Ganya too. General Yepanchin was probably more upset by the news than anyone else; the string of pearls he had presented that morning had been accepted with glacial politeness and even a particular sort of derision. Ferdyshchenko alone of all the guests was in an exuberant festive mood, laughing loudly now and then at nothing in particular, solely because he had undertaken to play the role of jester. Afanassy Ivanovitch himself, who had a reputation as a witty and polished raconteur and who had on past evenings usually led the conversation, was visibly out of sorts and somehow troubled, which was unlike him. The rest of the guests, who were not numerous (a poor old schoolteacher, invited no one knew why; a certain young man, unknown and terribly shy, who said nothing the entire time; a spirited woman of forty who seemed to be an actress; and a young lady who was very beautiful, richly and elegantly dressed, and extraordinarily taciturn), were not merely incapable of brightening the conversation but at times very simply did not know what to talk about.

In these circumstances the appearance of the prince was opportune. The announcement of his arrival caused some surprise and evoked a number of odd smiles, especially when it became evident from Nastassya Filippovna's look of astonishment that she had not dreamed of inviting him. But after her initial surprise Nastassya Filippovna suddenly displayed such pleasure that the majority present at once prepared to greet the guest with laughter and gaiety.

"We may assume this is his innocence," decided Ivan Fyodorovitch Yepanchin, "and as a general rule it's rather dangerous to encourage such tendencies, but at the moment I must say it's not such a bad thing he happened to come, even in such an original manner. He may possibly cheer us up, at least if I'm any judge of him."

"All the more because he's invited himself!" Ferdyshchenko hastened to add.

"What does that matter?" asked the general dryly, who hated Ferdyshchenko.

"It means he'll have to pay for his admission," explained the latter.

"Well, Prince Myshkin is not Ferdyshchenko, after all," blurted the general, who still could not reconcile himself to the thought of being in the same company and on equal terms with Ferdyshchenko.

"Oh, General, spare Ferdyshchenko," replied the latter, smirking. "I have special privileges here."

"What sort of special privileges?"

"Last time I had the honor of explaining it to this company in detail, but I don't mind repeating it again for Your Excellency. Please observe, Your Excellency, everyone has wit, but I have no wit. In compensation I have asked and been granted leave to tell the truth, for as everyone knows, the truth is told only by those who have no wit. Besides, I am a very vindictive man—this also because I am deprived of wit. I put up meekly with every insult, but only until he who insulted me comes to grief. When that first happens I remember and I take my revenge; I lash out, as Ivan Petrovitch Ptitsyn has said of me, having never lashed out at anyone himself, of course. Do you know Krylov's fable, 'The Lion and the Ass,' Your Excellency? Well, that's you and me. It was written about us."

"It seems to me you're talking nonsense again, Ferdyshchenko," said the general, furious.

"Why take it like that, Your Excellency?" pursued Ferdyshchenko, who had been counting on the opportunity to aggravate the matter and make the most of it. "Have no fear, Your Excellency, I know my place. If I said you and I were the Lion and the Ass from Krylov's fable, I am, naturally, in the role of the Ass, and Your Excellency—is the Lion, since it says in Krylov's fable:

> The mighty Lion, terror of the woods,
> With advancing years had lost his strength.

And I, Your Excellency, am the Ass."

"With that last I am in agreement," said the general incautiously.

All this was, of course, crudely and deliberately done, but it was generally agreed that Ferdyshchenko had the right to play the fool.

"The only reason I'm accepted here," Ferdyshchenko had once declared, "is that I talk exactly the way I do talk. How else would it be possible, after all, to receive a person like me? I quite understand this. How would it be possible for the likes of Ferdyshchenko to be asked to sit down next to such a perfect gentleman as Afanassy Ivanovitch? There is only one explanation: I am allowed to do so simply because such a thing is inconceivable."

But while all this was crude, it was also vitriolic, sometimes extremely so, and this, it appeared, was what appealed to Nastassya Filippovna. Those who desired to visit her had to make up their minds to tolerate Ferdyshchenko. He had perhaps guessed the truth in assuming that he was received because from the very first his presence had been insufferable to Totsky. Ganya, for his part, had endured from him an endless succession of torments, and in all this, Ferdyshchenko had learned how to make himself very useful to Nastassya Filippovna.

"I would like to have the prince begin by singing a popular ballad," concluded Ferdyshchenko, watching Nastassya Filippovna to see what she would say.

"I don't think so, Ferdyshchenko," she remarked dryly. "And please don't get so excited."

"Ah-ha! If he is under special protection I too will be sweetness and light."

But Nastassya Filippovna got up without listening and went to meet the prince herself.

"I am sorry," she said, appearing suddenly before him, "that in my haste this afternoon I forgot to invite you to my party, and I'm very glad you have now given me the opportunity to thank you and to congratulate you on your initiative." Saying this, she looked intently at the prince, trying to discover for herself some explanation of his action.

The prince would doubtless have said something in reply to her cordial greeting, but he was so dazzled and overwhelmed he could not utter a word. Nastassya Filippovna observed this and was pleased. Tonight she was in an evening dress and produced a very striking impression. She took his arm and led him toward the guests, but at the door of the drawing room the prince suddenly stopped and in great agitation whispered hurriedly to her:

"Everything about you is perfection—even that you're pale and thin—one wouldn't want to imagine you any other way —I wanted so much to come to you—I—forgive me."

"Don't apologize," laughed Nastassya Filippovna. "That would spoil all the quaintness and originality. So it's true, then, what they say about you, that you are a strange man. You take me for perfection, do you?"

"Yes."

"Well, you may be a master at guessing, but in this case you're mistaken. I shall remind you of this tonight."

She introduced the prince to the guests, more than half of whom knew him already. Totsky promptly said something courteous. Everyone became more animated, everyone began to talk and laugh. Nastassya Filippovna had the prince sit down beside her.

"But, look here," shouted Ferdyshchenko louder than anyone else, "what's so amazing about the prince turning up? It's plain as day. It speaks for itself."

"It's all too plain and speaks too much for itself," said Ganya, who had been silent until then.

"I've been observing the prince almost constantly today, right from the time this morning when he first looked at the portrait of Nastassya Filippovna on Ivan Fyodorovitch's table. I remember very well thinking even then what I am now entirely convinced of, and which, I might add, the prince confessed to me himself."

Ganya said all this in the most serious manner, without the slightest levity, indeed in a rather morose tone, which seemed somewhat strange.

"I have made no confessions to you," replied the prince, blushing. "I simply answered your questions."

"Bravo! Bravo!" cried Ferdyshchenko. "At least this is honest. Shrewd—but honest!"

Everyone laughed loudly.

"Don't shout like that, Ferdyshchenko," Ptitsyn remarked to him in an undertone, in disgust.

"I wouldn't have expected such enterprise from you, Prince," said Ivan Fyodorovitch. "Do you know the kind of person that makes you? And here I took you for a philosopher. Ah, these quiet fellows!"

"And to judge from how the prince blushes at an innocent joke, like an innocent young girl, I conclude that, like an honorable young man, he harbors in his heart the most honorable intentions," said, or rather mouthed, the toothless seventy-year-old schoolteacher suddenly and quite unexpectedly, who had been perfectly silent until then and whom no one expected to say a word the entire evening. Everyone laughed even harder. The old man, probably thinking that they were laughing at his wit, looked at them and laughed all the harder, causing him to begin coughing cruelly, which led Nastassya Filippovna, who was for some reason extremely fond of such original old men, old ladies, and even inspired fools, at once to begin making up to him, kissing him, and ordering more tea served to him. She asked the serving-woman who had entered for her shawl, wrapped herself in it, then ordered more logs for the fireplace. She asked for the time, and the servant answered that it was half past ten.

"Ladies and gentlemen, would you care for some champagne?" Nastassya Filippovna suddenly asked. "I have it ready. Perhaps it will make you more gay. Please don't stand on ceremony."

The invitation to drink, especially as it was phrased in such a naïve way, seemed very strange coming from Nastassya Filippovna. Everyone knew of the exceptional decorum of her previous evenings. On the whole the party was becoming livelier, but not in the usual way. The wine, however, was not refused, being accepted first by the general, then by the spirited woman, the old man, Ferdyshchenko, and after them, everyone else. Totsky, too, took his glass, hoping to alter the new tone of the party by lending it, insofar as was possible, the character of an amusing diversion. Ganya alone did not drink. Nastassya Filippovna too took a glass and declared that she would drink three this evening. But it was difficult to make any sense at all of her strange and sometimes very sudden and very shrill outbursts or her hysterical and pointless laughter that would abruptly turn to silent and even sullen depression. Some guests suspected she was feverish; at length they noticed that she seemed to be waiting for something, that she would often look at her watch and was becoming more impatient and preoccupied.

"Could you be a little feverish?" asked the spirited lady.

"Not a little—very. That's why I wrapped my shawl around me," answered Nastassya Filippovna, who indeed appeared paler and as if she was trying not to shiver.

Everyone became alarmed and stirred uneasily.

"Shouldn't we give the hostess some rest?" said Totsky, glancing at Ivan Fyodorovitch.

"Absolutely not, my friends! I ask you particularly to stay. Your presence is especially necessary for me tonight," declared Nastassya Filippovna, significantly and emphatically. And since almost all the guests knew that this was the evening a very important decision was to be made, her words carried particular weight. Again the general and Totsky exchanged glances, and Ganya made a convulsive movement.

"It would be nice to play some sort of game," said the spirited lady.

"I know a marvelous new game," put in Ferdyshchenko. "In any case it's a game that was played only once in the world, and even then it was not successful."

"What was it?" asked the spirited lady.

"Once a group of us got together—it's true there'd been some drinking—and suddenly someone suggested each one of us would, sitting right there at the table, tell whatever he honestly felt in his conscience was the worst of all the bad actions he ever committed in the whole course of his life. But it was to be done honestly, that was the point; it was to be done honestly, and no lying!"

"A strange idea," said the general.

"What could be stranger, Your Excellency, that's why it's so good."

"A droll idea," said Totsky, "but then quite understandable: it's just a way of bragging."

"Perhaps that was what we wanted to do, Afanassy Ivanovitch."

"But such a game would have us crying, not laughing," remarked the spirited lady.

"A completely absurd and impossible undertaking," declared Ptitsyn.

"But was it a success?" asked Nastassya Filippovna.

"Well, that's just it, you see. It wasn't. It turned out quite badly. Everyone did tell something or other, and many told the truth, and would you believe it, some actually enjoyed it, but afterward everyone was ashamed; they couldn't carry it through! On the whole, though, it was most amusing—in its own way, of course."

"Yes, it would be good!" said Nastassya Filippovna, suddenly brightening. "Let's try it, ladies and gentlemen! We need some livening up. If each one of us agreed to tell something—of that sort—voluntarily of course, quite freely. Perhaps we will bring it off? In any case it's terribly original—"

"A brilliant idea!" exclaimed Ferdyshchenko. "By the way, ladies are excused. The men will begin, and we'll cast lots as we did the other time. That's how we'll do it! Of course anyone who really doesn't want to, doesn't have to tell anything, but he would be particularly unobliging not to! Put your names in my hat here, gentlemen; the prince will draw. The game is very simple—just tell the very worst thing you've done in your entire life—it's terribly easy, gentlemen! Here, you'll see in a moment! If anyone has a lapse of memory, I'll try to remind him at once!"

The idea was an exceedingly strange one and almost no one liked it. Some frowned, others smiled shrewdly. Some protested, but not strenuously—Ivan Fyodorovitch, for instance, who did not wish to oppose Nastassya Filippovna and who noticed how greatly stirred she was by the strange idea, perhaps for the very reason that it was strange and almost impossible. Once she had made up her mind to express them, Nastassya Filippovna was always relentless and inexorable in her desires, however capricious, even if they were of no advantage to her. And now she seemed hysterical, excessively agitated, laughing in convulsive fits, especially at Totsky's alarmed protests. Her dark eyes sparkled, and two spots of color appeared on her cheeks. No doubt the sad, fastidious manner of some of the guests further stimulated her derisive impulses; no doubt the very cynicism and cruelty of the idea appealed to her. Some were even persuaded that she had some special object in it. However, in the end they agreed. It was, in any event, a curious idea, and for many of them a very enticing one. Ferdyshchenko was the most excited of all.

"And what if it's something that can't be told—in the presence of ladies," said the taciturn young man timidly.

"Then don't tell it," replied Ferdyshchenko. "As if there weren't enough bad actions without that. After all, young man!"

"As for me I don't know which of my actions is the worst," said the spirited lady.

"Ladies are not obliged to tell a story," repeated Ferdyshchenko, "but only not obliged. Any personal inspirations of theirs will be gratefully received. And gentlemen who strongly prefer to be excused will be excused."

"All right, but how can it be proved I'm not lying?" asked Ganya. "And if I do lie, the whole point of the game is lost. And who wouldn't lie? Naturally everyone is going to lie."

"Yes, and the interesting thing is just how a man will lie! But you, my dear Ganya, need have no particular fears about lying, since your own worst action is already well known to everyone. But think, gentlemen," cried Ferdyshchenko, suddenly inspired, "just think how we will look upon one another afterward, tomorrow, for instance, after we've told these stories!"

"But is this possible?" asked Totsky with dignity. "Are you really serious about this, Nastassya Filippovna?"

"If you're afraid of wolves, you don't go into the forest," Nastassya Filippovna observed with a mocking smile.

"But look here, Ferdyshchenko, how can you make a parlor game out of this?" pursued Totsky, more and more alarmed. "I can assure you that things of this sort never do work out. You told us yourself that it has been unsuccessful once already."

"Unsuccessful! Why, the last time I told them how I had stolen three roubles. I came right out with it."

"No doubt. But you couldn't possibly have told it in a way that it would sound like the real truth. Gavril Ardalionovitch observed quite correctly that with the least hint of falsehood the whole spirit of the game is lost. Truth is only possible here by accident, through a certain kind of bragging in the worst possible taste, unacceptable and completely out of place here."

"But what a subtle man you are, Afanassy Ivanovitch! You really astonish me!" exclaimed Ferdyshchenko. "Consider, ladies and gentlemen, that in remarking that I couldn't have told the story of my theft so that it would carry the truth,

Afanassy Ivanovitch suggests in the subtlest possible way that I could not in fact have stolen the money (because it would have been improper to admit it out loud), although it may very well be that he is personally convinced that Ferdyshchenko is perfectly capable of stealing! But to business, my friends, to business. The lots are collected, and you, Afanassy Ivanovitch, have put yours in too, which must mean no one has refused! So, Prince, draw."

Without a word the prince put his hand into the hat, and the first lot he drew was Ferdyshchenko's, the second Ptitsyn's, the third the general's, the fourth Afanassy Ivanovitch's, the fifth his own, the sixth Ganya's, and so on. The ladies had not put in their names.

"Good Lord, what a calamity!" cried Ferdyshchenko. "And here I was thinking the prince would be first and after him the general. But thank God at least Ivan Petrovitch comes after me and I'll have my reward. Now, ladies and gentlemen, of course I must set a noble example, but what I regret most at this moment is that I am a person of no consequence and not remarkable in any way. Even my rank is the lowest possible. Of what interest can it be, indeed, if Ferdyschenko has done something awful? And which is my worst action? There is an *embarras de richesse* here. Must I tell the same story of the theft again, to convince Afanassy Ivanovitch that it is possible to steal without being a thief?"

"You are also convincing me, Mr. Ferdyshchenko, that it is actually possible to experience intense pleasure in relating one's vile actions, even when one is not asked about them. However— Forgive me, Mr. Ferdyshchenko."

"Do begin, Ferdyshchenko," ordered Nastassya Filippovna irritably and impatiently. "You talk on and on and never finish what you're saying."

Everyone noticed that after her late fit of hysterical laughter she had suddenly become sullen, peevish, and irritable; yet she stubbornly and imperiously persisted in her caprice. Afanassy Ivanovitch was suffering agonies. He was also infuriated by Ivan Fyodorovitch, who sat there sipping his champagne as if nothing was the matter, even thinking, no doubt, of some story to tell when his turn came.

Chapter FOURTEEN

◄══❦══►

"I have no wit, Nastassya Filippovna; that's why I talk too much!" cried Ferdyshchenko. "If I had the wit of Afanassy Ivanovitch or Ivan Petrovitch I'd have kept quiet this evening like Afanassy Ivanovitch and Ivan Petrovitch. Prince, tell me, what do you think? It seems to me there're a great many more thieves in the world than nonthieves and that even the most honest man has stolen something at least once in his life. This is my opinion, from which I don't conclude, however, that all men are thieves, though, God knows, one is terribly tempted to think so. What do you think?"

"Oh, what a stupid way to tell a story," said Darya Alexeyevna, the spirited lady. "And what nonsense! It can't be true that everyone's stolen something. I've never stolen anything."

"You've never stolen anything, Darya Alexeyevna. But what will the prince say? He's blushing from head to toe."

"I think what you say is true, except that you're exaggerating a great deal," said the prince, who was in fact blushing for some reason.

"And you, yourself, Prince, have you stolen anything?"

"Bah! How ridiculous this is!" intervened the general. "Pull yourself together, Mr. Ferdyshchenko."

"The simple fact is that when you get down to cases you're ashamed to tell your story, so you want to drag the prince in because he can't reply for himself," snapped Darya Alexeyevna.

"Ferdyshchenko," said Nastassya Filippovna sharply and irritably, "either tell your story or be still and mind your own business. You're exhausting everybody's patience."

"At once, Nastassya Filippovna. But if the prince has confessed—for I insist that the prince has as good as confessed —what would anyone else—not to mention names—say if he wanted to tell the truth for once? As for me, ladies and gentlemen, there is no more than this to tell: it's very simple, stupid, and nasty. But I assure you, I am no thief, I have no idea how I came to steal. It happened three years ago, one

Sunday at the country house of Semyon Ivanovitch Ishchenko. He had friends dining with him. After dinner the men lingered over their wine. It occurred to me to ask his daughter, a young lady called Marya Semyonovna, to play the piano. On my way through the corner room I saw a green three-rouble note lying on Marya Ivanovna's worktable; she'd taken it out for some household expense. There wasn't a soul in the room. I took the little note and put it in my pocket—I don't know why. What came over me I can't understand. I just went right back and sat down at the table. I sat there waiting, in a state of great excitement, chattering away, telling funny stories and laughing, then went in and sat with the ladies. After a half hour or so they discovered the money was missing and questioned the maids. The suspicion fell on a certain Darya. I showed enormous interest and sympathy, and I even remember that when Darya became completely confused, I started persuading her to confess, swearing that she could count on Marya Ivanovna's kindness, and this aloud, in front of everyone. Everybody was watching, and I got extraordinary pleasure from it, particularly from preaching while the note lay in my pocket. I spent those three roubles that same evening for wine in a restaurant. I went in and asked for a bottle of Château Lafitte. Never before had I ordered just a bottle like that, without anything else. I wanted to spend the money as fast as possible. I didn't feel any particular remorse, either then or afterward. I certainly wouldn't do it again—you can believe me or not, as you choose; it makes no difference to me. Well, ladies and gentlemen, that's all."

"Except, of course, that this isn't at all your worst action," said Darya Alexeyevna with disgust.

"It's not even an action, it's a psychological case," observed Afanassy Ivanovitch.

"And the servant girl?" asked Nastassya Filippovna, not disguising her utter disgust.

"The servant was dismissed the next day, it goes without saying. It's a strict household."

"And you let it happen?"

"That's marvelous! You didn't expect me to go and confess, did you?" chuckled Ferdyshchenko, who was however rather struck by the extremely unpleasant impression his story had produced on the assembly.

"How vile!" exclaimed Nastassya Filippovna.

"Oh, you want to hear a man's worst actions and yet expect something shining and bright! Worst actions are always very vile, Nastassya Filippovna; we will shortly hear this

167

from Ivan Petrovitch. As if there weren't enough people already who positively glitter with respectability because they own their own carriage. Plenty of people have carriages of their own— And think how they got them—"

In a word, Ferdyshchenko completely lost his composure and suddenly became so enraged that he forgot himself and overstepped all bounds; his whole face was distorted. Strange as it may seem, it is very likely that he expected an entirely different success for his story. Such lapses of taste and this "way of bragging" as Totsky had referred to it, occurred quite often with Ferdyshchenko and were completely in his character.

Nastassya Filippovna trembled with rage and stared hard at Ferdyshchenko. He was suddenly swept with fright and fell silent. He had gone too far.

"And what if we put an end to this?" asked Afanassy Ivanovitch craftily.

"It's my turn, but I am exercising my right to abstain and will not tell anything," said Ptitsyn decisively.

"You don't want to?"

"I can't, Nastassya Filippovna. And on the whole I find such *petit-jeu* impossible."

"Then, General, I believe it's your turn," said Nastassya Filippovna, turning to him. "If you refuse too, you'll spoil the whole thing, and I shall be sorry, because I was counting on telling an incident from my own life as a conclusion. But I only wanted to tell it after you and Afanassy Ivanovitch, because you must give me courage," she added, laughing.

"Oh, if you promise to," the general cried warmly, "then I'm ready to tell you the whole story of my life. But I confess that as I was waiting my turn I already prepared my story."

"And just from the way His Excellency looks one may judge with what particular literary satisfaction he has worked out his anecdote," Ferdyshchenko ventured to remark with a sarcastic smile, though he was still somewhat ill at ease.

Nastassya Filippovna glanced quickly at the general, and she too smiled to herself. But it was obvious that her depression and irritability were increasing with every moment. Afanassy Ivanovitch was more alarmed than ever at her promise to tell something herself.

"Like everyone else," began the general, "I have done things in my life which were not exactly nice, but the strange thing is that I regard the little incident which I am about to relate to you as the foulest action of my entire life. It was almost thirty-five years ago, yet I can never recall it without experiencing a certain—pang in my heart, so to speak. It was, however, an extremely stupid business. I was at the time only a second lieutenant struggling along in the army. Well, we all know what a second lieutenant is: all blood and thunder and watching every kopeck. I had an orderly at that time named Nikifor, and he looked after me terribly well. He skimped and saved, sewed, scrubbed and scoured, and he even stole things wherever he could to add to our larder. He was a most faithful and honest man. I was strict, of course, but fair. For quite some time we were stationed in a small town. I was billeted on the outskirts in the house of the widow of a retired sub-lieutenant. This little old lady must have been eighty or thereabouts. Her little wooden house was run-down and wretched, and she didn't even keep a servant on account of her being so poor. The notable thing about her was that in the past she had had a numerous family and many relatives, but some had died, others had gone away, and still others had forgotten about her. Her husband she had buried forty-five years before. For a number of years a niece of hers had lived with her, a hunchback, and wicked as a witch, people said; one time she even bit the old lady on the finger, but she had died too, and for three years the old lady had been struggling on completely alone. I was terribly bored there, and she was so empty-headed it was impossible to get anything out of her. She finally stole a cock of mine. The matter has never been cleared up to this day, but there wasn't anyone besides her who could have done it. We had a quarrel over the cock, a violent quarrel. And it so happened that as soon as I put in my request I was transferred to other quarters, on the opposite side of the town, in the house of a merchant with a large family and a big beard. I can still see him. Nikifor and I were delighted to move, and I left the old lady with a great show of indignation. Three days later when I returned from drill Nikifor reported, 'Your Excellency, you shouldn't have left your bowl at the old lady's, I have nothing to serve soup in.' I naturally was astounded: 'How did the soup bowl happen to stay behind at the landlady's?' Nikifor, quite surprised, went on to report that when we were leaving, the landlady did not return the bowl for the reason that I had broken her pot, that she was keeping our bowl in place of her pot, and that she pretended I had suggested this arrangement myself. Such pettiness on her part naturally threw me into a rage. Young lieutenant that I was, it made my blood boil. I jumped up and flew out. When I arrived at the old woman's place I was, so to speak, already beside myself. I looked at her. She was sitting there in the corner of the entryway all alone, as if to be out of the sun, with her cheek resting on

169

her hand. I promptly poured a torrent of abuse on her, calling her this and calling her that, in the best Russian style. Except that as I looked, I noticed something odd: she is sitting there facing me with her eyes wide open, not answering a word, and she is looking at me very strangely and swaying slightly. At last I calmed down and looked at her more closely and asked her a question without getting any answer. I hesitated there, the flies were buzzing, the sun was setting, it was very still; and at last in a state of complete bewilderment I left. I didn't get home, because I was summoned by the major, and then I had to stop by the company, so that I didn't get home until quite late in the evening. Nikifor's first words were, 'Did you know, Your Excellency, that our old landlady died?' 'When?' 'This evening, about an hour and a half ago.' In other words she was dying at the very time I was swearing at her. This, I assure you, made such an impression on me I couldn't get over it. I really began to think about it, you know, and dream about it at night. Naturally I'm not superstitious, but two days later I went to church to the funeral. In a word, the more time goes by the more I think about it. Not about any one thing in particular, but sometimes my imagination starts working and I feel uneasy. What conclusion did I finally come to? In the first place, here was a woman, a fellow human being, as we say nowadays, who had lived, and lived long, outlived her time. Once she had had children, a husband, family, relations, all this, as you might say, bubbling around her, all this, you might say, smiling, and suddenly: zero, everything up the chimney; she is left alone, like some—fly, carrying the curse of the ages. And then at last God brought her to the end. At sunset on a quiet summer evening my old lady, too, passes away—there is certainly a moral here—and just at that very moment, instead of a tear of farewell, so to speak, a reckless young lieutenant full of swagger, hands on his hips, sees her off the face of the earth with some choice Russian language over a lost bowl! Without doubt I am to blame, and though, with the passage of the years and the changes in my nature, I have for some time regarded my action as being that of a stranger, I still feel sorry. To the point that, I repeat, it all seems positively odd to me, particularly since if I am to blame I am not entirely to blame. Why did she make up her mind to die just at that moment? There is one excuse, to be sure, that my action was in a certain sense psychological; nevertheless I could not find peace with myself until fifteen years ago, when I provided for two chronically ill old ladies, so that their last days in the public hospital would be adequately supported. I am thinking of making this a permanent endowment by providing a capital fund. Well, there you have it, ladies and gentlemen. As I say, I have probably been guilty of much in my lifetime, but in my conscience I consider this affair the worst action of all my life."

"Instead of your worst action, Your Excellency," said Ferdyshchenko, "you have told one of your good ones. You have cheated Ferdyshchenko!"

"Yes, General," said Nastassya Filippovna casually, "I never imagined you had such a good heart. It's rather a pity."

"A pity? Why?" asked the general with a genial laugh, taking a sip of champagne, not without a touch of self-satisfaction.

But now it was Afanassy Ivanovitch's turn, and he too had prepared himself. Everyone guessed he would not refuse as Ivan Petrovitch had done, and for several reasons his story was awaited with particular interest and they all were casting furtive glances at Nastassya Filippovna. With extraordinary dignity entirely in keeping with his stately appearance, Afanassy Ivanovitch began one of his "charming stories" in his soft, gentle voice. He was, by the way, a fine-looking man of stately bearing, quite tall, a trifle bald, a trifle gray, and rather heavy, with soft, pink, rather pendulous cheeks and false teeth. His clothes were full-cut and elegant, his linen extraordinary. One could not help noticing his plump white hands. On the index finger of his right hand he wore an expensive diamond ring. All the time he told his story Nastassya Filippovna examined intently the lace frill of her sleeve, pinching at it with two fingers of her left hand, and did not once glance up at the speaker.

"What makes my task easier," began Afanassy Ivanovitch, "is the express obligation of telling nothing else but the worst action of my whole life. In this there can of course be no hesitation: conscience and the promptings of my heart dictate at once exactly what I must tell. I avow with bitterness that among the no doubt innumerable frivolous and—thoughtless actions of my life there is one which weighs all too heavily upon my memory. It happened about twenty years ago. At that time I was visiting in the country with Platon Ordynsev. He had just been elected marshal of nobility and had come with his young wife, Anfisa Alexeyevna, to spend the winter holiday on his estate there. Her birthday happened to be then, and two balls had been arranged. At that time there was a terrific vogue for that delightful novel of Dumas *fils*, *La Dame aux Camélias*, which was just making a great sensation in the best society—a sheer poem in my opinion, not destined to die or dim with age. All the provincial ladies were in ecstasies over it—at least those of them who had read it. The charm of the tale, the originality of the heroine's situation, all that alluring world, so subtly dissected, and of course all those charming little details scattered through the book (for instance, the significance of alternating white camelias and red); all those delightful details, and all of it taken together, produced something almost like an earthquake. Camelias became extraordinarily fashionable. Everyone was begging for them and trying to get them. Now I ask you, how many camelias can you get in a provincial district when everyone is insisting on them for dances, even if there aren't many dances? Petya Vorhovsky, poor fellow, was breaking his heart over Anfisa Alexeyevna at the time. I don't really know if there was anything between them—I mean whether he could have had any sort of grounds for serious hope. The poor fellow was going out of his mind to obtain camelias for the evening of Anfisa Alexeyevna's ball. Countess Sotsky, from Petersburg, who was a guest of the governor's wife, and Sofya Bezpalov were definitely known to be coming with bouquets of them, white ones. Anfisa Alexeyevna, for some sort of special effect, wanted red ones. Poor Platon was almost driven to distraction, naturally—he was the husband. He promised to get her a bouquet—but what to do? The very day before the ball, Katerina Alexandrovna Mytishchev, a great rival of Anfisa Alexeyevna's in everything, had snapped up all the camelias there were. They were at dagger points. Naturally—hysterics and fainting spells. Platon was a wreck. Understandably, if Petya could at that interesting moment turn up a bouquet somewhere his affair could be considerably advanced, for woman's gratitude in such instances is virtually unlimited. He rushed around like a madman, but of course it was impossible, not even worth talking about. Then suddenly at eleven o'clock the evening before the birthday and the ball, I ran into him at the house of Marya Petrovna Zubkov, a neighbor of the Ordynsevs'. He was radiant. 'What's wrong with you?' 'I've found out where some are! Eureka!' 'Well, my friend, you amaze me! Where?' 'In Yekshaisk—a little town fifteen miles from here, out of our district. There's a merchant there, Trepalov, with a beard and very wealthy, he lives there with his old woman and a lot of canaries instead of children. Both of them have a passion for flowers, and he has camelias.' 'But it might not be true, and what if he doesn't give them to you?' 'I'll get down on my knees and grovel at his feet until he does give them to me. I won't leave until he does!' 'When are you going?' 'Tomorrow at dawn, at five o'clock.' 'Well, God be with you!' And, you know, I was very happy for him. I went back to the Ordynsevs'. Finally, about one o'clock, I was still thinking about it all. I was about to go to bed when suddenly I had a most original idea! I immediately made my way to the kitchen, woke up Savely the coachman, handed him fifteen roubles, and said, 'Get the horses ready in half an hour!' So a half hour later the sledge was at the gate. Anfisa Alexeyevna, I was told, had a headache; she was feverish and delirious. I got in and off I went. Towards five o'clock I was at Yekshaisk, at the inn. I waited until dawn, but only till dawn; I was at Trepalov's well before seven. I said to him, 'My dear sir, have you camelias? My friend, help me, save me, and I will bow down at your feet!' The old man was tall, gray-haired, severe—a dreadful old man. 'No, no! By no means. I can't do it!' I got down at his feet—stretched right out on the ground. 'What are you doing, sir? What are you doing?' He even became frightened. 'It's a matter of a man's life!' I cried out to him. 'If that's so, take them, and God be with you.' Then if I didn't cut those red camelias! It was a joy, a miracle, he had a whole little greenhouse full of them. The old man was sighing. I took out a hundred roubles. 'No, sir, please don't insult me in this manner.' 'If that's how it is,' I said to him, 'kindly do me the favor of presenting these hundred roubles to the hospital here to improve the patients' food and care.' 'That, sir,' he said, 'is another matter. That is a good and noble thing and pleasing to God. I shall give them for your health.' And you know, I rather liked that old Russian; he was Russian all the way through, you might say, *de la vraie souche*. Delighted at my success, I set off on the way back, but by a roundabout way so as not to meet Petya. As soon as I arrived I sent the bouquet in to Anfisa Alexeyevna to greet her when she woke up. You can imagine yourself her delight, her gratitude, her grateful tears. Platon, yesterday as good as dead, sobbed on my chest. Alas! All husbands have been that way since the creation of—legal marriage! I will only venture to say that from this episode onward poor Petya's affair collapsed completely. At first I thought he would kill me when he found out, and I even prepared to meet him; but something happened which I never would have even expected. He fainted. By nightfall he was delirious, and by the morning he was in a raging fever and was sobbing like a child and in convulsions. A month later, as soon as he had recovered, he volunteered for the Caucasus. It was exactly like something that happened in a story. It ended by his being killed in the Crimea. At that time his brother, Stepan Vor-hovsky, was in command of a regiment and distinguished himself. I confess I had feelings of remorse about it, even many years afterward. Why, for what purpose, did I deal him such a blow? If at least I had been in love myself at this time? But it was only a simple escapade, for the sake of a gallantry, nothing more. And if I hadn't snatched that bou-quet away from him—who knows—the man might be alive today; he might be happy, he might be successful, it might never have entered his head to go off and fight the Turks."

Afanassy Ivanovitch fell into the same stately and silent at-titude of dignity with which he had begun his tale. It was ob-served that Nastassya Filippovna's eyes flashed with a partic-ular brilliance and her lips actually trembled when Afanassy Ivanovitch finished. Everyone was watching both of them with curiosity.

"Ferdyshchenko has been cheated! Cheated! Oh, but he has really been cheated!" cried Ferdyshchenko in a lachry-mose voice, understanding that he could and in fact should say something.

"And who's to blame if you don't understand? You should learn from clever people," Darya Alexeyevna told him cut-tingly and sententiously. (She was an old and faithful friend and social ally of Totsky's.)

"You're right, Afanassy Ivanovitch, the game is a very dull one, and we must end it quickly," Nastassya Filippovna re-marked casually. "I'll tell what I promised to tell, and you can all play cards."

"But the story you promised first of all!" cried the general approvingly.

"Prince," Nastassya Filippovna addressed him suddenly in a sharp voice, sitting rigidly in her chair, "my old friends here, the general and Afanassy Ivanovitch, are anxious to have me married. Tell me what you think: shall I get married or not? Whatever you say I shall do."

Afanassy Ivanovitch turned pale, the general stiffened; ev-eryone was staring, craning their necks. Ganya froze in his chair.

"To— To whom?" asked the prince in a sinking voice.

"To Gavril Ardalionovitch Ivolgin," said Nastassya Filip-povna, still speaking in a sharp, firm, and very distinct voice.

Several seconds of silence followed; the prince appeared to be struggling to speak but could say nothing, as though a ter-rible weight was pressing on his chest.

"No—no— Don't marry him!" he whispered at last, and managed to draw a breath.

174

"Then so it will be! Gavril Ardalionovitch!" she addressed him authoritatively, almost triumphantly. "You heard what the prince has decided? Well, that's my answer, and let that end the matter once and for all!"

"Nastassya Filippovna!" said Afanassy Ivanovitch in a quavering voice.

"Nastassya Filippovna!" said the general in a persuasive yet alarmed voice.

Everyone stirred uneasily.

"What is the matter, my friends?" she went on, looking at her guests as if in surprise. "Why are you so upset? And what faces you are all wearing!"

"But, remember, Nastassya Filippovna," said Totsky faltering, "you have made a promise, quite voluntarily, and you might at least be considerate of—I'm at a loss and of course —perplexed, but— After all, now, at such a moment, and— in front of people, and like this to—end in a little parlor game an affair as serious, an affair of honor and sentiment— on which depends—"

"I don't understand you, Afanassy Ivanovitch; you don't know what you are saying. First, what does 'in front of people' mean? Aren't we in a wonderful company of intimate friends? And why 'parlor game'? I really meant to tell my story, and, well, I did tell it. Isn't it a nice one? And why do you say it isn't serious? Isn't this serious? You heard: I said to the prince 'Whatever you say I shall do.' If he had said yes, I would have consented at once, but he said no, and I have refused. Isn't that serious? My whole life was hanging in the balance. What could be more serious?"

"But the prince—what has the prince to do with it? And what is he, after all?" muttered the general, almost unable to control his indignation at the offense of authority being conferred upon the prince.

"The prince is the first man I have ever met in my whole life whose sincerity and devotion I have believed in. He believed in me at first sight, and I believe in him."

"It only remains for me to thank Nastassya Filippovna for the extreme delicacy with which she has—treated me," pronounced Ganya at last in a trembling voice and with twisted lips, turning pale. "This was, of course, how it had to be— But the prince—the prince in this affair is—"

"—is after the seventy-five thousand roubles, is that what you mean?" said Nastassya Filippovna, cutting him short. "Don't deny it, you were certainly going to say that! Afanassy Ivanovitch, I had forgotten to add that you may take back those seventy-five thousand and that I am setting you

175

free, for nothing. Enough! It's time you too should breathe freely! Nine years and three months! Tomorrow will be—new, but today is my birthday, and I'm my own mistress for the first time in my whole life! General, you take your pearls back too, give them to your wife, here they are. And tomorrow I shall be leaving this apartment for good, and there will be no more parties, my friends!"

Having said this she suddenly got up as if she meant to leave.

"Nastassya Filippovna! Nastassya Filippovna!" was heard on all sides.

Everyone was excited; everyone stood up; everyone crowded around her; everyone listened uneasily to her abrupt, feverish, frantic words; everyone sensed that something was wrong; no one could make it out; no one could understand anything. At this moment there was a sudden violent ring of the doorbell, exactly as there had been at Ganya's apartment that afternoon.

"Ah! Ah-ha! The denouement! At last! Half past eleven," cried Nastassya Filippovna. "Please be seated, ladies and gentlemen. This is the denouement."

Having said this, she sat down herself. A strange smile trembled on her lips. She sat silently, in feverish expectation, looking toward the door.

"Rogozhin and his hundred thousand, not a doubt of it," Ptitsyn murmured to himself.

Chapter FIFTEEN

Katya, the maid, came in very frightened.

"Goodness knows what's going on out there, Nastassya Filippovna! There're about ten men who've broken in, and they're all drunk. They want to come in. They say it's Rogozhin and that you know about it."

"That's right, Katya. Show them all in at once."

"All of them, Nastassya Filippovna? They're completely disorderly. It's terrible!"

"All of them, every one of them, Katya; don't be fright-

176

ened. Every single one of them or they will come in anyway. Listen to the racket they're making, just like this afternoon. Ladies and gentlemen," she said turning to the guests, "perhaps you are offended that I receive such company in your presence? I'm very sorry and beg your pardon, but it can't be helped; and I would very much appreciate it if you'd all be witnesses of this final scene; though, of course, you may do as you like."

The guests continued to express their amazement, to whisper to each other, and to exchange glances; but it was perfectly plain that all this had been contrived beforehand and that Nastassya Filippovna—though she had certainly taken leave of her senses—would not now be stopped. Everyone was suffering agonies of curiosity, and there was nothing in particular to be frightened of. There were only two ladies among the guests, Darya Alexeyevna, the spirited individual who had seen everything there was to be seen and was difficult to upset, and the beautiful but silent stranger. But then the silent stranger could hardly have understood anything. She was a German who had recently arrived and did not know a word of Russian. Moreover, it appeared that she was as stupid as she was beautiful. She was a novelty and it had become the fashion to invite her to certain parties, sumptuously attired with her hair done up as if for exhibition, and to seat her in one's drawing room as an attractive ornament to enhance the occasion—just as some people borrow for a single evening a picture, a vase, a statue, or a fire screen. As for the men, Ptitsyn was a good friend of Rogozhin, Ferdyshchenko was completely in his element, like a fish in water, Ganya had not yet collected himself but felt a vague burning need to stay at his shameful pillory to the bitter end. The old teacher, who had only a dim notion of what was happening, was near tears and actually trembling with fear, sensing some sort of unusual agitation in those around him, including Nastassya Filippovna, whom he adored like his own grandchild; and he would rather have died than abandon her at such a moment. As for Afanassy Ivanovitch, he had no desire to compromise himself in such adventures but he was too intrigued by the situation, in spite of the mad turn it had taken, to withdraw; and then Nastassya Filippovna had let fall two or three little remarks for his benefit, which made it impossible for him to leave until they were clarified. He had resolved to stay to the end, keeping perfect silence, solely as an observer, as was of course required by his dignity. General Yepanchin, so lately offended by the unceremonious and absurd return of his present, could now of course feel further insulted by these extraordinary eccentricities, or, for instance, by the appearance of Rogozhin. And indeed a man in his position had already gone too far in consenting to sit next to Ptitsyn and Ferdyshchenko. But though his passion might sway him it could finally be mastered by his sense of duty, of moral obligation, of rank, of his importance, and of the question of self-respect in general; so that, whatever the case, the presence of Rogozhin and his band before His Excellency was an impossibility.

"Ah! General, I'd forgotten!" said Nastassya Filippovna, the moment he turned to her in protest. "But you may be sure I had thought of you before. If you're really so offended I shan't insist you stay, though it would please me to have you, in particular, hear me now. In any case I am very grateful for your friendship and flattering attention, but if you are afraid—"

"Please, Nastassya Filippovna!" exclaimed the general in an outburst of chivalrous feeling. "Whom are you saying this to? Why, out of simple devotion to you I shall stay at your side, and if by any chance there is any danger— Besides, I must confess that my interest is aroused. I only meant to say they will ruin your carpets and probably smash something. And I don't think you should see them at all, Nastassya Filippovna!"

"Rogozhin in person!" proclaimed Ferdyshchenko.

"What do you think, Afanassy Ivanovitch?" the general whispered rapidly to Totsky. "Has she lost her mind? I don't mean figuratively, but in the medical sense. Eh?"

"I have told you she has always had a tendency toward it," Afanassy Ivanovitch whispered back wisely.

"And she's feverish too—"

Rogozhin's following was almost the same as it had been in the afternoon. There were only two additions to the company: one was an elderly libertine who in his day had been the editor of some salacious scandal sheet, who was said to have pawned his gold false teeth for drinking money; the other was a certain retired sub-lieutenant who made it his profession to be the rival and antagonist of the individual with the fists, and who was completely unknown to any of Rogozhin's following. He had been picked up on the sunny side of Nevsky Prospect, where he had been stopping passers-by and in the florid style of Marlinsky* begging for assistance, under the cunning pretext that in his day he had given fifteen roubles to anyone who asked. The two rivals promptly behaved in a hostile manner toward one another. The two-fisted gentleman went so far as to consider himself

178

offended by the admission into the company of a "beggar" and being taciturn by nature only growled occasionally, like a bear, and looked with profound contempt upon the efforts of the obsequious "beggar," who turned out to be a man of the world and a diplomatist, to play up to him and curry favor. When it came down to "business" the sub-lieutenant showed more promise of adroitness and agility than of strength, and he also happened to be shorter than the gentleman with the fists. Delicately, without actually starting anything, though boasting outrageously, he had already hinted several times at the superiority of English boxing; in other words, he showed himself to be a thoroughgoing Westerner. At the word "boxing" the two-fisted gentleman merely smiled in pained contempt, and for his part, as if he did not regard his rival worthy of a direct threat, he silently and apparently accidentally allowed a thoroughly native object to be seen—an enormous fist, sinewy, knotted, and overgrown with a sort of reddish fuzz, and it became evident that should this profoundly national object descend upon anything it would leave nothing after it but a damp spot.

Nevertheless none of them was entirely drunk, thanks to the efforts of Rogozhin, who had had his visit to Nastassya Filippovna in mind all day. He himself was now almost completely sober, yet nearly dazed by the various impressions he had experienced on this hideous day which resembled no other day in all his life. One thing alone was constantly before his mind and in his heart every minute, every instant. For this one thing alone he had spent the entire time from five until eleven that night in constant misery and anxiety, occupied with the Kinders and the Biskups, who were themselves almost distracted, rushing around like madmen on his behalf. Nevertheless they had raised the one hundred thousand in hard cash, the sum Nastassya Filippovna had vaguely and sarcastically hinted at in passing, against interest rates which Biskup himself was too ashamed to mention to Kinder above a whisper.

As in the afternoon, Rogozhin walked ahead, the others in the band followed him with a full sense of their advantages, though certainly with some apprehensions as well. For some reason they were most afraid of Nastassya Filippovna. Some of them actually thought that they would all promptly be "kicked downstairs," among them the dandy and lady-killer Zalyozhnev. But others, and notably the two-fisted gentleman, regarded Nastassya Filippovna, silently in their hearts, with profound contempt and even hatred, and they approached her house as they would approach a city under siege. But the splendid appointments of the first two rooms, the objects they had never seen nor heard of before, the rare furniture, paintings, and the enormous statue of Venus, all this inspired in them a feeling of respect and almost of fear. This uneasiness did not of course prevent them from shoving their way, little by little, after Rogozhin into the living room; but when the two-fisted person, the "beggar," and several of the others noticed General Yepanchin among the guests, they were at first so overcome that they actually started to turn back into the other room. Lebedev, however, was among those who kept up their spirits and resolution, and he walked almost at Rogozhin's side, understanding the full significance of one million four hundred thousand in available cash of which a hundred thousand was there in Rogozhin's hand. Yet it must be observed that all of them, even the expert Lebedev, were in a state of confusion over the exact extent of their power and whether they were now free to do anything they pleased, or not. At certain moments Lebedev was ready to swear that they could, but at others he felt, uneasily, the need to remind himself of several eminently encouraging and reassuring articles of the civil code.

Upon Rogozhin, Natassya Filippovna's drawing room produced an effect opposite from that made on his followers. The moment the portiere was raised and he saw Nastassya Filippovna, all else ceased to exist for him, as had happened in the afternoon, though now more completely. He turned pale and for a moment stopped dead; it was plain to see that his heart was beating violently. For several seconds he gazed timidly and distractedly at Nastassya Filippovna, never taking his eyes from her. Then suddenly, as if he was losing his reason, almost staggering, he went toward the table. On the way he stumbled against Ptitsyn's chair and stepped with his great dirty boots on the lace trimming of the silent German beauty's magnificent blue dress; he did not apologize or, indeed, notice. Having reached the table, he placed upon it the strange object which he had entered the room with, holding it before him in both hands. It was a thick package about eight inches long and six inches through, tightly and securely wrapped in a copy of *The Stock Exchange News,* tied both ways and twice across with the sort of cord used to tie sugar loaves. Then he stood without uttering a word, letting his hands fall slack, as if he was awaiting sentence. He was dressed exactly as before, except for a brand-new green and red scarf around his neck, fastened with an enormous diamond pin in the form of a scarab, and a massive diamond ring on a dirty finger of his right hand. Lebedev stopped short three paces from the table; the rest, as has been said, were slowly filing into the drawing room. Katya and Pasha, Nastassya Filippovna's maids, had also come running to watch from behind the raised portiere, in great amazement and fear.

"What is this?" demanded Nastassya Filippovna, having surveyed Rogozhin with intent curiosity and indicating the "object" with a glance.

"A hundred thousand!" replied Rogozhin almost in a whisper.

"Ah, he has kept his word! What a fellow! Here, sit down, please, right in this chair. I'll have something to tell you later. Who is with you? The same crowd? Well, let them come in and sit down. They can sit there on that couch. And there's another couch. Here are two armchairs— What's the matter? Don't they want to?"

Indeed, some of them were positively overcome with confusion and had retreated into the other room to sit down there to wait; but others stayed and seated themselves as they were invited to do, except farther from the table, mostly in the corners of the room, some apparently desiring to make themselves invisible, while others recovered their audacity with incredible rapidity. Rogozhin, too, sat down as he had been bidden, but not for long; he soon got up and did not sit again. Little by little he began to single out individual guests and scrutinize them. Seeing Ganya, he smiled venomously and whispered under his breath, "Well, look!" He glanced at the general and at Afanassy Ivanovitch without embarrassment and indeed without particular interest. But when he caught sight of the prince beside Nastassya Filippovna he could not take his eyes off him for a long time; he was extremely surprised and seemed powerless to account for his presence. At some moments one could imagine he was actually delirious. Besides all the emotional shocks of that day, he had spent all of the previous night on the train and had not slept for almost forty-eight hours.

"This, ladies and gentlemen, is a hundred thousand roubles," said Nastassya Filippovna, addressing them all in a sort of feverish, impatient challenge. "Right here in this dirty package. A while ago he screamed like a madman that he would bring me a hundred thousand this evening, and I've been waiting for him all the time. He bargained for me: he started with eighteen thousand, jumped to forty, and now here's this hundred. He has kept his word! My, how pale he is! This was all at Ganya's this afternoon. I had paid a call on his mamma, on my future family, and there his sister

181

shouted right in my face, 'Isn't this shameless creature going to be thrown out?' and she spat right in her brother Ganya's face. She has temperament, that girl."

"Nastassya Filippovna!" cried the general reproachfully. He was beginning, in his own way, to understand the situation.

"What's the matter, General? Do you find that improper? Enough of these pretenses! Here I've sat in a box in the French theater like some inaccessible paragon of fashionable virtue, and I've been running away—like a wild creature— from everyone who's been pursuing me for the last five years, looking the picture of proud innocence, and this is where all this nonsense has gotten me! Here in your presence he comes and lays a hundred thousand roubles on the table, after my five years of innocence, and I have no doubt they have troikas outside waiting for me. He sets my price at a hundred thousand! Ganya, I see you are still angry with me? Could you really have meant to make me one of your family? Me? Rogozhin's woman? What did the prince say just now?"

"I did not say you were Rogozhin's woman. You're not!" said the prince in a trembling voice.

"Stop, Nastassya Filippovna, please stop, darling," said Darya Alexeyevna, unable to restrain herself. "If they make you so miserable, why pay attention to them? How could you possibly want to go off with a fellow like that, even for a hundred thousand! It's true, a hundred thousand is something to consider. So, why not take the hundred thousand and send him packing. That's the way to treat people like that. Ah! In your place I'd send the whole lot of them— The very idea!"

Darya Alexeyevna was becoming quite angry. She was a kindhearted woman and highly impressionable.

"Don't be angry, Darya Alexeyevna," said Nastassya Filippovna, smiling at her. "I didn't speak to him in anger. I didn't reproach him, did I? I simply can't understand how I could have been so foolish as to want to enter a proper family. I saw his mother, I kissed her hand. And if I carried on at your house this afternoon, Ganya, I did it on purpose to see how far you would go. Well, you have really amazed me! I expected a lot, but not this! And could you really have married me knowing that this man here was giving me such pearls, almost on the eve of our wedding, and that I was accepting them? And Rogozhin? Why, he was bidding for me right in your own home, in front of your mother and your sister, and yet even after that you came to ask me to marry you—and you almost brought your sister! Perhaps Rogozhin told the truth about you when he said that for three roubles you'd crawl on all fours to the Vassilyevsky district?"

"He would!" said Rogozhin suddenly, in a quiet voice that carried extreme conviction.

"If at least you were starving to death, but they say you get quite a good salary! And on top of everything else, apart from just the shame of it, to bring a wife you hate into your house (because you do hate me, I know that!). No, I believe now that a man like you would kill for money! Nowadays everyone is so driven by this greed for money it's as if they had lost their minds. Even children are becoming usurers. And a man winds a razor in silk and silently, from behind, slits his friend's throat like a sheep's. I read about that recently. Well, you are a shameless man! I am shameless, but you are far worse. I won't speak of this bouquet-holder——"

"Is this you, Nastassya Filippovna? Can this be you?" said the general, wringing his hands in genuine distress. "You, so delicate, with such refined thoughts, and now! Such language! Such expressions!"

"I'm a little drunk now, General," laughed Nastassya Filippovna suddenly. "I want to have a good time! Today is my day, my holiday, my special day; I've been waiting for it a long time. Darya Alexeyevna, do you see this bouquet-holder, this *monsieur aux camélias*? There he sits laughing at us."

"I am not laughing, Nastassya Filippovna, I am merely listening with the greatest attention," replied Totsky with dignity.

"Well, why have I been tormenting him for five years without letting him go free? Was it worth it? He is simply the sort of person he is, the person he has to be. And besides, he'll put all the blame on my side. He has given me an education, kept me like a countess, and spent so much money, so much money on me, and found an honest husband for me in the country, and now dear little Ganya here. And what do you think? I haven't lived with him for five years now, but I've taken money from him, and I thought I was right to do it! So completely have I lost my senses! You say take the hundred thousand and send him packing, if it's so disgusting to go with him. And it is disgusting. I could have married long ago, and not just Ganya, but that too would have been very disgusting! And why have I spent five years of my life in spiteful rage! Believe it or not, four years ago there were times when I wondered whether I shouldn't really marry my Afanassy Ivanovitch! I thought about it out of spite then, my head was full of all sorts of ideas then—but I really could have had him marry me! He proposed it himself, believe it or not. It's true he was lying, but he is very susceptible and couldn't have resisted. And later, thank God, I decided he wasn't worth all that anger! Suddenly I was so disgusted with him that even if he'd begged me I wouldn't have married him. And for a whole five years I've been playing this game! No, I'd rather be out in the street, where I belong! Or carousing with Rogozhin, or become a washerwoman tomorrow! Because I've nothing that belongs to me. If I leave I'll leave everything of his behind, to the last rag. And who will take me when I have nothing? Ask Ganya here, would he take me? Why even Ferdyshchenko wouldn't!"

"Perhaps Ferdyshchenko would not, Nastassya Filippovna. I am a candid person," said Ferdyshchenko. "But then the prince would take you! You sit here and complain, but do have a look at the prince. I've been watching him for a long time."

Nastassya Filippovna turned to the prince with curiosity.

"Is it true?" she asked.

"It's true," murmured the prince.

"You will take me as I am, with nothing?"

"I will, Nastassya Filippovna."

"Now there's something new!" muttered the general. "I might have expected it!"

The prince looked with a stern, mournful, and penetrating gaze into the face of Nastassya Filippovna, who continued to watch him.

"Here's a new one!" she said suddenly, addressing herself to Darya Alexeyevna. "And yet he does it out of the goodness of his heart, I know him. I have found a benefactor! Yet perhaps it's true what they say about him, that he's a little—*off*. What will you live on if you're so much in love? Are you ready to marry Rogozhin's woman—you, a prince?"

"I shall be taking you as an honest woman, Nastassya Filippovna, not as Rogozhin's," said the prince.

"Me, an honest woman?"

"You."

"Well, that's—out of novels! That, darling Prince, is all old-fashioned illusions. Nowadays the world is wiser, and all that is nonsense! And how can you get married when you still need a nurse to look after you?"

The prince got up and in a shaking, timid voice, though at the same time with intense conviction, said:

"I know nothing, Nastassya Filippovna. I have seen nothing of life, you are right about that, but I—I consider you will be doing me an honor, and not I you. I am nothing, but you have suffered and come out pure from that hell, and that

184

is a great deal. What are you ashamed of that you're ready to go off with Rogozhin? This is your fever. You have given Mr. Totsky back his seventy-five thousand, and you say that you will leave everything here behind. No one else here would do that. I—love you, Nastassya Filippovna. I would die for you, Nastassya Filippovna. I won't let anyone say a word about you, Nastassya Filippovna. If we are to be poor I will work, Nastassya Filippovna—"

At these last words Ferdyshchenko and Lebedev sniggered, and even the general cleared his throat loudly with great displeasure. Ptitsyn and Totsky could not help smiling, but they restrained themselves. The others simply gaped in astonishment.

"But perhaps we shall not be poor, but very rich, Nastassya Filippovna," continued the prince in the same timid voice. "However, I cannot be sure, and I am sorry I haven't been able to learn anything all day, but I received a letter in Switzerland from Moscow, from a certain Mr. Salazkin, and he informs me that I might receive a very large inheritance. Here is the letter—"

The prince produced a letter from his pocket.

"Well, is he raving?" muttered the general. "This is a real madhouse."

For a moment there was silence.

"Did you say, Prince, that the letter to you was from Salazkin?" asked Ptitsyn. "This is a man very well known in his own circle, a well-known lawyer, and if he was really the person who let you know you can believe it implicitly. Fortunately I know his handwriting because I've had dealings with him lately. If you would let me have a glance at it I might be able to tell you something."

The prince silently offered the letter to him with a trembling hand.

"What's this? What's this?" cried the general, looking at them all with a half-crazed stare. "Is there really an inheritance?"

They all fixed their eyes on Ptitsyn, who was reading the letter. The general curiosity had received a new and powerful stimulus. Ferdyshchenko could not sit still; Rogozhin stared in astonishment and terrible anxiety, first at the prince, then at Ptitsyn. Darya Alexeyevna was on tenterhooks of expectation. Even Lebedev could not bear it and coming out of his corner, he craned and stretched and finally managed to peer over Ptitsyn's shoulder, with the air of a man who expected an immediate beating for doing so.

Chapter SIXTEEN

∽◦∾

"It's quite correct," declared Ptitsyn finally, folding the letter and handing it back to the prince. "By the incontestable will of your aunt you will receive, without any formal difficulties, an extremely large sum of money."

"Impossible!" exploded the general like a pistol shot.

Again everyone was agape with amazement.

Ptitsyn, addressing himself chiefly to Ivan Fyodorovitch, explained that five months previously an aunt of the prince, whom he had never actually known, had died. She was the elder sister of the prince's mother and the daughter of a Moscow merchant of the third guild,* Papushin, who had died bankrupt and in poverty. But Papushin's elder brother, who had also died recently, had been a rich and well-known merchant. About a year before this his only two sons had died almost in the same month. The old man was so shocked by their deaths that not long afterward he himself became ill and died. He was a widower and had no heirs at all, except the prince's aunt, his niece, a poor woman with no home of her own and who lived with others. At the time she came into the fortune this aunt was dying of dropsy but she had at once taken steps to find the prince, entrusting Salazkin with this task, and she had had time to make her will. It appears that neither the prince nor the doctor with whom he lived in Switzerland saw fit to wait for an official notification or to make inquiries, and the prince, with Salazkin's letter in his pocket, decided to set off himself.

"I can only tell you one thing," concluded Ptitsyn, addressing the prince, "all this is indisputably in order, and all that Salazkin writes you about the legality and certainty of your fortune you may take for money in your pocket. I congratulate you, Prince! Possibly you will have a million and a half, and perhaps more. Papushin was a very rich merchant."

"To the last of the Prince Myshkins!" bellowed Ferdyshchenko.

"Hurrah!" croaked Lebedev in a drunken voice.

"And I'm the one who lent him twenty-five roubles this morning, the poor man. Ha! Ha! Ha! This is fantastic!" said the dumbfounded general. "Well, my congratulations, my congratulations!" And rising from his place he went to the prince and embraced him. Others got up too and approached the prince. Even those who had withdrawn to the other side of the portiere now began to drift into the drawing-room. A confusion of voices filled the room, marked by exclamations, and there were even calls for champagne. Everyone was crowding and shoving in a great state of agitation. For a moment they almost forgot Nastassya Filippovna and the fact that she was, after all, the hostess of the occasion. But gradually the idea dawned on them all at about the same time that the prince had just made her a proposal of marriage. The whole thing therefore was already three times as mad and extraordinary as it had appeared at first. Totsky, profoundly astonished, shrugged his shoulders; he was almost the only one sitting; the rest of the company was crowding around the table in great disorder. Everyone asserted afterward that it was at this exact moment that Nastassya Filippovna went mad. She continued to sit there and for some time gazed at everyone with a strange, wondering expression, as if she could not understand what had happened and was trying to make sense of it. Then she suddenly turned to the prince and glared at him with a menacing frown; but for only a moment; perhaps she had imagined for an instant that it was all a joke, a deception; but the sight of the prince's face told her at once that it was not. She reflected a moment, then smiled again, as if she herself did not really know what she was smiling at.

"Then I really am a princess!" she whispered to herself, as if mockingly, and catching sight of Darya Alexeyevna she laughed. "An unexpected ending. I—I didn't expect it to turn out like that. But why are you all standing, ladies and gentlemen? Please sit down and congratulate me and the prince! I believe someone called for champagne. Ferdyshchenko, please have some brought in. Katya, Pasha." She suddenly noticed her maids in the doorway. "Come over here. I'm getting married, have you heard? To the prince. He has a million and a half—he's Prince Myshkin and he's marrying me!"

"And God bless you, darling, it's high time! It's not a chance to miss!" shouted Darya Alexeyevna, deeply moved by what had occurred.

"Do sit down beside me, Prince," Nastassya Filippovna went on. "That's right. Now they are bringing the wine. Congratulate us, ladies and gentlemen!"

Hurrah! shouted many voices. Many of the guests crowded toward the wine, including almost all of Rogozhin's followers. But though they shouted and were prepared to shout all the more, many of them, despite the strangeness of the circumstances and the surroundings, realized that the scene had changed. Others were bewildered and waited mistrustfully. And a number whispered to one another that it was after all a perfectly natural thing, for princes marry all sorts of women, sometimes girls out of Gypsy camps. Rogozhin himself stood and stared, his face twisted into a fixed, uncomprehending smile.

"Prince, my dear fellow, come to your senses!" whispered the general in horror, approaching the prince from one side and pulling his sleeve.

Nastassya Filippovna noticed it and laughed.

"No, General! I am a princess myself now, didn't you hear? And the prince will not let me be insulted! Afanassy Ivanovitch, do congratulate me. Now I can sit right beside your wife anywhere at all. What do you think? Isn't it an advantage to have such a husband? A million and a half, and a prince, and, they say, an idiot into the bargain. What could be better? Only now is my real life beginning! You are too late, Rogozhin! Take back your package, I am marrying the prince, and I am richer than you are!"

But Rogozhin had grasped the situation. There was a look of unutterable suffering on his face. He wrung his hands and a groan broke from his breast.

"Give her up!" he shouted to the prince.

Everyone around them laughed.

"Give her up for someone like you!" Darya Alexeyevna declared triumphantly. "For this lout who throws money on the table! The prince is marrying her, while you only came to make a scene!"

"I shall have her, too! I'll marry her at once, this moment! I'll give her everything—"

"Here, listen to the tavern drunk! You ought to be thrown out!" insisted Darya Alexeyevna with indignation.

The laughter grew louder than ever.

"Listen, Prince," said Nastassya Filippovna turning to him, "that's how a peasant bargains for your bride."

"He's drunk," said the prince. "He loves you very much."

"But won't you feel ashamed later that your bride almost ran off with Rogozhin?"

"You were in a fever. You're in a fever now, almost delirious."

"And won't you feel ashamed when they tell you later that your wife lived with Totsky as his mistress?"

"No, I won't be ashamed. You didn't live with Totsky of your own free will."

"And you'll never reproach me?"

"Never."

"Be careful! Don't answer for your whole lifetime."

"Nastassya Filippovna," said the prince softly and with compassion, "I told you before I would take your consent as an honor, and that you are doing me an honor, I am not doing you one. You smiled at those words, and I heard people around us laughing. Perhaps I expressed myself very comically and was indeed comical myself, but I thought all along that I—understood the meaning of honor, and I'm certain I spoke the truth. Just now you wanted to ruin yourself, irrevocably, since you'd never have forgiven yourself for it afterward: but you are not to blame for anything. Your life must not be utterly ruined. What does it matter that Rogozhin came to you and that Gavril Ardalionovitch tried to deceive you? Why do you keep insisting on these things? Few people could do what you have done, I repeat this; and as for your wanting to go off with Rogozhin, you made up your mind to do this when you were delirious with fever. And you're ill now and you'd be better off in bed. You would have gone off and become a washerwoman tomorrow, you wouldn't have stayed with Rogozhin. You are proud, Nastassya Filippovna, but perhaps you are so terribly unhappy that you really do think you're to blame. You need to be looked after, Nastassya Filippovna. I'm going to look after you. I saw your portrait this morning and it was as if I recognized a familiar face. I felt immediately as if you had already called to me—I—I will respect you as long as I live, Nastassya Filippovna," the prince concluded abruptly, blushing as if he had suddenly become aware of the sort of people before whom he was saying these things.

Ptitsyn had actually bowed his head out of delicacy of feeling and was staring at the floor. Totsky thought to himself, "He's an idiot, yet he knows that flattery is the best way to get what a person wants. It's instinct!" The prince noticed Ganya glaring at him from his corner with blazing eyes, as if he wanted to reduce him to ashes.

"What a good man he is!" declared Darya Alexeyevna, deeply touched.

"A cultivated man," whispered the general in an undertone, "but doomed!"

Totsky took his hat and was ready to get up and slip away

189

quietly. He and the general exchanged glances, intending to leave together.

"Thank you, Prince," said Nastassya Filippovna. "No one has ever talked to me like that before. They've always tried to bargain for me, and no decent man has ever asked to marry me. Did you hear, Afanassy Ivanovitch? What did you think of all the prince had to say? It's almost indecent, isn't it? Rogozhin! Don't leave yet. But I see you're not leaving. Perhaps I'll go away with you after all. Where did you want to take me?"

"To Yekaterinhof," Lebedev announced from his corner, while Rogozhin only gave a violent start and gazed wide-eyed, as if he could not trust his senses. He had become completely stunned, as though from a violent blow to the head.

"What are you saying, my dear? What are you saying?" cried Darya Alexeyevna in alarm. "Are you really delirious? Have you lost your mind?"

"You didn't really believe it, did you?" said Nastassya Filippovna, jumping up from the couch and bursting out laughing. "You didn't really think I'd ruin a child like that? That's all very well for Afanassy Ivanovitch—he's the one who is fond of young people! Come on, Rogozhin! Get your money ready! Never mind about wanting to marry me, give me that money anyway. I still may not marry you after all. Did you think if you married me, you'd keep the money? Not a chance! I'm a shameless person myself. I was Totsky's concubine. Prince! You ought to marry Aglaya Yepanchin and not Nastassya Filippovna, or else—Ferdyshchenko will be pointing his finger at you! You may not be afraid, but I'd be afraid of ruining you and of you reproaching me afterward! And as for your saying I'm doing you an honor, Totsky knows all about that. And, Ganya dear, you've spoiled your chances with Aglaya Yepanchin, did you know that? If you hadn't bargained with her, she'd most certainly have married you! That's the way you all are! You've got only one choice —disreputable women or reputable women! Otherwise you get into a hopeless mess. Look! The general is staring. His mouth has fallen open!"

"This is Sodom, Sodom!" said the general over and over again, shrugging his shoulders. He, too, got up from the couch. Everyone was standing again. Nastassya Filippovna seemed to be in a state of wild exaltation.

"Can it be?" moaned the prince, wringing his hands.

"Did you think it wasn't possible? Perhaps I too am proud, shameless as I am! You called me perfection just now; a fine perfection who goes into the streets just so as to boast of having trampled on a million roubles and a princess's title! What kind of a wife would I make you after that? Afanassy Ivanovitch, you see I really have thrown a million out the window! How did you suppose I'd marry Ganya for your seventy-five thousand and count myself happy? Take back your seventy-five thousand, Afanassy Ivanovitch; you didn't go to a hundred thousand, and Rogozhin has outbid you! And as for dear Ganya, I'll comfort him myself; I've an idea. But right now I want to have a good time, I'm a girl who belongs in the streets! I've spent ten years in prison, and now it's time to be happy! What are you waiting for, Rogozhin? Come on, let's go!"

"Let's go!" roared Rogozhin, overcome by delight. "Hey, you there—wine! Ah!"

"Be sure that there's wine, I want a drink. And will there be music?"

"There will! There will! Don't come near!" Rogozhin cried out in frenzy, seeing Darya Alexeyevna approaching Nastassya Filippovna. "She's mine! Everything's mine! My queen! This is the end!"

He was gasping with joy. He walked around Nastassya Filippovna shouting to everyone, "Don't come near!" His whole following had by now crowded into the drawing room. Some were drinking, others were shouting and laughing, all were in a state of high excitement and completely uninhibited. Ferdyshchenko was trying to join in with them. Totsky and the general made another attempt to slip out unobtrusively. Ganya also had his hat in hand, but he stood there in silence, as if unable to tear himself away from the scene that unfolded before him.

"Don't come near!" shouted Rogozhin.

"What are you bellowing for?" Nastassya Filippovna said, laughing at him. "I'm still the mistress here. If I like, I can still throw you out. I haven't taken that money of yours yet, there it lies. Now, give it to me, the whole package! Is there a hundred thousand in this package? Ah! how disgusting! What's the matter, Darya Alexeyevna? Would you have had me ruin him?" (She pointed to the prince.) "How can he marry? He still needs a nursemaid himself. The general there will be his nurse—see how he's making up to him! Look, Prince, your fiancée has taken money because she's a bad woman, and here you wanted to marry her! But why are you crying? Is it as bitter as that? You should laugh, as I do," went on Nastassya Filippovna, though two large tears shone on her own cheek. "Trust in time—everything will pass! It's better you come to your senses now than later— But why are

191

you all crying? Here Katya is crying too! What's the matter with you, Katya dear? I'm leaving quite a lot to you and Pasha, I've already made the arrangements. And now goodbye! I've made an honest young girl wait on a depraved woman like myself— It's better this way, Prince, really much better, afterward you would have begun to despise me, and we would not have been happy! Don't deny it, I don't believe you. And it would have been so stupid! No, it's better for us to say good-bye nicely, for I am a dreamer too and nothing good could have come of it. Haven't I dreamed of you? There you are right. I dreamed of you long ago, when I was still in the country with him, five years completely alone. I would think and think, sometimes, and dream and dream, and I always imagined someone like you, kind, honest, and good, and silly, so silly that he would suddenly appear and say, 'You are not to blame, Nastassya Filippovna, and I adore you!' Yes, I used to dream like that until I nearly went out of my mind. And then this man would come, stay for two months every year, and shame me, insult me, excite me, corrupt me, and then go away—so that a thousand times I wanted to throw myself into the pond; but I was too low for that, I lacked the courage to do it. Well, and now—Rogozhin, are you ready?"

"Ready! Don't come near!"

"Ready!" shouted several voices.

"The troikas are waiting with their bells!"

Nastassya Filippovna took the package in her hands.

"Ganya, I've had an idea. I want to compensate you. Why should you lose everything? Rogozhin, would he crawl on all fours to the Vassilyevsky district for three roubles?"

"He would!"

"Well then, listen, Ganya. I want to have a last look into that soul of yours. You have been tormenting me for the last three months, and it's my turn. Do you see this package? There are a hundred thousand roubles in it! I am now going to throw it into the fire, before everyone, they will all be witnesses! As soon as the fire has set it aflame, you must reach into the fireplace, without gloves, with your bare hands, and turn back your sleeves, and pull the package out of the fire. If you pull it out, it's yours, the whole hundred thousand! You'll only burn your fingers a little bit—but it's a hundred thousand, think of it! It won't take long to get it out. And I'll be having a good look at your real nature as you crawl into the fireplace after my money! Everybody is witness that that money will be yours. And if you don't crawl after it, it will burn; I won't let anyone else touch it. Stand back! Everybody stand back! This is my money! I took it for a night with Rogozhin. Is this my money, Rogozhin?"

"Yours, my delight! Yours, my queen!"

"Very well, then! Everyone stand back. I do as I please! Don't interfere! Ferdyshchenko, stir up the fire."

"Nastassya Filippovna, my hands will not do it," replied the dumbfounded Ferdyshchenko.

"Bah!" cried Nastassya Filippovna, and seizing the tongs, she separated two smoldering logs, and as soon as the fire blazed she threw the package of notes on it.

There was a general outcry; many actually crossed themselves.

"She has lost her mind! She has lost her mind!" they shouted back and forth.

"Shouldn't we— Shouldn't we—tie her up?" whispered the general to Ptitsyn. "Or send for the— She has lost her mind. She has, hasn't she?"

"No," said Ptitsyn, pale as a sheet and trembling, "perhaps this isn't entirely madness." He was unable to take his eyes off the smoldering package of bills.

"She's mad. Isn't she?" persisted the general to Totsky.

"I did tell you she was a *colorful* woman," muttered Afanassy Ivanovitch, who had also turned rather pale.

"But look here; after all, it's a hundred thousand roubles!"

"Good Lord!" people cried on all sides. Everyone was crowding around the fireplace, everyone was pressing forward to see, everyone was shouting. Some had even jumped up on chairs to look over the others' heads. Darya Alexeyevna had dashed into the other room and was frantically whispering something to Katya and Pasha. The beautiful German woman had fled.

"Madam! Royal lady! All-powerful lady!" wailed Lebedev, walking on his knees before Nastassya Filippovna, his arms outstretched toward the fire. "A hundred thousand roubles! A hundred thousand! I saw the bills myself, I saw them wrapped up! Dear lady! Bountiful lady! Order me into the fireplace! I'll get all the way in! I'll put my gray hair in the flames! My wife is sick and crippled. I have thirteen children, all orphans. I buried my father last week—starved to death —Nastassya Filippovna!" And with this outcry, he started to crawl into the fireplace.

"Get back!" cried Nastassya Filippovna, pushing him aside. "Everyone step aside! Ganya, what are you standing there for? Don't be ashamed! Go after it! There is your happiness!"

But Ganya had already been through too much that day and evening, and he was not prepared for this last, unexpected trial. The crowd parted before him, and he stood facing Nastassya Filippovna, three steps from her. She was standing near the fireplace, waiting, her intent, blazing eyes fixed upon him. Ganya, in evening dress with his arms folded, hat in his hand and wearing gloves, stood before her, silent and resigned, staring at the fire. An insane smile wandered over his chalk-white face. It is true he could not take his eyes from the fire, from the smoldering package, but now something new seemed to have risen in his very soul; as if he had made a vow to endure this ordeal. He did not move from his place, and after several moments it became clear to everyone that he was not going after the package, that he did not wish to go after it.

"Look out, it will burn, and they'll put you to shame!" Nastassya Filippovna shouted at him. "And afterward you will hang yourself. I mean it!"

The fire which had at first flared up between two smoldering logs had almost gone out when the package fell and smothered it. But a tiny blue flame crept from under one corner of the lower log. At last a long thin tongue of flame licked at the package and, catching, ran along the paper to the corners, and suddenly the whole package flared and burst into bright flame. Everyone gasped.

"Dear lady!" Lebedev wailed again, trying once more to rush to the fireplace, but Rogozhin dragged him back and pushed him away again.

Rogozhin's whole being was now in his unwavering stare. He could not take his eyes off her, he feasted his gaze upon her, he was in seventh heaven.

"Just like a queen!" he kept repeating to everyone around him. "This is how we do things," he would shout, quite beside himself. "Which of you pinch-pennies would do a trick like that, eh?"

The prince looked on sadly and in silence.

"I'd pull it out with my teeth for just one thousand!" proposed Ferdyshchenko.

"I'd pull it out with my teeth too!" cried the two-fisted gentleman from the rear, in genuine despair. "Damn it, it's burning! It's all burning up!" he shouted, seeing the flame.

"It's burning! It's burning!" they all cried in one voice, pushing together to get nearer the fireplace.

"Ganya, stop this nonsense! I'm telling you for the last time!"

"Get it!" roared Ferdyshchenko, rushing to Ganya in an absolute frenzy and pulling him by the sleeve. "Get it, you conceited fool! It will burn! Oh, damn you!"

Ganya pushed Ferdyshchenko violently away, turned, and

started toward the door, but before he had gone two steps, he swayed and fell to the floor.

"Fainted!" everyone around cried.

"Dear lady, it will burn!" howled Lebedev.

"It will burn for nothing!" they were shouting from all sides.

"Katya! Pasha! Get water for him, spirits!" cried Nastassya Filippovna, and seizing the fire tongs she pulled the package out of the fire. Almost all the paper wrapping was burned and smoldering, but it was evident at once that the contents were untouched. The bills had been wrapped in three layers of newspaper, and the money itself was intact. Everyone sighed with relief.

"Only one paltry little thousand note might be spoiled, but the rest is safe," said Lebedev with tender feeling.

"It's all his! The whole package of notes is his! Do you hear, my friends?" declared Nastassya Filippovna, laying the package near Ganya. "He didn't pull it out, he held firm! Which means his vanity is even greater than his lust for money. Don't worry, he'll come to. Otherwise he might have killed me—there, he's already coming around. General, Ivan Petrovitch, Darya Alexeyevna, Katya, Pasha, Rogozhin, do you hear? The package is his—Ganya's. I give it to him outright in compensation for—well, for what has been. Tell him. Let it lie there by him. Rogozhin, let's go! Good-bye, Prince, in you I've seen what a human being is for the first time in my life! Good-bye, Afanassy Ivanovitch, *merci!*"

With great clamor and shouting Rogozhin's whole crowd rushed through the rooms toward the front door, following Rogozhin and Nastassya Filippovna. In the large drawing room the maids held her fur coat for her; the cook Marfa ran in from the kitchen. Nastassya Filippovna kissed them all.

"You can't be leaving us forever, dear lady?" wondered the tearful girls, kissing her hands. "Where are you going? And on your birthday, too, on such a day!"

"I'm going on the streets, Katya, you heard me, that's my proper place, or I'll be a washerwoman. I've had enough of Afanassy Ivanovitch! Give him my regards, and don't think badly of me "

The prince rushed toward the street door, beyond which everyone was taking places in four troikas with bells The general managed to overtake him on the stairs.

"Good heavens, Prince, be sensible!" he said, catching him by the arm. "Let her go! You see what she is! I speak as a father."

The prince looked at him, but without saying a word broke away and ran downstairs.

At the street entrance, from which the troikas had just pulled away, the general saw the prince hail the first fiacre that passed and shout to the driver, "To Yekaterinhof—after those troikas." Then the general's gray trotter drew up his own fiacre and took him home, full of new hopes and schemes, and with the string of pearls, which in spite of everything he had not forgotten to take with him. Once or twice, among his schemes, the alluring image of Nastassya Filippovna danced. The general sighed.

"A pity! A real pity! A lost woman! A mad woman! Well, it isn't Nastassya Filippovna the prince needs now. So after all it's perhaps just as well things have turned out as they have."

Two other guests of Nastassya Filippovna's, who had decided to walk a certain distance together, exchanged a few parting words in the same edifying tone.

"Did you know, Afanassy Ivanovitch, they say the same sort of thing happens among the Japanese?" said Ivan Petrovitch Ptitsyn. "It seems that a man who has been insulted goes to the one who insulted him and says, 'You have insulted me and for this I have come to cut my stomach open in front of you,' and, when he has said this, he really does cut his stomach open before the eyes of his offender and feels, no doubt, a vast sense of satisfaction, as if he had really avenged himself. There are strange people in this world, Afanassy Ivanovitch."

"And you think something of that sort happened here?" Afanassy Ivanovitch replied with a smile. "Hm. You've put it rather cleverly—the comparison is splendid. But you've seen for yourself, my very dear Ivan Petrovitch, that I've done all I could; I can't do the impossible, can I? But you'll agree, I trust, that the woman has capital qualities—some brilliant features. Just now I felt tempted to call out to her—if only I could have brought myself to do it in that disgusting atmosphere—that she herself was the best reply I had to all her accusations. Who would not sometimes be captivated by this woman to the point of losing his reason and—all the rest? Look at that lout Rogozhin throwing a hundred thousand at her feet! Allow that all that happened there just now is flimsy, romantic, and unseemly; yet you must admit it was colorful; original, too. My God, what might have been made of a woman with such character and such beauty. But in spite of all efforts, in spite even of her education—it's all lost! A rough diamond—I've said so a number of times—"

And Afanassy Ivanovitch sighed deeply.

PART

TWO

〜〜〜

Chapter ONE

Two days after the strange adventure at Nastassya Filippovna's party, with which we concluded the first part of our story, Prince Myshkin hastened to Moscow to settle the matter of his unexpected inheritance. It was said at the time that there might have been other reasons for his precipitous departure, but about this, and about the prince's adventures in Moscow and during the whole time of his absence from Petersburg, we can provide little information. The prince was away for exactly six months, and even those who had reasons to be interested in his fate could learn very little about him during all that time. Certain rumors, it is true, did reach them, though quite rarely; and they were for the most part strange ones and almost always contradicted each other. Of course the Yepanchin family took the greatest interest in the prince, who in leaving had not even had time to bid them good-bye. The general however did see him beforehand, two or three times in fact; and they conversed very seriously about something or other. But while Yepanchin did see the prince, he did not inform his family of the fact. And indeed at first, that is for almost a whole month after the prince's departure, it was not considered acceptable in the Yepanchin house to speak of him. Only once did Madame Yepanchin declare at the very beginning that she had been "cruelly disappointed in the prince." Then two or three days later she had added, this time without naming the prince, in an abstract way, that the "main feature" in her life was her "continual mistaking of people." And finally a full ten days later, exasperated with something her daughters had done, she summed up the whole affair with the declaration, "Enough mistakes! We shall have no more of them!" We should observe that for quite some time an unpleasant atmosphere had prevailed in their house. There was a feeling of oppression, of strain, of repressed ill-temper; they all wore frowns. The general was busy day and night, absorbed in business affairs; seldom had they seen him busier or more active—especially with administrative matters. His household hardly caught a glimpse of him. As for the Yepanchin daughters, they of course did not express themselves openly. Perhaps even when among themselves they said very little. These were proud, haughty girls, sometimes reserved even with each other, though they understood one another not merely at a word but at a glance, so that it was often unnecessary for them to say very much.

One conclusion alone could have been drawn by a disinterested outsider, had there been such a person there: that judging by the above-mentioned indications, slight as they are, the prince had succeeded in making a particular impression on the Yepanchin household, though he had appeared among them only once, and then for a brief time. Possibly this effect was produced by simple curiosity, easily explained by certain eccentric adventures of the prince. Be that as it may, the impression remained.

Little by little the rumors which had spread through the town were obscured by uncertainty. It is true that a story was told of some dim-witted little prince (no one could be sure of his name) who had suddenly come into a huge fortune and had married a visiting Frenchwoman, a famous cancan dancer from the Château-de-Fleurs in Paris.* But others said that the inheritance had gone to some general or other, and that the man who had married the visiting Frenchwoman and famous cancan dancer was a young Russian merchant, immensely rich, and that at his wedding he had burned in the flame of a candle, out of pure drunken bravado, lottery tickets to the exact value of seven hundred thousand roubles. But all these rumors died away very soon, largely as a result of certain particular circumstances. All of Rogozhin's crowd, for example, many of whom could have had something to tell, left in a body for Moscow, with Rogozhin at the head, almost exactly a week after a dreadful orgy at the Yekaterinhof Vauxhall, at which Nastassya Filippovna had also been present. Through rumors it became known to the few who were interested that on the day following the Yekaterinhof orgy Nastassya Filippovna had run off, disappeared; and it was finally assumed that she had left for Moscow; so that Rogozhin's departure for Moscow seemed a sort of confirmation of these rumors.

There were also rumors specifically about Gavril Ardalionovitch Ivolgin, who was also rather well known within his own circle. But something happened to him which quickly tempered and finally stopped all the unkind things that were being said against him: he fell seriously ill and was unable to appear not only in society but at work. After about a month's illness he recovered, but for some reason resigned his post in the joint stock company, and someone else took his place. Neither did he appear once at General Yepanchin's house; so that the general had to engage another clerk. Gavril Ardalionovitch's enemies might have concluded that he was so embarrassed by all that had happened to him that he was ashamed to go out in the street, but he was really ill and fell into a state of morbid depression; he became moody, reflective, irritable. Varvara Ardalionovna married Ptitsyn that same winter, and all who knew them attributed the marriage directly to the fact that Ganya was unwilling to return to his job and not only ceased to support his family but actually began to be in need of assistance himself and almost of care.

Let us note in parentheses that Gavril Ardalionovitch was never mentioned in the Yepanchin household either—just as if such a man had never existed in the world, much less in their house. And yet everyone did learn (and rather quickly too) one very remarkable fact about him: on that fatal night after the unpleasant adventure at Nastassya Filippovna's, Ganya upon returning home did not go to bed but waited up for the prince with feverish impatience. The prince, who had gone to Yekaterinhof, returned at six o'clock in the morning. Then Ganya went into his room and put on the table before him the scorched package of bills which Nastassya Filippovna had presented to him while he lay on the floor in a fainting spell. He begged the prince to return this present to Nastassya Filippovna at the very first opportunity. When Ganya came into the prince's room he was in a hostile and almost desperate mood; but it seemed that certain words passed between them, after which Ganya spent two hours with the prince, sobbing bitterly the entire time. They parted on the most friendly terms.

This news, which reached every one of the Yepanchins, was afterward found to be absolutely accurate. Of course it was strange that information of this sort could be known so quickly; everything that had happened at Nastassya Filippovna's, for instance, became known at the Yepanchin household almost the next day, and in rather exact detail. As for the reports on Gavril Ardalionovitch, it might be assumed that they were conveyed to the Yepanchins by Varvara Ardalionovna, who had suddenly begun to pay visits to the Yepanchin girls and had very quickly become intimate friends of theirs, to the great amazement of Lizaveta Prokofyevna. But while Varvara Ardalionovna found it necessary, for some reason, to become so friendly with the Yepanchins, she certainly would never have discussed her brother with them. Too, she was also a rather proud woman in her own way, despite the fact that she had started friendships in a house from which her brother had virtually been turned out. Although she had been acquainted with the Yepanchin young ladies before this, she had seen them only rarely. And even now she hardly ever appeared in the drawing room but would go in, or, rather, slip in, by the back door. Lizaveta Prokofyevna had never liked her, neither before or then, though she held her mother, Nina Alexandrovna, in high esteem. She was bewildered, she was angered, and she attributed the acquaintance with Varya to the capricious and self-seeking natures of her daughters, who, she said, had nothing to think about except opposing her wishes; but Varvara Ardalionovna continued to come to them anyway, both before and after her marriage.

A month after the prince's departure, Madame Yepanchin received a letter from the old Princess Belokonskaya, who had left two weeks before to stay with her eldest married daughter in Moscow, and this letter had had a visible effect on her. Although she never communicated anything in it to her daughters or to Ivan Fyodorovitch, it became evident to them from various signs that she was particularly aroused and even disturbed. She opened strange conversations with her daughters, on all sorts of extraordinary topics; she clearly wanted to speak openly but for some reason restrained herself. On the day she received the letter she was nice to everyone and even kissed Aglaya and Adelaïda, by way of apology to them for something, though they could not make out what it was. Even toward Ivan Fyodorovitch, who had been in disgrace for an entire month, she suddenly became indulgent. Of course the very next day she was infuriated by her own sentimentality and managed to quarrel with everyone, even before dinner, but by evening the horizon once again cleared. For a whole week she continued to be in a fairly good frame of mind, which had not happened in a long time.

But a week later another letter was received from Belokonskaya, and this time the general's wife decided to express herself. She solemnly declared that "old Belokonskaya" (she never called the princess anything other when speaking of her behind her back) had given her very comforting news about that "queer fellow—you know—that prince." The old lady had found out about him in Moscow, made inquiries, and learned something very good; the prince had at last come to see her himself and had made an extraordinary impression on her. "That's clear from the fact that she invited him to come to see her every afternoon between one and two o'clock, and every day he drags himself over to her house and she hasn't got sick of him yet," Madame Yepanchin concluded, adding to this that through the "old woman" the prince had been received in two or three good houses. "It's a good thing he doesn't sit around at home like a fool." The young ladies, to whom this all was communicated, noticed immediately that their mamma was keeping a great deal in the letter from them. Perhaps they learned this through Varvara Ardalionovna, who could know, and of course did know, everything Ptitsyn knew about the prince and his stay in Moscow. And Ptitsyn could very well be in a position to know more than anyone else. However, he was exceedingly close-lipped as far as business matters were concerned, though of course he did confide in Varya. Madame Yepanchin immediately began to dislike Varvara Ardalionovna all the more on account of it.

Be that as it may, the ice was broken, and it suddenly became possible to speak of the prince aloud. Moreover it again became evident what an extraordinary impression the prince had made on the Yepanchin household and what great interest he had aroused concerning himself. The general's wife was in fact astonished by the effect upon her daughters of the news from Moscow. And the daughters were themselves surprised by their mother, who having solemnly declared that the principal feature of her life was her constant mistaking of people had at the same time recommended the prince to the attention of the "powerful" old Belokonskaya in Moscow, a thing which of course required much imploring and beseeching, since the "old woman" was notoriously hard to budge in such cases.

But no sooner had the ice been broken and there had been a change of the wind than the general too hastened to express his views. It seemed that he also had been extraordinarily interested in the prince. However, he referred only to "the business side of the matter." It seemed that, in the interests of the prince, he had asked two very reliable and, in their own way, influential persons in Moscow to keep an eye on him and in particular on his business agent, Salazkin. Everything that had been said about the inheritance, "that is, about the fact of the inheritance," turned out to be true, but the inheritance itself was in the end not nearly so large as had been reported at first. The estate was partly entangled, it appeared there were debts, other claimants turned up, and moreover the prince, against all advice, had conducted himself in a most unbusinesslike manner. "Of course, God bless him"; now that the ice had been broken the general was happy to say this "in all sincerity," because "though the fellow isn't quite *all there*" he still deserved it. On the other hand he had done stupid things; for instance creditors of the late merchant had appeared with documents which were questionable or of no value, as well as others who, sensing what sort of person the prince was, appeared with no documents at all. And what do you think? The prince gave satisfaction to almost all of them despite the warnings of friends that these were all unimportant people, small creditors quite without rights; and his sole reason for satisfying them was that it had appeared that some of them had really been treated unfairly.

The general's wife observed to this that Belokonskaya had written something of the sort to her, and that it was "stupid, very stupid; you can't cure a fool" as she added sharply; but it could be seen from her face how pleased she was by the conduct of this "fool." In the end the general noticed that his spouse took an interest in the prince almost as if he was her own son, and that she had begun to show great tenderness toward Aglaya. Seeing this, Ivan Fyodorovitch assumed an extremely businesslike air for some time.

But again this pleasant state of affairs did not last for long. Two weeks went by and once more there was a sudden change; the general's wife knitted her brows, and the general, after shrugging his shoulders several times, again resigned himself to "icy silence." The fact was that only two weeks before, he had received a certain confidential communication, which, though brief and therefore not completely clear, was quite authentic, that Nastassya Filippovna, who had at first disappeared in Moscow, had subsequently been found in Moscow by Rogozhin, had again disappeared somewhere, been found again, had then practically given her promise to marry him. And then, only two weeks later His Excellency had learned suddenly that Nastassya Filippovna had run away for the third time, almost from her own wedding, and that this time she had disappeared somewhere in the provinces, and that meanwhile Prince Myshkin had vanished from Moscow, leaving Salazkin in charge of all his affairs; "Whether with her or simply running off after her is not known—but there is something going on here," concluded the general. For her part, Lizaveta Prokofyevna also had received some unpleasant news. In the end, two months after the prince's departure almost every rumor about him had finally died down in Petersburg, and in the house of the Yepanchins the "icy silence" was again unbroken. Varvara Ardalionovna, however, continued to visit the girls anyway.

To make an end of all these rumors and reports we will add that there were a great many changes at the Yepanchins' in the spring, so that it was hard not to forget the prince, who sent no news of himself and perhaps had chosen not to do so. During the winter they gradually came to the decision to spend the summer abroad, Lizaveta Prokofyevna and the daughters, that is; it was, needless to say, quite impossible for the general to waste time on "idle amusement." The decision was taken because of the extreme and stubborn insistence of the young ladies, who were convinced that their parents did not wish to take them abroad because of their constant preoccupation with finding husbands for them and marrying them off. Possibly the parents were finally convinced that husbands could be found abroad, and that travel for one summer, far from spoiling matters, "might actually help." Here it should be mentioned in passing that the projected alliance of Afanassy Ivanovitch Totsky and the eldest Yepanchin girl had come to nothing and the formal proposal of marriage had never been made. This had somehow happened of itself, without much discussion and without any family quarrel whatever. After the departure of the prince nothing further had been said on either side. And this circumstance might be partly accountable for the mood of depression prevailing in the Yepanchin household, though the general's wife had declared herself at the time so pleased by it that she could have "crossed herself with both hands." Though the general was out of favor and though he himself felt he was to blame, he nevertheless sulked for quite some time; he regretted losing Afanassy Ivanovitch, "such a rich and clever fellow!" Not long afterward the general learned that Afanassy Ivanovitch had been captivated by a visiting Frenchwoman of the highest society, a marquise and a *légitimiste,* that they were to be married, and that Afanassy Ivanovitch would be taken off to Paris and then to somewhere in Brittany. "Oh well," decided the general, "marriage to a Frenchwoman will be the finish of him."

The Yepanchins were making preparations to leave by the beginning of summer. Then suddenly something happened which again changed everything anew, once again the trip was postponed, to the great delight of the general and the general's wife. From Moscow there arrived in Petersburg a certain prince, Prince S., a well-known man, well-known in the most creditable way. He was one of those men, one might say one of those men of the times, active, honest, modest, and sincerely and earnestly desirous of making themselves useful, who are always busy at work, and who are distinguished by that rare and happy quality of always finding something to do. Without putting himself to the fore, without ostentation and avoiding irritating and meaningless factional controversy, this prince understood contemporary events extremely well. He had been in government service and afterward had taken part in rural administration. Besides this, he was a useful corresponding member of several Russian learned societies. Together with a certain engineer of his acquaintance, he had collected information and done surveys which led to an improvement in the plan for one of the most important railroads then projected. He was about thirty-five. He was a man of the "very highest society" with, moreover, a fortune which was "good, serious, and indisputable," as it was described by the general, who had met and become acquainted with the prince at the home of the count, his superior in the service, in connection with some rather important business. This prince had a particular curiosity about Russian "men of affairs" and never avoided encounters with them. It so happened that the prince was introduced to the general's family. Adelaïda, the second of the three sisters, made a considerable impression on him. As springtime approached the prince declared himself. Adelaïda liked him very much and so did Lizaveta Prokofyevna. The general was very pleased. Of course the trip abroad was postponed. The wedding was fixed for that spring.

The trip, however, might still have been made in the middle or at the end of summer, if only as an excursion for a month or two to console Lizaveta Prokofyevna and the two daughters remaining to her for the loss of Adelaïda. But again something arose in the way. Toward the end of spring (Adelaïda's wedding had been postponed until midsummer) Prince S. introduced the Yepanchin household to one of his distant relatives, to whom he was, however, quite close. This was a certain Yevgeny Pavlovitch Radomsky, a young man of twenty-eight, an aide-de-camp to the Tzar, strikingly handsome and of excellent family, a man of wit and brilliance, "modern" ideas, extreme "cultivation" and quite fabulously rich. On this last point the general was always very careful. He made inquiries: "There does seem to be something to it —though of course it will have to be checked." This young aide-de-camp with a brilliant "future" was highly recommended by old Belokonskaya from Moscow. Only one aspect of his reputation was somewhat bothersome: one heard of liaisons and one was told of "conquests" over unhappy hearts.

On seeing Aglaya he became assiduous in his visits to the Ye-panchin house. True, nothing so far had been said, no hint had even been dropped, nevertheless it appeared to the parents that a trip abroad that summer was out of the question. Aglaya herself was perhaps of a different opinion.

All this happened just before the second appearance of our hero on the scene. Before that time, to judge by appearances, poor Prince Myshkin had been completely forgotten in Petersburg. Had he now appeared suddenly among those who had known him, it would have been as if he had dropped from the sky. However, we must report one more fact by way of conclusion to our introduction.

After the prince's departure Kolya Ivolgin had at first led the same life as before; that is to say, he went to school, visited his friend Hippolite, looked after the general, and helped Varya with the house by running errands for her. But the lodgers soon disappeared: Ferdyshchenko moved away somewhere three days after the episode at Nastassya Filip-povna's and soon vanished completely and nothing further was heard of him; it was said that he was drinking somewhere, but there were no grounds for this assertion. The prince had gone away to Moscow: there were no more lodgers. Subsequently, when Varya was married, Nina Alexandrovna and Ganya moved with her to Ptitsyn's house in the Izmaylovsky Regiment district. As for General Ivolgin, something quite unexpected happened to him at just about this time: he was put into the debtors' prison. He was sent there on the request of his friend, the captain's widow, on her presentation of notes he had given her at various times to the value of two thousand roubles. All this came as a complete surprise to him, and the poor general was "completely the victim of his boundless faith in the generosity of the human heart, speaking generally." Having adopted the habit of signing I.O.U.'s and bills of exchange, he had never conceived they might be in any way used against him, at any time whatever, always thinking that when he signed them that was *that*. It did not turn out this way. "How can you trust people after that? How can one show a generous confidence toward them?" he used to exclaim bitterly, sitting over a bottle of wine with his new comrades in the Tarassov debtors' prison, telling them tales of the siege of Kars and of the soldier who rose from the dead. Indeed, the life suited him quite well. Ptitsyn and Varya said that it was just the place for him; Ganya agreed entirely. Only poor Nina Alexandrovna quietly wept (which astonished the rest of the household), and though she was constantly ill, she dragged herself as often as she could to visit her husband. But since "what happened to the general," as Kolya expressed it, and, indeed, since his sister's marriage, Kolya had gotten completely out of hand, to the point that lately he seldom even slept at home. According to rumor, he had made a number of new acquaintances; besides which, he had become all too well known at the debtors' jail. Nina Alexandrovna could not manage there without him; at home now no one bothered to find out what he was doing. Varya, who had been so strict with him before, now did not trouble him with the slightest question about his wanderings; and Ganya, to the great surprise of the others in the house, sometimes talked and got on with him in a perfectly friendly way, despite his depression; and this was something quite new, because the twenty-seven-year-old Ganya had naturally never shown any friendly interest in his fifteen-year-old brother, treating him rudely and insisting that the others in the family be severe with him, always threatening to "pull his ears," a menace which had brought Kolya to the "ultimate limit of human endurance." Now one could believe that at times Kolya was almost indispensable to Ganya. He had been quite struck by Ganya's returning the money, and for that he was ready to forgive him a great deal.

About three months after the prince's departure, the Ivolgin family heard that Kolya had suddenly become acquainted with the Yepanchins and had been very well received by the young ladies. Varya soon learned of this; Kolya, however, had not made their acquaintance through Varya but "all on his own." Little by little, the Yepanchins grew quite fond of him. At first the general's wife had been very displeased by him, but she soon began to treat him with affection "because of his frankness and because he doesn't flatter people." That Kolya did not flatter was entirely true; he managed to put himself on a completely equal and independent footing with them, though he did sometimes read books and newspapers to the general's wife, but then he had always been ready to oblige. Twice, however, he quarreled seriously with Lizaveta Prokofyevna, declaring that she was a tyrant and that he would not set foot in her house again. The first time, the quarrel grew out of the question of "woman's rights" and the second time from a discussion of the best time of year to catch greenfinches. Unlikely as it may seem, two days after that quarrel Madame Yepanchin sent a note to him by a servant asking him to please come; Kolya did not stand on his dignity and went at once. Only Aglaya for some reason did not care for him and treated him haughtily. And yet she was the one he was destined to surprise. Once—during Easter week—finding a moment alone with her, Kolya handed her a letter, saying only that he had been asked to give it to her privately. Aglaya stared menacingly at the "presumptuous boy"; however Kolya did not stay but left the room. She opened the letter and read:

> There was a time when you honored me with your confidence. Perhaps you have completely forgotten me now. How does it happen that I am writing you? I don't know; but I have had an irresistible desire to remind you of me —you in particular. How many times I have been badly in need of all three of you, but of all three I saw only you. I need you, I need you very much. I have nothing to write you about myself, nothing to tell you. I did not wish this, I terribly want you to be happy. Are you happy? This is all I wanted to say to you.
>
> > Your brother,
> > Prince L. Myshkin

After she had read this brief and rather incoherent note, Aglaya blushed and then fell into thought. It would be hard to say what she was thinking. She asked herself among other things whether she should show the note to anyone. She somehow felt ashamed. However, she finally threw the letter into the drawer of her table with a strange ironic smile. She took it out again the next day and put it in a thick, solidly bound book (she always did this with her papers that she might find them more quickly when she wanted them). And not until a week later did she notice what book it was. It was *Don Quixote de la Mancha.* Aglaya burst out laughing—for reasons unknown. Nor is it known whether she showed the letter to either of her sisters.

But as she read over the letter she had a thought: could the prince have chosen this impertinent little braggart as his correspondent, perhaps indeed his only correspondent in Petersburg? Though she assumed an extremely scornful attitude she nevertheless took to questioning Kolya. But the "boy," who was always so quick to take offense, this time paid no attention to her scornful manner. Very briefly and rather dryly he explained to Aglaya that while he had given his permanent address to the prince before the latter's departure from Petersburg and had offered to be of any service he could, this was the first request he had received from him, and the first letter; and as proof of his words he handed her a letter addressed to himself. Aglaya had no hesitations about reading it. The letter to Kolya was as follows:

Dear Kolya,

    Would you be so kind as to give the enclosed sealed note to Aglaya Ivanovna? Keep well.

                        Fondly,
                        Prince L. Myshkin

"All the same, it's rather ridiculous to put such faith in a brat like you," said Aglaya, handing Kolya back his note and walking contemptuously by him.

This was more than Kolya could stand: for this occasion he had expressly asked Ganya, without explaining why, to lend him his brand-new green scarf. He was deeply hurt.

Chapter TWO

It was the beginning of June, and for a whole week the weather in Petersburg had been unusually good. The Yepanchins had a luxurious villa at Pavlovsk.* Lizaveta Prokofyevna had suddenly grown agitated and bestirred herself and before two days had passed they had moved there.

 Two or three days after the Yepanchins' departure, Prince Lev Nikolayevitch Myshkin arrived on the morning train from Moscow. No one met him at the station, but as he descended from the train the prince suddenly had the feeling that a pair of strange, burning eyes were staring at him from the crowd gathered to meet the passengers. He looked more attentively but now could see nothing more. Surely it was only his imagination, yet he was left with an unpleasant impression. And as it was, the prince was already sad and thoughtful and seemed worried about something.

He took a cab which brought him to a hotel not far from Liteyny. The hotel was not a particularly good one. The prince took two small rooms, dark and poorly furnished; he washed, changed, asked for nothing, and left hurriedly, as if he was afraid of being late or of not finding someone at home.

If anyone who had known him six months before, on his first arrival in Petersburg, had seen him now, such a person might have found a remarkable improvement in his appearance. But this was not altogether true. Only his clothes were completely different; everything he wore was new and had been cut in Moscow by a good tailor, but even these clothes had something wrong about them: they were cut too fashionably (as clothes always are by conscientious but not very talented tailors), and cut this way for a man who had not the slightest interest in fashion; so that a person inclined to mockery, upon careful observation of the prince, might have found reason to smile. But then people find all sorts of things amusing.

The prince took a cab to the Peski district. Along one of the streets there he soon found a small wooden house. To his surprise the house turned out to be quite pretty, clean, excellently kept, with a front garden planted with flowers. The street windows were open, and through them could be heard a strident voice talking uninterruptedly, almost shouting, as if someone was reading aloud or perhaps making a speech; now and then the voice was interrupted by resounding bursts of laughter. The prince entered the yard, mounted the steps, and asked for Mr. Lebedev.

"He's in there," answered the cook who had opened the door. Her sleeves were rolled up to her elbows. She pointed to the "drawing room." This room was papered in dark blue and neatly arranged, not without a certain pretension to elegance; that is, with a round table and a sofa, a bronze clock in a glass case, a narrow mirror on the wall, and a small and very ancient glass chandelier suspended from the ceiling by a bronze chain, while in the center of the room stood Mr. Lebedev himself, his back to the door as the prince entered, in waistcoat but no jacket in deference to the summer weather, pounding himself on the chest as he disclaimed bitterly on some subject or other. The audience consisted of a boy of fifteen with a rather cheerful and not unintelligent face and a book in his hands, a girl of twenty dressed all in mourning holding a baby in her arms, a thirteen-year-old girl, also in mourning, who was laughing very hard and opening her mouth very wide to do so, and finally, an uncommonly strange auditor stretched out on the sofa: a rather handsome young man of twenty, with thick long dark hair, large dark eyes, and faint traces of a beard and sideburns. This listener seemed to be interrupting Lebedev's oratory and frequently interfering and arguing with him; and this was apparently what made the rest of the group laugh.

"Lukyan Timofeyitch! Oh, Lukyan Timofeyitch! This way. Look this way! All right, don't if you like."

And the cook left, waving her arms in the air, so angry that she had turned quite red.

Lebedev turned around and, seeing the prince, stood there a moment as if thunderstruck, then he rushed toward him with an obsequious smile, but before reaching him he again stopped in his tracks, simpering:

"Il-il-illustrious Prince!"

But suddenly, as if still incapable of rising to the occasion, he turned around and for no reason at all suddenly rushed up to the girl in mourning holding the child in her arms, causing her to jump back in surprise, but immediately he turned from her and rushed over to the thirteen-year-old girl, who hung in the doorway of the next room with traces of laughter still on her lips. She was frightened by his shout and ran into the kitchen; Lebedev stamped his feet after her so as to frighten her more; but noticing the prince's look of bewilderment, he said in explanation:

"To instill respect. Heh, heh, heh!"

"You shouldn't do that," began the prince.

"One moment! One moment! Quick as the wind!"

And Lebedev disappeared from the room. The prince looked with astonishment at the girl, at the boy, and at the individual on the sofa. They were all laughing. The prince laughed too.

"He's gone to put his evening coat on," said the boy.

"What a bother," began the prince, "because I thought— Tell me, is he—"

"Drunk, you mean!" cried a voice from the sofa. "Not in the least! Three or four glasses, maybe; five at the most. And with him that's strict discipline."

The prince turned toward the voice on the sofa, but the girl began speaking and, with a most forthright expression on her pretty face, said, "He never drinks much in the morning. If you've come to him about business of some kind you should speak to him now. It's the best time. When he comes back in the evening, he's sometimes drunk; but now he mostly cries at night and reads aloud to us from the Bible, because our mother died five weeks ago."

"He ran off because he found it hard to answer you," said the young man on the couch, laughing. "I'll bet anything he's already cheating you and he's planning right this moment how to cheat you more."

"Five weeks! Only five weeks ago!" said Lebedev, coming back into the room in a frock coat, blinking, and pulling a handkerchief from his pocket to wipe his tears. "Orphans!"

"But why have you come out all in rags?" said the girl.

"You have a new coat right behind the door there. Didn't you see it?"

"Be quiet, grasshopper!" Lebedev shouted at her. "Oh—you!" And he started stamping his feet at her, but she only laughed.

"Why do you try to frighten me? I'm not Tanya. I won't run away. And if you carry on like this you'll waken Lubotchka and scare her into convulsions—shouting like that!"

"No, no, no! Don't say that!" said Lebedev, suddenly alarmed, and rushing up to the baby sleeping in the girl's arms he swiftly, with a very frightened face, made the sign of the cross over it several times. "God save her and protect her! That is my own infant daughter, Lubov," he said to the prince, "born in most lawful wedlock to my lately deceased wife, Yelena, who died in childbirth. And this little bird in mourning is my daughter Vera. And that one, that one, oh and that one—"

"Why don't you go on?" cried the young man. "Go on, don't be embarrassed."

"Your Excellency!" exclaimed Lebedev with sudden intensity, "have you read in the papers about the murder of the Zhemarin family?"

"Yes," said the prince, somewhat surprised.

"Well then, there's the real murderer of the Zhemarin family, right there in person!"

"What are you saying?" said the prince.

"That is—allegorically speaking—he is the next murderer of the next Zhemarin family, if there's going to be one. He's preparing for it—"

Everyone laughed. It occurred to the prince that Lebedev might really be clowning and performing because he anticipated the prince's questions and, not knowing how to answer them, was trying to play for time.

"He's a conspirator! He's hatching plots!" cried Lebedev, as though unable to control himself. "Tell me, how can I, how can I really consider such a foulmouthed fellow, such a —fornicator and monster as my own nephew, as the only son of my late sister Anisya?"

"Oh, shut up, you drunkard! Would you believe it, Prince, he has now taken to acting like a lawyer and he goes around pleading in the courts, making eloquent speeches, and at home is always talking to the children in a high-flown style. Five days ago he spoke before the tribunal of local judges. And who do you think he defended: the old lady who begged and pleaded with him to defend her against a miserable moneylender who had robbed her of five hundred roubles, all

213

she had in the world? But no. He defended the moneylender, a Jew by the name of Zeidler, because the Jew promised him fifty roubles—"

"Fifty roubles if I won, only five if I lost," explained Lebedev, in a completely new tone of voice, as if he had never been shouting.

"Well, in the end he made an ass of himself of course, but things aren't as they once were, and they only laughed at him. But even at that he was terribly pleased with himself. 'Remember, impartial judges,' he said, 'that an unhappy old man, deprived of the use of his legs and living by his honest toil, is being robbed of his last crust of bread. Remember the wise words of the lawgiver: "Let there be mercy in the court."'* And would you believe it, he keeps repeating that speech to us here every morning, word for word, just as he said it? It's the fifth time today. He was reciting it just before you arrived, he's so pleased with it. He's smacking his lips over it. And now he wants to defend somebody else. You are Prince Myshkin, aren't you? Kolya told me he'd never met anyone more intelligent than you in the whole world—"

"Yes! Yes!" Lebedev promptly joined in. "No one more intelligent in the whole world!"

"Well, we may take that for a lie. Kolya loves you and then this one tries to ingratiate himself with you. As for me, I won't flatter you, you might as well know that. But you have a certain amount of sense; so judge between him and me. Well," he addressed himself to his uncle, "do you want him to judge between us? As a matter of fact, I'm glad you turned up, Prince."

"Yes, I do!" cried Lebedev resolutely, casting an involuntary glance at his audience, which began crowding around him again.

"What is this all about?" asked the prince, with a slight frown.

He definitely had a headache, and he was growing more and more convinced that Lebedev was playing with him and was all too glad to delay the matter at hand.

"This is what it's about: I'm his nephew, that part wasn't a lie, even though he is always lying. I haven't finished my studies at the university, but I want to finish them, and I will, because I have it in me to do it. Meanwhile, since I have to live somehow, I've taken a job with the railways at twenty-five roubles a month. And what's more, I admit that he has helped me two or three times. I had twenty roubles and I lost them gambling. Can you believe it, Prince? I was so low and despicable that I lost them gambling!"

214

"To a scoundrel, to a scoundrel who should never have been paid!" cried Lebedev.

"A scoundrel, yes—but who had to be paid," the young man continued. "I can testify that he is a scoundrel, and not just because he gave you a beating. He's an army officer who's been dismissed from the service, Prince, a former lieutenant who was one of Rogozhin's group, and who teaches boxing. Now they are all scattered around, since Rogozhin got rid of them. But the worst of it is I knew the man was a scoundrel, a good-for-nothing, and a petty thief, and still I sat down and played with him, and as I bet my last rouble—we were playing 'sticks'—I was thinking to myself: 'If I lose I'll go to Uncle Lukyan and I'll act nice to him, he won't refuse me.' That was low, that really was low! That was deliberately vile!"

"It certainly was!" echoed Lebedev.

"Well, don't crow too soon, just wait a minute," shouted the nephew indignantly. "He's pleased. I came here to him, Prince, and admitted everything; I behaved honorably, I didn't spare myself; I castigated myself, everyone here was witness. To take that job with the railway I simply have to have some decent clothes, because I'm going around in rags. Just look at my boots! I can't possibly turn up at the job like this, and if I don't turn up at the proper time someone else will get the job, then I'll be high and dry again, and when will I ever find another job? Now I am asking him for only fifteen roubles and I promise that I'll never again ask for anything more, and in addition I will pay the whole debt within three months, to the last kopeck. I'll keep my word! I can live on bread and kvass for whole months on end, because I have will power. In three months I will get seventy-five roubles. With what I borrowed before, the whole debt will be thirty-five roubles, so I'll have enough to pay him. So let him charge any interest he likes, damn him! As if he didn't know me. Ask him, Prince: before, when he helped me out, did I pay him back or not? Why won't he help me now? He's angry because I paid that lieutenant, there's no other reason. That's the sort of man he is—a dog in the manger."

"And he won't go away!" cried Lebedev. "He just lies there and he won't go away."

"I've told you. I won't leave until you give it to me. You're smiling, Prince? You seem to think I'm in the wrong."

"I am not smiling, but in my opinion you are rather in the wrong," replied the prince unwillingly.

"Then say right out that I'm wrong. Don't beat around the bush. What does 'rather' mean?"

"If you like, you're wrong."

"If I like! That's funny! Do you really think I don't realize that the way I'm acting is ticklish, that it's his money, that it is for him to decide, and that on my part it looks like I'm forcing him? But you, Prince, you—you don't know life. If you don't teach people they'll never learn anything. They must be taught. My conscience is clear. In all frankness, I won't make him lose anything, I'll repay him with interest. He has gotten moral satisfaction out of it, too; he has seen my humiliation. What more does he want? What good is he if he isn't any use to anyone? Look at what he does himself. Ask him how he treats others and how he takes them in. How did he happen to get possession of this house? I'd stake my life that he's already cheated you and deceived you and that he's preparing to cheat you again! You smile. You don't believe it?"

"It seems to me that all this has very little to do with your business," observed the prince.

"I've been lying here for three days now, and you wouldn't believe the things I've seen!" shouted the young man, paying no attention. "Can you imagine it: he suspects this angel, this young orphaned girl here, my cousin, his own daughter, and every night he searches her room for lovers? He sneaks into my room and looks under my sofa too. He's gone mad with suspicion, he sees a thief in every corner. He jumps out of bed every minute of the night, looks if the windows are tightly shut, tries the doors, looks in the oven; and he does this as much as seven times a night. He defends crooks in the court, but he gets up three times in the night to pray, right here in this room, on his knees, banging his head on the floor for a half an hour. You should hear him praying for everyone and invoking everything when he's drunk! He prayed that the soul of Countess du Barry would rest in peace—I heard that with my own ears; Kolya heard it too. He has gone quite mad."

"You can see, you can hear how he would like to shame me, Prince!" cried Lebedev, reddening and quite beside himself. "The thing he doesn't know is that, drunkard, philanderer, swindler, and good-for-nothing though I may be, one thing I did do was wrap this insulting fellow in his diapers when he was a baby, and washed him in his bath, and I sat up for nights on end without sleep at my penniless widowed sister Anisya's—when I was as poor as she—looking after both of them when they were sick, stealing logs from the janitor downstairs for them, singing songs to him and snapping my fingers to amuse him, and on an empty stomach, nursing him—and this is what it's come to! Look, he's laughing at me! And what does it matter to you if I once did cross myself for the soul of the Countess du Barry? Four days ago, Prince, for the first time I read the story of her life in the encyclopedia. Do you know what sort of a person she was, Du Barry? Tell me, do you know or don't you?"

"I suppose you're the only one in the world who does know?" the young man muttered sarcastically though, it seemed, half-heartedly.

"She was a countess who, risen from shame, ruled almost as a queen, and to whom a great empress wrote in her own handwriting *'ma cousine.'* At a *lever du Roi* (do you know what a *lever du Roi* is?), a cardinal, a papal nuncio, volunteered to put her silk stockings on her bare legs, and what's more considered this an honor—this high and saintly personage! Do you know about this? By your expression I see that you don't! Well, then how did she die? Answer, if you know!"

"Oh, go away. Stop bothering me!"

"This is how she died: after such honor this great lady who had all but ruled the country was dragged to the guillotine by the executioner Samson, innocent as she was, for the amusement of the fishwives of Paris, and she so terrified she didn't know what was happening to her. She saw he was bending her neck down under the knife, kicking her along, while the people around were laughing, and she started to scream, *'Encore un moment, monsieur le bourreau, encore un moment!'* which means, 'Just one moment, Mr. *bourreau*, just one moment!' And perhaps for the sake of that moment the Lord will perhaps forgive her, for it is impossible to imagine a greater *misère* for a human soul than that. Do you know what the word *misère* means? Well, that's exactly what *misère* is. When I read about the countess' cry for 'just one moment' I felt as if my heart had been seized in a vise. And what is it to you, worm, if I thought of her in my prayers as I was going to bed, sinner that she was, and mentioned her? And perhaps I mentioned her because no one since the world began, probably, has ever crossed himself for her, or ever even thought of crossing himself for her. And it may be nice for her in the other world to know that a sinner like herself has turned up on earth and, once, prayed for her. Why are you laughing? You don't believe, atheist! And how do you know? Besides, if you were really listening to me, you lied. I didn't only pray for the Countess du Barry; I prayed this: 'Give rest, O Lord, to the soul of the great sinner Countess du Barry and everyone like her,' and this is something quite different, for there are many such sinful women who have known the changes of fortune, and who have suffered, and who are now in torment there, moaning and waiting. And what's more, I was praying for you, and for people like you, who are insolent and offensive—since you bother to eavesdrop on how I pray."

"Well, all right, that's enough! Pray for whomever you like, damn it, but don't shout like that!" interrupted the young man in vexation. "And he's so well read—Prince, did you notice that?" he added with forced sarcasm. "He's always reading books and memoirs of that sort now."

"Yet your uncle—is not a heartless man," the prince observed with reluctance. He was beginning to feel an intense aversion to this young man.

"You'll spoil him for us if you praise him like that! Look, he's already got his hand on his heart and a simpering smile on his face, waiting for more! Maybe he isn't heartless, but he is a rascal, that's what the trouble is, and he's a drunkard besides, gone all to pieces like anyone who's been drinking for years; that's why he creaks like that. He does love his children, I admit that, and he respected my late aunt—he even loves me too, and, by God, he's left me something in his will."

"I'm l-leaving you nothing!" cried Lebedev in exasperation.

"Listen, Lebedev," said the prince firmly, turning away from the young man. "I know by experience that you can be serious and businesslike when you choose. I have very little time now, and if you— What is your first name and your patronymic? I have forgotten."

"T-T-Timofey."

"And?"

"Lukyanovitch."

Again everyone in the room burst out laughing.

"A lie!" shouted the nephew. "Even now he's lying! His name isn't Timofey Lukyanovitch, at all, Prince, it's Lukyan Timofeyevitch! Look, tell us, why are you lying? Isn't it just the same to you if it's Lukyan or Timofey? And what does it matter to the prince? He tells lies from pure habit, I assure you."

"Can that be true?" asked the prince impatiently.

"It is Lukyan Timofeyevitch, as a matter of fact," admitted Lebedev, becoming embarrassed, humbly dropping his eyes and again putting his hand to his heart.

"But, good heavens, why do you do this?"

"Out of self-depreciation," murmured Lebedev, bowing his head more humbly than ever.

"Oh, but what kind of self-depreciation is that? If only I

218

knew where to find Kolya now!" said the prince and turned to leave.

"I'll tell you where Kolya is," offered the young man.

"No, no, no!" cried Lebedev, highly excited.

"Kolya spent the night here, but in the morning he went out to look for his general, whom you, Prince, have brought out of prison, God only knows why. The general promised yesterday to spend the night here but he didn't come. Most likely he spent the night at the hotel, 'The Pair of Scales,' which is quite near here. So Kolya is probably either there or in Pavlovsk at the Yepanchins'. He had the money and he meant to go yesterday. So he must be at the 'Scales' or in Pavlovsk."

"Pavlovsk! He's in Pavlovsk! Here we are, this way, out to the garden and—we'll have some coffee."

And Lebedev led the prince away by the arm. They went out of the room, crossed a small yard, and passed through a little gate. Here indeed was a tiny and delightful garden, in which all the trees, thanks to the fine weather, were already in leaf. Lebedev made the prince sit down on a green wooden bench before a green table implanted in the ground and seated himself facing him. A minute later coffee actually did arrive. The prince did not refuse. Lebedev continued to stare avidly and obsequiously into his eyes.

"I had no idea you had such a big household," said the prince, with the air of a man thinking of something else altogether.

"Or-orphans," began Lebedev, then squirmed his shoulders and stopped short. The prince was staring in front of him and had undoubtedly forgotten his own remark. Another minute passed, Lebedev watched and waited.

"Well?" said the prince, as if awakening from a trance. "Oh, yes! But of course, Lebedev, you know what our business is. I have come in response to your letter. So speak."

Lebedev became embarrassed, was about to say something, but only coughed; nothing came forth. The prince waited, then smiled sadly.

"I think I understand you quite well, Lukyan Timofeyevitch. You probably didn't expect me. You never thought I would come in from the country at your first message, and you wrote me to clear your conscience. But here I have come. So, now, please don't try to deceive me. Do stop trying to serve two masters. Rogozhin has been here for three weeks, I know everything. Have you succeeded in selling her to him as you did the other time? Tell the truth."

"The monster found out himself—himself."

219

"Don't insult him. He has treated you badly, of course—"

"He beat me! He beat me!" Lebedev interrupted with great vehemence. "And in Moscow he set his dog on me, all the way down the street. A borzoi bitch. A ferocious beast."

"You take me for a child, Lebedev. Tell me, has she really left him now in Moscow?"

"Yes, she really did, she really did, and right before the wedding again. He was counting the minutes, and she came here to Petersburg straight to me, 'Save me, protect me, Lukyan, and don't say anything to the prince—' She's even more afraid of you than of him, Prince, and that's what's so mysterious!"

And Lebedev put his finger shrewdly to his forehead.

"So now you have brought them together again?"

"Most illustrious Prince, how could I—how could I prevent it?"

"Well, all right, I shall find out everything for myself. Just tell me where she is now. At his place?"

"Oh, no. No, no! She's still by herself. 'I am free,' she says, and you know, Prince, she makes a great point of that. 'I am still completely free!' she says. She is still living at my sister-in-law's on Petersburg Street, as I wrote you."

"And she's there now?"

"She's there, unless she's gone to Pavlovsk on account of the good weather and staying at Darya Alexeyevna's little country place. 'I am completely free,' she says. Only yesterday she was going on about her freedom to Nikolai Ardalionovitch. That, sir, is a bad sign!"

And Lebedev grinned.

"Is Kolya with her often?"

"Thoughtless and unpredictable, that boy, and he can't keep things quiet."

"Is it long since you were there?"

"Every day, every day."

"So you were there yesterday?"

"N-no. Three days ago."

"What a pity you have been drinking, Lebedev. Otherwise I might have asked you something."

"No, no, no. Not a drop!" Lebedev pricked up his ears.

"Tell me, how did you leave her?"

"Hunting."

"Hunting?"

"As if she was always hunting for something, as if she had lost something. As for the marriage she gets disgusted at the thought of it and looks on it as an insult. As for *him* she cares no more about him than an orange peel. I mean,

220

though, she does care more than that, for she thinks about him with fear and trembling; she won't even have his name spoken, and they only see each other when it's absolutely necessary—and he certainly feels this! But there's nothing to be done, sir! She is restless, sarcastic, two-faced, quick-tempered—"

"Two-faced and quick-tempered?"

"Quick-tempered. She almost grabbed me by the hair during one conversation. I was reading the Apocalypse to her."

"What did you say?" the prince asked, thinking he had misunderstood.

"I was reading the Apocalypse. She's a lady of restless imagination, heh-heh! And I have discovered too that she's exceedingly fond of serious subjects, however irrelevant they happen to be. She really loves such talk and in fact takes it as a mark of respect for herself. Yes indeed, I am very good at interpreting the Apocalypse, and I've been interpreting it for fifteen years now. She agreed with me that we're living in the age of the third horse, the black one, whose rider carries the scales in his hand; for everything in our century is weighed on scales and settled by agreement, and people are seeking only for their rights: 'A measure of wheat for a penny and three measures of barley for a penny,' yet they still want to have a free spirit, a pure heart, a sound body, and all the gifts of God. But they won't hang on to these things just by rights alone, and the pale horse will follow, and he who is named Death behind whom is Hell— This is what we talk about when we meet and—it made quite a strong impression."

"Do you believe it yourself?" asked the prince, looking at Lebedev with a strange expression.

"I believe it and I interpret it. For I am naked and a pauper and an atom in the vortex of mankind. Who respects Lebedev? Everyone gets the better of him and everyone kicks him around. But when I interpret revelation I am equal to the greatest lord in the land. Because of intellect! And there was a great man trembling before me, sitting right in his armchair, as he grasped it with his intellect. His Excellency Nil Alexeyevitch heard of me two years ago just before Easter—when I was still serving in his department—and he expressly had Pyotr Zaharitch bring me from the office into his study; and when we were alone he asked me, 'Is it true you are an expounder of Antichrist?' And I made no secret of it, I said, 'I am,' and I expounded it and I laid it before him and I didn't soften down the horror but deliberately increased it as I unrolled the allegorical scroll before him and computed the figures. And he had been smiling, but at the figures and the correspondences he began to tremble, and he asked me to close the book and go away. He gave me an Easter bonus, but the following week he gave up his soul to God."

"What do you mean, Lebedev?"

"Just that. Fell out of his carriage after dinner—hit his head on a post and—like a child, like a little child—he gave up the ghost on the spot. Seventy-three years old according to the civil register. Ruddy face, white hair, always sprinkled with scent, always smiling, like a little child. Then Pyotr Zaharitch remembered: 'You predicted it,' he said."

The prince started to get up. Lebedev was surprised and in fact amazed that the prince would be getting up just then.

"You've gotten very indifferent to things, sir. Heh-heh!" he ventured to observe obsequiously.

"I really don't feel very well," replied the prince, frowning. "My head aches, perhaps from the trip."

"Maybe the country would do you good, sir," Lebedev hazarded timidly.

The prince stood lost in thought.

"Another three days and I'm going to the country myself with my whole family, for the good of the new nestling and so I can have this little house put in order. Also to Pavlovsk."

"You're going to Pavlovsk, too?" the prince asked suddenly. "What is this? How is it that everyone here is going to Pavlovsk? And you say you have a house there?"

"Not everyone is going to Pavlovsk. Ivan Petrovitch Ptitsyn let me have one of the houses he bought up cheaply. It's nice and it's high up and it's green and cheap and *bon ton* and musical—that's why everyone goes to Pavlovsk. However, I am living in a little lodge, and the house itself—"

"Rented?"

"N-no. No, not quite."

"Rent it to me," the prince proposed suddenly.

This appeared to be what Lebedev had been leading up to. The idea had occurred to him three minutes before. And yet he had need of a tenant; he had already found someone who told him he would, perhaps, take the house. Lebedev knew for a fact that there was no question of "perhaps" but that he would certainly take it. But now the sudden and by his reckoning profitable thought had struck him that he might rent the villa to the prince, taking advantage of the fact that the earlier tenant had not given his final word. Before his imagination there arose what he thought of as clash of interests and a whole new turn of events. He accepted the prince's offer with enthusiasm and went so far as to dismiss the question of price with a wave of his hand.

"Well, it's just as you like. I'll inquire. You won't lose anything by it."

They were both on their way out of the garden.

"And I could—if you like—I could tell you something very interesting, most honored Prince, something having to do with the same subject," muttered Lebedev, squirming with pleasure at the prince's side.

The prince stopped.

"Darya Alexeyevna has a little house in Pavlovsk too."

"Well?"

"And a certain person who is a friend of hers evidently intends to visit her quite often in Pavlovsk. With an object."

"Well?"

"Aglaya Ivanovna—"

"That's enough, Lebedev!" interrupted the prince, with an unpleasant feeling as if he had been touched on a tender spot. "All that—that's not how it is. Tell me rather when will you be moving? The sooner the better for me, since I'm at a hotel."

As they talked they left the garden, and without going back through the house, they crossed the yard and reached the gate.

"Well, what could be better?" said Lebedev after some hesitation. "Come straight over here from the hotel today, and the day after tomorrow we'll all go to Pavlovsk together."

"I'll see," said the prince thoughtfully, and he went out the gate.

Lebedev watched him go. He was struck by the prince's sudden air of vagueness. In leaving he had even forgotten to say good-bye, he had not even nodded, and this did not match what Lebedev knew of the prince's graciousness and courtesy.

Chapter THREE

∽∾∾∽

It was already past eleven o'clock. The prince knew that at the Yepanchin house he would now find only the general, who would be kept in town by his duties, and even that was not certain. It occurred to him that the general would probably take him along to Pavlovsk at once, and he was most anxious to pay one other call beforehand. At the risk of being late at the Yepanchins' and delaying his trip to Pavlovsk until the following day, the prince decided to look for the house he so particularly wished to visit.

This visit however was in a certain respect a risky one. He was perplexed and he hesitated. He knew that the house was on Gorokhovaya Street, not far from Sadovaya Street, and he decided to go there, hoping that by the time he reached the place he would at last have made up his mind.

As he came to the crossing of Gorokhovaya and Sadovaya he was surprised by his own extreme state of emotion; he had not expected that his heart would be pounding so hard. One house, no doubt because of its peculiar appearance, attracted his attention from a distance, and the prince later remembered saying to himself, "That must be the house." With great curiosity he walked toward it to see if his conjecture had been correct; he felt that he would for some reason be particularly distressed if he had guessed right. It was a large, gloomy house of three stories, of no particular architectural style, and of a dirty green color. A few such houses, a very few, built at the end of the last century, are still standing almost unchanged in these streets of Petersburg (where everything changes so rapidly). They were built solidly with thick walls and very few windows; sometimes the windows on the ground floor have iron bars. More often than not there is a moneychanger's shop below. The Scopéts* sitting in this shop rents an apartment upstairs. Outside and inside, everything about the house seems inhospitable and forbidding, as if everything about it was dissembling and guarding secrets; and it would be hard to explain why one has this impression from the very look of the house. Architectural lines have, of course, a secret of their own. These houses are occupied almost exclusively by tradespeople. On reaching the outer gate and noticing an inscription on it, the prince read, "The house of the hereditary burgess* Rogozhin."

Hesitating no longer, he opened the glassed door, which slammed noisily behind him, and started up the staircase to the main floor. The staircase was roughly made of stone and dark; the walls were painted red. He knew that Rogozhin and his mother and brother occupied the entire second floor of this dismal house. The man who had opened the door to the prince admitted him without taking his name and led him a long way. They passed through a large drawing room with

224

walls of imitation marble, an oak block floor, and furniture of the 1820's, crude and heavy, and through several indeterminate little rooms, zigzagging and turning corners, mounting two or three stairs, then descending as many, until at last they knocked at a door. The door was opened by Parfyon Semyonovitch himself. Seeing the prince, he turned so pale and was so stupefied that for a time he was like a stone statue, staring with a fixed and frightened expression, his mouth twisted into a strange smile of utter bewilderment, as if the visit of the prince struck him as something inconceivable and almost miraculous. Though the prince expected something of the sort, he was still surprised.

"Parfyon, perhaps I've come at the wrong time," he said finally, in embarrassment. "I can leave, if you like."

"Not at all! Not at all!" said Parfyon, recovering himself at last. "You are welcome. Come in."

They spoke to each other the familiar form of address like intimate friends. In Moscow they had met often and spent much time together, and there were certain moments during their meetings which had left a lasting impression in their hearts. Now however they had not seen each other for more than three months.

Rogozhin's face was still pale and twitched slightly in tiny spasms. Though he invited his visitor in, he continued to be extraordinarily embarrassed. As he was showing the prince to an armchair in front of the table, the prince happened to turn and was stopped dead by Rogozhin's strange, heavy gaze. Something seemed to transfix the prince, and at the same time some memory came back to him—something recent, something painful and somber. Not sitting down but standing there motionless, he kept looking directly into Rogozhin's eyes for some time; and those eyes seemed at first to glare more intensely. Finally Rogozhin smiled, but at once became disconcerted and more at a loss than ever.

"Why are you staring at me like that?" he muttered. "Sit down."

The prince sat down.

"Parfyon," he said, "tell me the truth. Did you know I was coming to Petersburg today or not?"

"I had an idea you might come, and as you see, I wasn't mistaken," said Rogozhin, and smiling sardonically he added, "But how could I know you'd come today?"

The harsh abruptness and strange irritability of the question were a new surprise to the prince.

"Even if you'd known I was coming today, why be so annoyed about it?" asked the prince gently, in confusion.

"But why do you ask that?"

"When I got off the train this morning I saw a pair of eyes looking at me just as you did just now, from behind."

"Oh, did you? Whose eyes were they?" said Rogozhin suspiciously.

It seemed to the prince that he gave a start.

"I don't know. They were in the crowd. Perhaps it was my imagination. I'm beginning to imagine things. Parfyon, my friend, I feel almost as I did five years ago when I still was having fits."

"Well," muttered Rogozhin, "perhaps it was your imagination, I have no idea."

The affectionate smile on his face did not suit him at all at that moment, it was as if it had become unfastened and he could not glue it together no matter how hard he tried.

"Well then, you'll be going abroad again, won't you?" he asked, then suddenly added, "You remember how we were on the train last fall, coming from Pskov. I was coming here, and you—in your cloak and those gaiters of yours—remember?"

And Rogozhin suddenly burst out laughing, this time with open malice, as if relieved that he could find some way to express it.

"Have you settled here for good?" asked the prince, looking around the study.

"Yes, I am at home. Where else should I be?"

"It's a long time since we've seen each other. I have heard things about you, as if they weren't about you at all."

"People will say anything," remarked Rogozhin dryly.

"And yet you've gotten rid of all your crowd. You stay here in your family house and don't carry on anymore. Well, that's good. Is the house yours, or do you have it in common?"

"It's Mother's house. Her rooms are right across the hall."

"And where does your brother live?"

"Semyon Semyonovitch is in the wing."

"Is he married?"

"He's a widower. What do you want to know that for?"

The prince looked at him and did not answer; he was suddenly lost in thought and did not seem to have heard the question. Rogozhin did not insist and waited. Both were silent for a moment.

"As I was coming here I guessed this was your house a hundred paces away," said the prince.

"How was that?"

"I have no idea. Your house has the look of your whole

family and your whole Rogozhin style of life, but if you ask me why I thought so I wouldn't be able to explain it. It was certainly a delirious fancy. I'm really frightened that it should trouble me so much. Before, it would never have occurred to me that you lived in such a house, but as soon as I saw it I thought immediately, 'This is exactly the house he ought to have!' "

"Did you?" Rogozhin smiled vaguely, without quite understanding the prince's unclear thought. "This house was built by my grandfather," he observed. "Scoptsi always lived in it, the Khludyakovs; they are still our tenants now."

"It's so dark, you live here in darkness," said the prince, looking around the study.

It was a big room, high-ceilinged and lightless, filled with all kinds of furniture, mostly large office desks, bureaus, cupboards, in which ledgers and all sorts of papers were kept. A long sofa covered in red morocco apparently served Rogozhin as a bed. The prince noticed on the table before which Rogozhin had seated him two or three books; one of them, Solovyov's *History*,* was open and had a book mark in it. Along the walls hung several oil paintings in tarnished gold frames, dark grimy paintings in which it was very difficult to make out anything at all. One life-size full-length portrait attracted the prince's attention: it represented a man of fifty in a frockcoat of German cut, but quite long, with two medals hanging from his neck, a short, very sparse, graying beard, a yellow, wrinkled face, and stealthy, suspicious, melancholy eyes.

"Isn't that your father?" asked the prince.

"In person," replied Rogozhin with an unpleasant smile, as if he expected to hear immediately some rude joke at the expense of his dead father.

"He wasn't an Old Believer,* was he?"

"No, he used to go to church; but it's true he said that the old faith was nearer the truth. He also respected the Scoptsi a great deal. This used to be his study. Why did you ask if he was an Old Believer?"

"Will you have your wedding here?"

"Y-yes," replied Rogozhin, almost with a start at the unexpected question.

"Will it be soon?"

"You know yourself it's not up to me "

"Parfyon, I am not your enemy and I have no intention of interfering with you in any way I tell you this as I told it to you once before, on an almost similar occasion When your wedding was to take place in Moscow, I didn't interfere with

227

you, you know that. The first time *she* came running to me herself, just before the wedding was to be, begging me to 'save' her from you. I am repeating her very word. Afterward she ran away from me too, you found her and were going to marry her again, and now they say she has run away from you again here. Is that true? Lebedev told me that, and this is why I have come. But I learned for the first time only yesterday that you had gotten together again here; I learned it in the train from one of your former friends—Zalyozhnev, if you care to know. I came here with a definite purpose: I wanted to persuade her to go abroad and recover her health; she is very ill, both in body and mind, but especially in her mind, and in my opinion she needs a great deal of care. I didn't intend to go abroad with her myself, I wanted to arrange all this without being a part of it myself. I'm telling you the absolute truth. If it's true that you're together again I won't even appear before her, nor shall I ever come to see you again. You know yourself I'm not deceiving you, because I have always been frank with you. I've never concealed from you what I thought about this, and I have always said that marriage to you would be the end of her. It would also be your end too—perhaps even more certainly than hers. I would be very glad if you were to part again, but I don't intend to disturb you or do anything to separate you myself. Be at ease and don't be wary of me. Yes, and you know perfectly well that I was never your *real* rival, even when she fled to me. Now you are laughing, I know what you're laughing at. Yes, we lived apart there, in different towns, and you know this *for a fact*. I explained to you before that I don't love her with love, but with pity. I believe that my definition is exact. You said then that you understood my words. Was that true? Did you understand? Here you are looking at me with such hatred! I've come to reassure you because you too are dear to me. I am very fond of you, Parfyon. And now I am leaving and I shall never come back. Good-bye."

The prince got up.

"Stay with me a little," Parfyon said softly, not rising from his place, his head resting in the palm of his right hand. "I haven't seen you for a long time."

The prince sat down. Both were silent again.

"When you aren't here before me I immediately begin to hate you, Lev Nikolayevitch. In all those three months I didn't see you, every minute I've been hating you, by heaven! I could have easily poisoned you! I could have. Now you haven't been sitting with me a quarter hour and already my hatred is disappearing, and you are dear to me as you were before. Stay here with me—"

"When I'm with you you believe me, and when I'm not you stop believing me at once and begin suspecting me again. You're like your father!" the prince replied, with a friendly smile and trying to conceal his emotion.

"I believe your voice when I'm with you. Of course I realize we can't be compared, you and I."

"Why do you say that? And now you're annoyed again," said the prince, wondering at Rogozhin.

"Yes, well, no one asks our opinion in the matter, my friend," he replied. "It's decided without us." He paused, then went on, speaking softly. "We love in different ways too—everything is different. You say you love her with pity. There's no such pity for her in me. And what's more, she hates me too, more than anything. I dream about her every night now: she's always with another man, laughing at me. Because this is the way it is, my friend. She's going to marry me, but she never gives me a thought; it's like she was changing her shoes. Would you believe it, I haven't seen her for five days, because I don't dare go to her. She'll ask, 'Why have you come?' She's put me to shame so often before."

"Put you to shame? What do you mean?"

"As if you didn't know! Well, she ran away from me, with you, right before the wedding, as you just said yourself."

"But you don't believe that—"

"And didn't she shame me in Moscow with that officer, Zemtuzhnikov? I know for a fact she did, and it was even after she set the date of our wedding."

"That's impossible!" cried the prince.

"I know for a fact," said Rogozhin with conviction. "You mean she isn't like that? There's no use saying she isn't like that, my friend. That's nothing but nonsense. With you she won't be like that, and she might even seem horrified at such things—but with me she's exactly like that. This is the way it is. She considers me the lowest of the low. She trumped up that affair with Keller, that officer, the fellow who boxes, simply to make a fool of me. You don't know the tricks she played on me in Moscow! And the money—oh, the money I've tossed away!"

"And—and so now you're marrying her! What will it be like afterward?" the prince asked in horror.

Rogozhin stared at the prince with a terrible, dark look and did not answer.

"I haven't been to her place for five days now," he went on after a minute's silence. "I'm afraid she'll throw me out. I'm still my own mistress,' she says. 'If I choose, I'll get rid of you for good and go abroad myself.' She's already told me she might go abroad," he observed parenthetically, looking with particular intensity into the prince's eyes. "It's true that sometimes she's just trying to scare me; I amuse her for some reason. But other times she will really frown and sulk and not say a word—that's what I'm really afraid of. The other day I realized I shouldn't be going to her empty-handed—but my gifts made her laugh at me, and then angry. She presented her maid Katya with a shawl I gave her, the likes of which she had probably never seen before, even though she has lived in luxury. As to the date of our wedding, I can't even mention the subject. What kind of a fiancé is it who's afraid to go to his future bride? Here I sit, and when I can't stand it any longer I go stealing past her house in secret or I hide in some corner. The other night I kept watch at her gates till almost dawn—and I got the idea something was going on. But she must have seen me through the window. 'What would you have done with me if you'd seen me deceiving you?' she said. I couldn't bear it, and I said, 'You know yourself!' "

"What does she know?"

"And how should I know?" Rogozhin laughed maliciously. "In Moscow I couldn't catch her with anyone, though I tried a long time. One time I took hold of her and said, 'You promised to marry me, you are entering a respectable family, and do you know what kind of a woman you are now? Well, I'll tell you, you're *that* kind of a woman!' "

"You told her that?"

"I did."

"And?"

"She said, 'Now I may not even take you as my servant, let alone as my husband.' And I said, 'And I'm not leaving, whatever happens.' And she said, 'In that case I'll call Keller immediately and ask him to throw you out of the house.' I threw myself at her and beat her black and blue."

"Impossible!" cried the prince.

"I tell you it happened," confirmed Rogozhin quietly, his eyes flashing. "For a day and a half I didn't sleep, or eat, or drink; I wouldn't leave her room, I stayed there kneeling before her. 'I will die,' I said, 'but I won't leave here till you've forgiven me, and if you have me thrown out I'll drown myself, because what would become of me without you now?' She was like a madwoman the whole day, first she cried, then she threatened to kill me with a knife, then she threw insults at me. She called Zalyozhnev, Keller, Zemtuzhnikov, and the rest of them, to show me to them and humiliate me in front of them. 'Let's all go to the theater today, gentlemen, and let him stay here if he doesn't want to go; I'm not tied to him. As for you, Parfyon Semyonovitch, they will serve you tea in my absence, since you must be hungry today!' She came back from the theater alone. 'They are worthless cowards,' she said. 'They are afraid of you, and they tried to frighten me too. They said, "He won't go away like that, he may very likely cut your throat." Well, I'll go to my bedroom and won't even lock the door—that's how frightened I am of you! You might as well see that and know it! Have you had tea?' 'No,' I said, 'and I won't.' 'If it was a question of honor, but this doesn't become you at all.' And she did as she had said, she didn't lock her room. In the morning she came out and laughed, 'Have you lost your mind? You'll die of hunger.' 'Forgive me,' I said. 'I don't want to forgive you,' she said. 'I won't marry you; I've said so. Have you really been sitting all night in that chair? You haven't slept?' 'No,' I said, 'I haven't slept.' 'Well, what a clever fellow you are! And you won't have any tea or dinner again either?' 'I said I wouldn't. Forgive me!' 'If you only knew how badly this suits you,' she said. 'It's like a saddle on a cow. Have you gotten the idea of frightening me? Because what does it matter to me if you sit there hungry? As if that could frighten me!' She got angry, but not for long, and soon she was taunting me again. And I was surprised that she showed no spite at all; for she is vindictive and for a long time she'll resent a wrong done her by someone else. Then I realized she thought so little of me that she couldn't feel resentment against me very long! And this was true. 'Do you know what the pope of Rome is?' she asked me. 'I've heard,' I said. 'You haven't studied universal history, have you, Parfyon Semyonovitch?' 'I haven't studied anything,' I said. 'Well then,' she said, 'I'll give you something to read. There was a pope once, and he got angry at a certain emperor, and that emperor knelt barefoot in front of his palace for three days without eating or drinking until the pope forgave him. What do you imagine the emperor was thinking about for three days, and what vows did he make while he was kneeling there? Wait,' she said, 'I'll read it to you myself.' She jumped up and brought over a book. 'It's in verse,' she said, and started reading me lines of poetry about how that emperor in those three days swore to avenge himself against the pope. 'Could it be that this doesn't appeal to you, Parfyon Semyonovitch?' she said. 'What you have read there is all true,' I said. 'Ah-ha, you yourself say it's true. Then maybe you too are making vows: "When she's married

231

to me I'll make her remember all this, then I'll make her regret it." ' 'I don't know,' I said, 'that could be.' 'What do you mean you don't know?' 'I don't know,' I said, 'I'm not thinking about that now.' 'And what are you thinking about now?' 'That when you get up from your chair and walk past me I look at you and follow you with my eyes; when your dress rustles, my heart stops, and when you go out of the room I remember every word you said and the way you said it; and all last night I thought of nothing, I listened the whole time to how you breathed in your sleep and how twice you stirred—' And she laughed and said, 'You probably don't think about how you beat me—you probably don't remember?' 'Maybe I do think about that,' I said. 'I don't know.' 'And what if I don't forgive you and don't marry you?' 'I told you. I'll drown myself.' 'You'll probably kill me before that—' She said this and then was thoughtful. Then she grew angry and left the room. An hour later she came back to me, very gloomy. 'I shall marry you, Parfyon Semyonovitch,' she said, 'and not because I'm afraid of you, but because I'm through anyway. Where is there anything better? Sit down,' she says, 'they'll bring your dinner right away. And if I do marry you I'll be a faithful wife to you; you need have no doubts or worries about that. I used to think that you were an absolute flunky.' Then she was silent. 'However,' she said, 'you're not a flunky. At first I thought you were an absolute flunky.' Right then she set our wedding day, and a week later she ran away from me to Lebedev here. When I came she said, 'I'm not refusing you altogether; I just want to wait some more, as long as I feel like, because I am still my own mistress. You wait too, if you like.' This is where we stand now. What do you think of all that, Lev Nikolayevitch?"

"What do you think yourself?" the prince asked in turn, looking sadly at Rogozhin.

"As if I was thinking anything!" blurted the other. He seemed to want to say something more, but faltered in hopeless dejection.

The prince got up, again meaning to leave.

"In any case I'm not going to interfere with you," he said softly, almost to himself, as if in reply to some inner, secret thought of his own.

"Do you know what I say?" cried Rogozhin with sudden animation, his eyes flashing. "I say I don't understand why you're giving in to me! Have you completely quit loving her? After all, before you were miserable; I saw it. How is it you've come running over here so fast? Out of pity?" His face was twisted into a malicious smile. "Ha! Ha!"

"You think I'm deceiving you?" asked the prince.

"No—I believe you; but I can't make it out. It seems that your pity is stronger than my love."

A certain malice and an urgent desire to make himself understood showed suddenly in his face.

"Well, there's no distinguishing your love from hatred," said the prince, smiling, "and when it passes, the trouble will be even greater, perhaps. I'm telling you, Parfyon, my friend—"

"What? That I'll murder her?"

The prince gave a start.

"You will hate her bitterly because of this love of yours, for all this suffering which you are accepting now. The strangest thing of all to me is that she would agree to marry you again. When I heard that yesterday, I could hardly believe it, and it made me so unhappy! For twice she has refused you and run away just before the wedding; so she must have some premonition. What can she find in you now? Your money? That's nonsense. Besides, you've probably wasted a lot of it by now. Can she just want a husband? She could find someone besides you. Anyone would be better than you, because you really may murder her, and perhaps she understands that all too well even now. Is it because you love her so intensely? It's true: that may be why—I have heard there are women who look for just that kind of love—only—"

The prince stopped, lost in thought.

"Why that little smile again when you look at my father's portrait?" demanded Rogozhin, who was closely watching every fugitive change of the prince's expression.

"Why did I smile? Well, it occurred to me that if you hadn't had this misfortune, if this love hadn't happened, you would have probably become just like your father, and in no time at all, too. You would have settled down quietly in this house with a silent and obedient wife, speaking seldom and then only sternly, trusting no man on earth and feeling no desire to, doing nothing but piling up money in solemn silence. At most, you would sometimes have praised old books and taken an interest in the Old Believers' custom of crossing themselves with two fingers, and that only in your old age."

"Laugh if you like. She said exactly the same thing not long ago, while she too was looking at that portrait! It's marvelous how you agree about everything now."

"She hasn't been here to see you, has she?" asked the prince with interest.

"She has. She looked at that portrait a long time, then asked me about my dear departed father. 'You'd be exactly

233

like that,' she said at last, laughing. 'You have strong passions, Parfyon Semyonovitch, such passions they might have landed you in forced labor in Siberia if you hadn't been intelligent too, for you do have a lot of intelligence.' (This, believe it or not, is what she said; it was the first time I'd heard anything like it from her!) 'You'd have soon stopped this running around, and since you're such a completely uneducated fellow, you'd have started putting away money, and you'd sit here in this house like your father, with your Scoptsi. Perhaps the time would come when you'd take up with their beliefs, and then you would come to love your money so well that you'd have stacked up not two million but probably ten million and died of starvation on your bags of gold. Because you're passionate in everything and turn everything to passion.' That's exactly what she told me, in almost exactly those words. She'd never spoken to me that way before! You see, she always talks lightly with me, or she jokes at me. Even this time she began by laughing, but then became very depressed; she went all through the house looking at everything, and seemed to be afraid of something. 'I'll change all this,' I said. 'I'll do it over, or maybe I'll buy another house before the wedding.' 'No, no,' she said. 'Don't change anything, we'll live here this way. I want to live near your mother when I'm your wife,' she said. I took her to my mother. She was as respectful to her as if she was her own daughter. For the last two years mother has not been quite in her right mind (she's an invalid), and after the death of my father she got just like a child; she doesn't talk or walk and she just sits in her chair and bows to everyone she sees. If she wasn't fed she'd probably sit there for three days without a word. I took Mother's right hand and folded her fingers. 'Bless her, Mother,' I said. 'She's going to marry me.' Then she kissed my mother's hand with real feeling. 'Your mother must have had a lot to bear,' she said. Then she saw this book I had. 'What's this?' she said. 'Have you started reading Russian history?' (She had herself said to me in Moscow once, 'You should try to learn something. You might at least read Solovyov's *Russian History*. As it is, you know absolutely nothing at all.') 'This is fine,' she said, 'go on reading it. I'll write you out a list of the books you should read first. Do you want me to or don't you?' And never, ever before had she said anything like that to me, so she really surprised me. For the first time I could breathe like a living person."

"I am very glad to hear that, Parfyon," said the prince with sincere feeling, "very glad. Who knows, perhaps God will bring you together."

"That will never be!" cried Rogozhin hotly.

"Listen, Parfyon, if you love her like this why shouldn't you want to win her respect? And if you want to do this, why shouldn't you hope to do it? I said just now it was very strange to me why she is marrying you. But while I can't understand it, I have no doubt that there must be a good, sensible reason. She's convinced of your love, but she must also be convinced you have certain good qualities. It can't be any other way! What you told me just now proves this. You said yourself she found it possible to speak with you entirely differently from the way she spoke to you and treated you before. You're suspicious and jealous, that's why you make so much of everything bad you notice. She certainly doesn't think so badly of you as you say. For if she did it would mean that in marrying you she was deliberately drowning herself or facing a knife. Can this be? Who would deliberately face drowning or being knifed?"

Parfyon listened with a bitter smile to the prince's intense words. His own conviction seemed unshakably firm.

"How grimly you're looking at me, Parfyon!" exclaimed the prince with a feeling of dread.

"Drowning or knifing!" said Rogozhin at last. "Ha! That's exactly why she's marrying me, because she knows my knife is waiting for her! Is it possible, Prince, that you still haven't understood what it's all about?"

"I don't understand you."

"Well, maybe you really don't understand. Ha, ha! They do say you're—*not all there*. She's in love with another man —try to understand that! Just the way I love her now, she loves someone else. And this other man, do you know who it is? It's *you!* What? You didn't know?"

"Me?"

"You. She has loved you ever since that time, since her birthday. Only she thinks she can't marry you because she would disgrace you and ruin your whole life. 'Everyone knows what I am,' she says. She still keeps saying the same thing even now. She's said it all straight to my face. She's afraid of disgracing and ruining you, but it doesn't matter in my case, she can marry me—that's what she thinks of me. Notice that too!"

"But then why did she run away from you to me and—from me—"

"And from you to me! Ha! What doesn't pop into her head! She's always in a kind of fever now. She'll shout at me 'Marrying you is like drowning myself—let's have the wedding quickly!' She rushes things herself, sets the day, but as

235

the time nears—she gets frightened, or she gets other ideas. God knows you've seen it: she cries, she laughs, she's seized with fever. What's so strange about her running away from you? She ran away from you then because she realized how much she loved you. She wasn't strong enough to stay with you. You said a while ago I 'sought her out' in Moscow: that's not so—she came running to me herself. 'Set the day,' she said, 'I'm ready. Give me champagne! Let's go to the Gypsies!' she screams. Well, if I hadn't been around she would have thrown herself in the water long ago, and I'm telling you the truth. The reason she doesn't do it now is that I just may be more frightening than the water. She's marrying me out of spite—if she does marry me, I tell you for sure, she'll be doing it out of pure spite."

"Then how can you—? How can you—?" cried the prince, and then hesitated. He looked at Rogozhin in horror.

"Why don't you go on?" demanded the other with a grin. "Would you like me to tell you what you're thinking right this minute? 'How can she marry him now? How can she be allowed to do this?' It's clear what you're thinking."

"I didn't come here for that, Parfyon. I tell you it wasn't that I had in my mind."

"You probably didn't come for that, and you probably didn't have that in mind, but you certainly have it in mind now. Ha, ha! Well, enough! Why are you so upset? Is it possible you really didn't know this? You amaze me!"

"This is all jealousy, Parfyon. This is all sickness. You are exaggerating everything terribly," said the prince softly, in great agitation. "What's the matter?"

"Leave it alone," said Parfyon and quickly snatched from the prince's hand the knife he had picked up from the table and put it back next to a book where it had been before.

"It's as if I knew it on the way to Petersburg," the prince went on, "as if I had a premonition. I didn't want to come here! I wanted to forget everything here, I wanted to tear it out of my heart! Well, good-bye—but what's the matter with you?"

As the prince was speaking he had again absentmindedly picked the knife up from the table, and once again Rogozhin had taken it from his hand and thrown it on the table. It was quite an ordinary knife with a horn handle and a fixed blade seven inches long.

Seeing that the prince had specially noticed that twice the knife had been taken from his hand, Rogozhin seized it and with vicious irritation put it inside the book and threw the book over on another table.

"Do you cut pages with it?" asked the prince, but rather mechanically, as if he was still absorbed in his thoughts.

"Yes."

"But this is a garden knife."

"Yes, it is a garden knife. Can't one cut pages with a garden knife?"

"Yes, but it's—it's quite new."

"And what if it is new? Can't I buy myself a new knife?" cried Rogozhin in a kind of frenzy, growing more irritated with each word.

The prince shuddered and looked intently at Rogozhin.

"Look, how foolish we are!" he suddenly laughed, completely regaining his composure. "Forgive me, my friend, when my head feels heavy, as it does now, and this sickness —I become terribly, terribly distracted and ridiculous. I didn't mean to ask you about this at all—I've forgotten what I did want to ask. Good-bye."

"Not that way," said Rogozhin.

"I've forgotten."

"This way, this way. Come, I'll show you."

Chapter FOUR

They went through the same rooms the prince had passed through before; Rogozhin walked a little ahead, the prince followed him. They entered the large drawing room. On the walls there were some pictures, all of them portraits of bishops or dark landscapes in which nothing could be seen. Over the doorway into the next room there hung an oddly shaped picture, about five feet wide and less than a foot high. It was of the Savior, who had just been taken down from the cross. The prince glanced narrowly at it as if he was trying to remember something, but he was about to pass through the door without stopping. He felt very depressed and wanted to get out of this house. But Rogozhin suddenly stopped in front of the painting.

"All these pictures were picked up at auctions for a rouble or two by my late father," he said. "He liked them. A man who knows paintings looked at all the paintings here. He said they were trash, all except this one, the one over the doorway; that one isn't trash, he said. My father paid a couple of roubles for that one too, and a fellow offered him three hundred and fifty for it; but Ivan Dmitrich Savelyev, a merchant who is a great collector, went to four hundred; and last week he offered my brother Semyon Semyonovitch five hundred. I kept it for myself."

"But it's—it's a copy of a Hans Holbein," said the prince, who had by now examined the picture. "And though I am no expert it strikes me as an exceptionally good copy. I've seen this painting abroad and I can't forget it. But—what's the matter?"

Rogozhin suddenly stopped looking at the painting and walked ahead. No doubt his distraction and the strangely irritable mood that had come over him so suddenly might explain this abruptness; nevertheless the prince found it odd that he would break off a conversation which he had started himself and not even answer him.

"Tell me, Lev Nikolayevitch," said Rogozhin suddenly, having walked on a few steps, "I've been meaning to ask you a long time, do you believe in God or not?"

"How strangely you ask that and—how strangely you look at me," observed the prince involuntarily.

"I like looking at that painting," Rogozhin murmured after a short silence, as if he had forgotten his question again.

"At that painting!" exclaimed the prince, struck by a sudden thought. "At that painting! Why, that's a painting that might make some people lose their faith!"

"Yes, faith may be lost too," assented Rogozhin unexpectedly. By now they had reached the front door.

"What do you mean?" said the prince, suddenly stopping. "What is the matter? I said it almost as a joke, but you're so serious! And why do you ask whether I believe in God?"

"Oh, like that, for no reason. I've meant to ask you before. Lots of people don't believe these days. And by the way, is it true—you've lived abroad—once a man told me while he was drunk that there are more people among us in Russia who don't believe in God than in all the other countries? 'It's easier for us,' he said, 'because we have gone farther than they.'"

Rogozhin smiled bitterly. After he had asked his question he suddenly opened the door and waited with his hand on the lock for the prince to go out. The prince was surprised, but he went out. Rogozhin went out on the landing with him and closed the door behind him. They stood facing each other, and it seemed as if both had forgotten where they were and what was now to be done.

"Good-bye, then," said the prince, holding out his hand.

"Good-bye," said Rogozhin, shaking the hand that was held out to him firmly but quite mechanically.

The prince went down one step and turned around.

"As for faith," he said, smiling—plainly not wishing to leave Rogozhin this way—and inspired by a sudden recollection. "As for faith, I had four different encounters in two days last week. One morning I was traveling on the new railway line and I talked for four hours with a certain S.; we had just become acquainted. I'd already heard a lot about him, among other things that he was an atheist. He is really a very learned man, and I was glad to have the chance to talk to such a person. Besides that, he is an unusually well-bred man, and he talked with me as if I was his equal in knowledge and understanding. He doesn't believe in God. Except one thing struck me: he didn't seem to be talking about that at all, the whole time, and this struck me precisely because whenever I've met disbelievers before, and no matter how many of their books I read, it has always struck me that they seem to be speaking and writing about something else, though on the surface it seems to be that. I told him this at the time, but I probably didn't say it clearly, or did not know how to express it, because he didn't understand a thing. That evening I stopped for the night at a provincial hotel where a murder had happened the night before, and everyone was talking about it when I arrived. Two peasants, older men who had known each other a long time and were friends, neither of them drunk, were having tea and were meaning to go sleep in the little room they had taken together. But for the past two days one of them had been noticing that the other wore a silver watch on a beaded ribbon, which apparently he had not known that he had before. The first was not a thief, he was in fact an honest man and for a peasant not at all poor. But he was so taken by this watch, so tempted by it that he finally could not restrain himself, he took a knife and when his friend's back was turned came up cautiously behind him, took aim, raised his eyes to heaven, crossed himself, and bitterly and silently prayed, 'Lord, forgive me for Christ's sake!' and he cut his friend's throat with one stroke like a sheep, and took his watch."

Rogozhin rocked back and forth with laughter. He laughed as if he was having a fit of some kind. It was indeed strange to see him laughing like this so soon after his somber mood.

"Oh, I like that! No, that really beats everything!" he

239

cried, gasping for breath. "One fellow doesn't believe in God at all, while the other believes in Him so much he murders people with a prayer on his lips. No, my dear Prince, you could never have just invented that. Ha, ha, ha! No, that beats everything!"

"Next morning I went out to walk around the town," continued the prince when Rogozhin had stopped laughing, though spasmodic laughter still burst from his lips, "and I saw a drunken soldier swaying along the wooden sidewalk in a terrible state. He came up to me and said, 'Buy this silver cross, sir. You can have it for twenty kopecks. It's silver!' I saw the cross in his hand—he must have just taken it off—on a dirty blue ribbon; but you could tell at first glance it was only made of tin, a big, eight-branched one, of a regular Byzantine design. I took out twenty kopecks and gave them to him, and at once put the cross around my neck; and I could see in his face how pleased he was to have cheated a stupid gentleman. He went off immediately to drink up the proceeds of the cross; there wasn't the least doubt of that. As for me, my dear friend, I was at the time tremendously impressed by everything that came pouring upon me in Russia; I had understood nothing about the country before, as if I had grown up unable to express myself; and my memories of it during my five years abroad were somehow fantastic. So I went away and I thought, 'No, it's too soon for me to condemn this peddler of Christ. God alone knows what is hidden in those weak and drunken hearts.' An hour later as I was going back to the hotel I came upon a peasant woman with a tiny baby. The woman was still quite young, the child about six weeks old. The child smiled at her for the first time in its life. I watched and suddenly she crossed herself with great devotion. 'What are you doing, my dear?' (I was always asking questions in those days.) 'There is joy for a mother in her child's first smile, just as God rejoices when from heaven he sees a sinner praying to Him with his whole heart.' This is what that peasant woman said to me, almost in those very words, such a profound, subtle, and truly religious thought, in which the whole essence of Christianity is expressed—I mean the whole conception of God as our own Father and of God's joy in man, like a father's in his own child—Christ's fundamental thought! A simple peasant woman! It's true she was a mother—and, who knows, perhaps she was the wife of that soldier. Listen, Parfyon, you asked me a question before, and here's my answer: the essence of religious feeling doesn't depend on reasoning, and it has nothing to do with wrongdoing or crime or with atheism. There is something else there
240

and there always will be, and atheists will always pass over it and will never be talking about *that*. But the important thing is that you will recognize it most quickly and clearly in the Russian heart—that's my conclusion! It's one of the main convictions I have received from our Russia. There is much to be done, Parfyon! There is much to be done in our Russian world, believe me! Remember how in Moscow we used to meet and talk then, you and I—no, I didn't want to come back here at all! And I never, never thought I'd be meeting you like this! Well, it's done! Good-bye for now. May God be with you!"

He turned and went down the stairs.

"Lev Nikolayevitch!" Parfyon shouted from above, when the prince reached the first landing. "That cross you bought from the soldier—do you have it with you?"

"Yes, I'm wearing it." And once again he stopped.

"Show me."

Again something strange! He thought a moment, then went up and showed him the cross without taking it off his neck.

"Give it to me," said Rogozhin.

"Why? Do you—" The prince did not want to part with the cross.

"I'll wear it, and I'll give you mine, for you to wear."

"You want to exchange crosses? By all means, Parfyon, if you want to I'm delighted. We will be brothers."

The prince took off his tin cross, Parfyon his gold one, and they exchanged. Parfyon was silent. With pained surprise the prince observed the same mistrust, the same bitter and almost sarcastic smile on the face of his adoptive brother; at least at times it could be plainly seen. Finally, in silence, Rogozhin took the prince's hand and stood for some time, as though he could not make up his mind about something. At last he suddenly drew him after him and, in a barely audible voice, said, "Come on." They crossed the first floor landing and rang at the door facing the one they had come out. It was soon opened to them. An old woman, all bent and dressed in black, wearing a kerchief over her head, silently bowed low to Rogozhin. He asked her something rapidly and without waiting for an answer led the prince inside. Again they went through dark rooms, of a somehow extraordinarily cold cleanliness, coldly and somberly furnished with ancient furniture under clean white covers. Without announcing himself, Rogozhin led the prince straight into a fairly small room like a drawing room, divided by a polished mahogany partition with doors at each end, behind which there was probably a bedroom. In the corner of the drawing room by the stove sat a little old woman in an armchair; she did not appear very old, and in fact she had a rather healthy and pleasant round face, but her hair was completely white and, as could be told at first glance, she had entered her second infancy. She wore a black woolen dress, a large black scarf around her neck, and a clean white cap with black ribbons. Her feet rested on a footstool. Near her sat another immaculate old woman, older than the first, also in mourning and also wearing a white cap, probably some sort of dependent, who was silently knitting a sock. It was likely that both kept silence all the time. The first old woman, seeing Rogozhin and the prince, smiled to them and nodded her head affably several times as a sign she was pleased.

"Mother," said Rogozhin, kissing her hand, "this is my great friend, Prince Lev Nikolayevitch Myshkin. We have exchanged crosses. He was like a real brother to me in Moscow at one time, he did a lot for me. Bless him, Mother, as you would bless your own son. Wait, old lady, like this; let me fix your fingers right."

But before Parfyon had time to do this, the old woman raised her right hand, with three fingers held up, and three times devotedly made the sign of the cross over the prince. Then, once again she nodded her head tenderly and affectionately to him.

"Well, let's be going, Lev Nikolayevitch," said Parfyon. "That's all I brought you here for."

When they came out on the landing again, he added, "She doesn't understand a thing, she didn't understand a word I said, and yet she blessed you. That means she wanted to do it herself. Well, good-bye, it's time for me to go, and you too."

And he opened his own door.

"But let me at least embrace you before we part, you strange fellow!" cried the prince, looking at him with tender reproach, and was about to embrace him. But Parfyon had barely raised his arms when he let them fall again. He could not bring himself to do it, he tried to avoid looking at the prince. He did not want to embrace him.

"Have no fear! Though I took your cross, I'm not going to knife you for your watch!" he muttered to himself indistinctly, and suddenly laughed in a strange way. But then his whole face changed: he turned terribly pale, his lips trembled, his eyes blazed. He raised his arms, embraced the prince warmly, and said in a breathless voice: "Well, take her, then, since it's fated to be! She's yours! I'm letting you have her. Remember Rogozhin!"

And turning away from the prince without looking at him, he went quickly inside and slammed the door behind him.

Chapter FIVE

❧❧❧

It was already late, almost half past two, and the prince did not find Yepanchin at home. Leaving his card, he decided to go to the hotel called "The Pair of Scales" and ask for Kolya, and if he was not there to leave him a note. At "The Scales" he was told that Nikolai Ardalionovitch "had already gone out in the morning but had said that if anyone came asking for him to tell them he would be back around three, possibly. But if he wasn't back by half past three it would mean he had taken the train to Pavlovsk where he would go to Madame Yepanchin's which would mean he would be dining there, sir." The prince sat down to wait for him and in the meantime ordered dinner.

It was half past three and then four and Kolya had not yet appeared. The prince left and walked on mechanically wherever his steps happened to lead him. In early summer in Petersburg there are sometimes lovely days—clear, hot, and still. As if on purpose, this was one of those rare days. For some time the prince wandered aimlessly. He did not know the city well. Sometimes he would stop and pause on street corners before certain houses, in squares, on bridges; once he entered a pastry shop to rest. Sometimes he would watch the passers-by with great interest, but most of the time he noticed neither the people nor where he was going. He was in a state of painful anxiety and his nerves were on edge and at the same time he felt an extraordinary craving for solitude. He wanted to be alone and give himself up completely passively to this agonizing tension, without seeking to escape it. He loathed the thought of resolving the questions that flooded his heart and soul, and he murmured to himself, hardly aware of what he was saying: "Can I be to blame for all this?"

Toward six o'clock he found himself on the platform of the Tsarskoye Selo railway station. Solitude had soon become unbearable to him, a new wave of fever seized his heart, and for a moment a bright light flared in the darkness in which his soul was languishing. He took a ticket to Pavlovsk and was impatient to leave, but of course now he felt he was being pursued by something—and yet it was not anything imaginary, as he himself inclined to believe, but something real. He was about to take a seat on the train when he suddenly threw the ticket to the ground and went out of the station again, disturbed and thoughtful. Some time later, in the street, he seemed suddenly to remember something, to seize hold of something very strange that had long been worrying him. He suddenly became conscious of doing something he had been doing for a long time, though he had not been aware of it until that moment: for several hours now, even at "The Scales," and even before he had gone to "The Scales," he had abruptly, from time to time, begun looking around him for something. He would forget about it for as much as a half an hour, then would suddenly start searching uneasily around him again.

But as soon as he noticed this sickly and until then quite unconscious impulse of his, which had taken possession of him for such a long time, he had another flash of recollection which interested him exceedingly. He recalled that at the instant he discovered that he was always looking around for something he had been standing on the sidewalk near a certain shop examining the merchandise in the window with the greatest attention. Now he felt he needed to be absolutely sure whether he had really been standing there in front of the shop window, perhaps five minutes earlier, or whether he had imagined it, whether he had become confused. Did that shop and that merchandise in fact exist? Indeed, today he felt particularly unwell, almost as he did long ago at the onset of an attack of his old illness. He knew that at some times he was unusually absentminded and often mixed up people and things, unless he looked at them with abnormally intense concentration. But there was a special reason why he wanted to find out whether he had actually stood before the shop. Among the goods displayed in the window there was one particular thing he had looked at and had even estimated would cost sixty kopecks—he remembered this in spite of his distraction and anxiety. Consequently, if the shop existed, he must have stopped on account of this object. Therefore that object must have held such fascination for him that it attracted his attention even at a time when he was in such distress and confusion, just after walking out of the railroad station. He now walked, looking to the right almost in anguish, and his heart was beating with restless impatience. But there was the store, he had found it at last! It was five hundred paces from the place he had had the notion of turning back. And there was the article which would be worth sixty kopecks. "It certainly must be sixty kopecks, and no more!" he assured himself and laughed. But his laughter was hysterical; he felt miserable. He clearly remembered now that it was precisely here, standing before this window, that he had suddenly turned around, just as earlier that day when he had caught Rogozhin's eyes fixed upon him. Having made sure he was not mistaken (though he had felt quite sure of it at once), he left the shop and walked rapidly away. He would have to think all this through carefully; it was now clear that it had not been his imagination at the train station either, that something absolutely real had happened to him that was certainly connected with all his former anxieties. But a kind of irrepressible inner revulsion again overcame him; he did not want to think anything through and he did not. He began thinking about something else altogether.

Among other things he fell to thinking that in his attacks of epilepsy there was a pause just before the fit itself (if it happened while he was awake) when suddenly in the midst of sadness, spiritual darkness, and a feeling of oppression, there were instants when it seemed his brain was on fire, and in an extraordinary surge all his vital forces would be intensified. The sense of life, the consciousness of self were multiplied tenfold in these moments, which lasted no longer than a flash of lightning. His mind and heart were flooded with extraordinary light; all torment, all doubt, all anxieties were relieved at once, resolved in a kind of lofty calm, full of serene, harmonious joy and hope, full of understanding and the knowledge of the ultimate cause of things. But these moments, these flashes were only the presage of that final second (never more than a second) with which the fit itself began. That second was, of course, unbearable. Thinking about this moment afterward, when he was again in health, he often told himself that all these gleams and flashes of superior self-awareness and, hence, of "a higher state of being" were nothing other than sickness, the upsetting of the normal condition and, if so, were not the highest state of being at all but on the contrary had to be reckoned as the lowest. And yet he came finally to an extremely paradoxical conclusion. "What if it is sickness?" he asked himself. "What does it matter if it is abnormal intensity, if the result, if the moment of awareness, remembered and analyzed afterward in health, turns out to be the height of harmony and beauty, and gives an unheard-of and till then undreamed-of feeling of wholeness, of proportion, of reconciliation, and an ecstatic and prayerlike union in the highest synthesis of life?" These cloudy expressions seemed very comprehensible to him, though too weak. That it was really "beauty and prayer," that it was really "the highest synthesis of life," he could not doubt and moreover could not even admit the possibility of doubt. For he did not see abnormal and fallacious visions during this moment, as from hashish, opium, or wine, debasing reason and distorting the soul. He could judge this sanely when his attacks were over. Those moments were nothing less than an extraordinary intensification of self-awareness—if the condition was to be described in one word—self-awareness and at the same time an extreme consciousness of existence. If in that second—that is, in the last lucid moment before the fit—he had time to say to himself clearly and consciously: "Yes, one might give one's whole life for this moment!" then that moment by itself would certainly be worth the whole of life. However, he did not insist on the dialectical aspect of his conclusion: for mental stupor, spiritual darkness, idiocy, appeared all too clearly as the consequences of those "higher moments"; he would not, of course, have seriously disputed this. In retrospect when he thought about that minute there was unquestionably a mistake in his conclusion, but the reality of the sensation somehow troubled him. What, after all, was to be made of reality? For that very thing had happened; he had actually had time to tell himself at that very second that the infinite happiness he had felt in it might indeed be worth a whole life. "At that moment," as he once told Rogozhin in Moscow when they used to see each other there, "at that moment somehow the extraordinary words 'there shall be time no longer'* become understandable to me. Probably," he added, smiling, "this is the same second the epileptic Mohammed's water pitcher had tipped and not yet spilled, and in that time he beheld all the dwellings of Allah." Yes, he had often met with Rogozhin in Moscow, and they had talked not only of this. "Rogozhin said just now I had been a brother to him then. He said it for the first time today," thought the prince to himself.

He thought of this as he sat on a bench under a tree in the Summer Garden. It was nearly seven o'clock. The garden was empty, a shadow passed over the setting sun for a moment. It was sultry, as if distant thunderstorms were approaching. He found a certain appeal in his present contemplative mood. He fixed his mind and memory on every object, and this pleased him; he wanted at all cost to forget something, something real and pressing; but from his first look around him he was immediately conscious of the gloomy thought which he wanted so badly to escape. He remembered he had talked to the waiter at the restaurant at lunch about an unusually strange recent murder, which had aroused a great sensation and much talk. But no sooner had he remembered this than something odd happened to him again.

An extraordinary, overwhelming desire, almost a temptation, suddenly numbed his will. He got up from the bench and walked straight from the garden to the Petersburg Side district. Earlier, he had asked a passer-by on the embankment along the Neva to point out to him the Petersburg Side across the river. It was pointed out to him, but he did not go there then. And in any case it would have been useless to go that day, he knew that. He had had the address a long time; he could have easily found the house of Lebedev's relative, but he knew almost for certain that he would not find her at home. "She must have gone to Pavlovsk, or Kolya would have left word at 'The Scales' as was agreed." And so if he went there now it was of course not to see her. A different kind of curiosity, somber and tormenting, now lured him. A sudden new idea had entered his mind. But it was quite enough for him that he had set off and knew where he was going; a minute later he was again walking along, hardly aware of his surroundings. To reflect further upon his "sudden idea" all at once seemed terribly repellent to him, and almost impossible. He looked with painfully strained attention at everything that met his eye; he gazed at the sky, at the Neva. He spoke to a little child he met. Perhaps his epileptic condition was becoming more and more acute. The storm seemed in fact to be drawing nearer, though slowly. It was beginning to thunder in the distance. The air was becoming oppressive.

For some reason the thought of Lebedev's nephew, whom he had seen that morning, kept running through his mind, just as a phrase of music sometimes keeps running through the mind, persistent and exasperating. The strange thing was that he kept seeing him as the murderer Lebedev had spoken of then, while introducing the nephew to him. Yes, he had read quite recently about this murderer. He had read and heard a great deal about such things since he had returned to Russia; he followed them intently. And in the evening he had been extremely interested in the waiter's conversation, precisely about that murder of the Zhemarins. The waiter agreed with him, he remembered that. He remembered the waiter himself; he was not at all a stupid fellow, but a solid man and careful, though "God only knows what he is really like;

it is hard to make out new people in a new country." Yet he was beginning to believe passionately in the Russian soul. Oh, in those six months he had been through a great deal—a great deal that was completely new to him, that he had never been told of, or heard of, or suspected! But another's soul is a darkness, and the Russian soul is a darkness—for many, a darkness. Here he had been seeing Rogozhin often, they had been close, they had become "brothers"—but did he know Rogozhin? And then what chaos and what confusion and what ugliness there was sometimes in all this! And what a disgusting and self-satisfied pimple of a boy that nephew of Lebedev's was! "But what am I saying?" wondered the prince. "Did he kill those creatures, those six people? I seem to have it all mixed up—how strange this is! My head seems to be turning round. But what a sweet, charming face Lebedev's eldest daughter has—the one standing with the baby, what an innocent, almost childlike expression! What almost childlike laughter!" It was odd he had almost forgotten that face and only remembered it now. Lebedev, who stamped his feet at them, probably adored them all. But it was as sure as two times two make four that Lebedev adored that nephew of his too!

But how had he come to pass such a final judgment on them, he who had arrived only that day? How could he reach such verdicts? And here Lebedev had been a riddle to him that day. Had he expected a Lebedev like that? Had he known a Lebedev like that before? Lebedev and Du Barry—Good Lord! Still, if Rogozhin did kill, at least he would not kill in such a slovenly way. There would not be the same chaos. A specially prepared weapon and six people slaughtered in a state of complete delirium! Had Rogozhin a specially prepared weapon? He had—but was it certain Rogozhin would kill? The prince suddenly gave a start. "Isn't it criminal, isn't it base of me to make a supposition like that with such cynical outspokenness?" he exclaimed, his whole face flushing with shame. He was astonished; he stood still as if rooted to the ground. He remembered all at once the Pavlovsk station that afternoon, and the Nikolayevsk station earlier in the day, and the question he had asked Rogozhin straight to his face about the *eyes*, and Rogozhin's cross, which he was wearing now, and the blessing from his mother, to whom Rogozhin had taken him himself, and the last convulsive embrace, Rogozhin's last renunciation, just before, on the stairs—and after all this to catch himself incessantly searching around for something, and that store, and that object—what baseness! And after all this he was going with a "special purpose," with a "sudden idea"! His whole soul was overwhelmed with despair and suffering. The prince wanted to turn back to his hotel at once, he actually did start back, but a minute later he stopped, thought it over, and went on in the direction he had been going.

Yes, he was already in the Petersburg Side, he was near the house, yet he was not going there for his former purpose, not with that "special idea"! And how could it be! Yes, his illness was coming back, there was no doubt of it, perhaps he would even have the fit today. Because of the fit there was all this darkness, because of the fit there was this "idea"! Now the darkness was dispersed, the demon banished, doubts did not exist, there was joy in his heart! And—he had not seen *her* for so long, he needed to see her, and—yes—he would have liked to meet Rogozhin now; he would have taken him by the hand and they would have gone along together. His heart was pure—was he Rogozhin's rival? Tomorrow he would go to Rogozhin himself and tell him he had seen her. Hadn't he rushed here, just as Rogozhin had said that afternoon, only to see her? Perhaps he would find her—it was not certain she was in Pavlovsk!

Yes, now it was necessary that everything be made clear, so that everyone might clearly read each other's hearts, and that there might be no more dark, passionate renunciations like Rogozhin's earlier that day; and let all this be done freely and—out in the light. Wasn't Rogozhin capable of that? He said he did not love her like that, that he had no compassion for her, that he had "no such pity." It was true he had then added that "your pity is perhaps stronger than my love"—but he was slandering himself. Hm! Rogozhin reading a book—was that not "pity," the beginnings of "pity"? Did not the very presence of this book prove he was fully conscious of his feelings toward *her*? And the story he had told him? No, that was deeper than mere passion alone. And did her face inspire no more than just passion? Yes, and could that face inspire passion now? It aroused suffering, it seized one's whole soul, it—and a poignant, agonizing memory suddenly passed through the prince's heart.

Yes, agonizing. He remembered how he had suffered not long ago when he first began to notice in her symptoms of insanity. Then he had been in almost complete despair. And how could he have left her when she ran away from him to Rogozhin? He should have run after her himself instead of waiting for news of her. But could it be that Rogozhin had not noticed her insanity even now? Hm—yes. Rogozhin saw different motives for everything, passionate motives! And what insane jealousy! What did he mean by that supposition of his? (The prince suddenly flushed and there was a shiver in his heart.)

But why should he recall all this? There was insanity on both sides. And for him, the prince, to love this woman with passion was almost unthinkable; it would have been almost cruel, inhuman. Yes, yes! No, Rogozhin was unfair to himself; he had a great heart capable of suffering and compassion. When he knew the whole truth, when he realized what a pitiful creature this hurt and half-demented woman was, would he not forgive her all the past, all his agonies? Would he not become her servant, her brother, her friend, her providence? Compassion would teach Rogozhin and give meaning to his life. Compassion is the chief and perhaps the only law of human existence. Oh, how unpardonably and dishonorably guilty he was before Rogozhin! No it was not that the Russian soul was darkness but that there was darkness in his own soul, if he could imagine such a horror. For a few warm, heartfelt words in Moscow, Rogozhin had called him his brother, and he— But this was sickness and delirium! It would all come out right! How gloomily Rogozhin had said that he was "losing his faith"! The man must be suffering terribly. He said that he liked looking at that painting; it was not that he liked it but that he felt a compulsion to look at it. Rogozhin was not only a passionate soul; he was, for all that, a fighter; he wanted to get his lost faith back by force. He suffers from the need of it now— Yes! To believe in something! To believe in someone! But what a strange picture that painting of Holbein's was! Ah, here is the street! And that must be the house—yes, No. 16, "The House of Madame Filissov." Here it is! The prince rang and asked for Nastassya Filippovna.

The mistress of the house herself told him that Nastassya Filippovna had left that morning to stay with Darya Alexeyevna, "and she might even stay there, sir, for several days." Madame Filissov was a small sharp-eyed and sharp-faced woman of about forty, who looked shrewdly and searchingly at the prince. When she asked his name—a question to which she seemed deliberately to impart a hint of conspiracy—the prince was at first unwilling to answer; but he turned back at once and urged her to give his name to Nastassya Filippovna. Madame Filissov received this insistent request with a new attentiveness and with an extraordinary air of secrecy, by which she evidently meant to say, "Have no fear, I have understood you." The prince's name obviously made a very strong impression on her. The prince looked at her absently, then left and went back to his hotel. But he went away looking quite different from the way he had looked when he rang at Madame Filissov's door. Again an extraordinary change had come over him in a single instant; again he walked along pale, weak, suffering, and agitated; his knees trembled and a vagrant smile wandered over his blue lips. His "sudden idea" had all at once been confirmed and justified and—he believed in his demon again!

But had it been confirmed? Had it been justified? Why was he again taken with this trembling, this cold sweat, this darkness, and this chill in his soul? Was it because he had once again seen those eyes? But he had gone out of the Summer Garden with the single idea of seeing them! That was what his "sudden idea" amounted to. He had intensely wanted to see "those eyes" again, so as to convince himself once and for all that he was sure to find them *there*, at that house. This had been his impulsive desire—so why was it he was now so crushed and overwhelmed now that he had actually seen them? As if he had not expected it! Yes, those were the same eyes (there was now no doubt that they were the same!) which had blazed at him in the crowd that morning as he was getting off the Moscow train at the Nikolayevsk railroad station; they were the same (absolutely the same!) he had caught looking at him from behind that afternoon as he was sitting down that afternoon at Rogozhin's. Rogozhin had denied it then; he had asked with a chilling twisted smile, "Whose eyes were they?" And quite recently, at the Tsarskoye Selo station when he was boarding the train for Pavlovsk to see Aglaya and had suddenly seen the eyes again, for the third time that day, he had felt a terrible urge to tell *him* whose eyes those were! But he had run out of the station and had only come to his senses in front of the cutler's shop at the moment he was standing there estimating the cost of an object with a deer-horn handle at sixty kopecks. A strange and hideous demon held him fast and would not leave him again. This demon had whispered to him in the Summer Garden, as he sat lost in thought under a lime tree, that if Rogozhin had had to follow him since morning and watch his every step, then he would certainly, on finding that he had not gone to Pavlovsk (which was of course fatal news for Rogozhin), have gone *there* to that house on the Petersburg Side and have watched there for him, the prince, who had given his word of honor that morning he would not see her, and that "he had not come to Petersburg for that." And there was the prince impulsively rushing to that house, and what if he did meet Rogozhin there? He had seen only an unhappy man whose state of mind was gloomy but not hard to understand. This unhappy man did not even conceal himself now. Yes, Rogozhin had for some reason that morning denied it and told a lie, but at the Tsarskoye Selo station he stood almost in the open. Indeed it was rather the prince who had concealed himself and not Rogozhin. And now at the house he stood on the opposite sidewalk about fifty paces away, waiting with his arms folded. There he was in full view, as if he wished to be seen. He stood like an accuser and like a judge and not like a—what?

But why had he, the prince, not gone up to him now, but turned away from him as if he had not noticed anything, though their eyes had met? (Yes, their eyes had met and they had looked at each other.) Had he not wanted earlier to take him by the hand and go *there* together with him? Had he not wanted to go to him the next day and tell him he had been to see her? Had he not renounced his demon, halfway there, when gladness had suddenly flooded his soul? Or was there really something in Rogozhin—that is, in the whole presence of this man *on that day*, in his whole aspect, his words, movements, actions, looks, taken together—that could justify the prince's dreadful apprehensions and the revolting whisperings of his demon? Something that was plainly there but difficult to analyze and put into words, impossible to justify by adequate reasons, but which in spite of all this difficulty and impossibility produced a perfectly complete and unavoidable impression, which then by itself became a conviction?

Conviction of what? (Oh, how terribly the prince was tortured by the hideousness, the "degradation" of this conviction, of this "base foreboding," and how he reproached himself!) "Say it if you dare, conviction of what?" he kept saying to himself, in challenge, in accusation. "Put it into words, dare express your full thought clearly, precisely, without hesitation! Oh, I am dishonorable!" he kept repeating with indignation and a flush in his face. "How am I to look this man in the face now for the rest of my life! Oh, what a day! Oh God, what a nightmare!"

There was a moment toward the end of that long and painful walk back from the Petersburg Side when the prince was suddenly seized by an irresistible desire to go directly to Rogozhin, to wait for him, to embrace him in shame, with tears, to tell him everything and put an end to it all at once. But he was already standing near his hotel. How he had loathed this hotel from the first! Those corridors, the whole building, his room, how he had hated it all from the very first! Several times during the day he had remembered with particular dis-

252

gust that he had to return here. "What's the matter with me today that, like a sick woman, I believe in all kinds of premonitions!" he thought with irritable sarcasm, stopping at the gates. One occurrence of today rose before his mind with particular clarity at this moment, but "coldly," "perfectly reasonably," "now not as a nightmare." He suddenly remembered the knife on Rogozhin's table. "But why, after all, shouldn't Rogozhin have as many knives on his table as he likes?" he asked, greatly surprised at himself, and just then, petrified with astonishment, he suddenly recalled how he had stopped in front of the cutler's shop. "But what connection could there be in that?" he cried, but stopped short. A new unbearable wave of shame, almost of despair, held him rooted just outside the gates. He stood still for a moment. It sometimes happens to people that a sudden unendurable memory, particularly when it is associated with shame, will stop them dead in their tracks for a moment. "Yes, I am a heartless man and a coward!" he repeated gloomily, and abruptly moved on, but only to stop again.

The entrance gateway, which was always dark, was particularly dark at that moment; the storm which had covered the sky and engulfed the evening light now broke just as the prince approached the house and the rain poured down When he moved on after his momentary halt he was almost at the gateway. And suddenly in the half-darkness he caught sight of a man inside near the stairs. The man seemed to be waiting there for something, but he quickly moved away and disappeared. The prince could not make out this man clearly and of course could not at all say for certain who it was. Besides, there were so many people who passed through there, it was a hotel and people were continually running in and out. But he suddenly felt an absolute, undeniable conviction that he had recognized this man, and that it was definitely Rogozhin. An instant later the prince rushed after him up the stairs. His heart stood still. "Everything will be decided now!" he said to himself with a strange certainty.

The stairs the prince ran up from the gateway led to the corridors of the first and second floors, along which were the hotel rooms. This stairway, as in all old houses, was of stone, dark and narrow, and it turned around a massive stone column. On the first half-landing there was a nichelike hollow in the column, no more than a yard wide and half a yard deep. But there was enough room there for a man to stand. Dark as it was, the prince, on reaching the landing, noticed immediately that a man was hiding in the niche. The prince suddenly wanted to walk by without looking to the right. He had taken one step past already, but he could not resist, and he turned.

Those two eyes—*the same two eyes*—suddenly met his own. The man hiding in the niche had meanwhile taken a step forward. For one second they stood facing each other and almost touching. Suddenly the prince seized him by the shoulders and turned him toward the staircase, nearer the light; he wanted to see his face more clearly.

Rogozhin's eyes flashed, and a smile of fury contorted his face. He raised his right hand, and something shone in it. The prince did not think of stopping it. He only seemed to remember he had shouted,

"Parfyon, I don't believe it!"

Then suddenly it was as if a gulf had opened before him, an extraordinary *inner* light flooded his soul. This moment lasted perhaps a half second, but he clearly and consciously remembered the beginning, the first sound of his own frightful cry, which broke from his breast of its own accord and which he could have done nothing to stop. Then his consciousness was instantly extinguished, and complete darkness followed.

It was an epileptic fit, the first in a very long time. It is well known that epileptic fits, the epilepsy itself, comes on instantaneously. At this moment the face is suddenly horribly distorted, especially the eyes. Convulsions and spasms seize the whole body and the features of the face. A terrible, incredible scream, unlike anything imaginable, breaks forth; and with this cry all resemblance to a human being seems suddenly to disappear; and it is impossible, at least very difficult, for an observer to realize and admit that the person screaming is the same. It is actually as if someone else was screaming, inside the person. At least this is how many people have described their impression. The sight of a man in an epileptic fit fills many with absolute and unbearable horror, which has even something mystical about it. It must be supposed that some such feeling of sudden horror—together with all the other frightful impressions of the moment—suddenly paralyzed Rogozhin and so saved the prince from the descending knife which would inevitably have stabbed him. Then, before he had time to realize it was a fit, and seeing that the prince staggered away from him and suddenly fell backward straight down the stairs, striking the base of his head violently against a stone step as he fell, Rogozhin rushed headlong down the staircase, avoiding the prostrate figure, and almost out of his senses ran out of the hotel.

With the convulsions and throbbing spasms, the sick man's

body slid down the steps, of which there were but fifteen, to the bottom of the staircase. Quite soon, no more than five minutes later, he was noticed and a group of people gathered. A pool of blood near his head made them wonder whether the man had fallen and injured himself or whether there had been "a crime of some kind." Soon, however, some of them recognized that it was a case of epilepsy; one of the hotel people identified the prince as a recently arrived guest. The confusion was finally ended very happily, thanks to a fortunate circumstance.

Kolya Ivolgin, who had promised to be back at "The Scales" around four and had instead gone to Pavlovsk, had on a sudden impulse refused to dine at Madame Yepanchin's, had come back to Petersburg and hurried to "The Scales," where he arrived about seven o'clock. Learning from the note the prince had left for him that he was in town, he went directly to find him at the address given in the note. Informed at the hotel that the prince had gone out, he went downstairs to the restaurant and waited for him there, drinking tea and listening to the organ. Happening to overhear something about someone having a fit, he ran directly to the spot, following a sure presentiment, and recognized the prince. The necessary measures were taken at once. The prince was carried to his room; and though he regained consciousness, he did not come fully to his senses for some time. The doctor sent for to examine his injured head prescribed cataplasms and declared that there was no danger to be feared from the wound. When, about an hour later, the prince began to understand fairly well what was going on around him, Kolya took him in a carriage from the hotel to Lebedev's. Lebedev received the sick man with extraordinary warmth and many bows. On his account he advanced the time of his move to the country; three days later they were all at Pavlovsk.

Chapter SIX

Lebedev's cottage was not large, but it was comfortable and even pretty. The part of it that was to be rented had been specially decorated. On the rather spacious veranda at the street entrance to the house were grouped a number of orange trees, lemon, and jasmine in large green wooden tubs which in Lebedev's estimation lent the house a most captivating appearance. He had acquired several of these trees with the house and was so enchanted by the effect they produced on the veranda that he decided to take advantage of an opportunity to buy more such tubbed trees at an auction, so as to make an ensemble. When all the trees were finally brought to the house and set in place Lebedev several times that day had run down the veranda steps into the street and from there admired his property, and each time he mentally raised the sum he proposed to ask from his future tenant.

The prince, worn out, depressed, and physically shattered, was very pleased with the house. Indeed, on the day of his arrival at Pavlovsk—that is, three days after his fit—he appeared almost in good health, though inwardly he still did not feel recovered. He was glad to see everyone around him in those days, glad to see Kolya, who scarcely left his side, glad to see the entire Lebedev family (minus the nephew, who had disappeared somewhere), glad to see Lebedev himself; he was even pleased to see General Ivolgin, who had visited him when they were still in the city. On the very evening of his arrival in Pavlovsk, a rather large number of visitors gathered around him on the veranda. First came Ganya, whom the prince hardly recognized, so changed was he in that period and so much thinner. Then Varya and Ptitsyn appeared, who were also summer residents of Pavlovsk. General Ivolgin had been staying almost all the time now at Lebedev's, and it seemed he had moved up with him as well. Lebedev tried not to let him near the prince and kept him with him; he treated the general as a friend, they appeared to have known each other for a long time. During those three days the prince noticed that they would sometimes enter into long conversations together and quite often would shout and argue, even about learned subjects, all of which apparently caused Lebedev great pleasure. One might even have thought he could not do without the general. As for the precautions he took regarding the prince, Lebedev applied them also to the members of his own family from the time they arrived at the house. On the pretext of not disturbing him he let no one close to him; he stamped his feet, ran around chasing off his daughters, even Vera with the baby, the moment he had the slightest suspicion they were going toward the veranda where the prince was, despite all the requests of the prince not to keep anyone away.

"In the first place," he replied at last to the prince's direct question, "they will show no respect whatever if they're let do as they please, and in the second place, it's just not proper."

"But why?" protested the prince. "Really, you're only annoying me with all this watching and supervision. I get bored alone, and you depress me all the more the way you keep on waving your arms and walking around on tiptoes."

The prince was alluding to the fact that while Lebedev kept his whole household away on the pretext that the invalid needed quiet, he himself had been coming in every other minute for the past three days, and every time he would poke his head in first and look around the room as if he wanted to assure himself the prince was really there and had not run away; then he would creep in slowly and stealthily and tiptoe up to the prince's armchair, so that he sometimes inadvertently startled his lodger. He was constantly inquiring whether the prince might not want something, and when the prince finally began asking him to leave him alone, he obediently turned around without saying a word and tiptoed back to the door, floating his arms in the air as he walked, as if he wanted to make clear that he was not saying a word, and that he was as good as gone, and that he would not come back; yet within ten minutes or at most a quarter of an hour he would be back again. The fact that Kolya had free access to the prince was for Lebedev a source of the deepest mortification and even hostile indignation. Kolya noticed that Lebedev would stand at the door listening for half an hour at a time to what he and the prince happened to be saying, and of course he informed the prince of this.

"You act as if you owned me, the way you keep me under lock and key," protested the prince. "In the country, at least, I want things to be different, and I assure you that I'll see anyone I like and go wherever I choose."

"Without the least little doubt," Lebedev replied, waving his arms.

The prince studied him intently from head to foot.

"Tell me, Lukyan Timofeyevitch, that little cupboard that was over the head of your bed in Petersburg—have you brought it with you?"

"No, I haven't."

"Could you have left it behind?"

"It was impossible to bring it. I'd have had to wrench it off the wall. It's firmly fixed—firmly!"

"Perhaps you have another one like it here?"

"A better one! A better one! That's why I bought the house."

"I see. Who was it you wouldn't let in to see me a while ago? About an hour ago."

"That? Oh, that was the general, sir. It's true I didn't let him in, he shouldn't be here to see you. I have the greatest respect for this man, Prince. This, sir—this is a great man. You don't believe me? Well, you shall see. But just the same, most illustrious Prince, it's better that you didn't receive him."

"And why is this, may I ask? And why are you standing on tiptoes now, Lebedev, and why are you always coming up to me as if you wanted to whisper a secret in my ear?"

"I am base and mean. I feel it," Lebedev replied unexpectedly, striking his breast with feeling. "But won't the general be too hospitable for you?"

"Too hospitable?"

"Yes, sir. Hospitable. To begin with he's intending to come and live at my house, and that's all right, but he's so impetuous, he wants to be a member of the family right away. We have gone into the question of our relationship several times already, it appears we are related by marriage. You too, you are a sort of nephew once removed on your mother's side, he explained this to me just yesterday. And if you are a nephew, then, most illustrious Prince, you and I must be related. That would be nothing, sir, just a little weakness, but he's been assuring me that his whole life from the time he was a subaltern until the eleventh of June last year there were never fewer than two hundred people eating at his house every day. It got to the point where they never got up; that is to say they took lunch, supper, had their tea for fifteen hours out of the twenty-four for close to thirty years on end without a break, so there was hardly time to change the tablecloths. One would get up and leave, another would come, and on holidays, particularly on the imperial holidays, there would be as many as three hundred, and on the thousandth anniversary of Russia there were seven hundred people. Well, sir, it's a passion with him—a story like that is a very bad sign and one hesitates to receive such hospitable people in one's own house, and I've been thinking: won't someone like that be too hospitable for you and me?"

"But you appear to be on excellent terms with him?"

"We're like brothers and I take it all as a joke. What if we are related by marriage—what do I care? If anything—it's an honor. I see in him, sir, for all his two hundred people and the thousandth anniversary of Russia, a most remarkable man. I say this in all sincerity. You spoke of secrets just now, Prince—I mean that I come up to you as if I was going to share a secret with you. Well, it just so happens that there is a secret: a certain person has just let me know that she'd like very much to have a secret interview with you."

"Why secret? Not at all. I'll go to her place myself—today even."

"Not at all, not at all!" said Lebedev, waving his arms. "And she's not afraid of what you think. By the way, the monster comes every day to find out about your health. Did you know that?"

"You call him a monster quite often. That makes me very suspicious."

"You need have no suspicions at all, none at all," Lebedev assured him hastily. "I merely wished to explain that a certain person was not afraid of him but of something entirely different, entirely different."

"Well, of what? Speak out," demanded the prince impatiently, watching Lebedev's mysterious pantomime.

"That's the secret." Lebedev snickered.

"Whose secret?"

"Yours. You have forbidden me yourself, most illustrious Prince, to speak of it in your presence," said Lebedev quietly, and having savored the pleasure of bringing his listener's curiosity to the point of exasperation, he suddenly concluded: "She's afraid of Aglaya Ivanovna."

The prince frowned and was silent for a moment.

"Lebedev, I swear I'm going to leave your house," he said suddenly. "Where are Gavril Ardalionovitch and the Ptitsyns? At your house? Have you lured them too?"

"They're coming, they're coming, sir. And even the general will be coming. I'll open all the doors, and I'll call all my daughters, every one of them—at once, at once." Lebedev whispered in a frightened voice, waving his arms about and rushing from one door to another.

At that moment Kolya appeared on the veranda from the street and announced that guests were just behind him—Lizaveta Prokofyevna and her three daughters.

"Shall I let Gavril Ardalionovitch and the Ptitsyns in or not? Shall I let the general in?" said Lebedev jumping up, overcome by the news.

"Why not? Let anyone come who likes. I assure you, Lebedev, you've somehow misunderstood my position from the very start; you are consistently wrong. I haven't the slightest reason for hiding and concealing myself from anyone," said the prince with a laugh.

Looking at him, Lebedev considered it his duty to laugh

too. In spite of his state of extreme agitation, he was visibly pleased also.

The news brought by Kolya was true. He had come just a few steps ahead of the Yepanchins, to announce their arrival, so that the guests arrived from two sides at once, the Yepanchins from the veranda and the Ptitsyns, Ganya, and General Ivolgin from the inner rooms.

The Yepanchins had only just learned from Kolya about the prince's illness and the fact that he was in Pavlovsk. Before this, Madame Yepanchin had been in a state of profound bewilderment. Two days earlier the general had conveyed to his family the prince's visiting card; the card inspired in Lizaveta Prokofyevna the firm conviction that the prince himself would be following it to Pavlovsk to call on them. In vain did the young ladies assure her that a man who had not written for half a year might be in no great haste to see them now and that he might have had a great deal to occupy him in Petersburg without them. Who knew anything about his affairs? The general's wife was definitely angered by these remarks, and she was ready to wager that the prince would arrive by the following day, and that that would be "at the latest." The next day she had been expecting him the whole morning, for lunch, in the evening, and when it fell completely dark Lizaveta Prokofyevna became cross with everything and fought with everyone, though of course the prince was never mentioned as the cause of the quarrels. On the third day not a word was said about him. When at lunch Aglaya unexpectedly made a remark that *Maman* was angry because the prince had not come—a remark to which the general immediately added that it was not his fault—Lizaveta Prokofyevna got up and left the table in a rage. Finally, toward evening, Kolya arrived with the whole story and a description of all the prince's adventures as he knew them. As a result, Lizaveta Prokofyevna was triumphant, but even so Kolya got a scolding from her: "There are times he's around here for days on end, and there's no smoking him out of the house, but in this case he could at least have let us know if he didn't see fit to call himself." Kolya was on the point of being angry over the words "smoking him out of the house," but he put it off for another time. If the phrase itself had not been so offensive, he would probably have forgiven it altogether—so pleased was he by the worry and concern shown by Lizaveta Prokofyevna at the news of the prince's illness. She insisted at length on the necessity of sending specially to Petersburg, immediately, to obtain some medical celebrity of the very first order and to have him brought down on the very first train. But her daughters dissuaded her; they did not wish however to be left behind when she got ready, as she did at once, to visit the invalid.

"He's on his deathbed," she kept saying as she flurried about, "and we're going to stand on ceremony now! Is he a friend of the family or not?"

"Yes, but we mustn't cross the river before we find the bridge," said Aglaya.

"Very well, then, don't come. As a matter of fact, it's better if you don't. Yevgeny Pavlovitch will arrive and there'll be no one to receive him."

Of course at these words Aglaya set forth immediately with the others, as indeed she had intended to do all along. Prince S., who had been sitting with Adelaïda, at her request instantly agreed to escort the ladies. He had already become extremely interested, when at the beginning of his acquaintance with the Yepanchins, he heard from them about the prince. It appeared he was acquainted with him, that they had met somewhere not long ago, and that they had spent two weeks together in some town. It was about three months before. Prince S. had in fact a great deal to say about the prince, and on the whole spoke of him in a friendly way, so it was with genuine pleasure that he was now going to call on an old acquaintance. General Ivan Fyodorovitch was not at home then. Yevgeny Pavlovitch had not arrived yet either.

It was not more than three hundred paces from the Yepanchins' house to Lebedev's. Lizaveta Prokofyevna's first disappointment was to find a whole group of visitors with the prince, not to mention that in this crowd were two or three individuals she positively detested. Her second surprise was to find a young man to all appearance completely recovered in health, elegantly dressed, and laughing as he came to greet them, instead of the invalid on his deathbed she had expected. She even stopped in bewilderment, to the intense delight of Kolya, who of course could have perfectly well explained as she was leaving her house that no one was dying and that there was no question of a deathbed. But he had not explained this, mischievously anticipating the comical wrath of the general's wife, when, as he reckoned, she would certainly be angry at finding her very dear friend the prince in good health. In fact, Kolya was actually so tactless as to express this conjecture aloud, provoking Lizaveta Prokofyevna still further, for he was always baiting her, sometimes quite maliciously, in spite of their affection for one another.

"Just wait, my dear, don't be in such a hurry. Don't spoil

your triumph!" countered Lizaveta Prokofyevna, sitting down in the armchair the prince had placed for her.

Lebedev, Ptitsyn, and General Ivolgin rushed to get chairs for the young ladies. The general offered a chair to Aglaya. Lebedev presented a chair to Prince S., managing to express respectfulness in the very curve of his back. Varya, as usual, greeted the young ladies with ecstatic whispers.

"It is true, Prince, that I expected to find you practically bedridden. In my fear I so exaggerated the prospect of it—I won't lie to you—that for a moment I was terribly vexed at the sight of your happy face. But I swear it was only a moment before I could reflect. I always act and speak more intelligently when I reflect, you certainly must do the same. The truth is I'd really be less pleased by my own son's recovery, if I had one, than I am by yours; and if you don't believe me, it's your fault and not mine. As for this nasty boy, he permits himself worse jokes than that at my expense. It seems he's a sort of protégé of yours, so I warn you that one fine morning, believe me, I shall deny myself the pleasure of his further acquaintance."

"But what have I done?" cried Kolya. "No matter how I might have tried to tell you the prince was almost recovered you wouldn't have believed me because it was much more interesting to imagine him on his deathbed."

"Are you here with us for long?" Lizaveta Prokofyevna addressed the prince.

"For the whole summer, and possibly longer."

"And you're alone? Not married?"

"No, not married." The prince smiled at the naïveté of this thrust.

"There is nothing to smile at—it sometimes happens. I'm asking because of our house here. Why haven't you come to us? We have a whole wing empty. But it's as you like. Are you renting from him? From that person?" she added in an undertone, nodding to indicate Lebedev. "Why is he making such faces?"

At that moment Vera came out of the inner rooms onto the veranda, carrying the baby in her arms as usual. Lebedev, who was gliding around the chairs at a complete loss over what to do with himself, but desperately anxious not to leave, suddenly rushed toward Vera, waved his arms at her to chase her off the veranda, and, completely forgetting himself, actually stamped his feet at her.

"Is he crazy?" demanded Madame Yepanchin abruptly.

"No, he's—"

"Drunk, perhaps? I can't say that your crowd is particularly attractive," she snapped, including the other visitors in her glance. "Yet, what a charming girl. Who is she?"

"That's Vera Lukyanovna, the daughter of Lebedev there."

"Ah! She is very charming. I should like to know her."

But Lebedev, having overheard Lizaveta Prokofyevna's words of praise, was already dragging his daughter forward to present her.

"Orphans! Orphans!" he cried in a melting voice as he approached. "And this little girl on her arm, her sister, my daughter Lubov, is also an orphan, born in the most lawful wedlock to my departed wife, Yelena, who died six weeks ago in childbirth by the will of God. Yes. Taken the place of the mother, though but a sister and no more. Like a sister and no more, no more."

"And you, my good man, you are no more than a fool, I regret to say. But enough!" she added shortly in great indignation. "I think you are aware of this yourself."

"The absolute truth!" agreed Lebedev with a low and respectful bow.

"Listen, Mr. Lebedev, is it true what they say about you, that you interpret the Apocalypse?" asked Aglaya.

"The absolute truth. For fifteen years."

"I have heard of you. There was something about you in the newspapers, it seems to me?"

"No, that was about another interpreter, another one. But that one is dead. I have taken his place," said Lebedev, beside himself with delight.

"Do me a favor, since we are neighbors, and interpret it for me some day soon. I don't understand a thing in the Apocalypse."

"I'm afraid I must warn you, Aglaya Ivanovna, that all that is nothing but charlatanism on his part, believe me," quickly put in General Ivolgin, who had been waiting on pins and needles in intense anxiety to enter the conversation. He had taken a place near Aglaya Ivanovna. "Of course," he went on, "country life has its privileges and its pleasures, and to receive such an outlandish person for an interpretation of the Apocalypse is a diversion like any other, indeed a remarkably ingenious diversion, but I— You seem to be looking at me with some surprise? Allow me to introduce myself. General Ivolgin. I used to carry you in my arms, Aglaya Ivanovna."

"I am very pleased to meet you," said Aglaya in a low voice, making a desperate effort not to break out laughing. "I am acquainted with Varvara Ardalionovna and Nina Alexandrovna."

Lizaveta Prokofyevna flushed. Something that had been boiling in her for some time had suddenly to be released. She could not stand General Ivolgin, with whom she had been acquainted, though only very long ago.

"You are lying, sir, as usual," she snapped in indignation. "You never carried her in your arms."

"You've forgotten, *Maman*," Aglaya suddenly asserted. "I swear he did carry me, in Tver. We were living in Tver then. I was about six years old then, I remember. He made me an arrow and a bow and taught me to shoot, and I killed a pigeon. Do you remember how we killed the pigeon together?"

"And you brought me a cardboard helmet and a wooden sword!" cried Adelaïda. "I remember too."

"I remember that too," said Alexandra. "You two had quarreled over the wounded pigeon, and you were made to stand in corners. Adelaïda stood there wearing the helmet and holding the sword."

When the general told Aglaya he had carried her in his arms, he said it for something to say, merely to join in the conversation and because whenever he wished to make the acquaintance of young people he almost always opened the conversation with that remark. But this time it happened that he was speaking the truth and, as it also happened, that he had forgotten it was the truth. So when Aglaya declared they had shot a pigeon together, his memory suddenly cleared and he remembered it all himself in the greatest detail, as a person of advanced years sometimes remembers something from the distant past. It is hard to say what there was in that memory which made such a strong impression on the poor general, who was as usual slightly drunk, but he was suddenly extraordinarily moved.

"I remember! I remember everything!" he cried. "I was a captain then. You were so little, such a sweet little girl. Nina Alexandrovna—Ganya—I was received in your house. Ivan Fyodorovitch—"

"And so you see what's become of you now!" said the general's wife. "That means you haven't completely drunk away your finer feelings, since this affects you so much! But you've made your wife suffer. Instead of looking after your children, you sit in a debtors' prison. Go away, my friend, stand in some corner behind a door somewhere, and have a good cry. Remember your past innocence and perhaps the Lord will forgive you. Go ahead, go ahead, I mean it seriously. Nothing improves a person like remembering the past with remorse."

But to insist she was speaking seriously was unnecessary:

like all drunken people, the general was very sentimental, and like all drunken people who have sunk very low, he could not endure memories of a happy past. He got up and walked docilely toward the door, so that Lizaveta Prokofyevna was at once sorry for him.

"Ardalion Alexandrovitch, my friend!" she called after him. "Stop a moment—we are all sinners. When you feel your conscience reproaches you less, come and see me. We shall sit and chat about the past. I may very well be fifty times more sinful than you. But for the time being, good-bye. Go along, there's no point in your staying here," she added, suddenly afraid that he was coming back.

"You'd better not go after him just yet," the prince said to Kolya, who had started to run after his father, "or he'll lose his temper in an instant and the whole moment will be lost on him."

"That is true," decided Lizaveta Prokofyevna. "Don't bother him. Go and see him in half an hour."

"That's what it is to speak the truth once in a lifetime. It moves him to tears!" Lebedev ventured to remark.

"You're a fine one yourself, my friend, if what I have heard is true," said Lizaveta Prokofyevna, at once putting him in his place.

The respective situations of all the guests gathered with the prince little by little became clear. The prince was certainly able to appreciate, and did in fact appreciate fully, the sympathy shown him by the general's wife and her daughters, and he of course told them truthfully that before their visit he had intended to stop by their house that very day, in spite of his illness and the late hour. Lizaveta Prokofyevna, glancing around at his visitors, replied that this could still be done. Ptitsyn, a man of great politeness and accommodation, very soon got up and withdrew to Lebedev's part of the house and was eager to bring Lebedev along with him. The latter promised to come soon. Varya, meanwhile, had fallen into conversation with the girls and remained. She and Ganya were very glad of the general's departure. Ganya himself soon withdrew after Ptitsyn. During the few minutes he had been on the veranda with the Yepanchins he had behaved modestly, with dignity, and was not the least disconcerted by the determined glances of Lizaveta Prokofyevna, who had twice surveyed him from head to toe. Indeed those who had known him before might have imagined that he had greatly changed. His behavior delighted Aglaya.

"Wasn't that Gavril Ardalionovitch who went out?" she suddenly asked, as she was sometimes pleased to do, loudly and brusquely, interrupting the conversation of others with her question, which was addressed to no one in particular.

"Yes," replied the prince.

"I hardly recognized him. He's changed a lot and—much for the better."

"I'm very glad for his sake," replied the prince.

"He was very ill," added Varya, with pleasurable commiseration.

"How has he changed for the better?" demanded Lizaveta Prokofyevna in angry bewilderment and almost in alarm. "Where did you get that idea? There's nothing better about him. Exactly what seems better to you?"

"There is nothing better than the 'poor knight,' " suddenly exclaimed Kolya, who had been standing near Lizaveta Prokofyevna's chair.

"I think so too," said Prince S. and laughed.

"I am of precisely the same opinion," Adelaïda solemnly declared.

"What 'poor knight'?" demanded Madame Yepanchin, looking around in bewilderment and vexation at all those who had spoken; but noticing that Aglaya had colored, she added in anger: "Some kind of nonsense! Who is this 'poor knight'?"

"It's not the first time this boy here, this favorite of yours, has twisted other people's words around, is it?" answered Aglaya with haughty indignation.

In each of Aglaya's angry outbursts (and she was very often angry) there was almost always, for all her apparent seriousness and implacability, something so childish, so schoolgirlish and candidly impatient that it was sometimes impossible to look at her and not laugh, to the great indignation of Aglaya herself, who did not understand what people were laughing at or "how they could dare laugh." And now her sisters were laughing, and Prince S., and even Prince Lev Nikolayevitch was smiling, though for some reason he was blushing also. Kolya roared triumphantly with laughter, Aglaya became angry in earnest, and looked twice as pretty. Her confusion was very becoming to her, and so was her indignation at her own confusion.

"As if he hadn't twisted your own words around too," she added.

"I'm only going by what you said yourself!" cried Kolya. "A month ago you were looking through *Don Quixote*, and you cried out those very words: that there was nothing better than a 'poor knight.' I don't know whom you were talking about, whether it was Don Quixote or Yevgeny Pavlovitch, or someone else. But you were talking of someone, and the conversation went on a long time."

"My dear young man, I see you let yourself go too far with your guesses," said Lizaveta Prokofyevna in vexation, cutting him short.

"But I'm not the only one," Kolya persisted. "They were all talking about it and they still are. Prince S. and Adelaïda Ivanovna declared just now that they were for the 'poor knight,' and so there must really be a 'poor knight,' and I think if it wasn't for Adelaïda Ivanovna, we would have found out long ago who this 'poor knight' is."

"What have I done?" laughed Adelaïda.

"You wouldn't draw his portrait—that's what you did! Aglaya Ivanovna asked you to draw the portrait of the 'poor knight' and even gave you the whole subject for the picture, which she'd made up herself. Remember the subject? You wouldn't do it."

"But how could I draw it? Of whom? According to the subject, that 'poor knight'

> His face from all was hid e're more
> Behind his steely visor.

So how could a face be drawn? What was I to draw? The visor? Some anonymous person?"

"I don't understand what you mean—what's this about a visor?" said Madame Yepanchin irritably, though she was beginning to have a very clear idea of who was meant by the name (doubtless agreed on long ago!) "poor knight." But what particularly outraged her was that Prince Lev Nikolayevitch appeared embarrassed too, and finally became completely disconcerted, like a boy of ten. "What is this?" she went on. "Are you going to stop this nonsense or not? Will I have an explanation of this 'poor knight' or won't I? Is it such a terrible secret we can't touch on it?"

But they only went on laughing. At last Prince S. intervened.

"It's simply that there's a strange Russian poem about a 'poor knight,'" he said, clearly anxious to close the subject and change the conversation, "a fragment with neither a beginning or an end. About a month ago we were all laughing together after dinner and, as usual, looking for a subject for Adelaïda Ivanovna's next picture. You know it's an old family enterprise to try to find subjects for Adelaïda Ivanovna's pictures. Then we hit on the 'poor knight'—which of us first I don't remember."

"Aglaya Ivanovna!" cried Kolya.

"I dare say it could be, but I don't remember," Prince S. went on. "Some of us laughed at this subject, others said that nothing could be greater, but that the 'poor knight' had to have a face. We began to run through the faces of all our friends, but no one seemed right. And that's how we left it. That's all. And I fail to understand why Nikolai Ardaliono-vitch has seen fit to remember it all and bring it up again? What was amusing and to the point before is completely un-interesting now."

"It's because there's some new foolishness back of it that's malicious and offensive," snapped Lizaveta Prokofyevna.

"There's no foolishness of any kind, nothing but the deep-est respect," Aglaya suddenly said, quite unexpectedly, in a grave and earnest voice.

She had overcome her embarrassment by now and had completely recovered herself. Moreover, just to look at her one could tell from certain signs that she was now delighted herself that the joke was going on and on. This whole rever-sal of her attitude had taken place in a single instant, when the prince's increasing embarrassment and distress had reached the point that it was obvious to everyone.

"First they laugh like crazy people, and now we have deep-est respect! They're mad! Why respect! Tell me at once why for no reason at all you suddenly drag in deepest respect?"

Aglaya replied to her mother's almost spiteful question in the same grave, earnest voice.

"Deepest respect because this poem presents a man who is capable of having an ideal and, what's more, who having set himself an ideal believes in it, and having believed in it blindly devotes his whole life to it. This does not always hap-pen in our days. The poem doesn't say exactly what the 'poor knight's' ideal was, but it's clear that it's some kind of bright vision, 'a vision of pure beauty,' and the enamored knight even wears, instead of a scarf, a rosary around his neck. It's true there is also some sort of obscure motto, which is unex-plained: the letters A.N.B., which he has drawn on his shield."

"A.M.D.*," corrected Kolya.

"But I say A.N.B., and that's what I want to say," said Ag-laya with vexation. "But however it is, it's clear that this poor knight did not care what his lady was or what she did. It was enough for him that he'd chosen her and believed in her pure beauty and then did homage to her forever. That's his merit: that if she became a thief, he would still be bound to believe in her and break lances for her pure beauty. The poet apparently wanted to unite in one striking figure the whole great conception of medieval courtly love, as experienced by a pure and high-minded knight. Of course it's all an ideal. In the 'poor knight' the feeling has reached its highest degree, asceticism. One has to admit that it means a lot to be capable of such a feeling, and that to have such a feeling implies a deep trait of character, one which is in a certain way laudable—not even to mention Don Quixote. The 'poor knight' is the same Don Quixote, but a serious one and not comic. At first I didn't understand and I laughed, but now I love the 'poor knight,' and, most of all, I respect his deeds of valor."

Aglaya finished and it was difficult to tell by looking at her whether she was serious or laughing.

"Well, he was some kind of fool, with his deeds of valor," decided the general's wife. "And you, young lady, are talking a lot of nonsense—a whole lecture. It doesn't become you if you ask me. In any case, it's not proper. What poem? Recite it. I'm sure you know it! I absolutely must know this poem. I've never in my life been able to stand poetry—as if I had a premonition. For heaven's sake, Prince, have patience. It seems that you and I must be patient together," she addressed Prince Lev Nikolayevitch. She was very irritated.

Prince Lev Nikolayevitch wanted to say something, but he was still too embarrassed to speak. Only Aglaya, who had taken such liberties in her "lecture," was not in the least embarrassed, but rather seemed pleased. She got up at once, all grave and serious as before, looking as if she was already prepared and was only waiting to be asked, went to the middle of the veranda, and stood before the prince, who remained sitting in his armchair. Everyone looked at her with surprise, and almost everyone—Prince S., her sisters, and her mother—looked on in discomfort at this new prank being played, which had somehow already gone too far. But it was clear that Aglaya delighted in the very affectation with which she began the ceremony of reciting the poem. Lizaveta Prokofyevna was about to chase her back to her seat, but at the instant Aglaya began to declaim the well-known ballad, two new visitors, talking loudly, entered the veranda from the street. They were General Ivan Fyodorovitch Yepanchin and, following him, a young man. Their arrival caused a slight commotion.

Chapter SEVEN

∽✹∾

The young man accompanying the general was about twenty-eight, tall and well built, with a handsome, intelligent face and large bright black eyes full of wit and mockery. Aglaya did not even look around at him but went on reciting the poem, still affecting to look at no one but the prince and addressing herself only to him. It became clear to the prince that she was doing all this with some special object. But at least the new arrivals somewhat lessened the awkwardness of his position. Seeing them, he got up, nodded amiably to the general from a distance, giving him a sign not to interrupt the reading, and managed to retreat behind the armchair, resting his left arm on the back of it, and continued listening to the ballad in a position which was, so to speak, more comfortable and less "funny" than before. For her part Lizaveta Prokofyevna twice motioned peremptorily to the newcomers to stand still. The prince, by the way, was greatly interested in this new visitor of his who accompanied the general. He guessed that he must be Yevgeny Pavlovitch Radomsky, of whom he had already heard a great deal and thought about more than once. He was perplexed only by his civilian dress; he had heard that Yevgeny Pavlovitch was a military man. A mocking smile played across the young man's lips the whole time the poem was being read, as if he too had heard something about the "poor knight."

"Perhaps it was his idea," thought the prince to himself.

But it was quite different with Aglaya. All the affectation and pomposity with which she had begun the recitation she now concealed under such seriousness and penetration into the spirit and meaning of the poetic work, speaking each word with such understanding, with such noble simplicity that at the end of the reading she not only held everyone's complete attention but by rendering the lofty spirit of the ballad had even partly justified that exaggerated and affected self-importance with which she had so solemnly stepped to the center of the veranda. Now this gravity might have been taken for no more than her unlimited and perhaps naïve respect for the poem which she had undertaken to render. Her eyes shone, and twice a faint, scarcely perceptible tremor of inspiration and ecstasy passed over her beautiful face. She recited:

Lived a knight once, poor and plain,*
Silent, simple, and pure;
His face was sorrowful and pale
But his spirit was bold and sure.

He had a vision before his eyes,
Mysterious and dark,
And deep did the mark of the vision lie
Graven in his heart.

Not a glance to women would he ever cast,
His soul burned like the sun,
He swore from his lips would never pass
A word to any one.

Around his neck a chaplet he wore
In place of a lady's favor;
His face from all was hid e're more
Behind his steely visor.

Full of pure love and always true
To his one exquisite dream,
N.F.B.—these letters he drew
In blood upon his shield.

And in the deserts of Palestine
From among the rocks there came
Rising to battle the paladins,
Calling their ladies' names.

Lumen coeli, sancta Rosa!
Wild and fierce he shouted;
As by a thunderclap his foes
The Musselmans were routed.

Returning to his distant castle,
He lived a lonely season,
Ever sad and ever silent,
And died, bereft of reason.

Recalling this moment afterward the prince was for a long time in doubt and troubled by a question he found it impossible to answer: how could such sincere and beautiful feeling be joined with such unmistakable malice and mockery? That it was mockery he had no doubt, he understood that clearly and for good reason during the recitation Aglaya had taken the liberty of changing the letters A.M.D. to N.F.B. That this was no mistake on her part and that he had not misheard her he could have no doubt (it was later proved). In any case Aglaya's performance—a joke of course, though too harsh and thoughtless—was premeditated. Everyone had been talking (and "laughing") about the poor knight for a month. And yet, as the prince was later to recall, Aglaya pronounced those letters with no trace of jest or derision, or any emphasis to set forth their meaning, but on the contrary she uttered them with the same imperturbable seriousness, the same innocent and naïve simplicity; so that one might have thought those were the very letters in the ballad printed in the book. The prince suddenly felt distressed. Lizaveta Prokofyevna of course neither noticed nor understood the change of letters, nor the allusion in it. General Ivan Fyodorovitch understood only that a poem had been recited. Many of the other listeners did understand and were surprised by the boldness of what she had done and the intention behind it, but they kept silent and tried not to show that they understood. But Yevgeny Pavlovitch (the prince was ready to wager his life on it) had not only understood but was trying to show that he understood; he smiled far too mockingly.

"What a lovely thing!" cried the general's wife with sincere delight as soon as the recitation was over. "Whose poem is it?"

"Pushkin's, *Maman!*" exclaimed Adelaïda. "Don't put us to shame, it's disgraceful!"

"With daughters like you around it's a wonder I'm not sillier than I am!" Lizaveta Prokofyevna replied bitterly. "Disgraceful! The moment we get home you will kindly give me that poem of Pushkin's."

"But I don't think we even have a Pushkin."

"I believe," said Alexandra, "that from time immemorial there've been two battered volumes lying around."

"Then we must immediately send someone to town to buy one—Fyodor or Alexey by the first train—Alexey would be best. Aglaya, come here! Kiss me, you recited that beautifully —but if you spoke it sincerely," she added almost in a whisper, "I feel sorry for you. If you read it to make fun of him, I don't approve of your feelings, so in either case it would

272

have been better not to have read at all. Understand? Run along, young lady, I have more to say to you, but we've stayed too long."

Meanwhile the prince was greeting General Ivan Fyodorovitch and the general was introducing Yevgeny Pavlovitch Radomsky to him.

"I met him on the way here, he was coming from the station and he heard I was coming here, and that the rest of us were here—"

"I heard you were here too," Yevgeny Pavlovitch interrupted, "and since I had long ago made up my mind to seek not only your acquaintance but your friendship I wanted to waste no time. You are ill? I only heard just now."

"I am perfectly well and very glad to meet you," Lev Nikolayevitch replied, offering his hand. "I have heard a lot about you and even spoken of you with Prince S."

Mutual courtesies were exchanged, they shook hands and looked intently into each other's eyes. A moment later the conversation became general. The prince noticed (he noticed everything now, quickly and avidly, and sometimes, possibly, what was not there at all) that Yevgeny Pavlovitch's civilian clothes excited a general and very marked surprise, so much in fact that for a while everything else was put out of mind. One might suppose that this change of dress implied something of great consequence. Adelaïda and Alexandra questioned Yevgeny Pavlovitch in bewilderment. His relative, Prince S., did so with much concern; the general spoke almost with emotion. Aglaya alone looked at Yevgeny Pavlovitch completely calmly, though with curiosity, as if she was simply trying to decide whether civilian or military dress suited him better, but after a minute she turned away and did not look at him again. Lizaveta Prokofyevna did not wish to ask any questions either, though she too was perhaps rather concerned. It appeared to the prince that Yevgeny Pavlovitch was not in her good graces.

"He amazed me, bowled me over," Ivan Fyodorovitch repeated in answer to all questions. "I couldn't believe it when I met him a little while ago in Petersburg. And why so suddenly? That's the mystery. He's the one who's always saying there's no point in going off the deep end."

From the talk that followed it appeared that Yevgeny Pavlovitch had been announcing his intention to retire for a long time but that each time he spoke of it so lightly that it had been impossible to take him seriously. But then he always spoke of serious things in such a joking manner that it was impossible to make him out, especially when he did not choose to be made out.

"It's only a certain time, a few months, a year at most, that I'll spend in retirement," said Radomsky laughing.

"But there was no need for it. That is, as far as I understand your situation," the general cried excitedly.

"But to visit my estates? You advised it yourself. Besides, I want to go abroad."

However, the subject was soon changed, though the prince was aware of continuing uneasiness so extraordinarily pronounced that he was certain there was some special reason for it.

"So the 'poor knight' is on the scene again," Yevgeny Pavlovitch asked, approaching Aglaya.

To the prince's surprise, she looked at him in a puzzled, questioning way, as if she wanted him to know that there could be no mention of the "poor knight" between them, and that she did not even understand his question.

"But it's too late, it's too late now to send to town for Pushkin! It's too late!" Kolya was arguing with Lizaveta Prokofyevna, urging the point as forcefully as he could. "For the thousandth time, it's too late!"

"Yes, in fact it is too late to send to town now," Yevgeny Pavlovitch intervened here too, hurriedly leaving Aglaya. "I believe the Petersburg shops are closed by now, it's after eight." He took out his watch to confirm this.

"We've gone this long without thinking about it, we can wait till tomorrow," put in Adelaïda.

"Besides," added Kolya, "it isn't proper for society people to be too interested in literature. Ask Yevgeny Pavlovitch. It's much more correct to care about a yellow charabanc with red wheels."

"You're talking right out of a book again, Kolya," said Adelaïda.

"But the only way he ever talks is out of books," said Yevgeny Pavlovitch. "He takes whole sentences from the periodicals. I've had the pleasure of knowing Nikolai Ardalionovitch's conversation for a long time, but for once he's not talking out of a book. Nikolai Ardalionovitch is obviously referring to my own yellow charabanc with red wheels. Except that I have exchanged it, and you are behind the times."

The prince was listening attentively to what Radomsky was saying. He thought he managed himself superbly—modestly and cheerfully—and he was particularly pleased to hear him reply as equal to equal and in a friendly manner to Kolya, who was trying to provoke him.

274

"What's this?" asked Lizaveta Prokofyevna, addressing Lebedev's daughter Vera, who stood before her holding several large books, handsomely bound and almost new.

"Pushkin," said Vera. "Our Pushkin. Papa asked me to present it to you."

"Did he? Did he really?" Lizaveta Prokofyevna demanded in surprise.

"Not as a present! Not as a present! I wouldn't take the liberty," cried Lebedev, jumping out from behind his daughter. "At cost price. This is our own family Pushkin, Annenkof's edition, impossible to find nowadays—at cost price. I offer it to you with reverence, wishing to sell it to you and so to satisfy the noble impatience of Your Excellency's noble literary feelings."

"Well, if you're selling them—thank you. You won't be the loser by it, I'm sure. But please don't play the clown, sir. I've heard about you, they say you're very well read, and we'll have a talk one day. Will you bring over the books yourself?"

"With veneration and respect!" said Lebedev with a smirking expression and—extraordinarily satisfied—he snatched the books away from his daughter.

"Just take care you don't lose them. Bring them—without the respect, for all I care—but only on condition," she added looking him over carefully, "that I only admit you as far as the door, since I don't intend to receive you today. You could send your daughter Vera at once, if you wish. I like her very much."

"Why don't you tell them about those people?" said Vera impatiently to her father. "If they're left as they are, they'll come in by themselves, they're making a racket already." She turned to the prince, who had already picked up his hat. "Lev Nikolayevitch, some people have come to see you some time ago, four men, and they're grumbling, but Papa won't let them see you."

"Who are these visitors?" asked the prince.

"They say they've come on business, but they're the kind who if you don't let them in now they'll stop you in the street. Lev Nikolayevitch, you'd better let them in and have it over with. Gavril Ardalionovitch and Ptitsyn are out there talking to them—but they won't listen."

"Pavlishchev's son! Pavlishchev's son! He's not worth it! He's not worth it!" cried Lebedev, waving his arms about. "There's no point in listening to them, and it's not right for you, illustrious Prince, to disturb yourself on their account. No indeed. They are not worth it!"

"Pavlishchev's son! Good Lord!" exclaimed the prince,

greatly perturbed. "I know—but I—I asked Gavril Ardalion-ovitch to take care of that Gavril Ardalionovitch told me just now—"

But Gavril Ardalionovitch had already come from inside onto the veranda, Ptitsyn followed him. In the next room there was an uproar, and General Ivolgin seemed to be trying to outshout several others. Kolya ran inside toward the source of the noise.

"This is very interesting!" observed Yevgeny Pavlovitch aloud.

"So he knows about it!" thought the prince.

"What son of Pavlishchev? And—how can there be a son of Pavlishchev?" General Ivan Fyodorovitch asked in bewilderment, looking at everyone with curiosity and finding to his amazement that he was the only one who knew nothing of this new affair.

For indeed the expectation and excitement were general. The prince was profoundly astonished that an entirely personal matter of his own had already aroused such strong interest in everyone present.

"It will be a very good thing if you settle this business at once *yourself* and let us all be your witnesses," said Aglaya, going up to the prince with particular earnestness. "They're trying to drag you through the mud, Prince, and you must acquit yourself triumphantly—and I'm terribly glad for you beforehand."

"I too would like to see a stop put to this odious claim at last," declared the general's wife. "Get after them, Prince. Don't spare them! My ears have been buzzing with this thing, and I've been spoiling my temper for your sake. Besides, it will be interesting to look at them. Call them in and we'll sit down. Aglaya has a good idea." She turned and addressed herself to Prince S. "Have you heard something about this, Prince?"

"Of course I have, and at your house," replied Prince S., "but I want particularly to have a look at these young people."

"These are the ones who are nihilists, aren't they?"

"No, madam, they are not what you'd call nihilists," said Lebedev, suddenly stepping forward shaking with excitement. "They're something else, madam—different altogether. My nephew has told me they have gone further than the nihilists. You are wrong if you think they will be intimidated by your presence, Your Excellency; they won't be intimidated. Nihilists are sometimes informed people, after all, learned; but these—they have gone further, madam, because before any-

276

thing else they're businessmen. This is actually a sort of result of nihilism, but not a direct one, more by hearsay and round-about ways; and they don't express themselves in any little newspaper articles but in direct action, madam; not in disputes over whether Pushkin was inept, for example, or the necessity of breaking up Russia into parts, there's no question of that; no, madam, they now take it as a right that if they want something bad enough there's no reason to stop at any limit, even if to achieve their aim they might have to do in eight or ten people along the way. In any case, Prince, I wouldn't advise you—"

But the prince had already gone to open the door for the visitors.

"You are slandering them, Lebedev," he said, smiling. "Your nephew has been worrying you about them. Don't believe him, Lizaveta Prokofyevna. I assure you that Gorskys and Danilovs are special cases, and these are only mistaken. But I would prefer not to see them here, with everyone. Excuse me, Lizaveta Prokofyevna, but they will come in, I'll present them, and then take them away. Come in, gentlemen!"

He was more worried by another thought which was painful to him. He wondered whether this whole thing had been prearranged, for this very time and hour, before these very witnesses, to bring about his disgrace and not his triumph? But then he was very saddened at his own "monstrous and evil suspiciousness." He felt he would have died had anyone known he had such a thought in mind; and just as his new guests were arriving he was sincerely ready to believe that he among all those around him was morally the very lowest of the low.

Five persons came out; four of them the new visitors and the fifth General Ivolgin, who was following them in a state of intense agitation and vigorous eloquence. "He is certainly for me," thought the prince with a smile. Kolya slipped in with the others. He was talking heatedly with Hippolite, who was one of the new arrivals; Hippolite listened with a grin.

The prince had his visitors sit down. They were all so young, hardly grown up in fact, that one could wonder about what had brought them there and at the formality of it all. Ivan Fyodorovitch Yepanchin, for one, who knew nothing about this "new affair," actually became indignant at the spectacle of so much youth, and certainly would have made some kind of objection had he not been stopped by his wife's ardent and unaccountable interest in the prince's private concerns. He remained, however; partly out of curiosity and partly out of the goodness of his heart, hoping in fact to be of help, and in any event to be on hand to exercise his authority. But General Ivolgin's bow to him, made from a distance when he came out, aroused his indignation anew. He frowned and made up his mind to say absolutely nothing.

Of the four young visitors there was one however who could have been thirty: the retired lieutenant who had been one of Rogozhin's gang, the boxer, "who had in his time given fifteen roubles to beggars." It could be surmised that he had come along with the others as a loyal friend, to stand by them and if the need arose to back them up. Of the rest, the foremost and most prominent was the one known as "Pavlishchev's son," though he introduced himself as Antip Burdovsky. He was a young man, poorly and slovenly dressed in a coat whose sleeves were shiny with grease, an equally greasy waistcoat buttoned to the top, with no trace of linen and an impossibly filthy black silk scarf twisted into a rope around his neck. His hands were unwashed, his face exceedingly pimply, he was blond, and he wore an expression, if one may so put it, of insolent innocence. He was fairly tall, thin, and about twenty-two. Not a sign of irony or introspection showed in his face; on the contrary, it expressed an absolutely blank enchantment with what he took for his rights and at the same time some sort of strange craving to be and to feel constantly insulted. He spoke emotionally, hurriedly, stumbling over words, not pronouncing some clearly, as if he had a speech defect or was a foreigner, though he was of pure Russian descent.

He was accompanied first by Lebedev's nephew, already known to the reader, and secondly by Hippolite. Hippolite was a very young man, of perhaps seventeen or eighteen, with an intelligent but constantly irritable expression on his face, on which illness had left terrible traces. He was thin as a skeleton, pale and sallow, his eyes glistened, and two hectic spots showed on his cheeks. He coughed incessantly; each of his words, almost every breath he took were accompanied by wheezing. He was obviously in an advanced stage of consumption. He looked as if he had only two or three weeks left to live. He was very tired and the first to sink into a chair. The others were stiff with ceremony as they entered, and embarrassed; they looked as important as they could, however, and were plainly in fear of losing their dignity somehow, a concern plainly out of keeping with their reputation for denying useless social observances, prejudices, and almost everything else in the world except their own interests.

"Antip Burdovsky," said "Pavlishchev's son" hurriedly, stuttering.

"Vladimir Doktorenko," Lebedev's nephew introduced himself, clearly and distinctly as though proud of the name Doktorenko.

"Keller," muttered the retired lieutenant.

"Hippolite Terentyev," squeaked the last in an unexpectedly shrill voice.

At last they were all seated in a row of chairs facing the prince, all having introduced themselves, frowned, and shifted their caps from one hand to the other, to keep their spirits up. All of them were ready to speak, but they all remained silent, waiting with an air of importance which seemed to say, "Nonsense, my friend, you won't take us in." One felt that the moment any one of them uttered a word they would all speak immediately, interrupting and trying to outtalk each other.

Chapter EIGHT

"Gentlemen, I was not expecting any of you," began the prince. "I have been sick until today, and a month ago I asked Gavril Ardalionovitch Ivolgin to deal with your business" (he turned to Antip Burdovsky), "as I informed you at the time. However, I have no objection to explaining myself personally, only you must agree that at this hour—I suggest you come with me into another room, if it won't be long—My friends are here now, and believe me—"

"Friends—as many as you like," interrupted Lebedev's nephew suddenly in an authoritative tone, though without raising his voice, "but allow us to say that you could have treated us more politely and not had us wait two hours in your servants' quarters."

"And of course—I too—it's just like a prince! And you—you must be the general! Well, I'm not your servant! And I, I—" suddenly sputtered Antip Burdovsky in a state of extraordinary emotion, his lips trembling, a hurt tremor in his voice, saliva flying from his mouth; but he was in such a rush to speak that after ten words it became impossible to understand him.

"This was just like a prince!" cried Hippolite in a shrill cracked voice.

"If this had happened to me," growled the boxer, "that is, if this had anything to do with me personally, if I was in Burdovsky's place, as a man of honor, I—"

"Gentlemen, I only heard this minute that you were here, I assure you," said the prince.

"We're not afraid of your friends, Prince, no matter who they are, because we're within our rights," Lebedev's nephew declared.

"Allow me to ask you, sir," cried Hippolite shrilly again, by now greatly excited, "what right you had to submit Burdovsky's case to the judgment of your friends? Perhaps we won't choose to accept their judgment. It's pretty clear what it might turn out to be!"

"But here now, after all, Mr. Burdovsky," the prince managed at last to get in a word, greatly amazed by such an overture, "if you don't wish to speak here, I'm telling you we can go at once into another room, and I repeat I only this minute heard of you all—"

"But you've no right, you've no right, you've no right! Your friends— There!" Burdovsky suddenly babbled again, looking around wildly and apprehensively, growing all the more excited as he became more fearful and mistrustful. "You've got no right." And having said this, he stopped abruptly as if he had been interrupted, and without a word opened wide his bulging, myopic eyes, with their heavy red veins, and leaning his whole body forward stared interrogatingly at the prince. This time the prince was so taken aback he too was speechless and only looked back at him wide-eyed without saying anything.

"Lev Nikolayevitch!" Lizaveta Prokofyevna suddenly called out, "read this at once, this very minute, it has directly to do with your affair."

She hastily held out to him a copy of a weekly humorous newspaper and pointed to an article. As the new visitors had been coming in, Lebedev had quickly sidled up to Lizaveta Prokofyevna, with whom he wished to ingratiate himself, and without a word drawn this paper from his side pocket and held it before her indicating a column circled in pencil. What Lizaveta Prokofyevna had had time to read aroused and upset her extremely.

"But wouldn't it be better not to read it aloud," protested the prince, very embarrassed. "I'd rather read it alone—later."

Lizaveta Prokofyevna turned to Kolya. "Then you'd better read it, at once, aloud!" Impatiently, she snatched the paper away from the prince, who had barely had time to touch it. "Read it aloud to everyone, so that everyone may hear."

Lizaveta Prokofyevna was a quick-tempered and impulsive lady, so that sometimes, without reflection, she would suddenly weigh all anchors and sail out into the open sea paying no attention to the weather. Ivan Fyodorovitch stirred uneasily. But while they all hesitated in perplexity in that first minute, Kolya unfolded the paper and began reading aloud at the place Lebedev had rushed over to indicate to him.

"PROLETARIANS AND NOBLE SCIONS, AN EPISODE OF DAILY AND EVERYDAY ROBBERY! PROGRESS! REFORM! JUSTICE!

"Strange things are happening in our so-called Holy Russia, in our age of reforms and capitalistic enterprises, a time of nationalism and hundreds of millions of roubles sent abroad each year, an age of encouragement of industry and the paralysis of work, etcetera, etcetera, it can't all be enumerated, gentlemen, and therefore straight to the point. A strange incident has happened involving one of the scions of our defunct landed gentry (*de profundis!*), one of those noble scions, however, whose grandfathers completely ruined themselves at roulette, whose fathers were forced to serve as subalterns in the army, and who usually died while on trial for some innocent deficiencies of money in their care, and whose children, like the hero of our story, either grow up as idiots or become involved in criminal cases, in which, however, they are acquitted by the jury on the pretext they have been warned and will mend their ways, or else they end up by creating one of these incidents which astound the public and disgrace our already disgraceful times. Our scion, wearing gaiters like a foreigner and shivering in an unlined overcoat, in wintertime, returned six months ago to Russia from Switzerland where he was being treated for idiocy (*sic!*). It must be admitted that he was blessed with good luck, for—to say nothing of the interesting illness for which he was being treated in Switzerland (though can there be any treatment for idiocy? just think of such a thing!)—his case could prove the exactness of the Russian proverb, 'Happiness is for fools.' Judge for yourselves: left as a baby after the death of his father, who as a lieutenant was said to have died while under trial for the disappearance of all his company's pay at cards, or possibly for excessive zeal in beating a subordinate (those were the good old days, remember, gentlemen!), our nobleman was taken out of charity to be brought up by a very rich

281

Russian landowner. This Russian landowner—let us call him P.—was the proud possessor in that golden time of four thousand souls—serfs (serfsouls! do you understand such expressions, gentlemen? I do not. I must depend on a good dictionary; 'a thing quite recent, but beyond belief!')—and was apparently one of these Russian idlers and parasites who spend their empty lives abroad, in the summer at spas and in the winter at the Château-de-Fleurs in Paris, where in the course of their lives they have left extraordinary sums of money. One may say with certainty that at least a third of the tribute paid in the old days by the serfs to their owners was diverted to the pockets of the proprietor of the Parisian Château-de-Fleurs (lucky man!). Be that as it may, the care-free P. brought up the little orphaned nobleman in the princely manner, hiring tutors and governesses for him (undoubtedly pretty ones), whom incidently he brought from Paris himself. But the last scion in the noble line was an idiot. The governesses from the Château-de-Fleurs could do nothing about it, and at the age of twenty our pupil had not learned to speak any language, not even Russian. Though the latter deficiency is of course excusable. Finally a fantastic idea entered P.'s serf-owning brain: that the idiot be taught some sense in Switzerland—an idea which while fantastic was logical: the parasite property-owner could naturally assume that intelligence could be bought on the market for cash, especially in Switzerland. Five years were devoted to treatment in Switzerland with a certain well-known professor, and thousands were spent. Obviously the idiot did not become intelligent, but they say he did unquestionably become more or less like a human being. Very suddenly P. died. There was no will, of course, and as usual his affairs were in disorder. There was a whole crowd of greedy heirs who cared nothing about the last scions of noble families who are cured out of charity for congenital idiocy in Switzerland. The scion, though an idiot, nevertheless tried to trick the professor, and for two years managed to have himself taken care of gratis, it was said, concealing from him the death of his benefactor. But the professor was something of a charlatan himself. Alarmed, at last, by the lack of payment and more than anything else by the appetite of his twenty-five-year-old parasite, he dressed him up in his old gaiters, made him a present of his worn-out coat, and, out of charity, sent him off on the third-class coach *nach Russland*—out of Switzerland and off his hands. It appeared that luck had turned its back on our hero. But not at all: fortune, which kills off whole provinces with famine showers her gifts at once on this little aristocrat, like the cloud in Krylov's fable that passed over the parched fields and emptied over the ocean. At almost the very moment of his arrival in Petersburg from Switzerland a relative of his mother (needless to say, of the merchant class) died in Moscow, a childless old bachelor, a bearded merchant and Old Believer, leaving a fortune of several millions in good, clean, hard cash (if it was only to you and me, dear reader!), all of it to our scion, all of it to our little nobleman who has been treated for idiocy in Switzerland! Well, now the tune changes. Suddenly a whole crowd of friends and acquaintances gathered around our lordling-in-gaiters, who had begun paying court to a certain notorious and beautiful kept woman; even relatives turned up, and most striking of all there were whole packs of noble—and nubile—young ladies all slavering after legal matrimony. And what could be better? An aristocrat, a millionaire, and an idiot—all the necessary qualifications at once; a husband such as is not to be found even with the aid of a lantern—or to be had on order!"

"That I simply do not understand!" cried Ivan Fyodorovitch, in great indignation.

"Stop, Kolya!" pleaded the prince. There were outcries on all sides.

"Read it! Read it, no matter what!" snapped Lizaveta Prokofyevna, evidently making a great effort to restrain herself. "Prince! If you stop him reading we shall quarrel."

Nothing was to be done. Kolya, all flushed and excited, began reading again in an agitated voice.

"But while our newly hatched millionaire was, so to speak, in seventh heaven, a completely unexpected development occurred. One fine morning a certain visitor called on him, a man with a calm, stern countenance, attired modestly but with distinction, courteous but dignified and of a clearly progressive turn of mind, reasonable in his speech, who in a few words explained the reason for his visit. He was a well-known lawyer and had been entrusted with a certain affair by a young man and was appearing on his behalf. This young man was no more or less than the son of the late P., though he bears another name. In his youth the lustful P. had seduced a virtuous young girl, a house-serf but with a European education (here, of course, he no doubt took advantage of the seignorial rights of the old serf-owning days); noticing the approach of the inevitable consequence of his liaison, he gave her to be married as soon as possible to a certain man of honorable character who was engaged in commerce and even had a civil service position, who had been in love with the girl for a long time. At first he helped the newlyweds, but soon his help was refused, owning to the honorable character of the husband. Some time passed, and little by little P. managed to forget about the young girl and the child he had had by her, and later, as we have seen, he died without having made provisions. Meanwhile, his son, who was born in legal wedlock but who had grown up under a different name, having been completely adopted owing to the honorable character of his mother's husband, who had however died subsequently, was thrown completely on his own resources with a suffering invalid mother who was crippled and lived in one of the remote provinces. He earned his living in the capital by respectable work, giving lessons in merchant families, supporting himself at first through school and then while he attended lectures with a view to his future advancement. But how much can one earn from a Russian merchant at ten kopecks an hour, especially with a crippled mother, whose eventual death in the remote province hardly relieved his situation at all? Now the question arises: how, in all justice, should our young scion have reasoned? Of course you are thinking, dear reader, that he said to himself, 'All my life I have enjoyed P.'s gifts, tens of thousands have gone to Switzerland for my education, my governesses, and my treatment for idiocy; and I have millions now, while P.'s son, honorable of character and in no way guilty of the actions of a wanton father who forgot him, is wasting away giving lessons. All that was spent for me should by rights have been spent for him. Those huge sums spent on me were not in reality mine. It was nothing but a blind error of fortune; they should have gone to P.'s son; they should have been used for his benefit and not for mine, as only happened through the fantastic caprice of the frivolous and forgetful P. Had I been perfectly honorable, considerate, and just, I would have given half of all my inheritance to his son, but since I am above all a prudent man, and know all too well that this is not a legal matter, I will therefore not give him half of my millions. But at the very least it would be too base and shameless (and, the scion had forgotten to add, imprudent) on my part not to give his son back those tens of thousands which P. spent on my idiocy. This is only right and proper! For what would have become of me if P. had not brought me up and instead of me taken care of his own son?'

"But no, gentlemen! Our scions of nobility do not reason this way. In spite of the representations of the young man's lawyer, who had come to speak for him solely out of friendship, almost against his will, almost under duress, in spite of his pointing out the necessity of honor, generosity, and even ordinary self-interest, the Swiss pupil remained unmoved—and what do you think? All this would be nothing, but here is something really unforgivable and which cannot be excused by any illness, however interesting: this millionaire who had only just stepped out of his professor's gaiters could not even understand that this noble person who was killing himself giving lessons was not asking for charity or assistance but for his own right and his due, though not by legal obligations, and that he was not even asking himself but that friends were intervening on his account. With a majestic air, and reveling in his power suddenly to be able to crush people with his millions, our scion pulls out a fifty-rouble bill and sends it to the noble young man as an insulting piece of charity. You don't believe it, gentlemen? You are shocked, you are pained, you utter outcries of indignation; but this is nonetheless what he did! It goes without saying that the money was immediately returned to him, flung back in his face so to speak. But what is to be done next? It is not a legal matter, there is no recourse but publicity! We pass this story along to the public with the guarantee of its authenticity. We learn that one of our better-known humorists has even come forth with a most delightful epigram, worthy not only of a place among sketches of provincial manners but also among those of the capital:

> Little Lyova five years stayed
> Snug in Schneider's cloak,
> Passing time the usual way
> With stupid little jokes.
> Returning in his gaiters tight,
> He inherited a million,
> He says his Russian prayers at night
> And next day robs schoolchildren.

When Kolya had finished he quickly handed the paper to the prince and, without a word, rushed to a corner of the room and huddled there, burying his face in his hands. He was unbearably ashamed, and his youthful sensitivity, not yet accustomed to filth, was outraged. It seemed to him that something extraordinary had happened, which had destroyed everything, and that he was almost the cause of it by the fact he had read the paper aloud.

But everyone else, too, seemed to feel something of the kind.

The girls felt very awkward and ashamed. Lizaveta Prokofyevna was struggling to contain her violent anger and was also, perhaps, regretting bitterly that she had meddled in the matter. Now she was silent. The prince was undergoing what excessively shy people often experience in such cases: he was so ashamed of the conduct of others, he was so ashamed for his guests, that at the first moment he did not even dare look at them. Ptitsyn, Ganya, Varya, even Lebedev—everyone appeared rather embarrassed. Strangest of all, Hippolite and "Pavlishchev's son" also appeared to be rather surprised; Lebedev's nephew, too, was obviously displeased. Only the boxer sat completely serene, twisting his moustache with an air of importance with his eyes lowered not from embarrassment but on the contrary, it seemed, out of superior modesty, his sense of triumph being all too apparent. From every indication it was obvious that he was delighted with the article.

"What a devil of a thing," muttered Ivan Fyodorovitch. "It's as if fifty lackeys had gotten together to compose it."

"But a-allow me to ask you, my dear sir," declared Hippolite, trembling all over, "how can you dare insult people with such suppositions?"

"That—that—that to an honorable man—you must agree yourself, General, that if it's an honorable man—it's insulting!" growled the boxer, who had suddenly for some reason become aroused, twisting his moustache as his body and shoulders began to twitch.

"In the first place I'm not your dear sir, and in the second I have no intention of giving you any explanations," replied Ivan Fyodorovitch sharply. He had become extremely irritated and got up from his place and without a word went to the entrance of the veranda and stood on the top step with his back to the company, highly indignant with Lizaveta Prokofyevna, who even then seemed not to have thought of stirring from her seat.

"Gentlemen, gentlemen, let me speak at last, gentlemen!" cried the prince in distress and agitation. "And I beg you, let us talk in a way we can understand each other. I say nothing, gentlemen, about this article; let it be. Except just one thing, gentlemen: what the article says is all untrue; I say this and you know it yourselves. It's shameful! So I'd be really surprised if one of you wrote it."

'I knew nothing about this article until this very moment," announced Hippolite. "I don't approve of this article."

"Though I knew it was written, still I—I wouldn't have advised it be published either, because it's too soon," added Lebedev's nephew.

"I knew, but I have the right—I—" muttered "Pavlish-chev's son."

"What! Were you the one who made all this up?" asked the prince, looking with curiosity at Burdovsky. "It can't be true!"

"One might not recognize your right to ask such questions," Lebedev's nephew interposed.

"I was only surprised that Mr. Burdovsky had managed to —but I mean to say, if you've already given publicity to the case, why were you so offended just now when I spoke of it to my friends?"

"At last!" muttered Lizaveta Prokofyevna indignantly.

"And in fact, Prince," said Lebedev, suddenly threading his way between chairs, almost feverish and unable to control himself, "in fact you are pleased to forget that it was only through your own good will and matchless kindness of heart that you received these people and listened to them, and that they have no right to demand anything, especially since you had already put the matter in the hands of Gavril Ardalion-ovitch, and that too you did out of your excessive goodness, and that now, most illustrious Prince, being among your chosen friends you cannot sacrifice their company to these gentlemen here, sir, and you could in fact have all these gentlemen, so to speak, shown to the front steps, a thing which I, sir, as master of the house, would do with the greatest pleasure."

"Absolutely right!" General Ivolgin suddenly roared from the end of the veranda.

"Enough, Lebedev, enough, enough," began the prince, but an outburst of indignation drowned out his words.

"No, I'm sorry, Prince, I'm sorry—now it is not enough!" Lebedev's nephew shouted over the din. "Now this matter must be made clear and definite, because it is obviously not understood. Legal quibbles are being brought in, and on the strength of these quibbles we are threatened with being thrown out in the street. But is it possible, Prince, that you consider us so stupid that we don't know ourselves we have no legal grounds, and that if it was on legal grounds we wouldn't have the right to demand even a single rouble from you? Yet we do understand precisely that if there are no legal rights there are still natural, human rights, the right of common sense and the voice of the conscience; and while this right may not be written down in any rotten human code, nevertheless an honorable and honest man, which is to say a right-thinking man, is bound to remain an honorable and honest man even on points which are not set down in codes.

This is why we've come here without fear of being thrown out (as you threatened just now), for the simple reason that we've come not to *beg* but to *demand,* and as for the impropriety of our visit at such a late hour (though we did not come at a late hour, it was you who kept us waiting in the servants' room), we have come, I tell you, without fear of anything, because we took you for a man of good sense, that is, a man of honor and conscience. Yes, it is true we did not come meekly, like followers or suppliants, but with our heads high, like free men, not with any petition, but with a free and proud demand (you hear, not with a petition but a demand —understand that). We put the question to you directly and with dignity: do you consider yourself right or wrong in Burdovsky's case? Do you admit you were the beneficiary of Pavlishchev and that he very likely saved your life? If you do (and it's undeniable), do you intend, or do you consider your conscience tells you, having received millions, to compensate in turn the son of Pavlishchev in his state of need even though he bears the name of Burdovsky? Yes or no? If it's yes, that is in other words, if you have within you what in your language you call honor and conscience, and which we more precisely call by the name of good sense, then give us satisfaction and the matter is closed. Give us satisfaction without requests for gratefulness on our part. Don't expect that from us, because you are not doing it for our sake but for the sake of justice. If you are unwilling to satisfy us, that is if you answer no, then we'll leave now and the affair is ended; but we tell you straight to your face and before all your witnesses that you are a man of gross mentality and low development, and that in the future you will not dare pretend to call yourself a man of honor and conscience, that you are trying to buy that right too cheaply. I'm through. I have stated the question. Throw us out, if you dare. You can do it, you have the power. But remember that we are demanding, not begging. We are demanding, not begging!"

And Lebedev's nephew, greatly excited, fell silent.

"We're demanding, demanding, demanding, not begging!" babbled Burdovsky, turning red as a lobster.

The words of Lebedev's nephew were followed by a general commotion and even a murmur of protest, though everyone in the party was obviously avoiding any involvement in the matter, with the possible exception of Lebedev, who was in a state of heated excitement. (Strangely enough, Lebedev, though clearly on the prince's side, now seemed to feel a glow of family pride after his nephew's speech. At least, he was looking around at everyone with a certain air of satisfaction.)

"In my opinion," began the prince in a quiet voice, "in my opinion, Mr. Doktorenko, you are half right in what you have said just now, I would even say more than half; and I would be completely in agreement with you if you had not left something out of your speech. Just what you've left out I'm unable to express to you exactly, but something is certainly lacking in your words for them to be perfectly true. But let's get down to business, gentlemen; tell me, why have you published this article? There isn't a word in it that isn't a slander; so that in my opinion, gentlemen, you have done something vile."

"Just a moment!"

"My dear sir!"

"This—this—this—" cried the excited visitors all at once.

"As for the article," replied Hippolite in a shrill voice, "as for the article I've already told you that I and the others don't approve of it! It was written by him" (he pointed to the boxer who was sitting beside him), "it's written disgracefully, I admit, it's written illiterately, and in the style of retired army people like himself. He's stupid, and on top of that he's a professional opportunist, I agree, I tell him that straight to his face every day. But all the same he was half in the right. Making matters public is everyone's legal right, and therefore Burdovsky's. Let him answer for his absurdities himself. As for my protest in the name of us all against the presence of your friends, I should explain to you, ladies and gentlemen, that I protested only to assert our rights but that essentially we prefer that there be witnesses, and also that before we came here all four of us agreed that whoever your witnesses might be, even if they were your friends, they could not help but recognize Burdovsky's right (because it is obviously a mathematical certainty), and so it's even better that these witnesses should be your friends; the truth will be even more clearly evident."

"That's true, we agreed about this," confirmed Lebedev's nephew.

"Then if that's the way you wanted it, why did you make such noise and disturbance when we started to talk?" asked the prince in surprise.

"As for the article, Prince," said the boxer, extremely anxious to get his word in and becoming pleasurably excited (it could be suspected that the presence of the ladies had a strong effect on him), "as for the article I admit that I am the author of it, though my sick friend here, who I'm used to forgiving on account of his feeble condition, criticized it just now. But I wrote it and I published it in the journal of a good friend of mine, in the form of a letter to the editor. Only the lines of verse aren't mine but are actually from the pen of a well-known satirist. I only read it to Burdovsky, and not all of it either, and he agreed at once to let me publish it. But you can see for yourself that I could have published it without his agreement too. An appeal to public opinion is everyone's right, a noble and beneficial right. I hope that you yourself, Prince, are progressive enough not to deny this."

"I won't deny anything, but you must admit that in your article—"

"A bit pointed, you mean? But this, you must agree, is for the public good, so to speak, and after all how could such a provocative case as this be overlooked? It's too bad for the guilty party, but public good comes before anything else. As far as certain inaccuracies are concerned, little hyperboles, you might say, you must agree that what matters most is the initiative, what matters most is the motive, the intention. What matters is the beneficial example, one can go into the individual case afterward. And besides there's the question of style, the question of, so to speak, humorous effect, and, after all, everyone else writes like that, as you must agree yourself. Ha! Ha!"

"But you are on a completely false track, gentlemen, I assure you!" cried the prince. "You have published that article on the assumption that I would never agree to satisfy Mr. Burdovsky, so you have tried to frighten me and somehow take revenge. But how could you know? Perhaps I have decided to satisfy Burdovsky. I am telling you plainly, before everyone gathered here now, that I will do so."

"Here, at last," proclaimed the boxer, "is the wise and noble statement of a wise and noble man!"

"Good God!" exclaimed Lizaveta Prokofyevna.

"This is intolerable!" muttered the general.

"Please, everyone, please allow me to explain all this," pleaded the prince. "Five weeks ago, Mr. Burdovsky, your agent and attorney Tchebarov came to see me in Z. You've described him rather flatteringly in your article, Mr. Keller." The prince turned suddenly to the boxer, laughing. "But I didn't care for him at all. I realized from the first that this Tchebarov was at the bottom of it, and that it was probably he, Mr. Burdovsky, who by taking advantage of your simplicity induced you to start the whole thing, if I may speak frankly."

"You have no right. I'm—not simple— This is—" Burdovsky stammered in a state of emotion.

"You have no right whatever to make such assumptions," Lebedev's nephew intervened sententiously.

"This is highly insulting!" Hippolite cried shrilly. "A most insulting assumption, both untrue and irrelevant!"

"I am sorry, gentlemen, I am sorry," apologized the prince. "Please forgive me. It's because I thought it might be better for us to be completely open with each other. But it's as you please, just as you like. I told Tchebarov that since I was not in Petersburg I would immediately empower a friend of mine to act in the matter, and that I would inform you, Mr. Burdovsky, of this fact. I will tell you frankly, gentlemen, that because of the presence of Tchebarov the whole affair struck me as an outright swindle— Oh, don't take offense, gentlemen! For heaven's sake don't take offense!" cried the prince in alarm, seeing that again Burdovsky was hurt and indignant and that his friends were aroused to protest. "It has nothing to do with you personally if I say that this affair was a swindle. I didn't know any of you personally then, not even your names. I judged only by Tchebarov. I speak in a general way because—if you only knew how terribly I have been deceived ever since I came into my inheritance."

"Yes, Prince, you are of course terribly naïve," said Lebedev's nephew sarcastically.

"And on top of it a prince and a millionaire! You may possibly be somehow good and kindhearted, but that certainly doesn't make you an exception to the general rule," proclaimed Hippolite.

"Possibly, gentlemen, very possibly," said the prince hastily, "though I don't understand what general rule you're talking about. But to continue, please don't take offense for no reason. I swear I haven't the slightest desire to offend you. And really, gentlemen, one can't say a single word without your immediately becoming insulted! Now, in the first place, I was greatly astonished to hear of the existence of 'Pavlishchev's son,' and that he existed in such dreadful straits, as Tchebarov explained to me. Pavlishchev was my benefactor and a friend of my father. Oh, why did you write such untrue things about my father in your article, Mr. Keller? There was no spending of the company's funds and no maltreatment of subordinates—I am absolutely convinced of this —and how could you lift your hand to write such a calumny? And what you wrote about Pavlishchev is absolutely intolerable. You have called that most noble-hearted man lecherous and frivolous with as much boldness and assurance as if you were actually speaking the truth, while in fact he was one of the most virtuous men ever on earth! He was also a very learned man; he corresponded with many distinguished scholars and spent a great deal of money for the advancement of science. As for his generous heart and his acts of charity, oh, you were no doubt quite right in saying that I was almost an idiot then and could not understand anything (though I did speak Russian and could understand it), but now I can appreciate everything I remember for what it was."

"Excuse me," squeaked Hippolite, "but isn't all this getting too sentimental? We aren't children. You wanted to get right to the point. It's going on ten, don't forget that."

"By all means, gentlemen, by all means," the prince agreed at once. "After my initial distrust I decided I might be mistaken and that Pavlishchev might really have had a son. But I was very amazed that this son should so readily, that is to say, so publicly, give away the secret of his birth and, most particularly, would disgrace his mother. Because even then Tchebarov was already threatening me with public exposure—"

"What nonsense!" exclaimed Lebedev's nephew.

"You have no right— You have no right—" cried Burdovsky.

"A son is not responsible for his father's dissolute conduct, and the mother's not to blame!" Hippolite shrieked angrily.

"All the more reason, it seems to me, for sparing her," said the prince mildly.

"You're not simply naïve, Prince; perhaps you go even far beyond that," Lebedev's nephew said with a malicious smile.

"And what right did you have!" screeched Hippolite in a most unnatural voice.

"None at all, none whatever!" the prince put in hastily. "You are right about that, I admit it, but I couldn't help it. And I immediately said to myself at the time that I shouldn't let my personal feelings have any bearing on the matter, because if I admit I am bound to satisfy Mr. Burdovsky's demands for the sake of my feelings toward Pavlishchev, then I must satisfy them in any case no matter whether I respect Mr. Burdovsky or whether I don't. I only went into this, gentlemen, because it did still seem unnatural to me that a son would make public his mother's secret. In short, it was mostly on account of this that I decided Tchebarov must be a scoundrel and had personally maneuvered Mr. Burdovsky by deceit into such a fraud."

"But this is intolerable!" shouted the new visitors, some of whom even leapt up from their seats.

"Gentlemen! It was because of this that I decided poor Mr. Burdovsky must be a simple man, helpless, easily manipulated by swindlers, and therefore I felt all the more obliged to help him, as 'Pavlishchev's son'—first, in opposing the influence of Mr. Tchebarov, secondly in offering my devoted friendship and guidance, and thirdly, by arranging to give him ten thousand roubles, which is by my reckoning the amount Pavlishchev must have spent on me."

"What! Only ten thousand!" shouted Hippolite.

"Look here, Prince, you're not very good at arithmetic. Either that or you're too good, though you pretend to be a simpleton," said Lebedev's nephew.

"I won't agree to ten thousand," said Burdovsky.

"Antip! Take it!" the boxer prompted in a rapid but quite distinct whisper, leaning forward across the back of Hippolite's chair. "Take it, and afterward we'll see!"

"L-listen here, Mr. Myshkin," shrilled Hippolite, "understand that we're not fools, not vulgar fools as all your guests probably think, including these ladies who are sneering at us so indignantly, and especially that fine gentleman"—he pointed to Yevgeny Pavlovitch—"whom I have not, of course, the honor to know, but about whom I believe I have heard something."

"Please, gentlemen, please, you have misunderstood me again!" the prince addressed them in agitation. "First of all, Mr. Keller, in your article you have described my fortune very inaccurately. I have received no millions. I have perhaps an eighth or a tenth of what you think I have. And in the second place, no tens of thousands were spent on me in Switzerland. Schneider got six hundred roubles a year, and that was only for the first three years, and he never went to Paris for pretty governesses, that is another calumny. In my belief a great deal less than ten thousand was spent on me, but I have decided on ten thousand, and you must admit that since I am paying a debt I cannot offer Mr. Burdovsky more, even if I was extremely fond of him, and could not do so out of simple decency for the very reason that I am repaying a debt and not making him a gift. I don't see, gentlemen, how you can fail to understand that! However, I intended to do more than that later, with my friendship and active interest in the destiny of the unhappy Mr. Burdovsky, who is obviously deceived, because he clearly could not otherwise have agreed to anything so low, for example, as the commentary on his mother we have heard today in Mr. Keller's article. But why are you getting exasperated again, gentlemen? We will end by completely misunderstanding one another! To think I should have been right all along! For from what I see with my own eyes I am convinced that my guess was right." The prince was excitedly trying to persuade his listeners, hoping to quiet them, not seeing that he only increased their agitation.

"What! What are you convinced of?" They came at him in a fury.

"In the first place, I had to take a good look at Mr. Burdovsky, and I now see the sort of person he is. He is an innocent man but taken in by everyone. A defenseless man, and this is why I must spare him. And in the second place, Gavril Ardalionovitch—to whom I entrusted this matter and from whom I have heard nothing for some time because I was traveling and ill for three days in Petersburg—has now suddenly about an hour ago during our first talk together told me that he has seen through Tchebarov's scheme and that he has proofs that Tchebarov is exactly what I took him to be. Of course I do know, gentlemen, that many people consider me an idiot, and Tchebarov, knowing my reputation for giving money away readily, thought he could easily deceive me, counting directly on my feeling for Pavlishchev. But the main thing is—do listen to me, gentlemen, hear me out!—the main thing is that it suddenly appears that Mr. Burdovsky is not Pavlishchev's son at all! Gavril Ardalionovitch informed me of this just now and assures me he has definite proof. Well, what do you think about that? Incredible after all the fuss that has been made, isn't it? And listen: definite proof! I still don't quite believe it, I don't quite believe it myself, I assure you; Gavril Ardalionovitch has not had time to give me all the details; but there can be no doubt whatsoever now that Tchebarov is a scoundrel! He has deceived poor Mr. Burdovsky and all of you gentlemen who have come here so nobly in support of your friend (who obviously needs support, I do understand!); he has deceived you all and involved you all in a swindle, because it is in fact an absolutely fraudulent swindle!"

"A swindle! Not Pavlishchev's son? How is that possible!" Exclamations were heard on all sides. All of Burdovsky's backers were in a state of inexpressible dismay.

"Yes, of course it's a swindle! For if Mr. Burdovsky turns out not to be the son of Pavlishchev, Mr. Burdovsky's claim in that case becomes a pure swindle (that is, of course, if he knew the truth!), but the fact is he has been fooled, and that is why I say he deserves to be pitied for his simplicity, and cannot be left without help, otherwise he too would come out of this affair as a swindler. But I am convinced he understands nothing! I was myself in the same state before my departure for Switzerland. I too stammered incoherently—you try to say something and you find you cannot. I understand this, I can be very sympathetic because I am almost the same way myself, so I'm able to speak about it! And in any case despite the fact that he is no longer Pavlishchev's son and that this has turned out to be nothing but humbug I still have not changed my mind and am prepared to give up ten thousand in memory of Pavlishchev. Before Mr. Burdovsky's appearance I wanted to use those ten thousand for founding a school in memory of Pavlishchev, but now whether it's for the school or for Mr. Burdovsky makes no difference, for if Mr. Burdovsky is not Pavlishchev's son he is almost as good as Pavlishchev's son because he has been so wickedly deceived; he honestly believed himself to be the son of Pavlishchev! Listen to Gavril Ardalionovitch, gentlemen; let's get this over with, don't be angry, don't be excited; sit down! Gavril Ardalionovitch will explain all this to you at once, and I confess that I am extremely anxious myself to know all the details. He says he has even been to Pskov to see your mother, Mr. Burdovsky, who is not dead at all as they had you say in that article. Sit down, gentlemen, sit down!"

The prince sat down and managed to have Burdovsky's friends, who had leaped up from their seats, sit down again. For the last ten or twenty minutes he had been talking loudly and heatedly, with impatient rapidity, carried away and trying to talk over the voices of the others, to outshout everyone, and of course now he could not help bitterly regretting some of the words and allegations that had escaped him. Had he not been aroused and almost beyond control he would never have allowed himself to express aloud so flatly and hastily certain conjectures and excessively candid statements. But no sooner had he sat down again than he was struck through the heart with a burning remorse: apart from having insulted Burdovsky, by suggesting so publicly that he suffered from the same illness for which he had been treated in Switzerland; apart from this, his offer of the ten thousand which had been destined for the school was, he felt, made grossly and carelessly as an act of charity, particularly because it had been made aloud in the presence of other people. "I should have waited and offered it tomorrow, in private," the prince thought immediately, "but now it probably can't be set right! Yes, I am an idiot, a real idiot!" he decided to himself, feeling ashamed and deeply distressed.

Meanwhile Gavril Ardalionovitch, who had until now stood aside keeping a persistent silence, stepped forward at the prince's invitation, stood beside him, and began a clear and concise account of the affair which had been entrusted to him by the prince. All conversation ceased instantaneously. Everyone listened with the greatest curiosity, especially every member of Burdovsky's group.

Chapter NINE

❧

"You will not of course deny," began Gavril Ardaliono-vitch, addressing himself directly to Burdovsky, who was listening to him as hard as he could, staring wide-eyed at him and obviously in a state of great consternation, "you will certainly not want to try seriously to deny that you were born exactly two years after the legal marriage of your respected mother with Burdovsky, your father. The date of your birth can be all too easily proved by evidence, so that the distortion of this fact, so insulting to you and your mother, in Mr. Keller's article can be explained only by Mr. Keller's own lively imagination, he thinking thereby to strengthen your claim and so to advance your interests. Mr. Keller says that he had read you this article beforehand, though not all of it —he undoubtedly did not read as far as this passage—"

"No, as a matter of fact," said the boxer, "but all the facts were given to me by a competent person, and I—"

"Excuse me, Mr. Keller," Gavril Ardalionovitch interrupted. "Let me speak. I assure you your article will come up in its turn, and then you can make your explanations, but now we had better proceed in the proper order. Quite accidentally, with the help of my sister Varvara Ardalionovna, I obtained from her intimate friend, Vera Alexeyevna Zubkov, a widow and landowner, a certain letter from the late Nikolai Andrey-evitch Pavlishchev, written to her twenty-four years before from abroad. Having become acquainted with Vera Alexey-evna, I addressed myself at her suggestion to the retired Colonel Timofey Fyodorovitch Vyazovkin, a distant relative and at one time a great friend of Mr. Pavlishchev. I succeeded in obtaining from him two more of Nikolai Andreyevitch's letters, also written from abroad. From these three letters, from the dates and facts indicated in them, it is proved with mathematical certainty, without the least possibility of denial or doubt, that Nikolai Andreyevitch had gone abroad—where he lived for three years—exactly one year and a half before your birth, Mr. Burdovsky. Your mother, as you know, has never been out of Russia. At the moment I won't read these letters. It is late, and for now I am only stating the fact. But if you care to set a time to see me at my house, Mr. Burdovsky, to-morrow morning if you like, and bring your witnesses—as many as you like—and experts to examine the handwriting, I have no doubt at all that you will be convinced of the obvious truth of what I am telling you. If that is so, then of course this whole affair collapses and comes to nothing."

Again there was a general commotion and intense excitement. Burdovsky himself suddenly got up from his chair.

"If that is so, I was deceived—not by Tchebarov but a long long time ago. I want no experts, I believe it, I renounce my claim. I want no ten thousand. Good-bye."

He took his cap and pushed his chair aside to go out.

"If you can, Mr. Burdovsky," said Gavril Ardalionovitch stopping him softly and gently, "stay another five minutes. Several other extremely important facts have come to light in this case, important especially for you, and in any case very interesting. In my opinion, you should certainly be acquainted with them, and perhaps it will be pleasanter for you if the matter is entirely cleared up."

Burdovsky sat down in silence, with his head bowed a little as if in deep thought. Lebedev's nephew, who had also got up to follow him, sat down too. Though he had not lost his composure or his boldness, he seemed greatly troubled. Hippolite was frowning, downcast, and apparently greatly amazed. At this moment, however, he had such a violent coughing fit that he stained his handkerchief with blood. The boxer seemed almost afraid.

"Eh, Antip!" he cried out bitterly. "I told you at the time —two days ago, that maybe you weren't really Pavlishchev's son!"

There was a sound of smothered laughter; two or three people laughed louder than the rest.

"The fact you have stated just now, Mr. Keller," continued Gavril Ardalionovitch, "is very valuable. Nevertheless I have every right to assert, on the most precise evidence, that while Mr. Burdovsky of course knew perfectly well the date of his birth, he was in complete ignorance of the circumstances of Mr. Pavlishchev's residence abroad, where he lived the greater part of his life, returning to Russia only for short periods. Besides, the fact of his departure then was not in itself remarkable enough to be remembered twenty years afterward, even by those who knew Pavlishchev well, not to mention Mr. Burdovsky, who was not even born at the time. Of course, it turned out to be virtually impossible to get information now, and I must admit that the information I did obtain came to me completely by chance, and might very well have not fallen into my hands at all. So this information was actually unavailable to Mr. Burdovsky and even to Tchebarov, even if they had thought of obtaining it. But they may never have thought of it—"

"If you don't mind, Mr. Ivolgin," said Hippolite, suddenly interrupting him in irritation, "what is all this nonsense about? The thing has been explained now, we agree to admit the main fact, so why drag out this tedious and offensive foolishness? Perhaps you want to brag about the cleverness of your investigations and demonstrate to us and the prince what a wonderful detective you are? Or is it your intention to excuse and justify Mr. Burdovsky by proving he got mixed up in this business through ignorance? But that's sheer impudence, my dear sir! Burdovsky has no need of your apologetics and justifications, and you may as well know it! He's hurt; it's painful enough for him now without this, you should see this and understand it—"

"Enough, Mr. Terentyev, enough!" said Gavril Ardalionovitch, managing to interrupt him. "Calm yourself, don't get excited. You're quite ill, aren't you? I sympathize with you. In that case, if you like, I've finished; that is I feel obliged only to state briefly these facts which should in my opinion be known to you in full detail," he added, noticing a general stir of impatience. "I simply wish to state for the information of everyone with an interest in this case—and I can give proof —that your mother, Mr. Burdovsky, was treated with kindness and consideration by Pavlishchev for the sole reason that she was sister of a serf-girl with whom Nikolai Andreyevitch as a very young man was in love, and whom he would have married had she not died suddenly. I have evidence that this family matter, which is absolutely correct and certain, is very little known and indeed has been completely forgotten. Furthermore, I could inform you how your mother was taken as a child of ten by Pavlishchev and brought up as if she was a relative of his, that a sizable dowry was set aside for her, and that all these attentions gave rise to extremely disturbing rumors among Pavlishchev's many relations. It was even thought that he was going to marry his ward, but by her own choice at the age of twenty (and this I can prove most incontestably) she ended by marrying a land-surveying official, a Mr. Burdovsky. Here I have collected certain precise facts which show that your father, Burdovsky, a completely un-businesslike person, left the civil service when he had received your mother's dowry of fifteen thousand roubles, entered into a commercial venture, was cheated, lost his capital, could not bear the blow, started drinking, grew very ill, and finally died prematurely, eight years after marrying your mother. Then, according to your mother's own testimony, she was left in utter poverty and would have been completely lost but for the constant and generous help of Pavlishchev, who aided her with as much as six hundred roubles a year. There is also ample evidence that he loved you very much as a child. From this evidence, confirmed by your mother, it appears that the main reason he loved you was that as a child you seemed tongue-tied, like a cripple, like a wretched unhappy child (and Pavlishchev, as I have determined from precise state-ments, had all his life a special tenderness for every creature afflicted and cheated by nature, particularly children—a fact which I am convinced is extremely important to our entire case). Finally, I can claim a precise discovery about this im-portant fact, that Pavlishchev's extreme fondness for you (he got you admitted to the gymnasium and taught under special supervision) little by little, toward the end, led Pavlishchev's relatives and the members of his household to the notion that you were his son and that your father was only a betrayed husband. But the main point is that this notion was firmly im-planted and became a general conviction only in the last years of Pavlishchev's life, when everyone was afraid of what would happen in his will, and when the original facts were forgotten and information impossible to find. No doubt this idea reached you too, Mr. Burdovsky, and took complete possession of you. Your mother, with whom I had the honor of becoming personally acquainted, knew of these rumors but to this day doesn't know (I hid it from her too) that you, her son, were taken in by this rumor. In Pskov I found your much respected mother, Mr. Burdovsky, ill and in extreme poverty, as she has been since the death of Pavlishchev. She told me with tears of gratitude that it was only because of you and your support that she was alive on earth; she expects a great deal from you in the future and firmly believes in your future success—"

"This is really intolerable!" Lebedev's nephew suddenly de-clared loudly and impatiently. "What's the purpose of this tale?"

"Disgusting and indecent!" said Hippolite with a violent gesture. But Burdovsky noticed nothing and did not move.

"What's the purpose? Why?" demanded Gavril Ardaliono-vitch in feigned astonishment, maliciously preparing to state his conclusions. "Well, first of all, Mr. Burdovsky may now be fully convinced that Mr. Pavlishchev loved him out of the goodness of his heart and not as a son. This fact alone was essential for Mr. Burdovsky to learn, since he upheld Mr. Keller and approved him just now when his article was read. I say this because I take you for an honorable person, Mr. Burdovsky. Secondly, it turns out that there was no question at all here of robbery or swindling, even on the part of Tche-barov; this is an important point, even for me, because the prince, speaking in heat just now, said something about me sharing his opinion concerning the robbery and swindling as-pect of this unhappy affair. On the contrary, there was com-plete conviction on everyone's part, and though Tchebarov is perhaps in fact a rogue, he appears in this case to be no more than a clever pettifogger seeking an opportunity. He hoped to make a lot of money out of it as a lawyer, and his calculation was not only cunning and masterful but well founded: it was based on the ease with which the prince gives away money and on his noble respect for Pavlishchev, and finally, and most important, on the well-known chivalrous views of the prince with respect to honor and conscience. As far as Mr. Burdovsky himself is concerned, it could even be said that because of certain convictions of his he was so led on by Tchebarov and by the people around him that he took up this affair quite without self-interest and virtually as a service to truth, progress, and humanity. Now that the facts have been stated, it is obviously clear to everyone that in spite of all ap-pearances Mr. Burdovsky is an honest man and that the prince may now, more readily and willingly than before, offer him his friendly assistance and that actual help he mentioned before when he spoke of schools and Pavlishchev."

"Stop, Gavril Ardalionovitch, stop!" cried the prince in real fear, but it was already too late.

"I have said, I told you three times already," shouted Bur-dovsky angrily, "I don't want money. I won't accept it—why —I don't want—I'm going!"

And he was running off the veranda, but Lebedev's nephew grabbed him by the arm and whispered something to him. He quickly returned and taking a large envelope out of his pocket threw it on the table near the prince. "Here's the money! How dared you? How dared you? The money!"

"The two hundred and fifty roubles you dared send him as charity through Tchebarov," explained Doktorenko.

"The article said fifty!" cried Kolya.

"It's my fault!" said the prince, going up to Burdovsky. "I've done you a great wrong, Burdovsky, but I didn't send it to you as a charity, believe me. And I'm to blame now— I was at fault just now." The prince was greatly distressed, he looked weakened and tired, and his words were disconnected. "I spoke of swindling—but I didn't mean you; I was mistaken. I said you were—sick—the way I am. But you are not like me, you—give lessons, you support your mother. I said you cast shame on your mother, but you love her. She says so herself—I didn't know—Gavril Ardalionovitch didn't tell me that earlier—I am at fault. I dared offer you ten thousand, but I am at fault, I shouldn't have done it that way, but now—it can't be done because you despise me."

"This is a madhouse!" exclaimed Lizaveta Prokofyevna.

"Of course it's a house of madmen!" Aglaya was unable to restrain herself from saying sharply, but her words were lost in the general uproar. Everyone was now talking loudly, some arguing, some laughing. Ivan Fyodorovitch Yepanchin was in the highest state of indignation and was awaiting Lizaveta Prokofyevna with an air of wounded dignity.

Lebedev's nephew had the last word: "Yes, Prince, one has to give you credit, you do know how to make use of your— well, illness (to put it politely). You have managed to offer your friendship and money in such a clever way that now no self-respecting man could possibly accept them under any circumstances. This is either a bit too innocent or a bit too clever. But you're the best judge."

"Please, gentlemen," cried Gavril Ardalionovitch, having meanwhile opened the packet of money, "there aren't two hundred and fifty roubles here, there're only a hundred. I say this, Prince, so that there will be no misunderstanding."

"It's all right, it's all right," cried the prince, waving in protest to Gavril Ardalionovitch.

"No, it's not all right," Lebedev's nephew picked up the words at once. "Your 'it's all right' is an insult to us, Prince. We don't hide back, we declare it openly; yes, there are only a hundred roubles here and not the whole two hundred and fifty, but doesn't it all come out to the same thing?"

"N-no, it isn't all the same thing," Gavril Ardalionovitch managed to put in, with an air of naïve bewilderment.

"Don't interrupt me. We are not such fools as you think we are, Mr. Lawyer," cried Lebedev's nephew in spiteful anger. "Obviously a hundred roubles are not two hundred and fifty roubles and therefore not the same thing, but it's the principle that's important; the gesture is the great thing, and the fact that a hundred and fifty roubles are missing is only a detail. What matters is that Burdovsky does not accept your charity, Your Excellency, that he throws it back in your face, and from this point of view it doesn't matter whether it's a hundred or two hundred and fifty. Burdovsky did not accept the ten thousand, as you've seen; he wouldn't have brought back the hundred roubles if he'd been dishonest. Those hundred and fifty roubles have gone to Tchebarov for his trip to see the prince. You may laugh at our lack of skill and experience in handling this affair—even without this you have done your best to make us ridiculous—but don't dare say we are dishonest. All of us together, my dear sir, will repay those hundred and fifty roubles to the prince; we'll pay it back if it has to be rouble by rouble, and we'll pay it back with interest. Burdovsky is poor, Burdovsky has no millions, but Tchebarov presented him with a bill after his trip. We hoped to win—who wouldn't have done the same thing in his place?"

"Who would have?" exclaimed Prince S.

"I'll go out of my mind here!" cried Lizaveta Prokofyevna.

"That reminds me," laughed Yevgeny Pavlovitch, who had been standing and watching the scene for some time, "of the famous defense of a lawyer recently who, pleading the poverty of his client as a justification for his having killed six people at once in order to rob them, suddenly concluded with something like this: 'It is natural,' said he, 'that his poverty gave my client the idea of killing six people—who wouldn't have had the same idea in his place?' It was something like that, but very amusing."

"Enough!" Lizaveta Prokofyevna announced suddenly, almost trembling with anger. "It's time to put an end to this nonsense!" She was in a state of terrible excitement; she threw her head back menacingly and with a fierce, haughty, impatient glare of defiance surveyed the entire company, hardly able at that moment to distinguish friend from foe. She was at that point of long-suppressed but at last uncontainable anger when the ruling impulse is toward immediate battle, an immediate need to attack someone. Those who knew Lizaveta Prokofyevna felt at once that something unusual had happened to her. Ivan Fyodorovitch told Prince S. the next day, "This does happen to her but very seldom to the degree it did yesterday—perhaps once every three years or so, never more often! Never more often!" he added sententiously.

"Enough, Ivan Fyodorovitch! Leave me alone!" exclaimed Lizaveta Prokofyevna. "Why are you offering me your arm now? You hadn't sense enough to take me away before! You're the husband, you're the head of the family, you should have dragged me off by the ear, fool that I am, if I didn't obey you and go. You might have at least thought of your daughters! But now we shall find the way without you! I've had enough disgrace for a whole year. Wait a moment, I've still got to thank the prince! Thank you, Prince, for this treat! And to think I stayed on to hear the young people. It's despicable, despicable! It's chaos, infamy, it's worse than a nightmare! Can there be many like them? Be quiet, Aglaya! Be quiet, Alexandra! This is none of your business! Stop fussing around me, Yevgeny Pavlovitch, I'm tired of you! So ask their forgiveness, my dear man," she continued, again addressing the prince. " 'I am terribly to blame for having offered you a large sum of money.' And as for you, you swaggering braggart, what are you laughing for?" She suddenly turned on Lebedev's nephew. " 'We refuse this, we demand, we don't ask that!' As if he didn't know this idiot will drag himself off to them again tomorrow and offer his friendship and his fortune! And you will, won't you? Won't you?"

"I will," said the prince in a meek and quiet voice.

"You heard! That's what you're counting on," she turned again to Doktorenko. "The money is as good as in your pocket, so you are swaggering around trying to put on airs. No, my dear fellow, find other fools, I see through you. I see your whole game!"

"Lizaveta Prokofyevna!" exclaimed the prince.

"Come away, Lizaveta Prokofyevna. It's high time we went, and let's take the prince with us," said Prince S. with a smile, as calmly as he could.

The young ladies stood back, on the verge of being afraid. The general was genuinely alarmed. Everyone present was amazed. Some of those standing farthest away grinned surreptitiously and whispered back and forth to each other. Lebedev's face bore a look of utmost rapture.

"You will find chaos and infamy everywhere, madam," declared Lebedev's nephew, looking greatly disconcerted nevertheless.

"But not like this! Not as you are displaying now, not like this!" pursued Lizaveta Prokofyevna with almost hysterical vindictiveness. "But leave me alone!" she shouted at those who were trying to reason with her. "No, since you yourself, Yevgeny Pavlovitch, told us just now that a defense lawyer at a trial declared that nothing is more natural than for a man to butcher six people because he was poor, then indeed the world is coming to an end. I hadn't heard about that. Now everything is all clear to me! And this stutterer, wouldn't he commit murder?" (She pointed to Burdovsky, who was staring at her in extreme bewilderment.) "I'd bet he would! Perhaps he won't take your money, the ten thousand, maybe, on account of his conscience, but he'll come back at night and murder you and take the money out of the cash box. And he'll do that with a clear conscience! That wouldn't seem dishonest to him! That would be 'an impulse of noble desperation,' that would be 'negation,' or heaven knows what— Foo! Everything is turned around backward, everything is upside down. A girl is growing up at home and suddenly in the middle of the street she jumps into a cab, 'Mama, I've just married some Karlitch or Ivanitch. Good-bye!' Do you think that's a good way to behave? Is that worthy of respect? Is that natural? The woman question? This young boy here—" she pointed to Kolya, "even he was trying to tell me that is what the 'woman question' means. Even if the mother was a fool, you still ought to treat her as a human being! Why did you come in earlier with your heads in the air? 'Make way— here we come!' 'Give us every right, but don't dare breathe a word in our presence. Pay us every kind of respect, such as has never even been heard of, and we shall treat you worse than the lowest of servants!' They are searching for truth, they stand on their rights, and like heathens they slander him in the article— 'We are demanding, we are not asking, and you will get no gratitude from us, because you will be acting to satisfy your own conscience!' What fine morality! Well, if he's to have no gratitude from you, the prince can answer you that he feels no gratitude toward Pavlishchev, because Pavlishchev also was doing good to satisfy his own conscience. And yet all you'd been counting on is his gratitude to Pavlishchev. He hasn't borrowed money from you, he doesn't owe you anything, so what are you counting on if not his gratitude? So how can you repudiate it? Lunatics! They regard society as savage and inhuman for holding a seduced girl up to shame, but if you regard society as inhuman you must think this girl can be hurt by society. And if she's hurt by it, why do you bring the matter up in the newspapers before this very society if she's not to be hurt? Lunatics! Conceited creatures! They don't believe in God, they don't believe in Christ! You are so devoured by pride and vanity that you will end by devouring each other, that's what I predict for you! Isn't that absurdity? Isn't that chaos, isn't that infamy? And after that this shameless creature goes after them and begs their pardon! Are there many like you? What are you grinning at? Because I've degraded myself in front of you? Well, I've done that already and there's nothing to do about it now! And don't you go grinning, you filthy fellow!"

She suddenly turned upon Hippolite. "He's hardly able to breathe, and he's corrupting others. You've corrupted this boy." She pointed at Kolya again. "He raves about you and you teach him atheism; you don't believe in God, but you are not too old for a whipping yourself, sir! And fie on you! So you are going to them, Prince Lev Nikolayevitch, you are going to them tomorrow?" she asked the prince again, almost out of breath.

"I will."

"Then hereafter I don't want to know you!" She turned quickly to leave but suddenly turned back. "And you'll go to this atheist?" she pointed to Hippolite. "Well, what are you laughing at me for?" she cried in an unnatural voice, and rushed at Hippolite, unable to endure his sarcastic laughter.

"Lizaveta Prokofyevna! Lizaveta Prokofyevna! Lizaveta Prokofyevna!" everyone was shouting at once.

"*Maman!* This is shameful!" Aglaya cried loudly.

"Don't worry, Aglaya Ivanovna," Hippolite replied calmly, though Lizaveta Prokofyevna had seized him by the arm and for some unaccountable reason was clutching it tightly, standing close to him fixing him with her frenzied look. "Don't worry, your *maman* will soon see that she can't attack a dying man. I'm quite ready to explain why I was laughing—I shall be very glad to be permitted to do so."

Here he was suddenly seized with a terrible coughing fit which for a full minute he could not control.

"He's dying, but he's still making speeches!" exclaimed Lizaveta Prokofyevna, letting go of his arm, and looking with some horror as he wiped the blood from his lips. "You shouldn't be talking! You should just go lie down."

"I shall do so," replied Hippolite in a low, hoarse voice that was almost a whisper. "As soon as I get home, I'll go to bed. In another two weeks I shall die, I know this. Dr. B——n* himself told me so a week ago. So if you will allow me I would like to say a few words to you in farewell."

"Are you crazy? Nonsense! You need looking after. This is no time for conversation. Go! Go along! Go lie down!" cried the frightened Lizaveta Prokofyevna.

"If I lie down I won't get up again until I die," said Hippolite, smiling. "I wanted to go to bed yesterday and not get up again, but I decided to put it off for two days, since I can still stand on my feet, so as to come here with them today. Except I am extremely tired—"

"But sit down, sit down! Why are you standing? Here's a chair," exclaimed Lizaveta Prokofyevna, offering him the chair herself.

"Thank you," Hippolite continued softly, "and do sit facing me and we can talk. We have to talk, Lizaveta Prokofyevna, I insist on it now," he smiled at her again. "Think that today is the last time I'll be out in the open and with people, and that in two weeks I will certainly be under the ground. So this will be a sort of farewell to people and to nature. And though I'm not very sentimental, would you believe it, I'm very glad all this happened here in Pavlovsk. At least you can see trees in leaf."

"But why talk now?" said Lizaveta Prokofyevna, becoming more and more alarmed. "You're all feverish. You were squealing and screeching just now, and now you can scarcely breathe. You're gasping!"

"I'll be better soon. Why do you want to deny me my last wish? Do you know I've dreamed of making your acquaintance for a long time, Lizaveta Prokofyevna; I have heard a great deal about you from Kolya—he is about the only one who hasn't given me up. You are an original woman, an eccentric woman, and now I've seen this for myself. Do you know that I was even a little bit in love with you?"

"Good heavens, and I was about to strike him!"

"Aglaya Ivanovna stopped you. I'm not mistaken, am I? This is your daughter Aglaya Ivanovna? She is so beautiful I recognized her at first glance just now, though I had never seen her. Let me at least look at a beautiful woman for the last time," Hippolite said with a sort of awkward, wry smile. "The prince is here, and your husband, and all the company. Why do you deny me this last wish?"

"A chair!" shouted Lizaveta Prokofyevna, but she seized one herself and sat down in front of Hippolite. "Kolya," she ordered, "you will leave with him immediately, take him, and tomorrow I will certainly come myself."

"If you allow me, I would ask the prince for a cup of tea. I am very tired. Do you know, Lizaveta Prokofyevna, I believe you wanted to take the prince back with you to tea; do stay here instead; let's spend the time together, and I'm sure the prince will have tea served to all of us. Excuse me for ordering things like this. But I know you, you are kind, and the prince too. We are all ridiculously kind people."

The prince busied himself. Lebedev flew headlong inside, followed by Vera.

"This is true," the general's wife decided abruptly. "Talk, but quietly, and don't get excited. You have touched me. Prince! You don't deserve to have me drink tea with you, but never mind. I shall stay, though I'm not going to beg anyone's pardon! No one's! Nonsense! However, if I've scolded you, Prince, forgive me; that is, if you wish to yourself. But I'm not detaining anyone," she suddenly addressed her husband and her daughters with an expression of extraordinary ferocity, as though they were guilty of offending her in some way. "I can find my way home by myself—"

But they did not let her finish. Everyone readily drew up a circle around her. The prince at once began pressing everyone to stay for tea and apologized for not having thought of it before. Even the general was so amiable as to mutter something reassuring and considerately asked Lizaveta Prokofyevna whether she wasn't a trifle chilly on the veranda. He almost asked Hippolite whether he had been at the university long, but did not. Yevgeny Pavlovitch and Prince S. suddenly became exceedingly amiable and gay. In Adelaïda's and Alexandra's faces something akin to pleasure began to mingle with their surprise. In short, everyone was visibly pleased that Lizaveta Prokofyevna's crisis had passed. Only Aglaya frowned and sat at a distance in silence. The rest of the party all remained, no one wanted to leave, even General Ivolgin, to whom however Lebedev whispered something in passing, probably something not particularly pleasant, because the general immediately disappeared into a corner. The prince also went up to Burdovsky and his friends and invited them to stay, omitting no one. They muttered in constrained voices that they would wait for Hippolite and at once moved away to the farthest end of the veranda where they sat down again in a row. The tea had probably been prepared some time before for Lebedev, since it was brought out at once. It struck eleven.

Chapter TEN

Hippolite moistened his lips with the tea Vera Lebedev handed him, put his cup down on a little table, and, suddenly becoming embarrassed, looked around in confusion.

"Look here, Lizaveta Prokofyevna," he began with a strange haste, "these cups, these are china cups, and I believe most excellent china. They are always locked up behind glass in Lebedev's sideboard and never used. That's how it has been. They are part of his wife's dowry. That's been the custom. But here he has brought them out for us—in your honor, of course, he is so pleased."

He wanted to say more but could not find the right words.

"He's embarrassed. I thought he would be!" Yevgeny Pavlovitch whispered suddenly in the prince's ear. "It's dangerous, isn't it? It's a sure sign that now he'll do something so eccentric out of spite that I'm afraid even Lizaveta Prokofyevna won't put up with it."

The prince looked at him questioningly.

"You're not afraid of eccentricity?" added Yevgeny Pavlovitch. "Well, I'm not either, I even look forward to it. All I want is for our dear Lizaveta Prokofyevna to be punished, and right now, this very day. I don't want to go away before it happens. You seem feverish."

"Later—don't bother me. No, I am not well," replied the prince carelessly and even impatiently. He had heard his name mentioned, Hippolite talking about him.

"You don't believe it?" Hippolite laughed hysterically. "You couldn't, but the prince will believe it at once and not be the least surprised."

"Do you hear, Prince?" said Lizaveta Prokofyevna, turning to him. "Do you hear?"

There was laughter all around them. Lebedev kept pushing forward and pirouetting in front of Lizaveta Prokofyevna.

"He says that this clown here, your landlord—corrected the gentleman's article—the one they read about you this evening."

The prince looked at Lebedev in surprise.

"Why don't you say something?" cried Lizaveta Prokofyevna, stamping her foot.

"I see already that he did," murmured the prince, looking steadily at Lebedev.

"Is it true?" demanded Lizaveta Prokofyevna, turning quickly to Lebedev.

"It's the honest truth, Your Excellency!" answered Lebedev firmly, unshakably, laying his hand on his heart.

"He's actually proud of it!" cried Lizaveta Prokofyevna, almost jumping out of her chair.

"I'm vile, vile," muttered Lebedev, pounding his chest and bowing his head lower and lower.

"What do I care if you're vile or not? He thinks if he says he's vile he's getting away with it. And aren't you ashamed, Prince, to have anything to do with such people? I ask you again. I shall never forgive you!"

"The prince will forgive me!" said Lebedev with conviction and deep emotion.

"Only out of good feeling, madam," Keller said suddenly in a loud ringing voice, jumping up and addressing himself directly to Lizaveta Prokofyevna, "only out of good feeling and so as not to betray a friend who has compromised himself. I said nothing just now about those corrections despite the fact that he offered to throw us down the stairs, as you heard yourself. To set the matter straight again, I admit that I did in fact apply to him and paid him six roubles, but not to correct the style but only, as one competent in this affair, to supply me with the facts, which were for the most part unknown to me. About the gaiters, about his appetite at the Swiss professor's, about the fifty roubles instead of the two hundred and fifty, that is to say all that part, that all belongs to him, and he got six roubles for it. But he did not correct the style."

"I must observe," Lebedev interrupted with feverish impatience and in a sort of crawling voice as the laughter became louder and louder, "that I corrected only the first half of the article, but since toward the middle we didn't agree and quarreled over a certain idea, I did not correct the second half, so that everything that's not grammatical there (and lots of it isn't) is not to be blamed on me."

"That is what he's worried about!" exclaimed Lizaveta Prokofyevna.

"May I ask," said Yevgeny Pavlovitch to Keller, "when the article was corrected?"

"Yesterday morning," replied Keller. "We met together and both gave our promise to keep the secret."

"That was when he was groveling before you and assuring you of his devotion. What people! I don't want your Pushkin, and don't let your daughter come see me!"

Lizaveta Prokofyevna was ready to leave but suddenly turned angrily to Hippolite, who was laughing.

"My dear young man, are you trying to make me the laughingstock here!"

"God forbid!" said Hippolite with a wry smile. "But what strikes me more than anything is your extreme eccentricity, Lizaveta Prokofyevna. I confess I brought up the subject of Lebedev on purpose, I knew how it would affect you and you alone, because the prince will certainly forgive him and has undoubtedly forgiven him already. Perhaps he has even thought up an excuse for him. Haven't you, Prince?"

He was breathing with difficulty; his strange excitement was increasing with every word.

"Well?" said Lizaveta Prokofyevna angrily, surprised at his tone. "Well?"

"I've heard a lot about you, of the same sort—with great pleasure—and I've learned to respect you very much," Hippolite went on.

He was saying one thing, but he was saying it as if he wished his very words to convey something quite different. He spoke with a touch of mockery but at the same time was extremely agitated, looked around suspiciously, obviously lost track of what he was saying at every other word; and all this, together with his consumptive appearance and strange, glittering, and somehow frenzied look, did not fail to hold the general attention.

"I might well be surprised—though I know nothing of the world (I am aware of this)—at your not only remaining in our company, which you find unfit for you, but at your allowing these young ladies to listen to this scandalous affair, though they have read everything in novels already. I don't know, though—because I'm somewhat confused, but who except you could have stayed—at the request of a boy (well yes, a boy, I admit this)—to spend the evening with him and —take part in everything—things one is ashamed of the next day (I'm aware that I'm not expressing myself properly). I find this highly commendable and I respect it deeply, though no one can see from the countenance of His Excellency, your husband, how unpleasant this all is for him— Ha, ha!" he chuckled, completely lost, and suddenly began to cough so hard that for about two minutes he could not continue.

"Now he's choking!" pronounced Lizaveta Prokofyevna coldly and sharply, studying him with solemn curiosity. "Well, dear boy, enough of you. It's time to go."

"Permit me, dear sir, to tell you on my part," said Ivan Fyodorovitch suddenly, having lost all patience, "that my wife is here visiting Prince Lev Nikolayevitch, our mutual friend and neighbor, and that in any case it's not for you, young man, to pass judgment on Lizaveta Prokofyevna's actions, nor to refer aloud and in my presence to what is written on my countenance. No, indeed, sir. And if my wife stayed on here," he went on, growing more irritated at each word, "it was rather out of astonishment, sir, and a perfectly understandable contemporary interest in the spectacle of peculiar young people. I stayed myself, as I occasionally stop in the street when I see something that one can look at as—as—"

"As a curiosity," suggested Yevgeny Pavlovitch.

"Exactly right," said His Excellency in relief, having been

at a loss for a comparison. "Precisely as a curiosity, but in any event, what seems to me most amazing and distressful—if I am expressing myself correctly—is the fact that you, young man, couldn't even understand that Lizaveta Prokofyevna has stayed with you now because you are sick—that is, if you really are dying—out of compassion, so to speak, on account of your pitiful speeches, sir, and that in any event no slur can be brought against her name, her character, or her position. Lizaveta Prokofyevna!" concluded the general, who had turned crimson, "if you mean to go, let's say good-bye to our good prince and—"

"Thank you for the lesson, General," Hippolite interrupted unexpectedly, speaking gravely and looking at him thoughtfully.

"Let's be going, *Maman*, this can go on forever!" said Aglaya angrily, getting up from her chair.

"Two minutes more, dear Ivan Fyodorovitch, if you don't mind," said Lizaveta Prokofyevna, turning with dignity to her husband. "It seems to me he's in a fever and quite simply delirious. I am sure of it from his eyes; he can't be left like this. Lev Nikolayevitch! Could he spend the night here, so he doesn't have to drag himself to Petersburg tonight? *Cher Prince*," she added, for some reason addressing Prince S., "are you bored? Come here, Alexandra, fix your hair, my dear."

She touched her daughter's hair, which was perfectly in order, and kissed her. That was why she had called her over.

"I thought you were capable of—development," said Hippolite, breaking out of his revery. "Yes! This is what I meant to say!" He was very pleased, as if he was suddenly recollecting something. "Burdovsky here sincerely wants to protect his mother, doesn't he? But it turns out he has disgraced her. The prince wants to help Burdovsky, and out of true good will offers him his tender friendship and a lot of money; he is perhaps the only one of us who doesn't feel an aversion toward him. And here they are, standing there face to face like real enemies. Ha, ha, ha! You all hate Burdovsky because, according to you, he behaved in an ugly and ungracious way toward his mother, isn't that it? Isn't it? Isn't it? For you all adore prettiness and formal elegance, and that's all you care about, isn't that so? (I've suspected a long time that's all it was!) Well, let me tell you that probably not one of you has loved his mother as Burdovsky has! I know, Prince, that you have secretly sent money through Ganya to Burdovsky's mother, and I'll bet"—he laughed hysterically—"I'll bet Burdovsky will now accuse you of bad form and disrespect to his mother, I swear he will. Ha, ha, ha!"

Again he choked and began coughing.

"Well, is that all? Is that all now? Have you said everything? Well, go to bed now, you have a fever." Lizaveta Prokofyevna interrupted impatiently, still looking at him anxiously. "Oh Good Heavens! He's still talking!"

"You seem to be laughing," he said irritably, suddenly addressing Yevgeny Pavlovitch. "Why are you laughing at me? I notice you keep on laughing at me."

Yevgeny Pavlovitch was indeed laughing. "I only wanted to ask you, Mr.—Hippolite—forgive me, I've forgotten your last name."

"Mr. Terentyev," said the prince.

"Oh, yes. Terentyev. Thank you, Prince, you told me before but it slipped my mind. I wanted to ask you, Mr. Terentyev, is it true as I've heard that you're of the opinion all you have to do is talk to the common people for a quarter of an hour out of your window and they will agree with you and follow you at once?"

"It's quite possible I said that," replied Hippolite, as if he was trying to recall something. "In fact I did say that!" he added suddenly, brightening again and looking steadily at Yevgeny Pavlovitch. "What about it?"

"Nothing at all. I only ask for information, to get everything straight."

Yevgeny Pavlovitch fell silent, but Hippolite was still looking at him with impatient expectation.

"Well, have you finished?" Lizaveta Prokofyevna asked Yevgeny Pavlovitch. "Get done with it quickly, my dear friend, it's time he went to bed. Or can't you?"

She was extremely annoyed.

"I'm tempted to add," continued Yevgeny Pavlovitch, smiling, "that everything I've heard from your friends, Mr. Terentyev, and everything you've said just now—and said with such brilliance—amounts as I see it to the theory of right over everything and in spite of everything and indeed to the exclusion of everything else, and very likely without a prior examination of what right consists of. Perhaps I am mistaken?"

"Of course you are mistaken. I don't even understand you. Go on."

There was also a protest from a corner of the veranda. Lebedev's nephew was muttering something in an undertone.

"There is not much to go on with," Yevgeny Pavlovitch continued. "I only want to point out that this theory can lead

312

directly to the notion that might makes right; that is, to the right of the individual first and of personal will, as it very often happens in the world. Proudhon arrived at the idea that right is might. In the American war, didn't many of the most advanced liberals declare themselves in favor of the plantation owners on the ground that Negroes are Negroes and inferior to the white race, and therefore that the right of might was on the white side?"

"Well?"

"Well, then you don't deny the right of might?"

"Go on."

"You're consistent, at least. I only wanted to say that from the right of might to the right of tigers and crocodiles and even Danilovs and Gorskys is only a step."

"I don't know. Go on."

Hippolite was hardly listening to Yevgeny Pavlovitch, and if he was saying "Well?" and "Go on," he was apparently doing it from old habits of argument and not out of attention or curiosity.

"There's nothing more. That's all."

"Anyway I'm not angry with you," concluded Hippolite suddenly and quite unexpectedly and, hardly aware of what he was doing, he held out his hand, even smiling.

Yevgeny Pavlovitch was surprised at first, but with a very serious air touched the hand held out to him as if he was accepting his forgiveness.

"I can only add my gratitude," he said in the same ambiguous tone of respect, "for your courtesy in allowing me to speak, because I have found from many observations that sometimes our liberal is incapable of granting anyone else his own convictions and immediately answers his opponent with abuse or something worse."

"You are absolutely right there," remarked General Ivan Fyodorovitch, and clasping his hands behind his back he retreated with an air of boredom to the veranda steps, where he yawned in annoyance.

"Well, enough of you, my friend," Lizaveta Prokofyevna declared suddenly to Yevgeny Pavlovitch. "I'm tired of you."

"It's time to go!" said Hippolite almost in a state of alarm, suddenly getting up and looking around in perplexity. "I have kept you, I wanted to tell you everything—I thought that everyone—for the last time—it was a fantasy."

It was evident that he became animated in fits and starts, that he would suddenly come out of a state very like actual delirium for a few moments, and in full consciousness he would suddenly remember and start to speak, mostly in disconnected phrases that he had undoubtedly thought out and rehearsed during the long weary hours of his sickness, in bed, alone, throughout sleepless nights.

"Well, good-bye!" he said sharply and abruptly. "Do you think it's easy for me to say good-bye to you? Ha, ha!" He laughed in annoyance at his own *awkward* question, and suddenly, as though angry with himself for not being able to say what he wanted, he said loudly and irritably: "Your Excellency, I have the honor of inviting you to my funeral, if you deem me worthy of the honor and—all of you, ladies and gentlemen, following the general!"

He laughed again, but now it was the laugh of a madman. Lizaveta Prokofyevna moved toward him in alarm and seized him by the arm. He looked at her steadily, the laugh now frozen on his face.

"Do you know that I came here to see the trees? Those there." He pointed to the trees in the park. "That's not absurd, is it? There's nothing funny in that, is there?" he asked Lizaveta Prokofyevna gravely, and suddenly was thoughtful. Then a moment later he raised his head and began searching among the people on the veranda. He was looking for Yevgeny Pavlovitch, who stood on his right, very near him where he had been before, but he had forgotten and was searching around. "Oh, you haven't left!" he said when he found him at last. "You were laughing at me just now for wanting to talk out the window for a quarter of an hour. But do you know I'm not yet eighteen? I've lain so long on that pillow and looked so long out that window and thought so much—about everyone—that— A person who is dead has no age, you know. I thought that last week, when I awoke in the night— But do you know what you are most afraid of? More than anything else you're afraid of our sincerity, though you despise us! I thought that too lying on my pillow at night. You think I meant to laugh at you just now, Lizaveta Prokofyevna? No, I was not laughing at you, I only wanted to praise you. Kolya said the prince called you a child—that's good. Yes, there was something else—I wanted to say." He buried his face in his hands and thought. "Yes, this is it: when you were saying good-bye just now, I suddenly thought 'Here are these people and they will never be anymore, never! And the trees too— There will be nothing but the wall, the red brick wall of Meyer's house—across from my window —well, tell them all about that. Try to tell them all about that—try to tell them. Here's a beautiful woman—but you of course are dead, introduce yourself as a dead man, tell her, 'A dead man can say anything' and Princess Marya Alexey-

314

evna won't object.* Ha, ha! You aren't laughing?" He looked around at them all mistrustfully. "But you know, many thoughts have come to me as I lie on my pillow. You know, for instance, I'm convinced that nature is ironical. You said just now I was an atheist, but you know that nature— Why are you laughing now? You're terribly cruel!" he declared suddenly with sorrowful indignation, looking around him. "I did not corrupt Kolya," he concluded in a completely different voice, earnest and convinced, as though suddenly remembering something again.

"Nobody, nobody here is laughing at you. Calm yourself!" said Lizaveta Prokofyevna in distress. "Tomorrow a new doctor will come, the other one was mistaken. Now sit down, you can't stand on your feet! You're delirious. Ah, what's to be done with him now?" She fussed over him, making him sit down in an armchair.

A tear shone on her cheek. Hippolite stopped in amazement, then raised his hand timidly and touched the tear. He smiled a childlike smile.

"I—" he began joyfully. "You don't know how I— He has always spoken of you to me with such enthusiasm. He, Kolya, there. I love his enthusiasm. I have not corrupted him! He's the only one I'm really leaving. I wanted to be leaving everyone, everyone—but there was no one, no one. I wanted to be a man of action, I had the right to be that. Oh, how I wanted it! I don't want anything now, I don't want to want anything, I have promised myself never to want anything again. Let them seek truth without me! Yes, nature is ironical! Why," he cried out suddenly, "why does she create her very best human beings only to make fools of them later? She takes the only creature recognized on earth as perfect— she does this, and having shown him to mankind she has him say words that have caused so much blood to flow that had it been shed at one time mankind would have drowned in it! Oh, it's good I'm dying! I too might have uttered some dreadful lie, nature would have had it happen! I have not corrupted anyone—I wanted to live for the happiness of all men, for the finding and the spreading of truth. I looked out the window at Meyer's wall and imagined I would speak for just one quarter of an hour and convince everyone, everyone, and for once in my life here I am—if not with everyone at least with you, and what has come of it? Nothing. What has come of it is that you despise me! So that means I am a fool, that I am unneeded, and that it is time for me to go! And I haven't managed to leave a memory behind! Not a murmur, not a trace, not one deed, I haven't spread a single truth! Don't

315

laugh at the fool! Forget him! Forget it all! Forget, please, don't be so cruel! Do you know that if this consumption hadn't come along I would have killed myself—"

He seemed to want to say much more, but he did not say it, he sank back into his chair and burying his face in his hands started to cry like a little child.

"Well, what are we going to do with him now?" cried Lizaveta Prokofyevna, and she ran up to him, took his head in her hands, and held him close to her bosom. He sobbed convulsively. "There, there, there! Come, don't cry. Here, that's enough, you're a good boy. God will forgive you because of your ignorance. Here, that's enough, be a man. Besides, you're going to feel ashamed of yourself."

"I have a brother and sisters at home," said Hippolite, trying to raise his head. "Little children, poor innocent little children. *She* will corrupt them! You are a saint, you—are a child yourself. Save them! Take them away from that woman —she—it's a disgrace. Oh, help them, help them! God will repay you a hundredfold. For God's sake, for Christ's sake!"

"Do tell us, after all, Ivan Fyodorovitch, what is to be done now!" cried Lizaveta Prokofyevna irritably. "Please be so good as to break your majestic silence! If you don't decide something you might as well know I'm going to spend the night here myself. I've had quite enough of your autocratic tyranny!"

Lizaveta Prokofyevna spoke with great feeling and anger and expected an immediate reply. But in such cases those present, even if there are many of them, will usually respond with silence and passive curiosity, unwilling to take anything upon themselves, and will express their opinions only a long time afterward. Among the assemblage on this occasion there were some who were capable of sitting there until the next morning without uttering a word. Varvara Ardalionovna for example had been sitting a little apart all evening, listening the whole time in silence and with extraordinary interest, for which she had perhaps good reasons of her own.

"My opinion, my dear," declared the general, "is that what is needed here rather than our emotionalism is, so to speak, a competent nurse—and perhaps a reliable, sober person for the night. In any event let us ask the prince and—leave the invalid in peace at once. And tomorrow we can do whatever more we can."

"It's now twelve o'clock, we are leaving," Doktorenko said irritably and angrily to the prince. "Is he coming with us or staying with you?"

"If you like, you can stay with him," said the prince. "There will be room."

"Your Excellency!" cried Mr. Keller with sudden enthusiasm, rushing up to the general, "if a satisfactory person is needed for the night, I am ready to sacrifice myself for a friend—he's such a rare person! I've long considered him a great man, Your Excellency! Me, of course, I may be lacking in education, but his criticisms—they are pearls, pearls, Your Excellency!"

The general turned away in desperation.

"I shall be very glad if he will stay," the prince was replying to Lizaveta Prokofyevna's irritable questions. "Of course it would be difficult for him to leave."

"But are you falling asleep? If you don't want him, my friend, I can take him home with me! My goodness, he can hardly stand up! Are you ill?"

Earlier in the evening Lizaveta Prokofyevna, not having found the prince on his deathbed, had in fact been misled by appearances into considerably exaggerating the satisfactory state of his health; however, his recent sickness and its painful associations, the fatigue following a strenuous evening, the "Pavlishchev's son" affair, and now the incident with Hippolite had so exacerbated the prince's morbid sensitiveness that he was in fact on the verge of fever. Besides this, still another anxiety, almost a fear, now showed in his eyes; he looked apprehensively at Hippolite as though expecting something more from him.

Suddenly Hippolite got up, terribly pale and with a frightful, almost despairing expression of shame on his face. It showed chiefly in his eyes, which stared at the company in hatred and fear, and in the vacant, abject smile that twisted his quivering lips. He lowered his eyes at once and walked slowly, staggering and still with the same smile, to Burdovsky and Doktorenko, who were standing by the veranda steps; he was leaving with them.

"Ah, this is what I was afraid of!" cried the prince. "This was bound to happen!"

Hippolite quickly turned to him in a frenzy of anger, and his whole quivering face seemed to be speaking.

"Oh, you were afraid of this. 'This was bound to happen,' you say. Then let me tell you that if there's anyone I hate here—" he was sputtering in a hoarse shriek, "and I hate you all, every one of you!—it's you, you treacly, Jesuitical soul, idiot, philanthropic millionaire, it's you I hate more than anyone or anything in the world! I've understood you and hated you ever since I first heard about you, I've hated you with all

317

the hatred in my soul. This has all been your doing! It's you who've brought on my attack of illness! It's you who've brought a dying man to shame—you, you, you are to blame for my final cowardness! I would kill you if I was going to live! I don't need your benefactions, I won't take them from anyone, do you hear, not from anyone, nothing! I was delirious and don't dare gloat over that! I curse every one of you, once and forever!"

At this point he choked up completely.

"He's ashamed of his tears!" Lebedev whispered to Lizaveta Prokofyevna. " 'This was bound to happen!' Ah, that prince! He saw right through him."

But Lizaveta Prokofyevna did not deign to glance at him. She stood proudly erect, her head thrown back, looking at "those people" with contemptuous interest. When Hippolite had finished, the general shrugged his shoulders; she looked him up and down angrily, as if demanding an explanation of his gesture, then immediately turned to the prince.

"Thanks very much, Prince, eccentric friend of our household, for the agreeable evening you have provided us. I have no doubt your heart must be pleased at having succeeded in involving us in your follies. This is enough, my dear friend of the family, but thank you anyway for the opportunity of really getting to know you at last." Indignantly she began to straighten her shawl, waiting for "them" to leave. At that moment a cab arrived for "them," for which Doktorenko had sent Lebedev's son, the schoolboy, a quarter of an hour earlier. Immediately after his wife, the general put in a word of his own as well.

"Really, Prince, I never would have expected—after everything—after all our friendly relations—and, after all, Lizaveta Prokofyevna—"

"Well, look here, how can you do that!" cried Adelaïda and went quickly up to the prince and shook his hand.

The prince smiled at her in bewilderment. Suddenly a hot, quick voice seemed to burn in his ear.

"If you don't throw out these revolting people at once, then all my life I shall hate you—all my life!" Aglaya was whispering.

She seemed to be in a state of frenzy but turned away before the prince had time to look at her. However, he no longer had anything or anyone to throw out: the ailing Hippolite had in the meantime, somehow, been put in the cab, and it had driven off.

"Well, Ivan Fyodorovitch, how long is this to go on?

What do you say? How long am I to suffer from these spiteful boys?"

"Yes, my dear, I—I am of course ready and—the prince—" Ivan Fyodorovitch held out his hand to the prince, but he did not have time to shake hands with him and ran after Lizaveta Prokofyevna, who was descending the steps of the veranda with much sound and fury. Adelaïda, her fiancé, and Alexandra took leave of the prince with sincere affection. Yevgeny Pavlovitch did the same, and he alone was in good spirits.

"It turned out as I thought!" he whispered, with a most charming smile. "Except it's a pity, poor fellow, that you have had to suffer too."

Aglaya left without saying good-bye.

But the adventures of that evening were not over yet. Lizaveta Prokofyevna had still to face one more very unexpected encounter.

Before she had descended the veranda steps to the road that circles the park, a magnificent carriage drawn by two white horses suddenly came dashing by the prince's house. Two splendidly dressed ladies sat inside. But suddenly the carriage pulled up abruptly not ten paces beyond the house, and one of the ladies turned around quickly as if she had caught sight of an acquaintance whom she absolutely had to speak to.

"Yevgeny Pavlovitch? Is that you, darling?" cried a beautiful, ringing voice, which startled the prince and perhaps someone else as well. "Well, how glad I am to have found you at last! I sent someone to your house in town—two people! They've been hunting all day for you!"

Yevgeny Pavlovitch stood on the veranda steps as if thunderstruck. Lizaveta Prokofyevna also stood still, though not like Yevgeny Pavlovitch in horror and stupefaction. She was looking at the audacious woman with the same cold contempt with which, five minutes before, she had been looking at "those people," and she promptly turned her glare on Yevgeny Pavlovitch.

"I have news!" the sonorous voice continued. "Don't worry about Kupfer's I.O.U.'s. Rogozhin has bought them up for thirty. I had him do it. You need have no worries for another three months. And we'll take care of Biskup and all those good-for-nothings through friends! So, you see? Everything is fine. Be cheerful. See you tomorrow."

The carriage drove off and quickly disappeared.

"It's a madwoman!" cried Yevgeny Pavlovitch at last, reddening with indignation and looking around him in bewilderment. "I haven't any idea what she's talking about. What I.O.U.'s? Who is she?"

Lizaveta Prokofyevna kept looking at him for a few seconds more. At last she set off abruptly and went quickly toward her house, and the others followed her. Exactly a minute later Yevgeny Pavlovitch came back to the prince on the veranda, extremely agitated.

"Prince, tell me the truth. Do you know what this means?"

"I know nothing about it," replied the prince, who was himself in a state of extreme tension.

"No?"

"No."

"I don't either," Yevgeny Pavlovitch suddenly laughed. "I never had anything to do with any I.O.U.'s, I swear it. Believe me, on my word of honor! What's the matter—are you fainting?"

"Oh, no, no, I assure you, no—"

Chapter ELEVEN

Only on the third day did the Yepanchins relent. Although the prince as usual assumed much of the blame and genuinely expected some punishment, he had been inwardly convinced from the first that Lizaveta Prokofyevna could not be seriously angry with him and was really more angry with herself. And so, such a long period of hostility had by the third day plunged him into the darkest perplexity. Other circumstances, too, accounted for this bewilderment, and one in particular. During the whole three days, it grew progressively in the prince's suspicious state of mind (and lately the prince had blamed himself for two extremes: an extraordinary "senseless and impulsive" trustfulness and at the same time a "morose, contemptible" suspiciousness). In short, by the end of the third day the incident of the eccentric lady who had spoken to Yevgeny Pavlovitch from her carriage had assumed in his imagination alarming and mysterious proportions. The heart of the riddle, apart from the other aspects of the affair, consisted in the dismal question: was he himself to blame for this new "enormity," or was it ——? But he did not say who else it might be. As for the initials "N.F.B.," that was as he saw it only an innocent prank, an absolutely childish prank, and it would have been unconscionable to pay any attention to it, and even, in a certain respect, almost dishonorable.

However, on the day after the disgraceful evening, in whose scandalous irregularities he was the principal "culprit," the prince had the pleasure of a morning visit from Prince S. and Adelaïda, out for a walk together. They had stopped by "principally" to inquire after his health. Adelaïda had just noticed a certain tree in the park, a splendid old tree with spreading, tortuous branches, and a huge crack and a hollow in it, and all covered with young green leaves. She had decided that she absolutely had to draw it. So during the whole half hour of their visit they talked of little else but this. Prince S. was as usual amiable and charming; he questioned the prince about the past and recalled the circumstances of their first meeting, so that almost nothing was said about the previous evening. Finally Adelaïda could restrain herself no longer and confessed with a laugh that they had come incognito; and though her confession went no further than this, it could be deduced from the word "incognito" that her parents —that is, principally, Lizaveta Prokofyevna—were particularly ill-disposed toward him. But neither Adelaïda nor Prince S. uttered a single word about her, about Aglaya, or even about Ivan Fyodorovitch throughout their visit. They did not invite the prince to continue their walk with them. There was not even a hint of inviting him to their house; indeed, a very characteristic phrase escaped Adelaïda as she was telling him about one of the water colors she was working on and suddenly expressed a great desire to show it to him. "How can we do it as soon as possible? Let's see! Either I'll send Kolya with it, if he's coming by, or I'll bring it tomorrow myself when I go for a walk with the prince," she concluded at last, glad that she had succeeded in resolving the difficulty so cleverly and conveniently for everyone.

Finally as they were about to say good-bye, Prince S. seemed suddenly to remember something. "Oh, yes," he said. "Perhaps, dear Lev Nikolayevitch, you might happen to know who that person was who was shouting to Yevgeny Pavlovitch from the carriage?"

"That was Nastassya Filippovna," said the prince. "Haven't you found out already it was she? But I don't know who was with her."

"I know, I did hear," said Prince S. quickly, "but what was

321

that shouting about? I must confess it's a complete mystery to me—to me and to others."

It was evident that Prince S. spoke with extreme perplexity.

"She spoke of some I.O.U.'s of Yevgeny Pavlovitch's," the prince answered very simply, "which Rogozhin had got hold of at her request from some moneylender, and she said that Rogozhin should await Yevgeny Pavlovitch's convenience."

"I heard, I heard, my dear Prince, but that couldn't possibly be true! Yevgeny Pavlovitch couldn't possibly have given any such I.O.U.'s. With a fortune like his! It is true that, being rather careless, he has done so in the past, and indeed I have even helped him out. But with a fortune like that to give I.O.U.'s to a moneylender and be worried about them—that is impossible. And he cannot be on such familiar and such friendly terms with Nastassya Filippovna—that's what is so mysterious. He swears he knows nothing about it and I completely believe him. But I wanted to ask you, my dear Prince, whether you knew anything about it? I mean has any rumor reached you by some miracle?"

"No, I know nothing about it, and I assure you I had nothing to do with it."

"Ah, how strange you've become, Prince! I simply don't know you today! How could I have imagined you would have had anything to do with such an affair? Well, but you must be out of sorts today."

He embraced him and kissed him.

"What do you mean had anything to do with 'such an affair'? I don't see any 'such an affair' here."

"There is no question," replied Prince S. rather dryly, "that that person wanted somehow or other to prejudice Yevgeny Pavlovitch by attributing to him before witnesses qualities which he does not and could not have."

Prince Lev Nikolayevitch was perplexed, but he continued to look steadily and inquiringly at Prince S.; but Prince S. said nothing further.

"But couldn't there simply be I.O.U.'s?" said the prince at last with a certain impatience. "Couldn't it literally be as she said yesterday?"

"But I'm telling you—judge for yourself—what can Yevgeny Pavlovitch have in common with—her and, even less, with Rogozhin? I repeat, his fortune is immense. I know this for a fact. And he is expecting another fortune from his uncle. It's simply that Nastassya Filippovna—"

Prince S. suddenly fell silent again, evidently because he

did not wish to say anything more to the prince about Nastassya Filippovna.

"Then at least he did know her, didn't he?" Prince Lev Nikolayevitch demanded suddenly, after a minute's silence.

"That appears to be so—he was frivolous enough! But if
he did, it was a long time ago, in the past, two or three years
ago. You see, he used to know Totsky. There could be nothing of this kind now, and they never could have been on such
intimate terms. You know yourself she has not been here.
She hasn't been anywhere. Many people don't know that she's
turned up again. I've noticed her carriage around for three
days, not more."

"A magnificent carriage!" said Adelaïda.

"Yes. The carriage is magnificent."

They both parted, however, on the most friendly and one
could say the most brotherly terms with the Prince Lev Nikolayevitch.

But for our hero there was an element of capital importance about this visit. Undoubtedly he had suspected a good
deal himself since the previous evening (and possibly even
earlier), but until this visit he had not permitted himself to
credit his apprehensions. Now it had become clear: Prince S.
had of course interpreted the incident incorrectly, yet he was
not far from the truth and had in any case sensed in it an
intrigue. "Perhaps, however, he understands it correctly,"
thought the prince, "but simply doesn't want to say what is
on his mind, and therefore interprets it falsely on purpose."
What was clearest of all was that they had come to see him
just now (Prince S. in particular) in the hope of learning
something; and if this was so then clearly they looked on him
as a participant in the intrigue. Moreover, if this was all true,
and if it was really of importance, it meant that *she* had some
dreadful object in mind. What object? It was terrible! "And
how is one to *stop* her? There is no possibility of stopping *her*
when she is resolved to carry out her purpose!" This the
prince knew already from experience. "She is mad! She is
mad!"

But far too many other unexplained circumstances had aris-
en that morning, all having come at once, all demanding
immediate solutions, and the prince felt very sad. He was
somewhat diverted by Vera Lebedev, who had come to see
him with little Lyuba and, laughing, had told a lengthy story.
She was followed by her sister, who had stood with her
mouth wide open, and then by Lebedev's schoolboy son, who
assured him that "the star called Wormwood" in the Apocalypse, that fell on the "fountains of waters," was according to

323

his father's interpretation the network of railroads spread over Europe. The prince did not believe that Lebedev interpreted it this way and decided to ask him about it himself at the first favorable opportunity. From Vera Lebedev the prince learned that Keller had moved into quarters with them the day before and from every indication would not be leaving them for quite some time, since he had found "people to talk to" and had struck up a friendship with General Ivolgin. He declared, however, that he was staying with them solely in order to complete his education. On the whole the prince was beginning to like Lebedev's children more and more every day. Kolya had not been there all day, he had left early for Petersburg. Lebedev too had left at dawn to transact certain little affairs of his own. But the prince was waiting impatiently for Gavril Ardalionovitch, who was sure to stop by that day.

He came toward six-thirty in the evening, immediately after dinner. At his first glance at him, the prince thought that this one gentleman, at least, must know everything there was to know about the affair thoroughly—and indeed how could he fail to know about it with such assistants as Varvara Ardalionovna and her husband? But the prince's relations with Ganya were rather peculiar. The prince had for instance entrusted the Burdovsky affair to him and made a special point of asking him to look after it, but despite this confidence, and despite something that had happened before, there were certain matters between them about which it was mutually agreed to say nothing. It sometimes seemed to the prince that Ganya for his part perhaps would have preferred the fullest and most friendly sincerity in their relations; now for example he had the feeling as Ganya came in that he was fully decided that the time had come to break the ice between them on all points. Gavril Ardalionovitch, however, was in a hurry, his sister was waiting for him at Lebedev's, they were both in a hurry to be off on some matter of urgency.

But if Ganya really was expecting a whole series of eager questions, impulsive communications and friendly confidences, he was of course very mistaken. During the twenty minutes of his visit, the prince was in fact rather pensive, almost abstracted. The questions Ganya expected—or rather the principal question he was waiting to hear, could not be asked. Then Ganya too decided to speak with greater reserve. He talked away the whole twenty minutes without stopping, laughed, carried on a light, charming and rapid chatter, but did not touch on the main point.

Among other things, Ganya told him that Nastassya Filippovna had only been four days here in Pavlovsk and was already attracting wide attention. She was staying at Darya Alexeyevna's place, a small, ramshackle house somewhere on Matrossky Street, but her carriage was almost the finest in Pavlovsk. A whole crowd of aspirants for her favor, young and old, had already gathered around her, her carriage was sometimes escorted by gentleman outriders. Nastassya Filippovna was, as she had been before, very discriminating and received only the people she wished to see. And yet a whole elite guard had formed around her, ready to stand behind her in case of need. A gentleman among the summer people had already broken his engagement on her account; and because of her one old general had come close to cursing his son. She often took driving with her a charming young girl, only sixteen, a distant relative of Darya Alexeyevna's. This girl sang well and their little house drew attention in the evenings. Nastassya Filippovna, however, behaved with extreme propriety, dressed simply but with extraordinary taste, and all the ladies envied "her taste, her beauty, and her carriage."

"Yesterday's curious incident was of course premeditated," Ganya allowed himself to say, "and must of course be passed over. To find any fault with her one would have to look hard for it, or invent it, which by the way will not be long in happening," he concluded, expecting the prince at this point to ask why he called yesterday's incident "premeditated" and why he predicted she would be slandered.

But the prince did not ask these questions.

Ganya talked in great detail about Yevgeny Pavlovitch without being especially asked, which was very strange inasmuch as he dragged him into the conversation without any reason at all. In Gavril Ardalionovitch's opinion Yevgeny Pavlovitch had not known Nastassya Filippovna and was only very slightly acquainted with her even now, having been introduced to her by someone only four days before while out walking; and it was doubtful whether he had ever been inside her house, even in the company of others. As for the I.O.U.'s, there might be something to this (Ganya was in fact certain there was); Yevgeny Pavlovitch's fortune was large of course, but "certain affairs connected with his estate were in some disorder." As soon as he touched on this interesting topic Ganya abruptly dropped it. He said not another word about Nastassya Filippovna's conduct on the previous evening, beyond his earlier passing reference to it. Finally Varvara stopped by for Ganya, stayed a minute, and declared (also without being asked) that Yevgeny Pavlovitch was in

Petersburg today and would perhaps be there tomorrow too, that her husband, Ivan Petrovitch Ptitsyn, was also in Petersburg, very likely on Yevgeny Pavlovitch's business, and that something had definitely happened there. As she was leaving, she added that Lizaveta Prokofyevna was in a fiendish mood today, but that, oddest of all, Aglaya had quarreled with her entire family, not only with her father and mother but even with both her sisters, and that "that is not at all good." Having communicated, as if in passing, this last piece of news (which was extremely meaningful to the prince), the brother and sister left. Ganya did not say a word about the "Pavlishchev's son" affair either, possibly out of false modesty, possibly to "spare the prince's feelings," but the prince nevertheless thanked him once more for the careful way he had brought the matter to a conclusion.

The prince was very glad to be left alone at last; he left the veranda, crossed the road, and went into the park; he wanted to think over and decide about a certain step. But this "step" was not the kind that can be thought over, but was precisely the kind one does not deliberate, but simply takes. He had suddenly a terrible longing to leave everything here and go back where he had come from, to some remote solitude, to leave at once without saying good-bye to anyone. He had a premonition that if he remained here even for only a few more days he would be irrevocably drawn into this world and his life would be bound to this world forever. But he did not consider this question even for ten minutes; he decided at once that it was "impossible" to run away, that it would almost be cowardice, that there were problems before him that he now had to solve or at least do everything he could to solve them. Absorbed in such thoughts, he returned home. His walk had taken less than a quarter of an hour. He was utterly unhappy at that moment.

Lebedev had not yet returned home, and toward evening Keller managed to burst in on the prince; he was not drunk, but overflowing with confidences and confessions. He told the prince flatly that he had come to tell him the whole story of his life, and that it was for this purpose he had stayed on in Pavlovsk. There was not the least chance of getting rid of him: he would not have left for anything in the world. Keller had come prepared to talk at great length and with great incoherence, but almost with his first word he skipped to his conclusion and declared that he had so completely lost "every vestige of morality" (solely because of his lack of faith in the Almighty) that he had actually turned to stealing.

"Can you imagine it!"

"Listen, Keller, if I were in your place I wouldn't confess this without some particular reason," the prince began. "But then, perhaps you do have some purpose in accusing yourself?"

"I'm telling this to you and only to you, and only in the interests of my own improvement! To no one else—I'll die and carry my secret to the grave! But, Prince, if you knew, if only you knew how hard it is in these times to get money! Where is one to get it, let me ask you? There's one answer: 'Bring in gold and diamonds and we'll lend you money against them.' That is, bring precisely the things I haven't got, can you imagine that? I finally lost my temper after I'd waited a while, and I said, 'And emeralds, do you lend money on emeralds?' And he said, 'Yes, we lend money on emeralds too.' I said, 'Well, that's excellent,' and I put on my hat and walked out. To hell with you bunch of rascals! Good Lord!"

"But did you have emeralds?"

"How would I have emeralds! Oh, Prince, what a simple, innocent, and, if I may say so, pastoral view you still take of life!"

The prince at last became less sorry for him than ashamed on his account. He even wondered whether someone's good influence couldn't do something for this man. For certain reasons he considered his own influence to be quite unsuitable, not out of self-depreciation but because of his special way of looking at things. Gradually they got to talking and before long they felt no desire to part from each other. Keller confessed with extraordinary readiness to actions of a sort that it was impossible to imagine how anyone could bring himself to speak of them. As he began each new story he assured the prince that he was repentant and inwardly "full of tears," and yet he told each one as if he was proud of his deeds, and sometimes so comically that both he and the prince ended by laughing like madmen.

"What matters," said the prince at last, "is that you have a child's trusting nature and extraordinary truthfulness. Do you know that a great deal can be forgiven you for that alone?"

"A noble nature, chivalrous and noble!" agreed Keller, greatly touched. "But you know, Prince, it's all only in dreams and, you might say, bluff. It never actually comes to anything! Why is that? I can't understand."

"Don't despair. Now it can definitely be said that you have shown me everything about yourself, haven't you? At least it seems to me impossible that anything could be added to what you have told me?"

"Impossible?" cried Keller in a pitying voice. "Oh, Prince, your way of understanding human nature is still, so to speak, completely Swiss!"

"Can you really have something more to add?" asked the prince with timid wonderment. "Well, what have you been expecting from me, Keller, tell me, please, why have you come to me with your confession?"

"From you? What have I been expecting? In the first place, it's a pleasure just to look at a person as simple as you, it's nice just sitting and talking with you. At least I know that before me is a very virtuous person, and secondly—secondly—" He fell into confusion.

"Perhaps you wanted to borrow money?" the prince suggested, very gravely and simply, even a little timidly.

Keller gave a violent start; he glanced up quickly with the same look of astonishment, looked directly into the prince's eyes, and brought his fist down loudly on the table. "Well, that's the way you completely throw a man off! Be merciful, Prince—such simplicity and such innocence as was never even heard of in the Golden Age, and at the same time you pierce a man through like an arrow, with such deep psychological insight! But, please, Prince, this calls for some explanation because I—I'm simply bowled over! Of course in the long run my object was to borrow money, but you asked about my wanting to borrow money as though you found nothing reprehensible in it, as if it was the most natural thing in the world."

"Yes—coming from you, it is."

"And you're not upset?"

"No. Why?"

"Listen, Prince, I've stayed on here since yesterday evening, first, out of special respect for the French Archbishop Bourdaloue (we were pulling corks at Lebedev's till three in the morning), but secondly and principally (I swear by all the signs of the cross I'm telling the truth!) I stayed because I wanted to impart to you, so to speak, my full, heartfelt confession—and in this way to promote my own improvement. With that idea I fell asleep toward four o'clock, drenched in tears. Will you, now, believe a man of noble nature? At the very moment I fell asleep, genuinely filled with inward and, so to speak, outward tears (because I finally was sobbing, I remember that!), a hellish thought occurred to me: 'And why not borrow some money from him after the confession, after all?' So I prepared my confession, you might say, like a sort of piquant little dish flavored with tears, so as to pave the way with those tears and, once you were softened up, have you hand over a hundred and fifty roubles. Don't you think that was dreadfully mean?"

"Yes, except that certainly wasn't the way it was, it was simply a coincidence. Two thoughts occurred at once, it happens quite often. With me it happens incessantly. However, I don't think it's a good thing, and you know, Keller, I blame myself for that more than anything. You might have been talking about myself just now. It has sometimes occurred to me," continued the prince very gravely, genuinely and profoundly interested by the question, "that everyone is like that, so I started making excuses for myself, for it is terribly hard to struggle against those *double* thoughts. I've tried. Heaven only knows how they come into being. And here you call them simply meanness! Now I'll begin being afraid of these thoughts again. Anyway, I am not your judge. But I don't think it can simply be called meanness, do you? You were acting deceitfully so as to obtain money with your tears, but you swear yourself that there was another motive for your confession, an honorable one and not simply a matter of money. As for the money, you need it for high living, don't you? And after such a confession, that is a weakness, of course. But then how is one to give up wild living in a single moment? It's not possible. So what's to be done? The best is to leave it to your conscience, isn't it?"

The prince looked at Keller with great interest. Apparently the question of double thoughts had been on his mind for some time.

"Well, after that I can't understand why they call you an idiot!" exclaimed Keller.

The prince reddened slightly.

"Even the preacher Bourdaloue wouldn't have shown a man such mercy, but you have shown mercy and judged me in a human way! So to punish myself and show you how touched I am, I don't want the hundred and fifty roubles—just give me twenty-five, and that will be plenty! At least that's all I'll be needing for the next two weeks. I won't come for money for two more weeks. I wanted to do something nice for Agashka, though she's not worth it. Oh, dear Prince, God bless you!"

Lebedev came in at last, having just returned from town, and, noticing a twenty-five-rouble note in Keller's hand, frowned. But Keller, in possession of the money, was already hurrying away and immediately disappeared. Lebedev proceeded at once to speak ill of him.

"You are unjust," said the prince at last, "he really did repent sincerely."

329

"Yes, but what is repentance? It's just like me yesterday. 'I'm vile, I'm vile'—nothing but words!"

"Then those were only words? I thought you—"

"Well, I'll tell you the truth, only you because you can see right through a man: words and actions and lies and truth are all mixed up together in me and all perfectly sincere. Truth and actions are my genuine repentance—believe it or not, I swear it—but I use words and lies in the infernal (and always present) thought of catching people up and drawing an advantage even from my tears of repentance! It's so, by God! I wouldn't have told anyone else—I'd be laughed at or spat at. But you, Prince, you judge things in a human way."

"Why, that's exactly what he said to me just now!" exclaimed the prince. "And both of you seem to be taking pride in it! You even surprise me, except that he is more sincere than you are—you have turned it into a regular profession. Come, that's enough, Lebedev, don't make such faces and don't lay your hands on your heart. Haven't you something to say to me? You haven't come in for nothing."

Lebedev made faces and began squirming.

"I have been waiting all day for you to ask you one question. For once in your life tell me the truth right from the start: did you have anything to do with that carriage coming by yesterday or not?"

Lebedev made more faces, began tittering, rubbing his hands, and even, at last, sneezing, but he still could not bring himself to speak.

"I see you did have something to do with it."

"But indirectly, only very indirectly! I'm telling you the absolute truth! The only part I had in it was to let a certain person know in good time that I had company at my house and that certain individuals were present."

"I know you sent your son *there*, he has told me so himself; but what sort of an intrigue is this?" the prince demanded impatiently.

"It's not my intrigue, it's not mine!" said Lebedev, waving his arms in protest. "There are others in it, others. And it's rather more a fantasy than an intrigue."

"But what is it all about? Explain it, for the love of Christ! Is it possible you don't understand that it concerns me directly? Why, they're trying to blacken Yevgeny Pavlovitch's character."

"Prince! Most illustrious Prince!" cried Lebedev, squirming again. "You won't let me tell you the whole truth. I've tried to tell you the truth more than once. You wouldn't let me go on with it."

The prince paused and thought for a moment.

"Well, all right," he said dejectedly, evidently after a great struggle. "Tell the truth."

"Aglaya Ivanovna—" began Lebedev promptly.

"Stop! Be still!" the prince shouted furiously, reddening with indignation and perhaps also with shame. "That can't be so, that's all nonsense! You made it up, all up yourself, or some madman like you did. Don't let me ever hear about that from you again!"

Late in the evening, toward eleven o'clock, Kolya arrived full of news. His news was of two kinds: of Petersburg and of Pavlovsk. He quickly covered the main Petersburg items (primarily about Hippolite and the affair of yesterday evening), intending to go into the details later, and hastily turned to the Pavlovsk tidings. He had returned from Petersburg three hours earlier and, without stopping to see the prince, had gone directly to the Yepanchins. "It's terrible what's going on there!" To be sure, the carriage incident was in the foreground, but something else had surely happened, something which neither he nor the prince knew anything about. "I didn't spy, of course, and I didn't want to ask anyone about it. However, I was well received, even better than I expected, but there wasn't a word about you, Prince!" The most important and interesting piece of news was that earlier Aglaya had had a quarrel with her family over Ganya. The details of the matter were unknown to him, except that the fight had been over Ganya (imagine!), that it had been violent, and that it was therefore something of capital importance. The general arrived late, frowning, with Yevgeny Pavlovitch, who was exceedingly well received, and had himself been wonderfully gay and charming. The most important piece of news was that Lizaveta Prokofyevna had quietly summoned Varvara Ardalionovna, who had been with the young ladies, and asked her to leave the house once and for all; in the most considerate manner, however. "I heard it from Varya herself." But when Varya came out of Lizaveta Prokofyevna's rooms and said good-bye to the girls, they had no idea she had been refused entry to the house forever and that she was saying good-bye to them for the last time.

"But Varvara Ardalionovna was here to see me at seven o'clock," said the prince in astonishment.

"She was turned out at eight or a little before. I'm very sorry for Varya. I'm sorry for Ganya. They always seem to have some kind of intrigue going on, they couldn't get along without that; I never could make out what they were plotting, and I don't want to know. But I assure you, my dear kind

331

Prince, that Ganya has a heart. Of course in many respects he's completely lost, but in many other ways he has good points that are worth seeking out, and I'll never forgive myself for not having understood him in the past—I don't know whether I should go on with them now, after this thing with Varya. It's true that I started off with them completely separately and independently, however, I have to think it over."

"You don't need to feel too sorry for your brother," the prince said to him. "If it has gone this far, Gavril Ardalionovitch must appear dangerous to Lizaveta Prokofyevna, and that means that certain hopes of his are being confirmed."

"What hopes?" cried Kolya in amazement. You don't think Aglaya—that's impossible!"

The prince said nothing.

Two minutes later Kolya added, "You're a terrible skeptic, Prince; I've noticed for some time you're getting to be an extreme skeptic. You're beginning to disbelieve everything and imagine all kinds of things. But have I used the word 'skeptic' correctly?"

"I think you have, though I'm not really sure myself."

"But I'm taking back the word 'skeptic,' I've found another explanation!" cried Kolya suddenly. "You're not a skeptic, you're jealous! You're infernally jealous of Ganya over a certain proud young lady!"

Having said this, Kolya jumped to his feet and began laughing as perhaps he had never laughed before. Seeing that the prince was blushing, Kolya laughed all the harder. He was delighted by the idea that the prince was jealous over Aglaya, but he stopped laughing at once when he observed that the prince was really hurt. After that they talked earnestly and anxiously for another hour or hour and a half.

The next day the prince had to spend the whole morning in Petersburg on a pressing matter of business. As he was starting back to Pavlovsk around five o'clock he met Ivan Fyodorovitch at the station. The general abruptly seized him by the arm and, looking all around him as if fearful of something, pulled the prince with him into a first-class carriage so that they might travel together. He was burning with impatience to discuss something important.

"First of all, my dear Prince, don't be angry with me, and if there's been any failing on my part, forget about it. I would have stopped by to see you myself yesterday, but I didn't know how Lizaveta Prokofyevna would take it. My house is simply hell. An inscrutable sphinx has settled in there, and I go around without understanding a thing. As for you, it seems to me you're the least to blame of anyone, though of course a great deal has happened through you. You see, Prince, it's nice to be a philanthropist, but not all that nice. You've probably found this out already. I like kindness, of course, and I respect Lizaveta Prokofyevna, but—"

The general went on a long time in this vein, but what he said was amazingly incoherent. It was evident that he was shocked and extremely disturbed by something utterly beyond his understanding.

"I have no doubt that you had nothing to do with it," he said, speaking out more clearly at last, "but don't come to visit us for a while, I beg you as a friend, not until there's been a change in the wind. And as for Yevgeny Pavlovitch," he cried in sudden heat, "it's all senseless slander—the slander of all time! It's a plot, it's nothing but an intrigue, an attempt to wreck everything and make us quarrel. You see, Prince, I'll tell you confidentially, there hasn't yet been a single word said between us and Yevgeny Pavlovitch, understand? We're not bound in any way, but this word might soon be said, and possibly very soon! So this is meant to spoil it all! And why—for what reason—that's what I do not understand! She's an extraordinary woman, an eccentric woman; I'm so afraid of her I can hardly sleep at night. And what a carriage! White horses. And all this *chic*—this is exactly what they call it in French—*chic!* Who gave it to her? I confess the day before yesterday I had the sinful thought that it might be Yevgeny Pavlovitch. But it turns out this is impossible, yet if it's impossible, what does she want to make a mess of everything for? That's the problem! To keep Yevgeny Pavlovitch for herself? But I tell you once more, and I'm ready to swear it, he doesn't know her and those I.O.U.'s are sheer invention! And the familiar way she shouted to him in the street! It's an obvious plot! It's clear that we must dismiss it with contempt and redouble our respect for Yevgeny Pavlovitch. That's what I told Lizaveta Prokofyevna. Now here is my private opinion: I am firmly convinced that she is doing this out of personal revenge against me for what happened quite a while ago—do you remember?—although I never did anything to be blamed for. I blush even at the thought of it. Now suddenly here she is again, I'd thought she disappeared for good. Where is this Rogozhin keeping himself? I thought she had become Madame Rogozhin a long time ago."

In short, the man was completely baffled. During the whole trip, which lasted almost an hour, he kept on talking, he asked questions, he answered them himself, he pressed the prince's hand, and he did at least convince the prince of one thing: that he hadn't the slightest suspicion of him. This was important to the prince. The general finished by telling him a story about Yevgeny Pavlovitch's uncle, who was the head of some government bureau in Petersburg, "highly placed, seventy years old, *viveur*, gourmet, and altogether quite an old tomcat. Ha, ha! I know he'd heard about Nastassya Filippovna, and in fact he even tried to have her. I called on him the other day. He wasn't receiving, he wasn't well, but he's rich, rich, and a man of consequence—may God give him many more good years, but in the end Yevgeny Pavlovitch will inherit everything. Yes, yes. Yet I'm afraid. I don't know what of, but I'm afraid. It's as if there was something in the air, something like a bat, trouble flying around, and I'm afraid, I'm afraid!"

And it was only on the third day, as we have said already, that the formal reconciliation took place at last between the Yepanchins and Prince Lev Nikolayevitch.

Chapter TWELVE

∽✺∾

It was seven o'clock in the evening. The prince was about to take a walk in the park. Suddenly Lizaveta Prokofyevna, alone, came up onto his veranda.

"In the first place," she began, "don't get the idea I've come to apologize to you. Nonsense! It was entirely your fault."

The prince said nothing.

"Was it your fault or not?"

"As much mine as yours. However, neither you or I did anything wrong intentionally. Three days ago I did think I was to blame, but now I have come to the conclusion that is not so."

"So that's the way you are! Very well, listen to me and sit down, for I don't intend to stand up."

They both sat.

"In the second place, not one word about those wicked young boys! I shall sit and talk with you for ten minutes. I've come to you for some information (Heaven knows what you thought I might be here for!), and if you say a single word about certain insolent boys I shall get up and leave and be through with you forever."

"Very well," replied the prince.

"Now let me ask you: about two or two and a half months ago, around Eastertime, did you write a letter to Aglaya?"

"I—I did."

"For what purpose? What was in the letter? Show it to me."

Lizaveta Prokofyevna's eyes were blazing, she was fairly trembling with impatience.

"I don't have the letter," said the prince, surprised and terribly ill-at-ease. "If it still exists intact, Aglaya Ivanovna has it."

"Don't trick your way out of it! What did you write about?"

"I'm not tricking my way out of it, and I'm not afraid of anything. I see no reason why I shouldn't write."

"Hold your tongue! You shall speak afterward. What was in the letter? Why are you turning red?"

The prince thought a moment.

"I don't know what you have in mind, Lizaveta Prokofyevna. I only see that this letter is displeasing to you. You must admit that I might refuse to answer such a question, but to show you I have no fears about this letter, and don't regret having written it, and am certainly not blushing on account of it," (here the prince blushed twice as hard as before), "I shall repeat that letter to you because I think I remember it by heart."

Having said this, the prince recited the letter almost word for word as he had written it.

"What a great lot of nonsense! What is the meaning of such nonsense according to you?" demanded Lizaveta Prokofyevna sharply, having listened with the closest attention.

"I don't completely know myself. I know that my feeling was sincere. There were moments then when I was intensely alive and full of extraordinary hopes."

"What hopes?"

"It's hard to explain, but not the kind you are undoubtedly thinking of now. Hopes—well, in a word, hopes for the future and joy that *there* I was perhaps not a stranger, not a foreigner. I was suddenly very glad to be in my own country. One sunny morning I took up a pen and wrote the letter to her—why to her, I don't know. Sometimes one wants a friend near at hand; I suppose I wanted a friend," the prince added after a hesitation.

"Are you in love, is that it?"

"N-no. I—I wrote to her as to a sister. I even signed as a brother."

"Hmm! On purpose. I understand."

"It's very painful for me to answer these questions of yours, Lizaveta Prokofyevna."

"I know it's painful, and it doesn't make the least difference to me that it's painful to you. Listen, tell me the truth as you would before God: are you lying to me or aren't you?"

"I am not lying."

"You're telling the truth that you're not in love?"

"I believe I am telling the complete truth."

"Oh, you 'believe,' do you? Did the little brat take it to her?"

"I asked Nikolai Ardalionovitch—"

"The brat! The little brat!" Lizaveta Prokofyevna interrupted in exasperation. "I don't know anything about any Nikolai Ardalionovitch! The little brat!"

"Nikolai Ardalionovitch—"

"The brat, I'm telling you!"

"No, not the brat—Nikolai Ardalionovitch," the prince answered at last, in a firm voice though rather softly.

"All right, my dear man, all right! I won't forget you for that!"

It took her a minute to contain her emotions and calm herself.

"And what does 'the poor knight' mean?"

"I have no idea. That was without me. Some sort of joke."

"How nice to find it out all at once! But could she really have been interested in you? She called you a 'freak' and an 'idiot.' "

"You needn't have repeated that to me," said the prince reproachfully but almost in a whisper.

"Don't be angry. The girl is willful, crazy, spoiled! If she falls in love with anyone she's certain to insult him in public and laugh in his face. I was just the same way. Only please don't go congratulating yourself, dear man, she's not yours. I refuse to believe it and it will never be! I am saying this so that you may take steps now. Listen, swear that you aren't married to that woman."

"What are you talking about, Lizaveta Prokofyevna? Good Lord!" said the prince, startled.

"But you almost did marry her, didn't you?"

"Yes, I almost did," answered the prince, bowing his head.

"Then aren't you in love with her? Haven't you come here now for *her?* For *that woman?"*

"I have not come here to get married," replied the prince.

"Is there anything sacred to you in the world?"

"Yes."

"Then swear that you have not come to marry her."

"I'll swear by anything you like!"

"I believe you. You may kiss me. I can breathe freely at last. But understand that Aglaya does not love you; take steps in time, for she won't marry you as long as I'm alive in this world! Do you hear?"

"I hear." The prince was blushing so much that he could not look directly at Lizaveta Prokofyevna.

"Be sure you remember it! I was waiting for you as one waits for Providence (you weren't worth it!); I have soaked my pillow at night with tears—oh, not for you, my dear, have no fear. I have my own sorrow, a different one, ever-lastingly the same. But here's why I've been waiting for you with such impatience: I still believe that God Himself sent you to me as a friend and brother. I have no one close to me, except old Belokonskaya, and even she has gone away—and besides she's gotten as stupid as a sheep in her old age. Now simply answer yes or no: do you know why *she* was shouting from her carriage the other night?"

"On my word of honor, I had nothing to do with it and I know nothing about it!"

"That's enough, I believe you. At present I too have other ideas about this myself, but only yesterday morning I blamed it all on Yevgeny Pavlovitch—all the day before yesterday and yesterday morning. Now, of course, I can't help agreeing with them. It's plain he's been made a fool of for some reason, for some purpose (that alone is suspicious! and not at all nice, either!)—but Aglaya won't marry him, I can tell you that! He may be an excellent man, but this is how it's going to be. I had hesitations before, but now I've definitely made up my mind: 'Lay me in my coffin and bury me in the earth, then marry off my daughter,' that's what I told the general today. You see that I'm trusting you, don't you?"

"I see and I understand."

Lizaveta Prokofyevna looked penetratingly at the prince. She seemed very eager to learn what impression her news about Yevgeny Pavlovitch made on him.

"You know nothing about Gavril Ivolgin?"

"That is—I know quite a lot."

"Did you or didn't you know he was in touch with Aglaya?"

"I had no idea," said the prince, surprised and even startled. "Do you mean that Gavril Ardalionovitch has been in touch with Aglaya? That can't be!"

"It's very recent. It's his sister who has been here paving the way for him all winter, she's been working at it like a rat."

"I don't believe it," the prince said firmly after a moment of troubled thought. "If this were so, I would certainly have known about it."

"Did you think he would come to you personally and confess it while weeping on your shoulder? Oh, you simpleton, you simpleton! Everyone fools you like a—like a— And aren't you ashamed to trust him? Can't you see that he's been cheating you at every turn?"

"I know very well that he does deceive me sometimes," the prince reluctantly admitted, in a low voice, "and he knows that I know it—" he added and broke off.

"He knows it and he trusts him! This is the limit! However, that's just the way it would be with you, so why am I surprised at it? Good heaven! Was there ever such a man? Pooh! And do you know that Ganya or else that Varya has put her in touch with Nastassya Filippovna?"

"Put whom?" cried the prince.

"Aglaya."

"I don't believe it! It's not possible. With what object?"

He jumped up from his chair.

"And I don't believe it either, though there is some evidence. The girl is headstrong, the girl is whimsical, the girl is crazy! The girl is wicked, wicked, wicked! I'll say it for a thousand years, she's wicked! All of mine are like that now, even that little hen Alexandra, but that other one has gotten quite out of hand. But I still don't believe it! Perhaps because I don't want to believe it," she added, as if to herself. "Why haven't you been coming to visit?" she suddenly demanded, turning again to the prince. "Why haven't you come for three whole days?" she shouted impatiently to him once more.

The prince began telling her his reasons, but she interrupted him again.

"Everyone looks on you as a fool and deceives you! You went to town yesterday, I'll swear you were down on your knees begging that rascal to accept your ten thousand!"

"Not at all, I never thought of it. I didn't even see him and, what's more, he is not a rascal. I had a letter from him."

"Show me the letter!"

The prince took a note from his portfolio and handed it to Lizaveta Prokofyevna. It was as follows:

Dear Sir,
I have, of course, in the world's eyes not the slightest

338

*right to any pride. In the world's opinion I am too insig-
nificant for that. But that is in the world's eyes and not
in yours. I am fully convinced that you, dear sir, are
perhaps better than other men. I do not agree with Doktorenko, and I differ with him in this matter. I shall
never take a kopeck from you, but you have helped my
mother and for this I am bound to be grateful to you,
though it be out of weakness. In any case I look on you
differently and feel I should tell you this. Whereupon I
assume that there can be no further relations of any sort
between us.*

Antip Burdovsky

*P.S. The difference between the two hundred roubles
and the sum I paid will be faithfully reimbursed to you
in the course of time.*

"What nonsense!" commented Lizaveta Prokofyevna, tossing back the note. "It wasn't worth reading. What are you
smiling at?"

"Admit that you were pleased to read it."

"What? That drivel, eaten through with vanity! Don't you
see they have all gone mad with pride and vanity?"

"Yes, but nonetheless he has admitted himself wrong, and
broken with Doktorenko, and the more vain he is the more
it must have cost to his vanity. Oh, what a little child you
are, Lizaveta Prokofyevna!"

"Perhaps you'd like me to slap your ears?"

"No, certainly not. It's only that reading the note gave you
pleasure, yet you hide it. Why are you ashamed of your feelings? You're like this in everything."

"Don't you dare set foot in my house now!" cried Lizaveta
Prokofyevna, jumping up and turning pale with anger. "Don't
ever let me see a sign of you there again!"

"In another three days you will come to me yourself and
ask me. Now, aren't you ashamed? These are your best feelings, why are you ashamed of them? You are only tormenting yourself."

"I'll die first. I shall never ask you! I'll forget your name! I
have forgotten it!!"

She rushed away from the prince.

"I have been forbidden to come to your house already,
without you telling me!" the prince called after her.

"Wh-what! Who has forbidden you?" She turned as if
pricked by a pin. The prince hesitated before answering. He
sensed that he had made a serious blunder.

339

"Who has forbidden you?" Lizaveta Prokofyevna cried furiously.

"Aglaya Ivanovna."

"When? Well, spe-eak!!!"

"She sent word this morning I was never to dare come to your house."

Lizaveta Prokofyevna stood as rigid as stone, but she was thinking hard.

"What did she send? Whom did she send? That little brat? A verbal message?" she suddenly exclaimed again.

"I received a note," said the prince.

"Where? Give it. At once!"

The prince thought a minute, then took from his waistcoat pocket a messy scrap of paper on which was written:

Prince Lev Nikolayevitch! If after all that has happened you intended to surprise me with a visit to our house, you may be assured that you will not find me among those who will be pleased to see you.

Aglaya Yepanchin

Lizaveta Prokofyevna reflected for a minute, then suddenly rushed up to the prince, seized him by the arm, and dragged him after her.

"Now! Come along, at once! It must be at once, this minute!" she cried in a fit of extraordinary excitement and impatience.

"But you're exposing me to—"

"To what? You innocent simpleton! It's as if you weren't even a man! Well, now I'll see it all myself, with my own eyes."

"But at least let me get my hat."

"Here's your revolting hat. Come on! You can't even choose a hat with taste! She did this—she did this after what had happened—in a rage," she muttered, pulling the prince after her without letting go of his arm for a moment. "I stood up for you this morning, I said out loud you were a fool for not coming. Otherwise she wouldn't have written such a silly note! An improper note. Improper for a noble, well-brought-up, clever young girl! Hmm!" she went on. "Or else—else perhaps—perhaps she became vexed herself at your not coming, only she didn't consider that one can't write like that to an idiot because he will take it literally, as has happened. Why are you listening to me?" she cried, realizing that she had said too much. "She needs a clown like you, to amuse her. She hasn't seen one for a long time. That's why she's asking you! And I'm glad, glad that now she'll make a laughingstock of you—glad! It's all you're worth. And she knows how to do it—oh, she knows how to do that!"

PART
THREE

Chapter Nine

PART

THREE

Chapter ONE

◦◦◦◦◦

We hear constant complaints that there are no practical people among us, that there are for instance plenty of politicians and plenty of generals, and that any number of managing directors of various sorts can be turned up at a moment's notice, but no practical people. At least, everyone complains that there are none. It is even said that on certain railroad lines there is no adequate service personnel. It is supposed to be altogether impossible to set up a tolerable administrative staff to manage a steamship company. You hear of trains colliding and newly opened railway bridges collapsing. You read of a train wintering in the middle of a snowfield, the passengers having set out on a trip of a few hours only to spend five days in the snow. They tell of hundreds of tons of merchandise lying rotting for two and three months before being dispatched, while elsewhere (though this is hard to believe) a certain administrator—that is, an inspector of some sort—has administered a punch in the nose to a merchant's agent who has been pressing him to dispatch the goods, and has moreover justified his administrative action on the ground that he became "hot under the collar." There are so many posts in government service that it is frightening just to think about them; everyone has been in the service, everyone intends to be in the service; so that you would think that from such an abundance of material it would be possible to form a decent administrative staff to manage a steamship line. A very simple answer is sometimes given for this—so simple that one hesitates to believe it. It is true, we are told, that everyone in the country has served or serves now and that this has been going on for two hundred years on the best German pattern, from grandfather to grandson; but the people in the civil service are precisely those who are the most impractical, and it

345

has reached the point where an abstract turn of mind and a lack of practical knowledge have even recently been considered by the civil servants themselves as being the highest of virtues and the best of recommendations. However, we did not mean to discuss civil servants, we set out to talk about practical people. There is no doubt that overcaution and a complete lack of initiative have always been regarded in our country as the hallmarks of a practical man—and are so regarded now. But why—if this opinion is to be taken as a disparagement—blame only ourselves? Lack of originality has from the beginning, the world over, always been considered the prime characteristic and the best recommendation of the businesslike, practical man of affairs, and at least ninety-nine percent of mankind (at the very least) has always gone along with that opinion, and only one percent at most, now or in the past, has ever thought otherwise.

Society has almost always regarded inventors and geniuses at the beginning of their careers—and very often at the end of their careers, too—as no better than fools; this is, to be sure, a platitude familiar to everyone. For example if everyone for decades put his money into a state savings and loan bank and millions had been invested in it at four percent, then quite obviously when the bank ceased to exist and everyone was left to his own devices, the greater part of these millions would inevitably be lost in frantic speculation and fall into the hands of swindlers—as required, indeed, by decency and propriety. Yes, propriety; for if a proper diffidence and a decent lack of originality have until now, in our society, been by common accord the inalienable qualities of a proper, well-regulated man, then it would be too disrupting, and even indecent, to change this state of affairs suddenly. What tender and devoted mother, for example, would not be horrified and sick with fear if her son or daughter took the slightest step off the beaten path. "No, better to be happy and live in comfort without originality," thinks every mother as she rocks her child to sleep. And from time immemorial our nurses, as they rock the children, have crooned, "Dressed in gold you'll go your way, and be a general one day." So, even to our nannies the rank of general represents the utmost in Russian bliss, and this has always been the most popular national ideal of quiet and gracious felicity. And indeed, once he has passed his examinations and served his time for thirty-five years, who in our country can fail to become a general eventually, and manage to pile up a tidy sum in the bank? This is how a Russian achieves almost effortlessly the reputation of being a capable and practical man. In fact, *not* to become a general is possible here only for an original man; in other words, a restless and searching man. Perhaps there is the possibility of error here, but on the whole it seems certainly true, and our society has been perfectly correct in defining its ideal of the practical person.

However, we have digressed too far; we only intended to say a few explanatory words about our friends the Yepanchins. That family, or at least the more reflective members of it, suffered from a common trait which was in exact opposition to the virtues we have been discussing above. Without clearly understanding the fact (for it is difficult to understand), they nevertheless suspected at times that things did not happen in their family the way things happened in other families. In other families everything went smoothly, in theirs everything was rough; other people stayed on the tracks, they were derailed at every turn; everyone else could be decorously timid, they could not. Lizaveta Prokofyevna, it was true, was subject to frights, but this was not that well-bred, worldly timidity for which they all longed. However, it was likely that only Lizaveta Prokofyevna was troubled; the girls were still young—though very knowing and ironical; and as for the general, he saw through to the bottom of things (not without some strain however), but confined himself to saying only "hmm" when the situation became perplexing, and in the end placed all his confidence in Lizaveta Prokofyevna. This meant that she bore the responsibility. It was not that this family was distinguished by any particular initiative or inclination to leave the beaten track in a conscious effort toward originality, which would have been utterly improper. No indeed! There was nothing of the sort really; that is, there was no such conscious aim; nevertheless, it worked out, in spite of everything, that while very respectable, the Yepanchin family was not quite everything a respectable family is expected to be. Of late, Lizaveta Prokofyevna had begun to place the blame entirely on herself and her "unfortunate" character—which only added to her suffering. She was forever reproaching herself for being a "foolish, uncouth old eccentric"; and, tormented by unfounded suspicions, she was constantly losing control of herself, she was at a loss when confronted by the most ordinary difficulties, and she invariably exaggerated every misfortune.

We have already mentioned at the beginning of our story that the Yepanchins benefited from an esteem which was both genuine and universal. Even General Ivan Fyodorovitch himself, a man of obscure origins, was unhesitatingly received everywhere with respect. And indeed he deserved respect;

first, as a man of wealth and a person "not to be over-looked," and secondly, as a man who was eminently decent, while not being impossibly intelligent. But it does appear that a certain dullness of mind is almost an essential quality, if not for every public man, at least for everyone who is seriously interested in making money. Finally, the general had proper manners, was modest, knew how to keep silent when he had to and, at the same time, how to keep from being trampled—and this was not only because he was a general but because he acted as an honest and honorable man. And what was more important, he had powerful protection. As for Lizaveta Prokofyevna, she was, as we have explained already, of good family, though this is not considered among us Russians to be of much importance unless it is backed up by good connections. But she did, after all, have such connections; she was respected and, in the end, liked by people of such consequence that, naturally, everyone followed them in respecting and receiving her. There was no doubt that her familial anxieties were groundless, the causes of them insignificant and ridiculously exaggerated; but of course if you have a wart on your forehead or on your nose it always seems that no one has a thing in the world to do but look at your wart, make fun of it, and condemn you for it, though you might be the discoverer of America. Nor was there any doubt that in society Lizaveta Prokofyevna was actually considered "eccentric," though this did not prevent her from being incontestably respected: but Lizaveta Prokofyevna ceased to believe, finally, that she was respected—and this was where the trouble lay. Looking at her daughters she was tormented by the suspicion that she was forever spoiling their prospects, that she had a ridiculous disposition, improper and unbearable, and because of this, quite obviously, she incessantly leveled accusations at her daughters and Ivan Fyodorovitch and fought with them for days on end, at the same time loving them selflessly and almost with passion.

What worried her most of all was the thought that her daughters were becoming as eccentric as she, and that such girls did not, and should not, exist in society. "They're growing up to be nihilists, that's all!" she said to herself every minute. In the past year, and particularly lately, this melancholy notion had become more and more anchored in her mind. "In the first place, why don't they get married?" she asked herself time and again. "So as to torment their mother —it gives them something to do with their lives; and it all comes from these new ideas, all this accursed women's rights question! Didn't Aglaya get it into her head six months ago to cut her magnificent hair? (Good Lord, I didn't even have such hair in my time!) She had the scissors in her hand, and I had to beg her on my knees! Well, she did it out of spite, if you please, to make her mother suffer, because she's a wicked girl, willful, spoiled, but above all wicked, wicked, wicked! But didn't that fat Alexandra try to copy her and cut off her locks too, and not out of spite or caprice, but in complete simplicity, like a fool, because Aglaya had convinced her that without hair she would sleep better and stop having head-aches! And the suitors, the countless, countless suitors they have had in the past five years! And they were truly good fellows; some of them even happened to be exceptional fellows! What are they waiting for? Why aren't they getting married? Only to torment their mother—there's no other reason—none, none whatever!"

At last the sun seemed to dawn in her maternal heart; at least one daughter, at least Adelaïda would finally be settled: "At least one off my hands," Lizaveta Prokofyevna would say whenever she had occasion to express herself on the subject (in her thoughts she was far more tender). And how well, how suitably the whole affair had worked out! Even in society it was talked of with respect. He was a man of excellent reputation, a man of property, a prince, a good man, and one who, on top of everything else, appealed to her daughter's heart. What, after all, could be better? But she had always in the past been less afraid for Adelaïda than for her two other daughters, though her artistic inclinations had sometimes troubled the ever-apprehensive heart of Lizaveta Proko-fyevna. "On the other hand she has a cheerful disposition, and a lot of good sense, too—she'll land on her feet, that girl!" she finally comforted herself. She was most afraid for Aglaya. As for her eldest, Alexandra, Lizaveta Prokofyevna did not know herself whether to be afraid for her or not. Sometimes it seemed she was a girl who had completely "lost her chances"; she was twenty-five, so she would certainly be an old maid. And "a beauty like that," too. Lizaveta Proko-fyevna sometimes even wept for her at night, while Alexan-dra Ivanovna herself slept soundly in perfect peace. "But what's the matter with her—is she a nihilist or simply a fool?" That she was no fool, however, even Lizaveta Proko-fyevna had no doubt: she had the greatest respect for Alex-andra Ivanovna's judgment and liked to have consultations with her. But that she was something of a "shrinking violet," of that there was no doubt: "She's so calm and collected there's no getting her moving! And yet shrinking violets aren't calm and collected! Ah! I can't make them out at all!"

Lizaveta Prokofyevna had a certain unaccountable feeling of sympathy with Alexandra Ivanovna, more than with Aglaya, who was her idol. But the rancorous outbursts (with which she chiefly expressed her maternal solicitude and sympathy), her taunts and names, such as "shrinking violet," only amused Alexandra. It sometimes reached the point that the merest trifles made Lizaveta Prokofyevna dreadfully angry and drove her into a fit. Alexandra Ivanovna, for instance, was fond of sleeping late and ordinarily had a great quantity of dreams, but her dreams were always remarkable for their extraordinarily vacuous and innocent character, like the dreams of a seven-year-old child; so that the very innocence of her dreams would somehow, once again, arouse the mother's irritation. Once Alexandra Ivanovna saw nine hens in a dream, and this led to a definite falling-out between herself and her mother—why, it would be difficult to explain. Once, and only once, had she managed to dream something that might be considered original: she dreamed of a monk who was alone in some sort of dark room which she was afraid to enter. The dream was immediately conveyed triumphantly to Lizaveta Prokofyevna by her two laughing sisters; but their mother became angry once again and called all three of them fools. "Hmm! She is placid, like a fool, and a regular 'shrinking violet,' there's no stirring her up, and yet she is sad, sometimes she looks quite sad! What is she moping about?" Sometimes she put this question to Ivan Fyodorovitch, and, as usual, she put it to him hysterically, peremptorily, expecting an immediate reply. Ivan Fyodorovitch said "Hmm," frowned, shrugged his shoulders, spread his arms wide, and declared:

"She needs a husband!"

"At least God let him not be like you, Ivan Fyodorovitch," Lizaveta Prokofyevna said at last, exploding like a bomb. "Not like you in his opinionated ideas and judgments, Ivan Fyodorovitch, not a crude vulgarian like you, Ivan Fyodorovitch—"

Ivan Fyodorovitch promptly retired from the field, and Lizaveta Prokofyevna quieted down after her "explosion." Needless to say, the same evening she became uncommonly attentive, soft-spoken, tender, and affectionate toward Ivan Fyodorovitch, toward the "crude vulgarian" Ivan Fyodorovitch, toward her kind, dear, and beloved Ivan Fyodorovitch, because all her life she had been fond of, and actually in love with, her Ivan Fyodorovitch, a fact of which Ivan Fyodorovitch himself was well aware, and for which he greatly respected his Lizaveta Prokofyevna.

But her chief and constant concern was Aglaya.

"She is exactly, exactly like me, the very image of me in every respect," Lizaveta Prokofyevna would say to herself. "A horrid, willful little devil! A nihilist, an eccentric, a crazy girl, and wicked, wicked, wicked! Good God, how unhappy she will be!"

But, as we have said already, the sun that had arisen within her had softened and illuminated all things for the moment. For almost a whole month of Lizaveta Prokofyevna's life she had a complete rest from her anxieties. As Adelaïda's marriage approached, Aglaya too was talked of in society, and Aglaya carried herself everywhere so beautifully, so serenely, so triumphantly, a little proudly, perhaps, but how it became her! She had been so affectionate and so friendly toward her mother for the whole month! ("It's true that Yevgeny Pavlovitch must be very, very closely watched, studied thoroughly, and Aglaya herself doesn't seem to be favoring him much more than the others!") Still, she had suddenly become such a delightful girl—and how beautiful! Good Lord, how beautiful! More beautiful every day! And then—

And then this dreadful little prince, this miserable little idiot had made his appearance, and everything was again in a turmoil, and everything around the house was topsy-turvy!

What had happened, though?

Nothing would have happened to other people, that was certain. But it was Lizaveta Prokofyevna's peculiarity that, with her inherent and ever-present anxiety, she managed to find in the combinations and interplay of the most ordinary things something that would alarm her, sometimes until it made her ill, filling her with fear that was all the more terrifying for being unfounded and irrational. What must she have felt when now suddenly, through all this tangle of absurd and groundless anxieties, there did begin to appear something that really seemed important, something that might in fact justify uneasiness, doubt, and suspicion?

"And how dared they, how dared they send me that accursed anonymous letter about that *creature* being in communication with Aglaya?"—Lizaveta Prokofyevna was thinking all the way home, with the prince in tow, and when she got home, as she made him sit at the round table where all the family was gathered: "How did they even dare think of it? I would die of shame if I believed a syllable of it, or if I showed that letter to Aglaya! Playing tricks on us, the Yepanchins! And it's all the fault of Ivan Fyodorovitch, it's all your fault, Ivan Fyodorovitch! Ah, why didn't we go to Yelagin Island, I said we should go to Yelagin! I know Varya probably wrote that letter, or perhaps— Ivan Fyodorovitch is to blame for the whole thing! He is the one that *creature* played this trick on, as a souvenir of their former relations, to show him up as a fool, just as she laughed at him for a fool before and led him around by the nose when he was still taking pearls to her. And so finally we're mixed up in it, your daughters are mixed up in it, Ivan Fyodorovitch, young girls, young ladies of the best society, marriageable girls; they were right there, they were standing there, they heard it all, and they are mixed up in that business of those dreadful boys too, rest assured, they were there too and they heard it! I will never forgive him, I will never forgive that miserable little prince, ever! And why has Aglaya been hysterical for three days? Why has she been ready to fight with her sisters, even with Alexandra, whose hand she always used to kiss, as a mother would—she respected her so? Why has she been talking in riddles to everyone for the last three days? What has Gavril Ivolgin to do with it? Why, yesterday and today, did she start praising Gavril Ivolgin and then burst into tears? Why is that accursed "poor knight" mentioned in that anonymous letter, when she never showed the prince's letter even to her sisters? And why—for what earthly reason did I go running to him like a scalded cat just now and drag him here myself? By heaven, I must have lost my mind—what have I done now? To talk about one's daughters' secrets to a young man, and—and about secrets that practically concern him! Thank God at least he's an idiot and—and—a friend of the family! But is it possible that Aglaya could be attracted to a little freak like that? Lord, what am I saying? Dear me! We are a set of originals—we ought to be shown off in a glass case—especially me—at ten kopecks' admission. I won't forgive you for this, Ivan Fyodorovitch, ever! And why doesn't she make fun of him now? She promised to make fun of him, and now she doesn't. There she is, staring at him wide-eyed, she doesn't say a word, she doesn't go away, she stands there, though she told him herself not to come. He sits there all pale. And that damned, accursed chatterbox Yevgeny Pavlovitch takes over the whole conversation! He runs on and on, not letting anyone get a word in edgewise. I could have found out everything at once, if only the conversation could have been brought to the point."

The prince was indeed quite pale as he sat at the round table and at the same time appeared to be in a state of extreme anxiety and, at moments, seized by a rapture he could not comprehend himself. Oh, how he feared to look toward the corner from which two familiar dark eyes were gazing at him, and at the same time how deliriously happy that he was there sitting among them all again, and that he would hear her familiar voice—after what she had written him. "Good Lord, what would she say now!" He had not uttered a word himself but listened with concentration to the "running on" of Yevgeny Pavlovitch, who had seldom been so pleased and excited as then, that evening. The prince listened to him and for a long time understood hardly a word. Except for Ivan Fyodorovitch, who had not yet returned from Petersburg, everyone was there. Prince S. was also present. Apparently they were gathered in order to go out and listen to the band a little later before tea. The conversation in progress had evidently begun before the prince's arrival. Soon, out of the blue, Kolya appeared on the veranda. "So he is received here as he was before," the prince thought to himself.

The Yepanchins' place at Pavlovsk was a sumptuous house in the style of a Swiss chalet, attractively framed with climbing blooms and foliage, with a small but charming flower garden all around it. They were all sitting on the veranda, as at the prince's, except that the veranda was rather larger and more luxuriously furnished.

The subject of conversation was apparently to the taste of only a few of those present; it had evidently arisen out of some heated argument, and of course everyone wanted to change the subject, but Yevgeny Pavlovitch seemed to pursue it all the more ardently for that reason, paying no attention to the effect it produced, and the arrival of the prince seemed to stimulate him even more. Lizaveta Prokofyevna was frowning, though she did not understand everything that was being said. Aglaya, sitting to one side, almost in a corner, did not leave, she remained listening, stubbornly silent.

"I beg your pardon," replied Yevgeny Pavlovitch heatedly. "I am not saying anything against liberalism. Liberalism is no sin, it is an essential component of the whole, which without the whole would fall to pieces or perish. Liberalism has as much right to exist as the most proper conservatism; but I am attacking Russian liberalism, and I say once again that I am attacking it precisely because the Russian liberal is not a *Russian* liberal, but an *un-Russian* liberal. Show me a Russian liberal and I will immediately kiss him in front of you all."

"That is, if he cares to kiss you," said Alexandra Ivanovna, who was greatly stirred, and even her cheeks were more flushed than usual.

"Well, there you are," thought Lizaveta Prokofyevna to herself. "She sleeps and eats and you can't rouse her, and then suddenly, once a year, she says something that makes you throw up your hands in amazement."

The prince noticed in a passing glance that Alexandra Ivanovna seemed very displeased that Yevgeny Pavlovitch was speaking so lightly on a serious subject, speaking as if he was moved and yet making a joke of it.

"I was saying just now, Prince, just before you arrived," Yevgeny Pavlovitch went on, "that up to now our liberals have come from only two levels of society, from the old landowning class—now abolished—and from the seminary. And since both classes have turned into absolute castes, entities completely separated from the nation and becoming more so from generation to generation, everything they have done and are doing is completely non-national."

"What? Do you mean that all that has been done—none of it is Russian?" protested Prince S.

"None of it is national; it may be Russian, but it is not national. Our liberals are not Russian, our conservatives are not Russian, none of them. And believe me, the nation will never accept anything that has been done by landowners and divinity students, either now or later."

"Well, that's just splendid!" Prince S. replied heatedly. "How can you maintain such a paradox, if you are even serious? I can't let such a statement about Russian landowners pass. You're a Russian landowner yourself."

"Yes, but I am not speaking of the Russian landowner in the sense you are taking it. It's a most respectable class, if only because I do belong to it—especially now when it has ceased to exist."

"Can it be that there is nothing national in our literature either?" Alexandra interrupted.

"I am no authority on literature, but it seems to me that in Russian literature, too, nothing is Russian, except perhaps Lomonosov, Pushkin, and Gogol."

"To begin with, that's already something, and in the second place, one of them was a peasant and the other two were landowners," said Adelaïda, laughing.

"Precisely, but don't be so pleased. Since of all Russian writers these three are the only ones so far who have been able to say something that was really *theirs*, something of their own not borrowed from anyone, therefore these three immediately became national. Let any Russian say or write or do anything of his own, anything which is incontestably *his* and not borrowed, and he will inevitably become national —even if he speaks Russian badly. I take this as an axiom. But we didn't begin by speaking of literature, we were speaking of socialists, and the discussion followed from that. Well, I hold that we haven't a single Russian socialist; there are none and there never have been, because all our socialists too have come from among landowners and divinity students. All our self-proclaimed and widely advertised socialists, both here and abroad, are nothing more than liberals from the landowning class of the days of serfdom. Why laugh? Show me their books, show me their doctrines, their memoirs, and, though I am not a literary critic, I shall write you a most convincing piece of literary criticism in which I'll show you as clear as day that every page of their books, their pamphlets, and their memoirs is first and foremost the work of a former Russian landowner. Their anger, their outrage, their wit belong to that class (even before Famusov!*); their raptures, their tears, may be real and sincere, but they are landowners' tears! Landowners' and divinity students'. You're laughing again, and you are laughing too, Prince? You don't agree either?"

Everyone was indeed laughing, and the prince smiled too.

"I can't tell you offhand whether I agree or not," said the prince, who suddenly stopped smiling and gave a start like a schoolboy caught doing wrong, "but I assure you that I am listening to you with the greatest pleasure."

As he said this he seemed at a loss for breath, and cold sweat broke out on his forehead. These were the first words he had uttered since he sat down. He was about to look around the table but didn't dare; Yevgeny Pavlovitch caught his movement and smiled.

"Ladies and gentlemen, I will tell you something," he went on in the same tone, that is, with extraordinary verve and warmth and at the same time as if he might be laughing at his own words, "a fact, an observation, and indeed a discovery which I have the honor of attributing to myself alone; at least, nothing has yet been said or written about it anywhere. This fact expresses the whole essence of Russian liberalism, the sort I'm speaking of. In the first place, what is liberalism, generally speaking, if not an attack (whether justified or not is another question) on the existing order of things? Isn't this so? Well, my fact is precisely that Russian liberalism is not an attack on the existing order of things, but an attack on the very essence of things, on the things themselves, not merely on their order, on the established order in Russia, but on Russia herself. My liberal has gone so far as to deny Russia herself; in other words, he hates his own mother and he beats her. Every Russian failure and misfortune stirs him to laughter and virtually delights him. He hates national traditions,

Russian history, everything. If there is any justification for him, it might be that he doesn't know what he's doing and takes his personal hatred of Russia for the most fruitful sort of liberalism (oh, how often you meet a liberal among us who is applauded by others and who is perhaps the most absurd, the most stupid, the most dangerous of conservatives, and who is unaware of it himself!) Not so long ago some of our liberals effectively took this hatred for Russia as sincere love for their country, and congratulated themselves on seeing better than others what that love should be; but now they have become more frank, and even the words 'love for country' have become an embarrassment to them, and the whole conception has been banished and dismissed as harmful and trivial. This fact is true, I guarantee it—and the time must come when the truth be told fully, simply, and openly. But it is a phenomenon that has never been known anywhere, at any time or among any other people, ever, and so it is something accidental and may pass, I will admit. For anywhere, a liberal who hates his own country is an impossibility. How can we explain it here? By what I have said before—that up to now the Russian liberal is an un-Russian liberal; that's the only explanation, as I see it."

"I take all you have said as a joke, Yevgeny Pavlovitch," said Prince S. earnestly.

"I haven't seen every liberal, so I can't judge," said Alexandra Ivanovna, "but I've listened to your ideas with indignation. You've taken a particular case and made a general rule out of it, and so you've spoken falsely and unfairly."

"A particular case? Ah-ha! That's what I was waiting to hear," said Yevgeny Pavlovitch. "Prince, what do you think, is this a particular case or not?"

"I must say too that I haven't seen many—liberals, or been with many," said the prince, "but it does seem to me you may be partly right in what you say, and that the Russian liberalism you are talking about is indeed rather inclined to hate Russia herself, and not merely the regime alone. Of course, this is only partly true. Certainly it cannot be true in all cases."

He broke off in confusion. In spite of his excitement he was extremely interested in the conversation. One of the prince's striking traits was a naïveté in the way he would always listen with great attention to anything that interested him and in the replies he would give when anyone addressed a question to him. His face and even the attitude of his body somehow reflected this naïveté, this faith, unsuspicious of either mockery or humor. But though Yevgeny Pavlovitch had

356

for some time persisted in addressing him with a special little smile, now, upon hearing his answer, he looked at him very gravely, as if he had not expected such an answer from him.

"Yes. But this is rather strange coming from you," he said. "Were you really answering me seriously, Prince?"

"Weren't you asking me seriously?" responded the prince in astonishment.

They all laughed.

"You can trust him!" said Adelaïda. "Yevgeny Pavlovitch always fools everyone! If you only knew the things he sometimes tells seriously!"

"I think this is a tiresome conversation and should never have started," said Alexandra sharply. "We wanted to go for a walk."

"And let's go, it's a lovely evening!" cried Yevgeny Pavlovitch. "But so as to show you that this time I was speaking in complete seriousness, and above all to show this to the prince (you have interested me very greatly, Prince, and I assure you I am not quite such an empty fellow as I certainly must seem to you—though I am in fact an empty fellow into the bargain!) and—if you will permit me, ladies and gentlemen —I shall ask the prince one last question, out of personal curiosity, and then we shall drop the matter. This question occurred to me, most auspiciously, two hours ago (you see, Prince, I too sometimes think about serious things); I have my own answer, but let's see what the prince will say. He referred to 'particular cases' just now. This is a very significant phrase among us, one hears it often. Recently everyone was talking and writing about that terrible murder of six people by that young man, and about the strange speech of the defense counsel, in which he said that because of the accused's impoverished condition it was *natural* for him to think of murdering those six people. Those are not the exact words, but that was apparently, in effect, the sense of what he said. My personal opinion is that in expressing such a curious idea the defense attorney was absolutely convinced that he was uttering the most liberal, the most humane and progressive thing that could possibly be said in our time. Well, what do you think? Is this perversion of understanding and convictions, this capacity to see the affair in such an extraordinarily distorted light, is this a particular case or a general one?"

Everyone laughed.

"Particular, of course, particular!" laughed Alexandra and Adelaïda.

"And may I point out to you again, Yevgeny Pavlovitch," added Prince S., "that your joke is beginning to wear thin."

"What do you think, Prince?" asked Yevgeny Pavlovitch, paying no attention, but aware that Prince Lev Nikolayevitch was gazing at him with grave interest. "How does it seem to you? Is this case general or particular? I confess that I made up this question especially for you."

"No, it is not a particular case," the prince said quietly but firmly.

"Oh my heavens, Lev Nikolayevitch," cried Prince S. with some vexation, "don't you see he's just trying to trip you up? He's obviously laughing at you and playing you for a fool."

"I thought Yevgeny Pavlovitch was speaking seriously," said the prince, blushing and lowering his eyes.

"My dear Prince," pursued Prince S., "do remember what we talked about once, about three months ago? We said then that in our newly opened law courts one could already point to a great many remarkable and talented lawyers, and how many highly remarkable verdicts have been handed down by our juries! How pleased you were, and how delighted I was, then, at seeing your pleasure! We said we had a right to be proud of this. But this clumsy defense, this strange argument is of course an accident, one out of thousands."

Prince Lev Nikolayevitch thought a moment, but replied with an air of perfect conviction, though softly and even, it seemed, rather timidly:

"I only wanted to say that the distortion of ideas and understanding (as Yevgeny Pavlovitch expressed it) is very often found, and is far more of a general than a particular occurrence, unfortunately. In fact if this distortion was not so general, perhaps there would not be such impossible crimes as these."

"Impossible crimes? But I assure you that exactly such crimes and perhaps far more terrible ones have existed in the past and at all times, and not only among us but everywhere, and in my opinion they will continue to occur for a very long time. The difference is that in this country they were less publicized before, while now everyone talks of them and even writes about them, so it seems as if those criminals have only appeared among us lately. That's where your mistake is, an extremely naïve mistake, Prince, I assure you," said Prince S. with a mocking smile.

"I do know there have been very many crimes in the past, and ones just as terrible. I have recently been in the prisons and managed to make the acquaintance of a few criminals and accused persons. There are criminals even more terrible than that one, men who have murdered a dozen people and feel no remorse at all. But this is what I noticed: the most hardened and unrepentant killer still knows that he is a 'criminal'; that is, he realizes in his conscience that he has not acted rightly, even though he is unrepentant. And they all were like that; but those Yevgeny Pavlovitch was speaking of refuse even to consider themselves criminals and they think they are in the right and—that they have even acted well, it almost comes to that. This seems to me where the terrible difference lies. And notice they are all young, I mean they are at an age at which one may fall most easily and helplessly under the influence of perverted ideas."

Prince S. was no longer laughing and listened to the prince with a puzzled look. Alexandra Ivanovna, who had been wanting to say something for some time, said nothing, as if some particular consideration had stopped her. Yevgeny Pavlovitch looked at the prince with distinct surprise and this time without mockery.

"But why are you surprised at him, my dear sir?" Lizaveta Prokofyevna suddenly broke in. "Did you think him stupider than you and that he couldn't reason as you do?"

"No, I didn't mean that," said Yevgeny Pavlovitch. "But, Prince, I only wonder—forgive the question—how, if you see it in this way, how—forgive me again—in that strange affair the other day, the Burdovsky affair, if I'm not mistaken, how you didn't observe the same perversion of ideas and moral convictions. Because, you see, it's exactly the same. I thought at the time that you didn't see it at all."

"My dear man," said Lizaveta Prokofyevna heatedly, "we all saw it, and we sit here feeling superior to him, when just today he got a letter from one of them, the main one, the pimply one, do you remember, Alexandra? He asks his forgiveness in this letter—in his own fashion, of course—and informs him that he has broken with that friend who kept urging him on—remember, Alexandra?—and that he now has more faith in the prince. Well, we haven't received any such letter, so we have no business sticking up our noses in front of him."

"And Hippolite just arrived at his house, too!" cried Kolya.

"What! Is he there already?" the prince asked in surprise.

"He arrived just after you had left with Lizaveta Prokofyevna. I brought him!"

"Well, I'll bet anything," said Lizaveta Prokofyevna, suddenly flaring up and completely forgetting that she had just been praising the prince, "I'll bet anything he went to him in his garret yesterday and got down on his knees and begged his pardon, so as to have that nasty little horror condescend to move into his house. Did you go yesterday? You admitted it yourself a little while ago. Was that how it was or wasn't it? Did you get down on your knees or not?"

"He didn't do that at all," cried Kolya. "Quite the contrary: yesterday Hippolite took the prince's hand and kissed it twice. I saw it myself. That's all that happened, except that the prince simply said he would be better off at the house in the country, and he immediately agreed to come here as soon as he felt better."

"You shouldn't, Kolya," murmured the prince, getting up and taking his hat. "Why are you telling that? I—"

"Where are you going?" asked Lizaveta Prokofyevna, stopping him.

"Don't bother, Prince," said Kolya, highly excited. "Don't go, don't disturb him, he's fallen asleep after his trip, he is very happy. And, you know, Prince, I think it will be much better if you don't see him today, and even put it off till tomorrow, or he'll be uncomfortable again. He said just this morning that he hadn't felt so well and strong for a full half year; he doesn't cough even half as much."

The prince noticed that Aglaya had suddenly left her place and come up to the table. He did not dare look at her, but he felt in his whole being that at that moment she was looking at him, perhaps threateningly, her face flushed, her black eyes showing indignation.

"But, Nikolai Ardalionovitch, I think you made a mistake in bringing him here," remarked Yevgeny Pavlovitch, "that is, if you mean that consumptive boy who wept and invited us to his funeral. He spoke so eloquently about the wall of the house next door that he will certainly miss it, believe me."

"That's exactly right! He will quarrel, have a fight with you, and go away—mark my words!"

And Lizaveta Prokofyevna pulled her work-basket to her with an air of great dignity, forgetting that they all were about to go for a walk.

"I recall he was bragging quite a lot about that wall," pursued Yevgeny Pavlovitch. "He can't die eloquently without that wall, and he is determined to die eloquently."

"What of it?" murmured the prince. "If you don't care to forgive him then he'll die without your forgiveness. He has come here this time on account of the trees."

"Oh, for my part I forgive him everything. You can tell him that."

"That's not the way to take it," the prince answered quietly and seemingly with reluctance, continuing to stare at a spot on the floor without raising his eyes. "You should be willing to receive his forgiveness too."

"What have I got to do with any of this? What have I done to him?"

"If you don't understand, then— But of course you do understand. He wanted to give us all his blessing and receive your blessing too, that was all."

"Dear Prince," Prince S. broke in rapidly, having exchanged apprehensive glances with some of the others present, "it is not easy to attain paradise on earth, and yet you seem to be counting on it. Paradise is a difficult matter, Prince, much more difficult than it appears to your beautiful heart. We had better drop the subject, or we may all feel uncomfortable again, and then—"

"Let's go hear the band," Lizaveta Prokofyevna said sharply, getting up from her place angrily.

Everyone else followed her example.

Chapter TWO

⌒⌒⌒

Suddenly the prince went up to Yevgeny Pavlovitch.

"Yevgeny Pavlovitch," he said with a strange warmth of feeling, seizing his hand, "believe me, I look on you as the most honorable and best of men in spite of everything, please believe me."

Yevgeny Pavlovitch actually drew back a step in astonishment. For a moment he had to fight to keep from laughing, but, looking closer, he saw that the prince was not himself, or at least that he was in a very unusual state.

"I would wager, Prince," he cried, "you didn't mean to say that, and perhaps it wasn't to me you meant to say it. But what's the matter with you? Are you feeling sick?"

"Possibly, yes, very possibly—and it was very clever of you to notice that perhaps it was not you I meant to address."

He said this with a strange and even somewhat comical smile, but then with sudden intensity he exclaimed:

361

"Don't remind me of what I did three days ago! I've been very ashamed since then. I do know that I was at fault."

"But—what did you do that was so terrible?"

"I see that you are probably more ashamed for me than anyone, Yevgeny Pavlovitch; you are blushing; this is the sign of a good heart. I am leaving at once, you needn't worry."

"What's the trouble with him? Is this how his fits begin?" Lizaveta Prokofyevna asked Kolya in alarm.

"Do not worry, Lizaveta Prokofyevna, I am not having a fit. I'm on my way now. I know that I'm—afflicted. I have been ill for twenty-four years, from my birth to my twenty-fourth year. You must take what I say now as the words of an invalid. I'll be on my way at once, at once, you can be sure. I'm not ashamed, for it would be strange to be ashamed for such a reason, wouldn't it? But in society I feel—superfluous. This isn't from vanity—I have thought it over for these three days and decided that I should explain things sincerely and honorably at the first occasion. There are certain ideas, certain great ideas, that I shouldn't start talking about because I would be sure to make everyone laugh. Prince S. reminded me of this possibility just now. My gestures are not right, I have no sense of measure, my words don't correspond with my thoughts, but only degrade them. And therefore I have no right—besides I am morbidly suspicious; I—I am convinced that no one in this house could wish to hurt me and that I am loved here more than I deserve, but I know (I know for certain) that after twenty years of sickness there must be some traces left, and that it is impossible not to laugh at me—sometimes—isn't it?"

He looked around as if he expected an answer and a judgment. Everyone stood in painful uncertainty at this unexpected, morbid, and, in any case, quite uncalled-for outburst. But the outburst did give rise to a strange episode.

"Why do you say that here?" Aglaya cried out suddenly. "Why do you say that to them? To *them!*"

She appeared to be moved to the highest indignation; her eyes blazed. The prince stood before her, silent, unable to speak, and suddenly turned pale.

"There is not a person here who is worth such words!" Aglaya burst out. "Not a single one who is worth your little finger—or your mind, or your heart. You are more honest, nobler, better, kinder, cleverer than any of them! There are people here who are unworthy to stoop and pick up the handkerchief you have just dropped. Why do you humble

362

yourself and put yourself beneath them all? Why have you twisted everything inside you? Why have you no pride?"

"Dear God, who could have ever imagined it!" said Lizaveta Prokofyevna wringing her hands.

"The poor knight! Hurrah!" cried Kolya, greatly elated.

"Be still! How dare they insult me in your house!" cried Aglaya, flying at her mother, having reached that state of hysteria where all caution and all obstacles disappear. "Why are they all, everyone without exception, torturing me? Why have they been after me for three whole days on your account, Prince? Not for anything will I marry you! I want you to know that I shall never marry you for anything in the world! Understand that! As if one could marry anyone as ridiculous as you! Look at yourself in the mirror, see what you look like standing there right now! Why, why do they tease me and say I will marry you? You should know that. You are in the plot with them too!"

"No one ever teased you!" Adelaïda murmured in alarm.

"It never entered anyone's head," cried Alexandra Ivanovna. "No such thing was ever said!"

"Who teased her? When was she teased? Who could have said this to her? Is she raving or what?" Lizaveta Prokofyevna demanded of everyone, trembling with anger.

"Everyone said it. Everyone! For the last three days! I will never, never marry him!"

Having said this in a loud voice, Aglaya burst into bitter tears, buried her face in her handkerchief, and sank into a chair.

"But he hasn't yet asked you."

"I haven't asked you, Aglaya Ivanovna," said the prince involuntarily.

"WH-A-AT?" said Lizaveta Prokofyevna in astonishment, indignation, and horror. "WHAT'S THA-A-T?"

She could not believe her ears.

"I mean—I mean," faltered the prince, "I only wanted to explain to Aglaya Ivanovna that I had no intention whatever of—I had no intention of asking for the honor of her hand in marriage—at any time. I am not at fault in this, I swear I am not, Aglaya Ivanovna. I never wanted to, it never entered my mind, I shall never want to, you will see for yourself—you can be sure of it! Some malicious person must have spoken ill of me to you. You need have no fear!"

As he said this, he approached Aglaya. She drew away the handkerchief she had covered her face with, glanced briefly at him and his terrified face, realized the meaning of his words, and suddenly burst out laughing in his face with such gay and irresistible laughter, such amused and mocking laughter, that Adelaïda could not restrain herself, especially when she too looked at the prince; she rushed to her sister, embraced her, and broke out in the same irresistible school-girlish laughter. As he watched them, the prince too suddenly began to smile, and with a happy and joyful expression he started saying over and over:

"Well, thank God! Thank God!"

Then Alexandra could not bear it either and began laughing wholeheartedly. It seemed as if the laughter of all three would never end.

"Well, they're quite mad!" muttered Lizaveta Prokofyevna. "First they frighten me, and then—"

But by now Prince S. was laughing too, Yevgeny Pavlovitch was laughing, Kolya laughed loudly without stopping, and the prince, looking at them all, laughed loudly too.

"Let's go for a walk! Let's go for a walk!" Adelaïda cried. "All of us together and the prince must come with us. Why should you leave, you dear man? What a dear man he is, isn't he, Aglaya? Isn't he, Mother? What's more, I positively must give him a kiss and a hug for—for his explanation to Aglaya just now. *Maman*, dear, will you let me kiss him? Aglaya! Please let me kiss your prince!" cried the mischievous girl, and she did rush over to the prince and kiss him on the fore-head. The prince seized her hands and squeezed them so hard that Adelaïda almost cried out; he looked upon her with infinite joy and suddenly raised her hand to his lips and kissed it three times.

"Do come on!" Aglaya called to them. "Prince, you will escort me. Is it all right, *Maman?* This fiancé who has refused me? For you have refused me once and for all, haven't you, Prince? No, not like that, that's not the way you offer your arm to a lady. Don't you know how to offer your arm to a lady? That's the way, come on, we'll go ahead of them all. Would you like us to go ahead of them all, *tête-à-tête?*"

She talked on without stopping, still laughing spasmodically.

"Thank God! Thank God!" repeated Lizaveta Prokofyevna, not knowing herself what she was rejoicing about.

"Extremely strange people!" thought Prince S. for perhaps the hundredth time since he had come to know them, but he was fond of these strange people. As for Prince Myshkin, he did not particularly care for him. Prince S. seemed moody and preoccupied as they all set out on their walk.

Yevgeny Pavlovitch appeared to be in most excellent spirits, and all the way to the railway station he entertained Alexandra and Adelaïda, who laughed so readily at his jokes that at times he suspected they were not listening to him at all. At this thought, he suddenly burst into loud and completely genuine laughter without explaining the reason (such was his nature!). Although the sisters were in a most hilarious mood, they kept casting glances at Aglaya and the prince, who were walking ahead. It was clear that their younger sister's conduct had presented something of a riddle to them. Prince S. was trying the whole time to engage Lizaveta Prokofyevna on other matters, no doubt in order to divert her mind, but only managed to bore her terribly. Her thinking was apparently unsettled, for she gave inappropriate answers and sometimes did not answer at all. But Aglaya Ivanovna was to pose further riddles that evening. The last one was reserved for the prince alone. When they had gone about a hundred paces from the house, Aglaya in a rapid half-whisper said to her obstinately silent escort:

"Look to the right."

The prince looked.

"Look more carefully. Do you see that bench in the park, where there are those three big trees—that green bench?"

The prince replied that he did.

"Do you like that place? Sometimes very early, about seven o'clock in the morning, when everyone is still asleep, I come and sit there alone."

The prince murmured that it was a lovely place.

"And now please leave me, I don't want to walk arm-in-arm with you anymore. Or, better yet, let's walk arm-in-arm but don't say a word to me. I want to think by myself."

This warning was in any case unnecessary: the prince would certainly not have uttered a word the whole day, even without such an order. His heart had begun pounding violently when she spoke of the bench. After a minute, with a feeling of shame, he dismissed his absurd thought.

As everyone knows, or at least, as everyone agrees, the public which frequents the park at Pavlovsk is more "select" on weekdays than it is on Sundays and holidays, when "all sorts of people" come there from the city. The dress of the ladies is not festive, but elegant. It is considered correct to listen to the music. The orchestra may indeed be the best of our park bands, and it plays new pieces. Propriety and decorum reign, despite a certain appearance of informality and even of intimacy. Those who are acquainted—all the summer people—gather to examine one another. Many fulfill this duty with sincere pleasure and come only for this purpose; but there are also those who go only for the music. Disagreeable incidents are exceedingly rare, though they do occur even on weekdays, as is of course inevitable.

It was a splendid evening, and there were a good many people in the park. All the places around the bandstand were taken. Our party settled in chairs somewhat to the side, not far from the left-hand exit from the railroad station. The crowd and the music raised Lizaveta Prokofyevna's spirits a little and diverted the young ladies; they had already exchanged glances with certain of their acquaintances and nodded amiably to others; they had examined the dresses and detected some oddities, which they had discussed with sarcastic smiles. Yevgeny Pavlovitch, too, bowed frequently to acquaintances. Aglaya and the prince, who were still together, had already attracted a certain attention. Soon several young men of their acquaintance came up to the young ladies and their mother; two or three stayed to converse with them; all of them were friends of Yevgeny Pavlovitch. Among them was a certain very young and very handsome officer, very gay, very talkative; he hastened to engage Aglaya in conversation and did his best to draw her attention to him. Aglaya was very gracious and exceedingly amused by him. Yevgeny Pavlovitch asked the prince to allow him to introduce this acquaintance; the prince hardly understood what was wanted of him, but the introduction did take place, both bowed and shook hands. Yevgeny Pavlovitch's friend asked a question, but the prince either did not answer him or else mumbled something to himself so strangely that the officer looked at him very hard, then glanced at Yevgeny Pavlovitch, understood at once the reason for the introduction, smiled faintly, and turned again to Aglaya. Only Yevgeny Pavlovitch noticed that Aglaya suddenly blushed deeply at this.

The prince did not even notice that other people were conversing with Aglaya and paying court to her, and he seemed to forget for minutes at a time that he was sitting next to her. Sometimes he felt like going away somewhere, like disappearing from there entirely, and even some dark, deserted place would have appealed to him if only he could have been alone with his thoughts and if no one would know where to find him. Or, at least, to be at his own house, on the veranda, provided no one was there, either Lebedev or the children, and throw himself down on the sofa, bury his head in the pillow, and lie that way for a day and a night and another day. At moments he dreamed of the mountains, and particularly of a certain spot he always liked to remember, and where he had always liked to go when he was still living there and look down on the village, at the barely moving white thread of a waterfall below, at the white clouds and the old deserted castle. Oh, how he longed to be there now and think of one thing only—oh, of nothing but this one thing his whole life long, for there was enough to think about for a thousand years! And let him be forgotten here, let him be utterly forgotten here! Oh, this had to be, and it would have been better indeed if they had not known him at all, and if all these appearances had been only a dream. And wasn't it the same, whether a dream or reality? Sometimes he would suddenly look carefully at Aglaya, not taking his eyes off her face for five minutes at a time, but his gaze was exceedingly strange: he seemed to be looking at her as at an object a mile distant from him, or as at her portrait, not at her.

"Why are you looking at me like that, Prince?" she said suddenly, interrupting her gay talk and laughter with the people around her. "I'm afraid of you. I have the feeling you want to reach out and touch my face with your fingers. Isn't it true, Yevgeny Pavlovitch, he looks that way?"

The prince listened to her as if he was surprised she should be talking to him, then appeared to be considering what she said, though without quite understanding her, and did not reply; but seeing that everyone was laughing he suddenly opened his mouth and began laughing himself. The laughter around him grew louder, and the officer, who must have been a very mirthful fellow, positively spouted laughter. Aglaya suddenly whispered angrily to herself:

"Idiot!"

"Good heavens! Could she be with a man like that! Had she completely gone out of her mind!" Lizaveta Prokofyevna muttered to herself.

"It's a joke," Alexandra whispered firmly in her ear. "It's the same as the joke about the 'poor knight'—and nothing more! She's making fun of him again, in her way. Only the joke has gone too far; it must be stopped, *Maman!* Just now she was playing a role like an actress and scared us all out of pure mischief."

"It's a good thing she happened to pick on an idiot like that," Lizaveta Prokofyevna whispered back to her. Nevertheless her daughter's remark relieved her.

The prince, however, heard that he had been called an idiot, and he gave a start, but not because he had been called an idiot. He forgot the "Idiot!" at once. But there at the edge of the crowd, not far from where he was sitting, he caught a rapid glimpse of a certain face—he could not have indicated the exact place—a pallid face, with dark curly hair, and a familiar, very familiar smile and expression; it vanished the moment he saw it. It was very possible that this was only an illusion; all that remained of his vision was a crooked smile, the eyes, and the stylish pale green necktie the apparition had been wearing. Nor could the prince determine whether this personage had disappeared in the crowd or slipped away into the station.

But a minute later he suddenly began looking around quickly and apprehensively; this first apparition might be the presage of a second. It had to be so. Could he have forgotten the possibility of an encounter when he had entered the gardens? It was true that when he went to the gardens he seemed completely unaware of going there—such was his state of mind. If only he had been more perceptive he would have already noticed fifteen minutes earlier that Aglaya too was looking around uneasily now and then, as if she too was looking for someone. Now, as his uneasiness became very marked, Aglaya's excitement and anxiety also increased, and as soon as he would look around she would instantly look too. The explanation of their troubled state followed quickly.

Suddenly, at the side entrance near which the prince and the Yepanchin party were seated, a whole group of people, ten at least, appeared. Three women headed the group; two of them were strikingly attractive, and it was no wonder that so many admirers followed them. But there was something special about the women and the admirers, about this whole party, a certain quality which set them apart from the rest of the public gathered for the music. They were immediately noticed by almost everyone, but most people tried to look as if they were not noticing them at all, and only some of the young people smiled in their direction and exchanged remarks in half-voices. Not to observe them at all was quite impossible, they were plainly putting themselves on show, talking loudly, laughing. One might have supposed that many of them were drunk, though some appeared dressed in fashionable and elegant clothes; but there were also some of very strange appearance, people in odd dress, with strangely flushed faces; there were several military people among them; some were not young; there were some comfortably attired in full-cut, well-made clothes, with rings and cufflinks, wearing magnificent wigs of pitch-black hair, side-whiskers, and with quite noble, though rather disgusted, expressions on their faces; but people of the sort, however, who in society are avoided like the plague. In our out-of-town centers there are of course people who are remarkable for their exceptional respectability and who enjoy particularly good reputations, but even the most careful person cannot defend himself at all moments from a brick falling from a neighbor's roof. Such a brick was now about to fall on the respectable public gathered to hear the music.

To go from the station to the esplanade where the bandstand was, it was necessary to descend three steps. The group stopped at the top of these steps; they hesitated whether to go down; but one of the women proceeded; only two of her entourage ventured to follow her. One was a middle-aged man of rather modest appearance who seemed in every way respectable but completely unrooted; that is, one of those people whom no one ever knows and who knows no one himself. The other who had not dropped back from his lady was a man of most ragged and equivocal appearance. No one else followed the eccentric lady, but as she went down the steps she did not even look back, as if it was a matter of complete indifference to her whether she was accompanied or not. She laughed and talked loudly as before, she was dressed with exceptional taste and richly but somewhat more splendidly than was required. She walked to the other side of the bandstand near the road where someone's carriage was waiting.

The prince had not seen *her* for over three months. Every day since his arrival from Petersburg he had been meaning to call on her; but perhaps some secret premonition had stopped him. At least, he could not imagine at all what it would be like to meet her, and he sometimes tried, with dread, to imagine it. It was only clear to him that this meeting would be painful. Several times during those six months he had remembered the first impression this woman's face had made on him when he had seen it only in the portrait; but even the impression her portrait had made on him had, he remembered, been painful. That month in the provinces when he had seen her almost every day had had a dreadful effect on him, to the point that the prince even tried to drive out the memory of this still recent time. There was always something in the face itself of this woman that tormented him; in talking to Rogozhin, the prince had interpreted this feeling as one of infinite pity for her, and this was the truth; her face in the portrait had filled his heart with an agony of pity; and this feeling of compassion, even of suffering, had never left his heart and did not leave it now. Oh no, it was stronger than ever! But the prince had remained dissatisfied with what he had said to Rogozhin; and only now, at the moment of her sudden appearance, did he perhaps realize in an intuitive feeling what had been lacking in his words to Rogozhin Nothing had been said which might have expressed horror— yes, horror! Now at this moment he felt it fully; he was convinced, he was completely convinced, for reasons of his own, that this woman was mad. If, loving a woman more than anything in the world, or foreseeing the possibility of such a love, one were suddenly to see her in chains behind iron bars under the stick of a jailor one would have felt very much as the prince did now.

"What's the matter with you?" Aglaya whispered rapidly, looking at him and ingenuously tugging at his arm.

He turned his head, looked at her, gazed into her black eyes, which at that moment were flashing in a way he could not fathom; he tried to smile at her, but suddenly, as if forgetting her instantly, he again looked to the right and again began watching that extraordinary apparition. Nastassya Filippovna was at that moment walking near the young ladies' chairs. Yevgeny Pavlovitch was telling something to Alexandra Ivanovna, something that must have been very interesting and amusing; he spoke fast and with great animation. The prince remembered that Aglaya had suddenly said in a half-whisper, "What a—"

The utterance was vague and incomplete; she immediately caught herself and said no more, but it was enough. Nastassya Filippovna, who was walking by as if she was paying no attention to anyone in particular, suddenly turned toward them as if she had only just now recognized Yevgeny Pavlovitch.

"Ah! But there he is!" she exclaimed, stopping suddenly. "Here we've been sending people everywhere for him, and there he sits where you'd never dream of finding him. And here I'd imagined you'd be at your uncle's!"

Yevgeny Pavlovitch reddened, glared angrily at Nastassya Filippovna, but quickly turned away from her again.

"What? Don't you know? Think of that, he doesn't know yet! He shot himself! Your uncle shot himself this morning! I'd heard it already at two o'clock, and half the town knows about it now. They say three hundred and fifty thousand roubles of state funds are missing, some say five hundred thousand. And here I was always counting on him leaving you a fortune, and he ate up everything. Really, aren't you going there? So you resigned from the service just in time, didn't you, you clever fellow? But nonsense, you knew, you knew it all beforehand. Very likely you knew it yesterday."

Though there was certainly some motive in her impudent provocation and her display of an intimacy of acquaintance which did not exist (there could be no doubt of this now), still Yevgeny Pavlovitch had thought at first that by persisting in paying no attention to his assailant he could get rid of her.

But Nastassya Filippovna's words hit him like thunderbolts. Hearing of his uncle's death he became pale as a sheet and turned toward his informant. At that moment Lizaveta Prokovyevna got up quickly, made everyone else get up after her, and fairly ran away. Only Prince Lev Nikolayevitch stayed seated for a second, as if in a state of indecision, and Yevgeny Pavlovitch still stood there, having not yet recovered. But the Yepanchins had not gone twenty paces when a terribly scandalous thing occurred.

The officer, Yevgeny Pavlovitch's great friend, who had been conversing with Aglaya, was highly indignant.

"All we need here is a whip, there's no other way to deal with such a creature!" he said almost out loud. (It appeared that he had been a confidant of Yevgeny Pavlovitch's in the past.)

Nastassya Filippovna instantly turned to him. Her eyes were blazing; she rushed up to a young man, a complete stranger who was standing a few steps from her holding a thin, plaited riding quirt; she seized it from his hand and lashed her offender with all her might across the face. It all happened in a single moment. The officer, beside himself, threw himself at her; Nastassya Filippovna's followers were no longer with her; the respectable middle-aged gentleman had managed to disappear completely, while the other gentleman, quite tipsy, was standing to one side laughing as hard as he could. Another minute and of course the police would have appeared, and just at that moment Nastassya Filippovna might have fared very badly if unexpected aid had not been at hand: the prince, who had also been standing a couple of paces away, managed to seize the officer's arm from behind. In wresting his arm away, the officer gave him a violent shove in the chest; the prince was flung three paces back and fell into a chair. But already two new defenders were protecting Nastassya Filippovna. Facing the attacking officer stood the boxer, author of the article already known to the reader and regular member of Rogozhin's old crowd.

"Keller, retired lieutenant!" he introduced himself forcefully. "If you want to fight, Captain, then in place of the weaker sex, I am at your service. I'm a master of the art of English boxing. Don't push, Captain, I sympathize with you for the *wounding* insult you have received, but I can't allow you to use your fists on a woman in full public view. If, as befits a proper gentleman, you'd care in another way to—But of course you probably understand me, Captain."

But the captain had already recovered himself and was not listening to him. At that moment Rogozhin appeared out of the crowd, quickly took Nastassya Filippovna by the hand, and led her away. Rogozhin too looked terribly shaken, he was pale and trembling. Still, as he was leading Nastassya Filippovna away, he found time to laugh maliciously in the officer's face and say in the triumphant voice of a vulgar shop-keeper:

"Whew! He really got it! His mug's all covered with blood!"

Recovering himself and realizing with whom he was dealing, the officer (covering his face with his handkerchief) politely addressed the prince, who had gotten to his feet.

"Prince Myshkin, to whom I have had the pleasure of being introduced?"

"She's mad! She's insane! I assure you!" replied the prince, for some reason reaching out his trembling hands to him.

"I, of course, have no such knowledge. But I must know your name."

He nodded and walked away. The police arrived exactly five seconds after the last actors in the scene had disappeared. However, the whole scandalous incident did not last more than two minutes. Some of the public left their chairs and walked away, others only moved from one place to another, a third element was delighted by the scene, a fourth talked volubly and with intense interest about it. In a word, the scene ended in the usual manner. The band started playing again. The prince followed the Yepanchins. If he had thought of it and managed to look to his left while he was sitting in the chair he had been pushed into, he would have seen Aglaya standing about twenty paces from him watching the disgraceful incident, paying no attention to the calls of her mother and sisters, who were farther away by now. Prince S. had run up to her and tried to persuade her to leave quickly. Lizaveta Prokofyevna remembered that Aglaya had come back to them in such a state of emotion that she probably had not heard them calling. But exactly two minutes later, just as they were entering the park, Aglaya said in her usual indifferent and capricious voice:

"I wanted to see how the comedy would end!"

Chapter THREE

∽≈∾

The occurrence at the gardens had impressed both mother and daughters with something close to horror. In her anxiety and excitement, Lizaveta Prokofyevna had almost literally run all the way home from the gardens with her daughters. In her view, as she understood the matter, so much had happened, so much had come to light in this incident, that in spite of all her confusion and fear certain definitive ideas were already forming in her mind. But then everyone realized that something special had happened and that perhaps, and very fortunately too, a secret of some sort was beginning to be revealed. Despite all Prince S.'s assurances and explanations, Yevgeny Pavlovitch had now been "driven out into the open," exposed, discovered, and "his relationship with that creature formally confirmed." This was what Lizaveta Prokofyevna thought and so, even, did her two elder daughters. The virtue of this conclusion was that still greater riddles loomed beyond it. The girls, though privately somewhat put out with their mother for her excessive alarm and all too obvious flight, still did not venture, in the heat of the commotion, to disturb her with questions. Besides, they for some reason felt that their sister, Aglaya Ivanovna, knew more about this affair than they and their mother together. Prince S. also looked somber as the night and very thoughtful. Lizaveta Prokofyevna did not utter a single word to him the whole way, and he did not appear to notice. Adelaïda tried to ask him: "What uncle were they talking about just now? And what happened in Petersburg?" But in reply he only muttered with a very sour face something vague about making some kind of inquiries and that the whole thing was of course only nonsense. "Well, that's certainly true!" Adelaïda had replied and asked nothing further of him. Aglaya remained extraordinarily quiet and only remarked on the way that they were going too fast. Once she turned around and saw the prince, who was hurrying after them. Noticing his efforts to catch up with them, she smiled sarcastically and did not look back at him again.

At last when they were almost back at their house they met Ivan Fyodorovitch, who was coming out to meet them, having just then returned from Petersburg. He inquired immediately about Yevgeny Pavlovitch. But his wife walked angrily past him without replying or even looking at him. From the expressions on the faces of his daughters and Prince S., he guessed at once that a storm was brewing in the household. But quite apart from this, his own face reflected uncommon distress. He at once took Prince S. by the arm, stopped him at the entrance of the house, and in a whisper exchanged several words with him. From the uneasy manner of them both as they went up on the veranda and approached Lizaveta Prokofyevna, one might have presumed that they had heard some sort of extraordinary news. Gradually everyone gathered in Lizaveta Prokofyevna's room upstairs, until finally the prince was left alone on the veranda. He sat in a corner as if he was expecting something, though in fact he had no idea why he was waiting there; it never occurred to him, in view of the disturbance in the house, to leave; he seemed oblivious of the entire universe and prepared to go on sitting a year or two wherever he might be put. Occasionally he heard anxious voices conversing upstairs. He could not have said himself how long he sat there. It was getting late and becoming quite dark. Suddenly Aglaya came out on the veranda; she appeared calm though rather pale. Seeing the prince, whom she had clearly not expected to find sitting there in a chair in a corner, Aglaya smiled as if in perplexity.

"What are you doing here?" she asked, going over to him. The prince murmured something in confusion and jumped up from his chair, but Aglaya immediately sat beside him, and he sat down again. She glanced at him briefly but very intently, then gazed out the window as if she hadn't a thought in her mind, then looked back at him. "Perhaps she feels like laughing," thought the prince. "But no, if that was so, she would laugh."

After a silence she said, "Perhaps you'd like some tea. I'll call for it."

"N-no. I don't know—"

"What? How can you not know that? Oh, yes, listen to me: if someone challenged you to a duel, what would you do? I wanted to ask you that before."

"But— Who would— No one will challenge me to a duel."

"But if they did? Would you be very frightened?"

"I think I would be—very frightened."

"Really? Then you are a coward?"

"N-no, perhaps not. A coward is somebody who is frightened and runs away, but someone who is frightened and does not run is after all not a coward," said the prince with a smile, after a moment's thought.

"And you wouldn't run away?"

"Perhaps I wouldn't," he said, finally laughing at Aglaya's questions.

"Even though I'm a woman I wouldn't run away for anything in the world," she observed, almost in annoyance. "But you're laughing at me and putting on airs like you always do to make yourself more interesting. Tell me, do they usually fire at twelve paces? And sometimes at ten? That means you would certainly be killed or wounded, doesn't it?"

"People rarely hit each other in duels."

"How rarely? Pushkin was killed."

"That might have been an accident."

"It wasn't at all an accident, it was a duel to the death, and he was killed."

"The bullet hit him so low that Dantes was certainly aiming higher, at his chest or his head. No one aims to hit him as he did, so it is more likely that the bullet hit Pushkin accidentally, by error. People who are expert in the matter have told me that."

"Well, a soldier I had a conversation with once told me that they have a regulation, an order, that when they're deployed for an attack they aim at mid-body. That's how they say it themselves: 'at mid-body.' So they are not ordered to aim at the chest or the head, they aim on purpose at the middle of the body. I asked an officer later and he said that this was exactly the way it was."

"That's probably because they shoot from a great distance."

"But can you shoot?"

"I never have."

"You mean you don't even know how to load a pistol?"

"No. That is, I know how it's done, but I have never done it myself."

"Well, that means you don't know how, because you need practice to do it! Listen and remember this: first, you must buy good gunpowder, not damp—they say it must be very dry and not damp—very fine powder, you must ask for that kind, and not the kind that is used in cannons. The bullets they say you mold yourself, somehow. Do you have pistols?"

"No, and I don't want any," said the prince laughing.

"Ah, what nonsense! Well, you'll have to buy a pair,

French or English ones, they say they are the very best. Then you take a thimbleful of powder, perhaps two thimblefuls, and you put it in the pistol. Too much is better than too little. Then you put in felt wadding—they say it has to be felt for some reason—which isn't hard to find, you can get some from an old mattress, and doors are sometimes stripped with felt. Then, when you've put the felt in, you put the bullet, the bullet last, the powder first, or it won't shoot. What are you laughing at? I want you to shoot several times every day so that you will positively know how to hit the target. Will you do that?"

The prince was laughing. Aglaya stamped her foot in vexation. Her serious air in such a conversation rather surprised him. He somehow felt that he should try to find out something, ask about something—something, in any case, more important than how to load a pistol. But all this had flown from his mind, everything except the one fact that she was sitting there beside him and that he was looking at her, and it made no difference to him then what she was talking about.

At last Ivan Fyodorovitch himself came downstairs and out on the veranda. He was going out somewhere and he was frowning, looking anxious and determined.

"Ah, Lev Nikolayevitch, it's you. Where are you going now?" he asked, despite the fact that Lev Nikolayevitch had not had the slightest thought of moving from his place. "Come along, I want a word with you."

"Good-bye," said Aglaya, holding out her hand to the prince.

It was already rather dark on the veranda, and at that moment the prince could not make out her face quite clearly. A minute later, when he and the general were leaving the house, he suddenly flushed deeply and clenched his right hand tightly.

It so happened that Ivan Fyodorovitch was going the same way as he. In spite of the late hour Ivan Fyodorovitch was hurrying off to confer with someone about something. But in the meantime he abruptly began talking to the prince, rapidly, urgently, and somewhat incoherently, with frequent references to Lizaveta Prokofyevna. If the prince could have been more attentive at that moment, he might perhaps have guessed that Ivan Fyodorovitch wanted, among other things, to learn something from him, or rather to ask him something openly and candidly, but somehow could not bring himself to the essential point. To his shame, the prince was so distracted that at first he heard nothing at all, and when the general stopped directly before him with some excited question, he was forced to admit to him that he had not understood a word.

The general shrugged his shoulders.

"What an odd lot you've all gotten to be, any way you look at it," he went on. "I tell you I can't comprehend Lizaveta Prokofyevna's notions and frights. She's in hysterics, she cries, and she says we've been shamed and dishonored. Who has? How? By whom? When? And why? I confess I'm to blame—I admit it—I am very much to blame, but the attempts of that—troubled woman—who is behaving very badly herself—can eventually be stopped by the police, and in fact I intend to see someone today to this effect and take steps. It all can be done quietly, gently and even tenderly, through friends, without a breath of scandal. I will admit too that a number of things may happen in the future, and that a great deal remains unexplained. There is an intrigue here, but if they know nothing of it here, they can't explain it anywhere else either. If I haven't heard anything, and you haven't, and someone else hasn't, and a fifth person hasn't either, who, after all *has* heard anything, will you please tell me? How do you suppose you can explain it except that half is a mirage, doesn't exist, is something like moonshine, for instance—or some other apparition."

"She is mad," murmured the prince, suddenly remembering with a feeling of pain all that had happened recently.

"That's exactly it, if you're talking about her. The same idea has occurred to me too—and let me sleep more peacefully. But now I see that their opinion here is right, and I don't believe in the madness. She's a preposterous woman, perhaps, but very subtle and not merely mad. Her outburst today about Kapiton Alexeyitch proves this all too well. There's some skulduggery of hers here. That is, at the very least, something Jesuitical, for a special purpose of her own."

"What Kapiton Alexeyitch?"

"Oh, Good Lord, Lev Nikolayevitch, you never listen to anything. I started by telling you about Kapiton Alexeyitch. I was so upset that I'm still shaking all over. That's why I stayed so long in town today. Kapiton Alexeyitch Radomsky, Yevgeny Pavlovitch's uncle—"

"What?" cried the prince.

"—shot himself this morning at dawn, at seven o'clock. A highly respected old fellow, seventy years old, an epicure, and —it's exactly as she said—a fabulous sum of state money is missing."

"Where could she have—"

"Heard about it? Ha, ha! You see, as soon as she arrived

377

here a regular general staff formed around her. You know what kind of people visit her now and seek 'the honor of her acquaintance.' She might naturally have heard something this morning from a visitor, because all Petersburg knows about it now, and half of Pavlovsk, perhaps all of Pavlovsk by now. But what a clever remark she made about the uniform—as I heard it—about how Yevgeny Pavlovitch managed to send in his resignation at the opportune moment! What a fiendish suggestion! No, that doesn't smack of madness. Anyway I refuse to believe that Yevgeny Pavlovitch could have known about the catastrophe beforehand—that is, that at seven o'clock on a certain day, and so forth. Of course he might have had a premonition about it. But I, and all of us, including Prince S., we all figured he would leave him a fortune! Terrible! Terrible! However, you understand that I'm not accusing Yevgeny Pavlovitch of anything, I hasten to make that clear—however, it certainly is suspicious. Prince S. is extremely shocked by it. It all happened so very oddly."

"But what is suspicious about Yevgeny Pavlovitch's behavior?"

"Nothing at all! He has behaved in the most honorable way. I wasn't suggesting a thing. His own fortune is, I believe, unaffected. Lizaveta Prokofyevna, of course, won't listen to anything. But the main thing is that all these family crises, these squabbles, one hardly knows what to call them. You are in a real sense a friend of the family, Lev Nikolayevitch, and, just imagine, it now appears—though it's not certain—that more than a month ago Yevgeny Pavlovitch proposed to Aglaya and apparently received a categorical refusal."

"Impossible!" cried the prince heatedly.

"Why? Do you know anything about it?" asked the general, startled and surprised, stopping as though rooted to the spot. "You see, my dear fellow, I may have told you more than I should, but, you see, it's because you are—you might say—the sort of person you are. Perhaps you know something in particular?"

"I don't know anything—about Yevgeny Pavlovitch," murmured the prince.

"I don't either! As for me, my friend, they want to see me dead and underground, and they refuse to see how hard it is on a man and that I can't bear it. There was such a scene just now, it was pure horror! I speak to you as if you were my own son. The worst is that Aglaya seems to be laughing at her mother. As for her apparent rejection of Yevgeny Pavlovitch a month ago and the rather formal conversation they had, it was a guess of her sisters—but a rather certain one. But she's such a willful and whimsical creature, there's no way to describe it! She has all the greatness of spirit, all the brilliant qualities of heart and mind—all this, it goes without saying, she has; but along with it there's caprice, sarcasm—in brief, she has a devilish disposition and is full of fantastic ideas besides. She was laughing right to her mother's face just now, and at her sisters, and Prince S., not to mention me, because she seldom does anything else but laugh at me, but of course I love her, you know, I love her even when she's laughing at me—and it does seem the little devil loves me specially for that; that is, she loves me more than the others do, apparently. I'll bet that in one way or another she's already been laughing at you too. I found you talking together right after the storm upstairs; she was sitting with you as if nothing had happened."

The prince blushed deeply and clenched his right hand, but said nothing.

"My dear, good Lev Nikolayevitch!" said the general with warmth and feeling. "I—and Lizaveta Prokovyevna too—though she's begun abusing you again, and me as well on your account, I don't understand why—we, however, love you, we love you and respect you, even in spite of everything, that is to say, in spite of all appearances. But you must agree, my friend, you must agree yourself how mystifying and how vexing it suddenly was to hear that cold-blooded little devil suddenly—because there she was standing in front of her mother with a look of profound contempt for all our questions, particularly for mine, because I, the devil take it, got it into my head to act sternly, seeing I'm the head of the family, and, well, I made a fool of myself—and that cold-blooded little devil suddenly declares with a laugh that that 'Madwoman'—that was her expression, and it does seem strange to me that she said the same thing you did: 'How could you have not seen it before?' she said—that that 'madwoman has gotten it into her head at all costs to marry me to Prince Lev Nikolayevitch, and for this she's trying to have Yevgeny Pavlovitch driven out of our house,' that's all she said, she made no further comment, she just laughed, and as we gaped at her she slammed the door and went out. Then I was told about what went on between you and her earlier today and—and—listen, my dear Prince, you're a very sensible fellow and not quick to take offense, I've noticed this about you, but—don't be angry, but, by heaven, she's only laughing at you. As a child does. So don't be angry with her, but that's the way it is. Don't get any ideas—she's simply making a fool of you, fools of us all, for having nothing better to do. Well, good-bye. You know of our feelings? Our sincere feelings toward you? They are immutable, and will never be otherwise—but now I must go in this direction. Good-bye. I've seldom ever felt so out of things—is that the expression?—as I do now. Ah, what a lovely summer holiday!"

Left alone at the crossroads, the prince looked around, quickly crossed the road and walked up under a lighted window in one of the houses, unfolded the little piece of paper which he had been holding tightly in his hand the whole time he had been talking with Ivan Fyodorovitch, and in the faint beam of light read it:

> *Tomorrow at seven in the morning I shall be on the green bench in the park, waiting for you. I have decided to speak to you about an extremely important matter, which concerns you directly.*
>
> *P.S. I hope you will not show anyone this letter. Though I am hesitant about writing such an instruction, I have made up my mind that you require it, and I wrote it blushing with shame for your peculiar character.*
>
> *P.P.S. This is the same green bench I showed you today. You should be ashamed of yourself! I have to write this too.*

The note had been written in haste and folded haphazardly, most likely just before Aglaya had come out on the veranda. With an indescribable emotion, very like terror, the prince again clenched the note tightly in his hand and quickly moved away from the window, out of the light, like a frightened thief; but as he did so he collided squarely with a gentleman who had been standing directly behind him.

"I have been following you, Prince," said the gentleman.

"Is that you, Keller?" cried the prince in surprise.

"I have been looking for you, Prince. I was waiting for you at the Yepanchins' house. I, of course, couldn't go in. I walked behind you while you were walking with the general. I am at your service, Prince. Keller is at your disposal. I am ready for any sacrifice, even to die, if necessary."

"But—why?"

"Well, there's sure to be a challenge. That Lieutenant Molovtsov, I know him, that is, not personally—he won't take an insult. The likes of us—that is, me and Rogozhin—he's inclined to look on as dirt, and perhaps for good reason, and

380

you will be the only one to answer. You'll have to pay the piper, Prince. He's been asking about you, I heard him, and a friend of his will certainly be calling on you tomorrow, if he isn't already waiting for you now. If you'll do me the honor of choosing me as your second, I'd be ready to go to prison for you. That's why I've been looking for you, Prince."

"So you're talking about a duel too!" the prince said and suddenly laughed, to Keller's great surprise. He roared with laughter. Keller, who had been on pins and needles until he experienced the satisfaction of offering to be the prince's second, was close to being offended at the sight of him laughing heartily.

"Prince, you did after all pin him by the arms this afternoon. For a man of honor that's hard to bear, especially in public."

"But he gave me a push in the chest!" cried the prince, laughing. "We have nothing to fight about! I'll apologize, that's all. But if we must fight, we'll fight! Let him shoot, I'd really like that. Ha, ha! I know how to load a pistol. Do you know how to load a pistol, Keller? First you have to buy the powder, the pistol kind, not damp and not so coarse as the kind for cannons, then you begin by putting the powder in, you get some felt off a door somewhere, and then you drop the bullet in, but not the bullet before the powder or it won't fire. Do you hear, Keller? Or it won't fire. Ha, ha? Isn't that a splendid reason, Keller my friend? Ah, Keller, I am going to kiss and embrace you this moment. Ha, ha, ha! How did you manage to turn up so suddenly, face to face with him this afternoon? Come to my house sometime soon and we'll drink champagne. We'll all get drunk! Did you know I have a dozen bottles of champagne in Lebedev's cellar? He offered them to me at a bargain the day before yesterday, the day after I moved into his house, and I bought them all! I'll get the whole crowd together! And you, are you going to sleep tonight?"

"As I do every night, Prince."

"Well, pleasant dreams, then. Ha, ha!"

The prince crossed the road and disappeared into the park, leaving a rather perplexed Keller to his thoughts. He had never seen the prince in such a strange mood, and until that moment could not have imagined him that way.

"A fever, perhaps, because he's such a nervous man, and all this has affected him, but of course he won't be a coward. His kind aren't fainthearted, by God!" Keller was thinking to himself. "Hmm. Champagne! An interesting piece of news, after all. Twelve bottles. A dozen. Not bad—a well-stocked garrison. And I'll bet Lebedev got that champagne as security from someone. Hmm. Still, he's rather nice, that prince, in fact I like that sort of fellow. But there's no time to lose, and if there's champagne, this is just the time for it."

That the prince was in a state resembling fever was of course quite true.

He wandered a long time in the dark park and finally "found himself" walking along a certain tree-lined alley. An impression remained with him of having once walked up and down this alley thirty or forty times, between the bench and a certain tall and very conspicuous old tree, a distance of about a hundred yards. He would not, even had he tried, have been able to remember what he had been thinking about during the full hour, at least, which he had spent in the park. However, he caught himself thinking of something which made him burst out laughing; he felt like laughing that is, though there was really nothing to laugh about. It occurred to him that the idea of a possible duel might have arisen in other heads than Keller's, and therefore that his lesson in pistol loading might not have been accidental.

"Ah!" he thought, suddenly struck by another thought. "She came out on the veranda when I was sitting in the corner, and was terribly surprised to find me there, and—laughing that way—spoke of tea; and all that time she had that piece of paper in her hand, so she must have known that I was sitting on the veranda. So why was she surprised? Ha, ha, ha!"

He took the note out of his pocket and kissed it, but stopped at once and became thoughtful.

"How strange! How strange!" he said a minute later with a sort of sadness: in moments of intense joy he always became sad, he did not himself know why. He looked around intently and was surprised he had come to this place. He was very tired, he went to the bench and sat down. There was an extraordinary stillness around him. The music in the gardens had stopped. There was perhaps no one else in the park—of course not, it was at least eleven-thirty. The evening was quiet, warm, clear, a Petersburg evening in early June, but in the dense, shadowy park, in the alley where he was, it was now almost dark.

If someone had told him at that moment that he was in love, passionately in love, he would have rejected the notion with surprise and possibly even with indignation. And if someone had gone on to say that Aglaya's letter was a love letter, arranging a lovers' rendezvous, he would have burned with shame for such a man and, perhaps, have challenged him to a duel. All this was perfectly sincere and not once did he have any doubt or admit the slightest "double" thought about the possibility of this girl loving him, or even of him loving her. He would have been ashamed of having such an idea! The possibility of love for him, for "a man like him," he would have found monstrous. It crossed his mind that, if there was anything to it at all, it was simply a prank on her part, but he was quite unconcerned by the whole matter and found it all too natural. He was absorbed and troubled by something entirely different. He fully believed the remark the general in his excitement had let fall a little earlier, about how she was laughing at everyone, at the general himself and at the prince in particular. He did not feel in the least offended by this; in his view it was as it should be. All that concerned him was to see her again tomorrow, early in the morning, to sit beside her on the green bench, and hear her tell him how to load a pistol and to look at her. He wanted nothing more than that. The question of what she intended to say to him, and what the important matter which concerned him directly was also crossed his mind once or twice. Moreover he did not for a single moment doubt that there really was some "important matter" for which he was summoned, but he put it almost completely out of his mind now and did not feel the slightest inclination to think about it.

The crunch of a soft step on the gravel of the alley made him raise his head. A man whose face was difficult to distinguish in the darkness approached the bench and sat down beside him. The prince quickly turned to him, nearly touching him, and recognized the pale face of Rogozhin.

"I knew you'd be wandering around here somewhere. I didn't have to look for you long," muttered Rogozhin through his teeth.

It was the first time they were together since their encounter in the corridor of the hotel. Astonished by Rogozhin's sudden appearance, the prince could not collect his thoughts for some time, and an agonizing sensation revived in his heart. Rogozhin apparently understood the effect he had produced, but though he was slightly disconcerted at first, speaking with what seemed to be affected casualness, the prince soon realized that he was neither affected or even particularly embarrassed. If there was any awkwardness in his words or gestures, it was only on the surface; deep down he was not a man who would change.

"How did you—find me here?" asked the prince for something to say.

"I heard from Keller you'd gone to the park—I was just at your house. Well, I thought—so that's how it is."

"How what is?" said the prince, anxiously picking up the remark.

Rogozhin laughed but gave no explanation.

"I got your letter, Lev Nikolayevitch. All that's no use— why do you bother? But now I've come to you from her. She's insisting you come to see her, she has something to tell you. She wants to see you today."

"I will come tomorrow. I'm going home now. Are you— coming with me?"

"What for? I told you all I had to say. Good-bye."

"Won't you stop by?" the prince asked gently.

"You're a strange fellow, Lev Nikolayevitch. One can't help being amazed at you."

Rogozhin smiled mockingly

"Why? Why do you hate me so much now?" the prince asked sadly and ardently. "You know yourself at this moment that all you have been thinking is untrue. And yet I had an idea you had not stopped hating me, and do you know why? Because you tried to kill me, that's why you have not stopped hating me. I tell you the only Parfyon Rogozhin I remember is the man I exchanged crosses with that day. I wrote you yesterday to forget all that madness and not to speak about it again with me. Why do you move away from me? Why do you keep your hand from me? I tell you I take all that happened then for nothing but madness. I know you as you were all that day, as if it were myself. What you imagined does not exist and could not exist. Why should there be this hatred between us?"

"How could you have any hatred?" said Rogozhin, laughing again in reply to the prince's sudden, heated speech. He had in fact moved two steps and had hidden his hands behind him. "It won't do for me to come to your house at all now, Lev Nikolayevitch," he added, slowly and sententiously, in conclusion.

"Do you hate me that much, then?"

"I don't like you, Lev Nikolayevitch, so why should I ome to see you. Ah, Prince, you're like a child: you want a y, you must have it at once, but you don't understand ngs. You wrote everything you're telling me now in your r. Do you think I don't believe you? I believe every word say, and I know you've never deceived me and never will future, and still I don't like you. Here you write that forgotten everything and only remember your brother in you exchanged crosses with, not the other Rogozhin who raised his knife against you. But how do you know my feelings?" Rogozhin smiled bitterly again. "Perhaps I've not once in all that time repented for what I did, and here you are presenting me with your fraternal pardon. Perhaps I was already thinking of something else that evening, but about that—"

"You forgot even to think about that!" the prince interrupted. "Of course you would! And I'll swear you went directly to the train station and came down here to Pavlovsk, and you looked for her in the crowd at the bandstand, and you saw her, just as you did today. That doesn't surprise me! If you hadn't been in a state where you were only able to think of one thing, perhaps you wouldn't have raised your knife against me. I had a premonition then, ever since morning, just from looking at you—do you know what you were like then? I think it was when we were exchanging crosses that the idea first came into my mind. Why did you take me to your mother then? Did you think you could stay your hand that way? No, you couldn't have thought that, and you only felt one thing, just as I did— We both felt the same thing then. If you hadn't raised your hand against me then (which God turned aside), how would I appear to you now? Anyway, I already suspected you: the sin was ours in common. (Don't scowl. Well, now what are you laughing at?) 'Not repented.' Even if you wanted to you probably couldn't repent, besides the fact that you don't like me. And even if I seemed as innocent as an angel to you, you still couldn't stand me as long as you thought she loved me and not you. That's what jealousy is. But now I've been thinking about that this past week, Parfyon, and I'll tell you. Do you know she probably loves you more than anyone else now, and loves you in a way that the more she torments you the more she loves you? She won't tell you this, you have to know how to see it. Why, at long last, is she going ahead and marrying you? Someday she'll tell you this herself. Some women want to be loved that way, and that's the kind of woman she is! The sort of person you are and your love must fascinate her! Do you know that a woman is capable of torturing a man with unspeakable cruelty and mockery and never once feel the slightest remorse, because as she looks at you she thinks to herself, 'Right now I'm tormenting him to death, but later I'll make up for it with my love.' "

Rogozhin heard the prince through, then broke into loud laughter.

"But tell me, Prince, haven't you been caught up with a woman like this? I heard something about you—is it true?"

"What—what could you have heard?" asked the prince, stopping in great confusion, suddenly startled.

Rogozhin kept on laughing. He had been listening to the prince not without interest and perhaps not without pleasure; the prince's joyous and ardent enthusiasm made an impression on him and lifted his spirits.

"It's not only that I heard something," he added, "now I can see for myself that it's true. Look here, when have you ever talked as you just did? Why, what you said didn't seem to come from you at all. If I hadn't heard this sort of thing about you I wouldn't have come here like this—and to a park, at midnight."

"I don't understand you at all, Parfyon Semyonovitch."

"She told me about you a long time ago, and now I saw it myself when you were sitting with that girl listening to the music. She swore to me yesterday and again today that you were wildly in love with Aglaya Yepanchin. It doesn't make any difference to me, Prince, and it's none of my business. If you don't love her anymore, she's still in love with you. You know she's set on marrying you off to that girl, she's promised she would, ha, ha! She told me, 'I won't marry you without that—they go to the church and we'll go.' What it's all about I don't understand and I never have: either she loves you more than anything or—but if she loves you why does she want you to marry someone else? She says, 'I want to see him happy.' That must mean she loves you."

"I told you and I've written you that she's not—in her right mind," said the prince, who had listened to Rogozhin with a feeling of great distress.

"Lord knows! It's you that might be mistaken about that. However, she did set a wedding day when I brought her back from the concert. She said for certain we'd marry within three weeks and perhaps even sooner. She swore to it. She took off her cross and kissed it. So now it's all in your hands, Prince. Ha, ha!"

"This is all insanity. What you are telling me now will never happen—never! Tomorrow I'll come to see you both!"

"How can you say she's mad?" said Rogozhin. "How can she seem sane to everyone else and mad only to you? How can she be over there writing letters? If she's mad they would have seen it in her letters."

"What letters?" the prince asked in alarm.

"She writes them to *her*, and *she* reads them. Don't you know that? Well, you will. She's sure to show them to you herself."

"That's impossible to believe!" cried the prince.

"Ah! It looks to me, Lev Nikolayevitch, as if you'd only gone a little way along that path. You're just starting out. Don't worry: soon you'll be hiring your own private detectives, and watching night and day yourself, and you'll know every step she takes, if only—"

"Stop it—don't ever speak of that again!" cried the prince. "Listen, Parfyon, just before you came I was walking here and suddenly I started laughing—why I have no idea, except that what started it was that tomorrow is my birthday—as if it was all intended. It's almost twelve o'clock now. Come on, let's celebrate the day! I have some wine, we'll drink wine. Wish for me what I don't know how to wish for myself now —I want you particularly to wish it for me, and I shall wish you all happiness. If not, give me back my cross! Because you didn't send my cross back the next day, did you! You're wearing it, aren't you? Aren't you wearing it right now?"

"Yes," said Rogozhin.

"Well then, let's go. I don't want to greet my new life without you, because my new life has begun today, hasn't it?"

"Yes. I see for myself now and I know it has begun. I will tell *her* so. You are not quite yourself, Lev Nikolayevitch!"

Chapter FOUR

As he and Rogozhin approached his house the prince noticed with great surprise that the veranda was brightly lit and a large and noisy company was gathered there. This lively assembly was laughing and shouting, some even arguing at the top of their voices; at first glance they all seemed to be having an exceedingly good time. And indeed as he went up on the veranda he saw that they were all drinking, and drinking champagne, and had evidently been doing so for quite some time, for many of the revelers had managed to become very pleasantly exhilarated. The guests were all known to the prince, but the strange thing was that they had all gathered together at once, as if by invitation, though the prince had invited no one and had himself only just remembered by chance that it was his birthday.

"You must have told someone you were setting out champagne, so they've all come flocking," muttered Rogozhin as he followed the prince onto the veranda. "That's how it happens, all you have to do is whistle," he added spitefully, no doubt remembering his own recent past.

Everyone greeted the prince with shouts and salutations and surrounded him. Some were very noisy, others much quieter, but, having heard of his birthday, they all hastened to congratulate him, everyone waiting his turn for the purpose. The presence of certain persons aroused the prince's interest; Burdovsky, for instance; but most surprising was that he suddenly noticed Yevgeny Pavlovitch among the company. When he saw him the prince could hardly believe his eyes, and was almost frightened.

At the same time Lebedev, quite red and ecstatic, ran up o offer explanations; he was rather "far gone." From his bbling it appeared that the party had assembled quite natu-ily and, as it were, by accident. First toward evening, Hip-polite had arrived and, feeling a great deal better, wanted to t the prince on the veranda. He settled on the couch, he was joined by Lebedev, and then by his entire house-d, that is to say, by his daughters and General Ivolgin. rdovsky had arrived with Hippolite, whom he had been ac-mpanying. It seemed that Ganya and Ptitsyn had dropped y a little later, their arrival having coincided with the inci-dent at the gardens. Then Keller had turned up, announced that it was the prince's birthday, and asked for champagne. Yevgeny Pavlovitch had arrived only a half an hour ago. Kolya too had insisted most energetically that the champagne be brought out and that there should be a celebration. Lebedev had readily produced the wine.

"But it's my own, it's my own!" he was babbling to the prince. "At my own expense to celebrate your birthday and congratulate you, and there'll be something to eat, some little snacks, my daughter is attending to that. But, Prince, if you only knew what they're discussing now! Do you remember Hamlet's 'To be or not to be'? A most contemporary theme, sir, most contemporary! Questions and answers. And Mr. Terentyev is completely— He doesn't want to go to bed! He only had a sip of champagne, only a sip, it won't hurt him. Come closer, Prince, and settle it! Everyone's been waiting for you, everyone's been waiting for your felicitous wit."

The prince noticed the kind, affectionate glance of Vera Lebedev, who was also making her way toward him through the crowd. He held out his hand to her, ahead of everyone else; she flushed with pleasure and wished him "a happy life *from this day on.*" Then she hurried back into the kitchen; she was preparing the food there; but even before the prince's arrival—whenever she could spare a moment from her work—she had come out on the veranda and listened with all her attention to the heated discussions of things which were to her most abstract and strange, being carried on by the slightly inebriated guests. Her younger sister had fallen asleep with her mouth open, on a chest in the next room, but the little boy, Lebedev's son, stood beside Kolya and Hippolite, and the look on his lively face showed that he was ready to stand there in that one place for another ten hours on end, listening and enjoying himself.

"I was waiting for you especially and I'm awfully glad you've come here in such a happy mood," said Hippolite when the prince came up to shake hands with him right after Vera.

"But how do you know I'm in a happy mood?"

"I can see it from your face. Greet your guests and come sit with us as soon as you can. I was waiting especially for you," he added, stressing the fact that he had been waiting. When the prince asked him whether it would be bad for him to stay up so late, he replied that he was surprised himself that three days earlier he had wanted to die, and that he had never felt better than on this evening.

Burdovsky jumped up and said that he had just happened to be there, that he had been accompanying Hippolite, and that he was also very glad that in his letter he had written "nonsense" and was now "glad simply to—" Without finishing his sentence he shook the prince's hand firmly and sat down in his chair.

Last of all the prince went up to Yevgeny Pavlovitch, who at once took him by the arm.

"I have only a couple of words to say to you," he said in an undertone, "about an extremely important matter. Let's step away for a minute."

"A couple of words," another voice whispered in the prince's other ear, and another hand took his other arm. In astonishment the prince observed a terribly unkempt figure with a red, winking, laughing face, whom he immediately recognized as Ferdyshchenko, who had appeared from nowhere.

"Remember Ferdyshchenko?" asked the latter.

"Where have you turned up from?" cried the prince.

"He's sorry!" cried Keller, suddenly coming up to them. "He was hiding, he didn't want to come up to you. He was hiding there in the corner. He's sorry, Prince, he feels guilty."

"But of what? What about?"

"I ran into him, Prince, I ran into him just now and I brought him along. He's one of my most particular friends. But he's sorry."

"I'm delighted, gentlemen. Do go sit with everyone. I'll be right along," said the prince, getting rid of them and hastily returning to Yevgeny Pavlovitch.

"It's very entertaining here in your house," remarked the latter, "and I've enjoyed the half hour I've been waiting for you. Now look here, my dear Lev Nikolayevitch, I've settled everything for you with Kurmyshov and I came to reassure you; you have nothing to worry about; he took the matter in a very, very sensible way, especially because, as I see it, he is the one more at fault."

"What Kurmyshov?"

"Why, the one you grabbed by the arms this afternoon. He was so furious he wanted to send his seconds tomorrow to demand satisfaction."

"Really! What nonsense!"

"Well, of course it's nonsense, and it certainly would have ended that way, but we have these people—"

"Haven't you come about something else as well, Yevgeny Pavlovitch?"

"Oh, certainly I have," said the other, laughing. "My dear Prince, I'm leaving tomorrow at daybreak for Petersburg about that unfortunate affair—about my uncle. Can you imagine, it's all true, and everyone knew except myself. It was all such a shock to me I haven't been able to go there—to the Yepanchins'. I won't tomorrow either because I'll be in Petersburg, you understand? Perhaps I'll be there three days —in a word, my affairs are in a mess. Although the thing isn't of the greatest importance I decided I had to have a frank conversation with you about something, and without delay; that is, before I leave. If you don't mind, I'll sit and wait until the party breaks up; besides, I have nowhere else to go. I'm so upset I won't try to go to bed. Anyway, even though it's unconscionable and improper to go after someone straightforwardly like this, I'll tell you frankly, my dear Prince: I've come here to seek your friendship. You are a unique person; that is, you don't lie every step of the way, and perhaps you don't lie at all. And I need a friend and an advisor in a certain matter, because I am one of the unfortunate ones now—"

He laughed again.

"The trouble is," said the prince after a moment's thought, "you want to wait until they've gone, but heaven only knows when that will be. Wouldn't it be better for us to go for a walk in the park now? They're sure to wait. I'll excuse myself."

"No, no. I have my reasons for not having them suspect we have anything special to talk about. There are people here who are very interested in our relations with one another. Didn't you know that, Prince? And it will be much better if they see we are ordinarily on the most friendly terms and not only for a special reason. Do you understand? They will leave in a couple of hours; I'll take twenty minutes or perhaps a half an hour of your time."

"Then by all means, do stay. I am very glad to have you even without your explaining anything, and I appreciate your kind words about our friendly relations. You must excuse me for being distracted today; you know, for some reason I can't concentrate just now."

"I see, I see," murmured Yevgeny Pavlovitch with a faintly mocking smile. He was very easily amused that evening.

"What do you see?" asked the prince, startled.

"But, my dear Prince," said Yevgeny Pavlovitch, smiling again but not answering the prince's direct question, "you don't suspect I've simply come to you to take you in and then worm something out of you, do you?"

"I haven't a doubt you've come to worm something out of me," said the prince, laughing at last, "and it may be that you've also decided to deceive me a little. But that's all right. Do you believe me? And—and—and I am as convinced as I was before that you are an excellent person, in fact we might perhaps end by becoming friends. I like you very much, Yevgeny Pavlovitch. You—you are a real person!"

"Well, in any case it's pleasant to have dealings with you, no matter what they are," concluded Yevgeny Pavlovitch. "Come, I'll drink a glass to your health. I'm terribly glad I got together with you. Oh," he stopped suddenly, "has that Mr. Hippolite come to live with you?"

"Yes."

"He's not going to die soon, I don't suppose?"

"Why do you ask?"

"Oh, for no reason. I spent a half hour with him here—"

Hippolite had all this time been waiting for the prince and casting glances at him and Yevgeny Pavlovitch as they were talking apart from the others. He became feverishly animated as they returned to the table. He was restless and agitated, sweat showed on his brow. His glittering eyes expressed a sort of wandering unrest and a vague impatience; his glance roved aimlessly from object to object, from one face to another. And although he had until that moment taken an active part in the noisy conversation, his animation was merely feverish. In fact he had been paying little attention to the conversation; his arguments had been incoherent, sarcastic, and offhandedly paradoxical; he would not finish his sentences and he would suddenly drop subjects he had begun with fervent intensity. The prince learned to his surprise and regret that that evening he had been permitted to drink two full glasses of champagne and that the half-empty one before him was his third. But he learned of this only later, at the moment he was not very observant.

"Do you know," cried Hippolite, "I'm awfully glad that today is your birthday."

"Why?"

"You'll see. Please sit down. Quickly. In the first place it's because all these—people of yours are gathered here. I was counting on there being people, and for the first time in my life something's happened the way I was counting it would! But it's too bad I didn't know it was your birthday or I would have come with a present. Ha, ha! Perhaps I have brought one! Is it long before daylight?"

"It's now two hours till sunrise," stated Ptitsyn, looking at his watch.

"What's the use of sunrise when one can read outside without it?" asked someone.

"Because I must see the rim of the sun. Can one drink the sun's health, Prince? What do you think?"

Hippolite put his questions brusquely, addressing everyone unceremoniously, as though he were giving orders, but apparently without being aware of it himself.

"Let's drink to it, if you like. But you should be quieter, Hippolite, shouldn't you?"

"You're always for sleep, Prince, you might as well be my nurse! As soon as the sun appears and 'resounds' in the heavens (Who wrote the verse, 'the sun resounded in the heavens'? It makes no sense but it's very good.), then we will go to bed. Lebedev! Isn't the sun the wellspring of life? What does 'water of life' mean in the Apocalypse? Have you heard of the 'star that is called Wormwood,' Prince?"

"I have heard that Lebedev understands that 'star Wormwood' as the network of railroads spread all over Europe."

"No, excuse me, that's not the way it is!" cried Lebedev, jumping up and waving his arms as if wishing to stop the rise of general laughter. "Please! With these people—all these people," he turned suddenly to the prince. "You see, on certain points, this is how it is—" and he rapped twice on the table, insistently, which brought on more laughter.

Though Lebedev was in his usual "evening condition," he was on this occasion particularly aroused and irritated by a long "learned" discussion that had taken place, and in such cases he always treated his opponents with infinite and quite undisguised contempt.

"That's not right. No, sir! Prince, half an hour ago we agreed not to interrupt and not to laugh while someone was talking, so that the person would be free to say what he had to say—and then let the atheists answer him if they cared to. We picked the general as chairman. Yes, sir! But what is this? This way anyone can be shouted down in the middle of a lofty idea, a profound idea, sir!"

"But speak, speak! No one is shouting you down!" said several voices.

"Speak but say something."

"What is this 'star called Wormwood'?" someone demanded.

"I haven't the slightest idea," responded General Ivolgin and with an important air resumed his place as chairman.

"I'm marvelously fond of all these discussions and arguments, Prince—learned ones of course," Keller was saying, fairly twitching in his chair with eagerness and enchantment. "Learned and political," he added, suddenly addressing Yevgeny Pavlovitch, who was sitting almost next to him. "Do you know I love reading about the English Parliament in the papers. I don't mean what they're discussing—I'm not a politician, you know—but how they talk among themselves and carry on, you might say, like politicians: 'the noble viscount seated opposite me,' 'the noble earl who shares my opinion,' 'my noble opponent who has astounded Europe with his proposal,' I mean all those fine little phrases, all that parliamentary procedure of a free people—that's what I like, I do! It delights me, Prince. I've always been an artist at the depths of my soul. I swear I have, Yevgeny Pavlovitch."

"So what you're saying is," said Ganya, who was arguing heatedly in another corner of the room, "the railroads are a curse, the ruin of mankind, a plague that has fallen on their earth to pollute the 'water of life.' Is that it?"

Gavril Ardalionovitch was in a particularly excitable mood that evening, a cheerful and almost exultant mood, it seemed to the prince. He was of course joking with Lebedev, egging him on, but he soon became aroused himself.

"No, not the railways, sir!" retorted Lebedev, simultaneously losing control of himself and experiencing an immense sensation of pleasure. "The railroads alone will not pollute the 'water of life,' but the whole thing is damned, sir, the whole trend of the past few centuries in its whole entirety, scientific and practical, may possibly really be damned, sir."

"Is it really damned or only possibly damned?" inquired Yevgeny Pavlovitch. "You see in this case it's important to know."

"Damned, damned, really damned!" Lebedev replied vehemently.

"Don't be in such a furor, Lebedev," remarked Ptitsyn with a smile. "You're really much better in the morning."

"But much more frank in the evening! Much more frank and convivial!" said Lebedev, turning to him heatedly. "More simple, more precise, more honest, more honorable, and though I do present my weak side to you, I don't give a damn! I challenge all of you, now, you atheists: how are you going to save the world and where are you going to find a proper path for it? You, men of science, of industry, cooperative associations, fair wages, and all that? How are you going to do it? With credit? What is credit? Where will credit take you?"

"Dear me, what a curiosity you have," remarked Yevgeny Pavlovitch.

"In my opinion anyone who's not interested in such questions is a fashionable good-for-nothing, sir!"

"But at least credit leads to general solidarity and a balance of interests," observed Ptitsyn.

"And that's all! That's all! Without allowing any moral basis except the gratification of individual egoism and material necessity! Universal peace, universal happiness—out of necessity! May I ask if this is how I am to understand you, my dear sir?"

"But the universal necessity of living, eating and drinking, and the complete conviction—a scientific one at that—that these necessities cannot be satisfied without universal association and a solidarity of interests, this it seems to me is a solid enough idea to be the basis and the 'water of life' for future centuries of humanity," said Ganya, now excited in earnest.

"The necessity of eating and drinking, that's nothing but the instinct of self-preservation—"

"And why isn't the instinct of self-preservation enough? After all, the instinct of self-preservation is the normal law of humanity."

"Who told you that?" Yevgeny Pavlovitch suddenly shouted. "It's true it is a law, but it's no more normal than the law of destruction, and perhaps even self-destruction. Is self-preservation alone the whole normal law of humanity?"

"Ah-ha!" exclaimed Hippolite, turning quickly to Yevgeny Pavlovitch and looking at him with wild curiosity; but seeing that he was laughing, he laughed too, nudged Kolya who was standing beside him, and again asked him what time it was, and even took Kolya's silver watch himself and looked avidly at the hands. Then, as though forgetting everything, he stretched himself out on the couch, placed his hands behind his head, and proceeded to stare at the ceiling. Half a minute later he was at the table again, sitting erect and listening to the babbling of Lebedev, who was at the highest pitch of excitement.

"This is a cunning and ironical idea, a most provoking thought!" said Lebedev, eagerly picking up Yevgeny Pavolovitch's paradox. "An idea expressed to provoke one's opponents to battle—but a true idea! Because you're a scoffing man of the world and a cavalry officer (though not without brains!) you yourself don't know what a true thought it is, what a profound thought! Yes, sir. The law of self-destruction and the law of self-preservation are equally strong in humanity! The devil holds equal dominion over mankind until some final time which is not yet known to us. You laugh? You don't believe in the devil? Not to believe in the devil is a French idea, a frivolous idea. Do you know who the devil is? Do you know his name? You don't even know his name and you laugh at the mere form of him, as Voltaire did, at his hoofs, his tail, his horns, which you invented; for the foul spirit is mighty and menacing and he hasn't the hoofs and horns you invented for him. But it's not a question of the devil now."

"How do you know it's not a question of the devil?" cried Hippolite suddenly and laughed as if he was having hysterics.

"A clever and suggestive thought!" said Lebedev approvingly. "But, once again, it's not to the point. Our question is whether the 'water of life' has been weakened by the increase of—"

"Railroads?" cried Kolya.

"Not railway communication, my young but impetuous lad, but the whole tendency of which the railroads may serve as, so to speak, the artistic representation. They speed around, clanking and rattling, all for the happiness, they say, of humanity! A certain thinker, secluded from the world, complained, 'Mankind has grown too noisy and industrial, there is little spiritual peace.' And another thinker always on the go replied triumphantly to him, 'That may be, but the rumble of railroad cars bringing bread to starving humanity is better, perhaps, than spiritual peace,' and walked proudly away from him. But I, the abominable Lebedev, do not believe in the cars that bring bread to humanity! For the cars that bring bread to humanity without a moral basis for doing so may be coldly excluding a considerable part of humanity from the enjoyment of what is brought, as has happened already."

"Those cars of yours can coldly exclude?" someone said.

"As has happened already," repeated Lebedev, not deigning to notice the question. "We've already had Malthus, a friend of humanity. But a friend of humanity with shaky moral principles is a devourer of humanity, not to speak of his vanity; for if you wound the vanity of one of these innumerable friends of humanity he's ready to set fire to the four corners of the earth to satisfy a petty revenge, like all of us would, and, to speak fairly, like I would, the vilest of all, for I might be the first to bring the kindling wood and then run away. But again that's not the point!"

"What is the point then?"

"He's boring!"

"The point lies in a little tale of long ago—for I find I do have to tell you a little tale of long ago. In our time, in our country—which I trust you love, gentlemen, as much as I do, for on my part I'm ready even to shed the last drop of my blood."

"Get on with it. Get on with it!"

"In our country, as in Europe, widespread and terrible famines visit humanity, as far as can be calculated and as far as I personally remember, no oftener nowadays than every quarter century, in other words once every twenty-five years. I don't vouch for the exact figure, but they are relatively rare."

"Relative to what?"

"To the twelfth century and the centuries immediately before and after it. For in those times, according to what the writers have written, general famines affecting all mankind occurred once every two, or in any case once every three years, so that in such circumstances men even had to resort to cannibalism, though they kept it quiet. One such parasite as he was approaching old age declared of his own free will and without being forced that in the course of a long and miserable existence he had personally and in the deepest secrecy killed and eaten sixty monks and several children of the laity —about six but no more, very few in comparison with the

396

number of ecclesiastics he consumed. Adult laymen, it appeared, he never laid a hand on for that purpose."

"That's impossible!" cried the chairman himself, the general, almost in a hurt voice. "I often discuss and argue with him, gentlemen, and always about things like this, but most of the time he comes forth with absurdities that would shrivel your ears, without a grain of truth to them."

"General! Remember the siege of Kars. And, gentlemen, you may be sure that my story is the unvarnished truth. For my part, let me say that almost every reality, though it may have its own immutable laws, is still almost always beyond belief and improbable. In fact, sometimes, the more real it is the more improbable."

"But can you eat sixty monks?" they were asking, laughing all around him.

"He didn't eat them all at once, obviously, but perhaps over a period of fifteen or twenty years, which is perfectly understandable and natural."

"Natural?"

"Yes, natural!" replied Lebedev with pedantic insistence. "Besides, a Catholic monk is by his very nature amenable and inquisitive, and it would be very simple to lure him into the woods or some secluded spot and deal with him in the aforesaid manner. But I don't deny that the number of persons consumed does seem excessive to the point of intemperance."

"Perhaps it is true, gentlemen," observed the prince suddenly.

Until then he had listened in silence to the disputants and had not entered the conversation, though often he had joined wholeheartedly in the general laughter. It was clear he was delighted that they were all so gay and so noisy, even that they were drinking too much. Possibly he might never have said a word all evening, but suddenly he had for some reason been moved to speak. He spoke with such extreme gravity that everyone turned to him attentively.

"What I mean, gentlemen, is that in those days such famines were frequent. I have heard of this too, though I don't know history well. But I rather think this is how it must have been. When I was up in the Swiss mountains I was amazed by the ruins of old feudal castles, built on the mountain slopes or on precipitous cliffs, at least half a mile high (which means several miles of footpath). You know what a castle is: a whole mountain of stone. It meant dreadful, impossible labor! And of course they were all built by those poor people, the vassals. Besides that, they had to pay all kinds of taxes and support the priesthood. How could they provide for themselves, then, and till the land! There must have been few of them then, they died off terribly from famine, they may literally have had nothing to eat. I have sometimes wondered how it happened that these people didn't become completely extinct then, how nothing befell them, how they could endure it and survive. Lebedev is certainly right in saying there were cannibals among them, and perhaps a great many—except I don't see why he brought monks into it or what he means by that."

"Undoubtedly because in the twelfth century one could only eat monks because only the monks were fat," observed Gavril Ardalionovitch.

"A magnificent thought and a true one!" cried Lebedev. "For he didn't even touch the laity. Sixty ecclesiastics and not a single layman, and that's an appalling thought! An historical thought! A statistical thought! And such facts make history for anyone who knows, for it proves with mathematical exactitude that the clergy in those days were at least sixty times happier and better off than the rest of humanity. And very likely at least sixty times fatter."

"An exaggeration! An exaggeration, Lebedev!" they were laughing all around him.

"I agree this is an historical thought, but what are you getting at?" pursued the prince. (He spoke with such seriousness and with such an absence of any mockery or jeering at Lebedev, at whom everyone else was laughing, that his words were in such contrast with the general tone of the company that they could only sound comical; a moment later they were beginning to laugh at him too, but he did not notice this.)

"Can't you see, Prince, that he's a madman?" Yevgeny Pavlovitch said, bending close to him. "I was told here earlier that he's obsessed with lawyers and lawyers' speeches and wants to take the examinations. I expect we'll have a splendid burlesque."

"I'm leading up to a tremendous conclusion," Lebedev was roaring in the meantime. "But first of all let's look at the psychological and juridical situation of the criminal. We see that the criminal—or as we might call him, my client—in spite of the impossibility of finding other food, several times during the course of his interesting career manifested a desire to repent and to abstain from ecclesiastics. We see this clearly from the facts: we are told that he did eat five or six infants, a number insignificant in comparison, yet meaningful in another respect. It is evident that, tormented by terrible pangs

398

of remorse (for my client is religious and a man of conscience, as I will presently show) and anxious to reduce his sin as much as possible, he as an experiment changed his diet six times from the clergy to the laity. That this was done as an experiment there can, once again, be no doubt; for had it been only for gastronomic variety the figure six would be too insignificant; why only six and not thirty? (I'm taking half, thirty of each.) But if it was only an experiment, inspired by despair and fear of sacrilege and offending the church, then the figure six becomes perfectly intelligible; for six attempts to appease one's conscience are quite enough, seeing they could not be successful in any case. And in the first place, in my opinion, an infant is too small—that is, insufficient—so that for a given period of time the demand for lay infants would be three times or five times greater than for clergy, so that while the sin might be lessened on one hand it would be in the end increased, not qualitatively so much as quantitatively. Reckoning thus, gentlemen, I am of course making allowance for the mental attitude of the twelfth-century criminal. As far as I'm concerned, a man of the nineteenth century, I might have reasoned differently, I can tell you. So, my friends, you have no reason to be grinning at me, and in your case, General, it's quite unbecoming. In the second place, in my own personal view an infant isn't sufficiently nutritious and might be too sweet and cloying, so that without satisfying the appetite would only leave pangs of remorse. Now for the conclusion, gentlemen, the finish, the finale, in which lies the solution to one of the greatest enigmas of those times and of ours! The criminal ends by going to the clergy and presenting evidence against himself and giving himself up to the authorities. One asks what tortures awaited him in those times—the wheel, the stake, the fire! Who made him inform against himself? Why didn't he simply stop at sixty and keep the secret until his dying breath? Why didn't he simply give up monks and live in penitence as a hermit? Why, after all, didn't he become a monk himself? Here's the answer! There must have been something stronger than the stake and fire, even stronger than a habit of twenty years. There must have been an idea stronger than all the calamities, the crop failures, torture, plague, leprosy, and all that hell which mankind could not have endured without that idea binding men together and guiding their hearts and fructifying the 'water of life'! Show me anything as strong as that in our age of vice and railroads —that is, one should say in our age of vessels and railroads, but I say in our age of vices and railroads because I'm drunk but right. Show me an idea that binds men together today with even half the strength as in those days. And dare say, then, that the 'water of life' has not been weakened and polluted under this 'star,' under this network that has entangled people. And don't try to scare me off with your prosperity, your wealth, the rarity of famine, and the rapidity of the means of communication! There's more wealth, but there's less strength; the binding idea doesn't exist anymore; everything has turned soft, everything is rotten, and people are rotten. We're all, all of us rotten! But that's enough, that's not the question now. The question now, most respected Prince, is whether we shouldn't be getting the food for our guests."

Lebedev, who had stirred some of his listeners to real indignation (it should be noted that bottles were being opened all during this time), at once appeased all his opponents by the unexpected conclusion of his speech. He called such a conclusion "a lawyer's clever twist." Merry laughter rang out again and the guests became cheerful, they all got up from the table to stretch their legs and wander about on the veranda. Only Keller was still dissatisfied with Lebedev's speech and was highly aroused.

"He attacks enlightenment, he preaches the fanaticism of the twelfth century, he makes faces and strikes attitudes, and not in any simple-hearted spirit either. How does he come to have this house, let me ask?" He spoke loudly, stopping everyone around him.

"I knew a real interpreter of the Apocalypse," the general was saying in another corner to other listeners, notably Ptitsyn, whom he had seized by one of his buttons, "the late Grigory Semyonovitch Burmistrov, he could set people's hearts on fire. First he'd put on his glasses, open a huge ancient book bound in black leather, yes, and besides that he had a gray beard and two medals for good works he'd done. He would begin very sternly, very severely; generals would bow before him and ladies would faint, yes—and here this fellow ends up with food for the guests! It beats anything!"

Ptitsyn listened to the general, smiled, and seemed to be ready to get his hat, but either could not quite make up his mind to leave or kept forgetting his intention. A little earlier, before they had gotten up from the table, Ganya had suddenly stopped drinking and pushed his glass away; a cloud seemed to cross his face. When everyone rose from the table he went over to Rogozhin and sat down next to him. One would have thought they were on the friendliest terms. Rogozhin, who at first had also been several times on the point of leaving quietly, now sat motionless, with his head bowed, as if he too had forgotten that he had wanted to leave. He had not drunk a drop of wine all evening and was very thoughtful. Every so often he would lift his eyes and gaze around at everyone. Now it seemed as if he was waiting for something to happen here, something extremely important to him, and that he had decided not to leave until it did happen.

The prince had drunk no more than two or three glasses and was feeling only a little light-hearted. As he got up from the table he caught Yevgeny Pavlovitch's eye, remembered the conversation they were to have, and smiled affably. Yevgeny Pavlovitch nodded and suddenly pointed to Hippolite, whom he had been watching intently just then. Hippolite was asleep, stretched out on the couch.

"Tell me, Prince, why has this wretched boy forced himself on you?" he said suddenly with such evident vexation, and even malice, that the prince was surprised. "I'll swear he's got some mischief in mind!"

"I've noticed," said the prince, "or, rather, it appears to me that you're especially interested in him today, Yevgeny Pavlovitch. Is this true?"

"And you could also say that in my own present situation I have enough to think about, so I'm amazed myself that I haven't been able to tear my eyes away from that loathsome face all evening!"

"He has a handsome face."

"There! There! Look!" cried Yevgeny Pavlovitch, pulling at the prince's arm. "There!"

Once again the prince gazed at Yevgeny Pavlovitch with astonishment.

Chapter FIVE

Hippolite, who had suddenly fallen asleep on the couch toward the end of Lebedev's harangue, now just as suddenly awoke; as if someone had jabbed him in the ribs; he gave a start, raised himself up, looked around and turned pale; he looked around with a sort of fear; and a look of horror came over his face when he remembered and began to consider everything.

"What? Are they leaving? It's over? It's all over? Has the sun risen?" he demanded in agitation, seizing the prince's hand. "What time is it? For God's sake what time is it? I've been sleeping. Have I been sleeping long?" he added, near desperation, as if he had slept through something on which, at the very least, his whole fate depended.

"You've been asleep seven or eight minutes," Yevgeny Pavlovitch replied.

Hippolite looked at him intently and reflected a few moments.

"Ah! That's all? Then I—"

And he drew a deep breath of relief, as if casting off a great weight. He realized at last that nothing was "over," that the sun had not risen, that the guests had only left the table, and that all that had ended was Lebedev's blabbering. He smiled and a hectic flush appeared in the form of two bright spots on his cheeks.

"And so you've been counting the minutes I've been asleep," he commented sarcastically. "You haven't taken your eyes off me all evening, I've noticed. Ah, Rogozhin! I've just been dreaming about him," he whispered to the prince, frowning and nodding toward Rogozhin, sitting at the table. "Oh, yes," he said suddenly, again with a fresh thought, "where's the orator, where's Lebedev? Is Lebedev really through? What was he talking about? Prince, is it true you once said that the world would be saved by 'beauty'? Gentlemen," he shouted loudly, addressing all of them, "the prince maintains that beauty will save the world. And I maintain that the reason he has such playful ideas is that he's in love. Gentlemen, the prince is in love. Just now, as soon as he came in, I was convinced of it. Don't blush, Prince, or I'll be sorry for you. What kind of beauty will save the world? Kolya told me— Are you a fervent Christian? Kolya says you call yourself a Christian."

The prince observed him attentively and made no answer.

"You're not answering me?" he said, then added suddenly as if the words had escaped him, "Perhaps you think I'm very fond of you?"

"No, I don't. I know you don't like me."

"What? Even after yesterday? Wasn't I honest with you yesterday?"

"I knew yesterday too that you didn't like me."

"You mean because I envy you? Because I envy you? You always thought that and you still do, but—but why am I telling you this? I want more champagne. Pour me some, Keller."

402

"You mustn't drink anymore, Hippolite, I won't let you."

And the prince moved the glass away.

"You're right," he agreed immediately, as though reflecting. "They might even say— But the hell with what they say! Am I right? Am I right? Let them say what they want afterward, eh, Prince? What does it matter to any of us what happens *afterward!* But I'm just waking up. What a terrible dream I had, it's just coming back to me now. I wouldn't wish such a dream on you, Prince, though perhaps I really don't like you. But even if you don't care for a person, why wish him harm, isn't that true? Why do I keep asking questions? I keep on asking questions! Give me your hand. I'll press it hard, like this. So you have held out your hand to me? That means you knew I would shake hands sincerely. All right, I won't drink anymore. What time is it? Never mind, I know what time it is. The hour is at hand. The time has come. What are they doing, setting out the food over there? This table is free? Splendid! Gentlemen, I—but all these gentlemen aren't listening—I intend to read an article, Prince; the food, of course, is more interesting, but—"

And suddenly, quite unexpectedly, he pulled from his inner pocket a large envelope, sealed with a large red seal. He put it down on the table in front of him.

This unexpected action produced a sensation among the company, which was by now fortified for anything, but not for that. Yevgeny Pavlovitch visibly jumped in his chair. Ganya moved quickly to the table; Rogozhin did too but with a sort of sullen irritation, as if he knew what it was all about. Lebedev, who happened to be nearby, came up and stared with his inquisitive little eyes at the envelope, trying to guess what it meant.

"What do you have there?" the prince asked uneasily.

"At the first ray of sun I'll go to bed, Prince. I've said so, and I promise; you'll see!" cried Hippolite. "But—but do you imagine I'm not in a state to open that envelope?" he added, glaring defiantly at everyone around him, as though not caring whom he was addressing. The prince noticed he was trembling.

"None of us thinks that," replied the prince for everyone. "And why do you suppose anyone would imagine such a thing? And what a strange idea to read to us. What have you there, Hippolite?"

"What has he got? What's the matter with him now?" they were asking on all sides. Everyone approached, some of them still eating; the envelope with the red seal attracted them all like a magnet.

"I wrote this myself yesterday, right after I'd given you my word I'd come to stay with you, Prince. I wrote it all day yesterday, and last night, and I finished it this morning. In the night, toward morning, I had a dream."

"Wouldn't it be better tomorrow?" the prince interrupted timidly.

"Tomorrow 'there will be no more time'!" Hippolite laughed hysterically. "But don't worry, I'll read it in forty minutes—an hour at most. And see how interested they all are; they've all come up, and they're all looking at my seal, and if I hadn't sealed the envelope there'd be no sensation! Ha, ha! That's what mystery is! Shall I break the seal or not, gentlemen?" he shouted, laughing his strange laugh and looking at them with glittering eyes. "A mystery! A mystery! But, Prince, do you remember who proclaimed 'there will be no more time'?" It was proclaimed by the great and mighty angel in the Apocalypse."

"Better not read it!" Yevgeny Pavlovitch cried suddenly, but with an uneasiness so unlike him that it struck many of them as strange.

"Don't read it!" the prince cried too, putting his hand on the envelope.

"Why read? It's time to eat," someone remarked.

"An article? For a periodical?" someone else inquired.

"Perhaps it will be dull," added a third.

"What's it all about?" the others were all asking.

But the prince's frightened gesture seemed to have alarmed Hippolite.

"So, I'm not to read it?" he whispered to him with a certain apprehension, a twisted smile on his blue lips. "I'm not to read it," he repeated, gazing around at everyone, at all their eyes and faces, as if he was trying to reach out to them again with his former expansiveness. "You are—afraid?" he said, turning to the prince again.

"Afraid of what?" the prince asked, his face altering more and more.

"Has anyone a twenty-kopeck piece?" Hippolite jumped from his chair as if he had been pulled up. "Or any coin?"

"Here!" Lebedev gave him one at once. The thought struck him that Hippolite had gone mad.

"Vera Lukyanovna!" Hippolite hurriedly called her over to him. "Take it, throw it on the table—heads or tails? Heads —I read it!"

Vera looked fearfully at the coin, at Hippolite, then at her father, and awkwardly, averting her head as if she felt she

404

should not look at the coin, she tossed it on the table. It came up heads.

"I read it!" whispered Hippolite, as though crushed by destiny's decision; he could not have turned paler if a death sentence had been read to him. "But what's this?" he said a half minute later, suddenly startled. "Have I really taken my fate in my hands?" He looked around at everyone with the same insistent frankness. "But this is an amazing psychological phenomenon!" he suddenly cried, addressing the prince with genuine astonishment. "It's—it's an incredible phenomenon, Prince!" he repeated, reviving, and seeming to come to his senses. "Make a note of this, Prince, remember it; aren't you collecting material about capital punishment? I was told that. Ha, ha! Oh God, what senseless absurdity!" He sat down on the couch, putting his elbows on the table, and clutched his head. "This is really shameful! But what do I care if it's shameful?" He raised his head almost at once. "Gentlemen! Gentlemen, I will break the seal," he announced with sudden determination. "I—I am not forcing you to listen!"

His hands trembling with excitement he opened the envelope, took out several sheets of notepaper covered with fine handwriting, placed them in front of him, and began to smooth them out.

"What is this? What's going on here? What's he going to read?" some were muttering somberly; others were silent. But everyone sat down and looked on with curiosity. Perhaps they were really expecting something extraordinary. Vera seized her father's chair and was almost in tears with fright; Kolya was almost as frightened. Lebedev, already seated, suddenly got up and moved the candles closer to Hippolite to give him more light to read.

"Gentlemen, this is—you will soon see what it's about," Hippolite added for some reason, and abruptly began to read, "My Essential Statement. The epigraph is *'Après moi le déluge.'* Damn it!" he exclaimed as if he had burned himself. "Could I seriously have put such a stupid epigraph? Listen, gentlemen! I assure you that this is all doubtless dreadful nonsense! There are only some thoughts of mine here. If you think that there's anything mysterious or—anything forbidden—that is—"

"If you'd just read it without the preamble," Ganya cut in.

"He's trying to get out of it!" said someone.

"Too much talk," put in Rogozhin, who had been silent until then.

Hippolite suddenly looked at him, and when their eyes met, Rogozhin grinned bitterly and spitefully at him, and slowly uttered these strange words:

"This isn't the way the thing should be done, lad, not like this."

No one, of course, understood what Rogozhin meant, but his words produced a rather strange impression on everyone; they all were fleetingly touched by a common thought. On Hippolite these words had a terrible effect; he trembled so much that the prince reached out to support him, and he would have certainly cried out if his voice had not suddenly failed him. For a whole minute he could not say a word, and, breathing heavily, he only stared at Rogozhin. At last, gasping for breath, with an extraordinary effort, he said:

"So it was you—it was you—you?"

"I was what? What did I do?" Rogozhin answered, looking bewildered. But Hippolite, flaring up, seized suddenly by fury, shouted sharply and vehemently:

"It was *you* who came to me last week, past one o'clock at night, on the same day I'd gone to see you in the morning—*you!!* Confess, it was you?"

"Last week, at night? Have you really gone out of your mind, lad?"

The "lad" was again silent, putting his forefinger to his brow, as though reflecting; but suddenly his pale, fear-distorted smile was overcome by a shrewd, almost triumphant look.

"It was you!" he repeated, almost in a whisper but with conviction. "You came to me and sat silently in my room on a chair near the window, for a whole hour; more; between twelve and two o'clock; then sometime after three you got up and walked out. It was you, you! Why you frightened me, why you came to torment me I don't understand—but it was you!"

And there was a flash of intense hatred in his eyes, even though he was still trembling with fear.

"You'll know all about this soon, gentlemen—I—I—listen—"

Again, and now with desperate urgency, he seized the sheets of paper, which had separated and gotten mixed up; he tried to arrange them; they shook in his trembling hands; for a long time he could not get them together.

"He's gone mad or delirious," Rogozhin muttered, almost inaudibly.

At last the reading began. For the first five minutes the author of the unexpected article was still short of breath and read unevenly and incoherently; but soon his voice became firmer and began to express the sense of what he was reading. Only now and then a strong fit of coughing overcame him;

halfway through the article he became quite hoarse; but his extraordinary animation, which grew greater and greater as he read, reached an intense pitch at the end, as did the painful impression it produced on his audience. Here is the whole "article."

MY ESSENTIAL STATEMENT
Après moi le déluge

"Yesterday morning the prince came to see me; among other things he persuaded me to move into his house. I knew that he would insist on this, and I felt sure that he would say right out that it would be 'better to die with people and trees around,' as he put it. But today he did not say *to die,* he said, 'it will be easier to live,' which amounts to almost the same thing for me, in my situation. I asked him what he meant with his everlasting 'trees' and why he forces 'trees' on me, and I learned from him to my surprise that I'd said on that evening that I had come to Pavlovsk to look at trees for the last time. When I remarked to him that it's the same to die under trees or looking out the window at my bricks, and that for a matter of two weeks there was no need for so much fuss, he agreed with me at once; but the greenness and fresh air will, in his opinion, certainly bring about some kind of physical change in me, and my overexcitement and *my dreams* will change and perhaps be relieved. I told him again, laughing, that he was talking like a materialist. He answered with his smile that he had always been a materialist. Since he never lies, his saying that must mean something. He has a nice smile, I've studied him carefully by now. I don't know whether I like him or not, I don't have time to worry about that now. The hatred I've felt for him for five months I must say has died down during the past month. Who knows, perhaps I came to Pavlovsk mainly to see him. But—why did I leave my room then? A man condemned to death must not leave his little cubbyhole; and if I had not made my final decision now, and decided instead to wait till the last minute, I never would have left my room for anything in the world and would not have accepted his invitation to come to his house 'to die' in Pavlovsk.

"I must hurry and finish all of this 'statement' before tomorrow without fail. That means I shall have time to read it over and correct it; I'll read it over tomorrow when I'll be reading it to the prince and the two or three witnesses I expect to find at his house. Since there will not be a single word of falsehood in it, but only the truth, the final and solemn truth, I am curious to know what impression it will make on me, at the hour and the very minute I'll be reading it over. However, I should not have written the words 'final and solemn truth'; it's not worth telling lies for two weeks, because it's not worth living two weeks; that's the best proof that I shall write nothing but the truth. (N.B. Not to forget the thought: am I not mad at this moment; that is, at certain moments? I was told positively that in the last stage of their illness consumptives sometimes go out of their minds for a time. Must check this tomorrow at the reading, by the effect on the audience. Must settle this question with the utmost precision; otherwise I can undertake nothing.)

"I think I have written something dreadfully stupid just now, but as I've said I have no time to correct it, and, besides, I promised myself expressly not to correct a single line in this manuscript, even if I notice I'm contradicting myself every five lines. What I want to find out tomorrow from reading this is whether the sequence of my thoughts is logically correct; whether I notice my mistakes, and whether everything I have been thinking over in this room for the last six months is true or only delirium.

"If two months ago I'd had to leave my rooms for good and say good-bye to Meyer's wall, I'm sure I would have felt sad. Now I feel nothing, and yet tomorrow I will be leaving my room and the wall *forever!* So my conviction that two weeks are not worth regretting or feeling anything about masters my whole nature and perhaps already dictates all my feelings. But is this true? Is it true that my nature is entirely subdued? If I was to be tortured now I would certainly scream and I wouldn't be saying it's not worth the trouble or screaming and feeling pain because I have only two weeks left to live.

"But is it true that I only have two weeks to live, and not more? I told a lie at Pavlovsk then: B——n said nothing to me and never saw me; but a week ago a student called Kislorodov was brought to me; by conviction he is a materialist, an atheist, and a nihilist, that's why I had him in particular come; I wanted someone to tell me the bare truth at last, without any softening or ceremony. This he did, and not only did it readily and without ceremony but with obvious pleasure (which I thought was going too far). He told me straight out that I had only a month left, perhaps a little more if circumstances were favorable, but perhaps much less too. In his opinion I could die suddenly, for example tomorrow. Such things have happened. Only the day before yesterday in Kolumna a young lady who was consumptive and in a situation similar to mine was starting off for the market to buy provisions when she suddenly felt ill, lay down on the couch, sighed, and was dead. Kislorodov told me all this with exuberant style and a heedless lack of feeling, as if he was giving me credit for being some kind of superior, all-negating creature like himself, for whom death would of course count for nothing. Anyway, one fact is established: it's a month and not more! I'm completely convinced he's not mistaken about that.

"I was very surprised when the prince guessed I had 'bad dreams'; he said, word for word, that at Pavlovsk 'my overexcitement and my *dreams*' would change. And why dreams? Either he is a doctor or an exceptionally intelligent man and can divine many things. (But that he is in the final analysis an 'idiot' there can be no doubt.) Just before his arrival, as if purposely, I had one pretty little dream (though of the sort I have now by the hundreds). I fell asleep—I think it was about an hour before he came—and dreamed I was in a certain room (but not my own). It was a larger room, with a higher ceiling, better furnished, with more light. There was a wardrobe, a chest of drawers, a couch, and my bed, which was big and wide and covered with a green silk quilt. But in the room I noticed a dreadful animal, a sort of monster. It was like a scorpion, but it was not a scorpion, but much more disgusting and much more horrible, precisely because nothing like it existed in nature, and there was a sort of mystery in the fact that it had come *expressly* to me. I examined it very carefully: it was brown and covered with a shell, a crawling reptile, about seven inches long, two fingers thick at the head, and narrowing toward the tail, so that the tip of the tail was less than a quarter of an inch thick. About two inches from the head, two legs, about three and a half inches long, one on each side, grew out at a forward angle of forty-five degrees, so that the whole creature was in the shape of a trident, when looked at from above. I couldn't make out the head clearly but I saw two short feelers, also brown, shaped like two sturdy needles. There were two feelers like this at the tip of the tail, and at the extremities of the legs, making eight feelers altogether. The beast was running around the room, very fast, supporting itself on its legs and its tail, and as it ran its body and tail wriggled like little snakes, with extraordinary speed, in spite of its shell, and it was very horrible to look at. I was terribly afraid it would sting me; I had been told it was poisonous, but what worried me most was who had sent it into my room, what they wanted to do to me, and what was behind it all. It hid under the chest of drawers,

409

under the wardrobe, and crawled into corners. I sat on a
chair and drew my legs under me. It ran quickly right across
the room and disappeared somewhere near my chair. I
looked around in terror, but as I was sitting with my legs
drawn up I hoped it would not climb up the chair. Suddenly
I heard right behind me near my head a sort of scraping rustle. I looked around and saw that the reptile was crawling up
the wall, and was already at the level of my head and was
actually touching my hair with its tail, which was twisting
and wriggling with extraordinary rapidity. I jumped up, and
the creature disappeared. I was afraid to lie down on the bed
for fear it should crawl under the pillow. My mother came
into the room with some man she knew. They began trying to
catch the beast, but they were much calmer than I and weren't
even afraid of it. But they understood nothing. Suddenly
the reptile crawled out again. This time it was crawling very
slowly and, it seemed, with some sort of special purpose,
writhing slowly, which was more revolting than ever, again
moving crabwise toward the door. At that moment my
mother opened the door and called Norma, our dog—a huge,
shaggy, black Newfoundland, who died five years ago. She
raced into the room and stopped in her tracks before the reptile. The reptile stopped too, but it was still writhing and
scraping the floor with its feet and tail. So far as I know, animals cannot fear the supernatural, but at that instant it
seemed to me that there was something extraordinary about
Norma's fear, as if there was something almost mystical in
it, and that therefore she too felt as I did that there was
something fatal about that creature, some mystery in it. She
was slowly moving back away from the reptile, which was
slowly and cautiously crawling toward her; it seemed that it
meant to leap at her suddenly and sting her. In spite of all
her fear, Norma looked at the animal with dreadful ferocity,
though she was trembling in all her limbs. Then slowly she
bared her terrible teeth, opened her huge red jaws, crouched,
got ready to spring, made her decision, and suddenly seized
the creature with her teeth. The reptile must have made a violent movement to escape, so that Norma had to catch it
again in midair, and twice got it all in her mouth, both times
in midair, as though she was gobbling it up. The shell
cracked between her teeth, the tail and legs which hung out
of the mouth were thrashing with terrifying rapidity. Suddenly Norma yelped piteously; the monster had managed to
sting her tongue. Whining and howling, she opened her
mouth wide with pain, and I saw that the creature, though
bitten in two, was still writhing in her mouth, and that from

410

her half-crushed body a quantity of white fluid, similar to the fluid of a squashed beetle, was oozing out on the dog's tongue. Then I woke up and the prince came in.

"Gentlemen," said Hippolite, suddenly looking up from his reading; he appeared rather embarrassed. "I haven't read this over, but it seems that in fact I have written a great deal that is unnecessary. This dream—"

"That's true enough," Ganya cut in.

"There's too much that's personal, I agree; specifically about me, that is."

As he said this, Hippolite looked tired and weakened, and he kept drying the sweat from his forehead with his handkerchief.

"Yes, sir, you're a bit too interested in yourself," hissed Lebedev.

"Gentlemen, let me repeat, I'm not forcing anyone to listen. Anyone who wishes can leave."

"He turns people out of someone else's house," Rogozhin grumbled, almost inaudibly.

"And what if we all suddenly get up and leave?" Ferdyshchenko said abruptly, having not ventured to say anything aloud until that moment.

Hippolite at once dropped his eyes and clutched his manuscript; but the next instant he raised his head again and, with glistening eyes and two patches of red on his cheeks, said, looking directly at Ferdyshchenko:

"You don't like me at all!"

There was some laughter; though most of the company did not laugh. Hippolite blushed violently.

"Hippolite," said the prince, "close your manuscript and give it to me, and please go to bed here in my room. We will talk before you go to sleep, and also tomorrow; but on condition that you never open those pages. Will you do this?"

"But is that possible?" said Hippolite looking at him in complete amazement. "Gentlemen!" he cried, becoming feverishly excited again. "This is just a stupid interruption. I behaved badly, and I won't interrupt the reading again. Whoever wants to listen may do so."

He quickly took a sip of water from the glass, hastily put his elbows on the table to shield his face from their glances, and began reading again, stubbornly. But his embarrassment soon disappeared.

"The idea that it's not worthwhile living for only a few weeks," he went on, "really began to take hold of me a month ago, I think, when I still had four weeks left to live, but it took possession of me completely only three days ago,

411

when I got back from that evening at Pavlovsk. The first time I felt the full, direct impact of that thought was on the prince's veranda, just at the very moment I had the idea of making a final effort at living, when I wanted to see people and trees (let's admit that I said that), when I got excited, insisted on the rights of Burdovsky, 'my neighbor,' and imagined that they would all fling wide their arms and embrace me and beg my forgiveness for something or other, and I would ask theirs; in short, I finished up like a miserable fool. And at this time a 'last conviction' was kindled in me. I'm surprised now how I could have lived a full six months without this 'conviction.' I knew positively that I had consumption and that it was incurable; I didn't deceive myself and I understood the matter clearly. But the more clearly I understood it the more convulsively I wanted to live; I clutched at life and I wanted to go on living no matter what. I admit I might well have resented the dark, deaf, and unheeding fate which had arranged that I be squashed like a fly and, of course, without my knowing the reason; but why didn't I stop at just resentment? Why was I actually *beginning* to live, knowing that I could not begin any longer? Why did I try, knowing there was no point in trying? And yet I couldn't read through a book, and I gave up reading: why read, why learn something for six months? This thought made me throw down my book more than once.

"Yes, that wall of Meyer's would have a lot to tell! I have written a great deal on it. There wasn't a spot on that dirty wall I didn't memorize. That damned wall! And yet it was dearer to me than all the trees of Pavlovsk, or at least it would be dearer if it made any difference to me now.

"I remember now with what avid interest I then began to watch *their* life; I had no such interest before. Sometimes I used to wait for Kolya with impatience and curses, when I was too sick to go out myself. I was so absorbed in trivial little things, so interested in every rumor that it seems to me I became a regular gossip. For instance, I didn't understand how people with so much life before them did not become rich (indeed, I don't understand that even now). I knew one very poor man, who I learned afterward died of hunger, and I remember that hearing this made me furious; had it been possible to bring that poor man back to life I believe I would have had him killed. Sometimes I felt better for weeks at a time, and I could go out in the street; but the street at last began to infuriate me so that I purposely spent days on end shut up inside, though I could have gone out like everyone else. I couldn't stand the scurrying, bustling people, forever

412

anxious, gloomy, and restless, darting all around me on the sidewalk. Why their eternal gloom, their eternal agitation and unrest, their eternal sullen meanness (because they are mean, mean, mean). Whose fault is it that they are unhappy and don't know how to live, even though they have sixty years of life before them? Why did Zarnitzin let himself die of hunger when he had sixty years of life before him? And each points to his own rags, to his own work-worn hands and cries in anger, 'We toil like cattle, we labor, we are hungry as dogs, and we are poor! Others don't work, and don't labor, and they are rich!' (The eternal refrain!) And among them, running and scurrying around from morning till night, a miserable weakling, Ivan Fomitch Surikov, born a 'gentleman' —he lives above in our building—forever out at the elbows, with his buttons falling off, running errands and doing services for all kinds of people from morning till night. Talk with him and he'll say, 'I'm poor, destitute, and miserable, my wife died, there was no money to buy her medicine, and my child froze to death in the winter; the older daughter is a kept woman—' He's forever whimpering and complaining! Oh, I never felt the slightest pity for those fools, neither then or now—I say this with pride! Why isn't he a Rothschild himself? Whose fault is it he doesn't have millions, as Rothschild does; why doesn't he have mountains of gold imperials and napoleons-d'or, towering mountains like you see at fairs at carnival time! Since he is alive, everything is within his power! Whose fault is it if he doesn't understand this?

"Oh, I don't care now, now I've got no time to be angry, but then—then I literally chewed my pillow at night and tore my quilt with rage. Oh, how I would dream then, how I wished, how I deliberately wished to be thrown out into the street, eighteen years old, almost without clothing, almost without covering, to be abandoned and utterly alone, without lodging, without work, without a crust of bread, without relatives, without a single acquaintance in the huge city, hungry, beaten (so much the better!), but in good health—then I would show them—

"What would I have shown?

"Do you imagine I don't know how I've already humiliated myself as it is with my 'statement'! Who now doesn't take me for a wretched little fool, a stranger to life, forgetting that I am not eighteen now, forgetting that to live as I have done for these six months means to reach grayhaired old age. But let them laugh and say that all this is fairy tales. I did indeed tell myself stories. I filled whole nights with them; I remember them all now.

"But must I tell them again now—now when the time for fairy tales is over even for me? And to whom? I amused myself with them when I saw clearly that I was even forbidden to study Greek grammar, as I once had the idea of doing. 'I shall die even before I reach the syntax,' I thought right at the first page and threw the book under the table. It's still there, I've forbidden Matryona to pick it up.

"Let anyone who gets hold of my 'statement,' anyone who has the patience to read it through, let him take me for a man condemned to death to whom it seems that everyone but him fails to value life enough, but rather expends it too cheaply, uses it too indolently, too unconscionably, so that no one, not one, is worthy of it! Let him. I declare that my reader will be mistaken and that my convictions have nothing to do with my death sentence. Ask them, just ask them what all of them, every one of them, understand by happiness? Oh, you may be certain that Columbus was happy not when he had discovered America but rather when he was just on the point of discovering it; you may be certain that his highest moment of happiness was perhaps three days before the discovery of the New World, when his mutinous crew in desperation almost turned back to Europe! It wasn't the New World that mattered, which could have slipped into the sea. Columbus died having hardly seen it and scarcely knowing what he had discovered. Life is what matters, life alone—the continuous, eternal process of discovering life—and not the discovery itself at all! But why go on talking? I expect that everything I am saying now is so much like the most common banality that I'll certainly be taken for a lower-form schoolboy handing in a composition on 'The Sunrise,' or it will be said that I perhaps had something to say, but, try as I would, I didn't manage to 'explain myself.' But I might add, however, that in every serious human thought born in anyone's brain there is always something left over which is impossible to communicate to others, even though one were to write whole volumes and explain the idea for thirty-five years; there will always be something left which cannot be coaxed out of your brain and which will remain with you forever; you will die with it, without ever communicating to anyone what is perhaps the essence of your thought. But if I too have failed just now to communicate everything that has been tormenting me for the past six months, at least it will be understood that I have perhaps paid too dearly for my present 'last conviction'; this is what I have felt necessary, for certain reasons of my own, to set forth in my 'statement.'

"But to continue."

Chapter SIX

~~~~~

"I don't want to lie: reality has been catching me too on its hook during these six months, sometimes even so that I forgot my death sentence, or rather I preferred not to think about it, and I even got some work done. A word, by the way, about my situation then. Eight months ago when I became very ill I broke all my ties and no longer saw my friends. Since I had always been a morose sort of person, my friends easily forgot me; of course they would have forgotten me in any case. My life at home, that is, 'in the family,' was also that of a recluse. About five months ago I shut myself up for good and cut myself off altogether from the rooms the family used. They always obeyed me and no one dared enter my room except at fixed times to clean and to bring meals. My mother trembled at my orders and didn't even dare whimper in front of me, whenever I decided to let her in. She was always spanking the children so they wouldn't make noise and disturb me; I complained so often about their shouting they must really love me now! I must have tormented 'faithful Kolya,' as I called him, pretty thoroughly too. Lately he was torturing me in turn, all that is natural, people are created to torture one another. But I noticed that he bore my irritability as if he had determined beforehand to humor the invalid. Naturally that annoyed me; but apparently he had taken it into his head to imitate the prince in 'Christian meekness,' which was quite funny. He's young and impassioned, and of course he imitates everything; but occasionally I felt that it was high time for him to be himself. I am very fond of him. I also tormented Surikov, who lives above us and runs errands from morning till night; I was always telling him he was personally to blame for his poverty, so that he finally became intimidated and stopped coming to see me. He's a very meek man, the meekest of creatures. (N.B. They say that meekness is a tremendous strength; I must ask the prince about that, it's something he says.) But in the month of March when I went upstairs to see how

415

they had let their little child 'freeze to death,' as he put it, and I inadvertently smiled at the corpse of the infant, since I had started again explaining to Surikov that he 'only had himself to blame,' the wretched fellow's lips suddenly began trembling and, laying a hand on my shoulder and pointing to the door with the other, he said softly, almost in a whisper, 'Get out, sir!' I went out; I was very pleased by all this, I was pleased even at the very minute he was showing me out; but for a long time his words left an impression with me whenever I recalled them, a painful impression, a sort of strange, contemptuous pity for him which I did not want to feel at all. Even at the moment of the insult (I did feel I had insulted him, though I had no intention of doing so), even at such a moment, this man could not become angry! His lips trembled then not at all from rage, I swear; he seized my arm and uttered his magnificent 'Get out, sir!' without a trace of anger. There was dignity, a lot of it, which didn't suit him at all (so that, in fact, there was quite a bit of comedy in it), but there was no anger. Perhaps he simply began to feel contempt for me, suddenly. From then on, the two or three times I met him on the stairs, he began taking off his hat to me, a thing he never used to do before, but without stopping, as he used to do, and would hurry past me in confusion. If he did despise me it was still in his own way; he despised me *meekly*. But perhaps he took off his hat out of simple fear, because I was the son of his creditor; for he always owed my mother money and could never manage to extricate himself from debt. And in fact that is the most likely explanation. I wanted to have it out with him, and I knew for certain that in ten minutes he would be begging my pardon; but I decided it was better to let him alone.

"At this time, that is, around the time Surikov 'let his baby freeze,' about the middle of March, I suddenly began to feel much better for some reason, and I continued to feel better for about two weeks. I began going out, most often toward dusk. I loved the March twilight, when it began to freeze, and when they lighted the gas; sometimes I walked a long way. Once, in the Street of the Six Shops, I was overtaken in the darkness by a 'gentleman' of sorts; I couldn't see him distinctly; he was carrying something wrapped in paper and he wore a miserable overcoat that was too short for him and too light for the season. When he passed under a streetlight, about ten paces ahead of me, I noticed something fall out of his pocket. I hastened to pick it up—just in time, because someone in a long kaftan was already lunging for it, but, seeing I had the thing in my hand, he didn't start an argument; he only glanced at what was in my hand and hurried past me. It was a large morocco billfold of old-fashioned style, stuffed full; but somehow from the first glance I guessed that it might be anything but not money. The man who had lost it was now forty or fifty paces ahead of me, and I soon lost him in the crowd. I ran and began shouting to him; but since all I could shout to him was 'Hey!' he did not turn around. Suddenly he darted to the left, through the gates of a house. When I reached the gateway, which was very dark, there was no one there. The building was huge, one of those enormous places speculators build for small tenement apartments; in some there are as many as a hundred. When I ran through the gate I had a feeling that in the far right-hand corner of the huge court there might have been a man walking, though in the dark I could scarcely tell. When I ran to that corner, I saw the entrance to a staircase; the stairs were narrow, extremely dirty, not lighted at all; but I could hear the man still running up them above me, and I rushed up after him, thinking that while a door was being opened for him somewhere I would catch up to him. And so it happened. The flights were short, there was an endless number of them, and I was terribly out of breath. A door opened and closed again on the fifth floor; I could tell this when I was still three flights below. While I was running up, catching my breath on the landings, and then feeling around for the bell, a couple of minutes passed. Finally, the door was opened by an old peasant woman, who had been occupied in blowing on the coals in a samovar in a tiny kitchen. She heard my question in silence and of course did not understand anything I said, and in silence she opened a door into the adjoining room, also tiny and terribly low, with the shabbiest and most rudimentary furniture and a great broad bed, with curtains, on which lay 'Terentyitch' (as the old woman called him), apparently drunk. On the table a candle stub was burning in an iron candlestick and a square bottle stood there, almost empty. Terentyitch grunted something to me, lying there, and waved toward another door, and the old woman left, so there was nothing for me to do but open that door. I did so and went into the next room.

"This room was even smaller and more cramped than the preceding one; I could hardly manage to turn around in it; a narrow single bed on one side took up a great amount of the space; the rest of the furniture consisted of three plain chairs, piled with all sorts of rags, and the plainest of kitchen tables, which stood in front of an oil cloth-covered sofa, allowing hardly room enough to pass between the table and the bed.

417

On the table was a lighted tallow candle in an iron candle-stick like the one in the other room, and on the bed a tiny baby was crying, not more than about three weeks old to judge by the sound it made. It was being 'changed' by a pale, sickly woman, who appeared to be young, negligently dressed, as if she was just starting to get around after child-birth, but baby was not soothed and went on crying for its mother's emaciated breast. Another child was sleeping on the couch, a little girl about three years old, covered, it appeared, with a man's dresscoat. By the table stood a gentleman in a very ragged coat (he had already taken off his overcoat and it was lying on the bed), and he was unwrapping a blue paper parcel which contained about two pounds of wheat bread and two little sausages. There was also a teapot on the table with tea in it and a few scattered crusts of black bread. From under the bed protruded a partly open suitcase and two large bundles containing rags of some kind.

"In a word, there was the greatest disorder. It seemed to me at first glance that both of them, the man and the woman, were quite decent people, but who had been reduced by pov-erty to that degrading state in which disorder finally defeats all efforts to combat it, and even drives people to the bitter need to find in the disorder itself, which increases each day, a sort of bitter and vengeful satisfaction.

"When I came in, this man, who had entered just before me and was unwrapping his provisions, was discussing some-thing rapidly and heatedly with his wife; she, though not yet finished changing the baby, had already begun whimpering; the news must have as usual been bad. The face of the man, who was twenty-eight or so, was dark and thin, framed by black sideburns, with a clean-shaven chin, and it struck me as a rather decent face and even agreeable; it was a somber face with a somber look to the eyes, but with some kind of sickly touch of pride, no doubt easily provoked. When I en-tered a strange scene occurred.

"There are people who derive extraordinary pleasure from their irritable susceptibility, especially (when as always hap-pens very quickly) it reaches its highest pitch; at that mo-ment it is apparently more pleasant for them to be offended than not offended. Such irritable people always suffer terrible remorse afterward—if they are intelligent, of course, and able to comprehend that they have been ten times more aroused than they need have been. That man looked at me for some time in amazement, and his wife in alarm, as if it was the greatest marvel that anyone would come to see them. But suddenly he flew at me almost in a rage. I had not had time to utter more than a word or two, but he must have felt deeply offended, especially when he saw that I was properly dressed, that I should so unceremoniously be peering into his hovel, seeing all around him the ugliness of which he was himself so ashamed. Of course he was glad for the opportunity to vent upon someone his outrage at his own bad luck. And for a moment I even thought he was going to fight me. He turned pale like a woman in hysterics and frightened his wife terribly.

"'How dare you come in like that! Get out!' he shouted, trembling and barely able to speak. But suddenly he saw his billfold in my hand.

"'I believe you dropped this,' I said, as calmly and dryly as I could in a way that was, in fact, appropriate.

"He stood before me in absolute fear, and for some time he did not seem to understand anything. Then he reached for his side pocket, his mouth fell open in dismay, and he clapped his hand to his forehead.

"'Good God! Where did you find it? How did you find it?'

"I explained in the briefest terms and, if that were possible, still more dryly than before how I had found the billfold, how I had run after him and called him, and how, at last, feeling my way, I had followed him up the stairs.

"'Oh, Lord,' he cried, addressing his wife. 'All our papers are there, the last of my documents, everything's there. Oh, dear sir, do you know what you've done for me? I would have been lost!'

"In the meantime I had grasped the door handle intending to leave without answering, but I was out of breath myself, and suddenly my emotion brought on such a violent fit of coughing that I could hardly remain standing. I saw that the man was running in all directions to find me a free chair, how, finally, he seized the rags from one and threw them on the floor, hurriedly offered me the chair and helped me sit down. But my coughing continued and did not subside for another three minutes. When I recovered myself he was then sitting beside me on another chair, from which he had thrown the rags to the floor, and was examining me closely.

"'You seem—ill,' he said in the tone a doctor ordinarily uses to a patient. 'I am myself a—medical man,' (he did not say 'doctor'), and as he said this he indicated the room with a wave of his hand as if he was protesting against his present position. 'I see that you—'

"'I have consumption,' I said as curtly as possible, getting up.

"He immediately jumped up too.

" 'Perhaps you're exaggerating and—with proper care—'

"He was very thrown off and still could not pull himself together, the billfold was still in his left hand.

" 'Oh, don't trouble yourself,' I interrupted again, seizing the door handle. 'B——n examined me last week,' (again I brought in B——n's name), 'and there's no question about my case. Excuse me——'

"Again I meant to open the door and leave my doctor, embarrassed, full of gratitude, crushed with shame, but again my cursed cough took hold of me. At this, my doctor insisted that I sit down to rest again; he turned to his wife, and she, without leaving her place, said a few grateful and courteous words to me. As she spoke she became so embarrassed that a flush appeared on her dry, sallow cheeks. I stayed, but I showed every second how terribly afraid I was of being in their way (which was the appropriate thing to do). My doctor was quite overcome by remorse. I could see that.

" 'If I—' he began, interrupting himself and jumping from one thought to another. 'I am so grateful to you and I behaved so badly to you—I—you see—' He indicated the room again. '—at the present moment I find myself in such a position—'

" 'Oh,' I said, 'there's nothing to see, it's nothing unknown. You've probably lost your job and you've come here to pursue the case and find a job again?'

" 'How—how did you know?' he asked in surprise.

" 'It's obvious from the first glance,' I replied with involuntary sarcasm. 'Many people come here from the provinces and run about full of hope, and then they live like this.'

"He suddenly began to speak with warmth, his lips trembling; he began complaining; he began telling me about himself, and I must admit he moved me; I stayed with him almost an hour. He told me his story, which was a very common one. He had been a doctor in the provinces, he had an administrative position, but he was the victim of all sorts of intrigues, in which even his wife had been involved. He had fallen back on his pride, had lost his temper, there was a change in the provincial government favorable to his enemies, someone worked underhandedly against him, lodged a complaint, he lost his post and with his last savings had come to Petersburg to explain his case. Of course in Petersburg he wasn't given a hearing for a long time, then he got a hearing, then they refused him, then they dangled promises, then they treated him harshly, then he was told to write something by way of a statement, then they refused to accept what he had written, he was directed to write a petition—in short he had

420

already been running around like this for five months and had used up all his savings, his wife's last rags were pawned, and then a child was born, and—'Today I received the final refusal of the petition I presented, and I have hardly any bread left, I have nothing, my wife has had a baby. I—I—'

"He jumped up from his chair and turned away. His wife was crying in a corner, and the baby started squealing again. I took out my notebook and began writing in it. When I finished and got up he stood before me, staring at me with timorous curiosity.

" 'I have taken your name,' I told him, 'and, well, all the rest of it: the place where you served, the name of the governor there, the dates. I have an old school friend named Bakhmutov, and he has an uncle who is Pyotr Maveyevitch Bakhmutov, an active state councilor serving as a director—'

" 'Pyotr Maveyevitch Bakhmutov!' cried my medico, practically trembling. 'Why, it all depends almost entirely on him!'

"And indeed everything in my doctor's story and its outcome, which I chanced to bring about, developed as if contrived beforehand, exactly as in a novel. I told those poor people to try not to build any hopes on me, that I was only a poor schoolboy myself (I deliberately exaggerated the humbleness of my situation—I finished my studies long ago and am not a schoolboy), that there was no need for them to know my name, but that I would go at once to Vassilyevsky Island to see my friend Bakhmutov, and that as I knew for certain that his uncle, an active state councilor and a bachelor with no children of his own, absolutely worshipped his nephew and was passionately fond of him, seeing in him the surviving descendant to carry on his name, 'My friend just might be able to do something for you and for me, of course through his uncle.'

" 'If only I could give my statement to His Excellency!' he cried, trembling as if he had fever, his eyes shining. 'If only I were permitted the honor of explaining in my own words!' That is how he said it: 'If only I were permitted.' Repeating once again that it would certainly fail and come to nothing, I added that if I did not come to see them the following morning it would mean that it was finished, and they had nothing to expect. They showed me out with bows, they were almost beside themselves. I will never forget the expression of their faces. I took a cab and went directly to Vassilyevsky Island.

"At school I had for several years been on poor terms with this Bakhmutov. We looked on him as an aristocrat, at least I used to call him one. He was very well dressed, came to school with his own carriage and horses, but he was not stuck-up, was always a good comrade, was always uncommonly bright and cheerful, and sometimes even very witty, though his intelligence was not particularly far-reaching, despite his being always at the top of the class. I was never at the top of anything. All my friends liked him, I was the only one who didn't. Several times during those years he would come up to make friends, but each time, sullenly and irritably, I would turn away from him. Now it was already a year since I had seen him, he was at the university. When at about nine o'clock I went in to see him at his house (after great formalities I was announced) he received me at first with amazement, and not at all cordially, but almost at once he brightened up and, looking at me, suddenly burst out laughing.

" 'Whatever possessed you to come and see me, Terentyev?' he cried with that unfailing easy good humor which was sometimes rather overbearing but never offensive, and which I so liked in him and so hated him for. 'But what's this?' he cried in alarm. 'You seem very ill!'

"My cough was racking me again. I sank into a chair and could hardly catch my breath.

" 'Never mind. I have consumption,' I said. 'I've come to you with a request.'

"He sat down, bewildered, and I immediately told him the whole story of the doctor, and I explained that he, having such influence over his uncle, could perhaps do something about it.

" 'I will. Certainly I will. I'll take it up with my uncle tomorrow. I'm really delighted to; and you told it all so well. But, Terentyev, how did you happen to think of coming to me?'

" 'So much depends on your uncle in this matter. Besides, we were always enemies, Bakhmutov, but since you're an honorable man,' I added with irony, 'I thought you wouldn't refuse an enemy.'

" 'Just the way Napoleon appealed to England!' he cried with a laugh. 'I'll do it! I'll do it! I'll go at once, if possible!' he added hastily, seeing that I was gravely and sternly getting up from my chair.

"And indeed the affair was settled in a most unexpected way and to our entire satisfaction. Six weeks later our medical man was appointed to another post in a different province and received financial assistance and even traveling expenses. I suspect that Bakhmutov, who had taken to visiting the doctor very often (while I purposely stopped visiting him and re-

422

ceived him coolly when he called on me), I suspect that Bakhmutov even persuaded the doctor to accept a loan from him. I saw Bakhmutov twice in those six weeks, and we were together a third time when we were saying good-bye to the doctor. Bakhmutov gave a farewell party at his own house, a dinner with champagne, which was also attended by the doctor's wife, though she left very early to go home to her baby. It was early May, a clear evening, and the great ball of the sun was sinking into the bay. Bakhmutov walked me home, we went by the Nikolayevsky Bridge, both a little drunk. Bakhmutov spoke of his delight that it had all turned out so well, thanked me for something or other, explained how fine he felt after the good deed, declared that the credit was all mine, and that people were wrong who were now professing and preaching that individual good action means nothing. I too felt terribly eager to talk.

"'Anyone who would attack individual charity,' I began, 'is attacking human nature and holding man's personal dignity in contempt. But the organization of "public charity" and the question of individual liberty are two separate questions, and one does not exclude the other. There will always be private good actions because they are one of man's personal needs, a vital need of one individual to influence directly another individual. In Moscow there was an old man, a "general"—that is, in fact, a state councilor—with a German name. He spent his whole life visiting prisons and seeing criminals; every party of convicts on their way to Siberia knew beforehand that "the Old General" would meet them on Sparrow Hills. He did his work with seriousness and devotion; he would appear, walk among the rows of condemned exiles, who crowded around him, stop before each one, questioning him as to his needs, would hardly ever lecture anyone, and called everyone "my poor dear friend." He gave them money, he sent the things they most needed—leg wrappings, underclothes, linen cloth, and sometimes he brought religious books and distributed them to those who could read, firmly persuaded they would read them on the way and that those who could read would read them to those who could not. He seldom asked a prisoner about his crime, but listened if a prisoner would start talking about it himself. He was on equal footing with all the criminals, making no distinctions among them. He spoke to them as if they were his brothers, but they finally came to look on him as a father. If he saw among the exiles a woman with a baby in her arms, he would come up, caress the child and snap his fingers to make it laugh. He went on doing all this for many years, until his death; so that he was known all over Russia and all over Siberia, that is, by the convicts. I was told by one who was there in Siberia that he had observed himself how even the most hardened criminals remembered the general, and yet at his visits with the convict parties he had seldom been able to give more than twenty kopecks to each prisoner. It is true that they didn't speak of him with any particular warmth or with any real seriousness. One or another of these "unhappy" creatures, who had murdered a dozen people or slaughtered six children solely for his own pleasure (I have heard there have been people like that), would suddenly, out of the blue, perhaps only once in all the twenty years, would suddenly heave a sigh and say, "What's that old general doing now? Is he still alive?" Perhaps he would even be smiling as he said it, and that would be all. But how do you know what seed might have been planted in his soul forever by that "old general," whom he had remembered over twenty years. How can you tell, Bakhmutov, what significance such a communion of one individual with another will have in the latter's destiny? For here you have a whole lifetime, with an infinity of ramifications which are hidden from us. The best chess player, the very cleverest, can think only a few moves ahead; a French player who could calculate ten moves ahead was written about as a marvel. But how many moves are there here and how much is unknown to us? In planting your seed, in offering your "alms," your good deed in whatever form, you are giving away part of your individuality and receiving part of another's; you are communing one with another already with a certain mutual consideration, and you will be rewarded by knowledge and by the most unexpected discoveries. You will certainly in the end come to look upon what you do as a science; it will absorb your whole life and perhaps fill it entirely. On the other hand, all your thoughts, all the seeds planted by you, which perhaps you have forgotten, will take root and grow; whoever received them from you will pass them on to another. And how will you know what part you will have played in shaping the destiny of mankind? If this knowledge and a whole lifetime of this work enables you at last to sow some great seed, to bequeath to the world some great thought, then—' And so on. I talked a great deal then.

" 'And to think you are the one who has to die!' Bakhmutov cried with heated reproach against someone.

"At that moment we were standing on the bridge, leaning on the rail, looking at the Neva.

" 'And do you know what just occurred to me?' I said, leaning even farther over the railing.

"'Not that you'll jump into the river?' cried Bakhmutov in alarm. Perhaps he had read the thought in my face.

"'No, for the time being I have only the following reflection: here I have about two or three months left to live, perhaps four; but when, for instance, I've only two months, and if I'm terribly anxious to do some good action which would take a lot of work and running around and trouble, as our doctor's affair did, then in that case I'd have to give it up for lack of time and look for some other "good deed," a more modest one which would be within my *means* (if I were still bent on good deeds). You must admit that this is an amusing idea!'

"Poor Bakhmutov was very worried about me; he walked me home and had the tact not to try even once to console me and was silent almost all the way. As he left me, he pressed my hand warmly and asked if he could come and visit me. I answered that if he came to me as a 'comforter' (because even if he was silent he would still be coming to comfort me, I explained to him), then each time he was there he would remind me a little more about death. He shrugged his shoulders but agreed with me; we parted quite civilly, which was more than I had expected.

"But that evening and later that night was sown the first seed of my 'last conviction.' I seized avidly at this *new* idea, and avidly examined it in all its facets, all its aspects (I did not sleep all night), and the more I considered it, the more I absorbed it, the more frightened I became. A most dreadful fear finally took hold of me and did not leave me in the following days. Sometimes, thinking of this continual fear of mine, I would freeze with new terror; and from this terror I could conclude that my 'last conviction' was too firmly implanted in me and must lead to its inevitable conclusion. But I lacked the determination for that conclusion. Three weeks later it was all over, the determination had come to me, but it was through a very strange circumstance.

"Here in my statement I note down all these figures and dates. Of course it will make no difference to me, but *now* (and perhaps only at this moment) I would like those who will judge my action to see clearly the logical chain of reasoning which led to my 'last conviction.' I have just written above that the ultimate determination, which I had lacked to carry out my 'last conviction,' came to me not from any logical conclusion at all but from a strange shock, a strange circumstance, perhaps quite unrelated to the rest of the course of the affair. About ten days ago Rogozhin came to see me about a certain matter of his own, which there is no reason

425

to enter into here. I had never seen Rogozhin before, but I had heard a great deal about him. I gave him the information he needed, and he soon left, and since he had only come for the information our relations might have ended there. But he interested me too much, and all that day I was under the influence of strange thoughts, so I decided to go to him the next day, to return the visit. Rogozhin was clearly not pleased to see me, and even hinted 'delicately' that there was no reason to pursue our acquaintance; nevertheless I spent a very interesting hour, as he probably did too. The contrast between us was such that we could not help being conscious of it, I especially; I was a man already counting his days, and he was living the fullest, most immediate existence, living for the present moment, with no care whatever for 'last' conclusions, numbers, or anything else which had nothing to do with—with—let us say, with the object of his madness. Mr. Rogozhin must forgive me that expression and blame it on a bad writer who doesn't know how to express his thought. Despite all his unfriendliness, he appeared to me as a man of intelligence and capable of understanding much, though he took little interest in what did not concern him directly. I did not give him any hint of my 'last conviction,' but somehow it seemed that, listening to me, he had guessed it. He said nothing, he is a dreadfully silent man. I hinted to him as I left that despite all the differences and all the contrast between us, *les extrémités se touchent* (I explained that to him in Russian), so that he was perhaps not at all so far from my 'last conviction' as it might seem. To this he replied with a very sullen, sour look on his face, got up, found my cap for me himself, making it seem as if I was leaving of my own accord, and simply led me out of his gloomy house on the pretext of accompanying me out of politeness. The house impressed me, it is like a graveyard, but he seemed to like it, which is indeed understandable; such a full, immediate life as he leads is too full in itself to require pleasant surroundings.

"This visit to Rogozhin exhausted me very much. Besides, I had not felt well since that morning; toward evening I was very weak and lay down on my bed, at times I felt extremely feverish and by moments even delirious. Kolya was with me until eleven o'clock. I do remember everything he said, however, and everything we talked about. But in the moments my eyes were closed I kept seeing Ivan Fomitch Surikov, who appeared to have received a fortune of millions. He had no idea where to put it all, and he racked his brains over his gold, trembling with fear lest it be stolen, and at last he seemed to have decided to bury it in the ground. Eventually I advised him that instead of burying such a great pile of gold in the ground he should melt it down into a gold coffin for the 'frozen' baby, which should be dug up for the purpose. Surikov appeared to receive this derisive suggestion with tears of gratitude and set about immediately to carry out the project. I seem to have made a gesture of disgust and left him. Kolya assured me when I recovered my senses that I had not been sleeping at all, and that all the time I had been talking to him about Surikov. At moments I was in great anguish and agitation, and Kolya was uneasy when he left me. When I got up to lock the door behind him, I suddenly remembered a painting I had seen at Rogozhin's, in one of the gloomiest rooms in his house over the doorway. He pointed it out to me himself as we passed through. I must have stood before it for five minutes. There was nothing good about it from an artistic point of view, but it caused a strange sort of uneasiness in me.

"The picture represented Christ just taken down from the cross. I believe that painters usually have a way of depicting Christ, either on the cross or being taken down from the cross, with a trace of extraordinary beauty still in His face; they strive to preserve this beauty in Him even during His most dreadful agonies. In Rogozhin's painting there was no beauty; it was a faithful representation of the corpse of a man who has borne infinite agony even before crucifixion, who has been wounded, tortured, beaten by guards, beaten by the people when he carried the cross and fell beneath its weight, and who, finally, has suffered the agony of crucifixion, lasting for six hours (by my calculation, at least). It is true this is the face of a man who has *just* been taken down from the cross; that is, a face which still retains much warmth and life; nothing is rigid in it yet, and the suffering seems to continue in the face of the dead man as if he was still feeling it (the artist has caught this very well); on the other hand the face has not been spared in the least; it is no more than nature itself, and the corpse of any man, whoever he may be, must really look like that after such suffering. I know that the Christian Church laid down, even in its early centuries, that Christ did not suffer symbolically but in fact, and that therefore His body on the cross was fully subject to the laws of nature. In the painting His face is dreadfully disfigured by blows, swollen, covered with terrible swollen and bloody bruises, the eyes open, the pupils turned up, the large open whites of the eyes bright with a sort of deathly, vitreous gleam. But, strange to say, when one looks at this corpse of this tortured man, a certain curious question arises:

if just such a corpse (and it certainly must have been like this) was seen by all His disciples, by those who were to become His chief apostles, by the women who had followed Him and stood at the foot of the cross, by all who believed in Him and adored Him, how could they believe, gazing on such a cadaver as that, that this martyr would be resurrected? Here one cannot help thinking that if death is so terrible and the laws of nature so powerful, then how can they be overcome? How can they be overcome when even He did not vanquish them, He who conquered nature in his lifetime, and whom nature obeyed, who cried *'Tailitha cumi!'* and the maiden arose, who cried 'Lazarus, come forth!' and the dead man arose? As one looks at that painting, one conceives of nature in the form of some huge, implacable, dumb beast, or to be more exact, to be much more exact, though it may seem strange, in the form of some huge machine of the latest design which, deaf and unfeeling, has senselessly seized, crushed, and swallowed up a great and priceless Being, a Being worth all of nature and its laws, all the earth, which was perhaps created solely for the advent of that Being! That picture expresses that notion of a dark, insolent, and stupidly eternal force to which everything is subject, and it conveys this to us unconsciously. The people surrounding the dead man, none of whom is in the picture, must have felt terrible anguish and dismay on that evening which crushed all their hopes at once and almost their belief. They must have parted in the most awful terror, though each carried away with him a tremendous thought which could never be taken away from him. And if on the eve of the crucifixion the Teacher could have seen His own image as He would be, would He then have mounted the cross and died as He did? That question too comes involuntarily to mind as one looks at the picture.

"For a full hour and a half after Kolya went away, all this drifted through my mind in fragments, sometimes even in vivid images, perhaps while I was actually delirious. Can something appear as an image that has no image? But I did imagine at times that I saw, in some kind of strange and impossible form, that infinite power, that deaf, dark, and speechless being. I remember that someone seemed to lead me by the hand and, holding a candle, show me an enormous and loathsome tarantula, assuring me that it was that very dark, mute, and all-powerful being, and laughing at my indignation. In my room at night there is always a little lamp lit in front of the ikon; it gives a dim and feeble light, yet one can make out everything and even read under that little lamp. I think it was already past midnight; I was wide-awake and lay

428

there with my eyes open. Suddenly the door of my room opened and Rogozhin came in.

"He came in, closed the door, looked at me in silence, and quietly went to a corner of the room where there was a chair just under the little lamp. I was very surprised and looked at him expectantly; Rogozhin leaned one elbow on a little table and began staring at me in silence. Two or three minutes passed in this way, and I remember that his silence offended and irritated me. Why wouldn't he speak? The fact that he had come so late did, of course, strike me as strange, but I remember that I was not particularly surprised by this. On the contrary, I knew that while I had not expressed my thought clearly to him that morning he had nevertheless understood it, and that thought was such that one might easily come to discuss it once more, even if it was very late. So I thought he had come for that. Our parting that morning had been rather unfriendly, and I remember that once or twice he had looked at me very sarcastically. I saw this sarcasm in his look now, and that was what offended me. That it really was Rogozhin and not an apparition, or a delirious vision, I did not in the least doubt at first. It never occurred to me to doubt it.

"Meanwhile he continued to sit there staring at me with that same sarcastic look. I turned angrily on my bed, leaned with my elbow on a pillow, and made up my mind to be silent too, even if we were to sit that way the whole time. For some reason I was absolutely determined that he would be the first to break the silence. I think about twenty minutes went by like this. Suddenly the thought occurred to me: what if it is not Rogozhin but a phantom?

"Neither in my illness or ever before it had I once seen a ghost, but I have *always* felt, even when I was a boy and even now—that is, quite recently—that if I ever did see a ghost, even once, I would die on the spot, though I don't even believe in ghosts. But when the thought struck me that this was not Rogozhin, but only an apparition, I remember I wasn't in the least frightened. In fact it even made me angry. Another strange thing was that the answer to the question whether it was Rogozhin or not somehow did not at all concern or disturb me, the way it should have; I believe I was thinking about something else then. For instance I was much more interested in why Rogozhin, whom I had last seen in a dressing gown and slippers, was now wearing a dresscoat, a white waistcoat, and a white tie. Also the notion crossed my mind that if this was a ghost and I was not afraid of it, then why didn't I get up and go over to it to make certain? Perhaps I did not dare and was afraid. But as soon as I had the thought that I was afraid, I suddenly felt as if my whole body had been touched with ice; a cold chill ran down my spine and my knees trembled. At that very moment, as if guessing that I was afraid, Rogozhin moved away the hand on which he had been leaning, straightened up, and started to open his mouth as if he was going to laugh; he was staring directly at me. I was seized by such a rage that I longed to fly at him, but as I had sworn that I would not speak first, I remained on the bed, particularly since I was still not sure whether it was Rogozhin or not.

"I don't remember for certain how long this went on, nor do I remember whether I lost consciousness at times or not. Finally Rogozhin got up, looked at me slowly and deliberately as he had done when he came in but not grinning at me now, and softly, almost on tiptoe, walked to the door, opened it, and closed it as he went out. I did not get up from the bed; I don't remember how long I lay there with my eyes open, thinking; God knows what I was thinking about; I don't remember dropping off to sleep either. The next morning I woke up when they were knocking at my door at ten. I have arranged that if I don't open the door myself by ten and call for my tea, Matryona should knock. When I opened the door to her, I was at once struck by the thought: how could he have come in when the door was locked? I made inquiries and concluded that the real Rogozhin could not possibly have come in, because all our doors are locked at night.

"It was this singular incident, which I have described in such detail, that caused me to make up my mind definitely. It was not logic which prompted my resolution; not a logical conviction, but repulsion. I could not go on living a life which could assume such strange and offensive forms. That apparition humiliated me. I haven't the strength to submit to the dark force which assumes the form of a tarantula. And it was only then, at dusk, when I sensed at last that I had definitely reached the moment of full decision that I felt better. This was only the first stage; for the second stage I went to Pavlovsk, but that I have already explained sufficiently."

Chapter SEVEN

⚬⚬⚬⚬

"I had a small pocket pistol: I bought it when I was still a young boy, at that ridiculous age when one suddenly becomes fascinated by stories of duels and holdups. I had imagined how I would myself be challenged to a duel and how nobly I would stand there facing the other pistol. A month ago I inspected it and got it ready. In the box where it lay I found two bullets, and in the powder bag enough powder for about three charges. It's a worthless pistol, it doesn't shoot straight or carry properly for more than about fifteen paces; but of course if placed against the temple it could take off the side of one's skull.

"I decided to die in Pavlovsk at sunrise, and to walk down to the park so as not to disturb anyone at the house. My 'statement' will explain the whole thing sufficiently to the police. People interested in psychology, and anyone else who cares to, are free to deduce from it what they like. However, I don't want this manuscript made public. I asked the prince to keep one copy himself and to give another to Aglaya Ivanovna Yepanchin. Such is my wish. I am bequeathing my skeleton to the Medical Academy for the use of science.

"I don't admit the right of anyone to judge me and I know that I am not beyond the power of the law. Not long ago I was amused by the idea that if it entered my mind, now, to kill someone, perhaps as many as ten people, or do something absolutely awful, something considered to be the most dreadful crime in the world, then the court would be in a difficult spot, faced with me and my two or three weeks left to live, now that torture and corporal punishment are abolished. I would die warm and comfortable in their hospital, with an attentive doctor, and very likely a lot more warmly and comfortably than I would at home. I don't see why such an idea doesn't occur to people in my situation, if only as a joke. Perhaps it does. We have our share of merry people too.

"But while I don't recognize the right of anyone to judge me, I do realize that I shall be judged when I am a deaf and

431

mute defendant. I don't want to go without leaving behind some word in reply—a free reply, not forced from me, not to justify myself—oh no! I have no one's forgiveness to beg—but just because I want to.

"First of all, there is a strange consideration: by what right and for what motive would anyone have the idea of questioning my right to dispose as I wish of these two or three weeks? What jurisdiction is involved? Who requires not only that I be condemned but also serve the full term of my condemnation respectably? Does anyone really demand this? For the sake of morality? I could understand that if in the flower of health and strength I took my life, which 'might be of use to my fellow man,' and all that, then morality might reproach me in the usual old way for having disposed of my life without asking permission, or for some such reason of its own. But now, now that my sentence has been pronounced? What morality demands not only your life but the last death rattle with which you surrender your life's last atom, listening to the consoling words of the prince whose Christian arguments inevitably lead to the happy thought that, on the whole, it's much better to be dying (Christians like him always arrive at this notion: it's their favorite recreation). And what are they getting at with their ridiculous 'trees of Pavlovsk'? To sweeten the last hours of my life? Can't they understand that the more I forget myself, the more I give myself up to this final illusion of life and love, with which they are trying to screen me from Meyer's wall and all that is so simply and openly written on it, the more unhappy they are making me? What use do I have for your nature, your Pavlovsk park, your sunrises and sunsets, your blue skies, your contented faces, when this whole festival, which is without end, has begun by excluding me from it? What is in all this beauty for me when every minute, every second I am obliged, forced to know that even this tiny gnat, buzzing near me in the sunlight now, is taking part in all this banquet and chorus, knows its place in it, loves it, and is happy, and I alone am an outcast and only through cowardice have I refused to realize this until now! Oh, I know how the prince and all of them would have liked it if, instead of all those 'evil and insidious' speeches, they had got me to sing, for the sake of propriety, and the glory of morality, the celebrated and classic stanza of Millevoye:*

> O, puissent voir votre beauté sacrée
> Tant d'amis sourds à mes adieux!
> Qu'ils meurent pleins de jours, que leur mort
> soit pleurée,
> Qu'un ami leur ferme les yeux!

432

"But believe me, believe me, dear innocents, that in that edifying stanza, in that academic benediction of the world in French verse, there lies so much hidden bitterness, so much irreconcilable malice, masquerading in rhyme, that perhaps even the poet himself was caught up and took this malice for tears of tender emotion—and thereupon died. God rest his soul! Let me tell you that there is a limit to the shame in the avowal of one's own insignificance and powerlessness beyond which a man cannot go, and at which he begins to feel a tremendous satisfaction in the shame itself. Oh, of course humility is a tremendous force in this sense, though not in the sense religion takes humility to be a force.

"Religion! I admit the existence of eternal life, and perhaps I always have granted that consciousness kindled by a higher power looked around the world and said, 'I am!' and granted that it is suddenly ordered by that higher power to annihilate itself because for some reason it must be this way—with no explanation of why it must be; granted, I admit it, but again the eternal question: why add to this necessity my humility? Can't I simply be devoured without being expected to sing praises to what is devouring me? Is it really possible that someone up there will be offended that I don't care to wait two weeks? I don't believe that; it's much more likely that my insignificant life, the life of an atom, is needed to fulfill some sort of universal harmony, some sort of plus and minus, to offset something, and so forth, just as a daily sacrifice is needed of a million individuals, without whose deaths the rest of the world could not endure (though I must say that that is not a very grand thought in itself). But let all that be so! I admit that it was impossible to arrange the world otherwise—that is, without the continual devouring of one another; I am even prepared to admit that I understand nothing of this organization; but one thing I do know for certain: if I have once been given the consciousness that 'I am,' what is it to me that the world has been constructed with faults and that it cannot exist otherwise? Who will judge me after that, and on what charge? Say what you like, it is all impossible and unjust.

"And yet despite all my efforts I have never been able to conceive that there is no future life and no Providence. Most likely they do exist, but we don't understand anything about future life and its laws. But if it is so difficult and even impossible to understand, how can I be responsible for understanding what is beyond comprehension? It is true, they tell me—and the prince among them of course—that this is where obedience is needed, obedience without reason, out of common decency, and that I shall certainly be rewarded in the next world for my humility. We degrade Providence too much by ascribing our ideas to it out of vexation at not being able to understand it. But there again, if it is not possible to understand it, then, I repeat, it is hard to be answerable for what is not given to man to understand. And if so, how am I to be judged for not being able to understand the will and the laws of providence? No, we'd better leave religion alone.

"Well, this is quite enough. When I reach these lines the sun will surely be rising and 'resounding in the heavens,' and in its vast and incalculable power will flow forth over all creation. Let it! I will die looking straight into the source of power and life, and I will not desire this life! If I could have never been born, I certainly would never have chosen existence on such ludicrous terms. But I still have the power to die, though the days I give back are numbered. It is no great power, and it is no great revolt.

"A final statement: I am not dying for lack of strength to endure those three weeks. Oh, I would have had strength enough, and if I wished I would have drawn sufficient consolation just from the awareness of the wrong done to me; but I am no French poet and I don't want such consolation. Finally, there is a temptation: nature has so limited my activity by its three-week sentence that suicide is perhaps the only thing I still have time to begin and bring to a conclusion of my own free will. Well, why shouldn't I take advantage of the last possibility to *act*? A protest is sometimes no small matter."

The "statement" was finished. Hippolite at last stopped. There is, in extreme cases, that final pitch of cynical frankness when a nervous person, exasperated and beside himself, is no longer afraid of anything and is ready for any kind of outrageous scene, even eager for it: he throws himself at people with an ill-formed but firm determination to fling himself from a belfry a minute later, and thereby all at once clear up any uncertainties which may exist. This condition is usually announced by the approach of complete physical exhaustion. The extreme, almost unnatural tension which had sustained Hippolite until then had reached that final pitch. This eighteen-year-old boy, worn out by illness, was as weak as a trembling leaf torn from a tree, but as soon as he brought himself to look around at his audience—for the first time in the past hour—the most haughty, the most contemptuous, the most offensive disgust was at once apparent in his smile and his whole expression. He pressed his challenge. But his audience also was highly indignant. They were all getting up from the table noisily and angrily. Fatigue, wine, and nervous tension

434

accentuated the disorderliness and, as it were, the foulness of their impressions, if one may so express it.

Suddenly Hippolite jumped up from his chair as if he had been wrenched from it.

"The sun has risen!" he cried, seeing the treetops alight and pointing them out to the prince as if he was showing him a miracle. "It has risen!"

"Did you expect it wasn't going to?" inquired Ferdyshchenko.

"Another scorching day," muttered Ganya with casual annoyance, stretching and yawning with his hat in his hands. "Will we have a month of this drought! Will we, Ptitsyn, or not?"

Hippolite listened with a surprise that approached stupefaction. Suddenly he turned terribly pale and began trembling.

"Your pretence of indifference so as to offend me is very clumsy," he said to Ganya, looking straight at him. "You're a good-for-nothing!"

"Well, what the devil is this? Letting himself go like that!" yelled Ferdyshchenko. "What phenomenal weakness!"

"He's just a fool," said Ganya.

Hippolite collected himself somewhat.

"I understand, gentlemen," he began, still trembling, his voice faltering at every word, "that I may deserve your personal resentment and—I'm sorry that I've—put you out with these ravings," (he pointed to the manuscripts), "or rather, I'm sorry I haven't put you out completely." (He grinned stupidly.) "Did I put you out, Yevgeny Pavlovitch?" he suddenly turned to him with the question. "Did I put you out or not? Tell me!"

"It was a trifle long, but—"

"Speak out! Don't lie for once in your life!" Hippolite demanded, trembling.

"Oh, it makes no difference to me at all! Please be so kind as not to bother me!" said Yevgeny Pavlovitch, turning away in disgust.

"Good night, Prince," said Ptitsyn, going up to the prince.

"But he's going to shoot himself! How can you? Look at him!" cried Vera, and rushing up to Hippolite in great alarm she seized him by the arms. "He said he'd shoot himself when the sun came up. How can you?"

"He won't shoot himself!" several voices, including Ganya's, muttered spitefully.

"Be careful, gentlemen!" cried Kolya, also grasping Hippolite by the arm. "Just look at him! Prince, Prince, what are you thinking of?"

Vera, Kolya, Keller, and Burdovsky crowded around Hippolite; all four had taken hold of his arms.

"He has the right! He has the right!" muttered Burdovsky, though he too seemed completely at a loss.

"Excuse me, Prince, but what do you intend to be done?" asked Lebedev, coming up to the prince, drunk and insolent with anger.

"Intend to be done?"

"No, sir. Excuse me, sir. I am the master of the house, sir, though I don't want to be lacking in respect to you—let's say you're the master too, but I don't want anything happening in my own house. No, sir!"

"He won't shoot himself—the lad is fooling!" General Ivolgin cried suddenly, with indignation and aplomb.

"Bravo, General!" acclaimed Ferdyshchenko.

"I know he won't, General, most honored General, but still —since I'm the master here."

"Listen, Mr. Terentyev," Ptitsyn said suddenly, having said good-bye to the prince and with his hand held out to Hippolite. "I think in your manuscript you mentioned your skeleton and about leaving it to the Academy? Is that your own skeleton? I mean your very own bones that you're leaving?"

"Yes, my own bones—"

"Well, good. Because there can be misunderstanding. They say there was such a case."

"Why do you tease him?" the prince cried suddenly.

"You've made him cry," Ferdyshchenko added.

But Hippolite was not crying at all. He started to move from his place, but the four people around him immediately seized him. There was a burst of laughter.

"That's what he's been after—people holding his arms; that's why he read his manuscript," remarked Rogozhin. "Good-bye, Prince. I've been sitting too long—my bones ache."

"If you really meant to shoot yourself, Terentyev," laughed Yevgeny Pavlovitch, "in your place—after such compliments —I would make a point of not shooting myself, just to provoke them."

"They're terribly anxious to see how I'll shoot myself," cried Hippolite, straining as if trying to attack him.

"They're annoyed they won't see that."

"So you think they won't?"

"I am not trying to stir you up; on the contrary, I think it is very possible you will shoot yourself. The great thing is not to lose your temper," said Yevgeny Pavlovitch in a patronizing drawl.

"I see only now that I made a dreadful mistake in reading the manuscript!" said Hippolite, looking at Yevgeny Pavlovitch with a sudden expression of trustfulness, as if he was asking the advice of a friend.

"Your situation is ridiculous, but—the fact is I don't know what to advise you," replied Yevgeny Pavlovitch, smiling.

Hippolite silently fixed him with a stern, unwavering look. It seemed as if at moments he was without consciousness.

"No, sir. Excuse me, but what a way to do things," said Lebedev. " 'I will shoot myself in the park so as not to disturb anyone!' So he thinks he won't be disturbing anyone if he goes down a flight of three stairs into the park."

"Gentlemen—" began the prince.

"No sir, excuse me, my most honored Prince," Lebedev persisted furiously, "but since you can see for yourself that this is no joke, and since at least half of your guests are of the same opinion, convinced that now, after what has been said here, he must certainly feel it a matter of honor to shoot himself, I, therefore, as master of the house and before witnesses, hereby call upon you to assist me."

"What is to be done, Lebedev? I am ready to assist you."

"This, sir: first he must immediately give up the pistol he was bragging to us about, with all the bullets and the powder. If he does this I will agree to let him spend the night in this house, in consideration of his state of illness; under my supervision, of course. But tomorrow he must be off wherever he wants to go. I'm sorry, Prince. If he doesn't give up the weapon I will at once take him by the arm, I will take one, the general will take the other, and send someone immediately to alert the police, and then, sir, the matter will be in the hands of the police. Mr. Ferdyshchenko, as a friend, will go."

An uproar began. Lebedev became highly excited and lost all restraint. Ferdyshchenko was preparing to go to the police. Ganya kept insisting frantically that no one was going to shoot himself. Yevgeny Pavlovitch was silent.

"Prince, have you at any time ever jumped off a belfry?" Hippolite asked him suddenly in a low voice.

"N-no," answered the prince naïvely.

"Do you think I didn't foresee all this hatred?" Hippolite continued in the same voice, looking at the prince with his eyes alight, as if he really expected an answer from him. "Enough!" he suddenly shouted to everyone present. "I am to blame—more than anyone! Lebedev, here is the key." (He took out his change purse and produced from it a steel ring with three or four keys.) "This one, the next from the last—

437

Kolya will show you—Kolya! Where's Kolya?" he cried, looking at Kolya and not seeing him. "Yes—he'll show you. He was helping me pack my bag. Take him, Kolya. In the prince's study, under the table—my bag—with this key—at the bottom in a little box—my pistol and the powder—he will show you. But on condition that early tomorrow when I leave for Petersburg you will give me the pistol back. Do you hear? I am doing this for the prince, not for you."

"Well, that's better," said Lebedev, seizing the key and, with a venomous smirk, he ran into the next room. Kolya stopped as if he had something to say, but Lebedev dragged him after him.

Hippolite gazed around at the laughing guests. The prince noticed that his teeth were chattering, as though he had a terrible chill.

"What worthless people they all are!" Hippolite said to the prince, again in a low voice. When he talked to the prince he would always lean over and whisper.

"Leave them. You are very weak."

"In a moment, in a moment—I'll be going in a moment." Suddenly he embraced the prince.

"Perhaps you think I'm mad," he said, looking at him and laughing strangely.

"No, but you—"

"In a moment—be quiet—don't say anything—stand still —I want to look you in the eyes. Stand like that and let me look. I am saying good-bye to a man."

He stood there motionless and silent looking at the prince for about ten seconds, his face pale, his temples damp with sweat, holding the prince in an odd way, as if he was afraid to let him go.

"Hippolite! Hippolite! What's the matter with you?" cried the prince.

"In a moment—enough—I'm going to bed. I shall drink one sip to the sun's health. I want to, I want to—leave me alone!"

From where he was sitting he quickly seized a glass, sprang from his place, and in one instant was at the veranda steps. The prince was about to run after him, but it so happened, as if purposely, that at that very moment Yevgeny Pavlovitch held out his hand to him to say good-bye. A second later there was suddenly a general outcry on the veranda. This was followed by a full minute of extreme confusion.

On reaching the steps down from the veranda, Hippolite had stopped, raised his glass in his left hand, and put his other hand into the right-hand pocket of his coat. Keller asserted later that Hippolite already had his hand in his right-hand pocket, even when he was talking with the prince, and that he had held him with his left and across his neck and shoulder, and that his right hand in his pocket was, according to Keller, the first thing that had aroused his suspicion. Whatever the case, some apprehension did make him run after Hippolite. But he was not quick enough. He only saw that suddenly something flashed in Hippolite's right hand, and that in the same instant the little pocket pistol was at his temple. Keller rushed forward to seize his hand, but at that second Hippolite pulled the trigger. There was a sharp, dry click, but no shot. When Keller seized Hippolite, the young man collapsed in his arms, as though unconscious, perhaps really imagining that he had been killed. The pistol was already in Keller's hand. Hippolite was supported, a chair was brought, he was seated, and everyone crowded around, shouting and asking questions. They had all heard the click of the trigger and they all saw the man alive without even a scratch. Hippolite himself sat there, not understanding what was happening, staring blankly at everyone around him. Lebedev and Kolya ran up at that moment.

"Did it misfire?" they were all asking.

"Maybe it wasn't loaded," others guessed.

"It's loaded!" Keller declared, examining the pistol, "but—"

"Was it a misfire?"

"There was no firing-cap in it," Keller revealed.

It is hard to describe the pitiful scene which followed. The general alarm of the first moment quickly gave way to laughter; some were even roaring with laughter, finding malicious delight in the situation. Hippolite sobbed as if in hysterics, wrung his hands, rushed up to everyone, even to Ferdyshchenko, clutching him with both hands and swearing that he had "accidently forgotten, not intentionally" to put the cap in, that he "had all the caps right here in my waistcoat pocket, about ten of them," (he showed them around to everyone), that he had not put one in before out of fear of the gun going off accidentally in his pocket, that he had counted all along on having time to put it in when it would be needed, and that he had suddenly forgotten. He rushed up to the prince, to Yevgeny Pavlovitch, he begged Keller to let him have his pistol back so that he could prove that "his honor, his honor—" that he was now "dishonored forever!"

He fell unconscious at last. He was carried into the prince's study, and Lebedev, completely sobered, immediately sent for a doctor, while he stayed by the sick man's bedside, with his daughter, his son, Burdovsky, and the general. When the unconscious Hippolite had been carried out, Keller stood in the middle of the room, and, spacing and stressing each word so that all might hear, declared with inspired resolution:

"Gentlemen, if any one of you ever again suggests out loud, in my presence, that the cap was forgotten intentionally, and asserts that this unhappy young man was only pretending, he will have me to deal with."

But no one answered him. The guests were at last leaving, in a group, and in haste. Ptitsyn, Ganya, and Rogozhin left together.

The prince was very surprised that Yevgeny Pavlovitch had changed his mind and was leaving without further conversation.

"Didn't you want to speak to me when the others had gone?" he asked him.

"So I did," said Yevgeny Pavlovitch, suddenly sitting down on a chair and having the prince sit next to him, "but now for the time being I've changed my mind. I'll admit that I'm rather upset, and you are too. My thoughts are confused, and, besides, what I want to discuss with you is too important a matter for me—and for you too. You see, Prince, for once in my life I want to do something completely honest—I mean something completely without ulterior motive, and, well, I think that at this moment I am not quite capable of a completely honest action, and perhaps you aren't either— So—and, well, we'll have our discussion later. Perhaps the matter will be more clear to me, and to you, if we wait for about three days, which I now intend to spend in Petersburg."

At this he again got up from his chair, so that it seemed odd that he had sat down in the first place. The prince also felt that Yevgeny Pavlovitch was discontent and irritated and that he was looking at him with a hostility that had not been there before.

"By the way, are you going to see our invalid now?"

"Yes—I'm rather afraid," said the prince.

"Don't be, he'll certainly live for another six weeks, and he might even recover here. But the best would be to send him off tomorrow."

"Perhaps I really did force his hand—by not saying anything. Perhaps he thought that I too was doubting he would shoot himself. What do you think, Yevgeny Pavlovitch?"

"Nothing of the sort. You keep worrying about it because you're too good and kind. I've heard of such things, but I've never seen in real life how a man could deliberately shoot himself to win praise, or out of anger because he did not receive it. Above all, I could not have believed such an authentic expression of a feeble will. Still you should chase him off tomorrow."

"Do you think he will shoot himself again?"

"No, he won't now. But beware these home-grown Lacenaires* of ours. I say it again, crime is all too often the haven of these mediocre, impatient, and greedy nonentities."

"Is he a Lacenaire?"

"Essentially the same—though their activities may be different. But you see whether this young gentleman isn't capable of murdering ten people just for the sake of the 'performance'; just as he himself read to us in his 'statement.' Now those words of his won't let me sleep."

"Perhaps your fears are exaggerated?"

"You're amazing, Prince. You don't believe he is capable of killing ten people *now*."

"I'm afraid to answer you. It's all very strange, but—"

"Well, as you please, as you please!" Yevgeny Pavlovitch concluded irritably. "Besides, you're such a brave man. Just try not to be one of the ten."

"It's not likely he'll kill anyone," said the prince, looking at him thoughtfully.

Yevgeny Pavlovitch laughed maliciously.

"Good-bye! It's time I was going. By the way, did you notice he bequeathed a copy of his 'statement' to Aglaya Ivanovna."

"Yes, I did and—I am thinking about that."

"I would—apropos of the 'ten.'" Yevgeny Pavlovitch laughed again and went out.

An hour later, well past three o'clock, the prince walked down into the park. He had tried to go to sleep in the house, but he could not because of the violent pounding of his heart. Things at the house had settled down, however, and as far as possible peace had returned: the invalid had fallen asleep and the doctor had declared that there was no particular danger. Lebedev, Kolya, and Burdovsky were lying down in the sick man's room to take turns looking after him; so there was nothing to fear.

But the prince's uneasiness increased from minute to minute. He wandered through the park, looking absently around him, and stopped in surprise when he reached the open area in front of the station and saw the rows of empty seats and the music-stands of the orchestra. This place made a strong impression on him and for some reason struck him as being hideous. He turned back and, following the path he had

441

walked the day before with the Yepanchins, came to the green bench which had been fixed as the meeting place, sat down on it, and suddenly laughed out loud, and this at once made him extremely annoyed with himself. His feeling of anguish persisted; he longed to go away somewhere— He did not know where. A bird was singing over his head and he started to look for it among the leaves; suddenly the bird flew out of the tree, and at the same instant he remembered the "gnat in the sunshine" which Hippolite had written about; and how it "knew its place and joined in the general chorus" while he alone was "an outcast." This phrase had struck him even at the time, and he recalled it now. A certain long-forgotten memory stirred in him and suddenly came back to him plainly.

It had happened in Switzerland during the first year of his treatment, in the first months of it, in fact. At that time he was still like an idiot, he could not even speak properly and sometimes did not understand what was wanted of him. Once, on a bright sunny day, he went up into the mountains and walked for a long time, tormented by a certain thought which he could not seize clearly in his mind. The brilliant sky was before him, below, the lake, all around the bright, boundless horizon which seemed to stretch endlessly. He gazed a long time torn by agony. He remembered now how he had stretched out his hand to that bright, infinite blue and had wept. The thing that tortured him was that he was a complete stranger to all this. What was this banquet, what was this great eternal festival without end, to which he had always, from childhood, been drawn, and in which he could never partake? Every morning the same bright sun rises, every morning there is a rainbow on the waterfall, every evening the highest snowcapped pinnacle, there on the horizon at the edge of the sky, burns with purple fire; every "little gnat that buzzes around him in the sunshine plays a part in this chorus; it knows its place, loves it, and is happy"; each blade of grass grows and is happy! Everything has its path, and everything knows its path, everything goes forth with a song and returns with a song; only he knows nothing, understands nothing, neither people nor sounds, a stranger to all things and an outcast. Oh, of course he could not speak then in those words, or state his question; he suffered dumbly, uncomprehendingly; but now it seemed to him that he had said all this at that time too, in these very same words, and that Hippolite had taken that "gnat" from him, from his own words and his tears of that time. He was sure of this, and for some reason the thought set his heart beating faster—

He dozed on the bench, but his anxiety persisted into his sleep. Just before falling asleep he remembered that Hippolite was supposed to kill ten people, and he smiled at the absurdity of the idea. All around him there was a magnificent clear silence, broken only by the rustling of the leaves, which seemed to make everything around him even more still and solitary. He had many dreams and they were all disturbed, and at moments made him start and tremble. At last a woman came to him; he knew her, he knew her and suffered in knowing her, he could always name her and point her out but, strange to say, her face seemed completely different from the one he had always known, and he felt a great revulsion against recognizing her as the same woman. There was such remorse and horror in this face that it seemed she must be a great criminal and had just committed a terrible crime. A tear trembled on her pale cheek; she beckoned to him and placed a finger on her lips, as if warning him to follow her silently. His heart stopped beating; not for anything, not for anything in the world did he want to admit that she was a criminal; but he felt that something dreadful was about to happen, something that would mark his whole life. She seemed to want to show him something, not far from there, in the park. He got up to follow her, and suddenly near him he heard a clear, fresh laugh; he felt someone's hand in his; he seized the hand, pressed it hard, and woke up. Aglaya stood before him. She was laughing out loud.

Chapter EIGHT

She was laughing, but she was also indignant.

"Asleep! You were asleep!" she cried in scornful surprise.

"It's you!" murmured the prince, not fully awake yet and recognizing her with amazement, "Oh, yes! We were to meet —I fell asleep."

"So I see."

"Did anyone besides you wake me? Was anyone besides you here? I thought there was—another woman here."

"There was another woman here?"

443

At last he was completely awake.

"It was only a dream," he said thoughtfully. "It's strange I should have such a dream just at this moment— Do sit down."

He took her hand and made her sit on the bench; he sat next to her and fell into thought. Aglaya did not open a conversation, she only looked at her companion intently. He too would look at her, but sometimes it was as if he was not seeing her beside him. She began to blush.

"Oh, yes," said the prince, startled, "Hippolite shot himself."

"When? At your house?" she asked, but without great surprise. "Because it seems to me he was still alive yesterday evening, wasn't he? How can you sleep here after that?" she cried with sudden animation.

"But he isn't dead. The pistol didn't go off."

At Aglaya's insistence the prince had to tell her immediately and in great detail all that had happened on the previous evening. She kept hurrying him on with his story, but she herself would interrupt with questions, almost all of them irrelevant. She took a particular interest in hearing what Yevgeny Pavlovitch had said, and even put several questions to him about that.

"Well, that's enough, we have to hurry," she concluded, having heard everything. "We have only an hour here, until eight o'clock, because at eight I absolutely must be home so they won't know I've been sitting out here. And I've come for a reason. I have a lot to tell you. Only now you've put me off completely. As far as Hippolite is concerned, I think the pistol was bound not to go off—that would be more like him. But you're sure he really wanted to shoot himself, that there was no trickery?"

"There was no trickery."

"Yes, that is more likely. And he wrote that you were to bring me his confession? Why didn't you bring it?"

"Well, because he didn't die. I will ask him for it."

"You must absolutely bring it to me, and you needn't ask anything. He will certainly be very pleased, because he was probably going to shoot himself so that I would read his confession afterward. Please don't laugh at what I am saying, Lev Nikolayevitch, because it might very well be so."

"I'm not laughing, for I too am convinced it might partly be true."

"You're convinced? Do you really think so too?" said Aglaya suddenly with great surprise.

She asked questions in quick succession and spoke rapidly

but sometimes seemed confused and did not finish her sentences; at times she seemed anxious to warn him about something. She was extremely disturbed and, while she seemed outwardly bold and defiant, she was probably a little frightened too. She was wearing a plain everyday dress which was very becoming to her. She often gave little starts and blushed, and she was sitting on the edge of the bench. The prince's agreement that Hippolite had tried to shoot himself so that she would read his confession had greatly surprised her.

"Of course," the prince explained, "he wanted all of us, as well as you, to admire him—"

"Admire him?"

"That is—how shall I explain it to you? It is very difficult. Except he certainly wanted everyone to gather around him and tell him they loved him very much and respected him, and he wanted everyone to beg him to stay alive. Very likely he had you in mind most of all, because he mentioned you at such a moment—though perhaps he didn't know himself that he had you in mind."

"I don't understand that at all: he had me in mind and he didn't know he had me in mind. But then perhaps I do understand it: do you know that even when I was only thirteen I thought of poisoning myself about thirty times, and I too thought of writing all about it in a letter to my parents, and I too thought how I would be there in my coffin and how everyone would weep over me and blame themselves for having been so cruel to me— Why are you smiling again?" she added quickly, frowning. "What do you think about when you are daydreaming all by yourself? Maybe you imagine yourself as a field marshal and dream you have defeated Napoleon?"

"Well," the prince laughed, "to tell you the truth I do think about that, especially when I'm just falling asleep. Only it's not Napoleon I defeat, it's the whole Austrian army."

"I don't feel at all like joking with you, Lev Nikolayevitch I shall see Hippolite myself, please tell him that. And as for you, I find all this very wrong, because it is very crude to look into a man's soul that way and judge him as you judge Hippolite. You have no tenderness; nothing but truth and so you are unfair."

The prince became thoughtful.

"I think you are unfair to me," he said. "For I find nothing wrong in his thinking that way, because everyone is inclined to think that way. Besides, maybe he didn't think that way at all, but only wanted to—he wanted one last time to meet with people and to win their respect and love. Those, you see, are very good feelings, only somehow it didn't turn out that way; it was his sickness and something else too! Also, with some people everything always goes right, but with others nothing ever does—"

"You are most surely saying that about yourself, aren't you?" remarked Aglaya.

"Yes, I was," replied the prince, aware of no malice in the question.

"Nevertheless I wouldn't have fallen asleep in your place. It seems that wherever you settle you fall asleep there. It's not at all very nice of you."

"But I didn't sleep all night. And then I walked. I walked and I went to where the music was."

"What music?"

"Where they were playing yesterday, and then I came here. I sat down, I thought and thought, and fell asleep."

"Oh, so that's how it was! That changes things in your favor— But why did you go where they play the music?"

"I don't know. I just did."

"All right, all right—afterward. You keep interrupting me. And what do I care if you went there? What woman was it you were dreaming about?"

"It was—you saw her—"

"I understand, I understand perfectly. You are very much — How did you dream of her? How did you see her? Anyway, I don't want to know anything about it," she snapped with vexation. "Don't interrupt me."

She waited a moment, as if trying to gather courage or overcome her annoyance.

"Now this is why I had you come—I want to offer to let you be my friend. Why are you suddenly staring at me like that?" she added, almost angrily.

The prince was indeed looking at her very intently at that moment, observing that she was blushing very deeply again. When this happened, the more she blushed, the more she seemed to become angry with herself, and this was apparent in her flashing eyes. Usually, a moment later, she would turn her anger against the person she was talking to, whether he was to blame or not, and would begin quarreling with him. Fully aware of her own shy, wild nature, she seldom entered readily into conversation and was more silent than her sisters, sometimes even too silent. But when, especially in delicate situations such as the present one, she was obliged to speak, she would open the conversation with extraordinary haughtiness and with a sort of defiance. She could always tell beforehand when she was starting to blush or was about to start.

"Perhaps you don't care to accept my offer?" She looked haughtily at the prince.

"Oh, yes, I do want to, except that it's quite unnecessary —that is, I never thought it necessary for you to make such an offer," said the prince in confusion.

"What did you think then? Why do you suppose I asked you to come here? What's in your mind? Perhaps you take me for a little fool, the way everyone does at home?"

"I didn't know you were taken for a fool. I—don't take you as one."

"Oh, don't you? How very clever of you. And how cleverly put."

"I think you are perhaps very clever at times," pursued the prince. "You said something just now that was very clever indeed. You said about my opinion of Hippolite that there was nothing but truth in it and therefore it was unfair. I shall remember that and think about it."

Aglaya suddenly flushed with pleasure. Such changes took place in her very openly and with extraordinary rapidity. The prince, too, was delighted, and even laughed with pleasure, looking at her.

"Then listen," she began again, "I've been waiting a long time to tell you all this—ever since you wrote me that letter and even before. You heard half of it from me yesterday: I consider you a most honest and a most sincere man, more honest and sincere than anyone, and if they say of you that your mind—I mean, that your mind is sometimes ill, that is unjust. I have decided this and I've argued about it because, even if you really are ill in your mind (you won't be angry about that, of course, I am speaking in a higher sense), what is important in your mind is far better than what is important in any of theirs, and they've never even dreamed of what it is like; for there are two sorts of mind: important ones and unimportant ones. Isn't that so? Well, isn't it?"

"Perhaps it is," the prince barely murmured; his heart was trembling and pounding violently.

"I knew you would understand," she went on gravely. "Prince S. and Yevgeny Pavlovitch understand nothing about there being two sorts of mind. Neither does Alexandra. But just imagine, *Maman* did."

"You are very like Lizaveta Prokofyevna."

"How so? Really?" asked Aglaya, surprised.

"Yes, really."

"Thank you," she said after a moment's thought. "I am very glad I resemble *Maman*. You have a great respect for

447

her, then?" she added, quite unaware of the naïveté of the question.

"A very great respect. And I am glad you understood this so well."

"And I'm glad, because I've noticed how people sometimes —laugh at her. But now listen to the most important thing; I've been thinking it over a long time and I've finally chosen you. I don't want them to laugh at me at home. I don't want to be taken for a little fool, I don't want to be teased. I realized all this at once and I refused Yevgeny Pavlovitch point-blank because I don't want them always marrying me off! I want—I want— Well, I want to run away from home, and I've chosen you to help me."

"Run away from home!" cried the prince.

"Yes, yes, yes! Run away from home!" she cried, suddenly flaring up with extraordinary anger. "I won't, I won't have them making me blush all the time. I don't want to blush in front of them, or in front of Prince S., or in front of Yevgeny Pavlovitch, or in front of anyone, and that's why I've chosen you. I want to talk to you about everything, everything, even about the most important things, when I want to; and on your part you must never hide anything from me. I want to talk about everything with at least one person just as I do with myself. They suddenly started saying I was waiting for you and that I loved you. That was even before your arrival, and I did not show them your letter, and now they are all saying it. I want to be brave and never be afraid. I don't want to go to their balls. I want to be useful. I've wanted to get away for such a long time. For twenty years I've been bottled up at home, and they're all out to marry me off. Even at fourteen, though I was a silly fool then, I thought of running away. Now I have it all worked out, and I've been waiting for you to tell me all about foreign countries. I have never seen a single Gothic cathedral, I want to go to Rome, I want to look into all the scientific academies. I want to study in Paris. I have been preparing myself all last year, and studying, and I have read a great many books. I have read all the ones that are forbidden. Alexandra and Adelaïda read any book, they're allowed to, but I'm not, they won't give them to me, they supervise me. I don't want to quarrel with my sisters, but I told Mother and Father long ago that I want to change my social position. I have decided to devote myself to teaching, and I've been counting on you because you said you liked children. Could we perhaps take up teaching together, if not now, at least later? We would be doing something useful together. I don't want to be a general's daughter. Tell me, are you a very learned person?"

"Oh, not at all."

"That's too bad, because I thought—what made me think that? But you will be my guide anyway, because I have chosen you."

"This is absurd, Aglaya Ivanovna."

"I do want to run away from home!" she cried, and again her eyes blazed. "If you don't agree to it, I'll marry Gavril Ardalionovitch. I don't want to be looked on as a horrid female at home and be accused of heaven knows what."

"Have you lost your senses?" cried the prince, almost jumping up from his seat. "What are you accused of? Who is accusing you?"

"Everyone at home. Mother, my sisters, Father, Prince S., even your nasty little Kolya! Even if they don't say it right out, that's what they're thinking. I told all of them that right to their faces, Mother and Father too. *Maman* was sick for a whole day, and the next day Alexandra and Papa told me I didn't understand what nonsense I was talking and even the words I was using. And I told them right out that I did understand everything, all the words, that I am not a little girl anymore, that two years ago I had purposely read two Paul de Kock novels to find out about everything. *Maman* almost fainted when she heard that."

A curious thought suddenly flashed through the prince's mind. He looked intently at Aglaya and smiled.

He could hardly believe that beside him sat the same haughty young lady who had read him Gavril Ardalionovitch's letter with such pride and disdain. He could not understand how such a disdainful, stern, beautiful young girl could be such a child, perhaps, indeed a child who did not understand "all the words."

"Have you always lived at home, Aglaya Ivanovna?" he asked. "I mean you have never gone away to school or any sort of academy to study?"

"I've never been anywhere. I've always sat there at home, corked up in a bottle, and I'm to be married right out of a bottle. Why are you smirking again? I notice that you too seem to be laughing at me and siding with them," she added, frowning menacingly. "Don't make me angry, I don't know what's the matter with me as it is—I'm sure you've come here fully persuaded that I am in love with you and that I have had you come here for a rendezvous," she snapped angrily.

"I was afraid of that yesterday," the prince blurted innocently (he was very confused), "but today I'm sure that you—"

"What!" cried Aglaya, and her lower lip suddenly began to tremble. "You were afraid that I—you dared to think that I —Good Lord! You suspected perhaps that I had you come here to lure you into my trap, so that then they would find us here and force you to marry me—"

"Aglaya Ivanovna! Aren't you ashamed? How could such a foul thought enter your pure, innocent heart? I swear you don't believe a single word of that yourself and—you don't know what you're saying!"

Aglaya sat there, looking steadily at the ground, as if frightened at what she had said.

"I'm not in the least ashamed," she murmured, "and how do you know I have an innocent heart? How dared you send me a love letter that time?"

"A love letter? My letter—a love letter! That was a most respectful letter, that letter came from the depths of my heart at a most difficult moment of my life! I thought of you then —as one thinks of a kind of light—I—"

"Yes, all right, all right," she suddenly interrupted, but in a completely different tone, as if she was full of remorse and almost frightened; she even leaned toward him, still trying not to look him in the face, and was ready to touch his shoulder so as to beg him more persuasively not to be angry with her. "All right," she went on, terribly ashamed, "I realize I used a very stupid expression. I did it—to test you. Take it as if it never was said. If I've offended you, forgive me. Please don't look straight at me. Turn away. You said that was a very foul thought—I said it on purpose to hurt you. Sometimes I'm myself afraid of what I'm going to say, and then suddenly I say it. You said you wrote that letter in a most difficult moment of your life. I know what moment it was," she said softly, looking at the ground again.

"Oh, if only you could know everything!"

"I do know everything!" she cried with fresh excitement. "You'd been living then for a whole month in the same apartment with that revolting woman you ran away with—"

She did not blush, but turned pale as she said this, and suddenly she got up as if she did not know what she was doing; then, recovering at once, sat down again; her lip continued to tremble for some time. The silence lasted a minute. The prince was astounded by the suddenness of her outburst and did not know what to attribute it to.

"I don't love you at all," she said suddenly, as if she were replying cuttingly to something he had said.

The prince did not answer; they were silent for another minute.

"I love Gavril Ardalionovitch," she murmured, speaking rapidly but barely audibly, bending her head still further.

"That's not true," said the prince, also almost whispering.

"So I'm lying? It is true; I promised to marry him the day before yesterday on this very bench."

The prince was startled, then thoughtful for a moment.

"That is not true," he repeated, decisively. "You have made all that up."

"How wonderfully polite of you. Well, let me tell you that he's reformed himself; he loves me more than his own life. He burned his hand in front of me just to show me that he loved me more than his own life."

"He burned his hand?"

"Yes, his hand. You may believe it or not—it makes no difference to me."

The prince was silent again. There was no trace of jesting in Aglaya's words; she was angry.

"Well, did he bring a candle with him, if he did it here? Otherwise I can't imagine how—"

"Yes, he brought a candle. What is so hard to believe about that?"

"A whole one or a burned one in a candlestick?"

"Well, no—a burned one—a stub—a whole one; what does it matter? Leave me alone! And if you must know, he brought matches too. He lit the candle and held his finger over it for a whole half hour. Isn't that possible?"

"I saw him yesterday. His fingers were all right."

Aglaya suddenly burst out in a peal of laughter, just like a child.

"Do you know why I said that lie just now?" she said, turning suddenly to the prince with childlike confidence, the laughter still on her lips. "Because when you are lying, if you skillfully put in something not quite ordinary, something peculiar, well, you know, something that very rarely if ever happens, then the lie becomes more believable. I've noticed this. Except in this case it didn't work because I didn't know how to—"

She suddenly frowned again, as if collecting her thoughts.

"When I read you about the 'poor knight' that time," she said, turning to the prince and looking gravely, even sadly at him, "I didn't want to—praise you, but at the same time I wanted to hold up your conduct to you and show you that I know everything."

"You are very unjust to me—and to the unhappy woman you just spoke of in such a horrible way, Aglaya."

"It's because I do know everything—everything—that I spoke like that! I know how six months ago you offered your hand to her in front of everyone. Don't interrupt. You see I'm speaking without comment. After that she ran off with Rogozhin; then you lived with her in the country somewhere, or in a town, and she left you for someone else." (Aglaya blushed deeply.) "After that she went back to Rogozhin again, who loves her like—like a madman. Then you—a very clever person yourself—have come galloping after her as soon as you learned she had returned to Petersburg. Last night you were in a great rush to defend her and just now you were dreaming about her. You see, I know everything. It's for her sake you came here, isn't it?"

"Yes, it was for her sake," the prince answered softly, bowing his head mournfully and pensively, not conscious of Aglaya's blazing glare upon him. "For her sake to find out—I don't believe she can be happy with Rogozhin, although— anyway, I don't know what I could do for her here or how I could help her, but I came."

He gave a start and looked at Aglaya; she was listening to him with a look of hatred.

"If you've come without knowing why," she said at last, "you must love her very much."

"No," replied the prince, "no, I don't love her. Oh, if you knew with what horror I recall the time I spent with her!"

A shudder passed through his body as he uttered these words.

"Tell me everything," said Aglaya.

"There's nothing you shouldn't hear about. Why I wanted to tell you and only you, about all this, I don't know; perhaps because I really did love you very much. That unhappy woman is deeply convinced that she is the most fallen, the most vicious creature in the whole world. Oh, don't hold her up to scorn, don't cast stones at her. She has tortured herself too much with her undeserved feeling of shame. And what in the name of heaven is she to blame for? Oh, she will cry out every minute, in her states of exaltation, that she is the victim of people, the victim of a depraved and evil man; but whatever she tells you, you may be sure she is the first to disbelieve it, and to believe with her whole heart that, on the contrary, she is hersef to blame. When I tried to dispel those dark feelings she suffered so that my heart will never recover as long as I remember that dreadful time. It's as if my heart was pierced forever. Do you know why she ran away from

452

me? Just to show me, just me, that she was a degraded creature. But the most terrible thing was that she probably didn't know herself that she only wanted to prove this to me, but ran away because she had an irresistible urge to something shameful, so she could then say to herself: 'There, you've done something shameful again, so you are a degraded creature.' Oh, perhaps you won't understand that, Aglaya. Do you realize she probably takes some terrible, unnatural kind of pleasure from that constant feeling of shame—a sort of revenge on someone. Sometimes I was able to make her see the light around her again, but she would become disturbed again at once, and would even accuse me bitterly of setting myself over her (when such a thought never occurred to me), and when I proposed marriage she would tell me in so many words that she was not asking for condescending pity or help from anyone, or to be raised up to anyone's level. You saw her yesterday. Do you think she is happy with that crowd, that that sort of society is for her? You don't know how educated and advanced she is and what she can understand! She would even surprise me sometimes!"

"Did you preach such—sermons to her then?"

"Oh, no," pursued the prince thoughtfully, not noticing the tone of the question, "I seldom spoke. Often I wanted to speak, but in fact I didn't know what to say sometimes. You know in some cases it's better not to say anything at all. Oh, I did love her; oh, I loved her very much, but later—later she guessed everything."

"What did she guess?"

"That I only pitied her, and that I—didn't love her anymore."

"How do you know? Perhaps she really did fall in love with that landowner she went off with?"

"No, I know all about it. She was only making a fool of him."

"And she never made a fool of you?"

"N-no. She would laugh maliciously. Oh, and then she would reproach me terribly, in a rage—and she was suffering herself! But—afterward— Oh, don't remind me, don't remind me of that!"

He buried his face in his hands.

"And do you know that she writes me letters almost every day?"

"Then it's true!" cried the prince in dismay. "I heard that, but I didn't want to believe it."

"Whom did you hear it from?" Aglaya asked, startled.

"Rogozhin told me yesterday, but only in vague terms."

453

"Yesterday? Yesterday morning? When yesterday? Before the concert or after?"

"After. At night, past eleven."

"Oh, if it was Rogozhin— And do you know what she writes me in those letters?"

"I wouldn't be surprised at anything. She's a madwoman."

"Here are the letters." Aglaya took three letters in three separate envelopes from her pocket and threw them down before the prince. "For a whole week now she's been begging, persuading, and coaxing me to marry you. She—well, she is intelligent, even though mad, and you are right in saying she's much more intelligent than I. She writes me that she's in love with me, that every day she looks for an occasion to see me, even from a distance. She writes that you love me, that she knows this, that she noticed it long ago, and that you used to talk to her about me when you were there. She wants to see you happy. She is sure that only I can make you happy. She writes so wildly—so strangely. I haven't shown those letters to anyone, I was waiting for you. Do you know what that means? Can you guess anything?"

"This is insanity, the proof of her madness," said the prince, and his lips trembled.

"You're not crying, are you?"

"No, Aglaya, I'm not crying." The prince was looking at her.

"What am I to do about it? What do you advise me? I can't go on receiving these letters!"

"Oh, leave her alone, I beg you!" cried the prince, "What can you do in this darkness. I'll do everything I can to prevent her writing you again."

"If so then you're a man of no heart!" cried Aglaya. "Don't you see that she's not in love with me, that she loves you, only you! Can you have really noticed everything about her and not noticed that? Do you know what it's about, what those letters mean? It's jealousy. It's more than jealousy! She—do you think she will actually marry Rogozhin, as she writes here in her letters? She would kill herself the day after your wedding!"

The prince gave a start, his heart stood still. But he was looking at Aglaya in amazement: it was strange to him to realize that this child had been a woman for a long time.

"God knows, Aglaya, that I would give my life to bring peace back to her and make her happy, but—I can't love her anymore, and she knows this!"

"Then sacrifice yourself—that would suit you so well! You're such a great philanthropist. And don't call me Aglaya.

You called me Aglaya a moment ago. You must, you are obliged to bring her back to life; you must go away with her again, to calm and pacify her heart. Yes, and you do love her!"

"I can't sacrifice myself, though I wanted to once and—perhaps I still do. But I know for *certain* that with me she would be lost, and that's why I leave her alone. I was to have seen her today at seven o'clock. I probably won't go now. Her pride will never let her forgive me for my love—and we shall both perish! This is unnatural, but then everything here is unnatural. You say she loves me, but is that love? Can there be such love after what I have suffered? No, there is something else here, but not love!"

"How pale you are!" Aglaya cried in sudden alarm.

"It's nothing. I haven't had much sleep. I'm very tired—We really did talk about you then, Aglaya—"

"So it's true? You really *could talk to her about me* and—how could you have fallen in love with me when you had only seen me once?"

"I don't know. In my darkness then I dreamed—had a vision, perhaps, of a new dawn. I don't know how I thought of you at first. It was the truth I wrote you then, that I didn't know. All that was only a dream, a way out of the horror of that time. Afterward I began to work. I wouldn't have come here for three years—"

"So you came here for her sake?"

There was a quiver in Aglaya's voice.

"Yes, for her sake."

For two minutes both of them fell into gloomy silence. Aglaya got up from the bench.

"Since you say—" she began in an unsteady voice, "since you believe yourself that that—woman of yours—is insane, I have nothing to do with her insane fantasies. I beg you, Lev Nikolayevitch, please take these three letters and throw them in her face for me! And if she ever dares," Aglaya suddenly screamed, "if she ever again dares write me a single line tell her that I shall complain to my father and have her put away in an asylum!"

The prince jumped up and stared in alarm at Aglaya's sudden rage; and suddenly a mist seemed to descend before him—

"You can't feel that way—it's not true!" he murmured.

"It is true! It's true!" screamed Aglaya, almost beside herself.

"What is? What is true?" they heard a frightened voice near them ask.

Lizaveta Prokofyevna stood before them.

"It's true that I'm going to marry Gavril Ardalionovitch! It's true that I love him and that I'm running away from home with him tomorrow!" Aglaya turned at her. "Did you hear? Is your curiosity satisfied? Are you pleased now?"

And she ran home.

"No, my friend, don't you go away now," Lizaveta Prokofyevna said, stopping the prince. "You'll do me the favor of coming home and giving me an explanation. Oh, what I have to suffer, and I haven't slept all night either."

The prince followed her.

Chapter NINE

On entering her house Lizaveta Prokofyevna stopped in the first room; she could go no further and sank down on a little couch, her strength completely gone, forgetting even to ask the prince to sit down. It was a rather large room with a round table in the center, a fireplace, quantities of flowers on shelves in the window, and another glass door in the far wall leading into the garden. Adelaïda and Alexandra came in at once and looked inquiringly and bewilderedly at the prince and their mother.

At the summer house the girls ordinarily got up at about nine o'clock; but for the past two or three days Aglaya had begun getting up by herself a little earlier and going for a walk in the garden; never at seven, but around eight or even a bit later. Lizaveta Prokofyevna, who in fact had not slept all night because of her various anxieties, got up at eight o'clock for the express purpose of meeting Aglaya in the garden, thinking that she was already up; but she did not find her either in the garden or in her bedroom. Becoming alarmed, she woke her other two daughters. They learned from the servant that Aglaya Ivanovna had gone out into the park before seven o'clock. The girls smiled at this new whim of their whimsical sister and remarked to their mother that Aglaya might well become angry if she went out looking for her in the park, and that she would surely be sitting now with a book on the green bench she had spoken of three days before and about which she had almost quarreled with Prince S. because he had found nothing remarkable about its location. Having surprised the couple in the park and listened to her daughter's strange words, Lizaveta Prokofyevna was greatly alarmed for a number of reasons, but now that she had brought the prince home with her she was uneasy about having taken the step: "After all, why can't Aglaya meet the prince and have a conversation with him in the park, even if they did arrange the meeting between them?"

"Don't think for a minute, dear Prince," she finally found the courage to say, "that I've dragged you here to interrogate you. After what happened yesterday evening, my friend, I might not have wanted to see you for quite some time—"

She hesitated.

"But you would still like very much to know how I happened to meet Aglaya Ivanovna this morning?" the prince very calmly finished her sentence for her.

"Well, it so happens I would!" said Lizaveta Prokofyevna, flaring up immediately. "I'm not afraid of speaking plainly. Because I'm not offending anyone and I've had no intention of offending anyone."

"Good heavens, you would naturally want to know; there's no offense in it: you are her mother. I met Aglaya Ivanovna this morning at the green bench at seven o'clock at her invitation of yesterday. She let me know yesterday by a note that she had to see me to discuss something of importance. We met and talked for a full hour about matters that concern only Aglaya Ivanovna, and that's all."

"Of course that's all, dear friend. There's absolutely no question there," Lizaveta Prokofyevna declared with dignity.

"Very well done, Prince," said Aglaya, suddenly coming into the room. "My heartfelt thanks for considering me incapable of stooping to a lie. That's enough, Mother, or do you mean to question him further?"

"You know that until now I've never had occasion to blush in front of you—though you might have been pleased if I had," replied Lizaveta Prokofyevna in an edifying tone. "Good-bye, Prince. And forgive me for having troubled you. I hope you will remain convinced of my unwavering esteem for you."

The prince at once bowed to the mother and then to the daughters and went out. Alexandra and Adelaïda smiled and whispered something between them. Lizaveta Prokofyevna looked at them sternly.

"*Maman,* it's just that the prince bowed so marvelously,"

laughed Adelaïda. "He's usually so clumsy, and here suddenly he's like—like Yevgeny Pavlovitch."

"Grace and dignity are learned from the heart, not from the dancing master," replied Lizaveta Prokofyevna sententiously, and she went upstairs to her room without so much as a glance at Aglaya.

When at about nine o'clock the prince got home he found Vera Lukyanovna and the maidservant on the veranda. They were sweeping and clearing up after the disorder of the previous evening.

"Thank goodness we've had time to finish before you came!" said Vera joyfully.

"Good morning. I feel a little dizzy. I slept badly. I think I'd like a nap."

"Here on the veranda, as you did yesterday? Good. I'll tell everyone not to wake you. Papa went out somewhere."

The maid left. Vera was about to follow her but turned back and went up to the prince with a worried look.

"Prince, have pity on that—poor young man. Don't send him away today."

"I wouldn't think of it. It's as he wishes."

"He won't do anything now, and—don't be severe with him."

"Oh, I won't. Why should I?"

"And—don't laugh at him. That's very important."

"Oh, certainly not!"

"I'm silly to mention such things to a man like you," said Vera, coloring. "And even if you are tired," she added, turning away to leave, "your eyes are nice, at this moment—so happy!"

"Are they really happy?" asked the prince earnestly, then laughed with delight.

But Vera, who was as simplehearted and unceremonious as a young boy, was suddenly overcome with confusion, blushed more deeply, and, still laughing, quickly left.

"What a—pleasant girl," thought the prince and promptly forgot about her. He went to a corner of the veranda where there was a sofa with a little table beside it, sat down, covered his face with his hands, and sat that way for some ten minutes; abruptly he put his hand in his side pocket and anxiously took out three letters.

But the door opened again and Kolya came in. The prince was evidently glad to put the letters back in his pocket and delay the moment of reading them.

"Well, what a thing!" said Kolya, sitting down on the sofa and addressing himself directly to the subject, as people of his kind always do. "What do you think of Hippolite now? You've lost your respect for him?"

"Why should I? But, Kolya, I'm tired. Besides, it's too sad to start in about that again. How is he, though?"

"He's asleep and he'll sleep another couple of hours. I understand: you didn't sleep at home, you went walking in the park—of course; the emotion—I'm not surprised!"

"How do you know I went for a walk in the park and didn't sleep at home?"

"Vera just said so. She was trying to persuade me not to come in, but I couldn't help coming in just for a minute. I've just spent the last two hours by his sickbed. Now I've had Kostya Lebedev take his turn. Burdovsky has left. Do lie down, Prince. Good—good day! Except, you know—I'm surprised."

"Of course. All this—"

"No, Prince, no. I'm amazed by his 'confession.' Mostly with the part where he talks about Providence and future life. There is a *tremendous* thought there!"

The prince looked affectionately at Kolya, who had of course come in to have a talk about the tremendous thought without delay.

"But the main thing is not just the thought itself but the whole setting of it! If that had been written by Voltaire, Rousseau, Proudhon, I would have read it and noticed it, but I wouldn't have been so struck by it. But a man who knows for sure he only has ten minutes more, and who speaks like that —why, that's real pride! Why, that's the highest assertion of one's independence and dignity—why, it's outright defiance! Yes, that's tremendous strength of mind. And then to say he purposely left the firing cap out—is mean, it's absurd! But you know he fooled us yesterday, he deceived us: I never helped him pack his bag and I never saw the pistol; he packed everything himself, so he had me all mixed up then. Vera says that you're letting him stay here; I swear there won't be any danger, especially since we are with him all the time."

"And which of you were with him last night?"

"Kostya, Lebedev, Burdovsky, and I. Keller was there a little while, but later he went to Lebedev's part of the house to sleep because there was nothing in the room for him to lie down on. Ferdyshchenko also slept on Lebedev's side, he left at seven. The general always sleeps at Lebedev's; now he's gone out too. Lebedev will probably be coming to see you presently. I don't know why, but he was looking for you, he asked for you twice. Shall we let him in or not, since you want sleep? I'm going to sleep too. Oh, yes, I do want to tell you one thing: I was surprised at the general just now. Burdovsky woke me after six, actually just at six; I went out for a moment and suddenly ran into the general and he was still so drunk he didn't recognize me; he stood there in front of me like a post. When he did recognize me he fairly flew at me. 'How's the patient?' he said. 'I came to ask about the patient?' I gave him a report, told him this and that. 'That's all very well,' he said, 'but I mainly came out to—what I really got up for was to warn you. I have reason to believe that one must not speak too freely in the presence of Mr. Ferdyshchenko and—one must watch one's step.' Do you understand this, Prince?"

"Really? Still, it doesn't concern us."

"No, of course it doesn't. We aren't Freemasons! That's why I was so surprised at the general's getting up in the night specially to wake me about this."

"Ferdyshchenko left, you say?"

"At seven. He came in to see me on the way. I was sitting up with Hippolite then. He said he was going to get some sleep at Vilkin's—there is a drunken person here called Vilkin. Well, I'm off! And here's Lukyan Timofeyitch. The prince wants to sleep, Lukyan Timofeyitch. Right about face!"

"Only a moment, most respected Prince, on a certain matter of consequence to me," Lebedev said in a forced tone of importance, bowing ceremoniously as he entered.

He had only just gotten back and had not been to his rooms, so he still held his hat in his hand. He looked concerned, and his face bore an extraordinary appearance of dignity. The prince asked him to sit down.

"You asked for me twice today? Perhaps you're still worried about what happened last night?"

"You mean on account of that boy, Prince? Oh, no, sir. My thoughts were quite confused yesterday—but today I don't intend to countercarry your intentions in any manner whatsoever."

"Countercar— What did you say?"

"I said 'countercarry'—a French word which like so many others has entered into the composition of the Russian language, but I don't especially insist upon it."

"What's the matter with you today, Lebedev? You look so important and dignified and you talk as if you were scanning each syllable," said the prince, laughing.

"Nikolai Ardalionovitch!" Lebedev addressed Kolya in a

voice approaching authentic feeling. "As I have to acquaint the prince with a matter touching principally—"

"Oh well, of course, it's none of my business! Good-bye, Prince!" said Kolya, leaving at once.

"I like that boy for his quick understanding," declared Lebedev, watching him go. "An alert lad, but intrusive at times. I have met with a grievous misfortune, most respected Prince, last night or early this morning—I am not yet certain of the exact time."

"What happened?"

"The disappearance of four hundred roubles from my side coat pocket, most respected Prince—snatched from me!" Lebedev added with a sour smile.

"You lost four hundred roubles? Why, that's too bad."

"Particularly for a poor man living honorably on the fruits of his own labor."

"Of course, of course. How did it happen?"

"On account of wine, sir. I present myself to you as I would to Providence, most respected Prince. I received the sum of four hundred roubles in silver from a certain debtor yesterday at five o'clock, and I took the train back here. I had my billfold in my pocket. I put it in my coat pocket when I changed from my uniform, with a view to keeping it with me, intending to give it that evening to someone who had requested it. I was waiting for a business agent."

"By the way, Lukyan Timofeyitch, is it true that you put an advertisement in the papers saying that you lend money on gold and silver objects?"

"Through an agent. My name is not mentioned, neither is my address. Having only a trifling capital, sir, and a growing family, you must admit that a fair rate of interest—"

"Oh, yes. Of course. I only asked for information. Pardon me for interrupting."

"The agent did not come. Meanwhile the unhappy young man was brought here. I was already in a rather advanced condition, having dined; those guests arrived, we drank—tea, and—I became quite merry—to my downfall, sir. When that Keller arrived, quite late, and announced it was your birthday and orders were given concerning champagne, then, my dear and most respected Prince, having a heart (as you must have noticed already, since I merit it)—having a heart, I will not say sensitive, but grateful—and I'm proud of that, sir—I had the idea that to honor the solemnity of the evening more properly and anticipating the opportunity to congratulate you personally I should change from that shabby old coat of mine into my uniform, which I had taken off on arriving—a thing

461

which I did, as you doubtless observed, Prince, having seen me the whole evening in my uniform. Changing my clothes, I forgot the billfold in the pocket of the coat. Truly when God wishes to punish a man He first deprives him of his reason. And only this morning at half past seven when I woke up, I jumped out of bed like a madman, grabbed my coat the first thing—the pocket was empty! Not a single trace of the billfold."

"Ah, how unpleasant!"

"Certainly it's unpleasant! And with true tact you have hit upon the perfect phrase, sir," Lebedev added, not without slyness.

"Well, but after all—" said the prince uneasily, pondering. "That's serious, isn't it?"

"Certainly it's serious. Another word you've found to describe—"

"Oh, look here, Lukyan Timofeyitch, what is there to find? Words are not what matter. Do you suppose you could have dropped the billfold out of your pocket when you were drunk?"

"I could have. Anything is possible when one is drunk, as you have said so plainly yourself, most respected Prince. But look at it this way, sir: if I did drop the billfold out of my pocket while changing my coat, then the dropped article would have stayed right there on the floor where it was dropped, wouldn't it? Where, then, is that article, sir?"

"You didn't put it away in a drawer, or in a table, did you?"

"I've gone through everything, I've looked everywhere. Besides, I didn't hide it anywhere and I didn't open any drawers, as I clearly remember."

"Did you look in the little dresser cabinet?"

"The very first thing, sir. Looked there several times already. But how could I have put it away in the cabinet, truly respected Prince?"

"I must admit, Lebedev, this does upset me. It means someone must have found it on the floor."

"Or lifted it out of my pocket! Two alternatives, sir."

"This distresses me very much indeed, because who could have done it? That's the question!"

"Without a doubt, that is the great question. You have a way of finding the word, the nuance, the very definition of a situation with amazing exactness, most illustrious Prince."

"Oh, Lukyan Timofeyitch, stop being sarcastic. This is—"

"Sarcastic!" cried Lebedev, clasping his hands together.

"Well, well, all right. I'm not angry. It's something else— I'm afraid for the people who— Whom do you suspect?"

"A most difficult and—complicated question! I can't suspect the servant: she was sitting in the kitchen. Nor my own children either—"

"No indeed."

"So it must be one of the visitors, sir."

"But that's not possible, is it?"

"Absolutely and totally impossible, yet that's the way it has to be. However, I'm prepared to admit, indeed I am convinced that if it's a case of theft it was committed not in the evening when everyone was together but in the night or even in the morning, by someone who stayed over."

"Oh, Good Lord!"

"Burdovsky and Nikolai Ardalionovitch I naturally exclude. They didn't even enter my part of the house."

"I should think you would! And even if they had gone there. Who did spend the night there?"

"Including me, four people did, in two adjoining rooms. Myself, the general, Keller, and Mr. Ferdyshchenko. So it was one of us four, sir!"

"Of the three, you mean. But which one?"

"I counted myself to be fair and orderly, but I agree with you, Prince, that I couldn't have robbed myself, though cases have been known—"

"Oh, Lebedev, how tiresome this is!" exclaimed the prince impatiently. "Come to the point. Why drag it out?"

"Therefore, three remain, sir. And first of all, Mr. Keller, an unstable fellow, a drunken fellow, and in certain respects a liberal; I mean concerning—pockets, sir; with tendencies in other respects, so to speak, more feudal than liberal. He slept here first, in the sick man's room, and only came over to us in the night on the pretext that it's hard to sleep on a bare floor."

"You suspect him?"

"I did suspect him. When sometime after seven I jumped up like a madman and struck my brow with my hand I at once awakened the general, who was sleeping the sleep of the just. Taking into account the strange disappearance of Ferdyshchenko, which in itself had aroused our suspicions, we both decided immediately to search Keller, who was lying stretched out there like—like—almost like a nail, sir. We searched him thoroughly, he hadn't a kopeck in his pockets, and in fact we couldn't find a single pocket that didn't have holes in it. There was a blue check cotton handkerchief in a perfectly disgusting state, sir. There was also a love letter, just one love letter, from some kind of housemaid with demands for money and threats, and some scraps of the article which you know about. The general decided he was innocent. To further our investigation we woke him up personally, which took some shaking, sir. He could hardly make out what it was all about, his mouth hung wide open, he looked drunk; the expression of his face was absurd and innocent, silly even— It was not he, sir!"

"Well, I'm very glad!" the prince sighed joyfully. "I was afraid for him."

"Afraid for him? Then you had reasons to be?" said Lebedev, narrowing his eyes.

"Oh, no. I just said that," faltered the prince. "I was terribly foolish to say I was afraid for him. Do me a favor, Lebedev, don't mention it to anyone."

"Prince! Prince! Your words are sealed in my heart—in the depths of my heart. As in a tomb, sir," said Lebedev rapturously, pressing his hat to his heart.

"All right, all right! Then—it's Ferdyshchenko? I mean to say: you suspect Ferdyshchenko?"

"Who else?" demanded Lebedev softly, looking intently at the prince.

"Well, yes, of course. Who else is there? That is, there again, what evidence is there?"

"There is evidence, sir. First, his disappearance at seven or even before seven o'clock in the morning."

"I know. Kolya told me he came to him and said he was going to finish sleeping at—I forgot whose house—some friend of his."

"Vilkin, sir. So Nikolai Ardalionovitch has already spoken to you?"

"He said nothing about the theft."

"He doesn't know, for I've been keeping the matter quiet for the time being. So, he went to Vilkin's. Well, what would seem so amazing about one drunkard going to see another drunkard, even before dawn and without any reason, sir? But here is just where we pick up his track: as he left, he left an address. Now, Prince, follow my question: why did he leave an address? Why did he purposely go out of his way to see Nikolai Ardalionovitch to tell him, 'Now I'm going to sleep at Vilkin's.'? Because who would possibly be interested in the fact he was leaving, and to Vilkin's in particular? Why does he announce the fact? No, there is cunning here, sir, the cunning of a thief. It's the same as saying, 'Look, I expressly don't cover my tracks, so how can I be a thief?' Does a thief announce where he's going? This is an excess of care to avert suspicion and, you might say, to obliterate his footprints in the sand. Do you understand me, most respected Prince?"

"I understand. I have understood you very well, but that's not enough, is it?"

"A second piece of evidence, sir: the trail turns out to be false and the address wrong. An hour later—at eight o'clock, that is—I was knocking at Vilkin's; he lives here on Fifth Street, in fact I know him, sir. No sign of Ferdyshchenko. However, I did get the information from a servant woman—stone deaf, sir—that an hour earlier someone had actually been rapping and ringing at the door, and quite energetically because he broke the bell. But the servant hadn't opened the door, not wishing to wake Mr. Vilkin, and probably not wishing to get up herself. This happens, sir."

"And that's all your evidence? It's not much."

"But, Prince, who else is there to suspect? Judge for yourself!" concluded Lebedev with feeling, and there was something crafty in his grin.

"You should search your room and in the drawers once more!" the prince said anxiously, after a moment's thought.

"I have, sir!" Lebedev said, sighing even more feelingly.

"Hm! And why, why did you have to change your coat?" cried the prince, pounding the table in vexation.

"That's a question from stock comedy, sir. But, most benevolent Prince, you take my misfortune too much to heart! I don't deserve it. I mean I alone don't deserve it; but you're suffering for the criminal too, aren't you? For worthless Mr. Ferdyshchenko."

"Yes, indeed, you have worried me," the prince interrupted him distractedly and with displeasure. "So what do you intend to do—if you are so sure it was Ferdyshchenko?"

"Prince, most esteemed Prince, who else could it be?" said Lebedev fairly squirming with ingratiation. "You see, the lack of anyone else to suspect and, you might say, the complete impossibility of suspecting anyone except Mr. Ferdyshchenko, this is, so to speak, still another piece of evidence against Mr. Ferdyshchenko, the third! For, once again, who else could it be? I can't suspect Mr. Burdovsky, now can I? Heh, heh, heh!"

"Look here, what nonsense!"

"Or the general either, of course? Heh, heh, heh!"

"What wild nonsense is this?" said the prince almost angrily, turning impatiently in his seat.

"Indeed it is nonsense! Heh-heh-heh! And how he made me laugh—I mean the general, sir! There we were following the hot trail to Vilkin's—and you must observe that the gen-

465

eral was struck even more forcefully than I was, when I woke him up the first thing after discovering my loss, so much so that his face changed; he turned red, he turned pale, and finally flew into such a state of noble outrage that it was quite beyond anything I would have imagined, sir. He is a most honorable man! He does lie constantly—out of weakness—but he is a person of the highest sentiments, a person who, though of no great intellect, inspires absolute confidence through his innocence. I've already told you, most honored Prince, I not only have a weakness for him but a real affection. Suddenly he stopped in the middle of the street, opened his coat, and bared his chest: 'Search me,' says he. 'You searched Keller, why don't you search me? I insist on it,' he says, 'justice demands it.' His arms and legs were trembling, he was all pale, and very threatening. I laughed and said, 'Listen, General,' I said, 'if anyone else had said such a thing about you, I would have cut off my head with my own hands, put it on a big platter, and carried it myself to all those who doubted you: "Here, do you see this head?" I would say. "I will swear by him with this head of mine, and not only that, I'll go through fire for him." That's how I would have answered for you,' I said. Here he threw himself into my arms, right in the middle of the street, burst into tears, trembling, and held me so tight to his chest that I almost choked from coughing. 'You are the only friend left to me in my misfortunes,' he said. A man of great sensibility, sir! Well then, of course, as we continued on our way he very appropriately told me a story about how once in his youth he was suspected of stealing five hundred thousand roubles. The next day he had thrown himself into a burning house and dragged the count who had been suspecting him out of the flames, also Nina Alexandrovna, who was still a girl at the time. The count embraced him, and that is how his marriage to Nina Alexandrovna came about. And the next day in the ruins of the house they found a box with the missing money; it was an iron box of English manufacture with a secret lock, and somehow it had fallen under the floor in such a way that no one had noticed it, and was only found thanks to the fire. A complete lie, sir. But when he spoke of Nina Alexandrovna he was positively blubbering. A most noble person, Nina Alexandrovna, though she is furious with me."

"But you're not acquainted with her, are you?"

"Hardly at all, sir, but with all my heart I'd like to be, if only to justify myself to her. She's put out with me because she thinks I lead her husband into drunkenness. But far from leading him into it, I hold him back. I undoubtedly keep him from more pernicious company. Besides he's my friend and, I confess to you, I won't give him up now. I mean it's like this: wherever he goes, I go, because the only way to manage him is through his feelings. He doesn't visit the captain's widow at all now, though he secretly longs to go to her, and he sometimes even moans for her, especially in the morning when he gets up and is putting his boots on. I don't know why just at that particular time. He has no money, that's the trouble, and he can't go to her without money. Hasn't he asked you for money, most respected Prince?"

"No, he hasn't."

"He's ashamed to. He wanted to. He even admitted to me he intended to trouble you, but he was embarrassed because you helped him out not long ago, and besides, he thinks you wouldn't give it to him. He told me this as his friend."

"And you don't give him money?"

"Prince! Most worthy Prince! For that man I'd not only give money, I'd give my life, so to speak— No, I won't exaggerate, not my life, but if it was a question of enduring fever, boils, or even a bad cough, then, by heaven, I'd be ready to bear it for him, providing only that it was absolutely necessary; for I look on him as a great man, though a ruined one. Yes, sir. Not merely money."

"So you do give him money?"

"No, sir. Money I have not given him, and he knows himself that I don't give him money, sir. But this is only with a view to moderating and improving him. Now he's insisting on coming with me to Petersburg; yes, I'm going to Petersburg, sir, to follow the hot trail after Mr. Ferdyshchenko, since I know for certain he's there by now. The general is very excited, sir, but I suppose once in Petersburg he'll desert me to visit the widow. I must confess I'm even letting him go intentionally, as we've already planned to separate immediately on arrival and go in different directions so as to catch Mr. Ferdyshchenko more easily. So I'll let him go and then suddenly, like a ton of snow on his head, I'll surprise him at his widow's place—just to put him to shame, as a family man, and as a man generally speaking."

"But just don't stir up a lot of trouble, Lebedev, for heaven's sake, don't stir up a lot of trouble," said the prince in a low voice full of concern.

"Oh, no, sir. Merely to put him to shame and to see the look on his face, for much can be learned from a person's face, most respected Prince, especially the face of a man like that! Ah, Prince! Great as my own misfortune is, I can't help thinking of him and of the reformation of his morals. I have a great favor to ask of you, most respected Prince, and I'll even admit that it was especially for that that I came to see you. You know their household, sir, you have even lived with them, so if you should decide to help me, excellent Prince, entirely for the sake of the general and his happiness—"

Lebedev actually folded his hands as if at prayer.

"Help you? How could I help you? Please be assured that I am very anxious to understand you, Lebedev."

"Entirely in that conviction have I come to you, sir! It could be done through Nina Alexandrovna, watching and, you might say, stalking His Excellency in the bosom of his family. Unfortunately, I don't know her, sir. Also we have Nikolai Ardalionovitch, who adores you, you might say, with every fiber of his youthful soul, who also might be of some use—"

"No. Nina Alexandrovna brought into this business—God forbid. Or Kolya either. But perhaps I still don't understand you, Lebedev."

"But there's absolutely nothing to understand!" Lebedev jumped out of his chair. "Sympathy and tenderness! That's all the medicine our invalid needs. You will allow me to consider him as a sick person, Prince?"

"Yes, it even shows your delicacy and intelligence."

"I will explain by an example taken from practice, for the sake of clarity. You see the kind of man he is, sir: his one weakness now is that captain's widow, whom he can't go to see without money, and at whose house I intend to surprise him today. For his own welfare. But suppose it wasn't just the captain's widow, suppose he had actually committed some crime, or at least some very dishonorable action (though he is quite incapable of it), even then, I say, one can only have his way with him through what you might call noble tenderness, because he is such a sensitive man! Believe me, he wouldn't hold out five days, he'd speak right out, weep, and confess everything—particularly if one was to act adroitly and with nobility, through his family's vigilance and yours over every small move he makes, so to speak— Oh, most benevolent Prince!" said Lebedev jumping up in a state of inspired feeling. "Of course I'm not asserting that he definitely — I am prepared to shed every drop of my blood for him this very moment, so to speak, though you must admit that his incontinence and drunkenness and the captain's widow and all that taken together—might lead him to anything."

"I am always ready to assist in such a cause, certainly," said the prince, getting up, "though I must tell you, Lebedev,

468

I'm terribly uneasy. Tell me, you still— In a word, you say yourself that you suspect Mr. Ferdyshchenko."

"And who else? Who else could it be, most sincere Prince?" Again Lebedev clasped his hands touchingly, and smiled ingratiatingly.

The prince frowned and got up.

"Look here, Lukyan Timofeyitch, a mistake here would be dreadful. This Ferdyshchenko—I would not want to say anything bad about him—but this Ferdyshchenko—that is, who knows, perhaps it was he! I mean perhaps he really is more capable of this than—than someone else."

Lebedev's eyes widened and his ears pricked up.

"Look here," said the prince, frowning all the more and becoming more and more confused as he paced up and down the room trying not to look at Lebedev, "I was given to understand—I was told about Mr. Ferdyshchenko that he would appear to be, besides, the sort of man one must be careful not to say too much in front of, do you understand? I say this because perhaps he really is more capable of it than anyone else—so as not to make a mistake—that's the important thing, do you see?"

"But who told you that about Mr. Ferdyshchenko?" demanded Lebedev.

"Oh, it was whispered to me. However, I don't believe it myself—I am very annoyed that I had to tell you that; I assure you I don't believe it myself—it's some sort of nonsense. Oh, how stupid of me to repeat it!"

"You see, Prince," said Lebedev, all trembling, "this is important. It is extremely important now—that is, not about Mr. Ferdyshchenko but about how this information reached you." (Saying this, Lebedev trotted behind the prince, trying to keep in step with him.) "Let me tell you something now, Prince: this morning when the general and I were going together to Vilkin's, after he told me about the fire, of course, he was boiling with rage, and suddenly he started hinting the same thing about Mr. Ferdyshchenko, but so oddly and incoherently that I couldn't help asking him certain questions, as a result of which I became convinced that the whole report was his own inspiration—the result, you might say, of His Excellency's magnanimity. For he only tells lies when he is unable to control his own lofty emotions. Now, look at it this way, sir: if he's been lying—and I'm sure he has—how did you come to hear of it? Please understand, Prince, that for him this was the inspiration of the moment—so who, therefore, might have informed you of it? It's important and —you might say—"

"Kolya told me just now, and he heard it from his father, whom he met in the hall sometime after six o'clock when he was going out for some reason or other."

And the prince told him everything in detail.

"Well, this is what you can call a lead, sir!" Lebedev was laughing to himself and rubbing his hands. "Just as I thought! This means that His Excellency arose from his innocent sleep at six o'clock in order to go wake his beloved son and warn him of the extreme danger of associating with Mr. Ferdyshchenko. What a dangerous man Mr. Ferdyshchenko must appear after this! And how great His Excellency's parental solicitude! Heh-heh-heh!"

"Listen, Lebedev," said the prince, utterly confused. "Listen, act quietly. Don't make a row! I'm asking you, Lebedev, I'm begging you— In that case I swear I'll help you, but only if no one is to know, no one is to know!"

"You may rest assured, most benevolent, sincere and noble prince," cried Lebedev, definitely inspired. "You may rest assured that all this will be buried in my own noble heart! We will tread softly. Together! Yes, we will tread softly—together! I would even give my life's blood— Most illustrious Prince, I am mean of soul and spirit, but ask any poor fellow, or even a scoundrel, whether he would rather deal with a scoundrel like himself or a man of most noble soul like you, forthright Prince? He will answer: with a man of most noble soul, and therein lies the triumph of virtue! Good-bye, most respected Prince. We'll tread softly—softly and—together!"

Chapter TEN

The prince understood at last why he turned cold every time he touched those three letters and why he had put off reading them until the evening. When, that morning, he had fallen into a deep sleep on the couch without having brought himself to open any one of the three envelopes, he again had an oppressive dream, and again the same wicked woman came to him. Again she looked at him with tears shining on her long lashes, again she beckoned him to follow her, and again he awoke, as before, with an agonizing remembrance of her face. He had wanted to go to her at once, but he could not; finally, almost in despair, he opened the letters and began reading them.

Those letters were also like a dream. Sometimes one dreams strange dreams, impossible and unnatural, and upon waking you remember them clearly and are amazed by a very strange thing. You remember before anything else that your reason did not desert you throughout the whole dream; in fact you remember that you acted with extreme cunning and logic throughout; the long, long time you were surrounded by murderers trying to outwit you, disguising their intentions, behaving amicably while holding their weapons in readiness, and only awaiting some sort of signal; you remember how cleverly you fooled them at last, hiding from them; then you realize that they had seen through all your deceptions and were only pretending not to know where you were hidden; but you were clever and fooled them again. You remember all this clearly. But how in the same space of time can your reason be reconciled with the manifest absurdities and impossibilities with which your dream was filled? One of your murderers changed into a woman before your eyes, and from a woman into a clever, loathsome little dwarf—and you accepted all this instantly as absolute fact with hardly any surprise at all, and precisely at a time when otherwise your reason was at its highest pitch and showed extraordinary power, cunning, clarity, and logic. And why, too, when you have awaked and completely returned to reality do you feel almost always, and sometimes with extraordinary intensity, that you have left behind in your dream a mystery you cannot solve? You laugh at your dream's absurdities, and at the same time you feel that in the fabric of those absurdities some thought is hidden, but a thought that is real, something belonging to your actual life, something that exists and has always existed in your heart. It is as if something new, prophetic, something you were awaiting, has been told you in your dream; your impression is very vivid; it may be joyful or agonizing, but what it is and what was said to you, you can neither understand nor remember.

This was very nearly how it was after he read the letters. Yet even before opening them the prince felt that the fact of their existence and the very possibility of it was like a nightmare. How could *she* ever have brought herself to write *her*, he asked himself as he was wandering alone that evening (at times hardly knowing where he was going). How could she write *about that,* and how could such a fantastic idea have arisen in her mind? But the fantastic idea had become reality, and to him the most astonishing thing of all was that after he read those letters he himself almost believed in the possibility of that idea, and even its justification. Yes, of course it was a dream, a nightmare, a madness; but there was in it something painfully real and agonizingly true which justified the dream, the nightmare, the madness. For several hours he seemed almost delirious from what he had read, by moments recalling fragments of it, brooding over them, pondering them. Sometimes he was even inclined to believe that he had had a presentiment of all this and foreseen it; it even seemed to him that he had already read all this a long, long time ago, and that everything he had been longing for ever since, everything he had suffered from and feared, everything was in these letters he had read long ago.

"When you open this letter," (the first one began), "look at the signature first. The signature will tell you everything and make everything clear, so I have no need to justify myself before you or make any explanation. If I were in any way your equal, you might be offended by such audacity. But who am I and who are you? We are two such opposites, and I am so far beneath you that I could not possibly offend you even if I wished to."

In another place, further on, she wrote:

"Don't take my words as the morbid ravings of a sick mind, but to me you are perfection! I have seen you, I see you every day. I don't judge you, it is not through reason I have come to believe you are perfection, I simply have faith that you are. But there is also a wrong I do you: I love you. And perfection must not be loved, perfection can only be looked upon as perfection, isn't that so? And yet I am in love with you. Though love makes people equal, don't be afraid, even in my most secret thoughts I have not made you equal to me. I wrote 'don't be afraid'; could you possibly be afraid? If that were possible I would kiss your footprints. Oh, I don't put myself on a level with you. Look at the signature, quickly look at the signature!"

"I notice, though," (she wrote in another letter), "that I think of you and him together and I have never once asked whether you love him. He loved you after seeing you only once. He remembered you as 'light,' that was what he said, I heard it from him. But even without words I knew that you were light for him. I lived near him for a whole month and I understood then that you loved him too; you and he are one to me."

"What does this mean?" (she wrote in another letter).

472

"Yesterday I passed you and you seemed to blush. It can't be, I only imagined it. If one was to take you to the filthiest den and show you naked vice, you ought not to blush; you cannot possibly resent an offense. You can hate everyone who is vile and mean, but not for yourself, for others, for those they wrong. No one can wrong you. Do you know I think you even love me. For me you are what you are for him—a bright spirit; an angel cannot hate, cannot help loving. Can one love everyone, all people, all one's neighbors? I have often asked myself that question. Of course not, it would even be unnatural. In an abstract love for humanity one almost always loves only oneself. But this is impossible for us, and you are something else altogether: how could you not love someone when you can't compare yourself with anyone, and when you are above every insult, every personal resentment? You alone can love without egoism, you alone can love not for yourself but for the sake of whom you love. Oh, how much better it would be for me to find that you feel shame or outrage on my account! That would be your undoing: you would at once put yourself on my level—

"Yesterday, after meeting you, I went home and contrived a picture. Artists always paint Christ according to the Gospel stories; I would show Him differently; I would show Him alone—His disciples must have sometimes left Him alone. I would leave only a little child with Him. The child would be playing beside Him, perhaps would be telling Him something in his childish language. Christ would have been listening to him, but now He would be thoughtful, His hand still resting, heedless, forgotten, on the child's fair head. He gazes into the distance at the horizon; a thought as great as the whole world dwells in His eyes; His face is sorrowful. The child, silent, is leaning on Christ's knees, resting his cheek in his hand, his head raised, looking intently at Him, pondering as children sometimes do. The sun is setting. That is my picture! You are innocent, and in your innocence lies all your perfection. Oh, only remember that! How can this passion matter to you? Now you are mine already, I shall be near you all my life—I shall soon be dead."

Finally in the very last letter:

"For God's sake, don't think anything about me; don't think either that I am degrading myself by writing you this way, or that I am one of those creatures who takes pleasure in abasing themselves, though the pleasure really be from pride. No, I have my consolations; but it is hard for me to explain this to you. It would be hard even to express clearly to myself, though this torments me. But I know that I cannot abase myself even out of pride. And as for self-abasement out of purity of heart I am incapable of it. And so I am not humiliating myself at all.

"Why do I want to bring you together—for your sake, or for my own? For my own, of course; it would solve everything for me, I told myself that a long time ago. I heard that when she saw my portrait your sister Adelaïda said that with such beauty one could overturn the world. But I have renounced the world. Does it amuse you to hear this from me, having met me dressed in lace and diamonds in the company of drunkards and rogues? Don't mind that, I have almost ceased to exist and I know it. God only knows what lives on inside me in place of myself. I read it every day in two terrible eyes which stare at me constantly even when they are not actually present before me. Those eyes are *silent* now (they are always silent), but I know their secret. His house is dark and dreary, and there is a secret in it. I am convinced that hidden in his drawer is a razor, wrapped in silk, like that murderer in Moscow; he too lived in the same house with his mother and had wrapped a razor in silk to cut a throat with. The whole time I was in their house I had the impression that somewhere under the floorboards there was a dead body hidden, perhaps by his father, and wrapped in oilcloth like the one in Moscow, and surrounded in the same way by bottles of Zhdanov's fluid. I could even show you the part of the room. He is always silent; and yet I know that he loves me to the point that already he can only hate me. Your marriage and mine will be at the same time; we arranged this. I have no secrets from him. I would kill him out of terror, but he will kill me first. He laughed just now and said I was raving. He knows I am writing you."

And there was much, much more such raving in these letters. One of them, the second, written in a small hand, covered two large sheets of notepaper.

At last the prince left the dark park, where he had been wandering a long time, as he had done the day before. The clear transparent night seemed to him brighter than usual. "Can it still be so early?" he thought. (He had forgotten to take his watch.) Somewhere in the distance he seemed to hear music. "It must be at the station," he thought. "They certainly didn't go there today." As he realized this he saw that he was standing near their house; he had known that he would surely find himself there finally, and with a sinking heart he went up on the veranda. No one met him, the veranda was empty. He waited, then opened the door into the main room. "They never close that door," it occurred to him, but the room was empty. It was almost completely dark. He stood in the middle of the room in bewilderment. Suddenly a door opened and Alexandra Ivanovna came in with a candle in her hand. Seeing the prince she was surprised and stopped before him as if to question him. Apparently she was only crossing the room, from one door to another, with no thought of meeting anyone.

"How did you get here?" she said at last.

"I—just came in."

"Maman isn't quite well, neither is Aglaya. Adelaïda is going to bed and so am I. Today we've been home alone the whole evening. Papa and the prince are in Petersburg."

"I've come—I've come to you—now—"

"Do you know what time it is?"

"N-no."

"Half past twelve. We always go to bed at one."

"I—oh, I thought it was—half past nine."

"It doesn't matter!" she laughed. "And why didn't you come earlier? Perhaps you were expected."

"I thought—" he murmured, starting to leave.

"Good-bye! Tomorrow I will make them all laugh."

He walked by the road that circled the park to his own house. His heart was pounding, his thoughts were mixed up, and everything around him seemed like a dream. And suddenly, just as before when he had twice awakened at the same apparition, that apparition appeared before him. The same woman came out of the park and stood before him as if she had been there waiting for him. He gave a start and stood still: she seized his hand and pressed it tightly. "No, it isn't an apparition!"

And here at last she was standing face to face before him the first time since their parting; she was saying something to him, but he stared at her in silence; his heart overflowed and ached with pain. Oh, never would he forget his meeting with her, and he always remembered it with the same pain. She got down on her knees before him, there on the street, like one demented; he stepped back in horror, and she tried to catch at his hand to kiss it, and just as earlier in his dream, tears now glistened on her long lashes.

"Get up! Get up!" he said in a frightened whisper, trying to raise her. "Get up at once!"

"Are you happy? Happy?" she asked. "Say only one word to me, are you happy now? Today, now? With her. What did she say?"

She did not get up; she did not listen to him; she questioned him hurriedly and spoke rapidly, as if she was being pursued.

"I'm leaving tomorrow as you told me. I'm not going to— I'm seeing you for the last time. The last time! Now it is absolutely the last time!"

"Calm yourself! Get up!" he said in despair.

She looked at him avidly, seizing his hands. "Good-bye," she said at last; she got up and quickly left him, almost running. The prince saw that Rogozhin had suddenly appeared at her side, had taken her arm, and was leading her away.

"Wait, Prince," called Rogozhin. "I'll be back in five minutes." Five minutes later he did return; the prince was waiting for him at the same place.

"I've put her in the carriage," he said. "A carriage has been waiting for her around the corner since ten o'clock. She knew you would spend the whole evening with the other one. I told her exactly what you had written me today. She won't write the other one anymore; she promised; and she'll be leaving here tomorrow, as you wished. She wanted to see you for the last time, though you refused her. We've been waiting here for you to return, right there on that bench."

"And she brought you with her?"

"Why not?" Rogozhin grinned. "What I saw I knew already. You've read those letters, have you?"

"And have you really read them?" asked the prince, struck by this thought.

"Certainly. She showed me each letter herself. Remember about the razor? Heh-heh!"

"She's mad!" cried the prince, wringing his hands.

"Who can tell? Perhaps not," said Rogozhin softly, as though to himself.

The prince did not reply.

"Well, good-bye," said Rogozhin. "I'm going tomorrow too. Don't think badly of me! And why is it, my friend," he added, turning quickly, "why is it you didn't answer her question? Are you happy or not?"

"No, no, no!" cried the prince with infinite sadness.

"I'd hardly think you'd say 'yes'!" Rogozhin said with a malicious laugh, and he went away without looking back.

476

PART

FOUR

Chapter ONE

⁓⦿⁓

About a week had passed since the two persons of our story met on the green bench. One bright morning at about half past ten Varvara Ardalionovna Ptitsyn, who had gone out to visit some friends, returned home in a state of sorrowful preoccupation.

There are people about whom it is difficult to say anything which would describe them immediately and fully in their most typical and characteristic aspects; these are the people who are usually called "ordinary" and accounted as "the majority," and who actually do make up the great majority of society. In their novels and stories writers most often try to choose and present vividly and artistically social types which are extremely seldom encountered in real life, and which are nevertheless more real than real life itself. Podkolyosin,* viewed as a type, is perhaps exaggerated, but he is hardly unknown. How many clever people having learned from Gogol about Podkolyosin at once discover that great numbers of their friends bear a terrific resemblance to Podkolyosin. They knew before Gogol that their friends were like Podkolyosin, except they did not know yet that that was their name. In real life bridegrooms very seldom jump out of windows before their weddings, because, apart from other considerations, it is inconvenient; yet how many grooms, even worthy and clever people, have at the bottom of their hearts been ready to admit just before their weddings that they were Podkolyosins. And not all husbands shout at every step, *"Tu l'as voulu, Georges Dandin!"* But Good Lord, how many millions and billions of times has this heartfelt cry been uttered by husbands the world over after their honeymoon, and—who knows?—perhaps the very day after the wedding!

Therefore, without entering more deeply into the matter,

we shall only say in real life typical characteristics seem to be watered down, and that all these Georges Dandins and Podkolyosins do exist and are running around before our eyes every day, but in a diluted state. Finally, with the qualification, for the sake of the whole truth, that the essential Georges Dandin as Molière created him can also be met in real life, though rarely, we conclude our discussion, which is beginning to resemble the criticism one finds in periodicals. Nevertheless the question remains before us: what is the novelist to do with absolutely "ordinary" people, and how can he present them to readers so that they are at all interesting? To leave them out of a story completely is not possible, because ordinary people are at every moment, by and large, the necessary links in the chain of human affairs; leaving them out, therefore, means to destroy credibility. To fill a novel entirely with types or, simply for the sake of interest, strange and unheard-of people, would be improbable and most likely not even interesting. In our opinion the writer must try to find interesting and informative touches even among commonplace people. When, for example, the very nature of certain ordinary persons consists precisely of their perpetual and unvarying ordinariness, or, better still, when in spite of their most strenuous efforts to lift themselves out of the rut of ordinariness and routine, they still end forever in the identical unvarying routine, then such persons acquire a certain character of their own—the typical character of mediocrity which refuses to remain what it is and desires at all costs to become original and independent, without having the slightest capacity for independence.

To this category of "commonplace" or "ordinary" people belong certain persons of our story who have until now, I must confess, been insufficiently explained to the reader. Such, namely, are Varvara Ardalionovna Ptitsyn, her husband Ptitsyn, and her brother Gavril Ardalionovitch.

There is, indeed, nothing more vexing than to be, for example, rich, of good family, of decent appearance, fairly well educated, not stupid, rather good-hearted even, and at the same time to possess no talent, no special quality, no eccentricity even, not a single idea of one's own, to be precisely "like everyone else." One is rich, but not so rich as Rothschild; of a good family, but one which has never distinguished itself in any way; of decent appearance, but an appearance expressive of very little; well educated, but without knowing what to do with that education; one is intelligent, but without one's own ideas; one is good-hearted, but without greatness of soul, and so on and so forth. There are a great number of such people in the world, far more than it appears. Like all people, they may be divided into two categories: some are mentally limited, others "much cleverer." The first are happier. For the "ordinary" person of limited intelligence nothing is easier than to imagine himself an exceptional and original person and to take delight in this delusion with no misgivings. It has been enough for some of our young ladies to cut their hair short, put on blue eyeglasses, and call themselves Nihilists for them to persuade themselves that, in putting on their spectacles, they immediately acquired "convictions" of their own. It is enough for a man to feel in his heart a droplet of humanitarian and benevolent emotion to be immediately persuaded that no one feels so deeply as he and that he stands at the very vanguard of civilization. It is enough for another to pick up some thought he has heard, or to read a page at random somewhere, to believe at once that it was "his own idea," engendered in his own brain. Naïve arrogance—if one may so express it—reaches extraordinary proportions in such cases; it is all quite unbelievable, yet very frequently met with. This naïve arrogance, this perfect confidence of the stupid man in himself and his own talent is superbly portrayed by Gogol in his marvelous character Lieutenant Pirogov.* Pirogov has no doubt that he is a genius, and even superior to all other geniuses; in fact, he is so certain of it that he never once questions himself on the matter; indeed, for him questions do not exist. The great writer was forced in the end to have him thrashed in order to appease his reader's outraged moral feelings, but, finding that the great man only shook himself off after the ordeal and consumed a small layered pastry to fortify himself, he threw up his hands in amazement and left his readers to make of him what they would. I have always regretted that Gogol gave the great Pirogov such a humble rank, for Pirogov is so self-satisfied that nothing would be easier for him than to imagine himself—as his epaulettes grew thicker and more tangled with the years and promotions—an extraordinary military leader; or rather not imagine it, but simply fail to doubt it: he was made a general, so he must be a great military leader! How many such warriors have afterward perpetrated dreadful fiascoes on the field of battle? And how many Pirogovs have there been among our men of letters, our savants, our propagandists? I say "have been," but of course they exist still.

One of the characters in our story, Gavril Ardalionovitch Ivolgin, belonged to the other category; he belonged to the category of "much cleverer" people; though from head to toe he was infected with the desire to be original. But this class of person, as we have observed above, is far less happy than the first. The difficulty is that the intelligent "ordinary" man, even if he does imagine himself at times (and perhaps all his life) a person of genius and originality, nevertheless retains within his heart a little worm of doubt, which sometimes leads the intelligent man in the end to absolute despair. If he does yield in this belief, he is still completely poisoned with inward-driven vanity. However, we have taken an extreme example: in the vast majority of cases in this *intelligent* category of people things do not end at all so tragically; the liver becomes more or less affected toward the end, that is all. However, before giving in and resigning themselves, these people sometimes play the fool for an extremely long time, from early youth to maturity, and all out of a yearning for originality. There are even strange instances of this: from the desire for originality an honest man is ready to do something base; it even happens that one of these wretched men is not only honest but good, and by his own labors provides not only for his own family but for strangers—and what happens to him? His whole life he can never be at peace! The thought that he has so well fulfilled his human obligation is no comfort or consolation to him; on the contrary, it even irritates him: "This," he says, "is what I've wasted all my life on. This is what has bound me hand and foot. This is what has prevented me from making a great discovery! If it wasn't for this, I certainly would have discovered something—gunpowder or perhaps America—I don't know precisely what, but I certainly would have discovered it!" What is most characteristic about these gentlemen is that all their lives they can never find out for certain precisely what it is they have to discover, what all their lives they are just on the point of discovering: gunpowder or America? But their suffering from the longing for discovery would have indeed satisfied a Columbus or a Galileo.

Gavril Ardalionovitch had started down this road, but he had only started. He still had a long time before him to play the fool. A profound and relentless awareness of his own mediocrity and, at the same time, an implacable wish to convince himself that he was a man of perfect independence had rankled in his heart since early boyhood. He was a young man of envious and impetuous cravings, and he seemed to have been born with his nerves overwrought. The impulsiveness of his desires he took for their strength. In his passionate yearning to distinguish himself he was sometimes prepared to take the most reckless step, but as soon as the moment came our hero was always too sensible to make the leap. That hurt him deeply. Perhaps, on occasion, he would have even made up his mind to do something ignominious, merely to attain something he dreamed of; but it happened, fatefully, that no sooner had the point of action been reached than he always found himself too honest to do anything ignominious. (He was always ready, however, to agree to a trifling base action.) He viewed poverty and the downfall of his family with loathing and hatred. He even treated his mother with haughtiness and contempt, though he knew very well that the character and reputation of his mother were for the moment the pivotal point of his own career.

When he entered General Yepanchin's service, he had promptly said to himself, "If I'm to be lowly, let me be really lowly, just so long as I come out on top"—and he was hardly ever really lowly. And why did he think he would necessarily have to be? At the time, he was simply frightened of Aglaya, but he kept on with her just on the chance—though he never seriously believed she would stoop to him. Afterward, at the time of his affair with Nastassya Filippovna, he suddenly imagined that money was the means of attaining *everything*. "If I'm to crawl then I'll crawl," he would repeat to himself every day with satisfaction, but also a certain fear. "If we're to be abject, let's make a good job of it," he spurred himself every other minute. "Ordinary people would be afraid, but we are not!" Having lost Aglaya and crushed by circumstances, he completely lost heart and actually brought the prince the money a madwoman had flung at him and which had been brought to her by a madman. Afterward he regretted returning the money a thousand times, though he prided himself as incessantly on having done so. He actually wept for three days while the prince was in Petersburg, but in those three days he came to hate the prince because the latter viewed him too compassionately for having returned such a sum of money, though "not everyone would have had the strength for such a deed." But the frank admission to himself that all his grief was due to nothing but his perpetually crushed vanity distressed him terribly. Only much later did he realize what a serious turn his affair with such a strange and innocent creature as Aglaya might have taken. He was consumed with remorse; he gave up his job and was plunged into anguish and despondency. With his mother and father he lived at Ptitsyn's at his host's expense, and he despised Ptitsyn openly, though at the same time he listened to his advice and almost always had the good sense to ask him for it. Gavril Ardalionovitch was for instance annoyed because Ptitsyn did not propose to become a Rothschild and had not set this goal for himself. "If one's a usurer, one should go all the way, squeeze people, wring money out of them, be somebody, be a king of Judea!" Ptitsyn was modest and quiet; he only smiled, but once he did find it necessary to speak seriously with Ganya, and he did so with a certain dignity. He proved to Ganya that he was not doing anything dishonest, and that it was unjust to treat him as a grasping Jew, that it was not his fault money was so dear, that he was acting honestly and justly, and that in actuality he was only an agent in these affairs, and that, finally, thanks to his exactness in business matters he was already very well regarded by the best people and his business was increasing. "I won't be a Rothschild," he said with a laugh, "and I don't want to be. But I'll have a house on Liteyny Avenue, and perhaps even two, and there I shall stop." "But who knows, perhaps even three!" he added to himself, but he never said it aloud, hiding his dream. Nature loves such people and cares for them tenderly: she will reward Ptitsyn not with three but with four houses, and precisely because he knew from childhood he would never be a Rothschild. But beyond four houses nature will not go, and for Ptitsyn that is where it will all end.

Gavril Ardalionovitch's sister was a completely different sort of person. She too had strong desires, but they were persistent rather than impulsive. She had a great deal of good sense whenever a crisis threatened. It is true that she too was one of the "ordinary" people who dream of being original, but she was able very early to realize that she had not the slightest shadow of originality, and she did not lament about this too much, perhaps—who knows?—out of a special sort of pride. She took her first practical step with great deliberation in marrying Ptitsyn, but in marrying she did not say to herself, "If I must demean myself I will do so, as long as I get what I want," as Gavril Ardalionovitch would have surely expressed himself in such circumstances (and indeed as he very nearly did say in her presence when, as her older brother, he approved her decision). In fact, quite to the contrary, Varvara Ardalionovitch married after having firmly assured herself that her future husband was a modest, pleasant, almost cultivated man who would never do anything really dishonorable. About minor acts of meanness Varvara Ardalionovna did not concern herself; they were trifles, and where were trifling meannesses not found? She was not searching for an ideal! Besides, she knew that by marrying she would provide a place for her mother, her father, and her brother. Seeing her brother in difficulty, she wanted to help him in spite of all their past family misunderstandings. Ptitsyn sometimes got after Ganya—in a friendly way, of course—to find another job in the administration. "Here you despise generals and the generalcy," he would sometimes say to him jokingly, "but watch out, 'they' will all end up being generals in their turns. Live long enough and you will see." "Where do they get the idea I despise generals and the generalcy?" Ganya thought to himself sarcastically. In order to help her brother, Varvara Ardalionovna decided to enlarge her field of action: she ingratiated herself with the Yepanchins, an endeavor greatly aided by childhood memories; both she and her brother had played with the Yepanchin girls as children. We may observe here that if Varvara Ardalionovna had been pursuing some sort of extraordinary dream in visiting the Yepanchins she would perhaps have at once emerged from that category of people in which she had decided she belonged; but she was not pursuing a dream; there was even a fairly well-grounded calculation on her part: she was counting on the particular character of this family. As for Aglaya's character, she never tired of studying it. She set herself the task of bringing these two, Aglaya and her brother, together again. Perhaps she actually did achieve something; perhaps, too, she blundered, counting too much, for instance, on her brother and expecting from him what he never possibly could have given. In any case she acted quite adroitly at the Yepanchins': for weeks at a time she made no allusion to her brother; she was always extremely truthful and direct; she behaved simply but with dignity. As for her conscience, she was not afraid to look into it and did not reproach herself for anything whatever. It was this that gave her strength. There was only one thing she sometimes noticed in herself, that she too was easily irritated, that she too had a great deal of pride, and indeed perhaps of smothered vanity. She noticed this especially at certain moments, almost every time she was returning home from the Yepanchins'.

And just now she was returning home from them, as we have already said, in a state of sorrowful preoccupation. There appeared to be a trace of bitter mockery in her distress. In Pavlovsk, Ptitsyn lived in an unattractive but spacious wooden house located in a dusty street, and of which he was shortly to have full ownership, so that he was already negotiating to sell it to someone. As she was going up the front steps Varvara Ardalionovna heard an exceedingly loud noise from upstairs and she made out the voices of her brother and her father, shouting. Upon entering the main room and seeing Ganya running back and forth, pale with

485

rage and nearly tearing his hair, she frowned and with a tired air sank into the sofa without taking off her hat. Knowing full well that if she kept silent any longer and failed to ask her brother why he was running around in such a state he would certainly be very angry with her, Varya hastened to ask, "The same thing?"

"The same thing indeed!" cried Ganya. "No! The devil only knows what's going on here, but it's not the same thing! The old man is going raving mad—Mother's wailing. By God, Varya, do as you like, but I'm going to turn him out of the house, or else I'll go away myself," he added, probably remembering that one could not turn a person out of someone else's house.

"One must make allowances," murmured Varya.

"Allowances? For what? For whom?" shouted Ganya, flaring up. "For his abominations? No, say what you please, that's impossible! Impossible, impossible, impossible! And what a way to behave: he's the one to blame and still he goes swaggering around! The gate won't do for him, take down the fence!— Why are you sitting there like that? You don't look yourself."

"I look the same as always," Varya answered, displeased.

Ganya looked at her more closely.

"You were there?"

"Yes."

"Listen, they're shouting again. It's a disgrace, and at such a time too."

"What sort of time? It's no special time." Ganya looked at his sister more intently than ever.

"Did you find out anything?" he asked.

"Nothing unexpected anyway. I found out that it's all true. My husband was more right than either of us, it's happened just as he predicted from the very beginning. Where is he?"

"He's not here. What's happened?"

"The prince is formally engaged to her, it's all settled. The older girls told me. Aglaya has consented; they're not even keeping it secret anymore. You know there was always such a mystery about it until now. Adelaïda's wedding will be put off again so they can have the two weddings on the same day —how romantic! It's like a poem. Yes, you'd do better to write a poem on the nuptial occasion than be pacing up and down the room like that. Belokonskaya will be with them this evening; she's come just in time; there will be guests. He will be presented to Belokonskaya, though he has met her already. I understand the engagement is to be announced. They're only afraid he'll drop or break something when he comes into the room with the guests, or that he'll fall down. It's the sort of thing he would do."

Ganya listened very attentively, but to his sister's surprise the news did not seem to have any striking effect on him at all.

"Well, it was clear enough," he said after a moment's thought. "So, that's the end!" he added with a strange smile, glancing slyly at his sister's face and still pacing the room, but more calmly now.

"It's a good thing you take it like a philosopher," said Varya. "I'm glad, really."

"Yes, it is a relief—for you, at least."

"I'd say I've done well enough by you, without arguing and without being any trouble to you. I didn't ask you what sort of happiness you were looking for with Aglaya."

"But was I looking for—happiness with Aglaya?"

"Now, please don't try to be philosophical about it! Of course you were. Of course you were, and it's all over for us; we've been made fools of and we've lost. I confess I never did take it seriously. I only took it up on the off chance, counting on her peculiar character, and mainly to please you; there were nine chances in ten it would fail. Even now I have no idea what you were trying to get out of it."

"Now you and your husband will be after me to look for a job, giving me lectures on perseverance and willpower and not despising small endeavors—I know it all by heart." Ganya burst out laughing.

Varya thought: "He has something new on his mind!"

"How are they taking it over there? The parents—are they pleased?" Ganya suddenly demanded.

"No, I don't think so. However, you can judge for yourself. Ivan Fyodorovitch is content enough. The mother is uneasy. She has always looked on him with loathing as a suitor. Everyone knew that."

"I don't mean that. He's an impossible, unthinkable fiancé, that's obvious. I mean what's happening there right now? Has she given her formal consent?"

"So far she hasn't said 'no,' that's all; but you wouldn't expect anything else from her. You know how madly shy and modest she still is. When she was a child she'd climb into a cupboard and sit there for two or three hours just to avoid coming out to the guests. She's grown like a weed now, but she's still the same. You know, I think there is really something serious there, even on *her* side. They say she laughs at the prince from morning to night, so as to conceal that she manages to say something to him in secret every day, as she must, because he seems to be walking on air. He is glowing with happiness. They say he's dreadfully funny. I heard it from them. I also had the impression they were laughing at me, the older girls."

Ganya at last began to frown; perhaps Varya was intentionally enlarging on the subject in order to find out what he was really thinking. But again there was shouting upstairs.

"I'll turn him out," roared Ganya, glad for something to vent his annoyance upon.

"And then he'll go out again and disgrace us everywhere as he did yesterday."

"Yesterday? What do you mean as he did yesterday? Could he have—" Ganya was suddenly terribly alarmed.

"Good Lord, don't you know?" said Varya.

"What! Could he really have been there?" cried Ganya, flushing crimson with shame and rage. "But you just came from there! Did you find out something? Was the old man there? Was he or not?"

And Ganya rushed for the door; Varya went after him and seized him with both hands.

"What are you doing? Where are you going?" she said. "Let him go out now and he'll do still worse, he'll go to everyone."

"What did he do there? What did he say?"

"They couldn't tell me themselves, they didn't understand; he only frightened them all. He went to see Ivan Fyodorovitch, he wasn't there; he demanded Lizaveta Prokofyevna. First he asked her for a job, to place him with the administration, and then he began complaining about us, about me, about my husband, particularly about you— He did say quite a lot."

"You couldn't find out what?" Ganya was trembling as if in hysterics.

"And how could I? He hardly knew what he was saying himself, and they probably didn't tell me everything."

Ganya clutched at his head and ran to the window; Varya sat down by the other window.

"Aglaya is very odd," she said suddenly. "She stopped me and said, 'Please give my special personal regards to your parents, and I will certainly find an opportunity to see your father one of these days.' And she said that seriously. It was very strange."

"Didn't she say it sarcastically?"

"No, not at all. That's what was so strange."

"Does she know about the old man or not? What do you think?"

"They don't know about it in the house, I'm sure of that. But you've given me an idea: perhaps Aglaya does know. She would be the only one to know because her sisters were also surprised when she sent regards to Father in that serious way. And why to him in particular? If she does know, the prince must have told her."

"It's not hard to guess who told her! A thief! That's all we needed. A thief in our family, 'the head of the family'!"

"That's nonsense!" shouted Varya, losing her temper. "A drunken story, that's all. And who thought it up? Lebedev, the prince—a fine lot themselves, a very wise lot. I don't give it any importance."

"The old man is a thief and a drunkard," Ganya went on bitterly. "I'm a beggar, my sister's husband is a usurer—that's enough to sweep Aglaya off her feet! No, really, it's lovely!"

"This sister's husband, this usurer—"

"Feeds me, is that it? Please don't hesitate to say it."

"Why are you so angry?" said Varya, restraining herself. "You don't understand anything, you're like a schoolboy. You think all this could hurt you in Aglaya's eyes? You don't know her. She'd turn away the most eligible suitor and run off happily with some student to die of hunger in a garret with him—that's her dream! You've never understood how interesting you would have been to her if you could have borne our situation with firmness and pride. The prince caught her because, in the first place, he wasn't trying to catch her and, in the second, because everyone regards him as an idiot. The very fact she's stirred up the family over him is what appeals to her now. Oh, you don't understand a thing!"

"Well, we'll see whether we understand or not," Ganya muttered enigmatically. "Still, I wouldn't want her to find out about the old man. I thought the prince would be able to keep his mouth shut. He kept Lebedev quiet, and, even when I insisted, he wasn't ready to tell me everything."

"So you can see for yourself that everything was already known without him. And what does it matter to you now? What are you hoping for? And even if you had a hope left, it would only make you look like a martyr in her eyes."

"Well, she'd be afraid of a scandal, in spite of all her romanticism. Everything within limits, everything within reason. You're all the same."

"Aglaya afraid?" Varya flared up, looking contemptuously at her brother. "What a mean little soul you have! You are all worthless. She may be peculiar and eccentric but she's a thousand times nobler than all of us."

"Well, never mind, never mind, don't be angry!" Ganya murmured again complacently.

"I'm only sorry for Mother," Varya went on. "I'm afraid this story about Father has reached her. Oh, I am afraid it has!"

"Certainly it has," remarked Ganya.

Varya had gotten up to go upstairs to Nina Alexandrovna, but she stopped and looked attentively at her brother.

"Who could have told her?"

"Hippolite probably. I suppose he took great pleasure in reporting it to Mother as soon as he moved in with us."

"But how does he know, please tell me? The prince and Lebedev decided not to tell anyone. Even Kolya doesn't know anything."

"Hippolite? He found out himself. You can't imagine what a clever creature he is, and what a gossip, and what a nose he has for smelling out anything bad, anything scandalous. Yes, believe it or not but I'm sure he's taken Aglaya in hand! And if he hasn't, he will. Rogozhin has been seeing him too. How is it the prince doesn't notice this? And how he wants to get at me now! He considers me a personal enemy; I found that out a long time ago. And why? What good will it do him, since he's dying? I can't understand it. But I'll fool him; you'll see, he won't get at me. I'll get at him."

"Why did you have him come here if you hate him so much? And is he worth getting at?"

"You advised me to have him come here."

"I thought he would be useful, but did you know he's fallen in love with Aglaya himself now and has been writing her? They were asking me—he may even have written to Lizaveta Prokofyevna."

"He's not dangerous that way," said Ganya with a malicious laugh. "Still, there must be something else to this. Most likely he's fallen in love, because he's only a boy! But—he wouldn't write anonymous letters to the old lady. He's such a nasty, insignificant, self-satisfied little mediocrity! I'm convinced, in fact I know for certain, he's presented me to her as a schemer—he began with that. But I must admit that like a fool I spoke too freely with him at first. I thought that out of a simple desire to revenge himself on the prince he would go along with my interests. He's such a clever creature! Oh, I've seen through him completely now. And as for that theft, he heard about it from his mother, the captain's widow. If the old man did bring himself to do it, it was for her sake. Suddenly out of the blue he told me that the 'general' promised his mother four hundred roubles; just like that, completely

490

out of the blue. Then I understood the whole thing. And there he was, staring me right in the face with a sort of delight; he must have told Mother about it too just for the pleasure of breaking her heart. And why on earth doesn't he die! He was going to die in three weeks, and here he is getting fatter! He's stopped coughing. Last night he said himself he hadn't coughed blood in two days."

"Send him away."

"I don't hate him, I despise him," Ganya declared proudly. "Well, no, I do hate him, I do!" he suddenly shouted with extraordinary fury. "And I'll tell him so to his face, even when he lies there dying on his bed! If you'd only read his confession—Good Lord, what naïve impertinence. He's a Lieutenant Pirogov, he's a tragic Nozdryov*—and, above all, he's a miserable little boy! Oh, how I'd have enjoyed giving him a thrashing, just to surprise him. Now he wants to get even with everyone because the other day he failed to— But what's that? More noise again! What is going on, for heaven's sake?" Ptitsyn came into the room. "I won't put up with this anymore!" he shouted to his brother-in-law. "What is it? What are we all coming to finally? This is— This is—"

But the noise was rapidly approaching them, the door suddenly flew open, and old Ivolgin, furious, purple in the face, beside himself with rage, also set upon Ptitsyn. The old man was followed by Nina Alexandrovna, Kolya, and, behind them all, Hippolite.

Chapter TWO

It was five days since Hippolite had moved to Ptitsyn's house. It had somehow happened naturally, without anything special being said and without any falling out between him and the prince; far from quarreling, they even seemed to have parted friends. Gavril Ardalionovitch, who had been so hostile to Hippolite on that earlier evening, came to see him himself, though not until three days afterward, probably directed there by some sudden idea. For some reason Rogozhin too had taken to visiting the invalid. At first the prince thought that it would actually be better for the "poor boy" if he moved out of his house. But when he was moving he stated that he was going to stay with Ptitsyn "who was so kind as to give him a little corner," and not once, as if expressly meaning not to, did he say that it was Ganya he was going to stay with, though it was Ganya who had insisted on his being received into the house. Ganya noticed this at the time and let the offense weigh on his heart.

He was right when he told his sister that the invalid was getting better. Hippolite was indeed somewhat improved, a fact which was evident at first glance. He came into the room, in no hurry, after everyone else, with a sarcastic and malevolent smile on his face. Nina Alexandrovna came in, very frightened. (She had greatly changed in the last six months; she was thinner; since she had married off her daughter and moved in with her, she seemed, outwardly, to have stopped partaking in her children's affairs.) Kolya was worried and looked bewildered; there was a great deal he did not understand in the general's "insanity," as he expressed it, being unaware, of course, of the real reasons for this new disturbance in the house. But it was clear to him that his father was quarreling, now, everywhere he went and that he had suddenly changed so much that he no longer seemed to be the same man. He was worried too by the fact that for the past three days the old man had completely stopped drinking. He knew that he had broken with and even quarreled with Lebedev and the prince. Kolya had just returned home with a half pint of vodka, paid for out of his own money.

"Really, Mother," he had assured Nina Alexandrovna upstairs, "really, it's better to let him drink. It's three days now since he's touched a drop, so he's feeling miserable. It would really be better. I used to take it to him in the prison."

The general threw the door wide open and stood on the threshold, trembling with indignation.

"My dear sir!" he shouted in a thunderous voice to Ptitsyn. "If you have actually decided upon sacrificing to a milksop and an atheist a venerable old man, your father, that is, at least, your wife's father, who has served his sovereign, then I will never again set foot in your house from this very hour. Sir. Choose! Choose at once: either me or this—screw! Yes, screw! I said it by accident, but he is a screw! Because he bores into my soul with a screw—and without the least respect. With a screw!"

"You don't mean a corkscrew, do you?" Hippolite put in.

"No, not a corkscrew. For I stand before you as a general, sir, and not a bottle. I have decorations, decorations for distinguished service. And you—you have nothing! It's either he or I. Make up your mind, dear sir, at once, this very minute," he shouted again frantically to Ptitsyn. Just then, Kolya placed a chair for him, and he sank into it exhausted.

"It would really be better—if you had a nap," murmured Ptitsyn, overwhelmed.

"And *he's* threatening!" said Ganya to his sister in an undertone.

"A nap!" cried the general. "I am not drunk, my dear sir, and you are insulting me. I can see," he went on, getting up again, "I can see that everything here is against me, everything and everybody. That does it! I'm leaving— But let me tell you, dear sir, let me tell you—"

He was not allowed to finish; they made him sit down and begged him to calm himself. Ganya, in a rage, retired into a corner. Nina Alexandrovna was trembling and weeping.

"What have I done to him? What's he complaining about?" cried Hippolite, grinning.

"What have you done?" Nina Alexandrovna said suddenly. "It's particularly shameful it should be you—it's inhuman to torment an old man—and in your position, too."

"First of all, what is my position, madam? I respect you very much, in particular, you, personally, but—"

"He's a screw!" cried the general. "He bores into my heart and soul! He wants to believe in atheism. Let me tell you, milksop, you weren't even born at a time I was being showered with honors. And you are nothing but an envious worm, racked with coughing and—dying of spite and lack of faith. And why did Gavril bring you here? Everyone's against me —from perfect strangers to my own son."

"Oh, stop acting out a tragedy!" cried Ganya. "Don't disgrace us all over town and everything would be better!"

"What? I disgrace you, milksop! You? I can only do you honor, I cannot disgrace you!"

He jumped up and they could not restrain him now, but Gavril Ardalionovitch obviously could not control himself either.

"You talk about honor!" he cried angrily.

"What did you say?" thundered the general, turning pale and taking a step toward him.

"I said that all I have to do is open my mouth for—" roared Ganya suddenly, then broke off. They stood facing each other, both terribly shaken, Ganya especially.

"Ganya, what are you doing?" cried Nina Alexandrovna, rushing forward to restrain her son.

"This is all nonsense!" Varya snapped in indignation. "Calm yourself, Mother," she said, taking hold of her.

"It's only for Mother's sake that I spare him," Ganya declared tragically.

"Speak!" roared the general, completely beside himself. "Speak on pain of a father's curse—speak!"

"So you think I'm afraid of your curse! And whose fault is it that for the past eight days you've been acting like a madman? Eight days—you see I keep track. Watch out you don't drive me too far. I'll tell everything. Why did you drag yourself off to the Yepanchins' yesterday? And you call yourself an old man, white-haired, the father of a family. It's too lovely!"

"Shut up, Ganya!" Kolya shouted. "Shut up, you fool!"

"And I? How have I offended him?" Hippolite persisted still in the same sarcastic tone of voice. "Why does he call me a screw? You heard him. He's the one who was bothering me. Came to me a while ago and started telling me about some Captain Yeropegov. I don't want your company, General; I've avoided it all along, you know that yourself. What is Captain Yeropegov to me? Admit it, sir. I didn't come here on account of Captain Yeropegov. I only expressed my opinion that this Captain Yeropegov probably never existed at all. And he started raising the devil."

"He certainly never existed!" Ganya cut in.

But the general stood there as if stunned and looked around in a dazed way. He was violently struck by the extraordinary frankness of what his son had said, and in the first instant he could not even find anything to reply. Finally, only when Hippolite had burst out laughing at Ganya's answer and cried out, "Well, there, you heard! Your own son too says there was no such person as Captain Yeropegov," the old man muttered, completely disconcerted:

"Kapiton Yeropegov, not Captain—Kapiton—the retired lieutenant colonel—Yeropegov—Kapiton."

"And there was no Kapiton either!" cried Ganya, thoroughly exasperated.

"Why—why wasn't there?" murmured the general, his face coloring.

"That's enough!" said Ptitsyn and Varya, trying to stop them.

"Shut up, Ganya!" Kolya shouted again.

But these interventions seemed to bring the general to his senses.

"What do you mean there wasn't? Why wouldn't there be?" he said menacingly to his son.

494

"Because there wasn't. He didn't exist, that's all. And he couldn't have existed. That's all there is to it. Leave me alone, I tell you."

"And this is my son, my own son, whom I— Oh, Lord! Yeropegov—Yeroshka Yeropegov didn't exist!"

"There you are!" put in Hippolite. "First he's Kapitoshka, now he's Yeroshka!"

"Kapitoshka, sir! Kapitoshka, not Yeroshka! Kapiton, Kapiton Alexeyevitch, I mean Kapiton—retired lieutenant colonel—married to Marya, to Marya Petrovna. Su—Su—a good friend and comrade-in-arms—Sutugov—from the time we were cadets together. I shed my—threw myself in front of him—he was killed. No such person as Kapitoshka Yeropegov? No such person indeed!"

The general was shouting vehemently, yet in a manner which suggested that what he was shouting about was not what really mattered. True, at some other time he of course would have tolerated a far greater insult than the assertion concerning Kapiton Yeropegov's utter nonexistence; he would have shouted, made a scene, lost his temper, and yet in the end he would have gone upstairs to bed. But now—such is the extreme singularity of the human heart—it happened that this particular offense, the doubt expressed about Yeropegov, was the very drop that overflowed his cup. The old man turned crimson, raised his arms and shouted:

"Enough! My curse! I'm leaving this house! Nikolai, bring my bag! I am going—away!"

He went out, precipitously, and in a towering rage.

"Look what you've done now!" said Varya to her brother.

"He'll probably drag himself over there again! The disgrace of it! The disgrace of it!"

"Well, he shouldn't steal!" shouted Ganya, almost choking with anger. Suddenly his eyes fell on Hippolite and he fairly trembled with fury. "As for you, my dear sir," he cried, "you ought to remember that you are in someone else's house, anyway, and—and enjoying his hospitality, and you ought not to provoke an old man who has obviously gone out of his mind."

Hippolite too seemed shaken with rage, but he at once controlled himself.

"I don't quite agree with you that your papa has gone out of his mind," he replied calmly. "It seems to me, on the contrary, that he's actually been showing more sense lately. Don't you think so? He's become so careful, so skeptical, he looks into everything, he weighs every word. He had some purpose in mind when he spoke to me about that Kapitoshka. Imagine, he wanted to lead me on to—"

"What the devil do I care what he wanted to lead you on to! Don't be clever and play tricks with me, sir!" shrieked Ganya. "If you, too, know the real reason the old man is in such a state (and you've been doing spying enough for the past five days so that you probably do), you should never have irritated that unhappy man and worried my mother by exaggerating what happened, because the whole thing is nonsense, nothing more than a drunken affair; nothing is even proved either, and I don't think it amounts to a rap— But you have to hurt people and spy because you are a—you are a—"

"A screw," said Hippolite, grinning.

"Because you are a good-for-nothing; you torture people for half an hour trying to frighten them by threatening you'd shoot yourself with that unloaded pistol of yours—you made such a shameful ass of yourself with—you suicide-pretender, you bag of bile—on two feet! I've shown you hospitality, and you've grown fat, you've stopped coughing, and now you are paying me back—"

"Just a word or two, if you'll allow me, sir. I am in Varvara Ardalionovna's house, not yours. You have shown me no hospitality at all, and I even rather suspect that you yourself are enjoying Mr. Ptitsyn's hospitality. Four days ago I asked my mother to find rooms for me in Pavlovsk and to move here herself, because I really do feel better here, though I have not grown fat and I do continue to cough. Mother let me know yesterday evening that the rooms are available, and I hasten to inform you on my part that, when I have thanked your mother and your sister, I will be moving to my own quarters today, as I decided to do last night. Excuse me, I interrupted you; I think you meant to say quite a lot more."

"Oh, if that's the way it is—" Ganya said, trembling.

"If that's the way it is, please let me sit down," added Hippolite, calmly sitting down in the chair in which the general had been sitting. "I am sick, after all. Now I'm ready to listen to you—especially since this will be the last conversation between us and perhaps even our last meeting."

Ganya suddenly felt a stab of conscience.

"You may be sure I won't demean myself by trying to settle scores with you," he said, "and if you—"

"There's no point taking such a lofty tone," interrupted Hippolite. "For my part I swore the first day I came here I wouldn't deny myself the pleasure of saying everything I had to say to you frankly the day we parted company. And I intend to do exactly that now—after you, naturally."

"And I am asking you to leave this room."

"You had better speak, since you'd regret not having had your say."

"Stop this, Hippolite," said Varya. "All this is terribly shameful. Do me the favor and please stop."

"Well, to oblige a lady," said Hippolite, laughing and getting up. "All right, Varvara Ardalionovna, for you I am ready to cut it short, but only to cut it short, because some accounting between myself and your brother has become absolutely essential, and I wouldn't want to go away leaving any uncertainty behind."

"In plain terms, you're a scandalmonger!" cried Ganya. "That's why you can't leave without spreading gossip."

"There, you see?" Hippolite observed with cold restraint. "You're losing control of yourself. Truly, you'll be sorry not to have spoken out. Once again: you have the floor. I'll wait."

Gavril Ardalionovitch said nothing and looked at him contemptuously.

"You won't speak—you mean to keep up your show of firm character—do as you please. As for me, I'll be as brief as possible. Two or three times today I have been reproached on account of the hospitality I've received. This is unfair. In inviting me to stay with you, you were trying to trap me; you thought I wanted to take revenge on the prince. You also heard that Aglaya Ivanovna had shown sympathy for me and had read my confession. Supposing for some reason I would give myself up completely to your interests, you hoped that you might perhaps find help from me. No need of further explanations! I don't ask for assurances or confessions from you either; it's quite enough that I leave you with your conscience, and that now we understand each other perfectly."

"Heaven knows what you will make out of the simplest things!" cried Varya.

"I told you he was a scandalmonger and a little brat," said Ganya.

"Let me continue, Varvara Ardalionovna. The prince, of course, I can neither love nor respect; but he is definitely a kindly man, though—rather ridiculous. But I certainly would have no reason at all to hate him. I didn't let on to your brother when he tried to stir me up against the prince; I was counting on having a good laugh at how it would turn out. I knew that your brother would talk too much and finally make a complete mess of it. And that's what happened. I'm ready to spare him now, but only out of respect for you, Varvara Ardalionovna. But having explained to you that it's not so easy to take me in, I shall also explain why I was so anxious to make a fool of your brother. Let me tell you that I did it out of hatred, I freely admit that. When I die (because I am dying even though, as you tell me, I've put on weight) —when I die I feel that I shall enter paradise far more peacefully if I succeed in making a fool of even one representative of that horde of people who have persecuted me all my life, whom I have hated all my life, and of whom your most estimable brother is such a striking example. I hate you, Gavril Ardalionovitch, because—and this may surprise you—*solely* because you are the type, the incarnation, the embodiment, and the acme of the most insolent, the most self-satisfied, the most trivial and odious mediocrity! Yours is a pompous mediocrity, a confident mediocrity Olympian in its serenity; you are the ordinary of the ordinary! Never will the smallest idea of your own take form in your mind or heart—never. But you are infinitely envious, you are firmly convinced you are the greatest of geniuses; but still sometimes doubt does visit you in your dark moments, and then you are both angry and envious. Oh, there are still dark clouds before you on the horizon; they will disappear when you have become quite stupid, and the day is not far off; however, a long and checkered path still lies before you, not a very cheerful one, I am happy to say. In the first place, let me predict that you will never come to have a certain person."

"Here, this is unbearable!" cried Varya. "Are you finished, you loathsome, spiteful little creature?"

Ganya turned pale, trembled, and was silent. Hippolite had stopped and was looking at him intently and with delight; he turned his gaze on Varya, grinned, bowed, and went out, without saying another word.

Gavril Ardalionovitch might with justice have complained of his fate and his lack of success. For some time Varya could not bring herself to say anything to him, she did not even look at him as he paced, taking long strides in front of her. Finally he walked to the window and stood with his back to her. Varya thought of the proverb about "a knife that cuts both ways." Again there was a commotion upstairs.

"Are you going?" Ganya asked her suddenly, hearing her get up from her place. "Wait. Look at this."

He went over to her and threw down on the chair in front of her a piece of paper folded as a note.

"Good heavens!" cried Varya, clasping her hands.

There were just seven lines to the note:

498

Gavril Ardalionovitch! As I am convinced of your friendly feelings toward me I have decided to ask your advice in a matter of great importance to me. I would like to meet you tomorrow morning at exactly seven at the green bench. It is not far from our house. Varvara Ardalionovna, who *must* accompany you, knows the place well. A. Y.

"Well, what is one to make of her after this?" Varvara Ardalionovna spread her hands in bewilderment.

Little as Ganya was disposed to be boastful at that moment, he could not help showing his feeling of triumph, especially after Hippolite's humiliating predictions. His face lit up with a self-satisfied smile, and Varya herself looked radiant with joy.

"And this on the very day they are to announce her engagement! Well, what is one to make of her after this!"

"What do you think? What does she want to talk about tomorrow?" Ganya asked.

"It doesn't matter. The main thing is she wants to see you for the first time in six months. Listen to me, Ganya: whatever has happened, whatever turn it takes, realize that this is *important!* It is very important. Don't show off again, don't make any mistakes again, but—look here—don't be afraid either. She must have understood why I have been going over there for the past six months. And imagine! She never said a word to me about it today, not a hint. I've had to smuggle myself into their house, you know; the old woman didn't know I was there or she would have ordered me out. I risked it for your sake, I wanted at all costs to find out—"

Again there was a noise and shouting overhead; several people were coming down the stairs.

"Now we mustn't let it happen for anything in the world!" cried Varya, flustered and alarmed. "Not a breath of scandal! Go on, apologize to him."

But the head of the family was already in the street. Kolya was dragging his bag after him. Nina Alexandrovna stood on the front steps, crying. She would have run after him, but Ptitsyn held her back.

"You'll only stir him up more," he said to her. "He has nowhere to go. He'll be brought back again in a half hour; I've already spoken to Kolya. Let him play the fool."

"What are you proving to us?" Ganya shouted from the window. "Where are you going? You have nowhere to go!"

"Come back, Papa," cried Varya. "The neighbors can hear."

The general stopped, turned around, raised his hand, and cried:

"My curse on this house!"

"He would have to be theatrical!" muttered Ganya, slamming the window shut.

The neighbors were in fact listening. Varya ran out of the room.

When Varya had gone, Ganya picked up the note from the table, clicked his tongue in satisfaction, and attempted an *entrechat*.

Chapter THREE

At any other time the general's performance would have come to nothing. He had had sudden wild outbursts of this sort before, though not often, because generally speaking he was a very mild-tempered man with a rather kindly disposition. A hundred times, perhaps, he had struggled to overcome the unruly habits which had gained mastery over him in late years. He would suddenly remember that he was "the head of a family," he would make peace with his wife, and he would shed genuine tears. He respected Nina Alexandrovna to the point of adoration because she had forgiven him so much without saying a word and even loved him in the degraded and ridiculous state into which he had fallen. But his high-minded struggle against dissolute habits usually did not last very long; the general was too "impulsive," though in his own particular way, to endure a life of penitence and idleness in the bosom of his family, and he would end by rebelling; he would fly into a passion, for which at the very same moment he would perhaps be reproaching himself, but he could not help himself; he would quarrel, he would begin talking pompously and eloquently, he would insist on being treated with an exaggerated and impossible respect; and finally he would vanish from home, sometimes staying away a long time. For the last two years he had known next to nothing, and mostly through hearsay, about the affairs of his family; he had stopped pursuing these matters, feeling not the slightest inclination to do so.

But this time there was something exceptional about the general's "performance"; it was as if everyone knew something and everyone was afraid to speak of it. The general had made a "formal" reappearance in the family, that is to Nina Alexandrovna, only three days earlier, but somehow not humbly or with the penitence which had always marked these "reappearances," but on the contrary, with extraordinary irritability. He was talkative and restless and entered into heated discussions with everyone he met, seeming to fly at people, yet always over subjects so diverse and unexpected that it was never quite possible to discover what really was disturbing him at any moment. Sometimes he was cheerful, more often he was thoughtful, without knowing himself exactly what he was thinking about. He would suddenly speak of something —the Yepanchins, the prince, Lebedev—then as suddenly break off and stop talking altogether, responding to further questions with a vacant smile, unaware that he was being questioned or that he was smiling. He had spent the previous night sighing and moaning and had exhausted Nina Alexandrovna, who had been up all night preparing hot compresses for him. Toward morning he had suddenly fallen asleep, slept for four hours, and awakened with a violent and uncontrolled attack of hypochondria, which had terminated with the quarrel with Hippolite and his "curse on this house." It was also noticed that during these three days he was subject to fits of self-glorification and was in consequence extraordinarily quick to take offense. Kolya insisted and assured his mother that it was all because he missed his drinking and, perhaps, missed Lebedev, with whom the general had become extremely friendly of late. But three days before, he had suddenly quarreled with Lebedev and had parted from him in a terrible fury. There had even been a scene of some sort with the prince. Kolya asked the prince about it and finally began to suspect that he too was keeping something from him. If, as Ganya had every good reason to believe, Hippolite and Nina Alexandrovna had had some private conversation, it was strange that this spiteful young man, whom Ganya had so openly called a scandalmonger, had not found the same satisfaction in initiating Kolya too into the secret. Very possibly he was not the malicious "little brat" Ganya made him out to be in speaking to his sister, but malicious in a different way; nor did it seem likely that he had informed Nina Alexandrovna of whatever he had observed for the sole purpose of "breaking her heart." Let us not forget that the motives behind human actions are usually infinitely more complicated and various than we assume them to be in our subsequent explanations, and they can rarely be defined clearly. Sometimes the narrator's best course is to confine himself to a simple presentation of events. And this is what we shall do in the rest of our narration of the present catastrophe concerning the general; for, do as we will, we are now under the absolute necessity of devoting to this secondary character in our story rather more space and attention than we originally had intended.

These events happened in the following order:

When Lebedev, after his trip to Petersburg to look for Ferdyshchenko, returned the same day with the general, he told the prince nothing in particular. If the prince had not been at that time too distracted and absorbed by other important preoccupations he might soon have noticed that during the following two days Lebedev, far from offering any kind of explanation, seemed for some reason to be avoiding encounters with him. When he finally did make this observation, the prince was surprised that in these two days he could not remember Lebedev, when he had run into him accidentally, being in any other but the most blissful disposition, and almost always in the company of the general. The two friends were never apart for a moment. The prince occasionally heard from upstairs loud and rapid conversations, merry, laughing disputes; and once, very late at night, the strains of a martial and bacchanalian song burst suddenly and unexpectedly on his ears and he recognized the husky bass voice of the general. But the song broke off suddenly and silence followed. Then a highly animated and, from all signs, drunken conversation went on for another hour. It could be guessed that the two convivial friends were embracing each other, and that one of them finally began to weep. Then a violent quarrel suddenly broke out, which also ceased almost at once. All this time Kolya seemed to be in a particularly troubled state of mind. The prince was usually not at home during the day and sometimes returned very late; he would always be told that Kolya had been looking for him all day and asking for him. But when they did meet, Kolya had nothing special to say to him except that he was decidedly "dissatisfied" with the general and his present behavior: "They roam around together, get drunk in a tavern near here, embrace each other, and quarrel on the street; they stir each other up and then they can't be parted." When the prince reminded him that the same thing had happened before, almost every day, Kolya had no idea what to answer or how to explain, exactly, the cause of his present uneasiness.

The morning after the bacchic song and the quarrel, the prince was leaving the house at about eleven o'clock when he was suddenly confronted by the general, who was greatly excited by something and seemed quite disturbed.

"For a long time I've been looking for a chance to see you, my dear Lev Nikolayevitch, a long time, a very long time," he muttered, squeezing his hand extremely hard, almost hurting him, "a very, very long time."

The prince invited him to sit down.

"No, I won't sit down; besides, I'm detaining you, I'll—another time. I believe I may take this occasion to congratulate you—on the fulfillment of your—heart's desire."

"What heart's desire?"

The prince was confused. He supposed, as do many people in his position, that no one saw, guessed, or understood anything about him.

"Please don't be uneasy! I'm not going to hurt your most delicate feelings. I've been through it myself and I know what it is when somebody—pokes his nose, as they say, where it isn't wanted. I feel this every morning. I have come about another matter, an important matter. A very important matter, Prince."

The prince again asked him to be seated and sat down himself.

"Perhaps just for a second. I have come for advice. Of course, you know I have no practical aims in life, but as I do respect myself and—business sense, which Russian men, as a rule, lack so conspicuously— I wish to place myself and my wife and my children in a position—in a word, Prince, I come for advice."

The prince warmly praised this intention.

"Well, all that's nonsense," the general suddenly interrupted. "That's not what I really came about, but something else, something important. I've decided to explain to you, Lev Nikolayevitch, as a man in whose sincerity of manner and nobility of feelings I have complete confidence, as—as— You are not surprised at my words, Prince?"

The prince was watching his visitor not perhaps with any particular surprise but with extraordinary attention and curiosity. The old man was rather pale, his lips quivered slightly at times, his hands seemed unable to find a place to settle. He sat only for a few minutes and twice now had suddenly got up from his chair for no reason, and just as suddenly sat down again, obviously not paying the slightest attention to what he was doing. There were books lying on the table; he took up one, continuing to talk, glanced at the page that fell open, and immediately shut it again and put it back on the table, picked up another which he did not open but held all the rest of the time in his right hand, waving it incessantly in the air.

"Enough!" he cried suddenly. "I see that I have been disturbing you."

"But not in the least, I assure you. Please do go on. On the contrary, I am listening and trying to guess—"

"Prince! I want to put myself in the position of respect—I want to respect myself and—my rights."

"A man with such a desire is worthy of respect on that account alone."

The prince uttered this copybook phrase with the firm conviction that it would have an excellent effect. He had guessed instinctively that some such empty but pleasant-sounding piety uttered at the right moment might at once subdue and soothe the mind of such a man, especially a man in the general's position. In any case it was necessary to send such a visitor away with his heart set at ease, and this was the problem.

The phrase flattered, touched, and greatly pleased the general: he was at once very moved, instantly changed his tone, and entered into long and enthusiastic explanations. But no matter how hard the prince tried, however intently he listened, he could not understand a single word. The general spoke for ten minutes, heatedly, rapidly, as if he had not sufficient time to utter all the thoughts that crowded his mind; toward the end tears actually glistened in his eyes, and still there were only fragments of sentences without beginning or end, chance words, chance thoughts bursting rapidly and unexpectedly forth and tumbling over one another.

"Enough! You have understood me and I feel much better," concluded the general suddenly, getting up. "A heart such as yours cannot fail to understand a man who suffers. Prince, you have the true nobility of an ideal! What are other men beside you? But you are young, and I bless you. The long and short of it is I came to ask you to fix an hour for an important conversation, wherein lies my greatest hope. I seek nothing but friendship and an understanding heart; for I have never been able to come to terms with cravings of my own heart, Prince."

"But why not right now? I am ready to listen."

"No, Prince, no!" said the general vehemently. "Not now! Now is an empty dream! This is too important, much, much too important. That hour of conversation will be the hour of fateful decision. It will be *my* hour and I don't want us to be interrupted at such a sacred moment by the first person coming in, some insolent fellow—and there are plenty of them." He suddenly bent down to the prince and said in a strange, mysterious, and almost frightened whisper, "So insolent as not to be worth the heel of your shoe, my very very dear Prince! Oh, I don't say the heel of my shoe! Observe particularly that I do not refer to my shoe; for I respect myself too much to say that out plainly, but only you are capable of understanding that by waiving, in this case, my shoe I am perhaps showing an exceptional pride in my own worth. Except for you, no one will understand—and *he* least of all. *He* doesn't understand anything, Prince; he is absolutely and totally incapable of understanding! One needs a heart to understand!"

In the end the prince was rather alarmed and he arranged to see the general on the same hour the following day. The latter strode out full of confidence, greatly comforted, and almost reassured. In the evening toward seven o'clock the prince sent to ask Lebedev to come to see him for a moment.

Lebedev made his appearance with extraordinary promptitude, "deemed it an honor," as he said immediately upon entering, with not the shadow of a hint that he had been in hiding for three days and obviously trying to avoid meeting the prince. He sat down on the edge of a chair, with smiles, with grimaces, with laughter and a watchful little squint, with much rubbing of hands, and with an air of the most innocent expectation of hearing some communication of capital importance, long expected and long guessed by everyone. The prince again winced; it became clear to him that everyone was suddenly expecting something from him, that everyone was glancing at him as if wishing to congratulate him for something, with hints, smiles, and winks. Three times already Keller had run in for a moment, also with a clear desire of congratulating him: each time he began to speak in an exalted and vague manner but never finished and quickly disappeared again. (He had been drinking particularly heavily for the past few days and was carousing loudly in some billiard room.) Even Kolya, in spite of his sadness, had also once or twice opened unclear conversations with the prince about something.

The prince asked Lebedev directly and somewhat irritably what he thought about General Ivolgin's present condition and why the latter was in such a state of anxiety. He told him briefly of the scene that morning.

"Everyone has his worries, Prince—and—especially in our strange and troubled age, sir. Yes, sir." Lebedev replied with a certain dryness, and fell into a hurt silence, with the air of a man whose expectations have been profoundly deceived.

"What a philosophy!" said the prince, laughing.

"Philosophy is needed, sir; the practical application of it would be very useful in our age, but it's neglected, that's the trouble, sir. For my part, most respected Prince, I've been honored by your confidence in a certain matter which you know of, but only to a certain point and never further than the circumstances relating to that matter in particular. This I quite understand. I am not complaining about it."

"Lebedev, you seem angry about something."

"Not at all, not in the least, most respected and resplendent Prince, not in the least!" Lebedev cried passionately, laying his hand on his heart. "On the contrary, I understood at once that neither my position in the world, nor my qualities of mind and heart, my fortune, nor my behavior in the past, nor my knowledge have made me worthy of the honor of your esteemed confidence, so far above my hopes; and that if I can serve you it is as your slave and a hireling, in no other way —I'm not angry, but I am sad, sir."

"Come, come, Lukyan Timofeyitch!"

"In no other way! This is how it is now, in the present case! My heart and my thoughts went with you when I met you, and I said to myself: 'I am unworthy of receiving amicable communications, but in the capacity of landlord I might, at the opportune moment and the proper time, so to speak, receive notification or at least an intimation in view of certain anticipated changes known to us—"

As he said this, Lebedev fixed his sharp little eyes on the prince, who was looking at him in amazement. He still hoped to satisfy his curiosity.

"I don't understand a single thing!" exclaimed the prince, almost angrily. "And—you are a dreadful intriguer!" He suddenly burst into heartfelt laughter.

Instantly Lebedev laughed too and his radiant expression showed that his expectations were confirmed and even redoubled.

"And do you know what I'm going to tell you, Lukyan Timofeyitch? Don't be angry with me, but I am amazed at your simplicity, and not only yours! Right now at this very moment you are waiting to hear something from me with such simplicity that I feel ashamed and embarrassed to have nothing to tell that would satisfy you; but I swear that I definitely have nothing to tell you. Can you believe that?"

The prince laughed again.

Lebedev assumed an air of dignity. It was true that sometimes in his curiosity he was too naïve and indiscreet, but at the same time he was a rather cunning and wily man and in certain cases even a little too calculatingly silent. The prince, by his incessant rebuffs, had almost made an enemy of him. But the prince rebuffed him not because he despised him but because the object of his curiosity was a delicate one. Whereas only a few days earlier the prince looked upon certain of his own dreams as criminal, Lukyan Timofeyitch took the prince's rebuffs only as signs of personal aversion and mistrust toward him and withdrew, cut to the heart and jealous on the prince's account not only of Kolya and Keller but even of his own daughter Vera Lukyanovna. Perhaps at this very moment he might have told the prince a certain piece of news of the highest interest to him, but he fell into gloomy silence and did not tell him.

"What, exactly, can I do for you, most respected Prince, since after all you did—summon me just now?" he said at last after a pause.

"Yes, it was really about the general," said the prince with a start, also after a reflective silence, "and—about that theft you were telling me about."

"What about it?"

"Now you pretend not to understand me! Oh, Good Lord, Lukyan Timofeyitch, you're always acting a role! The money, the money! The four hundred roubles you lost that day in your billfold, and that you came to tell me about in the morning before you left for Petersburg. Do you understand now?"

"Oh, you're talking about those four hundred roubles!" drawled Lebedev as if he had just guessed.

"Thank you, Prince, for your sincere sympathy. It's all too flattering to me but—I found it, and quite some time ago."

"You did? Oh, thank God!"

"A most generous exclamation on your part, sir, as four hundred roubles is no small matter for a poor man who lives by hard work, with a large family of motherless children—"

"But I'm not talking about that! Of course, I'm glad you found them," the prince hastily corrected himself. "But how did you find them?"

"Extremely simply, sir. I found them under the chair where I had hung my coat. Apparently the billfold had slipped out of the pocket onto the floor."

"Under the chair? But that can't be, because you told me

507

yourself you had searched everywhere. How could you have overlooked the most obvious place?"

"But that's just it—I looked there, sir! I remember only too well that I did look there! I crawled around on all fours, felt the place with my hands, moved the chair, unable to believe my own eyes: I saw there was nothing there, just a bare and empty place, just as smooth as the palms of my hands, sir, and still I kept feeling around for it. That's a weakness which always overcomes a man when he really wants to find something, whenever important or distressing losses occur; one sees there is nothing there, the place is bare, and still one looks over it a dozen times or more."

"Yes, I suppose so, but, still, how did it happen? I can't understand," murmured the prince, completely at a loss. "You told me first it wasn't there, that you had looked, and then suddenly it turned up there!"

"Suddenly it did turn up there, sir."

The prince looked at Lebedev in an odd way.

"And the general?" he suddenly asked.

"What do you mean, 'and the general,' sir?" said Lebedev —not understanding again.

"Oh, good heaven! I am asking you what the general said when you found the billfold under the chair. You first searched for it together, didn't you?"

"We did look together the first time, sir. But this time, I admit, I didn't say anything to him, preferring not to tell him that the billfold had been found by me, alone."

"But—why? And the money? Was it all there?"

"I opened the billfold. It was all there—to the very last rouble, sir."

"You might have come and told me," observed the prince thoughtfully.

"I was afraid to disturb you, Prince, in the midst of your personal preoccupations, which are perhaps, so to speak, of exceptional interest. Besides, I myself acted as if I had found nothing. I opened the billfold, examined it, then closed it, and put it back under the chair."

"But what for?"

"Oh, just like that, sir. Out of—supplementary curiosity," Lebedev suddenly chuckled and rubbed his hands.

"So it's been lying there since the day before yesterday?"

"Oh, no. It was only lying there for twenty-four hours. You see, I partly wanted the general to find it. Because since I eventually found it why shouldn't the general notice an object that fairly leaped to the eye, so to speak, sticking out from under the chair? I moved that chair several times, putting it back so the billfold would be in plain sight, but the general simply refused to notice it, and so it went for a whole twenty-four hours. He seems to be very lost and absent-minded these days, and there's no making him out; he talks, he tells stories, he laughs, even roars with laughter, and then suddenly he gets terribly angry with me, I have no idea why. Finally we were going out of the room, I left the door open on purpose; he hesitated, seemed to want to say something, obviously worried about leaving a billfold with so much money in it, then suddenly he flew into a terrible rage and said nothing. We hadn't gone more than a couple of steps down the street when he left me and walked off in another direction. We only met that evening in a tavern."

"But you did finally pick up the billfold from under the chair, didn't you?"

"No, sir. That same night it disappeared from under the chair."

"Then where is it now?"

"Why, it's here, sir," said Lebedev, laughing suddenly, drawing himself up to his full height, and looking amiably at the prince. "It suddenly turned up here in the skirt of my coat. Here, see for yourself, sir. Feel it."

And indeed, there was a bulge in the left skirt of his coat, right in front, in plain view; and by touching it one could tell there was a leather billfold there which had fallen through a torn pocket.

"I took it out and looked, sir; it's all there. I put it back again and I've been walking around like this since yesterday morning, carrying it in the skirt of my coat. It even knocks against my legs."

"And you pay no attention to it?"

"I pay no attention to it, heh, heh! And would you believe it, most respected Prince, though the subject is not especially worthy your attention, my pockets have always been perfectly sound, and here all of a sudden, in one night, we have a hole like that! I started looking at it more closely; it's as if someone had slit it with a penknife. Isn't that almost unbelievable?"

"And—the general?"

"He's been angry all day long, both yesterday and today; he's terribly distressed, sir. One moment he's full of high spirits and so bacchanalian he flatters you, and then he gets so sentimental he actually weeps, and then suddenly he's angry, but so very angry that even I am frightened, by God, sir. After all, I'm not a military man, sir. Yesterday we were sitting at the tavern and as if by accident the skirt of my coat was sticking out in full view, big as a mountain. He kept glancing at it out of the corner of his eye, very angry. He hasn't looked at me straight in the eye for a long time now, except when he's very drunk or sentimental; but yesterday he looked at me twice in a way that sent a chill up my spine. Tomorrow, though, I intend to find the billfold, but before tomorrow I'll be spending another amusing evening with him."

"Why do you torment him like this?" cried the prince.

"I'm not, Prince, I'm not tormenting him," replied Lebedev warmly. "I sincerely love him, sir, and—respect him; and now, believe it or not, he's dearer to me than ever; I've come to appreciate him even more!"

Lebedev said all this in such a sincere and serious manner that the prince was positively indignant.

"You love him and you torment him like this! Why, just by putting the missing billfold back under the chair and in your coat where you could see it, just by that he shows you clearly that he doesn't want to deceive you, but straightforwardly asks for your forgiveness! Do you hear? He is asking for your forgiveness! That is, he is counting on the delicacy of your feelings, which means he believes in your friendship for him. But you humiliate such a man, such a—very honest man!"

"Very honest, Prince! Very honest!" agreed Lebedev, his eyes sparkling. "And only you, most noble Prince, only you would be capable of saying something so true! This is why I'm so devoted to you, even worship you, though I am rotten with all sorts of vices! That settles it! I shall find the billfold now, at once, and not tomorrow. Here, I take it out before your eyes, sir; here it is; here is all the money untouched; here, take it, most noble Prince; take it and keep it till tomorrow. I'll get it tomorrow or the next day. But, you know, Prince, the money must have been lying hidden under a stone somewhere in my garden that first night it was missing. What do you think?"

"Take care not to tell him to his face that you've found the billfold. Just let him see there's nothing in the skirt of your coat anymore; he will understand."

"Is that the best way? Wouldn't it be better to say I found it and pretend I never guessed where it was till now?"

"N-no," said the prince thoughtfully. "No, it's too late. That would be more dangerous. You really had better not say anything! And be kind with him, but—don't overdo it, and —and—you know—"

"I know, Prince, I know. I mean I know that I probably

won't do it, because for this one needs a heart like yours. And besides, he's irritable and susceptible himself; one moment he looks down on me, the next he's whimpering and embracing me, and then suddenly he starts humiliating me and mocking. Well, right then I make a point of showing him the skirt of my coat, heh, heh! Good-bye, Prince, for it's clear I'm keeping you and, one might say, disturbing your most interesting feelings—"

"But for goodness' sake, the same secrecy as before!"

"Treading softly, sir, treading softly!"

But though the matter was settled the prince was almost more troubled than ever. He awaited with impatience his interview with the general the next day.

Chapter FOUR

∽✦∾

The hour fixed was twelve, but quite unexpectedly the prince was late. On his return home he found the general waiting for him. He saw at the first glance that he was displeased, and probably for the very reason that he had been kept waiting. Apologizing, the prince hastened to sit down, but he felt oddly intimidated, as if his visitor were made of porcelain and he was at each instant fearful of breaking him. He had never felt intimidated with the general before, and it had never occurred to him that he might. The prince soon perceived that he was a completely different man from what he had been the day before: in place of confusion and distraction there was an extraordinary reserve, and it was evident that here was a man who had taken some irrevocable decision. This composure, however, was more apparent than real. In any event the visitor displayed a sort of courtly nonchalance, though with reserved dignity. At first he even treated the prince with a certain air of condescension, in exactly the way proud people who have been unjustly insulted are sometimes loftily at their ease. He spoke affably, but with a certain rhetorical touch of melancholy in his voice.

"The book I borrowed from you the other day," he said,

nodding significantly at a book he had brought which was lying on the table. "Thank you."

"Oh, yes. Did you read that article, General? How did you like it? Interesting, isn't it?" said the prince, delighted at the opportunity to open the conversation on an indifferent topic.

"It's interesting, perhaps, but crude and, of course, absurd. It's probably packed with lies."

The general spoke with great self-assurance, and even drawled his words a little.

"Oh, but it's such a simple straightforward story: the story of an old soldier who was an eyewitness of the arrival of the French in Moscow; some of the things in it are charming. Besides, any account by an eyewitness is precious, whoever the person is. Don't you think?"

"If I'd been the editor I wouldn't have printed it. As for eyewitness accounts in general, people are more ready to believe crude liars who are amusing than a man of worth and merit. I know of certain accounts of the year 1812 which—I've made a decision, Prince, I am leaving this house—Mr. Lebedev's house."

The general looked meaningfully at the prince.

"You have rooms of your own in Pavlovsk at—at your daughter's—" remarked the prince, not knowing what to say. He remembered that the general had come to him for advice about a most important matter, on which his fate depended.

"At my wife's. In other words, at my home, in my daughter's house."

"Excuse me, I—"

"I am leaving Lebedev's house, dear Prince, because I have broken with that man. I broke with him last night with no other regret but that I had not done so earlier. I demand respect, Prince, and I expect to receive it even from those I give, so to speak, my heart. Prince, I am often giving my heart and I am almost always deceived. That man was unworthy of my gift."

"There's something very—unsettled about him," observed the prince discreetly, "and also certain traits—but with all that one can perceive a good heart and a sly and sometimes amusing mind."

The refinement of these expressions and their respectful tone clearly flattered the general, though he still would sometimes glance at the prince with sudden mistrust. But the prince's tone was so natural and sincere it was impossible to suspect it.

"That he has good qualities," pursued the general quickly, "I was the first to declare, when I almost bestowed my

512

friendship on that individual. I have no need of his hospitality, having a family of my own. I don't excuse my vices; I am intemperate; I have drunk wine with him and now maybe I regret it. But it was not for the sake of drink alone (forgive, Prince, the crude frankness of an exasperated man), not for drink alone that I made friends with him. What attracted me was exactly, as you say, his good qualities. But there's a limit to everything, including qualities; and if he suddenly has the impertinence to tell me to my face that in the year 1812, when he was still a child, he lost his left leg and buried it in the Vagankovsky cemetery in Moscow, well, that's going too far and it shows disrespect and it is impertinent."

"Perhaps it was just a joke to make people laugh."

"I see. An innocent lie to make people laugh, even though crude, does not offend the human heart. Some people, if you like, will lie merely out of friendship to please the people they talk to; but if there's disrespect there, and if by this disrespect one wishes to show precisely that he is weary of a friendship, then an honorable man has no choice but to turn away and break off the friendship, thus putting the offender in his proper place."

The general actually reddened as he spoke.

"But Lebedev couldn't have been in Moscow in 1812. He's too young for that. It's ridiculous!"

"That, first of all. But even supposing he could have been born then, how can he assert to a person's face, sir, that a French chasseur pointed a cannon at him and blew his leg off just for fun, that he picked up the leg and carried it home and afterward buried it in the Vagankovsky cemetery, and then tell me that he put a monument over it with an inscription saying: 'Here lies the leg of Collegiate Secretary Lebedev,' and on the other side, 'Rest in peace, beloved ashes, until the joyous morn'; and finally that he has a requiem service read over it every year (which is a sacrilege) and that every year he goes to Moscow for this occasion. To prove it he asks me to come to Moscow to show me the tomb, and even the very same cannon, captured from the French and now in the Kremlin. He assures me it is the eleventh from the gate, a French falconet of an early design."

"And still he has both his legs intact and in plain sight!" laughed the prince. "I assure you this is an innocent joke. Don't be angry."

"Allow me my own opinion, sir, concerning his having legs in plain sight. What he says is not all that improbable. He declares that he got a leg from Chernosvitov."

513

"Oh, yes. They say it's possible to dance with a Chernosvitov leg."

"I'm quite aware of that, sir. When Chernosvitov invented his leg, the first thing he did was to run and show it to me. But the Chernosvitov leg was invented much later. Besides, he also assured me that even his late wife in the whole course of their married life never knew that he, her own husband, had a wooden leg. When I showed him how foolish all this was, he said, 'If you were a page of Napoleon's in 1812, you might as well let me bury my leg in Vagankovsky.'"

"But were you really—" the prince began, then broke off in embarrassment.

The general too seemed a trifle embarrassed, but in the next instant he looked at the prince with resolute disdain and a trace of irony.

"Go on, Prince," he drawled very calmly. "Go right ahead. I don't mind; speak freely: please admit you are amused by the very idea of seeing before you a man in his present degradation and—uselessness, and at the same time hearing that this man was a witness of—great events. Hasn't *he* already been gossiping to you?"

"No, I have heard nothing from Lebedev, if you are talking about Lebedev."

"Well—I thought the contrary. Actually that conversation we had yesterday began in connection with that—strange article in *Archives*. I remarked upon its absurdity, and since I myself had been an eyewitness— You are smiling, Prince, you are looking at my face."

"N-no, I—"

"I am young-looking," said the general, drawling out his words, "but I am somewhat older in years than I look. In 1812 I was ten or eleven. I don't know my age exactly. In the service record it's less, and all my life it has been my weakness to make myself out younger than I am."

"I assure you, General, I don't find it strange that you were in Moscow in '12 and—of course you are able to tell us things—just as everyone who was there does. One of our writers begins his autobiography saying that when he was a nursing infant in Moscow in 1812 the French soldiers fed him bread."

"There, you see?" said the general with indulgent approval. "Of course my own case was quite out of the ordinary, but there is nothing really unusual about it. Truth very often appears impossible. A page! Of course that seems strange. But a ten-year-old's adventure may perhaps be explained precisely by his age. The same thing wouldn't have happened to a fifteen-year-old boy, because at fifteen I would not have run away from our wooden house in Old Basmanaya Street on the day of Napoleon's entry into Moscow; I would never have run away from my mother, who was too late to leave Moscow and was shaking with fear. At fifteen I too would have been afraid, but at ten I feared nothing, and I pushed my way through the crowd to the foot of the palace steps just as Napoleon was dismounting from his horse."

"Undoubtedly you are right that at ten one might not be afraid," the prince assented, distressed and fearful that he was about to blush.

"Undoubtedly, and it all took place as simply and naturally as things do happen in reality. If a novelist got to work on it he'd build up all sorts of nonsense and improbabilities."

"Oh, that's true!" cried the prince. "I was struck by the same thought, and quite recently. I know of a real case of murder that happened over a watch—it's in the papers now. If some author had invented it, the critics and our authorities on the life of the people would have immediately cried that it was improbable; but reading it in the papers as a fact one feels that the reality of Russian life is made of precisely such facts. You have observed this very clearly, General!" concluded the prince warmly, terribly glad to have escaped his blushes.

"Yes, haven't I? Haven't I?" cried the general, his eyes sparkling with pleasure. "The boy, the little child, knowing nothing of the danger, makes his way through the crowd to see the shining pageant, the uniforms, the emperor's suite, and finally the great man everyone has been telling him about. Because at the time, for several years, no one talked of anything but him. The world was full of that name. I drank it, you might say, with my mother's milk. Napoleon, passing a couple of paces from me, happens to catch my eye. I was dressed as a gentleman's son, they dressed me well. I, the only one dressed like that in that crowd, you may believe—"

"It undoubtedly must have struck him forcibly and shown him that not everyone had left and that some noblemen had stayed on with their children."

"Yes! Exactly! He wanted to win over the boyars! When he fixed his eagle gaze on me, my own eyes must have flashed in reply. *"Voilà un garçon bien élevé! Qui est ton père?"* I replied at once, almost breathless with excitement: 'A general who died on his country's battlefield.' *'Le fils d'un boyard et d'un brave par-dessous le marché! J'aime les boyards. M'aimes-tu, petit?'* To this rapid question I answered as quickly: 'A Russian heart can recognize a great man even in his country's enemy!' That is, of course, I don't remember if I expressed myself in those exact words—I was a child—but that certainly was the gist of it! Napoleon was very struck, he thought for a moment, then said to his suite: 'I like the pride of this child. But if all Russians think as this child does, then —' He did not finish and went into the palace. I at once joined with the suite and ran after him. They made way for me and already looked on me as a favorite. But all that happened in the wink of an eye. I only remember that when he entered the first room the emporor suddenly stopped before the portrait of Empress Catherine, looked at it thoughtfully for some time, and finally declared, 'That was a great woman!' and walked on. Within two days everyone in the palace and in the Kremlin knew me and called me *Le petit boyard.* I only went home to sleep. At home they were in a state about it. Two days after that one of Napoleon's pages, Baron de Basencour, worn out by the rigors of the campaign, died. Napoleon remembered me. They took me and brought me to him without telling me what it was about; they fitted me with the uniform of the dead boy, a child of twelve, and when they took me in my uniform before the emperor and he had nodded, they told me I had found favor and was appointed page-in-waiting to His Majesty. I was glad, I had felt attracted toward him for a long time—and, well, besides, as you can imagine, a spendid uniform means a lot to a child. I wore a dark green coat with long narrow tails, gold buttons, red facings stitched with gold on the sleeves, a high, erect open collar embroidered with gold, and embroidery on the tails; white, tight-fitting chamois leather breeches, a white silk waistcoat, silk stockings, buckled shoes—and whenever the emperor went forth on horseback if I was one of the suite I wore high-top riding boots. Although the military situation was anything but brilliant and great disasters were to be foreseen, etiquette was observed as much as possible, and indeed all the more scrupulously, as the sense of approaching calamity increased."

"Yes, of course," murmured the prince, quite at a loss. "Your memoirs would be—extremely interesting."

The general was of course repeating what he had already told Lebedev the day before, and therefore he was repeating it fluently; but at this point he again looked mistrustfully at the prince.

"My memoirs," he declared then with redoubled pride. "Write my memoirs? Doesn't tempt me, Prince! If you want to know, my memoirs are already written, but—they are lying in my desk. When my eyes are closed in the grave, let them be published then, and no doubt they will be translated into other languages, not on account of their literary merit, no, but for the importance of the tremendous events of which I was a witness, though a child; indeed, all the more, since as a child I could enter even into the private bedchamber of the 'great man'! At night I heard the groans of that 'Titan in adversity'; he could not feel ashamed to moan and weep before a child, though even then I understood that the cause of his suffering was the silence of the Emperor Alexander."

"Yes, he wrote letters—with proposals of peace," agreed the prince timidly.

"We don't know exactly what specific proposals he wrote, but he wrote every day, every hour, letter after letter! He was terribly agitated. One night when we were alone I flew to him in tears (oh, I did love him!): 'Please, please beg Emperor Alexander to forgive you!' I cried out to him. Of course, I should have said, 'make peace with Emperor Alexander,' but, like a child, I naïvely expressed my full thought. 'Oh, my child!' he replied—he was pacing back and forth in the room. 'Oh, my child!' He never seemed to notice that I was only ten, he loved to talk to me. 'Oh, my child, I am ready to kiss Emperor Alexander's feet; however, for the King of Prussia and for the Emperor of Austria my hatred is everlasting and—but then you know nothing of politics!' He suddenly seemed to remember whom he was talking to and fell silent, but his eyes were flashing fire a long time afterward. Well, if I was to describe all these facts—and I was an eyewitness to the greatest events—if I was to publish them now, all those critics, all the literary vanities, the envy, the cliques and—no, sir, no thank you!"

"As for cliques your observation is certainly true, and I agree with you," the prince replied quietly after a moment's silence. "I just read not long ago a book by Charras* about the Waterloo campaign. The book is obviously a serious work, and experts say it is written with an extremely thorough knowledge of the subject; but on every page one detects a feeling of joy at Napoleon's humiliation; and if it had been possible to deny Napoleon all trace of ability in his other campaigns as well, Charras would evidently have been happy to do so. And that's not a good thing in such a serious work, because it's the cliquish spirit. Were you kept very busy in your service with—with the emperor?"

The general was extremely pleased. The gravity and simplicity of the prince's remark had dispersed the last traces of his suspicion.

"Charras! Oh, I was outraged myself! I even wrote him at the time, but—I don't remember now— You ask whether I kept very busy in his service? Oh, no! I was called a page-in-waiting, but even at the time I didn't take it seriously. Besides, Napoleon soon lost all hope of winning over the Russians, and of course he would have also forgotten about me, whom he had taken only for the sake of policy, had he not taken a personal liking to me—I say this boldly now. As for me, my heart was drawn to him. The duties were not demanding; I sometimes had to be present at the palace and—to attend the emperor when he went out on horseback; that was all. I rode fairly well. He used to ride out before dinner. In his suite there were usually Davoust, myself, the Mameluke Roustan—"

"Constant," said the prince almost involuntarily.

"N-no," Constant was not there then. He was away with a letter—to the Empress Josephine; but a couple of orderlies replaced him and a few Polish uhlans— Yes, that was the whole suite, except of course for the generals and the marshals whom Napoleon took with him to study the terrain, the troop dispositions, and for consultations. Davoust was the one most often with him, as I remember it now; a huge, heavy, cool-headed man who wore glasses, with a strange look in his eyes. The emperor consulted with him more often than with anyone else. He valued his ideas. I remember once they were conferring together for several days; Davoust went to him in the morning and in the evening; often they even argued; finally Napoleon seemed to be coming around. They were together in the study, I was the third, almost unnoticed by them. Suddenly Napoleon's glance chanced to fall on me and a strange thought was reflected in his flashing eyes. 'Child!' he said to me suddenly. 'What do you think? If I adopt the Orthodox faith and free your serfs, will the Russians come over to me or not?' 'Never!' I exclaimed in indignation. Napoleon was dumbfounded. 'In the eyes of this child, gleaming with patriotism,' he said, 'I read the verdict of the whole Russian people. Enough, Davoust! All that is a fantasy. Tell me your other plan.' "

"Yes, but there was a great idea in that plan too!" said the prince, visibly interested. "So you attribute the proposal to Davoust?"

"At least they consulted together. Of course, the idea was Napoleonic, the idea of an eagle, but there was also a good idea in the other plan—this was the famous *'conseil du lion,'* as Napoleon himself called this advice of Davoust's. The idea was that they should shut themselves up in the Kremlin with all the troops, build barracks and fortifications, place cannon so as to kill as many horses as possible and then salt the meat, appropriate as much grain as possible, and winter there until spring, and in the spring fight their way through the Russians. This plan fascinated Napoleon. Every day we would ride around the Kremlin walls; he would show where to break down walls, where to build a lunette, a ravelin, a row of blockhouses—a glance, a swift look, a decision! Finally everything was arranged. Davoust was insisting on a final decision. Again they were together and I was the third. Again Napoleon was pacing the room with his arms folded. I couldn't look away from his face, my heart was pounding. 'I am going,' said Davoust. 'Where?' asked Napoleon. 'To salt the horses,' said Davoust. Napoleon trembled slightly—destiny was being decided. 'Child!' he said to me suddenly. 'What do you think of our plan?' Of course he asked me this as sometimes a man of the greatest intellect will, at the last moment, leave everything to the turn of a coin. Instead of replying to Napoleon, I turned to Davoust and said as if I was inspired: 'Take to your heels, General; go home!' The plan was abandoned. Davout shrugged and as he went out muttered: *'Bah! Il devient superstitieux!'* And next day the retreat was ordered."

"This is all extremely interesting," said the prince in a very low voice, "if that's how it was—that is," he hastened to correct himself, "I mean to say—"

"Oh, Prince!" cried the general, so enraptured by his own story that he probably would not have been stopped even by the most flagrant indiscretion. "You say 'that's how it was.' But there was more, I assure you there was a great deal more! These are all only paltry political incidents. But I repeat I was witness to the nightly tears and groans of that great man, no one but me saw that! Toward the end, it's true, he didn't weep anymore, he had no more tears, he only moaned at times; yet his face was more and more clouded with darkness. It was as if eternity had already cast its somber wing over him. Sometimes at night we spent whole hours alone together in silence—sometimes the Mameluke Roustan would be snoring in the next room—the fellow slept fearfully soundly. 'And yet,' Napoleon would say of him, 'he is devoted to me and my dynasty.' Once when I was in terrible distress he suddenly noticed the tears in my eyes; he looked at me deeply touched: "You feel sorry for me!" he cried. 'You, a child, and perhaps another child will feel sorry for

519

me too, my son, *le roi de Rome.* All the rest, they all hate me, yes, and my brothers will be the first to betray me in adversity!' I burst into sobs and flew to him; he could contain himself no longer; we embraced and our tears intermingled. 'Please,' I sobbed, 'please write a letter to the Empress Josephine!' Napoleon gave a start, though for a moment, and said to me: 'You have reminded me of the one other heart that loves me. Thank you, my friend!' Then he sat down and wrote that letter to Josephine. Constant was sent off with it the next day."

"You did very well," said the prince. "In the midst of bad thoughts you made him have a good feeling."

"Exactly, Prince, and how beautifully you do put it, and how very like that good heart of yours!" the general cried rapturously and, strange to say, real tears shone in his eyes. "Yes, Prince, that was indeed a sight! And, do you know, I almost went with him to Paris, and I would of course have shared his exile on the 'tropical prison isle,' but, alas, destiny parted us! We went our separate ways, he to that sultry island where perhaps more than once in his hours of dreadful tribulation he may have remembered that poor boy who had embraced him and forgiven him in Moscow. I was sent to the cadet corps, where I found nothing but harsh discipline, boorish comrades, and—alas! Everything turned to ashes! 'I don't want to take you away from your mother, and I am not taking you with me,' he said to me on the day of the retreat, 'but I want to do something for you.' He was about to mount his horse. 'Write something for me in my sister's album, as a memento,' I asked him timidly, for he was very gloomy and troubled. He turned back to me, asked for a pen, took the album. 'How old is your sister?' he asked me, raising his pen. 'Three years old,' I replied. *'Petite fille alors,'* he said. And he wrote in the album

> *Ne mentez jamais.*
> *Napoleon, votre ami sincère.*

Such advice and at such a moment—just think of it, Prince!"

"Yes, that is remarkable."

"That leaf hung in a gold frame under glass in the most conspicuous place in my sister's drawing room until the time of her death—she died in childbirth; where it is now I don't know, unless—but, good heavens! It's two o'clock already! How I have kept you, Prince! It's inexcusable."

The general got up from his chair.

"Oh, on the contrary," mumbled the prince, "you've quite

fascinated me and—after all, it's so interesting; I am quite grateful to you."

"Prince!" said the general, again squeezing his hand until it hurt and fixing him with gleaming eyes, as though coming to his senses and suddenly struck by an unexpected thought. "Prince! You are so kind, so forthright that sometimes I actually feel sorry for you. I am deeply touched when I look at you; oh, God bless you! May your life begin and flower—in love. Mine is finished. Oh, forgive me! Farewell!"

He went out quickly, covering his face in his hands. The prince could not doubt the sincerity of his emotion. He realized too that the old man had gone away elated at his success; yet he also felt somehow that he was one of that class of liars who, though they lie almost voluptuously, to the point of self-forgetfulness, still even at their most elated moments suspect they are not being believed and, indeed, that they cannot be believed. In his present disposition the old man might recover his senses, be overwhelmed with shame, suspect the prince of taking too much pity on him, and feel insulted. "Wasn't it worse to let him go on that way?" the prince wondered uneasily; suddenly he could not restrain himself and broke into an uncontrollable fit of laughter which lasted ten minutes. He began to reproach himself for his laughter but then realized he had nothing to blame himself for, because he felt infinite pity for the general.

His apprehensions proved true. That evening he received a strange note, brief but firm. The general informed him that he was parting from him too, that he respected him and was grateful to him, but that even from him he would not accept "evidence of a compassion humiliating to a man who was already miserable enough without that." When the prince heard that the old man had secluded himself with Nina Alexandrovna he felt almost reassured on his account. But we have already seen that the general had caused some sort of trouble at Lizaveta Prokofyevna's too. Here we cannot go into the details, but let us observe briefly that the upshot of the interview was that the general had frightened Lizaveta Prokofyevna and by his bitter references to Ganya had roused her to indignation. He was dismissed in disgrace. This is why he had spent such a night and such a morning, become completely unhinged, and run out into the street almost in a state of insanity.

Kolya still did not understand the matter fully and even hoped to manage him by severity.

"Well, where do you suppose we go now, General?" he said. "You don't want to go to the prince's, you've quarreled

521

with Lebedev, you have no money, and I never have any, and here we are in a nice mess, out in the middle of the street."

"Better to be in a nice mess than a mice nest," muttered the general. "I made that pun—with huge success at the—officer's mess—in forty-four. In the year eighteen hundred and—forty-four, yes! I don't remember— Oh, don't remind me, don't remind me! 'Where is my youth, where is my freshness?' as—who said that, Kolya?"

"That's in Gogol, Father, in *Dead Souls*," Kolya replied, with an anxious glance at him.

"Dead souls! Oh, yes, dead! When you bury me, write on the tombstone, 'Here lies a dead soul!' 'Disgrace is pursuing me!' Who said that, Kolya?"

"I don't know, Father."

"Yeropegov never existed! Yeroshka Yeropegov!" he cried wildly, stopping in the middle of the street. "And this from my son, my own son! Yeropegov, a man who for eleven months took the place of a brother, and for whom I fought a duel—Prince Vygoretsky, our captain, said to him over a bottle, 'Look here, Grisha, where did you ever get your Saint Anne's medal, tell me that?' 'On the battlefields of my country, that's where I got it!' I shouted, 'Bravo, Grisha!' Well, that led to a duel, and afterward he married—Marya Petrovna Su—Sutugin and was killed in action. A bullet glanced off the cross I wore on my chest and went straight into his forehead: 'I shall never forget!' he cried and fell dead. I—I have served with honor, Kolya, I have served nobly, but disgrace—'disgrace is pursuing me!' You and Nina will come to my grave—'Poor Nina!' I used to say that to her, Kolya, a long time ago in the old days, and she loved it so—Nina, Nina! What have I done to your life? What can you love me for, long-suffering soul? Your mother has the soul of an angel, Kolya, do you hear, of an angel!"

"I know that, Father. Father dear, let's go back home to Mother! She was running after us. Well, why are you standing there? As if you didn't understand— Well, what are you crying for?"

Kolya was in tears himself and kissing his father's hands.

"You are kissing my hands—my hands!"

"Well, yes, your hands! What's surprising about that? Here, why are you crying in the middle of the street? And you call yourself a general, a military man. Come along, let's go."

"God bless you, dear boy, for being respectful to a disreputable—yes, to a wretched and disreputable old man, your father. May you too have such a boy—*le roi de Rome*— Oh a curse, a curse on this house!"

"But what's going on here?" cried Kolya, flaring up. "What has happened? Why don't you want to go home now? Why have you gone out of your mind?"

"I'll explain, I'll explain to you—I'll tell you everything. Don't shout, people will hear—*le roi de Rome*—oh, I am sick, I am miserable! 'Nurse, where is thy grave?' Who said that, Kolya?"

"I don't know, I don't know who said that! Let's go home now—at once! I'll give Ganya a beating if necessary—where are you going now?"

The general was pulling him toward the front steps of a house.

"Where are you going? That's a stranger's house."

The general sat down on the steps, still drawing Kolya toward him.

"Bend down, bend down!" he murmured. "I'll tell you everything—disgrace—bend down—your ear, your ear, I'll whisper in your ear—"

"But what is it?" Kolya cried, terribly alarmed, yet turning his ear to listen.

"*Le roi de Rome,*" whispered the general again, appearing to tremble all over.

"What? Why do you keep saying *le roi de Rome?* What is it?"

"I—I—" the general whispered again, clutching "his boy's" shoulder more and more tightly. "I want—I want to tell you everything. Marya—Marya Petrovna Su—Su—Su—"

Kolya tore himself free, seized the general by the shoulders, and looked at him wildly. The old man had turned purple, his lips were blue, faint tremors passed over his face. Suddenly he lurched forward and began to sink gently into Kolya's arms.

"A stroke!" Kolya shouted aloud in the street, seeing at last what was the matter.

Chapter FIVE

❦

The fact was that Varvara Ardalionovna had in her conversation with her brother rather exaggerated the certainty of the news concerning the prince's engagement to Aglaya Yepanchin. Perhaps, being a perceptive woman, she had foreseen what was bound to happen in the near future; perhaps, disappointed because her dream (which in truth she had never really believed in) had gone up in smoke, she being human, could not deny herself the satisfaction of magnifying the disaster and pouring a little more bitterness into her brother's heart, even though she sincerely loved him and felt sorry for him. But in any case she could not have received such precise information from her friends the Yepanchin girls; there were only hints, half-uttered words, silences, riddles. And perhaps Aglaya's sisters had intentionally let fall some indiscretion so that they might learn something from Varvara Ardalionovna; perhaps in the end they could not forgo the feminine pleasure of teasing a friend a little, though they had known one another since childhood: they could not over such a long time have failed to notice certain little hints of her intentions.

On the other hand the prince, too, though he was in perfectly good faith when he assured Lebedev that he had nothing to tell him and that nothing special had happened to him, was perhaps also mistaken. In reality something very strange seemed to have happened to all of them: nothing had happened, and at the same time a great deal had happened. This fact Varvara Ardalionovna had guessed with her sure feminine instinct.

However, it is very difficult to explain in an orderly fashion how it came about that everyone at the Yepanchins' was suddenly struck by the identical thought that something of capital importance had happened to Aglaya and that her fate was being decided. But as soon as this thought flashed through their minds they had all immediately insisted that they had supposed something of the kind long ago and had seen it all clearly ever since the "poor knight" episode and perhaps even before, only at the time they had simply refused to believe anything so absurd. So did the sisters assert. Lizaveta Prokofyevna, of course had also foreseen it and known it all before anyone else, and she had been "heartsick" about it for a long time, but—whether she had known it long before or not—the thought of the prince now became intolerable to her, simply because it threw off her thinking. Here was a question which required an immediate solution, but not only could she not solve it but, no matter how hard she struggled, poor Lizaveta Prokofyevna could not even grasp it clearly. It was a difficult matter: "Was the prince a good match or not? Was it all a good thing or not? If it wasn't (which seemed certain), then why wasn't it? And if by any chance it was (which was also possible), then, there again, why was it?" The head of the family himself, Ivan Fyodorovitch, was of course at first surprised, but then he suddenly confessed, "I had an inkling of something of the sort all along; I'd put it out of my mind and then, by Jove, there it was again!" He relapsed into silence under the menacing glare of his spouse, but that was in the morning; in the evening, alone with her and compelled to speak he suddenly, and with unusual heartiness, gave voice to several unexpected reflections: "After all, what is it really all about?" (Silence.) "Of course, it's all very strange, if true, and I certainly don't dispute it, but—" (Another silence.) "And on the other hand, if one faces it squarely, the prince is, after all, by George, an excellent fellow and—and—and—well, after all, our name, our own family name, all this will have the effect of keeping up the family name, which has fallen in the eyes of the world, looking at it from that point of view, that is, because—after all there is the world! And the world is the world. But even so, the prince is not without a certain fortune, even though not a very great one. He does have—and—and—" (Prolonged silence and complete collapse.) When Lizaveta Prokofyevna had heard her husband out, her outrage surpassed all bounds.

In her opinion all that had taken place was "unpardonable and really criminal folly, a sort of fantasy, stupid and absurd!" In the first place, "This little princeling is a sickly idiot," and the second, "He is a fool, he knows nothing of the world and has no place in it. Whom is he to meet? What is to be done with him? Here is some impossible sort of democrat or other, without even a post in the Service, and—and—and—what would Belokonskaya say? Was this the sort of husband they had imagined and planned for Aglaya?" The last argument was, of course, the most important. Her mother's heart shuddered at this reflection, bled and wept, though at the same time something within it stirred and suddenly said to her: "In what way is the prince unacceptable to you?" Well, it was these objections of her own heart which troubled Lizaveta Prokofyevna more than anything else.

For some reason Aglaya's sisters liked the notion of the prince. It did not even strike them as particularly strange; in short, they might suddenly have gone over to his side altogether. But they both decided to say nothing. It had been observed in the household that, invariably, the more stubborn and insistent Lizaveta Prokofyevna's opposition and objections became on any point in a family dispute the more surely it could be taken as a sign that she was probably ready to give in on this point. However, Alexandra Ivanovna did not find it possible to be perfectly silent. Her mother, having for some time acknowledged her as her counselor, was calling on her every minute now, demanding her opinions and, above all, her recollections. "How has all this come about? Why didn't anyone see it? Why was nothing said at the time? What was the meaning of that horrid 'poor knight'?" And why was she alone, Lizaveta Prokofyevna, "doomed to look after everyone, to notice everything, to see everything ahead, while all the rest of them did nothing but count blackbirds?" And so forth and so on. Alexandra Ivanovna was guarded at first and only mentioned that she found her father's idea rather correct, that the marriage of Prince Myshkin with one of the Yepanchin girls might appear quite satisfactory. Becoming steadily more heated, she added that the prince was "no fool" and never had been; and that as for his social importance, God only knew what a decent person's importance would depend on in a few years here in Russia; whether on his successes in the Service, which were essential hitherto, or on something else. To all this her mother promptly retorted that Alexandra was "a freethinker and that it was all the result of the horrid woman's question." A half an hour later she went off to town, and from there to Kamenny Island to see Belokonskaya, who happened to be in Petersburg just at the time, but was soon leaving. Belokonskaya was Aglaya's godmother.

The "old woman" listened to all Lizaveta Prokofyevna's fervent and desperate confessions and was not in the least moved by the tears of the distraught mother. She even looked at her ironically. The old lady was a terrible despot; she could not bear having her friends on an equal footing with her, even her oldest ones, and she resolutely looked upon Lizaveta Prokofyevna as her protégée, as she had done thirty-five years before; and she could not reconcile herself to the sharpness and independence of her character. She observed among other things that "it appeared that in their customary fashion they had run ahead of themselves and made a mountain out of a molehill," that she was not convinced from anything she had heard that there was anything really very serious the matter, that it might be better to wait and see what else developed, that the prince was, in her opinion, a perfectly decent young man, though sickly, peculiar, and of little consequence. And, worst of all, he was openly keeping a mistress. Lizaveta Prokofyevna understood very well that Belokonskaya was rather cross about the failure of Yevgeny Pavlovitch, whom she had introduced to them. She returned home to Pavlovsk in an even greater state of irritation than when she had left, and immediately everyone fell afoul of her, chiefly on the grounds that "they had lost their minds," that in no other family were affairs conducted as in theirs. "Why were they in such a hurry? What has happened? So far as I can see, nothing has really happened! Wait until something happens!" Ivan Fyodorovitch was always imagining things, and weren't they making a mountain out of a molehill? And so on and so forth.

The upshot of it was that they had to keep calm, look on coolly, and wait. But, alas, the calm did not last even ten minutes. The first blow to their coolness was the news of what had happened during her absence on Kamenny Island. (Lizaveta Prokofyevna's visit had taken place the morning after the prince had paid his call after midnight instead of at nine o'clock.) The sisters replied to their mother's impatient questions in detail, saying first that "nothing special" seemed to have happened in her absence, that the prince had called, that Aglaya had not come down for quite a long time, for perhaps half an hour, and that then when she had come down had at once asked the prince to play chess, that the prince had not known the first thing about chess and Aglaya had immediately beaten him, that she had then been in very high spirits and made the prince feel terribly ashamed of his ignorance, had laughed at him dreadfully, until the prince was a very sorry sight to behold. Then she suggested that they play cards, "fools." But this time it turned out the other way: the prince was so good at "fools" that he played like a master, a veritable professor of the game. Aglaya even cheated and changed cards, and stole tricks from under his nose, and still he made her the "fool" five times in a row. Aglaya became furious, quite forgot herself, in fact, and said so many caustic and horrid things to the prince that he soon stopped laughing; and he turned quite pale when she told him at last that she would "never set foot in this room as long as he was sitting there," and that it was quite disgraceful of him to come calling on them, "particularly at night, past midnight, *after all that had happened.*" Then she went out and slammed the door. Despite all their consolation the prince had left as if he were leaving a funeral. Suddenly, fifteen minutes after the prince had left, Aglaya had run downstairs to the veranda in such haste that she had not dried her eyes, which were still wet with tears. She had run downstairs because Kolya had come and brought a hedgehog. They had all begun looking at the hedgehog, and in reply to their questions Kolya explained that the hedgehog was not his and that he was out walking with a schoolfriend of his, Kostya Lebedev, who had stayed out in the street too embarrassed to come in because he was carrying a hatchet; and that they had just bought both the hedgehog and the hatchet from a peasant they had met. The peasant was selling the hedgehog and took fifty kopecks for it, and they had persuaded him to sell the hatchet because it seemed like a good thing to do and also because it was a very fine hatchet. At this, Aglaya suddenly began pestering Kolya to sell her the hedgehog at once; she got very excited about it and even called him "dear." For a long time Kolya would not agree but at last gave in and called Kostya Lebedev, who did, in fact, come with a hatchet and looked very embarrassed. But then it had suddenly come to light that the hedgehog was not theirs at all, but actually belonged to a third boy, Petrov, who had given them both money to buy Schlosser's *History** for him from a fourth boy who being in need of money was selling it cheap; that they had gone out to buy Schlosser's *History* but could not resist and had bought the hedgehog; so that both the hedgehog and the hatchet belonged to that third boy, and they were taking them to him now, instead of Schlosser's *History*. But Aglaya was so insistent that they finally decided to sell her the hedgehog. As soon as Aglaya had the hedgehog she had promptly put it, with Kolya's help, into a wicker basket. covered it with a table napkin, and begun pleading with Kolya to take the hedgehog at once to the prince, in her name, with the request that he accept it as a "token of her most profound respect." Kolya agreed gladly and promised to do it but immediately began pestering her to know: "What did the hedgehog signify and what did making such a present mean?" Aglaya replied that it was none of his business. He answered that he was certain there was some allegory to it. Aglaya had then been angry and told him cuttingly that he was nothing but a silly boy. Kolya retorted at once that if he hadn't respected her as a woman and, beyond that, respected his own principles, he would have proved to her then and there that he knew how to answer such an insult. However, it had ended in Kolya's carrying off the hedgehog in great delight, and Kostya Lebedev had also run off after him. Aglaya, seeing that Kolya was swinging the basket too hard, could not help calling after him from the veranda: "Please don't drop him, Kolya darling!" as if she had not been quarreling with him just before. Kolya had stopped and, also as if they had not quarreled, shouted with the utmost readiness, "Don't worry, Aglaya Ivanovna, I won't," and again ran off as fast as he could run. After that Aglaya had burst into a fit of laughter and run up to her room, extremely pleased, and had been in high spirits all the rest of the day.

Lizaveta Prokofyevna was completely stunned by this news. One might wonder why, but this was, quite plainly, the sort of mood she was in. Her anxiety was aroused to the highest pitch—chiefly over the hedgehog. What did the hedgehog mean? What had been concocted? What lay behind it? What sign? What hidden message? Moreover, poor Ivan Fyodorovitch, who happened to be present during this interrogation, completely spoiled the whole thing by his reply. In his opinion there was no hidden message whatsoever and the hedgehog was "purely and simply a hedgehog"—unless it might also be taken to mean friendliness and the patching up of differences; in short, there was nothing here but an innocent and harmless prank.

Let us note in parentheses that he had guessed right. The prince, having returned home after being ridiculed and chased away by her, had been sitting for a half an hour in the darkest despair when Kolya suddenly appeared with the hedgehog. The skies immediately cleared; the prince seemed to have arisen from the dead; he questioned Kolya, hanging on his every word, asked the same questions ten times over, laughed like a child, and kept pressing the hands of the two laughing boys looking at him with their bright eyes. It was certain that Aglaya was forgiving him and the prince might go to see her again that very evening, and for him this was not merely the most important thing in the world but everything.

"What children we still are, Kolya! And—and how nice it is that we are," he cried joyfully at last.

"The plain fact is she's in love with you, Prince, and that's all there is to it!" Kolya replied with impressive authority.

The prince blushed but this time said nothing, and Kolya

just laughed and clapped his hands; a minute later the prince laughed too, and from then on he glanced at his watch every five minutes to see how much time had passed and how long it was until evening.

But Lizaveta Prokofyevna's mood got the better of her, and at last she could not help giving way to a moment of hysterics. In spite of all the protests of her husband and daughters she sent at once for Aglaya in order to put a definite question to her and receive from her a perfectly clear and definite answer. "So as to settle it once and for all, to be done with it, and to have it off our minds so we can forget about it. Otherwise," she declared, "I won't live through till evening." And only then did everyone realize to what an absurd pass the matter had reached. They got nothing from Aglaya except feigned surprise, indignation, loud laughter, and derisive remarks about the prince as well as all who were questioning her. Lizaveta Prokofyevna took to her bed and did not appear again until the tea hour, when the prince was expected. She awaited him with many a palpitation and when he did appear almost went into a fit.

And the prince too came in with trepidation, almost feeling his way, smiling oddly and searching everyone's eyes as though questioning them all because Aglaya was not in the room, a circumstance which alarmed him at once. This evening there were no other guests, only the members of the family. Prince S. was still in Petersburg occupied with the affairs of Yevgeny Pavlovitch's uncle. "If only he could have been here and said something," said Lizaveta Prokofyevna, referring to him. Ivan Fyodorovitch sat looking extremely troubled; the sisters were serious and, as though purposely, silent. Lizaveta Prokofyevna did not know how to open the conversation. At last she burst out in a vigorous attack against the railways and glared with determined challenge at the prince.

Alas! Aglaya still did not come, and the prince felt completely lost. Disconcerted and hardly able to utter a word, he ventured the opinion that it would be a very good thing if the railroad was improved, but Adelaïda suddenly laughed and the prince was again crushed. At that very moment Aglaya came in, looking calm and dignified, bowed ceremoniously to the prince, and solemnly seated herself in the most prominent place at the round table. She looked inquiringly at the prince. Everyone realized that the moment had come when all their doubts would be removed.

"Did you receive my hedgehog?" she asked firmly and almost angrily.

"Yes, I did," said the prince blushing, his heart failing him.

"Then please explain at once what you think about it. This is essential for Mother's peace of mind and everyone else's in the family."

"Look here, Aglaya—" said the general, suddenly uneasy.

"This is beyond all bounds!" cried Lizaveta Prokofyevna, suddenly alarmed by something.

"There are no bounds at all here, *Maman*," her daughter answered sternly at once. "I sent the prince a hedgehog today and I want to know his opinion. What about it, Prince?"

"What sort of opinion, Aglaya Ivanovna?"

"About the hedgehog."

"That is—I imagine you want to know—how I received the hedgehog—or rather how I looked upon the—sending of the hedgehog, I mean—if that's the case I would say that—in fact—"

He choked and fell silent.

"Well, you haven't said very much," said Aglaya after about five seconds. "All right, I'll say no more about the hedgehog; but I am very glad I can at last put an end to all the misunderstandings that have been accumulating. Let me at last find out from you yourself, personally, are you asking me to marry you or not?"

"Good heavens," cried Lizaveta Prokofyevna.

The prince gave a start and drew back; Ivan Fyodorovitch was rigid with astonishment; the sisters frowned.

"Don't lie, Prince, tell the truth. Because of you I am tormented by strange questions. Is tnere any foundation to these questions? Well, is there?"

"I have not asked you to marry me, Aglaya Ivanovna," answered the prince, suddenly reviving, "but you know yourself how I love you and believe in you—even now."

"What I asked you was—are you asking for my hand or not?"

"I am," replied the prince faintly.

There was a profound stir in the room.

"This won't do at all, my dear fellow," said Ivan Fyodorovitch, greatly agitated. "This—this is practically impossible if it's like this. Aglaya—I'm sorry, Prince, I'm sorry, dear friend!—Lizaveta Prokofyevna!" he turned to his wife for assistance. "It's got to be—looked into."

"I refuse! I refuse!" cried Lizaveta Prokofyevna, waving her hands.

"Please, *Maman*, let me speak too, for I count for something in this matter; the extreme moment in my life is being decided," (Aglaya expressed herself exactly this way), "and I want to find out for myself, and, what's more, I'm glad it's in front of everyone. Let me ask you, Prince, if you 'harbor such intentions' how do you propose to assure my happiness?"

"I don't know, truly, Aglaya Ivanovna, how to answer you. What answer is there to give? And—and is it necessary?"

"You seem to be embarrassed and out of breath. Rest a little and pull yourself together. Drink a glass of water, though you'll soon be given some tea."

"I love you, Aglaya Ivanovna, I love you very much, I love only you, and—don't joke, please—I love you very much."

"But this is a serious matter; we are not children and we must look at things from a practical point of view. Would you be so good as to explain now what your fortune is?"

"No, no, no, Aglaya," muttered Ivan Fyodorovitch in alarm. "What are you doing? That's not the way it's done, not like that!"

"Disgraceful!" Lizaveta Prokofyevna said in a loud whisper.

"She's mad!" Alexandra whispered just as loudly.

"My fortune? You mean—money?" said the prince in surprise.

"Precisely."

"I have—I have now one hundred and thirty-five thousand roubles," the prince murmured, blushing.

"Is that all?" Aglaya demanded in open surprise, not blushing in the least. "But never mind, it doesn't matter, especially if we live economically. Do you intend to enter the Service?"

"I was thinking of taking the examination to become a private tutor."

"A very good idea; that of course will augment our income. Were you thinking of becoming a court chamberlain?"

"A court chamberlain? I never thought of it, but—"

But at this point the two sisters could not restrain themselves and burst into laughter. Adelaïda had for some time noticed in Aglaya's twitching features the signs of imminent and irrepressible laughter, which she was then doing her best to control. Aglaya glared at her laughing sisters, but she could not contain herself even a second, and she too burst into mad, almost hysterical laughter. Finally she jumped up and ran out of the room.

"I knew it was all a joke and nothing more!" cried Adelaïda. "From the very beginning—from the hedgehog!"

"No, I won't stand for this! I won't stand for it!" cried Lizaveta Prokofyevna in sudden anger, and rushed out after

Aglaya. The sisters followed right after her. The prince was left alone in the room with the head of the family.

"This—this is— Could you ever have imagined such a thing, Lev Nikolayevitch?" cried the general sharply, apparently not knowing himself exactly what he meant to say. "No, I mean seriously; seriously speaking."

"I see that Aglaya Ivanovna is making fun of me," replied the prince sadly.

"Wait a minute, my dear friend. I'll go and see and you wait—because—will you, Lev Nikolayevitch, will you, at least, explain how this all happened and what it all means, all of it, so to speak, as a whole? You must admit, my boy, I am the father. I am the father, so I don't understand a thing that's going on. You, at least, explain it to me!"

"I love Aglaya Ivanovna. She knows this and—I think she has known it a long time."

The general shrugged.

"Strange, very strange—and you love her very much?"

"Very much."

"Strange, it all does seem very strange to me. I mean it's such a surprise and a blow that—you see, dear boy, it's not the fortune (though I did expect you had more than that) but—my daughter's happiness—after all—are you capable of assuring her—happiness? And—and—what is it: a joke on her part or is it real? I mean on her part; not yours."

From the other side of the door Alexandra Ivanovna was heard calling her father.

"Wait here, dear friend, please wait! Wait here and think it over, and I'll be right back," he said hurriedly and rushed off in alarm to answer Alexandra's call.

He found his wife and daughters in each other's arms, weeping tears of joy, tenderness, and reconciliation. Aglaya was kissing her mother's hands, cheeks, lips; both were hugging each other ardently.

"Here, look at her, Ivan Fyodorovitch, this is how she really is!" said Lizaveta Prokofyevna.

Aglaya raised her happy, tear-stained little face from her mother's breast, looked at her father, laughed aloud, ran over to him, hugged him tightly, and kissed him several times. Then she rushed back to her mother and hid her face in her bosom so that no one could see her and again burst into tears. Lizaveta Prokofyevna covered her with part of her shawl.

"Well, here, what are you doing to us, you cruel girl, for after all that's what you are!" she said, but joyfully, as if she could suddenly breathe freely again.

"Cruel! Yes, cruel!" Aglaya suddenly said. "Spoiled! Worthless! Tell that to Papa. Oh, yes, he's here. Papa, are you here? Do you hear?" she said, laughing through her tears.

"My dear, my idol!" said the general kissing her hand and beaming with happiness. (Aglaya did not take her hand away.) "So you do love this young man then?"

"No! No! No! I can't stand—your young man, I can't stand him!" cried Aglaya tossing back her head in sudden rage. "And if you ever dare say that again—I really mean it, Papa, I mean it. Do you hear?"

And evidently she really did mean it; she had flushed all over and her eyes were blazing. Her father was startled, but Lizaveta Prokofyevna made a sign behind Aglaya's back, and he took it to mean "don't ask questions."

"If that is so, my angel, it's as you wish; do as you please. He's waiting there alone; shouldn't he be given a delicate hint to leave?" The general, in his turn, winked significantly to his wife.

"No, no, that's not necessary; especially a 'delicate' hint. Go out to him yourselves; I'll come in right afterward. I want to beg this—young man's pardon, because I've hurt his feelings."

"You have indeed," Ivan Fyodorovitch affirmed gravely.

"Well, then, if that's so, you had better stay here, and I'll go in first alone, and you right after me, a second later. That will be better."

She had reached the door, but suddenly she turned back.

"I'll laugh! I'll die laughing!" she told them sadly.

But in the next instant she turned and rushed out to the prince.

"Well, what is all this? What do you make of it?" Ivan Fyodorovitch said quickly.

"I am afraid to say," replied Lizaveta Prokofyevna as quickly. "But it's clear to me."

"It's clear to me too. Clear as day. She loves him."

"More than loves him—she's in love with him!" put in Alexandra Ivanovna. "And with someone like that, imagine!"

"God bless her, if that's to be her fate!" said Lizaveta Prokofyevna, crossing herself devoutly.

"That's what it is—fate," the general agreed. "There's no escaping fate."

And they all went into the drawing room, where a new surprise awaited them.

Aglaya, far from laughing as she had feared to do, had gone up to the prince and said to him almost timidly:

534

"Please forgive a wicked, stupid, spoiled girl," (she took his hand), "and believe me that we all respect you immensely. And if I've dared make fun of your lovely good nature please forgive me as you would forgive a mischievous child. Forgive me for persisting in this foolishness which cannot of course have the slightest consequence."

The last words Aglaya spoke with special emphasis.

Father, mother, and sisters reached the drawing room in time to see and hear all this, and they were all struck by the words "foolishness which cannot of course have the slightest consequence," and even more by the serious way in which Aglaya had spoken of this foolishness. Everyone exchanged wondering glances, but the prince had apparently not understood these words and was at the very summit of happiness.

"Why do you talk like that?" he murmured. "Why do you —ask forgiveness?"

He even wanted to tell her he was unworthy of being asked forgiveness. Who knows, perhaps he did see the meaning of those words, "foolishness which cannot of course have the slightest consequence," but being such a strange man perhaps he was even pleased by them. There was no doubt that it was a supreme happiness to him just to know that he could come to see Aglaya again without hindrance, that he would be allowed to talk to her, sit with her, take walks with her; and, who knows, he would perhaps have been satisfied with no more than that for the rest of his life! (This was just the sort of contentment which Lizaveta Prokofyevna seemed secretly to be dreading; she had hit upon it instinctively; there was much that Lizaveta Prokofyevna secretly dreaded which she could not have put into words herself.)

It is difficult to describe how animated and high-spirited the prince was on that evening. He was so gay that one could feel gay just looking at him—as Aglaya's sisters expressed it afterward. He became talkative, and that had not happened to him since the morning six months before when he had first made the acquaintance of the Yepanchins. On his return to Petersburg he was conspicuously and deliberately silent, and had very recently said to Prince S., in the presence of everyone, that he had to control himself and say nothing because he had no right to degrade an idea by his way of expressing it. He was almost the only one who talked all that evening; he told them many things and gladly answered questions clearly and fully. But there was no hint of love-talk in his words. He was expressing earnest and sometimes quite abstruse ideas. The prince even presented some of his own views, his own private observations, so that it all could have been ridiculous if it had not been so "well put," as all who heard him agreed afterward. Although the general liked serious subjects of conversation, both he and Lizaveta Prokofyevna found it far too learned, and toward the end of the evening they had grown melancholy. However, toward the last the prince went so far as to tell several very amusing stories, which he was the first to laugh at, so that the others laughed more at his delighted laughter than at the stories themselves. As for Aglaya she said almost nothing the whole evening but was listening to Lev Nikolayevitch with unwavering attention, and even more than listening, gazing at him.

"The way she looks at him, can't take her eyes off him, hangs on every word he says, catching everything, everything!" Lizaveta Prokofyevna said later to her husband. "But tell her she loves him and the house falls in!"

"What can you do? It's fate!" said the general with a shrug, and for some time afterward he kept repeating this phrase. We may add that for him, as a man of business, there was a great deal about the present state of affairs which he, too, disliked—above all its lack of clarity; but for the time being he had also decided to keep silent and just look—into Lizaveta Prokofyevna's eyes.

The family's cheerful mood did not last long. The very next day Aglaya quarreled with the prince again, and things went on like this for several more days. For hours on end she would ridicule the prince and almost make a clown of him. It is true they would sometimes sit for an hour or two together under the arbor in the garden, but it was observed that at such times the prince was almost always reading the papers to Aglaya, or a book of some kind.

"Do you know," Aglaya said to him once, interrupting his reading of the newspaper, "I've noticed that you are terribly uneducated. You don't know anything really well. When someone asks you who someone is, or what year something happened, or the name of a treaty—you're quite pitiful."

"I told you myself I didn't have much education," answered the prince.

"Well, what have you besides that? How can I respect you after that? Go on reading. Or rather, don't go on reading. Stop reading."

And there was another brief incident that same evening which struck them all as enigmatic. Prince S. returned. Aglaya was very friendly with him, she asked him all sorts of questions about Yevgeny Pavlovitch. (Prince Lev Nikolayevitch had not arrived yet.) Suddenly Prince S. permitted himself an allusion to the "new change about to take place in the family," alluding to something Lizaveta Prokofyevna had let drop to the effect that it might be necessary to put off Adelaïda's wedding again so that both weddings would take place together. Aglaya flared up in an almost incredible way at "all these stupid ideas" and went so far as to say, among other things, that "she had no intention, just yet, of replacing anyone's mistress."

These words amazed everybody, but particularly her parents. In a secret conference with her husband, Lizaveta Prokofyevna insisted that he obtain a definite explanation from the prince concerning Nastassya Filippovna. Ivan Fyodorovitch swore that it was all nothing but an "outburst" resulting from Aglaya's "modesty," that the outburst would never have happened if Prince S. had not referred to the marriage, because Aglaya herself knew, and knew for certain, that all this was only slander on the part of malicious people, and that Nastassya Filippovna was going to marry Rogozhin, that the prince had nothing to do with it, let alone an affair with her, and never did have, if the real truth was to be told.

The prince however was not troubled by anything and continued to be blissfully happy. Oh, of course, he too occasionally noticed a gloomy and impatient look in Aglaya's eyes, but he believed more strongly that it was something else and the gloom disappeared of itself. Once he had put his faith in something, nothing could sway him. Perhaps he was a little too complacent; at least so it appeared to Hippolite, who happened to meet him accidentally in the park.

"Well, wasn't it true when I told you you were in love?" he began, going up to the prince and stopping him.

The prince shook hands with him and congratulated him on "looking so well." The invalid seemed to be in an optimistic frame of mind, as is so often the case with consumptives.

He had gone up to the prince to say something sarcastic about his happy expression but almost at once began talking instead about himself. He began complaining, he complained a great deal and for a long time, and rather incoherently.

"You wouldn't believe," he concluded, "how irritable, petty, vain, egotistical, and ordinary they all are there. Can you imagine? They took me only on the condition I would die as soon as possible, and now they're all furious because I'm not dying but that, on the contrary, I'm much better. What a comedy! I'll bet anything you don't believe me!"

The prince did not feel like answering.

"Sometimes I even consider moving back with you," Hippolite added casually. "So I suppose you don't believe them capable of taking in a person only on the condition that he dies as quickly as possible?"

"I thought they invited you with other things in mind."

"Ah-ha! So you're not so simple as you're made out to be! Now is not the time, or I would have told you a few things about dear old Ganya and those hopes of his. They are getting at you, Prince, mercilessly, and it's a pity you are taking it so calmly. But, too bad—you can't help it!"

"So that's what you're sorry for me about!" laughed the prince. "Do you imagine I'd be happier if I were more worried?"

"Better to be unhappy and *know* than to be happy and—fooled. You don't seem to believe you have a rival—and in that quarter?"

"What you are saying about a rival is rather cynical, Hippolite; I'm sorry I haven't the right to answer you. As for Gavril Ardalionovitch, you can see for yourself he can't very well be calm after all he has lost, that is if you know the first thing about his affairs. It seems to me better to look at it from this point of view. He can still change; he has a long life ahead of him, and life is rich—besides—besides—" the prince broke off abruptly. "As for getting at me, I don't even understand what you're talking about. We had better drop this conversation, Hippolite."

"Let's drop it for now. Besides, no question of your not acting nobly. Yes, Prince, you have to touch it and still you don't believe it. Ha, ha! And don't you despise me right at this moment, what do you say?"

"What for? Because you have suffered more than we and you go on suffering?"

"No, because I'm unworthy of my suffering."

"Whoever can suffer more is worthy of suffering more. When Aglaya Ivanovna read your confession she wanted to see you, but—"

"She's putting it off—she can't. I understand, I understand," interrupted Hippolite, as if anxious to close the subject as quickly as possible. "By the way, they say you read all that nonsense aloud to her yourself; really, it was written and—done in a state of delirium. And I don't understand how anyone could be so—I won't say cruel (that would be humiliating to me), but so childishly vain and vengeful as to reproach me with that confession and use it as a weapon against me! Don't worry, I'm not saying this about you."

"But I'm sorry you repudiate what you wrote, Hippolite; it's sincere and, you know, even the most absurd parts of it, and there are many," (Hippolite frowned), "are redeemed by suffering; for to avow them is also suffering and—perhaps an act of great courage. Certainly the idea that inspired you was basically noble, no matter how it might appear. I see that more clearly as time goes by, I swear to you. I'm not judging you, I'm saying this to tell you what I think, and I'm sorry I kept silent at the time—"

Hippolite reddened. It crossed his mind that the prince was pretending and trying to catch him up, but looking into his face he could not help but believe in his sincerity; his expression cleared.

"And still I have to die!" he said, nearly adding: "a man like me!" "And you can't imagine how that Ganya of yours plagues me; he objected that probably three or four of those who heard my confession would die before I do! Imagine! He thinks that will console me. Ha, ha! In the first place they haven't died yet; and even if these people did die, what sort of consolation do you suppose that would be for me? He judges according to himself, but now he's gone farther than that and he simply insults me. He says a decent man in this situation dies quietly, and that the whole thing was nothing but egoism on my part! Imagine! No, but really what egoism on his part! What refinement, or you might just as well say, what crude pigheaded egoism—that they can't even see in themselves! Have you read, Prince, of the death of a certain Stepan Glebov in the eighteenth century? I happened to read it yesterday."

"What Stepan Glebov?"

"He was impaled under the reign of Peter."

"Oh, Good Lord, I do know! He was fifteen hours on the stake, in the frost, in a fur coat, and he died with extraordinary greatness of spirit. Yes, I have read it. What about it?"

"God does grant such deaths to people, but not to us! But perhaps you think I'm not capable of dying like Glebov?"

"Oh, no, I don't think that," said the prince in confusion. "I only meant to say that you—I mean not that you wouldn't be like Glebov, but—that you—you'd be more likely to be—back in those days—"

"I see. I'd be Osterman,* not Glebov. That's what you mean."

"What Osterman?" asked the prince in surprise.

"Osterman, the diplomat Osterman, Peter's Osterman," Hippolite muttered, suddenly disconcerted.

A perplexed silence followed.

"Oh, no!" said the prince emphatically, after a moment, "that's not what I meant. I don't think you ever would have been an Osterman."

Hippolite frowned.

"However, the reason I say that," the prince suddenly continued, apparently wishing to make amends, "is that the people of those days (I assure you I've always been struck by it) were not at all like the people of today; it wasn't the same race as it is now, it was really like a different species. People then somehow all shared the same idea, but nowadays they are more nervous, more evolved, more sensitive, capable of having two or three different ideas at a time—modern man is broader, I assure you, that's what prevents him from being of a whole piece as they were in those days. I—I only meant to say that, and not to—"

"I understand. Because you disagreed with me so naïvely, now you're going out of your way to comfort me. Ha, ha! You are a complete child, Prince. Still, I notice you all treat me like a china teacup. Never mind, never mind, I'm not angry. Anyway, we've had a terribly funny conversation; you're sometimes a perfect child, Prince. You should know, though, it's just possible I'd like to be something better than Osterman; no, it wouldn't be worth rising from the dead to be an Osterman. However, I see that I must die as quickly as possible, or I too might— Leave me. Good-bye! Well, all right, then tell me what in your opinion would be the best way for me to die? I mean so that it would be as—virtuous as possible. Well, tell me!"

"Pass on by us and forgive us our happiness," said the prince in a low voice.

"Ha, ha, ha! Just what I thought. I expected something like that! And yet you are—you are— Well, well! You eloquent people! Good-bye, good-bye!"

Chapter SIX

Varvara Ardalionovna had also been quite correct in what she had told her brother about the evening party at the Yepanchins' at which Belokonskaya was expected: the guests were due to arrive that very evening; but here again she had expressed herself rather too strongly. It is true that the affair had been arranged with excessive haste, and even with quite unnecessary fussing, precisely because in that family "they could never do anything the way other people did." It could all be explained by the impatience of Lizaveta Prokofyevna, who did not want to be "kept guessing" any longer, as well as by the tender stirrings of both parental hearts over the happiness of their most beloved daughter. Moreover, Belokonskaya really was going away soon, and since her patronage actually did mean a great deal in society, and since it was hoped that she would be favorably disposed toward the prince, the parents were counting that "the world" would accept Aglaya's fiancé straight from the hands of the all-powerful "old woman," and that therefore, if there was anything strange about it, it would appear considerably less strange under such sponsorship. The crux of the matter was that the parents were themselves quite unable to decide whether there was anything strange about it, and, if so, how strange, or whether it simply was not strange at all. The friendly and candid opinion of people of authority and competence would have been just what was needed at the present moment when, thanks to Aglaya, nothing was as yet finally settled. In any case, the prince sooner or later would have to be introduced into society, about which he had not the slightest notion. In short, they intended to "show" him. Nonetheless the evening was planned to be quite simple; only "friends of the family" were expected, and not very many of them. One other lady besides Belokonskaya was coming, the wife of a most important dignitary. Among the young people only Yevgeny Pavlovitch was counted on, and he was to escort Belokonskaya.

The prince had heard that Princess Belokonskaya was coming almost three days before, but that there was to be an evening party he learned only the previous day. Of course he had noticed an air of anxiety among the members of the family, and from certain hints and worried remarks they let fall in his presence, he realized that they were afraid he might not make the right impression. But all the Yepanchins, without exception, had somehow formed the notion that because of his simplicity he would never be able to guess that everyone was so uneasy on his account. And therefore, looking at him, everyone was inwardly troubled. The fact was, however, that he attached almost no importance to the approaching event; something quite different preoccupied him: with every passing hour Aglaya was growing more capricious and gloomy—that was destroying him. And when he learned that Yevgeny Pavlovitch was expected, he was delighted and said he had been wishing to see him for a long time. For some reason no one liked this remark; Aglaya left the room in a state of pique, and it was only late in the evening, toward twelve o'clock, when the prince was leaving, that she took the occasion to say a few words to him in private, as she saw him out.

"I would like you not to come during the day tomorrow. Come in the evening when all these—guests are here. Did you know there will be guests?"

She spoke impatiently and with marked severity: it was the first time she had spoken to him of this "party." To her, too, the thought of the guests was almost unbearable; everyone noticed it. Possibly she wanted very much to quarrel with her parents about it, but pride and modesty prevented her from mentioning it. The prince understood at once that she too had fears on his account (and did not wish to admit she had), and he too suddenly felt frightened.

"Yes, I have been invited," he replied.

She evidently found it difficult to go on.

"Can one talk about something serious with you—for once in your life?" She was suddenly extremely angry, without knowing why herself, yet not able to control herself.

"You can, and I'm listening to you—I'm very glad to," murmured the prince.

For a minute Aglaya was again silent, then she began speaking with obvious repugnance:

"I did not want to argue with them about it, they won't listen to reason about some things. Some of the principles *Maman* has sometimes have always been revolting to me. I say nothing about Papa, you can't expect anything from him. Of course, *Maman* is a noble woman; if you were to suggest anything unworthy to her, you'd see. Yet she kowtows before these—wretched people! I'm not talking about Belokonskaya: she's a dreadful little old woman with a dreadful nature, but she's clever and she keeps them all wrapped around her little finger—at least there's that to say for her. Oh, the baseness of it! And the absurdity! We have always been middle-class people, as middle-class as can be. Why should we try to climb into these high social circles? My sisters are doing it; it's Prince S. who's mixed them up. Why are you pleased that Yevgeny Pavlovitch is coming?"

"Listen, Aglaya," said the prince, "I think you're afraid for me that I'll botch the test tomorrow, in that company?"

"Afraid for you?" cried Aglaya, turning crimson. "Why should I be afraid for you, even if you do—even if you do disgrace yourself completely? What is it to me? And how can you use such expressions? What does 'botch the test' mean? It's a wretched expression, vulgar."

"It's a—schoolboy expression."

"Yes, it is a schoolboy expression! A wretched expression! You apparently intend to use such expressions tomorrow evening. You can look up some more of them in your dictionary at home; you'll make a sensation! It's a pity you know how to come into a room properly; where did you learn that? Will you know how to take a cup of tea and drink it properly, when everyone will be watching to see?"

"I think I will."

"That's too bad, I would have laughed if you didn't. At least, be sure you break the Chinese vase in the drawing room! It's a very expensive one. Please do break it, it was a present. Mother would go out of her head and start crying in front of everyone—it's so precious to her. Make some sort of gesture with your hands, as you always do; knock it over and break it. Make a point of sitting next to it."

"On the contrary. I'll sit as far from it as possible. Thank you for warning me."

"So you're already afraid of making wild gestures. I'll bet anything you'll start talking about some serious topic, something serious and learned and elevated. It will be something so—proper!"

"I think that would be stupid—if it wasn't to the point."

"Listen, once and for all," said Aglaya, losing patience at last, "if you start talking about anything like the death penalty, or Russia's economic situation, or how 'beauty will save the world,' then I'll—of course I'll be delighted and I'll laugh a lot but—I warn you beforehand, don't let me ever see you again after! Listen, I'm serious! This time I'm serious!"

She did in fact utter her threat seriously, and there was something unusual in the way she said these words, something that showed in her eyes, something the prince had never noticed before, something which was certainly not a joke.

"Well, you've made it so that I'm sure to start talking about something serious and perhaps even break the vase. Just now I had no fears at all, and now I'm afraid of everything. I'm sure to botch the test."

"Then don't say anything. Sit down and don't say anything."

"I won't be able to. I'm sure that from fear I'll start saying something, and from fear I'll break the vase. Perhaps I'll fall on the slippery floor or something like that, because it's hap-

543

pened to me before. I'll dream about it all night. Why did you say all that?"

Aglaya looked at him gloomily.

"You know," he said at last, "it's better if I don't come at all tomorrow! I'll report sick and that will be that!"

Aglaya stamped her foot and turned pale with anger.

"Good Lord! Has anyone ever seen anything like this? He is not coming when it's just for him that— Oh, God, what a pleasure to deal with a—nonsensical creature like you!"

"Well, I'll come, I'll come!" the prince said quickly. "And I give you my word I'll sit the whole evening and not say anything. That's what I'll do."

"You'll do well. You just said, 'I'll report sick.' Where do you pick up such expressions? Why do you talk to me like that? Could you be trying to tease me?"

"I'm sorry. That was a schoolboy expression too. I won't use it again. I understand perfectly that—you're afraid for me—don't be angry!—and I'm terribly glad that you are. You can't believe how frightened I am now and—how glad for what you've said. But all this fear is trivial and absurd, I swear it is. Oh yes, Aglaya! But the joy will remain. I'm so glad you are such a child, such a good kind child— Oh, how lovely you can be, Aglaya!"

Aglaya was of course about to become very angry, but suddenly a feeling she herself did not expect took possession of her in a single instant.

"And you won't reproach me for the rude things I've just said—sometime—later?" she suddenly asked.

"Don't say such a thing! And why are you flaring up again? And now you're looking gloomy again. You look much too gloomy sometimes, Aglaya; you never used to look that way. I know why it is—"

"Be quiet!"

"No, it's better I say it. I've wanted to say this for a long time; I have said it but—it wasn't enough, because you didn't believe me. However, there is a person who stands between us—"

"Be quiet! Be quiet! Be quiet! Be quiet!" Aglaya suddenly interrupted, gripping his hand tightly and looking at him almost in dread. At that moment someone called her. As if greatly relieved, she broke away from him and ran off.

All night the prince was in a fever. Strange to say, he had been feverish for several nights in a row. This time, when he was half delirious, the thought occurred to him: what if he should have a fit tomorrow in front of everyone? For he had had fits when he was with people. He turned cold at the

544

thought. All night long he imagined himself in a weird and incredible company, among people of a strange kind. The important thing was that he "began talking"; he knew he ought not to be talking, but he talked all the time, he was trying to talk them into something. Yevgeny Pavlovitch and Hippolite were also among the guests, and they seemed to be on extremely good terms.

He woke up toward nine o'clock with a headache and confused thoughts and strange impressions. For some reason he badly wanted to see Rogozhin, to see him and talk to him at great length—about what, he did not know himself. Later he made up his mind to go to see Hippolite for some reason. His heart was so troubled that though the events of the morning made an extremely strong impression on him it was an impression which was somehow incomplete. One of these events was Lebedev's visit.

Lebedev appeared rather early, shortly after nine, almost completely drunk. Although the prince had not been observant of late, he could not help noticing that ever since General Ivolgin had moved out of their house, three days now, Lebedev had been behaving very badly. He had suddenly appeared dirty; his clothes were spotted, his tie askew, his coat collar torn. He even took to shouting and raging in his part of the house, and this commotion could be heard across the little courtyard. Vera had come in once in tears and had spoken about it. As he made his appearance now, he began talking very strangely, pounding himself on the chest, and blaming himself for something.

"I've been paid back—I've been paid back for my treachery and meanness—a slap in the face!" he concluded at last in a tragic tone.

"A slap in the face! From whom? And so early in the day?"

"So early in the day?" Lebedev smiled sarcastically. "Time has nothing to do with it—even with physical reprisals. But I have received a moral slap, not a physical one!"

Suddenly, without further ceremony, he sat down and began to tell his story. It was a very incoherent one. The prince looked pained and was about to leave but suddenly certain words caught his attention. He was struck dumb with amazement. Lebedev was telling him curious things.

He started by talking, apparently, about some letter. Aglaya Ivanovna's name was mentioned. Then suddenly Lebedev began bitterly accusing the prince of something; it seemed that he had been offended by the prince. At first, he said, the prince had honored him with his confidence in dealings with a certain "personage" (with Nastassya Filippovna), but had later broken with him completely and had dismissed him in an ignominious manner, and had indeed been so offensive the last time as to avoid with great rudeness "an innocent question about coming changes in the house." With drunken tears Lebedev confessed that after that he could bear it no longer, especially as he "knew a great deal—a very great deal—from Rogozhin, from Nastassya Filippovna, and from Nastassya Filippovna's friend, and from Varvara Ardalionovna—herself—and from—and even from Aglaya Ivanovna herself—can you imagine it, sir—through Vera, through my beloved daughter Vera, my one and only child —yes, sir—though in fact she is not my one and only child, since I have three. And who was informing Lizaveta Prokofyevna by letters, in the greatest of secrecy, sir, heh, heh? Who has been writing her about all the doings and—movements of the personage Nastassya Filippovna, heh, heh, heh? Who, who is this anonymous writer, let me ask?"

"Could it be you?" asked the prince.

"Exactly," replied the drunkard with dignity, "and today at half past eight, only a half hour ago—no, it was three-quarters of an hour ago—I informed that most noble mother that I had news of a certain incident—of consequence—to communicate to her. I informed her by a note through a maid at the back door, sir. She received me."

"You've just been to see Lizaveta Prokofyevna?" the prince asked, hardly able to believe his ears.

"I've just been to see her, and I've just received a slap in the face—a moral one. She returned the letter, she actually threw it at me, unopened—and threw me out on my ear—morally of course, not physically—though not very far from it!"

"What unopened letter did she throw at you?"

"But could I have—heh, heh, heh! Haven't I told you yet? I thought I had already. I'd received a certain little letter to pass on to—"

"From whom? To whom?"

But some of Lebedev's "explanations" were extremely hard to make out, or to understand anything from them whatever. The prince could only gather that the letter had been brought early in the morning to Vera Lebedev by a servant girl, to be delivered to the person to whom it was addressed—"just as before—just as before to a certain personage and from the same person, sir (for one of them I designate as a "person" and the other only as a "personage," to set her in her place; for there's a great difference between the innocent and most noble daughter of a general and—a kept woman, sir), and so, the letter was from a 'person' whose name begins with the letter 'A.' "

"How is it possible? To Nastassya Filippovna? Nonsense!" the prince exclaimed.

"It was, it was. Or if not to her, to Rogozhin—it's the same thing, to Rogozhin—and there was even one from the person whose name begins with the letter 'A' to Mr. Terentyev, to be passed on, sir," said Lebedev, winking and smiling.

As Lebedev often wandered from one subject to another and forgot what he had started to say, the prince kept silent to let him finish. However, it was all very obscure: did he pass on the letters or did Vera? Since he said himself it was the same if the letters were to Rogozhin or to Nastassya Filippovna, it seemed more likely that the letters had not passed through his hands, if there actually had been letters. How this particular letter had come to him remained completely unaccountable; the most likely explanation was that he had somehow taken it from Vera—taken it on the sly and brought it to Lizaveta Prokofyevna with some object in view. This was what the prince finally pieced together and understood.

"You've gone out of your mind!" he cried in extreme agitation.

"Not completely, most respected Prince," Lebedev replied, not without malice. "It's true that my first thought was to give it to you, into your own hands, as a favor—but I then thought it better to do the favor there and reveal everything to the noble mother—since I had informed her before by anonymous letter; and when I wrote her the note asking her to see me at twenty minutes past eight I also signed myself 'your secret correspondent.' I was admitted at once, and in fact with the utmost haste by the back door, into the presence of the noble mother."

"Well?"

"Well, you already know, sir, she almost beat me; came very close to it; so that you might almost say that she did beat me, sir. And she threw the letter in my face. It's true she wanted to keep it—I saw this, noticed it, but she reconsidered and threw it in my face: 'Since a fellow like you has been entrusted to deliver it, then deliver it.' She really was offended. Since she wasn't ashamed to say that in front of me, it means she was really offended. She has a fiery temper!"

"Where is that letter now?"

"Why, I still have it. Here it is."

And he handed the prince Aglaya's note to Gavril Arda-

547

lionovitch, which the latter showed to his sister so triumphantly two hours later.

"This letter mustn't remain with you."

"It's for you! For you! I'm bringing it to you, sir," Lebedev said ardently. "Now I'm yours again, all yours, from head to heart, your servant, sir, after my momentary treachery! 'Pierce my heart but spare my beard,' as Thomas More said —in England and Great Britain, sir. *Mea culpa, mea culpa,* as the Romish pope says—I mean he's the pope of Rome, but I call him the Romish pope."

"This letter must be passed on at once," said the prince anxiously. "I'll deliver it."

"But wouldn't it be better, most well-bred Prince, wouldn't it be better—to do this!"

Lebedev made a strange, obsequious face, began fidgeting violently in his chair as if he had suddenly been pricked by a needle, and, winking craftily, made a meaningful gesture with his hands.

"What do you mean?" demanded the prince severely.

"Wouldn't it be better to open it first?" he said in a low, ingratiating voice intended to be confidential.

The prince jumped up in such a rage that Lebedev took to his heels, but stopped in the doorway to see whether he would be pardoned.

"Ah, Lebedev, is it possible to sink to such a state?" the prince cried bitterly.

Lebedev's face brightened.

"I'm low! I'm vile!" he said, returning at once, with tears in his eyes, beating himself on the chest.

"Why, this is detestable!"

"Yes, it is detestable! That's just the word for it!"

"And why this habit of acting so—strangely? Because you're—nothing but a spy! Why have you written anonymously and worried such a—noble and kind-hearted woman? And why, after all, doesn't Aglaya Ivanovna have the right to write whomever she pleases? Did you go there to complain today? What did you hope to get out of it? What made you turn informer?"

"Merely out of friendly curiosity and—to be of service to a noble spirit. Yes, sir!" Lebedev said. "Now I am all yours, all yours again! Even if you were to hang me!"

"And you went to Lizaveta Prokofyevna in the state you're in now?" the prince inquired, his curiosity mingled with disgust.

"No, sir. I was fresher. And, in fact, more decent. It was only after my humiliation that I got into—this state."

"Well, very well, leave me now."

However, this request had to be repeated several times before the visitor at last made up his mind to go. He had the door wide open but came back in again, on tiptoe, into the center of the room and again began making motions with his hands to show how a letter could be opened; however, he dared not put his advice into words; then he went out with a gentle and affectionate smile.

All this had been extremely painful to hear. Out of it all appeared one striking and significant fact: that Aglaya was in a state of great anxiety, great uncertainty, and great distress for some reason ("from jealousy," the prince whispered to himself). It also appeared that she was being upset by ill-meaning people, and it was very strange that she trusted them as she did. Of course, in her inexperienced but proud, hot little head she was no doubt hatching all sorts of special schemes, perhaps ruinous ones, wild and unheard-of. The prince was greatly alarmed and in his troubled state he did not know what course to take. There was something he absolutely had to prevent from happening—he felt that. Once again he looked at the address on the sealed letter. Oh, he had no doubts or concern on this score, because he trusted her; something else made him uneasy about this letter; he did not trust Gavril Ardalionovitch. And yet he decided to deliver the letter to him himself and had already left his house to do so, but on the way he changed his mind. Almost at Ptitsyn's door, as if it was planned that way, he met Kolya and asked him to deliver the letter into his brother's hands, just as though it had come directly from Aglaya Ivanovna. Kolya asked no questions and delivered it, so that Ganya had no idea that the letter had stopped so many times on its way. When he returned home, he asked Vera Lebedev to come to him, told her what was necessary and reassured her, for she had been all this time searching for the letter and in tears. She was horrified when she learned that her father had carried off the letter. (The prince found out from her later that she had more than once helped Rogozhin and Aglaya Ivanovna in secret; it never occurred to her that she might be doing anything harmful to the prince.)

And the prince at last became so distressed that when, two hours later, a messenger from Kolya ran in with the news of his father's illness, for a while the prince could scarcely make out what it was all about. But this event restored him, for it completely distracted his attention. He went to Nina Alexandrovna's (where of course the sick man had been carried) and stayed right up until the evening. He was hardly of any use, but there are people whom one somehow likes to have around one in moments of grief. Kolya was terribly affected, he cried hysterically and yet was always off running errands: he ran for a doctor and turned up three, he ran to the chemist's and to the barber's. The general was resuscitated, but did not regain consciousness. The doctors declared that the patient was, at all events, "in danger." Vera and Nina Alexandrovna did not leave the sick man's side for a moment. Ganya was upset and shaken, but he did not want to go upstairs and was even afraid to see the invalid; he wrung his hands and in a broken, almost incoherent conversation with the prince he managed to say, "What a calamity—and to have to happen at just such a time!" The prince thought that he understood what particular time Ganya was referring to. The prince did not find Hippolite at Ptitsyn's. Toward evening Lebedev rushed in, having slept the whole day after the morning's "explanation." He was now almost sober and shed genuine tears over the sick man, as if he had been his own brother. He blamed himself loudly, not explaining, however, just how he was at fault, and he kept after Nina Alexandrovna, assuring her every moment that he, he alone was the cause of it, he and no one else, that he had only acted out of "friendly curiosity," and that the "deceased" (as for some reason he persisted in calling the still-living general) was a "man of genius!" He made a special point of stressing his genius, as if this reflection might be of some extraordinary utility just then. Seeing his sincere tears, Nina Alexandrovna finally told him, without a trace of reproach and even with a certain affection, "Well, God bless you. Don't cry, now. Here, God will forgive you!" Lebedev was so struck by these words and the tone in which they were said that for the rest of the evening he was unwilling to leave Nina Alexandrovna's side (and he spent all the following days, until the general's death, in their house almost from morning till night). Twice during the day a messenger came from Lizaveta Prokofyevna to inquire about the invalid's health. When at nine o'clock in the evening the prince made his appearance in the Yepanchins' drawing room, already filled with guests. Lizaveta Prokofyevna immediately began questioning him about the sick man, sympathetically and in detail, and she replied with great gravity to Belokonskaya's question, "Who is this sick person and who is Nina Alexandrovna?" This pleased the prince very much. In his own explanation of the case to Lizaveta Prokofyevna the prince himself spoke "beautifully," as Aglaya's sisters declared afterward: "modestly, quietly, without too many words, without gestures, and with dignity; he came in beautifully, he was dressed perfectly," and not only did he not "fall down on the slippery floor," as he had feared the evening before, but on the contrary he clearly made a favorable impression upon everyone.

For his part, having sat down and looked around, he immediately noticed that the company bore no resemblance whatever to the specters with which Aglaya had frightened him the evening before, or to the nightmare figures he had dreamed of in the night. For the first time in his life he saw a tiny corner of what was known by the awesome name of "society." For some time now certain particular inclinations, considerations, and purposes of his own had made him extremely anxious to penetrate into this charmed circle of people, and therefore he was greatly interested in his first impression of it. This first impression was indeed fascinating. At once it seemed to him that all these people had been born to be together; that the Yepanchins were not having a "party" that evening, that no outside guests had been invited, that these were all "their intimate friends," and that he himself had long been their devoted friend and shared their feelings and convictions, and that he was rejoining them now only after a short separation. The charm of the elegant manners, the simplicity, the apparent candor was almost magical. It could never have entered his mind that all this forthrightness and nobility, this wit and high personal dignity, were perhaps no more than a magnificent artistic veneer. Indeed, the majority of the guests, despite their imposing appearance, consisted of rather empty people, who in their self-satisfaction were themselves unaware that much of their superiority was only a fine surface for which they were not responsible, having received it unwittingly and through inheritance. The prince, under the spell of his first exquisite impression, had no inclination to suspect this. He saw, for example, that this old man, an important dignitary, who was old enough to be his grandfather, actually stopped his conversation in order to listen to a young and inexperienced man like himself, and not only to listen but visibly to value his opinion, be so friendly with him, so genuinely cordial to him, though they were strangers meeting each other for the first time. Perhaps it was this refined courtesy which most impressed the prince's warm and sensitive nature. Perhaps he was all too predisposed and even determined toward this favorable impression.

And yet all these people—though they were of course "friends of the house" and of each other—were far from being such friends of the house or of each other as the prince took them to be when he met them and was presented to them. There were people here who would never have recognized the Yepanchins as their equals in any manner. There were people here who absolutely detested one another; all her life old Belokonskaya had "despised" the wife of the "old dignitary," and that lady in turn was far from being fond of Lizaveta Prokofyevna. Her husband, the "dignitary," who had for some reason been looking out for the Yepanchins since their youth and was the leading figure present, was such a consequential personage in Ivan Fyodorovitch's eyes that the latter could feel nothing but veneration and awe in his presence, and he would have genuinely despised himself had he for one moment regarded him as his equal and not as the Olympian Jove. There were people here who had not met each other for years and felt nothing for one another but indifference if not dislike, but they greeted each other now as if they had seen one another only yesterday in the most friendly and agreeable company. Yet the group was not a large one. Besides Belokonskaya and the "old dignitary" —who was in fact an important person—and his wife, there was first of all a very solid army general, a baron or a count with a German name, an extremely taciturn man, who had an extraordinary reputation for his knowledge of governmental affairs and even something of a reputation for learning— one of those Olympian administrators who know everything, "except perhaps Russia itself," a man who made some "extraordinarily profound remark" once every five years, but which inevitably would become proverbial and reach even into the very highest circles; one of these leading functionaries who usually, after an extraordinarily long career (indeed phenomenally long), die with great rank in magnificent circumstances, with great fortunes, though they have served without ever performing great deeds and even with a sort of distaste for great deeds. This general was Ivan Fyodorovitch's immediate superior in the service, and the latter, out of warm-hearted gratitude and from a special form of vanity, considered him to be also his benefactor; but this general did not by any means consider himself Ivan Fyodorovitch's benefactor; indeed, he treated him with placid indifference; and though he gladly availed himself of his multitudinous good services he would have immediately replaced him with another administrator had any consideration, however trivial, demanded it. There was also an elderly and important gentleman who was said to be a relative of Lizaveta Prokofyevna, though this was quite untrue, a man of good rank and title, wealthy, well born, stout and in the best of health, a great talker, and who even had the reputation of being a discontented person (though of course in the most legitimate sense of the term), even a disgruntled man (but this too, in him, was agreeable), with the manners of an English aristocrat and English tastes in matters of rare roast beef, harness, footmen, and so on. He was a great friend of the "dignitary" and diverted him, and moreover Lizaveta Prokofyevna for some reason entertained the curious idea that this elderly gentleman (a rather frivolous man and at times a great admirer of the fair sex) would suddenly take it into his head to make Alexandra happy by proposing marriage. Just beneath this highest and most solid stratum of the assembly came a layer of much younger people, though they were, too, conspicuous for their extremely elegant qualities. Besides Prince S. and Yevgeny Pavlovitch, this group included the well-known and very charming Prince N., who had once seduced and ravished female hearts all over Europe, now a man of forty-five, but still of splendid appearance, a wonderful raconteur, a man of wealth, though his affairs had fallen into a certain disorder, and who by habit spent most of his time abroad. There were, finally, people there who might be said to make up a third special layer, who did not themselves belong to the "charmed circle" of society but who, like the Yepanchins, could sometimes, on occasion, be met within that circle. Out of a certain tact, which they had adopted as a rule, the Yepanchins liked on the rare times they gave large invitational parties to mix the highest society with people of a somewhat lower level, with selected representatives of "the average sort of people." The Yepanchins were indeed praised for doing this, and it was said of them that they knew their place and were people of finesse; and the Yepanchins were proud of this opinion of themselves. One of the representatives of the average sort of people that evening was an engineer with the rank of colonel, a serious man, a particularly close friend of Prince S., by whom he had been introduced to the Yepanchins, a man, however, taciturn in company and who wore on the index finger of his right hand a large and conspicuous ring which had probably been given to him. There was also present a poet of German origin, but a Russian poet, and perfectly presentable, so that he could be introduced into good society without apprehensions. He was of handsome appearance, though for some reason rather repulsive, about thirty-eight, impeccably dressed, from an extremely bourgeois though highly respectable German family; he knew how to make the most of every opportunity, to fight for the protection of high-placed people and keep in their good graces. At one time he had translated into verse an important work of some major German poet, and he had been clever in dedicating his translation, and in boasting of his friendship with a certain celebrated but dead Russian poet (there is a whole category of writers who are extremely fond of maintaining, in print, their friendships with great though deceased writers), and he had quite lately been introduced to the Yepanchins by the wife of the "old dignitary." This lady had the reputation of being a patroness of literary and learned people and in fact had actually obtained pensions for one or two writers through persons in high places with whom she had influence. And she did have a certain sort of importance. She was a lady of about forty-five (a very young wife for a man so old as her husband), a former beauty who now, like so many forty-five-year-old ladies, had a mania for dressing far too elegantly; she had no great intelligence and her knowledge of literature was quite dubious. But the patronage of literary men was as much a mania with her as elegance of dress. Many original works and translations were dedicated to her; two or three writers had with her permission printed letters they had written to her on subjects of the greatest importance.

And this was the society the prince took for the truest coin, for pure unalloyed gold. Besides, it happened, as if expressly, that on this evening all these people were in a most happy frame of mind and particularly pleased with themselves. All without exception knew that they were doing the Yepanchins a great honor by their visit. But, alas, the prince had no suspicion of such subtleties! For instance he did not suspect that the Yepanchins, having undertaken such an important step as a decision about their daughter's future would not have dared fail to exhibit him, Prince Lev Niko-layevitch, to the old dignitary who was the acknowledged patron of the family. The old dignitary on his part, though he would have borne with the most perfect tranquility the news that the most dreadful of calamities had befallen the Yepanchin family, would have been offended had the Yepanchins betrothed their daughter without his advice and without, so to speak, his blessing. As for Prince N., this charming, unquestionably witty, and wholly forthright man, was absolutely convinced that he was something in the nature of a sun which had risen that night to shine down upon the Yepanchins' drawing room. He regarded them as infinitely beneath him, and it was precisely this artless and generous notion which prompted his marvelously charming ease of manner and friendliness with the Yepanchins. He knew quite well that on this occasion he would be obliged to tell some story to enchant the company, and he was preparing for this moment with positive inspiration. When, a little later, Prince Lev Nikolayevitch had heard the story, he felt he had never heard such brilliant humor and such wonderful gaiety and ingenuousness, something which was touching, coming from such a Don Juan as Prince N. And yet had he only known how old and hackneyed that story was, how everyone knew it by heart, and how sick and tired every drawing room was of it, and how only at the innocent Yepanchins did it reappear as a novelty, as an impromptu, genuine, and brilliant reminiscence of a brilliant and marvelous man! At last even the German poet, though he behaved with extraordinary politeness and modesty, was ready to believe that he was conferring an honor on the household by his presence. But the prince did not notice this other side of the coin, he did not see what was underneath. This was the calamity Aglaya had not foreseen. She looked particularly beautiful that evening. All three young ladies were dressed well but not ostentatiously, and their hair was done in a special style of their own. Aglaya was sitting with Yevgeny Pavlovitch and was talking and joking with him with exceptional friendliness. Yevgeny Pavlovitch was behaving more sedately than usual, perhaps out of respect for the dignitaries present. He was, however, already well known in society; he was there quite in his own right, even though he was a young man. This evening he had arrived at the Yepanchins' wearing crepe on his hat and Belokonskaya had praised him for it: not every fashionable young man under similar circumstances would have worn crepe for such an uncle. Lizaveta Prokofyevna, too, was pleased by it, but on the whole seemed rather excessively preoccupied. The prince noticed that twice Aglaya had looked at him intently, and he thought she seemed satisfied with him. Gradually he began to feel terribly happy. His earlier "fantastic" thoughts and apprehensions (after the conversation with Lebedev) seemed to him now, in his sudden and frequent recollections of them, an inconceivable, impossible, and even ludicrous dream! (And his principal, though unconscious, impulse and desire had all day been to do anything to make himself disbelieve this dream!) He spoke little and only in answer to questions, and at last was silent altogether; he sat and listened to everyone, but was obviously overcome with pleasure. Little by little something like inspiration was gathering within him, ready to break forth at the first occasion. He began talking quite by chance, in answer to a question, and apparently without any special object.

Chapter SEVEN

❦

While the prince was gazing in admiration at Aglaya as she talked gaily to Prince N. and Yevgeny Pavlovitch, suddenly the elderly Anglophile, who was entertaining the "dignitary" in another corner, telling him something with great animation, uttered the name of Nikolai Andreyevitch Pavlishchev. The prince turned quickly toward them and began to listen.

They were discussing public affairs and some sort of disorders on estates in a certain province. There was apparently something amusing in the Anglophile's accounts, for the old man finally began laughing at the speaker's ill-humored vehemence. He spoke smoothly, drawling out his words peevishly, caressing the vowels, telling how he had been obliged as a direct result of current regulations to sell and at half price a splendid estate of his in that province, although he was in no particular need of money, and at the same time to keep an estate that had fallen into ruin, was losing money and under litigation, and how he had even had to spend money on it. "To avoid another lawsuit over the Pavlishchev estate, I ran away from them. One or two more inheritances like that and I'll be ruined. And yet there were nine thousand acres of excellent land to come from it!"

Ivan Fyodorovitch, who happened to be near the prince and had noticed his marked attention to the conversation, said to him in an undertone: "Well, there—that Ivan Petrovitch is a relative of the late Nikolai Andreyevitch Pavlishchev. I believe you were searching for his relatives." Until then he had been entertaining the general who was his superior in the Service, but he for some time had been noticing Lev Nikolayevitch's extraordinary isolation and was becoming uneasy. He wanted to introduce him in some measure into the general conversation and in this way to exhibit him a second time and bring him to the attention of "eminent persons."

"Lev Nikolayevitch was brought up under the care of Nikolai Andreyevitch Pavlishchev after the death of his own parents," he put in, catching Ivan Petrovitch's eye.

"De-lighted," remarked the latter. "And I remember very well. Just now when Ivan Fyodorovitch first introduced us I recognized you at once, from your face. In fact you've changed little in appearance, though I only saw you as a child of ten or eleven. There is something in your face I remember."

"You saw me as a child?" the prince asked in great astonishment.

"Oh, yes, a long time ago," Ivan Petrovitch went on, "in Zlatorverkhov, where you were living at my cousin's house. I used to go quite often to Zlatorverkhov in those days—don't you remember me? Quite possibly you don't. At that time you —had an illness of some kind. I was very much struck on one occasion."

"I don't remember at all!" said the prince ardently.

A few more words of explanation, perfectly calm on the part of Ivan Petrovitch and arousing extraordinary agitation in the prince, and it appeared that the two elderly maiden ladies, relatives of the late Pavlishchev, who lived on his Zlatorverkhov estate on which the prince had been brought up, were also cousins of Ivan Petrovitch. Ivan Petrovitch was, like everyone else, unable to explain why Pavlishchev took so much trouble over his ward, the little prince. "In fact I didn't interest myself in the matter then." And yet he did have an excellent memory, because he even remembered how severe his elder cousin, Marfa Nikitishna, had been with her little pupil, "to the point that once I stood up for you and had a dispute with her about her method of upbringing, because to be always caning and caning a sick child—that, you must admit—" and how tender, on the contrary, the younger cousin, Natalya Nikitishna, had been to the poor little child. "Now," he went on to explain, "they are both living in —— province, except I don't know if they're still alive, where Pavlishchev left them quite a nice little estate. I think Marfa Nikitishna wanted to enter a convent; however, I'm not sure about that; perhaps it was someone else I heard about—yes, I heard that the other day about a doctor's wife—"

The prince listened to all this with delight and emotion. With extraordinary warmth he declared that, for his part, he could never forgive himself for not having taken the opportunity during his six months' travels in the central provinces to look up and visit the ladies who had once brought him up. He had been meaning to go every day but he was always put off because of circumstances. But now he had promised himself—most certainly—even if it meant going to —— province. "So you really know Natalya Nikitishna? What a fine, what a saintly person! But Marfa Nikitishna too—excuse me, but I think you are mistaken about Marfa Nikitishna! She was severe but—it was impossible not to lose patience with —such an idiot as I was then. Ha, ha! Because I was a complete idiot then. Ha, ha! And yet—and yet you did see me then and— How is it I don't remember you, tell me? So you —my Lord! Are you really a relative of Nikolai Andreyevitch Pavlishchev?"

"I as-sure you I am," said Ivan Petrovitch with a smile, studying the prince.

"Oh, I didn't mean to say I—doubted it—and anyway, could it be doubted—ha, ha!—I mean at all? I mean could it really be doubted at all? But I meant the late Nikolai Andreyevitch Pavlishchev was such a splendid man! A most magnanimous man, truly; I assure you!"

The prince was not so much out of breath as "choked up with good-heartedness," as Adelaïda expressed it the next morning to her fiancé, Prince S.

"Well, good heavens," said Ivan Petrovitch with a laugh, "can't I even be a relative of a mag-nanimous man?"

"Oh, dear me!" cried the prince in confusion, growing more and more hurried and animated. "I—I said something foolish again, but—it had to happen because I—I—I'm off the point again! And what do I amount to, please tell me, in comparison with such interests, such vast interests? And in comparison with such a very magnanimous man, because, by heaven, he was a most magnanimous man, wasn't he? Wasn't he?"

The prince was trembling all over. Why he was suddenly so excited, why he had become so transported for no reason at all and, it appeared, in a matter quite out of keeping with the subject of conversation, it would have been difficult to tell. But he was in that state of mind and at that moment seemed almost to feel the very warmest and most tender gratitude toward someone on some account—perhaps even toward Ivan Petrovitch, and toward everyone in the room. He was "brimming over" with happiness. At last Ivan Petrovitch began looking at him much more attentively, the "dignitary" too was staring at him fixedly. Belokonskaya cast an angry glance at the prince and tightened her lips. Prince N., Yevgeny Pavlovitch, Prince S., the young ladies, all stopped their conversations and listened. Aglaya appeared to be frightened. As for Lizaveta Prokofyevna, she simply lost heart completely. They too had acted strangely, the mother and the daughters; they had foreseen and determined that it would be best for the prince to sit through the evening in silence, but as soon as they saw him in the corner, completely alone and perfectly content, they had at once become anxious. Alexandra had been about to go over to him and discreetly bring him across the whole room to their group, that is to Prince N.'s group, near Belokonskaya. And as soon as the prince began talking they became more anxious than ever.

"You are right there, he was a most excellent man," declared Ivan Petrovitch impressively, no longer smiling. "Yes, yes, he was a splendid man! A splendid man and a worthy one," he added after a pause. "Worthy, one might say, of every respect," he added still more impressively, after a third pause. "And—and it is very agreeable to find on your part—"

"Wasn't it that Pavlishchev there was a strange story about —with an abbé—an abbé—I've forgotten which abbé, except I do recall everyone was talking about it at the time," said the "dignitary," trying to remember.

"Abbé Goureau, a Jesuit," Ivan Petrovitch reminded him. "Yes, indeed, sir, there you have our most excellent and worthy people! Because after all he was a person of good birth, with a fortune, a court chamberlain, and if he had—if he had gone on in the Service— And there he suddenly threw up everything to go over to Catholicism and become a Jesuit, and quite openly, in a spirit of enthusiasm. It's true he died just in time—yes. Everyone said so then."

The prince was beside himself.

"Pavlishchev—Pavlishchev went over to Catholicism? That's impossible!" he cried in horror.

"Well, 'impossible' is saying quite a lot," said Ivan Petrovitch in a low, firm voice, "you must admit youself, my dear Prince. However, you do have such a high opinion of the deceased—he was indeed a most good-hearted man, a fact to which I chiefly attribute the success of that rascal Goureau. But just ask me what fuss and trouble I had over this affair later—and especially with that Goureau! Can you imagine," he turned suddenly to the old man, "they even tried to put a claim on the will, and I actually had to resort to the most—to the most energetic measures—to bring them around—because they're masters at such things! A-mazing! But, thank heavens, this was all happening in Moscow. I went right to court and we—brought them to reason—"

"You wouldn't believe how you've shocked and saddened me!" cried the prince again.

"I regret it, but as a matter of fact all this was essentially a trifling matter and would have come to nothing in the end, as always happens. I'm quite sure of that. Last summer," he said, turning again to the old man, "Countess K., too, they say, entered some Catholic convent abroad. Our people somehow never seem to stand up against those—cunning rogues—especially abroad."

"It all comes from our—fatigue, I should say," the little old man mumbled authoritatively. "Yes, and they have their way of preaching—very elegant and—quite their own—they do know how to scare a person. They even gave me a good scare, I can tell you, in Vienna, 1832. But I wouldn't give in and I ran away from them. Ha, ha! I really ran away from them."

"I heard that on that occasion, my dear sir," Belokonskaya put in suddenly, "you gave up your post in Vienna and ran off to Paris with the beautiful Countess Levitsky, not from a Jesuit."

"Well, it was from a Jesuit, all the same it was from a Jesuit!" the old man replied, amused by the pleasant recollection. He turned to Prince Lev Nikolayevitch, who was listening open-mouthed and still dumbfounded, saying amiably, "You seem to be very religious, which is something so rarely found in young men nowadays." The old man evidently wished to know more about the prince. For some reason he had begun to interest him very much.

"Pavlishchev was a clear-headed man and a Christian, a true Christian," the prince declared suddenly. "How could he submit to a faith—that is unchristian? Catholicism," he added suddenly, his eyes flashing and looking around as if he was trying to glare at everyone at once, "is no more than an unchristian faith!"

"Well, that's going too far," muttered the little old man, and he looked with surprise at Ivan Fyodorovitch.

"How can Catholicism be an unchristian religion?" demanded Ivan Fyodorovitch, turning in his chair. "What is it, then?"

"It's an unchristian religion, in the first place!" the prince said again, in great agitation and with unwarranted sharpness. "That's in the first place; secondly, Roman Catholicism is even worse than atheism—that's my opinion! Yes! That's my opinion! Atheism only preaches nullity, but Catholicism goes further; it preaches a distorted Christ, a Christ it has calumnied and defamed, the opposite of Christ! It preaches the Antichrist, I swear it does, I assure you it does! This is my own opinion, I've had it for a long time, and it has caused me distress myself—Roman Catholicism believes the Church cannot remain on earth without universal temporal power, and cries out: *Non possumus!* In my opinion, Roman Catholicism is not even a religion but very definitely the continuation of the

Holy Roman Empire, and everything in it is subservient to that idea, beginning with faith. The pope usurped the earth, an earthly throne, and took up the sword, and since then everything has been going on that way, except that to the sword they have added craft, deceit, fanaticism, superstition, villainy. They have trifled with the most sacred and truthful, the purest and most ardent feelings of the people; they have bartered everything, everything for money, for base earthly power. And isn't that the teaching of Antichrist? How could they fail to create atheism? Atheism has come from them, directly from Roman Catholicism! Atheism began, first, with themselves: how could they believe themselves? It has strengthened by revulsion from them; it has grown from their lies and their spiritual impotence! Atheism! Among us only exceptional classes of people don't believe, those, as Yevgeny Pavlovitch put it so splendidly the other day, who have lost their roots. But there, in Europe, awesome masses of the people themselves are beginning to lose their faith—first from darkness and lies, and now from fanaticism, from hatred of the Church and Christianity!"

The prince paused for breath. He had been talking terribly fast. He was pale and breathless. Everyone was exchanging glances, but at last the little old man burst out laughing openly. Prince N. drew out his lorgnette and stared for some time at the prince. The German poet crept from his corner and moved closer to the table, with a malicious smile on his face.

"You exaggerate a lot," drawled Ivan Petrovitch in a rather bored manner, and as if he was even embarrassed by something. "There are representatives of that church too who are virtuous and worthy of ev-er-y respect."

"I never said anything about individual representatives of the Church. I was speaking of Roman Catholicism in its essence, I was speaking of Rome. Can a church disappear entirely? I never said that!"

"Agreed, but all that is well known and even—there's no need to—it's a question of theology."

"Oh, no, no! It's not just a question of theology, I assure you it's not! It concerns us far more closely than you think. Our whole mistake is that we are still unable to see that this is not merely a question of theology! For socialism too is an offspring of Catholicism and the essential Catholic idea! It too, like its brother atheism, springs from despair in opposition to Catholicism as a moral presence, to replace the lost moral power of religion, to quench the spiritual thirst of parched humanity, and to save it not through Christ but also

561

through violence! This too is freedom through violence, this too is union through the sword and blood! 'Dare not believe in God, dare not have property, dare not have individuality —*fraternité ou la mort*, two million heads!' By their works ye shall know them—as it is said. And don't think this is so innocent and without danger to us. Oh, we must resist, and soon, soon! Our Christ, whom we have preserved and they have not even known, must shine forth in opposition to the West! Not by falling like slaves into Jesuit traps but by carrying our Russian civilization to them, we must now stand before them. And let it not be said among us that their preaching is elegant, as someone did just now—"

"But allow me, allow me!" said Ivan Petrovitch, growing terribly uneasy, looking around and even beginning to show signs of alarm. "Of course all these ideas of yours are praiseworthy and full of patriotism, but they are still extremely exaggerated and—we'd best drop the matter."

"No, it is not an exaggeration, it's rather an understatement, definitely an understatement, because I can't express it fully, but—"

"Al-low me—please!"

The prince fell silent. He sat erect and motionless in his chair, glaring at Ivan Petrovitch.

"It seems to me," remarked the little old man gently, without losing his composure, "that you have been too affected by what happened to your benefactor. You are overardent—perhaps because of your solitude. If you lived more among people—and you would, I trust, be welcomed in society as a remarkable young man—you would of course become less ardent and you would see that all this is much simpler—and besides, in my opinion, such rare cases occur partly because we are blasé and partly because we are—bored."

"Exactly, that's exactly it," cried the prince. "A splendid idea! Because of boredom, out of boredom, not because we are blasé, but on the contrary from thirst, not from surfeit; there you are mistaken! Not just from thirst, but from fever, from feverish thirst! And—don't think it's such a slight matter that we can merely laugh. Forgive me, but one must see ahead! As soon as our people reach the shore, as soon as we are certain it is the shore, we are so delighted that we immediately rush to its extreme end. Why is that? Here you are surprised at Pavlishchev, putting it all down to his madness or his goodness, but that's not the way it is! And it is not just we who are surprised by our strange Russian intensity in such cases, but all Europe. If one of us becomes a Catholic, he is bound to become a Jesuit, and one of the most subterranean. If one of us becomes an atheist he is bound to demand the uprooting of faith in God by force, that is, of course, by the sword! Why is this? Why such frenzy? Don't you know? Because he has found the homeland he has been missing here and he is rejoicing; he has found the shore, he has found land, and he rushes to kiss it! It is not only vanity, not only bad vain feelings that make Russian atheists and Russian Jesuits, but also spiritual agony, spiritual thirst, an anguished longing for something higher, for firm ground, for a fatherland in which they have lost faith because they have never even known it! It is so easy for a Russian to become an atheist, easier than for anyone else in the world! And our people don't simply become atheists, they infallibly *believe* in atheism as though it was a new religion, without being aware they are believing in nothingness. Such is our thirst! 'Whoever has no firm ground beneath his feet has no God either.' That's not my saying. It's the saying of a merchant, an Old Believer, whom I met while I was traveling. It's true he didn't say it that way. He said: 'Whoever has renounced his fatherland has also renounced his God.' Just to think that some of our most cultivated people have joined the sect of flagellants! But then in what way are flagellants worse than nihilists, Jesuits, or atheists? Perhaps it's even more profound! But this is where their anguish has brought them! Show the thirsting and burning companions of Columbus the shores of the New World, show a Russian the 'Russian world,' let him find this gold, this treasure hidden from him in the earth! Show him the future renewal of all humanity and its resurrection perhaps by Russian thought alone, by a Russian God and Christ, and you will see what a mighty, truthful, wise, and gentle giant he will grow into before the eyes of the astonished world, astonished and frightened, because from us they expect only the sword, the sword and violence, because, judging us by themselves, they cannot imagine us except as barbarous. And this has always been, and will be so more and more! And—"

But here suddenly something happened that stopped the orator's speech in the most unexpected manner.

All this feverish tirade, all this outpouring of impassioned and agitated words, confused and exalted ideas, which seemed to be jarring each other and tumbling over each other in confusion, all this foretokened something dangerous, something particular about the mental state of the young man who had so unexpectedly flared up, and for no apparent reason at all. Those in the drawing room who knew the prince wondered apprehensively (and some of them with shame) at this outburst, which was so at odds with his usual restraint and, indeed, his timorousness, his rare and particular tact in certain circumstances, and his instinctive feeling for true propriety. They could not understand why it had happened: the news about Pavlishchev could not possibly have been the cause of it. The ladies, in their corner, stared at him as at a madman, and Belokonskaya admitted later that one minute more and she would have "run for her life." The old gentlemen were almost totally confounded from the first moment of astonishment; from his chair General Yepanchin's superior glared with severity and displeasure. The colonel of engineers sat completely motionless. The little German actually turned pale, but he still smiled his false smile, looking at the others to see how they were reacting. However, all this, the whole scandalous scene, might have terminated in the most ordinary and natural way perhaps in another minute. General Yepanchin, greatly astonished but having recovered himself sooner than the others, had already made several efforts to stop the prince, but having failed was now making his way toward him with firm and decisive intentions. Another minute and, had it appeared necessary, he probably would have determined to lead the prince out of the room in a friendly way on the pretext of his illness, which was perhaps a valid reason, and one which Ivan Fyodorovitch himself believed firmly. But the affair took a very different turn.

At first, when the prince had entered the drawing room, he had sat as far as possible from the Chinese vase about which Aglaya had so frightened him. It seems incredible but, after Aglaya's words of the day before he was filled with an indelible conviction, an astonishing and incredible sort of premonition, that he would surely break this vase the next day, no matter how he tried to stay away from it, no matter how he tried to avoid the disaster! But so it was. In the course of the evening other impressions, as strong yet more bright and lucid, filled his heart: we have already spoken of this. He forgot his premonition. When he heard Pavlishchev mentioned and Ivan Fyodorovitch had led him to Ivan Petrovitch and presented him again, he had then drawn nearer the table and had sat in an armchair directly beside the large and beautiful Chinese vase, which stood on a pedestal just at his elbow and a little behind him.

As he said his last words he suddenly got up from his chair, waved his arm carelessly, somehow moving his shoulder and—there was a general outcry of horror! The vase swayed, as if hesitating whether to fall on the head of one of the elderly gentlemen, then suddenly inclined in the opposite direction, toward the little German poet, who just managed to leap out of the way in terror, and it crashed to the floor. The crash, the cry of horror, the precious fragments scattered on the carpet, the alarm, the astonishment—oh, it is difficult to describe what the prince felt then, and perhaps almost unnecessary! But we cannot fail to mention one strange sensation which came over him at that very moment and suddenly stood forth clearly amid all the other confused and terrible sensations: it was not the shame, nor the scandal, nor fright, nor the suddenness of it that had most struck him, but the realization that the prophecy had come true! Just what was so overpowering about this thought he could not explain to himself; he only felt struck to the heart and he stood still in an almost mystical terror. Another moment and everything seemed to open around him and in place of horror there was light and joy and ecstasy; his breath was about to fail him—but the moment passed. Thank God, it was not that! He caught his breath and looked around.

For a long time he seemed unable to understand the commotion around him; or rather he understood it perfectly and saw everything, but he stood there like a person apart, who had no place in any of it, and who, like an invisible man in a fairy tale, had stolen into the room and was watching people who were strangers to him yet who interested him. He saw them picking up the broken pieces, he heard the rapid conversations, he saw Aglaya, who was pale and looking at him strangely, very strangely: there was no hatred in her eyes, no anger; she looked at him with a frightened expression, yet with so much affection in it, and she looked at the others with such flashing eyes, that his heart suddenly ached with sweet pain. At last he saw to his amazement that everyone had sat down again, and they were actually laughing, just as if nothing had happened! In another moment the laughter grew louder; they were looking at him, laughing at his mute stupefaction, but their laughter was friendly and gay; many were starting to speak to him and speaking so affectionately, Lizaveta Prokofyevna most of all: she spoke laughingly and was saying something very, very kind. Suddenly he felt Ivan Fyodorovitch patting him on the shoulder in a friendly way; Ivan Petrovitch too was laughing; but the little old man did even better, was still more appealing and engaging: he took the prince's hand and, pressing it lightly and patting it with his other hand, urged him to collect himself as if he were talking to a small frightened boy, which pleased the prince greatly; and at last the old man had him sit down beside him. The prince was gazing into his face with a look of delight, still somehow unable to speak and short of breath; he liked the little old man's face so much.

"What?" he murmured at last. "You really forgive me? And—you too, Lizaveta Prokofyevna?"

The laughter grew louder than ever. Tears came to the prince's eyes; he could not believe it and he was enchanted.

"Of course, it was a superb vase. I remember it being there for fifteen years, yes—fifteen years," began Ivan Petrovitch.

"Well, what a tragedy!" said Lizaveta Prokofyevna loudly. "A person's life too must come to an end, and all this fuss about a clay pot. You're not really that startled about it, are you, Lev Nikolayevitch?" she added in a concerned voice. "Don't be, my dear boy, don't be. You'll really frighten me."

"And you forgive me for *everything*? For *everything*, besides the vase?" The prince started to get up from his chair, but the old man promptly drew him back by the arm. He was unwilling to let him go.

"C'est très curieux et c'est très sérieux!" he whispered across the table to Ivan Petrovitch, though rather loudly, and the prince may have heard.

"So I've not offended any of you? You have no idea how happy that makes me—but it had to be like that! How could I possibly offend anyone here? I would be offending you again if I thought as much."

"Calm yourself, my friend, this is all exaggeration. And you have no cause to be so thankful. It's an excellent sentiment, but exaggerated."

"I'm not thanking you, I'm only—admiring you. I am happy looking at you. What I say may be foolish, but I must speak, I must explain—even if only out of self-respect."

He was all fits and starts, confused, feverish; very likely the words he uttered were often not the ones he wanted to say. His eyes seemed to be begging permission for him to speak. His glance fell upon Belokonskaya.

"Never mind, dear fellow, go on, go on, only don't get out of breath," she observed. "You began just now out of breath and look where it got you. But don't be afraid to speak. These ladies and gentlemen have seen stranger things than you, you won't surprise them. And Lord knows how wise you may be, though here you've broken the vase and frightened us all."

The prince listened to her, smiling.

"But wasn't it you, sir," he said suddenly addressing the little old man, "wasn't it you who saved the student Podkumov and the clerk Shavbrin from deportation three months ago?"

The little old man blushed a little and muttered that he should calm himself.

"And wasn't it about you," he said turning abruptly to Ivan Petrovitch, "that I heard you gave your peasants timber when their huts had burned down, though they were free and had been causing you trouble?"

"Well, that's an ex-ag-ger-ation," muttered Ivan Petrovitch, looking very pleased and dignified.

This time, however, it was quite true that it was an exaggeration: the rumor which had reached the prince was false.

"And you, Princess," he said suddenly addressing Belokonskaya with a bright smile, "did you not entertain me six months ago in Moscow as if I was your own son, after Lizaveta Prokofyevna's letter? And just as if I really was your own son you gave me a piece of advice which I shall never forget. Do you remember?"

"What's gotten into you?" said Belokonskaya in annoyance. "You're a nice fellow, but absurd. Someone gives you a penny and you thank him as if he'd saved your life. You think it's praiseworthy, but it's disgusting."

She was about to become angry with him in earnest, but suddenly she laughed, and this time her laughter was good-natured. Lizaveta Prokofyevna's face also brightened, and Ivan Fyodorovitch beamed.

"I told you Lev Nikolayevitch was a man—a man—in short, if only he wouldn't get out of breath, as the princess observed," the general murmured in joyous rapture, repeating Belokonskaya's words, which had impressed him.

Only Aglaya appeared to be sad, but her face was still flushed, perhaps with indignation.

"He is really quite nice," the old man murmured again to Ivan Petrovitch.

"I came here with anguish in my heart," the prince went on, still with mounting agitation, speaking more and more rapidly, more queerly and animatedly. "I—I was afraid of you, and afraid of myself too. Most of all of myself. On my way back here to Petersburg, I determined that I would see our leading people, those of the oldest families, of ancient lineage, among whom I myself belong, being among the first by birth myself. For now I am sitting among princes like myself, am I not? I wanted to know you; it was necessary—very, very necessary! I have always heard too much said that was bad about you, more than what was good, about your pettiness, your limited interests, your backwardness, your shallow education, your ridiculous habits—oh, so much is written and said about you! I came here today curious, and disturbed. I had to see for myself, make up my own mind whether this whole upper level of Russian society is really worthless, whether it has outlived its time, whether the old life has withered and is now fit only to die yet still goes on in a petty, envious struggle with men—of the future, hampering them, never noticing that it is dying itself. Even before, I didn't fully believe this opinion, because we have never had an upper class, except for courtiers, by uniform or—by chance, and now it has disappeared completely, hasn't it?"

"Well, it hasn't at all," said Ivan Petrovitch, laughing sarcastically.

"There, he's off again!" said Belokonskaya, losing patience.

"*Laissez le dire*, he's trembling all over," the little old man warned them again in a low voice.

The prince was quite beside himself.

"And what do I find? I find people who are forthright and intelligent. I find an old man who listens to a boy like myself and is kind to him. I see people ready to understand and to forgive, Russian people, good-hearted people, almost as good —and warm-hearted as those I met there—hardly worse than they You can imagine how pleasantly I was surprised! Oh, do let me tell this! I have heard it said often and I've fully believed that society was all manners, antiquated forms, not real anymore; but now I see for myself that this cannot be so among us. Anywhere else but not among us. Could you all be Jesuits and frauds? I heard the story Prince N. was telling just now: isn't that plain but inspired good humor, isn't that true good nature? Could such words fall from the lips of a man—who is dead, whose heart and talent have dried up? Could dead people have treated me as you have? Isn't this substance—for the future, for hope? Could such people fail to understand and fall behind the times?"

"Once more, dear friend, I beg you, calm yourself. We will talk about all this another time, and for my part with pleasure," said the old "dignitary" with a smile.

Ivan Petrovitch made a sound in his throat and turned around in his chair; Ivan Fyodorovitch stirred restlessly; the ranking general was talking to the old "dignitary's" wife, no longer paying the slightest attention to the prince; but the "dignitary's" wife kept listening and glanced at him often.

"No, it's better if I speak, you know!" the prince went on, in a new burst of feverish excitement, addressing himself to the little old man with particular trustfulness and indeed a confidential manner. "Yesterday Aglaya Ivanovna told me not to talk, and even told me what subjects not to talk about. She knows I'm absurd when I do! I'm twenty-seven, and yet I know I'm like a child. I have no right to express my opinion. I've said so a long time. It's only with Rogozhin in Moscow I've spoken openly. We read Pushkin together, all his works. He didn't know anything, not even the name Pushkin. I'm always afraid that my ridiculous manner will betray my thought, and the *main idea*. I have no sense of gesture. My gestures are always exactly wrong, and that makes people laugh and degrades the idea. I have no sense of proportion either, and that's the most important thing, the most important of all. I know that it's better if I sit and say nothing. When I persist and do keep quiet, I appear quite reasonable, and what's more I think things through. But now it's better if I talk. I began talking because of the way you are looking at me—you have such a beautiful face! I promised Aglaya Ivanovna yesterday I'd keep still the whole evening."

"Vraiment?" said the little old man, smiling.

"But sometimes I think I'm wrong in thinking that. Sincerity is worth more than mere gestures, isn't it?"

"Sometimes."

"I want to explain everything, everything, everything! Oh, yes! You think I'm a utopian, an ideologist? Oh, no, my thoughts are all so simple. You don't believe it? You smile? I'm sometimes contemptible, you know, because I lose my faith. As I was coming here just now, I thought, 'How shall I talk to them? What words shall I start with so they will understand even a little?' How frightened I was—but I was more frightened for you, terribly frightened! Still, how could I be afraid, wasn't it shameful to be afraid? What does it matter that for one progressive man there is such a world of backward and wicked men? My joy is that I am now convinced there is no such world at all, but that the substance of life is in everyone! There is no reason to be troubled because we are absurd, is there? For we really are: we are absurd, frivolous, we have bad habits, we're bored, we don't know how to look around ourselves, we don't know how to understand; we are all like this, all of us, you, and I, and everyone! And you aren't offended by my telling you straight to your faces that you are absurd? There is the basic stuff of life in you, isn't there? You know, I believe it's sometimes even good to be ridiculous. Yes, much better. People forgive each other more readily and become more humble, we can't understand everything at once, we can't begin with perfection! To reach perfection there must first be much we do not understand. And if we understand too quickly we will probably not understand very well. I tell this to you who have been able to understand so much and and—do not understand. I am not afraid for you now. For you can't be angry that such a boy as I should be telling you such things. Of course not! Oh, you will know how to forget and to forgive those who have offended you, as well as those who have not offended you at all; because it's always harder to forgive those who have not offended you, for the very reason they have done you no wrong and your complaint is groundless. This is what I expected of superior people. This is what I was anxious to tell them, as I was coming here, and didn't know how— You are laughing, Ivan Petrovitch? You think I was afraid for *them*, that I was *their* champion, a democrat, an advocate of equality?" He laughed hysterically (he had been often breaking out in short, ecstatic bursts of laughter). "I am frightened for you, for all of you, for all of us together. I am a prince of ancient family myself, and I am sitting with princes. I am saying this to save us all, so that our class shall not disappear meaninglessly into darkness, without realizing anything, decrying everything, and losing everything. Why disappear and give place to others when we might remain in the lead and first in rank? Let us be men of progress, then we shall lead. Let us be servants so as to be masters."

He started to get up from his chair, but the little old man kept holding him back, though looking at him with growing uneasiness.

"Listen! I know it's not right to talk. Better to set an example, better just to start—I have already started—and—and can one really be unhappy? Oh, what do my grief and my misfortune matter if I have the strength to be happy? You know, I don't understand how one can walk by a tree and not be happy at the sight of it! Or to speak with a man and not be happy in loving him? Oh, it's just that I can't express it— and yet there are so many things at every step so beautiful that even the most desolate of men find them beautiful. Look at a child, look at God's sunrise, look at the grass, how it grows, look into eyes that look at you and love you—"

He had for some time been standing as he spoke. The little old man was now looking at him in great alarm. Lizaveta Prokofyevna cried "Oh, my God" and clasped her hands together, the first of all of them to guess what was wrong. Aglaya quickly ran to him, just in time to catch him in her arms, and in horror, her face contorted with pain, she heard the wild shriek of "the spirit that shook and cast down" the unhappy man. The sick man lay on the carpet. Someone had hastily put a pillow under his head.

No one had expected it. Fifteen minutes later Prince N., Yevgeny Pavlovitch, and the little old man tried to revive the evening, but in another half hour everyone was leaving. Many words of sympathy and regret were uttered, and sundry comments. Ivan Petrovitch expressed the opinion, among others, that "the young man is a Slav-o-phile or something like that, however, there is nothing dangerous about it." The little old man expressed no opinion. It is true that two or three days afterward everyone became rather annoyed. Ivan Petrovitch even felt offended, though not seriously. The general in charge of the department was for a time rather cold toward Ivan Fyodorovitch. As the "patron" of the family, the old dignitary muttered something by way of admonition to its head, though in flattering terms he expressed the greatest interest in Aglaya's future. He was in fact a rather kind man, but one of the reasons he had taken an interest in the prince that evening was the old story of the prince and Nastassya Filippovna. He had heard something said about this affair and was quite intrigued by it, and had even meant to inquire into it.

Belokonskaya said to Lizaveta Prokofyevna as she was leaving that evening:

"Well, there's good and bad there, but if you want to know my opinion there's more bad than good. You can see for yourself what sort of man he is—he's a sick man!"

Lizaveta Prokofyevna made up her mind once and for all that as a fiancé he was "impossible," and that night she vowed to herself that as long as she lived the prince would never be Aglaya's husband. She got up next morning with the same opinion. But at the midday meal at one, she contradicted herself in a surprising way.

In reply to an extremely guarded question from her sisters, Aglaya suddenly said coldly but haughtily, as if she wanted to put a stop to such questions:

"I never gave him any sort of promise. I've never in my life considered him as my fiancé. He's as much of a stranger to me as to anyone else."

Lizaveta Prokofyevna suddenly flared up.

"I didn't expect that from you," she said in dismay. "He is an impossible husband, I know that, and I thank the Lord it's turned out as it has, but I didn't expect such words from you! I expected something quite different from you. I'd have turned everyone out last night and kept him—that's the kind of man I think he is!"

Here she suddenly stopped, frightened by her own words. But if only she had known how unjust she was being to her daughter at that moment! Everything was already settled in

Aglaya's mind. She, too, was awaiting the hour which would be decisive for her, and every allusion, every incautious touch made a deep wound in her heart.

Chapter EIGHT

❧

For the prince, too, that morning began under the influence of painful forebodings; they could be explained by his state of illness, but his sadness was quite undefined, and that was what made it most tormenting to him. It is true he was faced with facts that were clear, painful, and incisive, but his sadness went beyond everything he remembered and could reflect upon; he understood that he could not set his mind at rest again by himself. Little by little the conviction grew in him that something special and decisive would happen to him that very day. The fit of the night before had been a light one. Except for a sense of depression, a certain heaviness in his head, and pain in his limbs, he felt no particular indisposition. His brain functioned quite accurately, though his soul was uneasy. He got up rather late and immediately recalled the previous evening clearly; he somehow remembered, too, though not quite distinctly, how he had been taken home about a half hour after his fit. He learned that a messenger from the Yepanchins had already come to inquire about his health. At half past eleven another came—that pleased him. Vera Lebedev was among the first to call on him and look after him. The first moment she saw him she burst into tears, but when the prince at once reassured her she started to laugh. He was suddenly struck by the strong compassion this girl felt toward him; he took her hand and kissed it. Vera blushed deeply.

"Oh, please, what are you doing!" she cried in alarm, quickly drawing her hand away.

She soon went away in a strangely troubled state. She did manage to tell him, among other things, that her father had hurried off at daybreak to see "the deceased," as he called the general, to find out whether he had died during the night, and that she had heard that he would certainly die soon. Toward twelve o'clock Lebedev himself returned to the house, but only for a minute, to inquire about his "precious health," and so forth, and also to visit his "special little cupboard." He did nothing but sigh and moan, and the prince soon let him go, but he did attempt to question the prince about his fit, though it was obvious that he already knew about it in detail. After him, Kolya ran in, also for only a minute; he was in fact in a great hurry and was in a state of intense and troubled agitation. He began by asking the prince, directly and insistently, for an explanation of everything they had been keeping from him, asserting that he had already found out almost everything the day before. He was deeply and violently moved.

With all the sympathy he was capable of, the prince told him the whole story, relating the facts fully and precisely, and the poor boy was thunderstruck. He could not utter a word and quietly burst into tears. The prince sensed that this was one of those impressions which remain forever and are turning points in a young boy's life. He hastened to give him his own view of the affair, adding that in his opinion the old man's death might be principally due to the horror left in his heart by his own action, and that not everyone was capable of such a feeling. Kolya's eyes flashed as he heard the prince through.

"Worthless little Ganya, and Varya, and Ptitsyn! I'm not going to quarrel with them, but our paths are separate from this moment on! Ah, Prince, I feel so many different feelings about things since yesterday; it was my lesson! And I consider my mother my direct responsibility now, even though she's taken care of at Varya's, but that's not the way—"

He jumped up, remembering that he was expected, hurriedly inquired about the prince's health, and, having heard his reply, added in haste:

"Isn't there something else? I heard yesterday—though I have no right—but if you ever for any reason need a faithful servant, he stands here before you. I don't think we are either of us quite happy, are we? But—I'm not asking, I'm not asking."

He went away and the prince fell even deeper into thought. Everyone was predicting disaster, everyone had already drawn some conclusion, they all were looking at him as if they knew something, something he did not know; Lebedev was asking pointed questions; Kolya was openly hinting something; and Vera was weeping. At last he dismissed the subject with a gesture of vexation: "My accursed morbid mistrustfulness," he thought. His face brightened when, past one o'clock, he saw the Yepanchins, who had come to visit him "for only a minute." They did in fact come only for a minute. Getting up from lunch, Lizaveta Prokofyevna had declared that they were all going for a walk, at once, all together. This announcement was issued in the form of an order, abruptly, dryly, without explanation. They all went out —that is, the mother, the girls, Prince S. Lizaveta Prokofyevna started off in a direction opposite the one they took every day. They all understood what this meant, they all kept silent for fear of irritating the mother, while she, as if to escape reproaches and objections, walked ahead of everyone without looking back. At last Adelaïda remarked that there was no point in running like that on a walk, and that it was impossible to keep up with their mother.

"Now then," said Lizaveta Prokofyevna, suddenly turning around, "we're just passing his house. Whatever Aglaya might think, and whatever might happen afterward, he's not a stranger to us, and what's more he's sick and miserable now; as for me I'm going to pay him a visit. Whoever wants to come with me, come; whoever doesn't, go on. No one is stopping you."

Needless to say, they all went in. The prince, as was fitting and proper, hastened to beg forgiveness once again for breaking the vase and for—the scandalous scene.

"Well, it doesn't matter," Lizaveta Prokofyevna replied. "I feel sorry for you, not the vase. So you realize now yourself that there was a scandal—this is what 'the morning after' means. But that doesn't matter either, because everyone now sees that no demands can be made upon you. Well, good-bye in any case. If you're feeling strong enough, take a walk and then go back to sleep. That's my advice. And if you should care to, come to see us as usual. Rest assured, once and for all, that whatever happens, whatever may come, you will still always be a friend of our family; of mine, at least. I can at least answer for myself."

They all responded to this challenge and echoed the mother's feelings. They went out, but in this good-natured readiness to say something kind and encouraging was concealed a lot that was cruel, and of which Lizaveta Prokofyevna was completely unaware. In her invitation to come to see them "as usual," and in the words "of mine, at least," there was another ominous note. The prince began remembering about Aglaya: it was true she had given him an astonishing smile as she came in and as she left, but she did not say a word, even when they had all made their pledges of friendship, though twice she had looked at him very intently. Her face was paler than usual, as if she had slept badly the night before. The prince decided that he would definitely go to see them in the evening "as usual," and feverishly he looked at his watch. Vera came in exactly three minutes after the Yepanchins had left.

"Aglaya Ivanovna has just given me a message for you in secret, Lev Nikolayevitch."

The prince trembled.

"A note?"

"No, a spoken message, and she hardly had time for that. She begs you urgently not to be away from your house for a minute all day today, until seven this evening, or maybe it was until nine, I didn't hear that part clearly."

"But—why this? What does it mean?"

"I know nothing about it, except that it was very imperative I pass on the message."

"Did she say 'imperative'?"

"No, she didn't say it. She hardly had time to turn and give me the message, as luckily I'd come up to her myself. But I could see clearly from her face it was imperative for her, whether she said it or not. She looked at me in a way that made my heart stop beating."

The prince asked a few more questions, and, while he didn't find out anything more, he became more disturbed than ever. Once alone, he lay down on the couch and set to thinking again. "Perhaps someone will be at their house until nine and she's afraid I might again do something silly with visitors there," he thought at last, and once again began waiting impatiently for evening and looking at his watch. But the answer to the riddle came long before evening, and again in the form of a new visit, an answer which was itself a new and agonizing mystery. A half hour after the Yepanchins' departure, Hippolite came in to see him, so tired and exhausted that, entering without a word, he literally collapsed, as if unconscious, into an armchair and at once broke into a dreadful coughing fit. He coughed until blood came. His eyes glittered and hectic spots appeared on his cheeks. The prince tried to say something softly to him, but he did not answer, and for a long time he only kept waving to tell the prince to let him alone. At last he recovered himself.

"I'm going!" he managed to say at last in a hoarse voice.

"I'll go with you if you like," said the prince, starting to get up, then sinking back, as he remembered that he had been forbidden to leave the house.

Hippolite laughed.

"I'm not going away from you," he went on, continually gasping and coughing. "On the contrary, I found I had to come to you about a certain matter—if it wasn't for that I wouldn't have disturbed you. I'm going *there,* and this time I think it is really so. I'm done for! I'm not here for sympathy, believe me—I lay down today at ten o'clock intending not to get up until that time came, but then I changed my mind and got up once more to come to you—so you see, I had to."

"I'm sorry to see you like this. You should have called me, instead of making the effort to come."

"Well, all right, that's fine. You've said you're sorry and that ought to take care of manners— Oh yes, I forgot, how are you?"

"I'm all right. But yesterday—not so well."

"I heard, I heard. The Chinese vase fared badly. I'm sorry I wasn't there! I've come on business. First, I had the pleasure today of seeing Gavril Ardalionovitch meeting Aglaya Ivanovna at the green bench. I was positively amazed to see how stupid a man can look. I mentioned this to Aglaya Ivanovna when Gavril Ardalionovitch had gone— But you don't seem to be surprised at anything, Prince," he added, looking mistrustfully at the prince's calm face. "They say that not to be surprised at anything is the sign of great intelligence. In my opinion, it might just as well signify great stupidity. However, I don't mean you, forgive me. I'm afraid my expressions are very unfortunate today."

"I already knew yesterday that Gavril Ardalionovitch—" The prince stopped short, obviously troubled, though Hippolite was annoyed at his not being surprised.

"You knew! Well, that's news! But don't bother to tell me— But you weren't a witness of their meeting today?"

"You saw I wasn't there, since you were there yourself."

"Oh, you may have been sitting behind a bush somewhere. Anyway I'm glad for your sake, of course, for I was beginning to think that Gavril Ardalionovitch was—the favorite!"

"I beg you not to speak of that to me, Hippolite, and in such terms."

"Especially since you know everything already."

"You are wrong. I know almost nothing, and Aglaya Ivanovna knows for certain that I know nothing. I didn't even know anything about this meeting. You did say there was a meeting? All right then, let's drop the subject."

"But how is this? First you know, then you don't know? You say, 'All right, let's drop the subject'? But really, don't be so trusting! Especially if you don't know anything. You are trustful because you don't know anything about it. And do you know what those two are counting on—the brother and the sister? That you do suspect, don't you? All right, all right, I'll drop it," he added, observing the prince's impatient gesture. "But I came here about a personal affair of my own and I want to—explain it. Damn it all, a person can't even die without making explanations; it's terrible how much explaining I have to do. Do you care to hear?"

"Go on. I'm listening."

"And anyway I've changed my mind again: I will begin with little Ganya. Would you believe that I too had an appointment at the green bench today? But I don't want to lie: I insisted on the meeting; I asked for it, I promised to reveal a secret. I don't know if I came too early (I think in fact I was early), but no sooner had I taken my place beside Aglaya Ivanovna than I saw Gavril Ardalionovitch and Varvara Ardalionovna approaching arm in arm, as though they were out for a walk. They both seemed very astonished to see me, they didn't expect it, and they were even embarrassed. Aglaya Ivanovna flushed crimson and, believe it or not, was even a bit disconcerted, whether because I was there or simply at the sight of Gavril Ardalionovitch—because he's just too handsome, you know—anyway she flushed crimson and put an end to the whole thing in a second, very absurdly. She got up, responded to Gavril Ardalionovitch's bow and Varvara Ardalionovna's ingratiating smile, and suddenly said sharply: 'I only wanted to tell you personally how pleased I am by your sincere and friendly feelings and that if I ever have need of them, believe me—' Then she bowed and the two of them went off—I don't know whether feeling like fools or in triumph; though dear little Ganya, of course, must have felt like a fool. He couldn't make out anything and he turned red as a lobster (he has wonderful expressions on his face sometimes!). But Varvara Ardalionovna seemed to understand that they had to get away from there quickly, and that that was already quite enough from Aglaya Ivanovna, and she dragged her brother away. She's cleverer than he is and I'm sure she's triumphant now. I came to talk to Aglaya Ivanovna about arranging a meeting with Nastassya Filippovna."

"With Nastassya Filippovna!" cried the prince.

"Ah-ha! You seem to be losing your coolness and beginning to show some surprise. I'm glad you're ready to act like a human being at last. In return I'll tell you something amusing. This is what it is to be obliging to young gentlemen and high-minded young ladies: today I got a slap in the face from her!"

"A—moral one?" the prince could not help asking.

"Yes, not a physical one. I don't think anyone would raise a hand against someone like me; even a woman wouldn't hit me now—even little Ganya wouldn't! Though for a time there yesterday I thought she was about to fly at me—I'll bet I know what you're thinking right now. You're thinking: 'Indeed he mustn't be beaten, but he might be smothered with a pillow or a wet rag in his sleep—in fact he should be.' It's written all over your face that that's what you're thinking at this very moment."

"I never thought that!" said the prince in disgust.

"I don't know. I had a dream last night that I was smothered with a wet rag by—a certain fellow. Well, I'll tell you who it was; imagine—it was Rogozhin! What do you think? Can a person be smothered with a wet rag?"

"I don't know."

"I've heard you can be. All right, let's drop it. Well, why am I a talebearer? Why did she accuse me of being a talebearer today? And, mind you, that was after she listened to every last word and even asked questions. But that's just like a woman! For her sake I got in touch with Rogozhin—an interesting man. In her own interest I arranged a personal meeting with Nastassya Filippovna for her. Was it that I hurt her feelings by hinting she was glad to have Nastassya Filippovna's leavings? Yes, in her own interest I did impress that on her. I won't deny it, I wrote her two letters in that vein, and now said it again, for the third time, at the meeting—I began by telling her it was humiliating for her— And anyway that word 'leavings' wasn't mine but someone else's; at least at Ganya's everyone was saying it, and she confirmed it herself. Well then, why does she take me for a talebearer? I see, I see, you're awfully amused as you look at me now, and I'll bet you're applying those stupid verses to me:

> And perhaps the sorrow of my sunset hour
> Love will brighten with a farewell smile.*

Ha, ha, ha!" He suddenly broke into hysterical laughter. "And notice," he gasped through his coughing, "what sort of person little Ganya is: he talks about 'leavings,' but what else would he like to profit by now?"

The prince was silent a long time. He was horrified.

"You spoke of a meeting with Nastassya Filippovna?" he said quietly at last.

"Ah, is it really possible you don't know that there's to be a meeting between Aglaya Ivanovna and Nastassya Filippovna today? And that for this purpose Nastassya Filippovna is specially asked to come from Petersburg, through Rogozhin, at the invitation of Aglaya Ivanovna and by my efforts, and that she is now here with Rogozhin in the same house she stayed before, not very far from you, at Darya Alexeyevna's—a very questionable lady, a friend of hers—and there, today, to this very questionable house Aglaya Ivanovna will go for a friendly conversation with Nastassya Filippovna to settle certain problems. They want to do some arithmetic. Didn't you know? Really?"

"It's incredible!"

"Well, it's a good thing it's incredible. Still, how would you know about it? In a little place like this if a fly buzzes by it's news to everyone! But I've warned you, and you may be grateful to me. Well, good-bye—until the next world, probably. And there's something else: though I've behaved badly toward you, because—why should I give up what's mine by right, tell me? For your benefit, perhaps? I've dedicated my 'Confession' to her—you knew that, didn't you? And how she received it! Ha, ha! But I didn't act badly toward her, I haven't done her any wrong; she's the one who's disgraced me and tricked me. And, besides, I haven't acted badly toward you either. If I did mention those 'leavings' and things like that, I'm telling you now the day and the hour and the address of their meeting; I've shown you the whole game— out of spite, of course, not generosity. Good-bye—I'm as talkative as a stammerer or a consumptive. Mind you take all necessary measures, and as soon as possible—if you deserve to be called a man. The meeting will take place this evening —it's true."

Hippolite went to the door, but the prince called to him and he stopped in the doorway.

"So, according to you, Aglaya Ivanovna will be going to Nastassya Filippovna?" demanded the prince. Patches of red appeared on his cheeks and his forehead.

"I don't know for an absolute fact, but she probably will," replied Hippolite, turning around. "Yes, because it can't be any other way. Nastassya Filippovna wouldn't go to her! And it wouldn't be at dear Ganya's—there's a man who's almost dead there. What do you think of the old general?"

"That alone makes it impossible!" the prince said. "How could she go out, even if she wants to? You don't know the —customs of that house; she couldn't go out alone to see Nastassya Filippovna. It's nonsense!"

"Look here, Prince, nobody jumps out of windows, but when there's a fire the finest gentleman and finest lady will jump out of a window. When necessity arises there's nothing else to do, and our young lady will go to Nastassya Filippovna. Aren't they allowed to go out anywhere, your young ladies?"

"No, that's not what I mean—"

"Well, if that's not it, all she has to do is walk down the front steps and walk away, and she needn't go back home again either. There are sometimes cases where one may burn one's bridges and not go home again: life is not made up just of luncheons and dinners and Prince S.'s. You seem to take Aglaya Ivanovna for a proper young lady or a boarding-school girl; I already told her that and she seemed to agree with me. Wait until about seven or eight o'clock. If I were in your place I'd send someone over there to know the exact minute she walks down the front steps. You might send Kolya; he'd be delighted to act as a spy, believe me—on your account, that is; because all that is relative. Ha, ha!"

Hippolite went out. The prince had no reason to ask anyone to spy for him, even had he been capable of doing such a thing. Aglaya's order for him to stay home was now almost explained: perhaps she meant to stop by for him. Of course, she might have not wanted him to appear there, and for that reason had asked him to stay home. That also might be so. His head was spinning; the whole room was turning. He lay down on the couch and closed his eyes.

One way or the other, it was decisive, final. No, the prince did not take Aglaya for a proper young lady or a schoolgirl: he felt now that he had been dreading something for a long time, something of exactly this kind. But why did she want to see him? A chill passed through the prince's whole body; he was in a fever again.

No, he didn't take her for a child! Certain looks she had given him of late, certain things she had said had terrified him. At times it seemed to him she was holding herself in far too much, controlling herself too much, and he remembered how this had alarmed him. It was true that all these past days he had been trying not to think about that, trying to ward off burdensome thoughts; but what lay hidden in that soul of hers? This thought had worried him for a long time, though he had faith in that soul. And now all this had to be settled and revealed this very day. A horrible thought! And once again—"that woman!" Why had he always imagined that that woman would appear at the very last moment and tear his life apart as if it were a rotted thread? He was now prepared to swear that he had always thought this, though he was half delirious. If he had tried to forget *her* lately it was solely because he was afraid of her. What was it? Did he love this woman or did he hate her? That question he did not ask himself once today; in this his heart was pure: he knew whom he loved. He was not so much afraid of the meeting of the two, not of its strangeness, not of the unknown reason for that meeting, not of its outcome, whatever it might be—he was afraid of Nastassya Filippovna herself. He remembered afterward, several days later, that in these feverish hours her eyes, her look, were before him almost the whole time, and he could hear the words she spoke, strange words, though his mind retained little of them after those fever-ridden and anguished hours. He barely remembered, for instance, how Vera had brought him dinner, and that he had eaten dinner, and did not recollect whether he had slept after dinner or not. All he knew was that he had only begun to make things out clearly that evening at the moment Aglaya suddenly came out to him on the veranda and he had jumped up from the sofa and gone to the middle of the veranda to meet her. It was a quarter past seven. Aglaya was all alone, simply and apparently hastily dressed, wearing a light hooded cloak. She was pale, as she had been that morning, and her eyes shone with a clear, dry light. He had never known such a look in her eyes before. She studied him attentively.

"You are all ready," she observed quietly and seemingly calmly. "Dressed and hat in hand. That means you've been warned, and I know by whom. Hippolite?"

"Yes, he did tell me—" the prince murmured, more dead than alive.

"Then let's go. You know you have to escort me there. I suppose you're feeling strong enough to go out?"

"Yes, I am, but—is this possible?"

He stopped himself at once and could say nothing more. This was his one attempt to stop the insane girl, and after that he followed her like a slave. However disturbed his thoughts were he still understood that she would go *there* even without him, and therefore that he had to follow her. He had guessed just how strong her determination was; it was quite beyond him to check this wild impulse. They walked in silence, hardly saying a word to each other the whole way. He only noticed that she knew the way very well, and when he wanted to take a long but more deserted road and proposed it to her, she listened with a sort of strained attention and replied abruptly, "It's all the same!" When they had almost reached Darya Alexeyevna's house (a big, old, wooden house), a splendidly dressed woman was descending the front steps and with her a young girl; both got into an elegant carriage waiting at the steps, laughing and talking loudly and not once glancing at the arriving couple, exactly as if they had not noticed them. No sooner had they driven off than the door opened a second time and Rogozhin, who had been waiting there, admitted the prince and Aglaya and closed the door behind them.

"No, there's no one in the whole house except the four of us," he said aloud, and looked strangely at the prince.

In the first room they entered, Nastassya Filippovna was waiting. She too was dressed simply and all in black. She got up to meet them but did not smile and did not offer her hand even to the prince.

Her intent and uneasy gaze fell upon Aglaya. They sat down at a distance from one another, Aglaya on a couch in a corner of the room, Nastassya Filippovna by the window. The prince and Rogozhin did not sit down, nor were they invited to do so. Again the prince looked uncomprehendingly and seemingly with pain at Rogozhin, but Rogozhin went on smiling as before. The silence lasted another few minutes.

Finally an ominous look crossed Nastassya Filippovna's face; her gaze hardened, became severe and almost touched with hatred, and did not leave her guest even for a moment. Aglaya was visibly disturbed, but not intimidated. Entering the room, she had scarcely looked at her rival, and now was sitting with downcast eyes, as though in meditation. Once or twice, as if casually, she glanced around the room; there was an unmistakable look of disgust on her face, as if she was afraid of contamination in this place. Mechanically she arranged her dress, and restlessly changed her seat once, moving to the far corner of the couch. She was probably not conscious of all her movements, but their very unconsciousness made them more insulting. Finally she looked firmly straight into Nastassya Filippovna's eyes and at once read clearly all the malice gathering in her rival's look. Woman understood woman. Aglaya sighed.

"You know, of course, why I asked you to be here," she brought out finally, but in a very low voice, hesitating once or twice even in this short sentence.

"No, I know nothing," replied Nastassya Filippovna, dryly and abruptly.

Aglaya blushed. Perhaps it had suddenly struck her as terribly strange and unbelievable that she should be sitting now with this woman, at "this woman's" house, attending her reply. At the first sound of Nastassya Filippovna's voice a tremor seemed to pass through her whole body. "This woman," of course, observed all this very clearly.

"You understand everything—yet you purposely pretend

not to understand," Aglaya said, almost whispering, looking morosely at the floor.

"Why should I do that?" Nastassya Filippovna asked with a faint smile.

"You want to take advantage of my position—my being in your house," Aglaya persisted, awkwardly and absurdly.

"For that position you're responsible, not I!" said Nastassya Filippovna, suddenly flaring up. "You're not here at my invitation, but I am here at yours, and up to now I don't know why."

Aglaya raised her head haughtily.

"Watch what you say! I didn't come here to fight you with that weapon of yours."

"Ah! So then you have come to 'fight' me? Just imagine, I thought you were—cleverer."

They looked at each other no longer concealing their malice. One was the woman who had been writing such incredible letters to the other. And here all that had vanished into thin air at their first encounter and at their first words. How could this be? At this moment no one of the four people in the room seemed to find it strange. The prince, who only yesterday would not have believed it possible even in a dream, now stood looking and listening as if he had foreseen it long ago. The most fantastic dream had suddenly turned into the most vivid and sharply defined reality. At this moment one of these women so despised the other and so wanted to tell her so (perhaps she had only come in order to do this, as Rogozhin said the next day) that however extravagant the other was with her disturbed mind and her sick soul no predetermined intention of hers could, it seemed, stand against the venomous, purely feminine contempt of her rival. The prince felt certain that Nastassya Filippovna would not mention the letters himself—from her flashing eyes he could guess what those letters must be costing her now—and he would have given half his life if Aglaya would not mention them either.

But suddenly Aglaya seemed to find strength and at once gain control of herself.

"You misunderstood me," she said. "I did not come here to fight you, though I don't like you. I—I came to you—to speak—as one human being to another. In asking to see you I had already made up my mind what I would say to you and I won't give up that decision, even if you don't understand me at all. This will be the worse for you, not for me. I wanted to answer what you have written me, and answer in person, because this way seemed more convenient to me. So hear my reply to all your letters: I felt sorry for Prince Lev

583

Nikolayevitch the very first day I became acquainted with him and afterward when I heard about all that happened at your party. I felt sorry for him because he is a man of such simple spirit and who in his simplicity believed he could be happy with a woman of—such a character. What I feared for him happened: you were unable to love him, you tormented him, and then you gave him up. You could not love him because you were too proud—no, not proud, I'm wrong, because you are too vain—and even that isn't it: you are filled with self-love to the point of madness, and to me your letters serve as the proof of this. You couldn't love him, a simple-hearted man, and you probably secretly despised him and laughed at him, you can love nothing but your own shame and the incessant thought that you have been abused, and dishonored. If your shame were less, or if you had none, you would be far more unhappy—" (Aglaya uttered these words with an intense delight, speaking too rapidly, though the words had been prepared and pondered long before, at a time when she had not even dreamed of today's encounter. With a venomous gaze she read the effect of them in Nastassya Filippovna's face, distorted with emotion.) "You remember," she went on, "he wrote me a letter then. He says that you know about that letter and even read it. From that letter I understood everything and understood it correctly. He recently confirmed all this himself, everything I am saying to you now, word for word. After the letter I began waiting. I guessed that you had to come here, because you can't do without Petersburg: you are still too young and too beautiful for the provinces. However, those aren't my words either," she added, blushing violently, and the blush did not leave her face until she finished speaking. "When I saw the prince again, I felt terribly hurt and offended on his account. Don't laugh—if you laugh you're not worthy of understanding that."

"You see I'm not laughing," said Nastassya Filippovna sadly and severely.

"It doesn't matter to me, laugh as much as you like. When I began to question him he told me he had not loved you for a long time, that even the memory of you was painful to him, but that he was sorry for you and that when he thought of you his heart seemed 'pierced forever.' I also must tell you that I have never in my life met anyone to equal him in noble simplicity of spirit and boundless trustfulness. I understood after what he said that anyone who wanted to could deceive him, and that anyone who deceived him he would forgive afterward, and that was why I began to love him"

Aglaya paused for a moment as though amazed, as though hardly able to believe that she could have said such a thing; but at the same time there was a look of boundless pride in her eyes; and it seemed that it would make no difference to her now, even if "that woman" should burst out laughing at the avowal which had escaped from her.

"I have told you everything, and I suppose you understand now what I want from you."

"Perhaps I do, but tell me yourself," Nastassya Filippovna answered softly.

Aglaya's face flared with anger.

"I wanted to find out from you," she said firmly and distinctly, "by what right you interfere with his feelings toward me? By what right have you dared write me letters? By what right have you been continually telling him, and telling me, that you love him, after leaving him and running away from him in such an insulting and—shameful way?"

"I have never told him or you that I love him," Nastassya Filippovna said with difficulty. "But you are right, I did run away from him," she added, barely audibly.

"What do you mean you never told him or me?" cried Aglaya. "What about your letters? Who asked you to start matchmaking and persuading me to marry him? Isn't that to say something? Why do you impose yourself on us? At first I thought that you were interfering with us to make me dislike him, so that I would give him up, and only later did I guess what it was all about: you simply imagined in this whole performance of yours that you were doing something noble and wonderful. Well, could you ever have loved him if you love your vanity so much? Why didn't you simply leave here instead of writing me ridiculous letters? And why don't you, now, marry the generous man who loves you so much and has honored you by offering his hand? It's all too plain: if you marry Rogozhin, what will happen to your grievances? You will have had far too much honor done you! Yevgeny Pavlovitch said you read too many poems and that you have 'too much education for your—position'; that you're a bookish and idle woman. Add to that your vanity, and there are your motives—"

"And you—aren't you an idle woman?"

All too quickly and too crudely the encounter had reached this unexpected point, unexpected because on her way to Pavlovsk Nastassya Filippovna still had had illusions of something different, though of course she assumed things would turn out badly rather than well. Aglaya however was completely carried away in a single moment, as if she were

585

tumbling down a mountainside, and she could not resist the terrible joy of revenge. It was indeed strange to Nastassya Filippovna to see Aglaya like this; she looked at her as though unable to believe her eyes, and was decidedly at a loss for the first moment. Whether she was a woman who had read too many poems, as Yevgeny Pavlovitch had supposed, or simply mad, as the prince was convinced, in any case this woman—though her behavior was sometimes so cynical and arrogant—was in fact far more modest, tender, and trusting than one might assume. It was true that there was in her a great deal that was bookish, dreamily romantic, capricious, and fanciful, but there was also much that was strong and deep. The prince understood that, there was a look of suffering in his face. Aglaya noticed it and trembled with hatred.

"How dare you speak to me like this?" she said with indescribable haughtiness in reply to Nastassya Filippovna's remark.

"You must not have understood me," said Nastassya Filippovna in surprise. "How have I spoken to you?"

"If you wanted to be an honest woman why didn't you give up your seducer Totsky simply—without theatrics?" said Aglaya suddenly, out of the blue.

"What do you know of my position that you dare judge me?" demanded Nastassya Filippovna, trembling and turning terribly pale.

"I know that you didn't go to work, but went off with a rich man, Rogozhin, so as to go on posing as a fallen angel. I'm not surprised Totsky was ready to shoot himself on account of that fallen angel!"

"Stop!" said Nastassya Filippovna with revulsion, seeming deeply pained. "You have understood me about as well as— Darya Alexeyevna's housemaid, who was just tried in court with her fiancé. She'd have understood better than you."

"She's probably a respectable girl who works for her living. Why do you have such contempt for a housemaid?"

"I have no contempt for work, but for you when you speak of work."

"If you'd wanted to be an honest woman you'd have become a laundress."

Both got up and, their faces pale, were glaring at one another.

"Aglaya, stop it! This is unjust!" the prince cried in dismay. Rogozhin was no longer smiling but listened with compressed lips and folded arms.

"Just look at her," said Nastassya Filippovna, trembling with anger, "look at this young lady! And I took her for an angel! Have you come to me without your governess, Aglaya Ivanovna? And—and do you want me to tell you right now, frankly and honestly, why you did come to me? You were afraid—that's why you came "

"Afraid of you?" demanded Aglaya, beside herself with naïve and arrogant surprise that this woman dared speak to her this way.

"Of course you were! You were afraid of me or you wouldn't have decided to come to see me. You don't despise someone you're afraid of. And to think that I respected you right up to this very moment! And do you know why you are afraid of me and what your main concern is now? You wanted to find out for yourself whether he loves me more than you or not, because you are terribly jealous—"

"He has already told me he hates you," Aglaya barely murmured.

"Perhaps. Perhaps I'm not worthy of him, except—I think you're lying! He can't hate me, and he can't have said such a thing! However, I am ready to forgive you—in view of your position—though I did think better of you: I thought you were cleverer and even prettier—I did, indeed! Well, take your treasure—here he is looking at you, quite dazed—take him, but on one condition: get out of here immediately! This minute!"

She dropped into an armchair and burst into tears But suddenly her eyes blazed anew; she looked steadily and intently at Aglaya and got up from the chair.

"But if you like I'll *order* him at once—do you hear?—I have only to order him and he'll give you up immediately and stay with me forever and marry me, and you will run along home alone! Shall I? Shall I?" she cried out like a madwoman, as if she was hardly able to believe that she was uttering such words.

Aglaya ran to the door in terror, but she stopped in the doorway, petrified, and listened.

"Shall I turn Rogozhin out? You thought I was going to marry Rogozhin to suit your purposes? Right here in front of you I'll shout, 'Get out, Rogozhin!' and I'll say to the prince, 'Do you remember what you promised?' Good Lord! Why have I humiliated myself so before them? Didn't you tell me yourself, Prince, that you would follow me whatever happened to me and never abandon me, that you loved me and you forgive me everything and you res—you res— Yes, you said that too! And I ran away from you only to set you free, but now I don't want to run away! Why has she been treating me as a loose woman? Ask Rogozhin if I'm a loose woman,

587

he'll tell you! Now that she has covered me with shame, and before your eyes too, will you turn away from me too, and take her off on your arm? Well damn you then, for you were the only one I trusted. Get out, Rogozhin, you're not needed here!" she cried, scarcely knowing what she was saying, bringing the words out with difficulty, her face distorted, her lips parched, and obviously not believing a word she was saying, yet at the same time wishing to prolong the illusion and to deceive herself if only for a second longer. Her outburst was so intense that she might have died from it, at least so it seemed to the prince. "There he is—look!" she cried at last to Aglaya, pointing to the prince. "If he doesn't come to me at once, if he doesn't take me and doesn't give you up, take him for yourself, I give him up, I don't want him!"

And she and Aglaya both stood still in expectation, staring at the prince like insane women. But he perhaps did not understand the whole force of the challenge; indeed, he certainly did not. He only saw before him the face, despairing and demented, which he had once told Aglaya had 'pierced his heart forever.' He could bear it no longer and he turned, imploringly and reproachfully, to Aglaya, pointing to Nastassya Filippovna:

"How can you? She's—so unhappy!"

But he said no more than this, stopped dead by Aglaya's terrible look. There was so much suffering in that look and at the same time such infinite hatred that he wrung his hands in despair, cried out and ran to her, but it was already too late She could not endure even his instant of hesitation, she covered her face in her hands, cried "Oh, my God!" and ran out of the room. Rogozhin followed her to unbolt the street door.

The prince ran too, but at the threshold a pair of arms seized him. The deadened, distorted face of Nastassya Filippovna stared at him, her blue lips moved, asking:

"You're following her?"

She fell senseless into his arms. He took her up and carried her back into the room, laid her in an armchair, and stood over her in dumb anxiety. There was a glass of water on the table; Rogozhin, coming back, seized it and sprinkled water on her face. She opened her eyes, not understanding anything for a moment, but suddenly she looked around, gave a start, got up and rushed to the prince.

"Mine! Mine!" she cried. "Has the proud young lady gone? Ha! Ha! Ha!" she laughed hysterically. "Ha, ha, ha! I was giving him up to that young lady? And why? For what reason? I was mad! Mad! Get out, Rogozhin! Ha, ha, ha!"

Rogozhin looked at them intently, said not a word and

took his hat and went out. Ten minutes later the prince was sitting next to Nastassya Filippovna, gazing at her and stroking her head and face with both hands, as if she were a little child. He laughed when she laughed and was ready to cry when he saw her tears. He said nothing but listened closely to her excited, incoherent outbursts, hardly understanding anything, but smiling gently, and as soon as he thought she was beginning to grieve or weep again, or to reproach or complain, he at once began caressing her head again, and tenderly drawing his hands over her cheeks, soothing and comforting her like a child.

Chapter NINE

Two weeks had passed since the events related in the last chapter, and the situations of the characters of our tale had changed so much that it is extremely difficult for us to continue without specific explanations. And yet we feel we must confine ourselves as much as possible to a simple account of the facts without such explanations, for a very simple reason· because we ourselves in many instances would be hard put to explain what happened. Such a preliminary statement on our part must seem exceedingly strange and obscure to the reader: how can we narrate events about which we have no clear understanding or personal opinion? To avoid putting ourselves in an even falser position, let us rather try to explain our difficulty with an example, and perhaps the kindly disposed reader will then understand what that difficulty is, especially since this example will not be a digression but, on the contrary, an immediate and direct continuation of our story.

Two weeks later—that is at the beginning of July as well as in the course of those two weeks—the story of our hero and particularly the last adventure in that story was transformed into a strange, highly entertaining, almost incredible, and at the same time glaring scandal which gradually spread through all the streets adjacent to the houses of Lebedev, Ptitsyn, Darya Alexeyevna, and the Yepanchins; in short, throughout the entire town and even its outlying districts. Almost everyone there—natives, summer people, and those who came up for the concerts—all began telling one and the same story, in a thousand versions, about how a certain prince, after causing a scandal in a respectable and prominent household and jilting a young girl of the family to whom he was engaged, became captivated by a well-known cocotte, broke all his former connections, and, heedless of everything, heedless of threats, heedless of public indignation, intended within a few days' time to marry the disreputable woman, right there in Pavlovsk, openly, in public, with his head high and looking everyone straight in the face. The story was so richly embroidered with scandalous details and so many well-known and important people were mixed up in it, so many fantastic and enigmatic meanings attributed to it, even as it was being presented with such incontestable and circumstantial facts, that the general curiosity and the gossip were, of course, very pardonable. The most subtle, shrewd, and at the same time probable interpretation of the event was left to a few dedicated gossips belonging to that category of reasonable people who always, in every society, are in haste to explain events for the benefit of others, finding in this pursuit their vocation as well as, often, a certain consolation. According to their interpretation the young man, who was of good family, a prince, almost wealthy, a born fool but a democrat who had lost his head over modern nihilism as revealed by Mr. Turgenyev, and scarcely able to speak Russian, had fallen in love with one of General Yepanchin's daughters and had succeeded in being received at the house as her fiancé. But like the French divinity student whose story had just appeared in print, who had purposely let himself be consecrated as a priest, had asked for this consecration, had gone through all the rites, the genuflections, the kissing, the vows, and so on, only so as the very next day to make public in a letter to his bishop that as he did not believe in God he considered it dishonest to deceive people and live at their expense and for this reason he rejected his sacrament of the day before and sent his letter to be printed in the liberal papers—like that atheist, the prince too had carried out a deception. It was said that he had purposely waited for the formal evening reception given by his fiancée's parents, at which he was introduced to quite a number of very prominent people, in order to state his views aloud in front of everyone, heap abuse on distinguished statesmen, reject his fiancée publicly and in an insulting manner, and, in resisting the servants who were ushering him out of the house, to break a magnificent Chinese vase. To this account it was added, as a commentary on modern manners, that the foolish young man was really in love with his fiancée, the general's daughter, but had broken with her entirely on the ground of nihilism and for the sake of the consequent scandal, so as to enjoy the satisfaction of marrying a fallen woman before the whole world and thereby prove that there are neither fallen women nor respectable women but only free women, that he did not believe in the old conventional distinction but had faith only in the "woman question," and finally that in his eyes a woman who had fallen was even rather better than one who had not. This explanation appeared highly plausible and was accepted by the majority of summer people, all the more so as it was substantiated by daily events. True, a great many things remained unexplained: it was said that the poor girl was so much in love with her fiancé—and, according to some, her seducer—that the day after he had broken with her she had run to him as he was sitting with his mistress. Others maintained that on the contrary she had been purposely lured by him to his mistress's house solely out of nihilism; that is, to shame and humiliate her. However it had happened, interest in the affair grew daily, especially since not the slightest doubt remained that the scandalous marriage would really take place.

And now, if we were asked for an explanation—not of the nihilistic aspects of the matter, oh no!—but simply of the extent to which the proposed marriage satisfied the prince's real desires, of exactly what those desires were at the moment, of how to define the prince's state of mind at this time, and so on and so forth, we would admittedly be hard put to reply. We know only that the wedding had actually been arranged and that the prince himself had authorized Lebedev, Keller, and a certain friend of Lebedev's who had been presented to the prince for the occasion, to undertake all the necessary arrangements, religious as well as secular, that he had told them that money was not to be spared, that Nastassya Filippovna was insisting on the wedding and that it take place as soon as possible, that Keller, at his own impassioned request, had been chosen as the prince's best man, while Burdovsky was appointed to give away the bride and had accepted the office with enthusiasm, and that the wedding day had been set in the beginning of July. But beyond these very precise circumstances, a number of other facts are known to us which completely throw us off, because they directly contradict the foregoing ones. We strongly suspect, for example, that once having given Lebedev and the others full powers to make all the arrangements the prince on that very same day nearly

591

forgot that he had a master of ceremonies, a best man, and a wedding, and that his hasty decision to turn over the arrangements to others was solely in order not to think about any of it himself and perhaps even to put it quickly out of his mind. In that case what was he thinking about? What was he trying to remember? What was he seeking? Nor is there any question that he was being coerced, by Nastassya Filippovna, for instance, nor that Nastassya Filippovna did in fact definitely want an early wedding, and that it was she and not the prince who had thought of the wedding. But the prince had freely agreed to it, even rather casually, as if he had been asked some quite ordinary thing. There are a great many such strange facts before us, but far from making things clearer they in our opinion only obscure the interpretation of the affair, no matter how many of them are brought forth. But let us cite yet another example.

We know for a fact that in the course of those two weeks the prince spent whole days and evenings with Nastassya Filippovna, that she took him with her on walks and to the band concerts, that he rode with her every day in her carriage, that he became worried about her if an hour passed without his seeing her (that is, by all indications he genuinely loved her), that he listened with a soft, gentle smile to whatever she said to him, for hours on end, rarely ever speaking himself. But we also know that several times during those same days, indeed quite a number of times, he would suddenly go off to the Yepanchins, making no secret of it to Nastassya Filippovna, though it had almost driven her to despair. We know that while the Yepanchins were still in Pavlovsk they did not receive him and consistently refused to let him see Aglaya Ivanovna, that he would go away without a word and the next day return again as if he had completely forgotten the refusal of the day before and, of course, be refused again. We also know that an hour after Aglaya Ivanovna had run away from Nastassya Filippovna, and perhaps even less than an hour afterward, the prince was already at the Yepanchins', confident of course of finding Aglaya there, and that his appearance at the Yepanchins' had produced extreme agitation and alarm in the household, because Aglaya had not yet returned home, and it was only from him that they learned for the first time that she had gone with him to Nastassya Filippovna's. It was said that Lizaveta Prokofyevna, her daughters, and even Prince S. had then treated the prince with extreme severity and hostility, and that they had then and there refused him, in the strongest terms, their friendship and acquaintance, especially when Varvara Ardalionovna had suddenly appeared and declared to Lizaveta Prokofyevna that Aglaya Ivanovna had been at her house for the past hour in a terrible state and that she seemed unwilling to return home. This last piece of news affected Lizaveta Prokofyevna more than anything else, and it was quite true upon leaving Nastassya Filippovna's Aglaya would truly have sooner died than have faced her own family then, so she had rushed over to Nina Alexandrovna's. For her part Varvara Ardalionovna had found herself obliged to inform Lizaveta Prokofyevna immediately of all this. And mother and daughters promptly rushed off to Nina Alexandrovna's, followed by the head of the family, Ivan Fyodorovitch, who had just re- turned home, and by Prince Lev Nikolayevitch, who trailed after them despite his banishment and the hostile words; but on Varvara Ardalionovna's orders he was not permitted, there either, to see Aglaya. However, the end of the matter was that when Aglaya saw her mother and sisters weeping over her and not reproaching her in the least, she rushed into their arms and at once returned home with them. It was said, though the rumor remained rather imprecise, that here too Gavril Ardalionovitch was extremely unlucky, that seizing the moment Varvara Ardalionovna had run off to Lizaveta Prokofyevna's and he was left alone with Aglaya, he had deemed it the proper time to begin talking of his love, and that as she listened to him Aglaya, in spite of her anguish and tears, had suddenly burst out laughing and abruptly put a strange question to him: would he, in order to prove his love, burn his finger at once in the candle flame? Gavril Ardalion- ovitch, it was said, was stunned by the suggestion, so dumb- founded, and showed such extreme amazement in his face that Aglaya had then started laughing at him as if she was in hysterics, and she had rushed away from him and upstairs to Nina Alexandrovna, where her parents found her. This anec- dote reached the prince through Hippolite the next day. No longer getting up from his bed, Hippolite sent expressly for the prince in order to pass it on to him. How this rumor reached Hippolite is unknown to us, but when the prince heard about the candle-and-finger episode he laughed so hard that he even surprised Hippolite; then suddenly he began to tremble and he burst into tears. During these days he was generally in a state of great anxiety and extreme perturbation that was both vague and tormenting. Hippolite bluntly de- clared that he was out of his mind, but it was then quite im- possible to say this with any certainty.

In presenting all these facts and refusing to explain them we do not in the least mean to justify our hero in the eyes of our readers. More than that, we are quite prepared to share the indignation he aroused even in his friends. Even Vera Lebedev was for a time indignant with him, even Kolya was indignant, even Keller was indignant, until he was chosen as best man, not to speak of Lebedev himself, who actually began to intrigue against the prince, also out of an indignation which was in fact quite genuine. But of all this we shall speak later. In general we are in complete sympathy with some quite forcible and indeed psychologically profound words uttered plainly and unceremoniously by Yevgeny Pavlovitch in friendly conversation with the prince on the sixth or seventh day after the incident at Nastassya Filippovna's. Let us observe, by the way, that not only the Yepanchins themselves but everyone who was directly or indirectly connected with the Yepanchin household found it necessary to break all relations with the prince. Prince S., for example, even turned away when he encountered the prince and did not return his greeting. But Yevgeny Pavlovitch was not afraid of compromising himself by going to see the prince, even though he had again begun visiting the Yepanchins daily and was even received with an evident increase of cordial feeling. He came to see the prince the day after all the Yepanchins had left Pavlovsk. He came in already aware of all the rumors that were circulating and indeed was perhaps partly responsible for spreading them. The prince was delighted to see him and began speaking at once of the Yepanchins. Such a simple and direct beginning completely disarmed Yevgeny Pavlovitch, and he too did not beat around the bush but went straight to the point.

The prince did not know that the Yepanchins had left; he was struck by the news and turned pale, but a minute later he shook his head, confused and thoughtful, and acknowledged that "it had to happen," then quickly inquired where they had gone.

Meanwhile Yevgeny Pavlovitch was observing him closely, and all this, the rapid questions, their naïve simplicity, his troubled agitation, and at the same time his strange outspokenness, his restlessness, his excitement, all this surprised him considerably. However, he informed the prince of everything, courteously and in great detail. There was a great deal the latter did not know, and this was the first person to bring news from the Yepanchin household. He confirmed that Aglaya had really been sick and had had a fever and not slept for three nights in a row, that she was now better and was entirely out of danger but was quite nervous and hysterical. "It's a good thing there is perfect peace in the house," he said. "They are trying to make no allusions to what has happened, either before Aglaya or even among themselves. The parents have already discussed a trip abroad in the fall, right after Adelaïda's wedding. Aglaya received the first hints of it in silence." He, Yevgeny Pavlovitch, also might possibly be going abroad. Even Prince S. might go for a couple of months with Adelaïda, if his affairs allowed. The general would remain. The family had now all moved to Kolmino, fifteen miles out of Petersburg, where they had an estate with a spacious manor house. Belokonskaya had not yet gone back to Moscow and was evidently staying on for some purpose. Lizaveta Prokofyevna insisted strenuously that it was impossible to remain in Pavlovsk after all that had happened. He, Yevgeny Pavlovitch, informed her daily about the rumors circulating in the town. Nor did they find it possible either to go to their small country house at Yelagin.

"And as a matter of fact," added Yevgeny Pavlovitch, "you'll admit the situation was hardly tolerable—especially knowing all that was going on here in your house, Prince, and after your daily visits *there,* in spite of being refused—"

"Yes, yes, yes, you are right," the prince said, again nodding his head. "I wanted to see Aglaya Ivanovna—"

"Ah, dear Prince!" Yevgeny Pavlovitch suddenly exclaimed fervently and sadly. "How could you have—allowed all that to happen? To be sure, to be sure, this was all so unexpected—I quite see that you must have been overcome and —you couldn't very well stop a madwoman, it wasn't in your power! But then you should have understood how strongly and intensely that girl—cared about you. She did not wish to share you with another woman, and you—you could leave her and shatter such a treasure!"

"Yes, yes, you are right. Yes, I am to blame," the prince said again in terrible anguish. "And you know only she, only Aglaya looked on Nastassya Filippovna that way. No one else looked on her like that."

"Yes, and that's why it's all so shocking—that there was nothing serious there!" cried Yevgeny Pavlovitch, decidedly carried away. "Forgive me, Prince, but—I—I've thought about this, Prince. I've given it a lot of thought. I know all that happened before, I know all that happened six months ago, everything, and—all that amounted to nothing! All that was only in your head, an image, a fantasy, smoke patterns, and only the frightened jealousy of a completely inexperienced young girl could have taken it for anything serious!"

At this point Yevgeny Pavlovitch, having already dropped the reserves of formality, now gave full vent to his indignation. Sensibly and clearly and, we repeat, with extraordinary psychological insight, he drew for him a vivid picture of all the prince's past relations with Nastassya Filippovna. Yevgeny Pavlovitch had always had a way with words but now he rose to positive eloquence. "From the very beginning," he declared, "there were lies between you, and whatever begins with lies must end with lies, for that is a law of nature. I don't agree and I even resent it when someone—when anyone—calls you an idiot. You are far too intelligent to be called that, you're so strange you are not like other people—you must admit it yourself. I have determined that the fundamental cause of all that has happened is what I might call your innate inexperience (note the word 'innate,' Prince), also your unusual simplicity of heart, and then too your phenomenal lack of any sense of proportion (as you yourself acknowledged several times), and finally the enormous mass of merely intellectual convictions which you, with your extraordinary honesty, have until now taken for sincere, natural, and spontaneous convictions! You must admit, Prince, that in your relations with Nastassya Filippovna there was from the very start something *conventionally democratic* (I put it this way for the sake of brevity), the fascination, so to speak, of the 'woman question' (to put it still more briefly). For you see I knew all about the curious and scandalous scene that took place at Nastassya Filippovna's when Rogozhin brought his money. If you like I shall give you a systematic analysis of yourself, I shall show you yourself as in a mirror, for I know precisely what this was all about and why it turned out as it did! You as a young man in Switzerland longed for your country, you longed for Russia as for a land which is unknown but full of promise; you read many books about Russia, superb books perhaps, but harmful to you. You arrive with your first ardent desire for action and, so to speak, you fling yourself into action! And then on the very day of your arrival you are told a sad and heartrending story of an injured woman, you, a virtuous knight, a story about a woman! On the very same day you see this woman, you are bewitched by her beauty, her fantastic, demoniacal beauty (for I do agree she is beautiful). Add to this your state of nerves, your epilepsy, add our Petersburg thaw that shatters the nerves, and that whole day in a city that is unknown and seems almost fantastic to you, a day of encounters and scenes, a day of making unexpected acquaintances, a day of most unexpected reality, a day of three lovely Yepanchin girls and, among them, Aglaya, add fatigue, light-heartedness, add Nastassya Filippovna's drawing room and its whole tone, and—

what could you expect of yourself at that moment? What do you think?"

"Yes, yes. Yes, yes," said the prince, nodding his head and starting to blush. "Yes, that's almost how it was. As you know, I really had hardly slept at all in the train the night before, and the night before that, and I was in a terrible state."

"Yes, of course. What do you think I'm getting at?" Yevgeny Pavlovitch continued ardently. "It's perfectly clear that you, in the heat of enthusiasm, so to speak, seized the opportunity to declare publicly the magnanimous notion that you, a prince and a man whose life is pure, do not consider a woman dishonored who has been put to shame not through her own fault but through the fault of a revolting aristocratic libertine. My Lord, how easy to understand! But that, dear Prince, is not the point. The point is, was this the truth, was your feeling genuine, was it a natural feeling or merely intellectual enthusiasm? In the temple a woman was forgiven, but do you think she was told that she had done well, that she was deserving of all honor and respect? Didn't good sense tell you three months later what the true state of affairs was? Let's grant that she's guiltless now—I have no desire to press that point—but can all her adventures justify such intolerable, diabolical pride, such arrogant, greedy egoism? Forgive me, Prince, I'm letting myself get carried away, but—"

"Yes, all that may be so," the prince agreed again. "You may be right. She really is very irritable, and you are right, of course, but—"

"She deserves compassion? Is that what you meant to say, my dear good Prince? But could you, out of compassion and to please her, put someone else to shame, a pure and noble-minded girl, and humiliate her in those haughty, those hating eyes? Where will your compassion stop after that? For this is past belief! How can you, loving the girl, humiliate her like that before her rival, reject her for the sake of someone else before the very eyes of that other—after you had made her an honorable offer—and you did make her a proposal, didn't you?—you did so in the presence of her parents and her sisters! Are you an honest man after that, Prince, may I ask you? And—and haven't you deceived that divine girl in telling her you loved her?"

"Yes, yes, you are right. Oh, I do feel I am to blame!" said the prince in inexpressible anguish.

"But is that enough?" Yevgeny Pavlovitch cried out indignantly. "Is it enough to cry, 'Oh, I'm to blame'? You are to blame, and yet you persist! And where was your heart then, your 'Christian' heart? Because you saw her face at that moment—was she suffering any less than *that other woman,* the one who has come between you? How could you see that and let it happen? How could you?"

"But—I didn't let it happen," murmured the unhappy prince.

"How is that?"

"Good Lord, I didn't let anything happen. Even now I don't understand how it all came about. I—I ran after Aglaya Ivanovna, but Nastassya Filippovna fainted. And since then they haven't let me see Aglaya Ivanovna."

"It doesn't matter! You should have run after Aglaya even if the other did faint!"

"Yes—yes, I should have—but she would have died! She would have killed herself, you don't know her, and—it didn't matter, I would have told Aglaya Ivanovna everything afterward and— You see, Yevgeny Pavlovitch, it appears to me you don't know everything. Tell me, why am I not allowed to see Aglaya Ivanovna? I'd explain everything to her. You see, neither of them talked about what they should have then, not what they should have at all, that's why it turned out the way it did. I can't possibly explain it to you—but perhaps I might have explained it to Aglaya. Oh dear, oh dear God! You speak of her face at that moment, as she was running out. Oh dear God. I do remember it! Let's go! Let's go!" he cried, suddenly jumping up and taking Yevgeny Pavlovitch by the arm.

"Where?"

"Let's go to Aglaya Ivanovna, let's go at once!"

"But she isn't in Pavlovsk, I told you that. And why go to her?"

"She will understand, she will understand!" the prince murmured, clasping his hands as if in prayer. "She will understand it isn't this way at all, it's completely, completely different."

"How is it completely different? You are getting married, aren't you? That means you're persisting. Are you marrying or not?"

"Well, yes, I am. Yes!"

"Then why isn't it this way?"

"Oh no, it isn't! It isn't. It doesn't matter that I'm marrying her. It doesn't matter."

"How can it not matter? It's no trifling thing. You are marrying the woman you love to make her happy, and Aglaya Ivanovna sees this and knows it, so how can it not matter?"

"Happy? Oh, no! I'm simply marrying her—that's all. She wants it. And what if I am marrying her? I— No, all that doesn't matter! Only she certainly would have died. I see now that her marriage with Rogozhin was insanity! I understand now everything I didn't understand before, and, you see, when they were standing there then facing each other I could not bear looking at Nastassya Filippovna's face— You don't know, Yevgeny Pavlovitch," he said, dropping his voice mysteriously, "I have never said this to anyone, never, even to Aglaya, but I cannot bear Nastassya Filippovna's face— It's true what you said just now about that evening at Nastassya Filippovna's, but there is something else you left out, because you don't know it. I looked at *her face!* Even that morning, looking at her portrait, I couldn't bear it— Now, Vera Lebedev has quite different eyes. I—I am afraid of her face!" he added in extraordinary terror.

"Afraid of it?"

"Yes. She is—mad!" he whispered, turning pale.

"You're sure?" asked Yevgeny Pavlovitch with extreme interest.

"Yes, I'm sure. Now I am sure. Now, during these past days, I have become quite sure."

"Then what are you doing, Prince?" Yevgeny Pavlovitch cried out in alarm. "So you're marrying her out of a kind of fear? This is impossible to understand! And even without loving her, perhaps?"

"Oh, no, I love her with all my soul! For she's—a child. She's a child now, a complete child. Oh, you know nothing!"

"And at the same time you assured Aglaya Ivanovna that you loved her?"

"Oh, yes, yes!"

"How is that? Do you want to love both of them?"

"Oh, yes, yes!"

"For heaven's sake, Prince, what are you saying? Come to your senses!"

"Without Aglaya I— I absolutely must see her! I— I shall soon die in my sleep. Oh, if only Aglaya knew, if she knew everything—I mean absolutely everything. For in this matter you have to know everything—that's what is most important! Why can we never learn *everything* about another person, when we have to, when that other person is at fault. But I don't know what I'm saying, I'm all mixed up. You've shocked me terribly. And could her face still be the same as when she ran out? Oh, yes, I am to blame! Most likely everything is my fault. I still don't know just how, but I am to blame— There's something here I can't explain to you, Yevgeny Pavlovitch, I have no words for it, but—Aglaya Ivanovna will understand! Oh, I always believed she would understand!"

"No, Prince, she won't understand! Aglaya Ivanovna loved you like a woman, like a human being, not like—a disembodied spirit. Do you know, my poor Prince? Most likely, you never loved either one of them."

"I don't know—perhaps, perhaps. You are right about many things, Yevgeny Pavlovitch. You are unusually intelligent, Yevgeny Pavlovitch. Ah, my head is beginning to ache again. Let's go to her! For God's sake—for God's sake!"

"But I tell you she isn't in Pavlovsk, she's in Kolmino."

"Let's go to Kolmino. Let's go at once!"

"That's im-possible!" Yevgeny Pavlovitch said emphatically, getting up.

"Listen, I'll write her a letter. Take a letter to her!"

"No, Prince, no! Spare me such errands. I can't!"

They parted. Yevgeny Pavlovitch went away with a strange conviction: in his opinion too the prince was not quite in his right mind. And what was the meaning of that *face* he was so afraid of and loved so much? And yet at the same time he might really die without Aglaya, so that perhaps Aglaya will never learn how much he loves her! "Ha, ha! And how can he love two women? With two different kinds of love at once? That's interesting—the poor idiot! And what will become of him now?"

Chapter TEN

❧

However, the prince did not die before his wedding, either while awake or "in his sleep," as he had predicted to Yevgeny Pavlovitch. Perhaps he did not sleep well and had bad dreams, but by day, in people's company, he seemed kind and even content, and if sometimes he was very thoughtful it was only when he was alone. The wedding was being moved up, it was set for about a week after Yevgeny Pavlovitch's visit. In the face of such haste, even the prince's very best friends, had he any, would have been forced to abandon their efforts to "save" the poor crazy fellow. There were rumors that General Yepanchin and his wife, Lizaveta Prokofyevna, were partly responsible for Yevgeny Pavlovitch's visit. But even if they both, out of the infinite kindness of their hearts, might have wished to save the pitiful lunatic from the abyss, they could not, of course, go beyond this one feeble effort; neither their position nor even, perhaps, their own inclinations (as was only natural) could be reconciled to any more serious undertakings. We have mentioned that even those closest to the prince had for the most part turned against him. Vera Lebedev, however, confined herself to shedding tears in solitude, staying more in her part of the house, and looking in on the prince less often than before. Kolya at this time was occupied with his father's funeral; the old man had died of a second stroke eight days after the first. The prince shared in the family's grief, and in the first days spent several hours daily with Nina Alexandrovna. He went to the funeral and to the service at the church. Many people noticed that the prince's arrival and departure provoked whispering among the crowd gathered at the church, and the same thing happened in the streets and in the gardens. Whenever he would pass on foot or ride by, talk was heard, his name was mentioned, he was pointed out, and Nastassya Filippovna's name was heard. People looked for her at the funeral, but she was not at the funeral. Nor was the captain's widow, whom Lebedev had managed to prevent from coming on time. The funeral service itself produced a strong and painful impression on the prince; when still in the church he whispered to Lebedev, in reply to a question of his, that he was attending an Orthodox funeral for the first time and that he remembered from childhood only one other funeral in some village church.

"Yes, sir, it's as if the man lying there in the coffin wasn't the man we chose as our chairman so recently—remember, sir?" Lebedev whispered to the prince. "Who are you looking for?"

"Oh, it's nothing. I just thought—"

"Not Rogozhin?"

"Is he here?"

"In the church."

"So that's why I thought I saw his eyes," murmured the prince in confusion. "But what— Why is he here? Was he invited?"

"They never thought to, sir. They don't know him at all. But then anyone comes here; the public, sir. Why are you so surprised? I often meet him now, I've met him in Pavlovsk four times in the past week."

"I haven't seen him even once—since that time," murmured the prince.

As Nastassya Filippovna too had never once mentioned meeting Rogozhin "since that time," the prince now concluded that Rogozhin was for some reason purposely keeping out of sight. All that day he was absorbed in deep thought, while that day and also in the evening Nastassya Filippovna was unusually gay.

Kolya, who had made up with the prince before his father's death, suggested that he should invite Keller and Burdovsky to officiate (since the matter was urgent and not to be put off). He guaranteed him that Keller would behave properly, and said that he might also be "of some use"; as for Burdovsky there was nothing to be said of him, since he was a quiet and retiring person. Nina Alexandrovna and Lebedev observed to the prince that even if the wedding was now decided upon, why at least did it have to be at Pavlovsk, and at the height of the summer season, and so public? Would it not be better to have it at Petersburg, and even at home? To the prince the drift of all these apprehensions was perfectly clear, but he replied briefly and simply that this was Nastassya Filippovna's express wish.

The next day Keller called on the prince, having been informed that he was to be best man. Before entering he stopped in the doorway as soon as he caught sight of the prince, raised his right hand with his forefinger pointing upward, and, as if taking an oath, cried: "I'm not drinking!"

Then he went up to the prince, pressed both his hands and shook them warmly, and declared that of course when he had first heard of the wedding he had been strongly opposed to it, and had announced that fact at billiards, and this was for no other reason than that he had hoped and with the impatience of a good friend daily expected to see the prince marrying no less a person than the Princess de Rohan, or at least De Chabot; but now he could see for himself that the prince was looking at things at least ten times more nobly than "all of them put together!" For he was not seeking pomp or wealth or even repute but only—truth! The sympathies of highplaced persons were all too well known, and the prince was too exalted by his education not to be a high-placed person, speaking loosely! "But the riffraff and the rabble are of another opinion. In town, in houses, at gatherings, at the summer cottages, at the band concerts, in the taverns and the billiard rooms they are talking and yelling about nothing else but the coming event. I heard that they were even planning to organize a shivaree under your windows—and on the first night, so to speak! If you should have need of an honest man's pistol, Prince, I am ready to exchange half a dozen shots as a gentleman even before you arise the next morning from your nuptial bed." He advised too that there would be a great outpouring of thirsty people from the church and that a firehose should be in readiness outside, but Lebedev objected. "They will take the house apart for kindling if there's a firehose," he said.

"That Lebedev is intriguing against you, Prince. I swear he is!" said Keller. "They want to place you under legal custody —can you imagine that?—with everything you have, your freedom of will and your money; that is, with the very two attributes that distinguish each one of us from a four-legged beast! I have heard that, I definitely have! It's the absolute truth!"

The prince seemed to remember that he too had heard something of the kind, but of course he had paid no attention. And now again, he only laughed and forgot about it. Lebedev had in fact been very busy for some time; the man's plans and calculations always seemed to be born of an inspiration of the moment, yet in his excessive ardor they would become complicated, ramify, and develop far out of sight of their point of departure; and that was why he had little success in his life. When, almost on the wedding day, he came to the prince to confess his guilt (it was his usual habit always to come and confess to those he had intrigued against, especially if the intrigue had not been successful), he declared to him that he had been born to be a Talleyrand but had for some unknown reason always remained a Lebedev. He then proceeded to reveal his whole game, and the prince was greatly interested by this. According to his story, he had begun by seeking the protection of highly placed persons, those on whom he could rely in case of need, and he had gone to General Ivan Fyodorovitch. General Ivan Fyodorovitch was thrown into perplexity, wished the very best for "the young man," but declared that "for all his desire to save him, it was not fitting for him to act in this case." Lizaveta Prokofyevna did not wish either to see him or to hear him. Yevgeny Pavlovitch and Prince S. only gestured to him to go away. But he, Lebedev, did not lose heart; he sought the counsel of a very shrewd lawyer, an eminently worthy little old gentleman, a great friend of his and almost a benefactor. The lawyer concluded that it all was perfectly possible, provided there were competent witnesses to testify to his mental derangement and complete insanity and, most important of all, that he had the support of high-placed people. Lebedev did not lose heart here either, and he had on one occasion actually brought a doctor to see the prince—also an eminently worthy old man, with a St. Anne ribbon, who was summering in Pavlovsk—for no other purpose than, as it were, to look over the terrain, to make the prince's acquaintance, and not officially but, so to speak, in a friendly way let him know what he thought. The prince remembered the doctor's visit; he remembered that Lebedev had the day before been pestering him with remarks about his being ill, and when the prince had positively refused medical assistance, Lebedev had suddenly appeared with the doctor on the pretext that they had just left Mr. Terentyev, who was in a very bad way, and that the doctor had something to tell the prince about the sick man. The prince commended Lebedev and received the doctor very cordially. They at once began talking of Hippolite; the doctor asked him to tell him all about the time the ailing man had attempted suicide, and the prince had completely fascinated him with his account and commentary of the event. They had talked on about the climate of Petersburg, about the prince's own illness, about Switzerland, about Schneider. His explanations of Schneider's methods of treatment and his stories had so interested the doctor that he stayed for two hours, smoking the prince's superb cigars, while Lebedev, for his part, produced a most delicious liqueur, which was brought in by Vera; whereupon the doctor, a married man with a family, paid her such pointed compliments that he aroused her intense indignation. They parted friends. After leaving the prince, the doctor declared to Lebedev that if such people were put into custody who would be left to be their custodians? In answer to Lebedev's tragical account of the forthcoming event, the doctor shrewdly and slyly shook his head and remarked that, not even to speak of the fact that there is no telling whom a person will marry, the ravishing creature possessed, at least so he had heard, not only incomparable beauty, which alone might captivate a man of wealth, but a fortune which had come to her from Totsky and Rogozhin, pearls and diamonds, shawls and furniture; and therefore the dear prince's choice, far from being a manifestation of, so to speak, glaring stupidity on his part, gave evidence to the contrary of subtle and worldly calculation and intelligence, and so led to the very opposite conclusion and one completely favorable to the prince. This idea struck Lebedev too—and remained with him. "And now," he added to the prince, "you will see noth-

ing from me but devotion and my readiness to shed my blood
—this is what I have come to tell you."

Hippolite too distracted the prince during those last days;
he sent for him all too often. The family was living in a little
house not far away. The little children, Hippolite's brother
and sister, were pleased to be at the house because at least
they could escape from the invalid into the garden. The poor
captain's widow was left at his bidding and was completely
victimized by him. The prince had to intervene and make
peace between them every day, and the sick man kept calling
him his "nurse," yet at the same time could only despise him
for his role as peacemaker. He was in a great state against
Kolya for scarcely visiting him at all, the boy having spent
his time first with his dying father and then with his widowed
mother. At last he made the prince's approaching marriage
with Nastassya Filippovna the object of his mocking remarks
and ended by offending the prince and finally making him
lose his temper completely. The prince stopped visiting him.
Two days later the captain's widow came over in the morning
and in tears begged the prince to come to them or else "he
will eat me alive." She added that he wanted to reveal a great
secret. The prince went. Hippolite wanted to make peace, he
burst into tears, and after his tears, of course, became more
spiteful than ever, except that he was afraid to show his spite.
He was very ill, and now it was plain from every sign that he
soon would die. There was no secret whatever, except certain
extraordinary appeals—gasped out, so to speak, with an emotion that was perhaps put on—"to beware of Rogozhin."
"This is not a man to give up what he thinks is his. You can't
judge him by us, Prince. If he wants something, he will never
hesitate—" And so forth. The prince began pressing for details, trying to get at some sort of facts, but there were no
facts at all, only Hippolite's personal impressions and feelings. To his own great satisfaction, Hippolite did give the
prince, finally, a terrible fright. At first the prince had not
wanted to answer certain questions of his and only smiled at
his advice "to get out of the country—there are Russian
priests everywhere, you could be married there." But in the
end Hippolite had expressed the following reflection: "I'm
only afraid for Aglaya Ivanovna; Rogozhin knows how much
you love her. A love for a love. You have taken Nastassya
Filippovna from him, he will kill Aglaya. And though she's
not yours now, you'd still feel badly about it, wouldn't you?"
He had achieved his goal; the prince was hardly himself
when he left him.

These warnings about Rogozhin came the day before the

wedding. That same evening the prince saw Nastassya Filippovna for the last time before the wedding, but Nastassya Filippovna was in no state to set his mind at rest; indeed on the contrary, she had of late made him more and more uneasy. At first, that is a few days before, whenever she saw him she had done everything she could to cheer him up. She was terribly afraid of his melancholy look and she even sang to him; most often she would tell him all the amusing things she could think of. The prince almost always pretended to laugh a great deal, and sometimes he really did laugh at the brilliant wit and feeling with which she told stories whenever, as often happened, she was carried away by her tale. Seeing the prince laugh, seeing the impression she made on him, she was delighted and began to feel proud of herself. But now her melancholy and pensiveness grew with every hour. His opinion of Nastassya Filippovna was firmly fixed in his mind, otherwise of course everything about her would now have seemed enigmatic and incomprehensible to him. But he genuinely believed that she could still be reborn. He had quite truthfully told Yevgeny Pavlovitch that he loved her sincerely and completely, and in his love for her there really was the sort of attraction one has toward a sick, pitiful child whom it is difficult and even impossible to leave to himself. He did not explain his feelings toward her to anyone, and in fact disliked talking about it at the times it became impossible to avoid the subject. When they were together he and Nastassya Filippovna never spoke of their "feelings," as if they had promised each other not to do so. Anyone might have joined in their bright and spirited conversation. Darya Alexeyevna would say afterward that all this time, as she watched them, she could only marvel and rejoice.

But these views of his toward Nastassya Filippovna's mental and spiritual condition saved him for the most part from many other perplexing considerations. Now she was completely different from the woman he had known three months before. He no longer wondered, for instance, why she had fled from marrying him then, in tears and with curses and reproaches, and now was insisting that the marriage be as soon as possible. "It means," thought the prince, "she's no longer afraid that our marriage would mean misery for me." Such a rapid growth of self-assurance could not, in his opinion, be natural in her. Nor, again, could this confidence be due only to her hatred for Aglaya: Nastassya Filippovna was capable of deeper feelings than that. And surely it could not come from dread of her fate with Rogozhin? In brief, all these reasons as well as others might enter into it, but what was clearest to him was what he had already suspected for a long time—that her poor, sickly soul had broken down. All this, while in a certain way freeing him from doubts, could not give him any peace of mind or rest during that whole time. Sometimes he seemed to be trying not to think about anything. He seemed indeed to look upon the wedding as a sort of unimportant formality; he valued his own future too cheaply. As for any objections, such as in the conversation he had with Yevgeny Pavlovitch, he could definitely have made no reply to them and he felt altogether incompetent, and therefore he avoided all conversations of this kind.

He noticed, however, that Nastassya Filippovna knew and understood all too well what Aglaya meant to him. She said nothing about it, but he saw how her face looked when she sometimes would find him, at the very beginning, preparing to go to the Yepanchins'. When the Yepanchins left she was positively radiant. Unobservant and unaware though he was, he began to worry at the thought that Nastassya Filippovna had determined upon some scandalous scene to get Aglaya out of Pavlovsk. The uproar about the wedding in all the summer houses was undoubtedly kept alive in part by Nastassya Filippovna in order to exasperate her rival. As it was difficult to meet the Yepanchins, Nastassya Filippovna on one occasion got the prince into her carriage and gave orders to drive past their windows. This was a dreadful surprise for the prince; he realized what was happening when, as was usually the case with him, it was too late to do anything about it, when the carriage was directly under the windows. He said nothing, but he was ill for two days afterward; Nastassya Filippovna did not repeat the experiment. During the last days before the wedding she would become very thoughtful and melancholy. She always ended by conquering her sadness and becoming cheerful again, but somehow more quietly, not so exuberantly, not so happily cheerful as she had been such a short time before. The prince redoubled his attention. He found it odd that she never spoke of Rogozhin. Only once, five days before the wedding, a message from Darya Alexeyevna suddenly summoned him to come at once, because Nastassya Filippovna was in a very bad state. He found her in a condition approaching complete insanity: she shrieked, she trembled, she cried out that Rogozhin was hidden in the garden, in their house, that she had seen him just now, that in the night he would kill her—cut her throat! The whole day she could not quiet down. But that very evening, when the prince had stopped to see Hippolite for a moment, the captain's widow, who had just returned from town, where she had gone on some little affairs of her own, told him that Rogozhin had come to her at her Petersburg apartment that day and questioned her about Pavlovsk. The prince asked her exactly when Rogozhin had come and the captain's widow said it had been almost the exact hour Nastassya Filippovna had supposedly seen him that day in her garden. The whole thing was explained as a single illusion. Nastassya Filippovna went to the captain's widow herself to question her in greater detail and was greatly relieved.

On the day before the wedding the prince left Nastassya Filippovna in a state of great excitement; the finery for the next day had arrived from the dressmaker's in Petersburg, the wedding dress, the bridal veil, and the rest.

The prince had not expected that she would be so excited over the fine clothes; he praised everything and his praise made her happier than ever. But she let slip that she had heard there was indignation in the town, and that certain rowdy people were actually planning some sort of shivaree, with music and possibly even the reading of verses composed for the occasion, and that the whole thing was being done more or less with the approval of the rest of Pavlovsk. And so now she wanted more than ever to hold her head high before them and to outshine them all with her taste and the richness of her attire. "Let them shout, let them whistle if they dare!" Her eyes flashed at the very thought of it. She had still another secret dream, but she did not express it aloud: she hoped that Aglaya, or at least someone sent by her, would also be in the crowd, incognito, in the church, would be watching and would see it all, and she inwardly prepared herself for this. She parted from the prince at eleven o'clock in the evening absorbed by these thoughts, but before it had struck twelve a messenger came running to the prince from Darya Alexeyevna asking him to "come at once, she's very bad." The prince found his fiancée shut up in her bedroom in tears, in despair, in hysterics. For a long time she would hear nothing that was said to her through the closed door, but at last she opened it, letting in only the prince, shut the door behind him, and fell to her knees before him (Such at least was the report of Darya Alexeyevna, who had managed to catch a glimpse of what was happening.)

"What am I doing! What am I doing! What am I doing to you!" she cried, embracing his legs convulsively

The prince spent a whole hour with her; we do not know what they said. Darya Alexeyevna recounted that they parted an hour later, reconciled and happy. Once again that night the prince sent to inquire about her, but Nastassya Filippovna had already fallen asleep. In the morning, before she had awoken, two more messengers from the prince arrived at Darya Alexeyevna's, and a third messenger was charged to report that "there's a whole pack of dressmakers and hair-dressers from Petersburg around Nastassya Filippovna now, no trace of last night's breakdown; she is as busy as only a beauty like her would be busy with dressing before her wedding, and at this very moment there is an extremely impor·tant conference in progress as to which of her diamonds she will wear and how she will wear them." The prince was completely reassured.

The whole account of the wedding which follows was given by people who were present, and it appears to be cor·rect.

The wedding was fixed for eight o'clock in the evening Nastassya Filippovna was ready by seven. Since six, a crowd of bystanders had begun to gather around Lebedev's house and even more around Darya Alexeyevna's; at seven the church too began to fill. Vera Lebedev and Kolya were dreadfully alarmed on the prince's account. But they had a great deal to do at the house; they were arranging the reception to be held in the prince's rooms. However, not much of a gathering was expected after the ceremony. In addition to the necessary persons taking part in the wedding, Lebedev had invited the Ptitsyns, Ganya, the doctor with the St. Anne around his neck, and Darya Alexeyevna. When the prince inquired of Lebedev why he had invited the doctor, whom he hardly knew at all, Lebedev replied complacently, "He has a decoration—he's a respectable man—it's for the appearance of the thing, sir." And the prince was amused. Keller and Burdovsky looked quite proper in their evening clothes and gloves, except that Keller still rather worried the prince and his followers by a certain open inclination to battle, and he glared in a very hostile manner at the crowd gathering around the house. Finally, at half past seven, the prince left for the church in a carriage. Let us observe, by the way, that he expressly wished to omit none of the usual customs and traditions; everything was done publicly, openly, and "as it was supposed to be done." In the church, having somehow made his way through the crowd, accompanied by incessant whispering and exclamations, escorted by Keller, who cast menacing glances right and left, the prince disappeared for a while behind the altar doors, and Keller went off to fetch the bride At the front steps of Darya Alexeyevna's house he found a crowd which was not only two or three times as large as the one at the prince's but fully three times as unconstrained. As he went up the front steps, he heard such exclamations that he could not control himself and had already turned to address the crowd with an appropriate speech when, fortunately, he was stopped by Burdovsky and Darya Alexeyevna herself, who had run out of the house and down the stairs. They got on either side of him and led him forcibly inside. Keller was irritated and in a great hurry. Nastassya Filippovna got up, glanced once more in the mirror, observed with a "twisted smile"—as Keller reported afterward—that she was "as pale as a corpse," bowed devoutly before the ikon, and went out on the front steps. A drone of voices greeted her appearance. It is true that at the first moment there was laughter, clapping, and perhaps even derisive whistling, but in another moment other voices were heard:

"What a beauty!" some in the crowd exclaimed.

"She's not the first, she won't be the last!"

"Marriage sets everything right, you fools!"

"You don't find another beauty like that. Hurrah!" cried those standing nearest.

"A princess! For a princess like that I'd sell my soul," some clerk cried out, and he sang, " 'For one night of love I'd give up my life.' " *

Nastassya Filippovna was indeed as white as a sheet as she stepped out, but her large black eyes blazed upon the crowd like burning embers. This look was too much for the crowd; indignation was transformed into cries of enthusiasm. The doors of the carriage were open, Keller had already offered the bride his arm, when suddenly she uttered a cry and rushed down the front steps and directly into the crowd. All who were accompanying her were stunned with amazement. The crowd parted before her and suddenly, five or six paces from the steps, Rogozhin appeared. It was his eyes that Nastassya Filippovna had seen in the crowd. She rushed up to him like a madwoman and seized him by both arms.

"Save me! Take me away! Anywhere you like—at once!"

Rogozhin seized her in his arms and almost carried her to the carriage. Then, in a flash, he drew a hundred-rouble note from his billfold and handed it to the driver.

"To the railroad station, and if you catch the train there's another hundred for you!"

And he jumped into the carriage after Nastassya Filippovna and shut the doors. The coachman did not hesitate an instant and whipped up his horses. Keller later laid the blame on the unexpectedness of it all: "Another second and I would have known what to do! I wouldn't have let it happen!" he explained, describing the adventure. He and Burdovsky were about to take another carriage, which was standing nearby, and rush off in pursuit, but just as they were starting off he gave up the idea, saying, "Anyway it's too late! You can't bring her back by force!"

"And besides, the prince wouldn't want it!" decided Burdovsky, very shaken.

Rogozhin and Nastassya Filippovna galloped up to the station in time. When he was out of the carriage and was about to step aboard the train, Rogozhin had time to stop a girl who was wearing an old but presentable shawl and a silk kerchief around her head.

"Let me have your shawl for fifty roubles!" he said, abruptly holding out the money to the girl. While she was still lost in amazement and had not yet quite understood, he had already pressed the fifty-rouble bill into her hand, pulled off the shawl and kerchief, and thrown them over Nastassya Filippovna's head and shoulders. Her splendid attire was too conspicuous and would have attracted attention on the train, and only later did the young girl understand why her old and worthless shawl had been bought at such a profit to herself.

The rumor of what had happened reached the church with extraordinary speed. While Keller was hurrying to the prince, a number of people whom he did not know rushed up to question him. There was loud conversation, shaking of heads, and even laughter. No one was leaving the church, all were waiting to see how the bridegroom would take the news. He turned pale but received the news calmly, saying in a barely audible voice, "I was afraid, yet I didn't think it would happen—" and then after a short silence he added, "Still—in her state—it could be expected." This remark Keller himself described afterward as "a piece of matchless philosophy." The prince went out of the church apparently calm and quite himself, at least so many people noticed and remarked afterward. It appeared that he was very anxious to get home as soon as possible and be left alone, but this he was not to be permitted. Some of the guests followed him into his room—Ptitsyn, Gavril Ardalionovitch, and the doctor, who like the others showed no inclination to leave. Besides, the whole house was literally besieged by a crowd of idlers. While he was still on the veranda, the prince heard Keller and Lebedev getting into a bitter dispute with some persons who were complete strangers, though they appeared to be functionaries of some rank, and who were intent on coming up on the veranda at all cost. The prince went out to the disputants, asked what the matter was, and politely waving aside Lebedev and Keller, he courteously addressed a gray-haired, portly gentleman who was standing on the steps at the head of a group of others who wished to enter, and invited him to honor him with his visit. The gentleman was somewhat embarrassed, but came up all the same; and after him came a second and a third. Out of the whole crowd seven or eight came in, trying to appear as much at ease as possible; but there were no more volunteers, and soon some of the same crowd began to criticize the intruders. Those who had come in were invited to sit down, conversation began and tea was served, all in the most correct fashion, modestly and decorously, to the considerable surprise of the visitors. There were of course several attempts to enliven the conversation and turn it toward the "essential" topic; a few indiscreet questions were asked, a few "pointed" remarks made. The prince answered everyone with such simplicity and good feeling, and at the same time with such dignity, with such confidence in the propriety of his guests that the indiscreet questions stopped of their own accord. Little by little the conversation became almost serious. One gentleman, picking up something which was said, suddenly swore with great indignation that he would not sell his property, no matter what happened; that, on the contrary, he would wait and hang on, and that "enterprise is better than money," and that "there, sir, you have my whole system of economics, and you might as well know it." Since he was addressing the prince, the prince praised him warmly, even though Lebedev whispered in his ear that this gentleman did not have a stick of property to his name and never had. Almost an hour passed, tea was finished, and after tea the guests felt ashamed to stay any longer. The doctor and the gray-haired gentleman bid the prince a warm farewell, and indeed they all said good-bye warmly and loudly. Good wishes were expressed and the opinion that "there is no use grieving and perhaps it's all for the best," and so forth. Attempts were made, it is true, to ask for champagne, but the older guests restrained the younger. When they all had gone, Keller leaned over to Lebedev and said, "You and I would have yelled and fought and disgraced ourselves and brought in the police and here he's been making new friends—and what friends! I know them!" Lebedev, who was already a little "elevated," sighed and declared, " 'Thou hast hid these things from the wise and prudent, and hast revealed them unto babes.' I said this about him before but now I will add that God has preserved the babe himself, saved him from the abyss, He and all His saints."

Finally, about half past ten, the prince was left alone. His head ached. Kolya helped him change from his wedding suit into his everyday clothes and was the last to leave. They parted warmly. Kolya did not discuss what had happened and he promised to come back very early the next day. He stated afterward that the prince had not warned him of anything at their last parting, and so was concealing his intentions even from him. Soon there was almost no one left at the house: Burdovsky had gone to Hippolite's, Keller and Lebedev had gone off somewhere together. Only Vera Lebedev remained for a time in the prince's rooms, hurriedly restoring them to their normal order. Before going, she looked into the room where the prince was. He was sitting with his elbows resting on the table, his head buried in his hands. Softly she went up to him and touched his shoulder; the prince looked at her in bewilderment and for almost a minute seemed to be trying to remember something; then, having remembered and realized everything, he suddenly became extremely agitated. All he did, however, was to beg Vera very urgently to knock at his door early the next morning at seven o'clock, in time to catch the first train. Vera promised. The prince beseeched her not to speak of it to anyone. She promised this too, and finally, when she had opened the door and was leaving, the prince stopped her a third time, took her hands, kissed them, and then kissed her on the forehead and in a rather "peculiar" way said, "Till tomorrow!" So, at any rate, Vera related afterward. She went away in great anxiety about him. She felt somewhat better the next morning when at about seven o'clock, as agreed, she knocked on his door and told him that the train for Petersburg would leave in fifteen minutes. It seemed to her that he was quite alert when he answered her, and had even smiled. He had hardly undressed that night, but he had slept. He thought he might be returning the same day. It appeared therefore that he had found it possible and indeed necessary to tell only her, at that moment, that he was going to town.

Chapter ELEVEN

❧

An hour later he was in Petersburg, and shortly after nine o'clock he was ringing at Rogozhin's door. He went in at the main entrance and for a long time there was no answer. At last the door of the apartment occupied by Rogozhin's mother opened and a proper-looking old maidservant appeared.

"Parfyon Semyonovitch is not at home," she announced from the doorway. "Whom do you want?"

"Parfyon Semyonovitch."

"He's not at home, sir."

The servant was studying the prince with extreme curiosity.

"At least tell me if he spent the night at home? And—did he come back alone yesterday?"

The servant went on looking at him but did not answer.

"Wasn't—Nastassya Filippovna with him—here—last night?"

"But allow me to ask who you might be?"

"Prince Lev Nikolayevitch Myshkin, we are very well acquainted."

"He's not at home, sir."

The servant dropped her eyes.

"And Nastassya Filippovna?"

"I know nothing about that, sir."

"Wait! Wait! When will he be back?"

"I don't know that either, sir."

The door closed.

The prince decided to come back an hour later. Looking into the courtyard, he saw the caretaker.

"Is Parfyon Semyonovitch home?"

"Yes, sir."

"Why was I just told he wasn't home?"

"They told you that at his apartment?"

"No, his mother's servant told me. I rang at Parfyon Semyonovitch's, no one came to the door."

"Then perhaps he went out," the caretaker decided. "He doesn't say what he does. Sometimes he takes the key off with him, and the rooms are locked up for three days at a time."

"Are you certain he was home yesterday?"

"Yes. Sometimes he comes in by the main entrance and then you don't see him."

"And was Nastassya Filippovna with him yesterday?"

"That I don't know, sir. She doesn't come very often. I think I would have known if she'd been here."

The prince went out, and for some time he walked up and down the sidewalk deep in thought. The windows of Rogozhin's apartment were all closed; almost all the windows of his mother's part of the house were open; it was a hot, bright day and the prince crossed the street to the other sidewalk and stopped again to look once more at the windows; they were not only closed but white blinds were pulled down at almost every window.

He stood there for a minute and—oddly—it suddenly seemed to him that a corner of one of the blinds was raised and Rogozhin's face appeared and then disappeared again in the same instant. He waited a little longer and then decided to go back and ring again; but he changed his mind and put it off for an hour. "And who knows? Perhaps I only imagined it."

What mattered to him now was to make his way as quickly as possible to the Izmaylovsky Regiment district, to the apartment lately occupied by Nastassya Filippovna. He knew that when, at his request, she had left Pavlovsk three weeks before, she had gone to live at the house of an old friend of hers, the widow of a teacher, a very respectable woman with a family, who rented out a good furnished apartment, which was almost her entire livelihood. It was very likely that when she returned again to Pavlovsk, Nastassya Filippovna had kept her rooms; at least it was highly probable that she had spent the night at this apartment, where undoubtedly Rogozhin had brought her that evening. The prince took a cab. On the way it occurred to him that he should have gone there in the first place, because it was very unlikely that she would have gone straight to Rogozhin's at night. He remembered too the caretaker's words that Nastassya Filippovna did not often pay visits. If she never came often, why should she be staying at Rogozhin's now? Encouraging himself with these consoling reflections, the prince at last arrived at the Izmaylovsky Regiment district more dead than alive.

To his utter amazement no one at the widow's had heard anything of Nastassya Filippovna either that day or the day before, but they all ran out to stare at him as if he was a sort of phenomenon. The widow's whole numerous family—all girls of every age between seven and fifteen—poured out after their mother and surrounded him, staring at him open-mouthed. After them came a lean and sallow aunt of theirs in a black kerchief, and finally the grandmother of the family appeared, a little old lady in spectacles. The widow insistently asked him to come in and sit down, which the prince did. He guessed at once that they knew perfectly well who he was, and that they were very well informed that his wedding was to have taken place yesterday and were dying to ask him about the wedding and about the marvelous fact that here he was inquiring about the woman who should have been with him then in Pavlovsk, but that out of delicacy they refrained. In brief terms he satisfied their curiosity about the wedding. Cries of wonder and consternation followed, so that he was obliged to tell almost everything that had happened, in general terms, of course. Finally the council of sage and agitated ladies determined that the first thing to be done was to knock at Rogozhin's and learn everything from him positively. If he was not at home (and he would ascertain this for certain), or if he refused to say anything, then he should go to the Sem-yonovsky Regiment district to a certain German lady, a friend of Nastassya Filippovna's, who lived with her mother: perhaps Nastassya Filippovna, in her excitement and anxiety to conceal herself, had spent the night with them. The prince got up completely overcome; they told later that he had looked terribly pale; and indeed his legs were almost giving way beneath him. Finally, through the shrill crackle of voices, he made out that they were trying to persuade him to act with them and were asking for his town address. He had no town address, so they advised him to stay at a hotel somewhere. The prince thought a moment and gave the address of his old hotel, the one where he had had an attack five weeks before. Then he set out again for Rogozhin's. This time he got no answer not only at Rogozhin's but at the old woman's door as well. The prince went in search of the caretaker and with some difficulty found him in the courtyard; the caretaker was busy and hardly answered him, barely even glanced at him; but he did however declare positively that Parfyon Semyonovitch "left very early in the morning, went to Pavlovsk, and will not be home today."

"I'll wait. Perhaps he'll be back in the evening?"

"And perhaps he won't be home for a week. Who knows about him?"

"So at least he did spend the night here?"

"Yes, he did spend the night."

All this was suspicious, there was something wrong about it. In the time that had passed, the caretaker had very likely received fresh instructions; he had been quite talkative before, but now he simply turned his back. However, the prince decided to come back once again, two hours later, and even to keep watch on the house if necessary; but for now there was still hope at the German lady's house, and he hastened to the Semyonovsky Regiment district.

But at the German lady's they did not even understand what he wanted. From certain things that were said, he was even able to guess that the beautiful German woman had had a quarrel with Nastassya Filippovna about two weeks before, and she had heard nothing of her in all these days and was now exerting herself forcibly to have him understand that she was not interested in hearing about her, "even if she had married all the princes in the world." The prince hastened to leave. Among other thoughts, it occurred to him that she might have gone off to Moscow, as she had done before, and Rogozhin had no doubt gone after her, or perhaps with her. "At least if I could find some trace of her!" He remembered, however, that he had to stop at a hotel, and he hurried to Liteyny Avenue; there he was at once given a room. The servant asked him if he wanted something to eat; he absent-mindedly said that he would, and then, furious with himself, realized that the meal was making him waste an extra half hour, and only afterward did it occur to him that nothing prevented him from leaving the food that was served without eating it. A strange sensation overcame him in that dark and stuffy corridor, a sensation which persistently sought some kind of form as a thought; but he had no idea what this new thought was which was seeking expression. He was hardly himself when he went out of the hotel; his head was turning, but—where was he to go now? He hurried off to Rogozhin's again.

Rogozhin had not returned, no one answered the bell; he rang at old Mrs Rogozhin's, the door was opened and he was told there too that Parfyon Semyonovitch was not at home and might not be back for three days. What disturbed the prince was that, as before, the servant woman stared at him with intense curiosity. This time he did not find the caretaker at all. He went out and, as he had done earlier, crossed to the opposite sidewalk, looked at the windows, and walked up and down in the oppressive heat for about a half hour and possibly more. This time nothing stirred, the windows did not open, the white blinds were motionless. He made up his mind that before he had only imagined it all, that indeed the windows were so dark and had not been washed for so long that it would have been difficult to see even if someone had been peering out. Relieved by this thought, he again drove back to the schoolteacher's widow in the Izmaylovsky Regiment district.

There they were expecting him. The widow had already been to three or four places and had even been to Rogozhin's, without finding a sign of anything. The prince listened in silence, went into the room, sat down on the sofa and began looking at them all as if he did not understand what they were talking about. It was strange but he could be extremely observant and then suddenly become incredibly absentminded. The whole family declared afterward that he was an astonishingly strange person that day, and that "perhaps it was clear what was to happen even then." At last he got up and asked them to show him Nastassya Filippovna's rooms. They were two, large, sunny, high-ceilinged rooms, well furnished and no doubt quite expensive to rent. The ladies all declared afterward that the prince had examined every object in the room and had seen on the table a library book lying open, the French novel *Madame Bovary,* turned down a corner of the open page, asked permission to take it with him, and not heeding the objection that it belonged to the library put it in his pocket. He then sat down at an open window and, noticing a card table with chalk marks on it, he asked who played. They told him that Nastassya Filippovna had played cards with Rogozhin every evening: Fools, Preference, Millers, Whist, Your Own Trumps, all the games, and that they had taken up card playing only lately, after she had come back from Pavlovsk to Petersburg, because Nastassya Filippovna kept complaining that she was bored and that Rogozhin would sit the whole evening without saying anything and that he couldn't talk about anything, and she often cried; and the next evening Rogozhin suddenly took a pack of playing cards out of his pocket; then Nastassya Filippovna had laughed and they had begun playing. The prince asked where the cards were they had played with, but there were no cards to be found; Rogozhin had always brought the cards in his pocket himself, a new pack every day, and then taken them away with him.

The ladies advised him to go once more to Rogozhin's and once more to knock loudly, not right away but in the evening: "perhaps something will develop." The widow herself offered in the meantime to go to Pavlovsk before the evening to see Darya Alexeyevna and find out if she knew anything.

They asked the prince in any case to stop by again at ten that evening to make plans for the following day. In spite of all their words of comfort and reassurance, the prince's soul was seized with absolute despair. He walked to his hotel in a state of inexpressible anguish. The dusty, stifling Petersburg summer weighed down on him like a press; he was jostled by grim-looking people, by drunken people; he stared aimlessly at the faces, and probably walked much farther than he had to; it was almost evening when he got to his room. He decided to rest a little and then go again to Rogozhin's, as they had advised him to do. He sat down on the sofa, rested his elbows on the table, and fell into thought.

God knows how long he sat there and what he thought. There was much that he feared and he realized painfully and agonizingly that he was dreadfully afraid. Vera Lebedev came to his mind; then it occurred to him that perhaps Lebedev knew something about these things, and that if he did not know that he could find out much more quickly and easily than he could. Then he remembered Hippolite and the fact that Rogozhin used to visit Hippolite. And then he thought of Rogozhin himself, as he had recently seen him at the funeral, then at the park, then—suddenly here in the corridor, when he had hidden and had waited for him with a knife. Now he remembered his eyes, his eyes as they had looked at him then in the darkness. He shuddered: the thought which before had been seeking expression now suddenly came to his mind.

It was partly that if Rogozhin was in Petersburg, though he might hide for a time, he would certainly end by coming to him, the prince, with good or with evil intentions, as he had done before. At least if Rogozhin found it necessary to come for any reason, he would have to come here, again to this corridor. He did not know his address, so he might very well think that the prince would stay at the same hotel as before; at least he would try looking for him here, if he needed him very badly. And who knows, perhaps he would need him very badly?

Thus he reflected, and for some reason the idea seemed to him entirely possible. Had he tried to pursue his thought, he could never have explained why, for instance, he would suddenly be so necessary to Rogozhin, and why it was impossible that they would not, finally, meet again. But it was an oppressive thought: "If he is all right, then he won't come," the prince went on thinking; "he will only come if he is unhappy, and he is certainly unhappy."

Of course with that conviction he should have waited for

619

Rogozhin in his room; but it was as if he could not bear his new thought, and he jumped up, took his hat and ran out. In the corridor it was already almost completely dark. "What if he suddenly stepped from that corner and stopped me by the stairs?" it flashed through his mind as he reached the familiar spot. But no one stepped out. He went down to the gateway, went out on the sidewalk, wondered at the dense crowds of people who had flocked into the streets at sunset (as they always do in Petersburg during the summer vacations), and walked in the direction of Gorokhovaya Street. About fifty paces from the hotel, at the first crossing, someone in the crowd suddenly touched his elbow and said in a low voice directly into his ear:

"Lev Nikolayevitch, follow me, brother, I want you."

It was Rogozhin.

Curiously enough, the prince began joyfully telling him—babbling away and barely getting the words out—how he had expected to see him just now in the corridor at the hotel.

"I was there," Rogozhin replied unexpectedly. "Let's go."

The prince was surprised by his answer, but he was surprised only two or three minutes later when he had fully taken it in. Having understood the answer, he became frightened and began looking intently at Rogozhin, who was walking almost half a pace ahead, looking straight ahead without glancing at the people approaching, and making way for them with mechanical care.

"Why didn't you ask for me in my room—if you were at the hotel?" the prince suddenly asked.

Rogozhin stopped, looked at him, thought a moment, and, as if he had not understood the question, said:

"Listen, Lev Nikolayevitch, you go straight on there—to the house—you know it, don't you? And I'll be walking on the other side. And see that we keep together."

Saying this, he crossed the street to the opposite sidewalk, looked back to see if the prince was coming, and seeing that he was standing still, staring at him wide-eyed, he gestured in the direction of Gorokhovaya Street, and went on, turning around every moment to see the prince and waving at him to follow him. He was obviously relieved to see that the prince understood him and did not cross over from the other sidewalk. It occurred to the prince that Rogozhin was watching for someone he did not want to miss on the way, and that that was why he had crossed to the other sidewalk. "Except why didn't he tell me whom he has to look out for?" They walked on this way for about five hundred yards and suddenly the prince for some reason began to tremble; Rogozhin was still looking back but less often; the prince could not bear it any longer and beckoned to him. At once Rogozhin crossed the street to him.

"Is Nastassya Filippovna at your house?"

"Yes."

"And was it you who looked at me from behind the curtain this morning?"

"Yes."

"How is it that you—"

But the prince did not know what more to ask or how to finish his question. Moreover his heart was beating so hard it was difficult for him to speak. Rogozhin too was silent and looked at him as before—that is, almost dreamily.

"Well, I'm going on," he said abruptly, starting to cross the street again, "and you go on by yourself. Let's go separately in the street—it's better for us—on different sides—you'll see."

When at last they turned on opposite sides of the street into Gorokhovaya Street and started toward Rogozhin's house, the prince's legs began to weaken again, and it was difficult for him to walk. It was already about ten o'clock in the evening. The windows in the old lady's part of the house were open as before, in Rogozhin's they were closed, and in the twilight the white blinds seemed even more conspicuous. The prince approached the house on the opposite sidewalk; Rogozhin from his side of the street started up the front steps and he was waving to him. The prince crossed over and joined him on the steps.

"Even the caretaker doesn't know I've come back, I said this morning I was going to Pavlovsk, and I left word with my mother too," he whispered with a shrewd and almost satisfied smile. "We'll go in and no one will hear us."

He already had the key in his hand. As he went up the stairs, he turned and gestured to the prince to warn him to walk more quietly, and he quietly opened the door to his apartment, let the prince in, cautiously followed him inside, closed the door behind him, and put the key in his pocket.

"Come," he said in a whisper.

He had been speaking in whispers ever since they had met on the sidewalk on Liteyny Avenue. Despite all his outward calm, inwardly he was deeply disturbed. When they went into the drawing room and were approaching the study, he went over to the window and mysteriously beckoned to the prince.

"When you began ringing this morning, I guessed right away it was you. I tiptoed up to the door and I heard you talking with Pafnutyevna. I had given her orders at daybreak this morning that if you or anyone you sent or anyone at all came knocking at my door, she was not on any account to say anything, especially if you came asking for me yourself, and I gave her your name. And later, when you went out, the thought struck me: 'What if he stands out there now and looks and keeps watch in the street?' I went up to this very window, raised the blind, looked out, and there you were, standing there looking directly at me. That's how it was."

"Where is—Nastassya Filippovna?" said the prince in a breathless voice.

"She's here," Rogozhin said slowly, after a slight hesitation.

"Where?"

Rogozhin raised his eyes and looked steadily at the prince.

"Come."

He was still speaking in a whisper and not hurriedly, still with the same strange sort of dreaminess. Even as he told about raising the blind, it was as if he wanted to tell him something else, despite his unconstrained way of speaking.

They went into the study. A certain change had been made in the room since the prince had been there: a green damask curtain that could be drawn open at either end had been stretched across the entire room, dividing the alcove where Rogozhin's bed was from the rest of the study. The heavy curtain was drawn closed at both ends. But it was very dark; the summer "white nights" of Petersburg were beginning to get darker, and were it not for the full moon, with the blinds down it would have been difficult to make out anything at all in Rogozhin's dark rooms. It is true they could still see each other's faces, though very faintly. Rogozhin's face was as usual pale; he fixed the prince with a blazing glare, which was somehow rigid.

"Why don't you light a candle?" asked the prince.

"No, there's no need," Rogozhin answered, and taking the prince by the hand he had him sit down in a chair. He sat down facing him, pulling up his chair so that his knees almost touched the prince's. There was a small round table to one side between them. "Let's sit, let's sit for a while!" he said, as if he was trying to persuade the prince to stay seated where he was. They were silent for a moment. "I knew you'd be staying in that hotel," he began, as people sometimes lead up to an important topic of conversation by a side issue which has nothing directly to do with it. "But as I got to the corridor, I thought to myself: well, what if he's sitting there waiting for me now, just as at this moment I'm waiting for him? Have you been to the teacher's widow?"

"Yes." The prince was hardly able to answer because of the violent beating of his heart.

"I thought of that too. There'll be talk, I thought— But then later I thought: I'll bring him here for the night, so that we can spend this night together."

"Rogozhin! Where is Nastassya Filippovna?" the prince whispered urgently, and he got up trembling in every limb. Rogozhin got up too.

"There," he whispered, nodding toward the curtain.

"Asleep?" whispered the prince.

Again Rogozhin looked at him steadily as before.

"Well, come on then! Only you— Well, come on!"

He drew back the curtain, stood still, and turned to the prince again.

"Go in," he said, motioning him to go inside the curtain. The prince went in.

"It's dark here," he said.

"You can see!" muttered Rogozhin.

"I can barely see—the bed."

"Go closer," Rogozhin suggested softly.

The prince took another step nearer, then another, and stopped dead. He stood there staring for a minute or two; neither of them uttered a word the whole time they were standing by the bedside; the prince's heart was beating so violently it seemed it could be heard in the room, in the deathly stillness of the room. But now his eyes had grown accustomed to the darkness and he could make out the whole bed; someone lay asleep on it in an absolutely motionless sleep; not the faintest stir was to be heard, not the faintest breath. The sleeper was covered from head to foot with a white sheet, but the limbs could be made out only vaguely; all that could be seen was that a human figure lay there stretched out at full length. All around, on the bed, at the foot of it, on the armchair nearby, even on the floor, clothes had been strewn in disorder, a rich white silk dress, flowers, ribbons. On a little table at the head of the bed diamonds which had been thrown there lay gleaming. At the foot of the bed there was a crumpled heap of lace, and on the white lace, protruding from under the sheet, appeared the tip of a bare foot; it looked as if it was carved out of marble and it was dreadfully still. The prince looked, and he felt that as he looked the room was becoming even more still and deathlike. Suddenly there was a buzz as a fly awakened and flew over the bed and settled at the head of it. The prince gave a start.

"Let's go out," said Rogozhin, touching his arm. They went out, they sat in the same chairs, again facing one another. The prince was shaking more and more and he kept looking steadily at Rogozhin with his questioning eyes.

"I see you are trembling, Lev Nikolayevitch," Rogozhin said at last, "almost as you do when you have your fits. Do you remember—in Moscow? Or as once you did just before a fit. And I can't imagine what I'll do with you now—"

The prince listened, straining with all his force to understand, and still his eyes were questioning him.

"Was it you?" he managed to say at last, nodding toward the curtain.

"Yes—it was," whispered Rogozhin, and he lowered his eyes.

They were silent for about five minutes.

"Because," Rogozhin went on suddenly, as if there had been no break in the conversation, "because if you are ill now and have a fit and scream someone may hear from the street or the yard and guess that people are spending the night in the apartment they'll start knocking and come in—because now they all think I'm not at home. I haven't lit a candle, so that they won't guess from the street or the yard. Because when I'm not home I take the key with me, and while I'm away no one comes in to make up the rooms for three or four days, that's the way I always do. So they wouldn't know we're spending the night here—"

"Wait," said the prince. "I asked the caretaker and the old woman this morning whether Nastassya Filippovna hadn't stayed overnight here. So they must know already."

"I know you asked them. I told Pafnutyevna that Nastassya Filippovna came yesterday and then went off to Pavlovsk and that she was here only ten minutes. And they don't know she spent the night here—no one does. We came in very quietly yesterday, just as I did with you today. I was thinking on the way that she wouldn't want to come in, but —not at all! She whispered, she tiptoed, she pulled her skirts around her and held them so they wouldn't rustle, she put her finger to her lips at me on the stairs—it was you she was afraid of. On the train she was mad with fear, and it was her wish to spend the night here. I thought first of taking her to the widow's place—but no! 'He'd find me there in the morning,' she said, 'but you'll hide me and early tomorrow we'll be off to Moscow.' And then she wanted to go to Oryol somewhere. And she went to bed still saying how we would go to Oryol—"

"Wait. What are you going to do now, Parfyon? What do you want to do?"

"Yes, I'm wondering about you, you keep on trembling.

624

We'll spend the night here, together. There's no other bed but that one but I thought we'd take the pillows from both sofas and I'll make a bed right here, near the curtain, for you and me, so that we can be together. Because if they come in they'll start looking around and searching, they'll see her at once and take her away. They'll start questioning me, and I'll say I did it, and they'll take me off at once. So let her lie there now beside us, beside you and me."

"Yes, yes!" the prince agreed ardently.

"So we won't confess and let them take her away."

"Not for anything in the world!" the prince decided. "No, no, no!"

"That's what I decided, lad, not to give her up for anything, not to anyone! We'll spend the night quietly here. I was only away from the house an hour today, in the morning; the rest of the time I was with her. And then in the evening I went out to find you. Another thing I'm afraid of is that it's so close and there'll be a smell. Do you notice a smell or not?"

"Perhaps I do, I don't know. There will certainly be a smell by morning."

"I covered her with oilcloth, good American oilcloth, and put the sheet over it, and I opened four bottles of Zhdanov's disinfectant and set them around; they're there now."

"Like they did there—in Moscow?"

"It's for the smell, my friend. And the way she is lying there— In the morning when there's some light, have a look at her. What's the matter? Can't you even get up?" Rogozhin asked with apprehensive surprise, seeing that the prince was shaking so much he was unable to stand up.

"My legs won't move," murmured the prince. "It's from fear, I know that. When the fear goes, I'll get up."

"Wait, then, while I make us a bed, and you can lie down —and I'll lie down beside you—and we'll listen—because, lad, I don't know yet—I don't know everything yet, so I'm telling you this beforehand, so that you'll know everything about it—"

Muttering these vague words, Rogozhin began to make up the beds. It was clear that he had thought about these beds, possibly even that morning. The night before he had lain on a sofa. But there was not room for two on the sofas, and he was determined that their beds would be side by side, and this was why he now, with great effort, was dragging cushions of all sizes from the two sofas across the room and placing them near the opening at the end of the curtain. He had more or less managed to make the bed, then he went up to the prince, took him tenderly and elatedly by the arm, raised him up, and led him to the bed; but it seemed that the prince could walk by himself; which meant his fear was passing, yet he still was trembling.

"For you see, my friend," Rogozhin suddenly began, after settling the prince on the best cushions on the left, and stretching out himself on the right, without undressing, his hands clasped behind his head, "it's hot now and, you know, the smell— I'm afraid to open the windows, but my mother has flowerpots with lots of flowers, and they have such a beautiful smell. I thought of getting them, but Pafnutyevna would guess something, because she's inquisitive."

"Yes, she is inquisitive," the prince agreed.

"We could buy some—put little bouquets and flowers all around her? But then I think, friend, it would be a pity to see her all covered with flowers!"

"Listen," said the prince, seeming uncertain, as if he was hunting for what exactly he had to ask and forgetting it immediately. "Listen, tell me: what did you kill her with? The knife? The same one?"

"The same one."

"Wait, there's something else! I want to ask you something else, Parfyon—I'm going to ask you a lot of questions, about everything—but first you'd better tell me, to begin with, so that I'll know: did you intend to kill her before my wedding, just before the ceremony, at the door of the church, with the knife? Did you or not?"

"I don't know if I did or not," Rogozhin replied dryly, as if he was rather surprised at the question and did not understand it.

"Did you ever bring the knife with you to Pavlovsk?"

"No, never," he said, then after a silence added, "All I can tell you about the knife is this, Lev Nikolayevitch: I took it out of a locked drawer this morning, because it all happened this morning, sometime before four o'clock. It was always here between the pages of a book. And—and there was something else that was strange: the knife seemed to go in three or four inches, just under the left breast, and no more than half a tablespoonful of blood came out of her chemise, no more than that."

"That—that—that—" the prince said, sitting up suddenly in great agitation. "I know about that. I read about it—it's called internal hemorrhage. Sometimes there's not even a drop. That's when the stab goes straight into the heart—"

"Shh, do you hear?" Rogozhin urgently interrupted him, suddenly sitting up in terror on the cushions. "Do you hear?"

626

"No!" said the prince as quickly and fearfully, looking at Rogozhin.

"Steps! Do you hear? In the drawing room."

They both listened.

"I hear," the prince whispered firmly.

"Someone's walking?"

"Yes."

"Shall we shut the door or not?"

"Yes."

They closed the door and both lay down again. They were silent a long time.

"Oh, yes!" said the prince suddenly, in the same hurried and excited whisper, and sitting up as if he had seized his thought again and was terribly afraid of losing it again. "Yes —I wanted—those cards! The cards— They said you played cards with her?"

"Yes, I did," said Rogozhin, after a pause.

"Where—where are the cards?"

"They're here," said Rogozhin after an even longer silence. "Here—"

He pulled from his pocket a used pack of cards, wrapped in paper, and held them out to the prince. The prince took them, but as if he did not realize what he was doing. A new feeling of melancholy and hopelessness weighed on his heart; he understood suddenly that at that moment and for a long time past he was not saying what he should have been saying, not doing what he should have been doing, and that these cards he held in his hands, and which he had been so pleased to see, were no use now, no use at all. He got up and wrung his hands in dismay. Rogozhin lay motionless, as if he did not see or hear his gesture, but his eyes shone brightly in the darkness and they were wide open and staring. The prince sat down on a chair and looked at him in terror. A half hour passed; suddenly Rogozhin uttered a loud cry and began laughing, as though he had forgotten that they had to speak in whispers.

"That officer—that officer—remember how she whipped that officer at the band concert—remember? Ha, ha! And the cadet too—the cadet that rushed up—"

The prince jumped up from the chair in new terror. When Rogozhin was quiet again (and he grew quiet suddenly), the prince gently bent over him, sat down beside him, and with his heart pounding, his breath coming heavily, he looked at him closely. Rogozhin did not turn his head toward him and seemed even to have forgotten about him. The prince watched and waited, time was passing, it was beginning to get

627

light. Now and then Rogozhin would suddenly begin to mutter, loudly, harshly, incoherently; he would cry out and begin laughing; the prince reached out his trembling hand then, and softly touched his head, his hair, and began stroking him and stroking his cheeks—he could do nothing more! He started to tremble again, and again his legs seemed to be failing him. Some completely new sensation oppressed his heart with infinite anguish. Meanwhile it had become quite light; at last he lay down on the cushions, as though now completely powerless and in despair, and laid his face against Rogozhin's pale, motionless face; tears flowed from his eyes onto Rogozhin's cheeks, but perhaps he did not notice his own tears and was not at all aware of them.

In any case, when after many hours the doors opened and people came in, they found the murderer completely unconscious and in feverish delirium. The prince was sitting motionless beside him on the cushions, and every time the sick man cried out or began raving, he hastened to pass his trembling hand gently over his hair and cheeks as though caressing and soothing him. But he understood nothing of what they were asking him and he did not recognize the people who had come in and were standing around him. And if Schneider himself had come from Switzerland then to look at his former pupil and patient, remembering the condition in which the prince had sometimes been during the first year of his cure in Switzerland, he would have thrown up his hands and said as he had done then, "An idiot!"

Chapter TWELVE

CONCLUSION

The schoolteacher's widow hurried to Pavlovsk and went straight to see Darya Alexeyevna, who was greatly disturbed by the events of the previous day, and, telling her everything she knew, she nearly frightened her out of her wits. The two ladies immediately decided to get in touch with Lebedev, who was also greatly upset, both as a friend of his lodger and as his landlord. Vera Lebedev told them all she knew. On Lebedev's advice they decided that all three of them should go to Petersburg to prevent, as quickly as possible, "what might easily happen." So it was that at about eleven o'clock the next morning Rogozhin's apartment was opened in the presence of the police, Lebedev, the ladies, and by Rogozhin's brother, Semyon Semyonovitch Rogozhin, who lived in a wing of the house. Matters were facilitated above all by the statement of the caretaker, who said that he had seen Parfyon Semyonovitch the evening before entering with a visitor by the front and apparently in secret. After this testimony there was no more hesitation about breaking in the door, at which they had been ringing in vain.

Rogozhin survived two months of brain inflammation, and after his recovery he was examined and tried. On every point he gave direct, exact, and fully satisfactory testimony, as a result of which the prince was kept completely out of it from the very beginning. Rogozhin otherwise kept silent during the trial. He did not contradict his adroit and eloquent attorney, who demonstrated clearly and logically that the crime was a consequence of brain fever, which had set in long before the crime was committed, as a result of mental suffering the accused had undergone. But he himself added nothing to support this opinion and, as before, recalled and confirmed, clearly and exactly, the smallest details of the crime. He was sentenced, in view of extenuating circumstances, to fifteen years of hard labor in Siberia, and heard the sentence grimly, silently, and "dreamily." All his huge fortune, with the exception of a comparatively small part of it squandered in the first period of debauchery, passed to his brother, Semyon Semyonovitch, to the vast satisfaction of the latter. Rogozhin's elderly mother is still living, and sometimes she seems to remember her favorite son, Parfyon, though not clearly: God has preserved her mind and her heart from knowledge of the horrible calamity which struck her melancholy house.

Lebedev, Keller, Ganya, Ptitsyn, and many other figures in our story go on living as before, little changed, and we have almost nothing to tell about them. Hippolite died in a state of terrible excitation, somewhat sooner than he had expected, two weeks after Nastassya Filippovna's death. Kolya was deeply affected by what had happened; he became closer than ever to his mother. Nina Alexandrovna is concerned about his being too thoughtful for his years; he may perhaps turn out to be a man gifted for practical affairs. By the way, it was partly through his efforts that the prince's future was satisfactorily settled; he had decided long before that Yevgeny Pavlovitch Radomsky was different from all the other people he had come to know of late, and he was the first to go to him and tell him all he knew about what had happened, and about the present condition of the prince. He was not mistaken: Yevgeny Pavlovitch showed the warmest possible interest in the fate of the unfortunate "idiot," and, as a result of his efforts and solicitude, the prince is once again in Schneider's Swiss clinic. Yevgeny Pavlovitch, who has gone abroad himself with the intention of spending quite a long time in Europe and openly refers to himself as a "completely superfluous person in Russia," often—at least once every few months—visits his sick friend in Switzerland. But Schneider frowns and shakes his head more and more each time; he hints at a complete breakdown of the intellect; he does not yet say positively that the illness is incurable, but he allows himself the most melancholy intimations of that possibility.

Yevgeny Pavlovitch takes this very much to heart, and he does have a heart, as is evident from the fact that he receives letters from Kolya, and even answers them sometimes. But, besides this, still another curious trait of his character has come to light, and since it is a good quality, we hasten to mention it: following each visit to Schneider's clinic, Yevgeny Pavlovitch, besides writing to Kolya, sends another letter to a certain person in Petersburg, with the most detailed and sympathetic account of the prince's condition at that moment. Beyond the most respectful expression of devotion, there has begun to appear in these letters (and more and more frequently) certain frank statements of views, ideas, and sentiments; in a word, there is a beginning of what appears to be an expression of friendly and intimate feelings. The person who is in correspondence with Yevgeny Pavlovitch (though they write rather seldom), and who has merited this attention and respect from him, is Vera Lebedev. We have been unable to discover just how such a relationship could have arisen between them; it began of course at the time of the misadventure which had befallen the prince, when Vera Lebedev was so grief-stricken that she had actually fallen ill; but we do not know under what exact circumstances they became acquainted and grew to be friends. We have referred to these letters chiefly because some of them contain information about the Yepanchin family, and particularly about Aglaya Ivanovna Yepanchin. Yevgeny Pavlovitch wrote about her in a rather rambling letter from Paris, saying that after a brief and extraordinary attachment to a certain *émigré,* a Polish count, she had suddenly married the man against the wishes of her family, who only gave their consent finally because there was a threat of the affair ending in a terrible scandal. Later, after almost six months of silence, Yevgeny Pavlovitch informed his correspondent, again in a long and detailed letter, of how on his last visit to Dr. Schneider's he had met there the entire Yepanchin family (except of course Ivan Fyodorovitch, who had stayed back in Petersburg on business) and also Prince S. It was a strange meeting: they all greeted Yevgeny Pavlovitch with transports of delight; Adelaïda and Alexandra were for some reason even grateful to him for "the angelic way he took care of the unhappy prince." Lizaveta Prokofyevna wept heartfelt tears at the sight of the prince in his sick and humiliated condition. Apparently everything had been forgiven him. Prince S. took the occasion to express a few felicitous and clever truths. It seemed to Yevgeny Pavlovitch that Adelaïda and he were not yet perfectly in harmony with one another, but that inevitably in the future Adelaïda would voluntarily and wholeheartedly let her tempestuous nature be guided by Prince S.'s sense and experience. Moreover the painful experiences the family had undergone had made a profound impression on them, particularly Aglaya's recent affair with the *émigré* count. Everything the family had dreaded in giving up Aglaya to this count had within six months' time come to pass, with the addition of certain surprises of which they had never even dreamed. It turned out that the count was not even a count, and if he was in fact an *émigré* it was because of some dark and dubious circumstances in the past. He had fascinated Aglaya by the extraordinary nobility of his soul, torn by anguish for his native land, and fascinated her to such a degree that even before she married him she had joined some sort of committee abroad for the restoration of Poland, and had moreover found her way to the confessional of a certain celebrated Catholic priest, who had inspired her and gained complete ascendancy over her mind. The count's colossal fortune, of which he had given Lizaveta Prokofyevna and Prince S. almost irrefutable evidence, turned out to be nonexistent. Beyond that, within six months after the wedding, the count and his friend the famous priest had managed to cause a violent quarrel between Aglaya and her family, and they had not seen her for several months. In brief, there was much that could have been said, but Lizaveta Prokofyevna, her daughters, and even Prince S. were so affected by all this "terror" that they were afraid even to mention certain things in conversation with Yevgeny Pavlovitch, though they were aware that he knew all about Aglaya's latest obsessions. Poor Lizaveta Prokofyevna longed to be back in Russia and, according to Yevgeny Pavlovitch, she was bitter and quite unfair in her criticism of everything abroad. "They don't bake decent bread anywhere, and in winter they freeze like cellar mice," she said. "At least here I've had a good Russian cry over this poor fellow," she added, pointing to the prince, who did not recognize her at all. "Enough indulging our whims, it's time to be reasonable. And all this being abroad, all this Europe of yours is only a fantasy, and all of us, when we're abroad, we are only a fantasy. Mark my words, you'll see for yourself!" she concluded almost angrily, as she parted with Yevgeny Pavlovitch.

1868–1869

NOTES

Page 29.
Prince: The title *knyaz* may apply to an independent feudal ruler or to a male member of the Tzar's family; however it may also be a lesser hereditary title conferred by a Tzar for services to the state.

Page 29
Karamazin's *History:* Nikolai Mikhaïlovitch Karamazin (1766–1826), Russian historian, author of a twelve-volume *History of the Russian State.*

Page 30.
hereditary burgess: In the nineteenth century many merchants were peasants who had earned their fortunes in trade or were descended from such peasants. "Hereditary burgess" is an approximate translation of one of the legal class designations intended to confirm and formalize the merchant's acquired rank.

Page 36.
devotion without flattery: The epitaph, composed by himself, of General Alexei A. Arakcheyev (1769–1834), Minister of War under Alexander I, often accused of servility, satirized by Pushkin.

Page 42.
the new criminal courts: The institution of trial by jury was among the sweeping reforms of Russian courts and judicial procedure introduced by the ukase of November 24, 1864.

Page 54.
Pogodin's edition: Mikhaïl Petrovitch Pogodin (1800–1875), Russian medievalist and archaeologist.

Page 78.
". . . have been painted long ago": From Lermontov.

Page 148.
Pirogov: Nikolai Ivanovitch Pirogov (1810–1881), a famous Russian surgeon.

Page 178.
Marlinsky: Pseudonym of Alexander A. Bestuzhev (1797–1837), a popular writer in the effusive Romantic mode.

Page 186.
third guild: In the early and mid-nineteenth century Russian law classified merchants into one of three guilds according to their capital worth; hence Papushin was a lesser merchant.

Page 200.
Château-de-Fleurs: In the nineteenth century a popular dancing and entertainment establishment on the Champs-Élysées.

Page 210.
Pavlovsk: A town about twenty miles south of Saint Petersburg, surrounded by vast parks. The musical concerts held near the railroad station attracted local summer residents and genteel Petersburg society.

Page 214.
". . . mercy in the court": A citation from the imperial ukase of November 24, 1864, which established the new judicial reforms.

Page 224.
Scopéts: A member of a dissenting religious sect which practiced castration. Many of the Scoptsi were money-changers.

Page 224.
hereditary burgess: See note, Book I, Chapter 1, page 300.

Page 227.
Solovyov's *History:* Sergei Mikhaïlovitch Solovyov (1820–1879), Russian historian whose *History of Russia* appeared between 1851 and 1879 in twenty-nine volumes.

Page 227.
Old Believer: A member of a schismatic movement which refused to accept the liturgical reforms introduced by Patriarch Nikon in the mid-seventeenth century.

Page 246.
"there shall be time no longer": From the Apocalypse.

Page 268.
A.M.D.: *Ave, mater Dei.*

Page 271.
"Lived a knight once, poor and plain": One of Pushkin's best-known verses, written in 1829.

Page 305.
Dr. B——n: Probably Dr. Sergei Petrovitch Botkin (1832–1889), Alexander II's physician.

Pages 314–15.
and Princess Marya Alexeyevna won't object: "What will Princess Marya Alexeyevna say?" was a comic line in the play *Woe from Wit* (1825) by Alexander S. Griboyedov, which came into current use.

Page 355.
Famusov: A character in *Woe from Wit.*

Page 432.
Millevoye: The stanza is not by Millevoye (1782–1816) but by Nicolas-Joseph-Florent Gilbert (1751–1780), the last lines of "Ode Imitée de Plusieurs Psaumes," the poet's best-known work, composed eight days before his death following a fall from a horse.

Page 441.
Lacenaires: Pierre-François Lacenaire (1800–1836), famous French murderer, for whom killing was an expression of revolt against society.

Page 479.
Podkolyosin: The comic hero of Gogol's play *Marriage* (1842), an indecisive character who resorts to desperate acts.

Page 481.
Pirogov: Principal character in the Gogol story "The Nevsky Prospect."

Page 491.
Nozdryov: A character in *Dead Souls,* "the cheat and bully, with the manners of a hearty good fellow" (D. S. Mirsky).

Page 517.
Charras: Lieutenant-Colonel Charras, *Histoire de la Campagne de 1815, Waterloo* (1864).

Page 528.
Schlosser's *History:* Frederick Schlosser (1776–1860), German historian, author of *Universal History.*

Page 539.
Osterman: Count Andrei Ivanovitch Osterman (1686–1747), German-born Russian diplomat under Peter the Great and Empress Anna. With the ascension of Empress Elizabeth, Osterman was sentenced to death on the wheel; however that sentence was commuted and the count and his family suffered exile in Siberia.

Page 578.
"And perhaps the sorrow . . .": Famous lines from Pushkin.

Page 610.
"For one night of love . . .": From a Pushkin story, "The Egyptian Nights."

SELECTED BIBLIOGRAPHY

Works by FYODOR DOSTOYEVSKY

Poor Folk, 1846
The Double, 1846
An Honest Thief, 1846
White Nights, 1848
Uncle's Dream, 1859
The Friend of the Family, 1859
The Insulted and the Injured, 1861
The House of the Dead, 1862
Notes from Underground, 1864 (Signet Classic 0451-514424)
Crime and Punishment, 1866 (Signet Classic 0451-514793)
The Gambler, 1866
The Idiot, 1868–69 (Signet Classic 0451-516184)
The Eternal Husband, 1870
The Possessed, 1871–72 (Signet Classic 0451-517474)
A Raw Youth, 1875
The Dream of a Ridiculous Man, 1877
   (Signet Classic 0451-514424)
A Diary of a Writer, 1873–81
The Brothers Karamazov, 1879–80
   (Signet Classic 0451-514645)
Letters of Fyodor Dostoyevsky

SELECTED BIOGRAPHY AND CRITICISM

Bakhtin, Mikhail. *Problems of Dostoyevsky's Poetics.* Trans. R. W. Rotsel. Ann Arbor: Ardis, 1973.

Berdyaev, Nicholas. *Dostoyevsky.* Trans. Donald Attwater. New York: Meridian Books, 1960.

Blackmur, R. P. *Eleven Essays in the European Novel.* New York: Harcourt, Brace & World, 1964.

Carr, Edward H. *Dostoyevsky, 1821–1881: A New Biography.* London: Allen and Unwin, 1949.

Coulson, Jessie. *Dostoyevsky: A Self-Portrait.* London: Oxford University Press, 1962.

Gide, André. *Dostoyevsky.* Trans. Arnold Bennett. New York: Knopf, 1926.

Grossman, Leonid. *Dostoyevsky: A Biography.* Trans. Helen Mackler. Indianapolis: Bobbs-Merrill, 1975.

Ivanov, Vyacheslav. *Freedom and the Tragic Life: A Study in Dostoyevsky.* Trans. Norman Cameron. Ed. S. Konovalov. New York: The Noonday Press, 1957.

Jackson, R. L. *Dostoyevsky's Underground Man in Russian Literature.* New York: Humanities Press, 1959.

————, ed. *Twentieth Century Interpretations of Crime and Punishment: A Collection of Critical Essays.* Englewood Cliffs, N.J.: Prentice-Hall, 1974.

Lavrin, Janko. *Dostoyevsky.* New York: Macmillan, 1947.

Magarshack, David. *Dostoyevsky.* New York: Harcourt, Brace & World, 1963.

Mirsky, Dmitri. *History of Russian Literature.* Ed. Francis J. Whitfield. New York: Knopf, 1949.

Mochulsky, Konstantin. *Dostoyevsky: His Life and Work.* Trans. Michael A. Minihan. Princeton, N.J.: Princeton University Press, 1967.

Modern Fiction Studies (Dostoyevsky Number), 4 (Autumn, 1958).

Muchnic, Helen. *Dostoyevsky's English Reputation.* New York: Octagon Books, 1969.

Seduro, Vladimir. *Dostoyevsky in Russian Literary Criticism: 1846–1956.* New York: Columbia University Press, 1957.

Simmons, Ernest J. *Dostoyevsky: The Making of a Novelist.* London: Oxford University Press, 1940.

Steiner, George. *Tolstoy or Dostoyevsky*. New York: Knopf, 1959.

Wasiolek, Edward, ed. *Crime and Punishment and the Critics*. San Francisco: Wadsworth Publishing Co., 1961.

———. *Dostoyevsky: The Major Fiction*. Cambridge, Mass.: M.I.T. Press, 1964.

———, ed. *The Brothers Karamazov and the Critics*. Belmont, Calif.: Wadsworth Publishing Co., 1967.

Wellek, René, ed. *Dostoyevsky: A Collection of Critical Essays*. Englewood Cliffs, N.J.: Prentice-Hall, 1962.

Yarmolinsky, Avrahm. *Dostoyevsky: His Life and Art*. New York: Criterion Books, 1957.

SIGNET CLASSICS by Russian Authors

(0451)

☐ **CHEKOV: SELECTED STORIES by Anton Chekov.** New translation by Ann Dunnigan with a Foreword by E.J Simmons.
(515277—$2.50)

☐ **WARD SIX and Other Stories by Anton Chekov.** New translation by Ann Dunnigan with an Afterword by Rufus W. Mathewson, Jr.
(516907—$3.50)

☐ **THE BROTHERS KARAMAZOV by Fyodor Dostoyevsky.** Translation by Constance Garnett, with Foreword by Manuel Komroff.
(514645—$2.75)

☐ **CRIME AND PUNISHMENT by Fyodor Dostoyevsky.** Translated and with Afterword by Sidney Monas. (517458—$2.25)

☐ **THE IDIOT by Fyodor Dostoyevsky.** A new translation by Henry and Olga Carlisle. Introduction by Harold Rosenburg.
(516184—$2.50)

☐ **NOTES FROM UNDERGROUND, WHITE NIGHTS, THE DREAM OF A RIDICULOUS MAN and Selections from House of the Dead by Fyodor Dostoyevsky.** New translation and Afterword by Andrew R. McAndrew. (514424—$2.50)

☐ **THE POSSESSED by Fyodor Dostoyevsky.** New translation by Andrew R. McAndrew, with an Afterword by Marc Slonim.
(517474—$4.50)

☐ **DEAD SOULS by Nikolai Gogol.** New Translation by Andrew R. McAndrew with a Foreword by Frank O'Connor. (515293—$2.50)

☐ **DIARY OF A MAD MAN and Other Stories by Nikolai Gogol.** New translation by Andrew R. McAndrew and Afterword by Leon Stilman. (515331—$2.25)

☐ **OBLOMOV by Ivan Goncharov.** Translation by Ann Dunnigan with a Foreword by Harry T. Moore. (515722—$3.95)